I0822419

THE ROYALS

VOLUME TWO

THE ROYALS

VOLUME TWO

CRAVE ME
COVET ME
CAPTURE ME
COMPLETE ME

GENEVA LEE

This is a work of fiction. Names, characters, businesses, places, events and incidents are either the products of the author's imagination or used in a fictitious manner. Any resemblance to actual persons, living or dead, or actual events is purely coincidental.

Quaintrelle Publishing + Media

www.GenevaLee.com

Crave Me, first published, 2015.

Covet Me, first published, 2015.

Capture Me, first published, 2015.

Complete Me, first published, 2017.

Cover design © Date Book Designs.

Image © vitaly tiagunov/Adobe Stock.

Print ISBN-13: 978-1-945163-53-1

For the girls who never lose hope...

CRAVE ME

PROLOGUE

Westminster Bridge stretched into oblivion, lost in the fog sitting like smoke over the Thames. Tourists straggled across, taking photos beside clinging lovers as runners jogged. One by one the haze swallowed each of them.

They disappeared from my sight, never to appear again—like people disappear from your life. There and gone.

I pressed my hands to the balcony railing to steady myself. A city of a million souls, and I had never felt more isolated. The hollow ache in my stomach spread through me with each breath I took, reminding me I was empty. I was alone.

An hour ago I hadn't been. An hour ago I had a plan and a future —and him. But now that life was gone.

"There you are." Clara stepped onto the balcony and moved beside me. She rested a hand gently over mine.

"I haven't gone anywhere," I said flatly. My whole future had, but I was still here. "Jilted fiancée sounds less glamorous than bride-to-be, don't you think?"

"Nobody is labeling you, and if they do they'll only call you the woman who clocked Pepper Lockwood, which in my book makes you fabulous," she said firmly.

It had felt pretty good to finally hit that tart. The only thing that would have been better was if I'd been able to hit her and Philip. "I should have seen it coming. Philip's been acting oddly for weeks."

"No one saw that coming," Clara assured me. "And this is in no way your fault. Philip cheated on you. He ended things."

The diamond ring on my hand grew heavy, as if it were an anchor, tying me to a past that I needed to be freed from. I slipped it off my hand and held it to Clara. "At least that will fetch a pretty sum. Enough to live on for a bit."

"Don't make snap decisions." She took the ring, clenching it in her fist, but her forehead wrinkled in concern. She didn't try to talk me out of selling it though. We both knew I would need the money while I looked for a job.

A job.

I told myself I had an excellent education—that I would have no trouble finding work. But I wasn't sure how a year of planning for a wedding that wasn't going to happen would look on a resume.

"We'll worry about that tomorrow," Clara said in a comforting tone. She tugged me away from the railing as the terrace door slid open to reveal a handsome, curly-haired man. "I have procured all the liquor in the world," Edward announced. The younger prince had proven himself a true friend and tonight, it seemed, would be no exception to that fact. "Literally. There is none left in the world. It's all ours."

He reached over and placed an ice pack on my knuckles then held up a bottle. "For your right hook. And vodka for the rest of you."

I took one last look at the city below and turned to my friends. "What are we waiting for? Let's get pissed."

CHAPTER ONE

London did not care that I had somewhere to be. That much was evident from the crowds herding themselves obliviously through Kensington. The few trees scattered along the busy thoroughfare had turned traitor, shifting from green into glorious shades of gold and rust, and it seemed every tourist in the city needed a picture of them. I pushed past a large group that had stopped for a photo op in front of Top Shop. Muttering an obligatory apology for ruining their shot, I dashed down a less crowded side street. I caught sight of a red-lacquered door that read Smith Price, Esq. on the other side of the street just as the alarm on my phone rang out to remind me I had an interview in five minutes. Jogging across as quickly as my impractical shoes would allow, I paused at the door and took a deep breath.

I ran a hand over my hair, pleased to discover it was still laying straight after the mad dash I'd made from my flat. I'd recently opted out of the long, wavy locks that I'd been growing out for my wedding. New life. New look. The shoulder-length bob I'd chosen—complete with a thick fringe that fell over my forehead—was easier to style and apparently immune to the frantic chaos of London streets. Briefly I considered checking to make sure my red lipstick didn't need freshening but thought better of it. There wasn't the time. I was due in his office in one minute. I smoothed my black pencil skirt down, prayed I hadn't snagged my stockings, and checked the top button of my fitted ivory blouse. I looked the part. Now all I had to do was land it. A steady job would be the final piece in getting my life back on track, and it might finally provide me with the extra money I needed for my own start-up company.

Inside, everything changed. I'd stepped from one of London's most sleek and modern streets into the past. The place dripped with rich mahogany and leather. Large bookshelves lined the walls of the small waiting room and behind an oak desk sat a very prim woman, guarding an office door. She pursed her lips and stared me down. Maybe I hadn't dressed the part after all. I guessed her to be in her mid to late forties, but then again, the giant stick up her ass might have made her look older. I smiled sweetly and strode toward her.

"I have an appointment with Mr. Price."

The disapproval on her face didn't budge, even as she nodded. "Right on time, Miss...?"

"Stuart," I offered, suspecting she already knew that. A woman had confirmed my interview time, and she was the only one here. It wasn't worth it to point this out, however, given that I'd spent the last six months bouncing between interviews and temporary jobs. Instead I swallowed my pride and waited. I'd gotten rather good at that since I'd caught my fiancé cheating on me. Perhaps I should consider listing the skill on my resume.

"Mr. Price is expecting you," she said as she stood and gestured for me to follow her through the door she guarded.

I stepped into his office and stopped dead in my tracks. I'd googled Smith Price yesterday, but it had never occurred to me to look up pictures of him. Considering the long list of accomplishments and the caliber of clients associated with his firm, I'd expected someone older. Much older. But the man sitting at the desk in front of me, looking like God's gift to three-piece suits, couldn't have been more than thirty years old. His dark hair had been combed carefully but couldn't quite hide a slight wave that cried out to be pulled. Dark lashes framed eyes that were stunningly bright green, even from this distance. But it was his jawline, smooth and strong, and his broad shoulders that oozed a primal masculinity. He was leaning back in a leather chair, his hand resting thoughtfully on a shapely set of lips. Something stirred inside of me, beating against the wall I'd built to protect myself from men, especially men like this. I squared my shoulders and forced a professional, and disinterested, smile onto my face.

Price didn't stand as his secretary led me into the room. He simply watched, his eyes traveling slowly up my body. The intensity of the gaze burned across my skin, sending a flush of heat over my cheeks. For one brief moment, I thought my knees were going to buckle, and it took all the composure I could muster to stay upright in my Louboutins. Thank God I'd gone with the more responsible heel, or I would have found myself arse over tits on his office floor. His eyes stopped on my mouth, and I suddenly regretted wearing such a suggestive shade of red. But I hadn't expected Smith Price to look like—well, a sex god. His own lips twitched, as if he guessed what I was thinking, but then his face returned to a stony mask. Completely unreadable. Completely disarming.

And worst of all, completely sexy.

This is not good! the high-pitched voice in my head shrieked in warning. You need this job and you'll never get it if you can't show you have a few brain cells. *Speak up!* I opened my mouth and took a deep breath. If he wasn't going to introduce himself, I needed to do the honors. But more than anything, I needed to refrain from sounding desperate. No vulnerability. I'd spent one whole minute in Price's presence, but I already knew what would happen if I showed any weakness. I'd be in his bed and out of a job.

"Mr. Price, it's a pleasure to meet you," I said in a smooth voice—too smooth and way too sexy.

Keep your knickers on your arse and off the floor, I commanded myself silently.

His fingers shifted to rest on his chin, revealing those chiseled lips that I couldn't tear my eyes from. This interview was going nowhere if we couldn't stop staring at each other's mouths.

"Smith." The simple correction was enough to break the spell, and my eyes flashed up, finally meeting his. The look was long and hard. The kind of look you share with someone you've known a long time—someone you've known intimately. His eyes weren't guarded like the rest of him, and I knew without a doubt that this was purposeful. He wanted me to see what he was thinking. I could drown in the green pools of his irises—lost to the turmoil reflected there. It mirrored my own. My belly constricted as desire wound itself tightly in my core. One pluck and it would unravel. I would unravel.

"Sit, Miss Stuart," he ordered, turning his attention to his desk. I seized the opportunity to look away and regain a bit of control as I slid into the chair opposite his. When our eyes met again, a curtain had descended, concealing his thoughts. "I suppose you have questions about the position."

I didn't actually. I'd expected to walk in here and be grilled. Fumbling to find my voice, I finally managed to force out the first one that came to mind. "What exactly are the expectations...for the position?"

It seemed silly to tack on the last bit, but Smith struck me as the type of man that needed clear boundaries and definitions.

"My private assistant."

He didn't elaborate further. Apparently, he was going to make me work for each shred of information.

"Here?" I asked, gesturing to the office around us. "Will I be assisting with cases?"

I wasn't certain I could actually help him with legal work, but I sure as hell could fake it until I figured out what I was doing.

"Do you have a legal background I'm unaware of?" His tone was low and cold.

I fought the urge to shrink back in my seat. Instead I squared my shoulders. At least if he was going to be an ass, it would cure me of my initial attraction to him. His head tilted, waiting for my answer.

He stroked the slight five o'clock shadow peppering the strong curve of his jaw. What would it be like to have that hand on me? How would it feel when his stubble scratched along my thigh?

Maybe I wasn't cured after all.

"I don't," I said, adopting a similarly cool attitude.

"That's just as well, because my private assistant does not assist with casework." He smirked as he spoke. He actually fucking smirked.

What kind of grown man smirked during a job interview?

The kind that knows exactly what you really want from him.

I ignored the voice, losing patience with myself as much as I was with him. "Then what do you want me to do?"

The smirk shifted into a crooked grin that vanished in seconds. "You will assist me in my private affairs. Obviously my secretary handles my schedules and court appearances. You will oversee my personal life as well as my personal relationships with clients. I'm a busy man, Miss Stuart—"

"Belle," I interrupted him, relishing the chance to correct him.

"Miss Stuart," he repeated. "I'm a busy man. I don't remember birthdays. I do not shop for wedding presents. And I never dine alone."

"I'm supposed to have dinner with you?" I choked out. This was starting to sound a lot like marriage without the benefit of his bank account—or orgasms.

"Not at all times," he continued. "I often have dinner plans. On nights that I do not—or on the occasion that my plans require an escort—you will be present."

"I had no idea this was going to be a lifestyle." The glib remark was out of my mouth before I'd thought it through.

Smith's jaw tensed but he didn't speak, which only made the air in the room feel heavier. This job was pressure. The question was whether or not doing the job would be more pressure than finding another opportunity. Despite my pedigree and education, I'd yet to receive a call back after an interview. But I couldn't let the feeling of inferiority those snubs elicited force me into making a mistake.

"May I ask you a question?" The time for being blunt was now—before I got in over my head.

"You already have," he pointed out, "and I didn't bite."

His answer sent my eyes to his lips, and my mind to fantasizing about what it would be like if he did bite. I had a sinking suspicion I wouldn't mind it if Smith Price bit me.

Now would be a really good time to run.

But I didn't want to. I felt locked to the chair, locked to this room and this man. I told myself it was the possibilities that the job offered, even though I knew it was more than that. He had already wormed his way under my skin. I could feel him there—an itch that I desperately wanted to scratch. Staying meant I'd have to fight that urge, but leaving felt impossible.

"Assuming you select me for the position"—I paused, wondering if he was going to call me out on my conjecture— "why would you choose me?"

"There are a number of reasons why you'd make an excellent candidate." He settled back in his chair, raising his arms to rest casually behind his head as he regarded me. "Your education, for starters."

I nodded, even though an Oxford education seemed wasted on running errands and being a dinner date.

"From the look in your eyes, you disagree."

"No, I—"

"Allow me to finish." The words he chose were considerate, but his tone was full of expectation. He expected my silence. He expected to speak uninterrupted. And I suspected that he expected me to agree with whatever he was about to say. "Your education will benefit me. I prefer a companion with which I can hold a conversation. I also prefer a well-bred escort for business affairs. Not all of my business associates share the same predilections."

I raised an eyebrow. "Predilections is a strong word."

"Not all whores stand on the street corners, Miss Stuart. Most of them simply find a man willing to purchase their favor in exchange for their pussies. While I'm certain it's comforting to have something to stick your cock in at home, such relationships are a liability that often end in embarrassment or blackmail," he finished.

He had a point, even if he'd ratcheted himself up on my knobhead meter. "But as you said, I'm educated. I'd be much more likely to understand what is and isn't blackmail worthy."

"You will have signed a nondisclosure agreement," he informed me, shifting in his seat so that his face fell into shadow. "And I promise you will find yourself very much bound to it—as well as bound to me."

The lump in my throat slid ominously as I swallowed this. Bound. Did I want to be bound to him? Legally, at least. It was difficult to consider, given the thoughts his choice of words had conjured. I wasn't going to need a drink after this. I was going to need the whole bloody bottle.

"There are other reasons," he continued. "It wasn't until I ran a background check on you that I discovered you were best friends with our new Queen. I found it quite impressive that you managed to stay out of the press. You must have some knack for flying under the radar."

"Or I'm really boring," I countered.

"I doubt that," he said in a low voice that sent a tingle rippling up my spine. "My business requires privacy. I need a person who comprehends that. You are intimately familiar with that obligation."

"I was friends with Clara long before she met Alexander."

"It's a compliment." Smith waited for me to challenge this interpretation. When I didn't, he continued, "And of course, you look the part."

"I look the part?" I repeated. Surely he didn't mean what it sounded like he meant.

"You are a beautiful woman. There's no need to pretend otherwise."

I tried to keep my cool and failed miserably. "That's dangerously close to harassment."

Smith Price was an enigma. Or maybe he wasn't. All he wanted was a pretty girl who wasn't dumb to attend to his every whim. When

I actually thought about it, it was what all men really wanted. Only he was willing to pay for it—without the expectation of sex in return. The realizations should have neither shocked nor disappointed me, and somehow it still did on both counts.

"Companies employ attractive individuals every day. It's hardly illegal when it's requisite to the position." Smith shrugged and leaned forward to rest his palms on his desk. His hands didn't move. His fingers didn't tap impatiently. He was completely in control of himself and this situation. That's what scared me.

It was also what excited me.

"As long as there is clear differentiation between my job and being your girlfriend." The implication was clear. Perhaps the way he'd been studying me since I walked into the room was simply him measuring me up, but it felt a lot more like he was fucking me with his eyes. I was used to that—used to men mentally screwing me. I just wasn't interested in actually getting screwed. I didn't need to be tempted to change my mind, and judging from the way my body responded to his penetrating gaze, I needed to make that crystal clear.

"I assure you I have no interest in romance. Another man might utilize his position of authority over you, bribe you with presents, or make unsavory proposals. Our relationship will be strictly professional." His voice trailed away as if he was leaving something out—a clause or an afterthought—but he didn't finish the thought. "Do you have more questions for me?"

I should, but I didn't. It was getting harder to think in his presence. All I could do was shake my head.

"Then I think we're finished here." It was an abrupt end to the interview, but one I had seen coming.

It was for the best. Of that much I was certain. But despite all the red flags and warning signs, I couldn't get past the lost opportunity. This job had paid. Well. I was doing okay financially, given the life-changing events of the last few months, but that largely had to do with my Aunt Jane refusing to take rent money and best friends who constantly picked up the tab.

I mustered up the shred of dignity I had left and forced a smile. "I'll look forward to hearing from you."

"You won't have to," he said dismissively, and my heart sank into the pit of my stomach. "I'll expect you here tomorrow at one to discuss my current agenda and needs."

I tried to look past the suggestiveness of those words and focus on the fact that I'd actually landed the job. "I'll be here."

"Be prompt, Miss Stuart. I'm not a man who likes to wait."

A sharp sting sang through my lower lip, and I realized I was biting it. Smith's eyes lingered on my mouth. He'd noticed before I had, and despite what he'd said about our relationship, the hunger burning in his gaze was anything but professional.

I needed to get out of here and clear my head. It was the only way I could decide if I would be in this office tomorrow at noon or sending a cowardly email. I popped out of my chair, relieved to be the one lording over the room in my four- inch heels. I paused, hovering in front of his desk. "Let's be clear on one thing. I'll attend these functions. I'll work from your home. But I'm not sleeping with you."

"Noted," he said, but his answer was anything but reassuring. I couldn't be certain if he viewed me as a challenge or a done deal. Either way, I knew one thing: keeping my legs shut in the presence of Smith Price was going to prove difficult. Maybe impossible.

But it was one challenge I was happy to accept.

CHAPTER TWO

Coco's was overrun by the time I made my way from Kensington to Notting Hill. The once quaint bistro had become a haven for curious tourists and paparazzi hoping to snap a picture of the Royal baby bump ever since the tabloids had run a story about the weekly dinner date I kept with Edward and Clara at the establishment. Pushing my way through the crowd, I caught sight of Clyde, Coco's manager. He dabbed a napkin across his forehead as he scanned the crowd. I couldn't help but notice that the lines on his forehead had deepened as his hairline had receded since he'd taken up crowd control. I'd grown fond of him, making a point to come in the front door to be sure I saw him each week.

"Clyde!" I called, waving my arm over my head. It was undignified, but so was being smashed between smelly wannabe photographers.

Clyde released a long breath and sprung into action, motioning for servers to help make a path for me. As soon as I was at his side, he whisked me through the kitchen and up the backstairs to a private dining room.

"The crowd is worse than ever." I shouldered my purse as I slowed my pace to match the weary restaurateur.

"They seem to be swellin' along with Clara's belly," he said in his thick Irish brogue. "I don't know how many more souls we can fit into this establishment. It's fixin' to burst."

"So is Clara," I said in a teasing whisper. "Once the baby comes, we'll be out of your hair." I suddenly wished I could take the comment about his hair back, but Clyde only nodded sadly.

"It's not been any trouble to have you here." He held open the door for me.

"We both know that's not true." I stepped inside and paused before planting a small kiss on his cheek. This might very well be the last time we saw him for a while. "Thank you for everything."

"It's been no trouble," he repeated gruffly before excusing himself.

"Flustering Clyde?" Edward tsked as he stood to give me a hug. "A kiss from a pretty girl? I'm not sure his heart can take any more stress. "

"I was simply thanking him." I swatted at his shoulder, but Edward only laughed and pulled out a chair for me. "She's not here yet?"

Edward took a long sip of his wine, sighing as he set the glass back down. "Alexander has gone into full-scale alpha mode."

"When isn't he in alpha mode?" I asked dryly as I poured my own glass from the open bottle.

"She's due in two weeks. He has a right to be protective." The response was dismissive. Edward, like most of us, had a tendency to forgive his older brother's need for control.

I might have argued with his logic if Clara hadn't been a magnet for trouble in the last year and a half. As it was, it made me feel better that Alexander kept such close tabs on her—most of the time. The rest of the time I wished I saw her more often. I doubted it had less to do with Alexander's protectiveness and more to do with the near obsession the two displayed toward one another.

"I guess we should all be so lucky." I shrugged my shoulders and settled back in my chair.

"I suppose." Edward's mouth twisted into a wry grin. "David isn't exactly the type."

I winked at him. "Maybe that's your job."

"What's his job?" a tired voice asked from behind me. A moment later, Clara was at the table, lowering herself slowly into the remaining chair with one hand cradling her ever-growing bump protectively. She might have sounded exhausted, but her fair skin glowed and her chestnut hair had even more bounce than normal. I might have hated her if I didn't love her so much.

"We're trying to decide who's the Alexander in my relationship."

Clara grimaced. "Hopefully neither of you."

"Trouble in paradise?" Edward's forehead crinkled in concern.

"He's just being a tad overbearing. You're lucky I convinced him to let me come at all tonight. Norris and half of the British Armed Forces are downstairs. What's the point of having a back entrance if you show up with a small army?" She patted her stomach and smiled grudgingly. "I imagine it will be even worse when she makes her appearance."

"We'll come to you," I promised her. "And it's not so terrible to have someone looking out for you."

Clara locked eyes with me and nodded, immediately sending a wave of guilt rushing through me. I hadn't meant it to sound like sour grapes but it had. The fact that she was happily married wasn't anything to feel badly about. I'd told her that a hundred times, but it never quite sunk in.

"So I have news." I unrolled my silverware as I quickly switched topics.

"Tell me you got laid!" Edward threw his hands up in a pleading gesture to the heavens.

"Very funny," I said, tossing the napkin at his head. "I have sworn off men, remember?"

"Then tell me you got a vibrator, love," he retorted.

"She had one long before she broke up with Philip," Clara said dryly.

I wagged a finger at her. "That is true. But sadly, this news doesn't end in an O. I merely got a job."

"That's fantastic." Edward's face split, as if this announcement was half as exciting as finding out I'd shagged someone.

"What happened to your idea for that clothing company?" Clara asked.

"Oh, I'll never get around to that," I lied. I'd only mentioned the idea once to my best friend, but Clara never forgot anything. There was no point in involving either of them in something that was likely a pipe dream. Especially because I knew they would both be all too eager to finance the venture, which was the last thing I wanted. "Office work is the boring stuff us mere mortals are made of."

"Uh-uh!" Clara mimicked my earlier finger wag. "You were aristocracy long before I was."

"Ah well, that hasn't really worked out too well for my family," I reminded her. I didn't add that my mother's perpetually failing estate was one of the many reasons that I needed said job. "A girl must eat."

"And eat we shall," Edward said as a waiter appeared with our standing order.

I reached for the serving spoon, and he batted away my hand.

"No, us immortals shall eat while you entertain us with tales of your lowly peasant existence. What is this job you speak of?"

Clara meanwhile grabbed the spoon and started ladling pasta onto my plate. "Eat, but do tell."

"I'm going to be a personal assistant." I twirled my fork in the pasta, my stomach rumbling as I watched the decadent Alfredo sauce coat the linguini.

"To a celebrity?" Edward asked.

"To a lawyer," I said before slowly slurping down the noodles.

"Distinctly less glamourous."

"You haven't seen the lawyer." It was out of my mouth before I'd really considered the ammunition I was giving them.

"Oh really?" Clara's voice peaked in excitement.

"She's going to sleep with him," Edward noted, as if it was already a proven fact.

"Don't get any ideas," I warned them. "He seems like a first-class knobhead."

Clara and Edward shared a knowing look.

"She's definitely going to sleep with him," Edward predicted. "She's already thinking about his knob."

THE LIGHTS WERE LOW IN MY FLAT WHEN I STEPPED INSIDE. Music drifted across the open space in a slow sensual melody that crackled slightly. I peeked around the corner, not wanting to disturb my aunt, and watched as she swayed softly, her loose kaftan swirling in a muted rainbow around her elegant form. I'd always idolized my aunt with her wild platinum hair and even wilder clothes. The fact that she was as spirited as she looked was an added bonus.

"Tell me about your day," she called without ever turning around.

"I can wait." I slid my purse onto the kitchen counter and lingered there, resisting the urge to drum my fingernails against the granite.

"Nonsense." Jane swooped to retrieve a bottle of wine from the cabinet. "Grab the glasses."

A sense of peace settled over me as I plucked two long-stemmed globes from the shelf and placed them on the counter. Most twenty-somethings would have minded living with a family member, but I had no such qualms. Jane was a hurricane of a woman, constantly shifting and moving from place to place—and man to man. I hadn't been ready to live on my own when Clara got married, especially not after ending my own engagement. Making the choice to move in with Jane had been simple, and given how hard it had been to find a stable job over the last few months, I'd become increasingly glad she had asked me to live with her.

"How was the interview?" she asked, passing me a full wine glass.

"Interesting." I tapped my finger on the delicate stem, watching as the thin crimson liquid swished along the sides of the globe, coating it for a moment before retreating back to the bottom.

Jane raised a penciled eyebrow. "How so?"

"Well, I got the job." I paused as I searched for the right words.

"But it scares you," Jane guessed.

"My boss scares me," I admitted.

"Is he an asshole? Or does he just have a stick up his ass like most lawyers?"

"I can't tell. He's direct." I continued to choose my words carefully. Not because I wanted to keep anything from Jane, but because I was trying to understand the emotions tumbling through me. Just thinking about the interview had produced tiny flutters of anxiety in my belly.

"And powerful?"

I nodded. He was definitely that. I knew very little about Smith Price, but that much I could sense. Power. Authority. He radiated those qualities. They emanated off him like rays from the sun, and I suspected that if I didn't have the good sense to protect myself, I was going to wind up burned.

"And handsome," Jane finished for me.

"Yes," I whispered as my stomach did a little flip. "I'm afraid that working for him is going to get me into trouble."

Jane reached over and took my hand, shaking her head as a bell-like laugh peeled from her. "You could use a little trouble."

"I've had enough trouble for a lifetime." It was the last thing I was looking for after Philip. But Jane always had a tendency to flit from love affair to love affair. It made her happy, but it wasn't what I was looking for in life. "I want to focus on me and work on my business plan, not get distracted by a man."

"The thing about distractions is that they're necessary. You can't work constantly. That's no life. Every woman needs a healthy dose of romance. You don't have to choose between a career and love," she said softly.

"Maybe I don't know what's healthy," I pointed out, my eyes darting to study the table. "I was going to marry a man who was in love with someone else."

"Belle." Jane's voice took on a gentle tone as she said my name.

"You were infatuated by the idea of love. The wedding. The lifestyle. You wanted stability, and God knows, after your childhood, no one could blame you for that."

"Now I want my own stability." I lifted my head and met her gaze.

"Then make that happen, but don't stop living. Not taking chances isn't stability, it's a slow way to die."

"So I should take the job?" I asked.

"Do you need the job?"

"That depends," I said, grinning despite myself, "how long can I keep paying rent in cheap wine?"

"Take the job and pay me in good wine." Jane winked. "I don't want rent from you, but I do want you to start this business. So unless you've had a change of heart about investors..."

I waved a hand. "I need to get it started by myself."

I had no idea if there was room for my company in the marketplace. So much had changed since I'd been at university, there was no way I was taking Jane's nor anyone else's money until I was standing on my own two feet.

"You know I won't pressure you, but the offer is always open."

"I know." I took a long sip of my wine before abandoning my glass. "I should get some sleep. It seems I have work tomorrow."

"Belle, have you told your mother...about the job?"

I tensed, my body responding automatically to the mere idea of calling her. "Not yet."

"Don't," Jane advised.

"She'll find out."

"Then that will be soon enough." Jane stood and wrapped her arms around my shoulders. "If you want to focus on you, that might be a good place to start."

"You might be right about that." But even though I knew she was, a heaviness had already descended on my chest. I shook my head, trying to clear the wave of guilt.

Jane gave me a small smile and pressed me close, hugging me until the guilt disappeared entirely. "I'm proud of you."

"Will you still be proud of me if I break down and throw myself at my boss?" I asked wryly.

"Darling, nothing would make me prouder."

CHAPTER THREE

It was five minutes past one—an inauspicious start to my new assistant's career. My fingertips drummed across the windowsill. I didn't appreciate waiting. I hadn't waited for any woman in the last three years. If Belle Stuart hadn't intrigued me so damn much, I'd have already left instructions with my receptionist to show her right back out the door when she deigned to show up. Doris, the old battle-axe that I'd employed for the last five years, would have no problem giving her the boot.

It was a mistake not to send her packing. I had finally settled on this fact when a soft knock that definitely didn't belong to Doris announced she was here.

I straightened up, clasping my hands behind my back, and waited a moment before I answered. "Enter."

The door opened, but I kept my back to her, training my eyes on the street outside. It was important that she learned early on that she didn't command my attention, rather that I would choose when to give it to her. That didn't mean I was immune to her presence though. Her soft breathing carried across the silent room, and my fingers tightened over my wrist.

A mistake.

Given my position by the window and given that my arms were crossed behind my back, the movement was in her line of sight. It didn't matter if she'd actually seen it. I'd make another mistake in the presence of Belle Stuart. My first might have been hiring her in the first place. I couldn't allow myself to be affected by her. She must only be permitted to see what I allowed. No more slip-ups. The fact that I was aware of the problem would presumably make it easier to contend with it in the future.

"Mr. Price." Her words were timid. Unlike the woman I'd interviewed the previous day. Perhaps she would prove a study in contrasts. Strong but vulnerable. Cold and still inviting. A lady in clothes and something dangerously wild out of them.

Time would tell.

Of course, it might be embarrassment over her tardiness.

I turned to her before I made another mistake. My hand curled into a fist, stifling the twitch that tingled across my palm. Maintaining control was going to prove a challenge around her, especially if she chose to blatantly ignore my instructions. For now, a simple correction was in order, but I had no doubt that eventually I'd have the pleasure of giving her a much more serious reprimand. "Smith."

"Smith." I enjoyed how it sounded as she tried it out. My name on her lips was familiar—intimate. Belle crossed one leg behind the other and rubbed it nervously along her calf. Shoes with red soles again. Some type of luxury brand. Normally I might ask my assistant to send a pair to the beautiful woman standing before me. A present that would grease the path to what I was really interested in. The right present cut through all the unnecessary shit—dinner, conversations, romance—and got straight to the point: my cock buried in warm pussy. The other things were necessary, at least the dinner and conversation, if I wanted more. In my experience, the right amount of attention and then a woman would do whatever I wanted.

I hadn't decided what I wanted from Belle Stuart yet.

"I'm not a man who likes to wait," I advised her. "You would do well to remember that."

"Of course." She inclined her head, but I caught her eyes flash.

Belle Stuart didn't like to be chastised. That was unfortunate given how much I enjoyed reprimands.

Extending my arm, I motioned to the leather cigar couch. "Join me. There's paperwork to discuss."

I found the folder that contained the various documents and contracts I required her to sign without taking my eyes from her. She lowered herself onto the couch, her hands smoothing down her backside as she sat. Her grey skirt was slightly too tight or had been altered to hug her ass in a way that made me want to find the tailor and give him a bonus. She crossed her legs as I took a seat next to her, her hands folded in her lap.

Mixed signals.

Dropping the papers on the oak coffee table, I leaned back, dropping one arm over the back of the couch. Her posture stiffened. I wasn't touching her. Not quite. But she had reacted all the same.

Interesting.

"Given that you will be accompanying me to a variety of business meetings, you'll be required to sign a nondisclosure agreement as well as an arbitration agreement."

"Arbitration?" Her eyebrow notched up.

"Basically it means you won't sue me without trying to work things out first." It was common new hire paperwork, but all of it was airtight. It protected me and my business.

"I think I'd just blackmail you instead." Her cherry red lips curved into a smile, and I realized she was joking.

"I wouldn't recommend that," I told her in a low voice.

The amusement vanished from her eyes, and she leaned down to gather the contracts, treating me to a glimpse down her blouse. Her tits were on the small side, B-cups maybe. Big enough for a mouthful.

I drew a pen out of my suit pocket and dropped it on the table. I could have handed it to her, but now she would be forced to lean over again.

"You mentioned dinners," she said as she scanned the pages. "Will they all be business-oriented or will some be for pleasure?" Her cheeks went pink and she gasped. "I mean, will we be dining with your friends or only your clients?"

"Some men believe in keeping business and pleasure separate."

"And you?" she asked breathlessly, her eyes lifting to mine.

"I've always enjoyed mixing them."

She broke the stare first, trying to cover her restless fidgeting by flipping to the next contract. "So you will need me frequently in the evenings?"

"And on weekends," I added. "Is that an issue?"

"A girl has to have a life." She shrugged, but I noticed color still stained her face.

"This position is more of a lifestyle. I think you'll find if you flip to the last page that the salary and benefits are more than adequate recompense for your time." I waited as she searched for the offer I'd purposefully placed at the end of the paperwork.

A desperate girl would have already asked what I was paying her.

A stupid girl would have signed the contracts before I told her.

Belle was neither desperate nor stupid, but she wasn't exactly trusting. That was why I had hired her in the first place, despite the dangerous attraction I'd felt toward her from the moment we met.

She studied the page silently, not speaking until her eyes had reached the end. "This is too much."

"Most people would already be signing the contracts and waiting for their first cheque," I said dryly. The salary I was offering her was part of a message: I expect loyalty. Six figures, a private driver, an expense account—that was the price I was willing to pay.

"I'm not a whore, Mr. Price. I can't be bought. This isn't the kind of money you pay an assistant."

"Perhaps not." It was my turn to shrug. "That's the second time you've referenced your unwillingness to sleep with me as part of the job. Let me assure you, Belle, I have no interest in fucking my employees. I don't need to pay a woman to spread her legs."

Her eyes found the floor. I leaned forward, dropping my elbows to my knees to find her downcast face.

"Are we clear?"

"Yes." Her jaw tensed as she nodded. "Now let me be clearer, I don't spread my legs, Smith."

I couldn't keep myself from grinning. Some men disliked a sharp tongue. I enjoyed the sting.

"I would be disappointed if you did," I said simply, surprising myself. "Regardless, it's a nonissue."

It was far from a nonissue. She wasn't trying to warn me away, she was attempting to convince herself. The flush on her cheeks had crept down her neck and blossomed over the swell of her breasts. She bit her lip, as if she was also picturing my mine sweeping over her collarbone and brushing up the curve of her neck until my own teeth sank into her plump lower lip.

Belle cleared her throat, effectively bringing us both back to reality. I lounged into the corner of the couch, shifting my leg so that it bumped against her knee. She shuffled the papers and sucked in a breath, but she didn't move. Our legs stayed pressed close, separated by the silk of her stockings and my wool slacks, but I could feel the heat radiating off of her.

The trouble was that Belle Stuart didn't want to sleep with me. She wanted to be taken. She wanted to be fucked hard. Her whole body screamed for it, but until her head caught up with the rest of her, I'd be happy to continue this little game of foreplay. And there was the fact that she'd been hired to assist me. Sex would complicate that. It would also break my only rule when it came to women: no strings. I preferred quick, clean one-night stands or a carefully screened escort. This woman was currently signing a contract that legally bound us together. It was almost as bad as marriage. Better to keep my distance.

I stood and noticed the room immediately felt cooler, but I loosened my tie anyway. There was no need to be completely formal around her. It would set a strange precedent. My last assistant had brought me my coffee in bed each morning. I chuckled as I considered the uppity Ms. Stuart having to bring me breakfast. She was going to appreciate that I slept nude, and I was going to enjoy her trying to hide her excitement.

"Is something funny?" she asked, her body turning to follow my movement as I crossed the office.

"A lark." I waved my hand dismissively. "Nothing important."

"I love a good joke." She called my bluff, tilting her head to watch me.

I opened my desk drawer and drew out a small white box. "I'm still deciding on the punch line."

"You're easily amused then."

"Hardly." I returned to her and held out the box. "It's merely that the subject fascinates me."

"Perhaps we share a common interest." Her hand skimmed over mine as she took it from me. Cool and soft—the velvet touch of a woman.

My cock stirred, drawing my mind to thoughts of that delicate hand wrapping around it. "I feel certain we do."

"But you still won't share." Each word was pointed—laced with a meaning that I understood instinctively. Whatever was passing between us was primal. An undeniable force of nature pulled us toward one another. I needed to shove my dick in her and fuck her until she was full of me. And she needed to be taken, held down—possessed.

Instead I waited as she lifted open the lid to reveal a new phone.

"I have a phone," she said, even as her fingers traced the champagne gold frame.

I'd chosen correctly. Even if she was going to pretend to be obstinate, it was obvious she liked it. Something had told me Belle liked the small touches—the hint of luxury. She was a woman with taste.

"This phone is for me. Only I will have the number, and you will keep it with you at all times."

"What's next? Are you going to take me home and chain me to your wall?" she asked in a flat voice, shoving it toward me.

Belle's slender neck collared and chained. It was going to prove difficult to hide my erection if she kept planting ideas like that in my head. Too late. I took a small step behind the couch, forcing her to swivel around. The tufted back wasn't nearly high enough to hide my rock hard dick.

She kept her hand thrust in the air, but I shook my head. "May I ask you a question?"

"Obviously."

Jesus, she was even sexy when she pouted.

"Why take this job if you so obviously loathe me?"

Her pretty little mouth fell open. "I don't...I'm not sure why...I don't even know you."

"And yet you've made plenty of assumptions," I pointed out. "You assume I want to sleep with you. You assume I think you're a prostitute."

"I didn't say that—"

"Actually you did."

"Correct me if I'm wrong, but you want a beautiful woman hanging off your arm." Her arms folded over her chest.

"It's nice to see a woman with confidence. Men grow tired of pretty girls acting ignorant of their looks. I don't dispute that's the case, but I also hired you because you're Oxford educated, are well-bred, and more than capable of meeting my demanding schedule. Or am I wrong about those things?" I asked, savouring the opportunity to call her out.

"I am all of those things." She stood and snatched the phone from me. "And much more. I simply don't want to be an expensive accessory."

"I assure you that I'll work you hard." I didn't bother to keep the insinuation out of my voice. "Harder than you've ever experienced before."

"I look forward to the challenge," she breathed.

Christ, did she have any sense of self-preservation? She'd spent the last half hour dangling herself like meat over the lion's den and poking the beast when it came near. She was lucky not to have been eaten alive. It was all I could do not to pounce.

"A driver will pick you up in the morning." I wanted to step closer to her—to see what she would do when she was riled up—but the sofa provided a solid barrier. I'd never been so grateful to a piece of furniture before.

"About that. I can take the Tube or catch a cab. I'm not certain a driver is necessary."

"I decide what's necessary." I ignored her protest. She'd learn soon enough that I wasn't one to make requests.

Her eyes narrowed, but her mouth clamped shut. It was a shame actually. I quite liked when it was open.

"Anything else?" she snapped, rounding the couch. She jerked her purse over her shoulder and stared me down.

"Yes. Keep your phone on."

Flashing me a fake smile, she pivoted and marched out of the room.

A breath I didn't know I'd been holding released, and I lumbered back to my desk. Sinking into my chair, I stared at the door she'd just walked through. Her perfume still hung in the air. Hiring her was a mistake. I knew that now. This was proving to be less a game than a test. One I was certain I was failing. I'd seen her file. I knew exactly why she was erecting a barrier between us. I'd always been able to do the same. She wasn't the first attractive woman I'd hired for this position. All of them had eventually offered themselves to me, and I'd refused each of them.

But I had no doubt that if Belle had wagged her finger, I'd have had her pinned to the wall five seconds later. Keeping this professional might prove impossible so long as my thoughts continued to center around breaking her. I wanted to dismantle her walls until I freed the wild creature she had locked away. I wouldn't be satisfied until I claimed her.

Which was why I never could.

I slid open my desk drawer and drew out a picture frame. Running a flannel cloth over the glass, I stared into the eyes looking back at me. They were so alive, so bright.

"Why haven't I fired her?" I asked the photo, but no one responded.

No one ever did.

CHAPTER FOUR

She moaned as I pushed her legs open, her teeth biting into her full bottom lip. Nice and slow—that's what she deserved. But as I sank inside her, burying myself deeper, my pace quickened until I was slamming into her. God, she felt fucking amazing. I wanted to tell her that, but there was no way she'd hear me over her screams. This was where I belonged. I knew that now.

Slipping my arm around her waist, I flipped her over, eager to get a view from behind. Instead, I jolted awake, drenched in sweat and facedown in my sheets. Alone. It was only a dream. The realization was as unwelcome as my empty bed. My hands fisted into the feather pillow over my head, ready to rip it apart in frustration. Immediately a sharp sting prickled through my palm. I fumbled for the remote I kept on my bedside table and hit the button to draw the curtains. Light seeped in as the blackout drapes that kept the room in absolute darkness automatically opened. The hollow shaft of a feather had poked through the pillow casing. I plucked it out and stared for a moment at its downy tuft. Softness with a hint of pain. There was a certain poetry to it. I blew it into the air. Then found my mobile on the nightstand.

SMITH: Coffee. Black. Garrison will pick you up in five minutes in front of your flat.

We hadn't discussed important items like my morning coffee yesterday, or what time I expected her at my house each morning. Personally, I'd been too distracted by wanting to fuck her. Now I didn't have coffee, and I still wanted to fuck her. I groaned as I rolled over, liberating the rock hard erection I'd awoken to. Maybe it was better that she hadn't been here to wake me up this morning. Then again, it was a shame not to put this to good use.

BELLE: Do you have any idea what time it is?

SMITH: Time for coffee.

My free hand stroked my shaft as I responded. There was no way I was getting off this easily. The only cure for morning wood was a warm pussy. Although I imagined her tight ass would do just as well.

BELLE: Tell this Garrison I'll be ready in twenty minutes.

SMITH: You have five.

BELLE: Go back to sleep and wake up on the right side of the bed.

I could hear the annoyance in her message. She definitely had the wrong stick up her ass. I had another one in mind. My cock twitched in agreement.

SMITH: Wake up and do your job.

BELLE: You can keep yourself occupied for half an hour.

I considered snapping a pic of my dick in hand to show her exactly how I would be occupying that half hour. It might actually get her here faster. Then again she might never show up at all. It was difficult to read her still. Generally that wasn't a problem I had around people, particularly women. It's what made me a good lawyer. I knew she wanted to fuck me. It was written all over her body. Of course, it shouldn't surprise me that she was going through a man-hating phase given the information the background check had revealed. It wasn't like I was going to be the man who would heal her, but that didn't mean I wouldn't help her rebound if I had the chance.

Thinking like that was going to get me into trouble.

In fact, I didn't need to be thinking about it all. She was my assistant. I'd never fucked assistants before. This was different. Our professional ties should reign me in, but I knew they wouldn't. If only I hadn't seen how responsive her body was during that interview. I was already imagining harnessing it—controlling it. Belle Stuart wouldn't be a simple fling. Not with the things I wanted to do to her.

Which is exactly why you need to take a cold shower.

I yanked the pillow from under my head and threw it across the room. Apparently I had a half hour to get my head—and my dick—under control.

She's a means to an end, I reminded myself as I started the water a few moments later. As long as I remembered that, I could keep myself from touching her. It was that simple.

"Who are you kidding?" I asked the empty bathroom. "It's that complicated."

Then I turned the heat down a few more notches and stepped inside.

CHAPTER FIVE

I needed to quit this job. That much was already clear. Smith Price might get his rocks off on ordering me around, but there was no way I was going to let him. The trouble was that I needed this job and its completely ludicrous salary.

The salary page from yesterday's contracts floated to mind. So many zeroes behind that two.

Okay, so I couldn't quit. Not yet. A few months of putting up with his bullshit, and I would have the capital I needed to finance my business plan. In the meantime, I would be setting up some clear boundaries, like more than a five-minute notice that he expected me dressed and ready to head out the door.

Jane appeared in her doorway and rubbed the back of her neck. "Starting this early? We shouldn't have had so much wine last night."

"Apparently I'm on call at all hours," I grumbled as I shoved bobby pins in my hair. There was no time to wash it. I had no intention of actually meeting my new driver outside in five minutes, but I didn't want to risk being later than ten minutes. Checks and balances. "I'm sorry I woke you up. Mr. Price needs his morning coffee in bed."

"A demanding man waiting for you in bed." Jane bit back a smile. "If you decide to quit, I'm available for the position."

I held up a finger in warning. "Don't. I'm not sleeping with him."

"That's a pity," she said with a yawn, "because you need to get laid."

"I'm not justifying that with a response." I planted a kiss on her cheek as I swooped past her.

"Have a lovely morning," she called out, her voice tinged with amusement.

I'm sure there were a lot of women who would jump at the chance to serve coffee to Smith Price in bed. They'd probably offer to serve him a lot more. I just didn't want to be one of them. Sex and Belle Stuart no longer mixed. I had a vibrator I wasn't afraid to use and a plan. Screwing Smith wasn't part of that equation.

But the site that greeted me at the door stopped me in my tracks. A sleek, silver Mercedes AMG idled in front of the building. Holy fuck, it was hot. I said a silent prayer that Smith hadn't been here to witness my reaction. He didn't need to know I had a penchant for luxury cars.

The driver side door opened and I braced myself. I half expected it to be Smith himself, come to drag me to his house to make him coffee. But the fiery red hair didn't belong to him. An unfamiliar face smiled in greeting.

"Garrison?" I asked, shouldering my purse as I fought to regain my composure.

"Miss." Garrison tilted his head in greeting and opened the back door.

I slid in, allowing my fingers to caress the buttery leather seats before I settled back. This car was power. And sex. Maybe it made me a gold digger, but I loved it.

"This is...nice," I said conversationally, aware that Garrison might be wondering if I was having some sort of fit in the back seat. "It's an AMG, right?"

"An AMG S-65. Mr. Price has excellent taste in cars." Garrison turned out slowly, making his way into the morning traffic of East London.

"Yes, he does," I murmured to myself. Expensive taste, inhuman good looks and an asshole to boot—it was the trifecta of hotness. And three big red flags. Smith Price was dangerous.

"Will you be requiring me for the rest of the day?" Garrison asked as we made our way toward Knightsbridge. I made a mental note to ask more about what area of law he practised as the houses grew larger.

"I don't know," I answered truthfully. "Do you drive Mr. Price?" I didn't think his excellency would want to be parted with his servant much today.

"Mr. Price drives his own car," Garrison informed me as he turned toward a gated drive. "I drive him to social functions in whatever car he puts me in. Today he asked me to pick you up in this car."

My thoughts jumbled together as I took in the house that loomed overhead. Maybe it was more than one flat. Surely, it was more than one flat. Deciding that, I was finally able to process Garrison's last statement.

"This isn't his personal car?" I asked in surprise.

Garrison shook his head as the gate opened to allow us entrance.

"I'm sorry. I assumed it was." It made sense that Smith would use a company to pick me up. I could only hope whatever Smith drove was somewhat less extravagant. I didn't want to think about riding shotgun with Smith manoeuvring a stick shift next to me. I might come on the spot.

"That's why I asked if you would require me the rest of the day." Garrison's kind eyes caught mine in the rearview mirror. "Mr. Price would prefer that your car be garaged privately overnight."

"My car? I don't have a car," I informed him.

"This is your car. Mr. Price acquired it yesterday," Garrison continued as if this wasn't a complete bombshell. "I will pick you up and drive you home each day. It's up to you if you would prefer I drive you throughout the day. He keeps me on retainer, so I will be available when you decide."

"I'll be sure to let you know," I managed to squeak. My car? I might have to have a few minutes alone with it in the garage. I shook my head, recovering some composure as Garrison pulled up next to a black Bugatti Veyron. One of just over four hundred models in the world. I ogled it as the driver popped out and opened the door for me. Smith and I clearly had one thing in common.

"The lift is to your right." He gestured to the side of the private garage.

"Thank you." My head was still swimming when I reached it and realized I had no idea where I was going. "Um, which flat is Mr. Price's?"

Garrison's eyebrows knit together. "This is his house, Miss. Kitchen's on the lower ground floor. His bedroom is on the second."

"Of course. That's what I meant." I beamed at him, wondering just how big of an idiot he thought I was.

A Mercedes for his assistant. A Bugatti for himself. And a house roughly the size of Harrods. I'd known a few lawyers in my lifetime. They didn't make this kind of money. Maybe I should ditch the business plan and go back to law school, I thought as I stepped out of the lift into the entrance hall. I'd been in palaces for heaven's sake, but this place was impressive. Traditional eighteenth century architecture blended with crisp, clean decor. Grey marble complimented the modern furniture. I dropped the keys Garrison had given me on an empty console table that stretched the length of the foyer. It was the opposite of his office. How many faces did Smith Price have, and which one hid the real man?

Now if I could just find the kitchen.

As it turned out, the coffee maker was the one item that was easy to find once I'd located the kitchen. It was the only item on his granite counter. I stared at it for a moment, wondering how to work the Impressa espresso maker.

"Use the auto mode. I'll teach you how to pull a proper shot sooner or later," a gruff voice instructed me.

I spun on my heels and nearly dropped the mug I was holding. I'd been worried about keeping my hands to myself when I brought

Smith coffee in bed. Now I would give anything to have him tucked under his covers. It seemed infinitely...safer.

Apparently Smith had occupied himself in the shower, and now he stood before me with a towel hanging loosely on his hips. Damp hair had fallen across his forehead, dripping down his face. Smith pushed it back with one hand, the other tightening over knotted fabric at his waist. Drops of water glistened over his broad shoulders and chest. Chiseled abs tapered into narrow hips. I'd guessed he was powerfully built when he was fully clothed, but I had no idea how much. He watched me, his eyes smoldering with a raw authority that unnerved me. He was temptation in a towel—a masculine trap that sent prurient thoughts flooding through me.

I had to push the brew button four times before I actually hit it. I was pretty certain I looked like I was drunk. My first official day of work was going to consist of confusion and incompetence. Fabulous.

Smith accepted the coffee without comment when I passed it to him a minute later. He cupped the mug with both hands, allowing his towel to hang suggestively off his hips.

Do not look at his abs, I ordered myself even as my eyes drifted to the perfect slab of muscles on display.

"Is your car acceptable?" he asked after he took a long, slow sip.

"Yes-s-s," I stammered. "Um, actually, I'm a little confused about that."

His eyebrow raised as he took another drink.

"When you say my car..." I trailed away as embarrassment overtook me. I'd had a proper British upbringing, which meant I'd been taught never to talk about money. Or ask questions, for that matter. I'd had no problem eschewing those rules until today. Now I twisted my fingers together and hoped he wouldn't make me continue.

"The car is part of your compensation package," Smith explained with a shrug.

The nonchalance with which he responded bolstered my confidence. "Daily transportation is part of my compensation package."

He smirked. "You're not driving my car."

My thoughts flashed to the sports car in the garage.

"The Bugatti?" I guessed.

"Yes," he said, surprise flitting over his features. He was impressed. "Need I say more regarding the possibility of you driving it?"

Not impressed enough.

"Maybe someday you'll trust me enough to change your mind on that," I countered.

"There's no one I trust that much." He took a step closer, bringing his nearly naked body too close for comfort. "But I'll take you for a ride."

Smith Price needed to be schooled on where I stood on cars—and him. "As long as you drive in manual, I'll consider. I'm not a girl who rides an automatic."

Smith's eyebrow cocked up at my blatant double entendre.

Oh God, I was flirting with him. Shamelessly flirting with him. So much for keeping my thing for cars under wraps. I might as well have stripped naked and climbed into his back seat as an offering.

Smith rubbed a hand over the stubble on his chin. "Let me get dressed, and I'll show you around. You'll need to know the entire house for when we have guests."

There was that we again. I couldn't quite figure out if this was standard personal assistant fare or if I'd been hired to play house. "You know a wife might be a cheaper option for you."

Lightning flashed across his green eyes, a fleeting thunderstorm of anger that was quickly replaced by calm. "Until she divorced me and took half of it."

"I believe that's why they have pre-nups." I crossed my arms over my chest and took a step away from him. This wasn't the first time Smith had displayed a volatile mood swing. At least, it had passed quickly. "But I'm not a lawyer."

"You seem intent on proving yourself unnecessary to me, Belle," he said, bypassing my jibe.

That wasn't my intention at all. Or was it? Why was everything so confusing in the presence of Smith Price? "You haven't fired me yet."

"Yet," he repeated with meaning.

My attitude hadn't gone unnoticed it seemed. Well, then I figured he was also aware of how often he was flirting with me, or rather, sexually harassing me. It was best to think of it in those terms. Flirtation was too welcome a concept.

"Follow me." He motioned toward the lift.

I stared at him, trying to comprehend. I couldn't handle Smith giving me the grand tour in that towel. "I thought you were going to get dressed."

"I am, but we have things to discuss. You'll find there isn't much downtime in my life. I already wasted half an hour waiting for my coffee."

"Maybe next time you could get up and make it yourself. You seem to know how." I shrugged but forced the haughty smirk on my face into a false smile.

"Don't do that," he ordered in a stern voice, catching my elbow and tugging apart my still crossed arms.

I swallowed hard and forced myself to be honest. "I tend to be a little snarky when I'm nervous."

"No, not the snark. Don't force yourself to smile. I didn't hire you to be a puppet. Although I would request a little less of the biting remarks in the presence of clients." His tone had softened, and my heart did a strange leap.

"I'm sure I won't be nervous then at all," I said dryly.

"Do you drink wine?" he asked as we stepped into the lift.

"Um, yes." Apparently we were changing floors and topics.

"Then I'll have some brought up from my private stock. You should have a glass or two before client dinners to help ease your nerves." Smith lounged against the mirrored glass of the lift.

Drinking around him seemed like a very bad idea, but I kept that to myself and nodded, determined to contain some of my snark. What I couldn't quite ignore was the way his towel had split open in the front, revealing too much of a muscular thigh. An inch or two higher and the towel would become obsolete. Smith crossed his legs, breaking the spell, and I looked sheepishly back up at him. A crooked grin carved across his face.

Suddenly the lift felt too small, as if it was closing in on me, pushing me closer and closer to him. I locked my legs into place and hoped for a miracle that didn't include me pinned against the control panel. His head tilted, studying me, and then he slowly licked his lower lip.

In that moment I had no doubt what he could do with those lips, and more than ever before, I wanted to find out. I needed to know how that tongue would taste in my mouth and what it would feel like on my skin—how it would feel between my legs. I took one step closer just as the lift dinged and the doors slid open.

"After you." He held an arm out past the door to prevent it from closing. The gesture did nothing to allay the steady pulse growing in my core. There was a promise in his words—a knowingness that hinted at an intimacy we hadn't yet shared but would.

I did my best to brush it off as I exited into a plush hallway.

Smith led me through a set of French doors into the master suite.

"Excuse me." He sauntered across the room to another door. My gaze followed the swagger of his hips. The towel was even more low-slung now, showcasing his taut back and perfectly carved tailbone. I nearly followed him through the closet door.

Instead I hung back until he reemerged carrying a slate grey suit and a precisely folded oxford. He laid them across the bed then tossed two ties on top.

"Choose one," he instructed me before he disappeared into the attached en suite.

I could no longer see him, despite the fact that the door was wide open. Forcing myself to get a grip, I picked up the silk ties and turned them over in my hands. The differences were subtle. Both blue. A slightly checked pattern to one, a thin red threading artfully embroidered in the other. I wrapped them around my hands, savouring the smoothness of the fabric. The strangest desire to press them to my lips came over me, but I threw one down and stepped away before I gave in to the urge.

A low buzzing vibrated from the loo as Smith called out, "Do you have your phone?"

I stepped closer, trying to hear him over the sound of the electric shaver. Movement caught the corner of my eye, and I realized he was now visible through the crack of the door. When I saw the towel puddled around his feet, I wanted to look away. Instead I drank in the pronounced curve of his ass matched along with the muscular arch of his thigh. He shifted, revealing more of his groin and the carved v that pointed down to the top of a dark patch of hair and the very root of his shaft.

I stumbled back and pressed a hand to my chest before he noticed me staring.

He called out again.

"Yes," I responded, mentally berating myself for peeping on my boss. Then again, he was the one who invited me into his bedroom.

Not a good reason! the persistent voice in my head screamed.

"We have a dinner tomorrow at seven."

Typing while in heat turned out to be more difficult than I expected. My fingers kept finding the wrong buttons, but I finally got it in the calendar on my mobile.

"We're running later than I thought," he continued, "so I'll show you around the house tomorrow morning. Can you be here with my coffee at seven-thirty?"

Was that actually a request? "Yes."

"This afternoon, I'll have you copy my date book for your own reference. Doris will see that you're listed on my important accounts." He strode through the bathroom door a moment later.

The only thing that registered was the lack of towel.

And wow.

He walked into the closet and returned slipping into a pair of black boxer briefs, seemingly oblivious to the fact that he was on display. I needed to look away. I couldn't be sure, but I was pretty certain staring at your boss's dick—his beautiful, perfect dick—on the first day on the job sent the wrong message. Then again, it would be an injustice to the female race if I didn't look. It hung low, brushing several inches down his thigh.

God, if it looked like that right now—

A warning bell rang in my head, cutting me off from that line of thinking. Nothing good would come out of it, although someone would probably come of it.

I blurted out the first question that came to mind. "What do I wear?"

"Come again," Smith said as the briefs slipped over his hips.

Good job, Belle. Mention clothes while he's naked. That's not obvious at all. "Tomorrow. What do I wear for dinner tomorrow? Is it formal? Cocktail?"

"Don't worry about it." He wandered closer to me and my breath caught. He'd seen me watching, and there was no way I was going to put up a fight. The only thoughts racing through my mind were whether to start on the bed or the floor. But he brushed past me and picked up his dress shirt. His fingers nimbly undid the buttons, and he slipped it over his broad shoulders.

"I need to know what to wear. If I show up in cowboy boots, no amount of wine will save me from my nerves." I planted my fists on my hips and stared him down.

"We have an appointment at Harrods tomorrow at ten sharp. I'll pick something out then."

Not this again. "I actually have an excellent wardrobe."

Smith turned on me, and before I could process it, his hand had covered the one on my hip. He tugged slightly, and I stumbled forward breathless—waiting—until he released me. He held up the second tie. I'd forgotten I had it wadded in my fist.

"I think I'll wear this one," he said in a low voice that shivered over my skin. "You have delicious taste, Belle. But given your financial portfolio, I imagine you don't have the latest pieces. We need to look like we're doing well at all times."

This time I ignored the we and went straight to the point. "My financial portfolio? You've been looking at my bank statements."

"And your debt," he said. "It's standard. I need to know who I'm getting in bed with—metaphorically speaking."

So he knew I was broke. Was that why he chose me? Because he knew I was desperate enough to do anything he asked? Worse yet, did he think I was desperate enough to sleep with him?

"I don't think any less of you," he added as if he could read my mind. "Most recent graduates have debt."

I didn't want to press the issue. I had no idea how far he had looked into my personal circumstances. Obviously he would know that I hadn't been gainfully employed previously. He would know about the engagement to Philip. He'd already admitted to knowing I had a relationship with Clara and Edward. It was a perfectly reasonable thing for a prospective employer to do a background check, but that didn't stop my stomach from tying into knots.

But there was one thing I needed to be clear about. "I don't want charity."

"I'm not offering it." He looped the tie around his neck and crossed it. "I told you I would work you hard."

Somehow I still suspected there was a double meaning there, but all I said was, "good."

"Did I choose correctly?"

It took me a moment to realize he was talking about the tie. My hand reached out absently and smoothed it down. Even through the layers, I could feel the hardness of his body underneath. "I chose."

"Ah yes. Beauty's privilege." His eyes sparked as he spoke, and I sensed he was looking past the words we exchanged and the few moments we had shared, searching for a place I'd locked away.

I turned away, afraid to let him find it.

CHAPTER SIX

Belle stood at my bedroom window, enveloped in the first light of dawn. The warmth of it wrapped around her, making her porcelain skin glow pink. Her simple ivory sheath dress hugged her body, revealing her slight curves. The ensemble was relatively chaste, if suggestive, save for the leopard print heels she'd chosen—yet another sign of a wild side that she tried to hide. As she stared, her expression changed from fascination to sadness. I still couldn't read her. She remained an enigma, but part of me empathized with the sudden bouts of melancholy that seemed to color her world.

I cleared my throat politely, not wanting to scare her. "Good morning."

She spun around to greet me, a look of relief crossing her face. "Oh, you're dressed!"

Had she hoped I wouldn't be? Was she as preoccupied with what was beneath my clothes as I was with what was beneath hers? Her gaze swept over me appreciatively. She liked suits, and I had a fucking closet full of them.

"We have lots to do today." I pointed to a coffee mug sitting on my bedside table. "Is that for me?"

"No, it's for me. I thought I'd drag myself across the city to make myself coffee." She rolled her eyes as she picked up the cup and brought it to me.

"Not a fan of coffee?"

A slight grin played at her lips, but she held it back. "I'm a Brit. I drink tea."

"I suppose us Scots are less discriminating," I said, before taking a hesitant sip. I hadn't been there to oversee her use of the machine.

"I didn't poison it." She twisted her hands, undermining her antagonistic facade.

She wanted to please me, even if she pretended otherwise. Things were getting interesting.

"It's good," I reassured her. "Precisely to my preference."

"Black coffee isn't that hard." She shook her head with a disapproving sigh.

"I suppose you take your tea with milk and sugar?"

"You suppose correctly. Do you find that repulsive?"

"No. I might bring you tea one morning." I made a mental note to have my housekeeper pick up bags.

She cast a dubious glance at me but said nothing.

"Let's get on with the tour," I snapped. Since she didn't respond to kindness, there was no point in operating under false pretenses. We both seemed to prefer when I was an asshole.

"Shall we start at the bottom?" she suggested.

Beautiful, you're staying bottom, I thought. Outwardly, I jerked my head and strode toward the lift, pleased that she had to run to catch me. You have no idea how hard it's going to be to keep up with me.

As soon as the lift doors shut, the space contracted and I had to inhale deeply.

She eyed me in concern. "Are you okay?"

"I'm fine," I replied in a clipped tone. I kept my gaze and thoughts on her tits until the doors slid back open.

Belle darted out and headed into the garage—the only area she was familiar with. I didn't bother to correct her. Instead I headed left, banking into a hallway. She didn't like to be told what to do. I appreciated that in a woman, but she needed to learn that I was the one in control.

"Where are we going?" she demanded when she finally caught up to me.

I smirked but didn't stop to acknowledge her. "On the tour."

"I thought maybe you would take me for that ride in the Veyron." She took a step closer, crossing her arms behind her back and drawing attention to her breasts.

A simpering request. Well-played. I'd been impressed that she knew the make and model of my personal car yesterday. This morning's initiative sealed what I already suspected.

I turned on her. "You like cars."

"I guess," she hedged, but it was written all over her body—flushed cheeks, quick, shallow breaths. Unrestrained lust practically dripped off her. She ran her tongue over her lower lip, leaving her sinfully red lipstick glistening while proving my point. An image of her mouth closing over my cock flashed to mind.

"You do." I stepped closer, noting how her body shifted toward mine. "I said I'd take you for a ride. Now you have to earn it."

I walked away, leaving her panting in the hall. Surreptitiously, I adjusted my hard-on before opening the door at the end of the passage. I could fuck her right here. Or take her back to the garage and screw her against the Bugatti. She'd like that. There'd be no fight. That car was a guaranteed leg-spreader. There would also be no chase—and I loved the pursuit.

I chose to start with my least favorite feature of the house. The faint aroma of chlorine seeped through the open door as I showed her my private lap pool. The smell made my stomach roil. but I'd learned to ignore that.

"You have a swimming pool?" she shrieked.

Despite myself, I grinned at her enthusiasm. "It was added in the seventies. You're welcome to use it."

We continued our progress through the house, which somehow felt more extravagant with Belle struck silent with awe at my side. I'd never looked at the property as anything more than a showpiece—a relic meant to project a familial grandeur that never was. Now I couldn't help seeing it through her eyes.

"We need to purchase some art," Belle said, noting the bare walls that accompanied most floors.

I allowed a tight smile. Perhaps I was being too encouraging of her enthusiasm. "I recently painted. I prefer an uncluttered space."

"That's a shame. This place is practically a gallery." She spoke wistfully as her eyes continued to scan the blank space. "Maybe—"

"Out here is the garden," I interrupted her. Watch out for the hole I'm currently digging myself into.

She took the hint and lapsed back into silence. My gaze darted to her periodically as I continued the tour. Her initial shock over my house had dissipated. I'd assumed that she'd been in grander estates, given the company she kept. Her amazement had been directed at me. No doubt she'd begin to ask unwanted questions soon.

On the third floor, I ushered her through a cluster of guest rooms.

"Does anyone actually use these?"

"My housekeeper sees they're kept fresh." It wasn't exactly a lie. Mrs. Andrews did dust and change the sheets purely out of compulsion. Most of the rooms hadn't been slept in for years.

"Do you have guests stay often?" Once again Belle seemed psychically in tune with my inner thoughts. I couldn't deny her mysterious insight made her more alluring. Perhaps that's why I kept her around. I was hoping to discover the trick behind the magic.

"Very rarely." I opened a door at the end of the hall. "This is your bedroom."

"My bedroom?"

I couldn't resist. "Unless there's another room you'd prefer to sleep in."

"I have a flat," she said, bypassing my insinuation.

"Believe me, I'm not asking you to move in." I couldn't think of anything I wanted less in the world. Mrs. Andrews nagged me enough during the hours we were both on premises. Two ladies of the house would be untenable. "There will be times when I need you until very late or I require you here very early. You may choose to use this room on those occasions if you prefer."

Belle stepped inside the suite and pivoted slowly around, taking it in. The room was decorated in hues of champagne, from the creamy silk curtains to the oversized king bed made up with a golden coverlet. Sunlight shimmered across the gilded damask wallpaper. It was an elegant space—understated while still opulent. She belonged here.

"There's a private bath attached." I motioned to a door in the corner. "You may keep anything you wish here."

"I'll consider your offer," she said as she exited. She paused in the corridor, her attention focused directly across from her on the only closed door in the hall. "Another guest room?"

I didn't look at the room "No."

She walked past me and jiggled the handle. "Locked?"

"I prefer that room remains undisturbed." I gestured toward the hall we had come down, trying to ignore the faint memories forcing themselves to the front of my mind.

"What's in there?" she pushed.

"Nothing that concerns you," I snarled.

"You've made it pretty clear that I need to know everything about your life, so I can only assume you keep your murder weapons in here!" She huffed as she finished her rant, waiting for me to respond.

I stalked away, laughing humorlessly at her suggestion.

"The tour's over," I called over my shoulder as I dashed off a list on my mobile. "I'm sending you a to-do list. Finish it and meet me at Harrods at ten sharp."

"Yes, sir," she hissed.

Sir. I'd pressed her buttons. "Garrison will drive—"

"I can drive myself," she yelled.

I knew she could, because she'd been driving me crazy since we met. "I don't care who drives you. Just leave."

"Gladly." Her tone was flat as she pushed past me and smacked the button for the lift.

She entered it and turned to glare at me. Neither of us made a move to prevent the doors from sliding closed. I stayed there, eyes transfixed on the lift. I was caught in limbo. All it would have taken was one act to move forward and away from the ghosts lingering at the end of this hall. I couldn't turn to face them and I couldn't walk away. Belle had seen that, but she didn't understand it. She never could.

I wouldn't let her.

CHAPTER SEVEN

I stepped through the glass door of Harrods and breathed in the familiar smell. Some people might not believe shoes and designer dresses had a scent, but they did. The rich aroma of soft-grain leather and linen mixed with floral notes from the department store's display of fine teas and the perfume counters. With any luck, I had a little credit on my account and could pick out a treat to celebrate my new job. I hadn't charged anything for months, not since I'd found myself suddenly single. But surviving my first days working for Smith Price deserved a reward.

Before the glass door had shut behind me, a woman swooped over, dressed in an unapologetically plum dress suit that matched her lipstick. A large Harrods' badge pinned to her lapel read Harriet. She offered me a tentative smile. "Miss Stuart?"

I froze in place before nodding.

"I've been waiting for you." The hesitancy in her expression vanished, replaced by a warmer, if slightly less than genuine, smile.

"I must be later on paying my charge account than I thought if you're meeting me at the door."

"What?" she asked, the joke whizzing right over her smooth black hair. She tilted her chin, as if to puzzle me out.

"I usually don't get met by name at the door somewhere unless I'm in trouble." I tried to sound light-hearted, but inside my stomach churned. There had been a time when I was met at restaurants and parties by people eager to introduce themselves. Or rather to meet Philip's fiancée. That time had passed.

"Oh! Nothing like that!" Her polite laugh tinkled like a bell—too high and practiced. She'd obviously been working here a long time. "Mr. Price informed us you would be arriving."

"Did he send over my mug shot?"

"You're so funny." She batted my arm as if we were lifelong friends.

I hated her already.

"Mr. Price described you—in perfect detail, I must say." Winking at me, she motioned for me to follow her toward the lift. "You're quite lucky to have a man who is so attentive."

"He's my boss," I said flatly, even though butterflies fluttered in my stomach as I spoke.

That revelation shut her up, and we enjoyed a blissful silence as the lift carried us to the fifth floor. The opening of the doors broke the magic spell, and she began to chatter again. Something about starting with the base pieces and building toward ensembles. I stopped listening to her. I had more important things on my mind.

Smith Price had described me in perfect detail. What did that mean? My height and build? Any stranger could do that. But I had hardly been the first petite blonde to walk through Harrods' doors this morning. He had to have told her more.

"Excuse me," I said, interrupting her blather about the rising importance of proper stockings. "How did Mr. Price describe me?"

She paused as if to recall. "I believe he referenced you as a sophisticated blonde. About eight stone with a 32B breast size. He also guessed you'd be wearing Louboutins."

This circus trick obviously impressed her, but it only surprised me. He'd perfectly sized me up, down to noticing my shoes.

"Of course, he didn't know they were Louboutins. He mentioned the red sole," she continued, adding, "He did ask that we pull a selection. I was truly sorry when I told him we didn't carry them."

"Me too." I didn't know what else to say. Not with my head swimming over the fact that Smith had been so attentive. Then again, after yesterday's show in his bedroom, I could guess his shirt size...amongst other things.

Harriet led me past the front desk of the Penthouse, where By Appointment, Harrods personal shopping service, was housed, to a private fitting room. Sleek leather armchairs clustered around a large turquoise ottoman, and against the wall not one rack, but three racks of clothing waited. They must have pulled every piece in my size that the store had. This was hardly the first time I had been to Harrods, but it was the first time I was treated like royalty—and I'd been here before with Clara.

"Does Mr. Price do this often?" I asked. The whole spectacle smacked of the sort of privilege afforded to wealthy men that readily flashed their wallets.

"I've never worked with him before, but my manager was very clear on Mr. Price's expectations. She was also clear that we meet them all."

Enough said. Then again, I'd thrown on clothes yesterday to attend him on a whim. Smith Price might simply be a man who got what he wanted.

Except me.

I wandered over to the racks, brushing my fingers across the silky fabrics. Shopping had been a luxury I couldn't afford the last few months after cutting up Philip's credit cards. Although he'd left me with a stocked closet in addition to my broken heart, I had grown tired of window shopping. Enough so that I'd hatched a business idea. A company that catered to women with tastes that exceeded their bank accounts. Women like me.

A tag snagged against my palm, and I flipped it over absent-mindedly. My mouth fell open when I saw the price. There was taste like mine and then there was taste like Smith Price's. I shouldn't be shocked given that I'd seen his house, but even I had never spent such an extravagant amount on a piece of clothing.

"Did he give you parameters?" I tucked the obscene price tag inside the neckline, unable to look at it.

"The most expensive pieces from our top lines," Harriet answered as she joined me. She pushed apart the gowns to reveal the one I'd just stumbled upon. I glanced over to tell her to take it away and spotted him. Harriet rattled off more particulars, but I didn't hear her.

Smith was in the doorway, his eyes studying me intently. He'd looked at me this way each time we met, as if I was a puzzle he was trying to lock into place. Or maybe he was hoping to fill a certain open slot. I turned back to the racks, my face burning. I told myself it was embarrassment that a man I barely knew thought I needed a new wardrobe. But that wasn't it. The heat I felt had nothing to do with my emotions. No, it came from somewhere deeper—a place I'd sealed away with my own psychological chastity belt.

I sensed him behind me before he spoke, his presence silently urging me to step back and close the space between us. It took a record-breaking amount of willpower not to do just that.

"Belle." He said my name softly, as though he was tasting it.

Closing my eyes, I took a steadying breath before I turned to greet him. "I thought you said ten sharp."

"A client needed a moment of my time." The answer was final and more than a tad bit dismissive.

"That reminds me." I switched the topic to business, eager to clear the tension in the air. "Exactly what area of law do you practice?"

"The gray area," he replied in a clipped tone.

A tingle danced up my spine. Suddenly the house, the cars, the extravagance made a little more sense. Terrible people needed lawyers who could be paid to look the other way. Before I could attach judgment to this revelation, I realized I was no better than he was. Not while I worked for him.

"Will you require a model, or do you want to try on the garments personally?" Harriet broke in. This time I was grateful for her obliviousness.

"She'll try them on," Smith decided for me.

It irked me that he'd made the call, even though I had the same preference. "Exactly what I was thinking."

"You two must have a wonderful working relationship," Harriet gushed.

I grabbed something from the rack and dashed into the attached dressing room before I laughed. Tense? Yes. Awkward? Yes. Sexually volatile? Hell yes. But wonderful? No. I hung the dress on a hook and sank against the wall, staring at it. Simple, black but with a cut that made it something more than a little black dress. No, this was a statement. It was exactly the kind of thing I would pick out.

Harriet poked her head through the curtain. "May I?"

I waved her inside. She bustled in, carrying an armful of other options and began to place them on the rack in the corner of the space. Meanwhile I stripped down.

"Do you require any special undergarments?" Harriet asked.

"I think I'm fine," I said, allowing a little sarcasm to slip through.

I caught her glancing up in the mirror and surveying the validity of my claim. Her mouth fell open a little when she saw the Lucille London garter set I was wearing. Lingerie as distinctive as this had that effect regardless of gender or sexual preference. My lips curved a little in challenge, and she quickly looked away, busying herself with removing the black dress from the hanger.

Philip's bank account might have supplied my shopping habits, but he had personally supplied my lingerie drawer. Each week he'd brought me something new, dressing me up like a paper doll. My belly tightened at the memory as a wave of nausea rolled through me. I'd been his plaything while he'd bided his time waiting for Pepper Lockwood. Now I was expected to do the same thing for Smith. By the time Harriet had helped me into the dress and zipped up the back of it, I was fuming. I barely had the presence of mind to slip my heels back on before I strutted out.

If Smith Price wanted a show, I would give him one.

He looked up from the business section of The Globe as I came closer, his expression changing from distracted to keenly interested instantly.

Planting my hand on my hip, I turned for him and then flourished my arms. The dress had been little more than a fitted black sheath on the hanger, but it dipped low in the front, revealing the valley between my breasts. It was understated but very sexy. "Does this meet your approval, sir?"

Smith frowned and motioned for me to turn once more.

So that was how he was going to play it. I remained still and stared him down.

"Most women enjoy shopping," he said, his voice so cool that I shivered.

"I enjoy shopping," I spit out. "I don't enjoy being a toy."

"I needed to be present to make certain we were on the same page regarding your appearance, given how often you'll be accompanying me and, at times, representing me." Smith paused to let this sink in.

"You gave me that line before."

"Do you like this dress?" he asked.

"Yes, but—"

"Enough." Tossing his newspaper aside, he stood. He tipped his chin toward the corner of the room, and Harriet scurried over. "Miss Stuart desires a private shopping experience. Please place her purchases on my account."

"Of course," Harriet said, a bit too eagerly. But then her eyes darted over to me like she was being left with a rabid animal.

Was it so crazy for a girl to want to try things on and consider them by herself?

Smith reached for the suit jacket he'd laid over the back of his seat. He slipped it on, buttoning it over the matching charcoal vest. As he adjusted his cufflinks, I realized he was actually going to leave. Heat crept over my cheeks and across my chest. This had to be the tenth time I'd blushed in front of him. If I were smart I'd lay outside until I had a sunburn that might hide future instances.

"Wait," I blurted out.

He stopped a few steps from the door. "Yes?"

"Stay." I managed to force out the request despite the rapid pounding of my heart. "I get a little defensive when I feel like a charity case."

"And when you feel like a toy," he added, a thoughtful gleam in his green eyes.

Most of my life had been spent occupying one of those two roles. If I was going to strike out on my own I wanted another option. "Can you blame a girl?"

His jaw visibly tensed. It took a moment for me to realize he wasn't angry, he was trying not to smile.

Taking a deep breath, I crossed the room and stuck out my hand. "Let's start over."

"Why would we do that?" he asked.

"Because I've been provoking you since the moment we met," I admitted.

Smith took my outstretched hand, but he didn't shake it. Instead he drew me slowly to him, close enough that I felt the heat radiating from his body. I'd never been this close to him before. I caught faint traces of leather and bergamot on the air around me, forcing me to fight the urge to melt against him and breathe in his warm, rich scent. Smith leaned closer until his breath tickled my ear and whispered, "Continue to provoke me, beautiful. I like it. But you're wrong about one thing: I don't look at you as a toy. Although I should be so lucky to play with you."

My eyes closed involuntarily as my body took over, but he didn't pull me closer. I ached for him to, caught up in the irresistible draw of his presence.

"You've been fighting me. This. We both have, and it's for the best. We have a professional relationship," he continued quietly. "I don't know if you like me, Belle, but you shouldn't."

"Do you like me?" The question slipped effortlessly off my tongue. I didn't want it to matter. I wished it didn't.

"Very much. Too much." His thumb rubbed circles on my palm as he admitted it. "You're smart to keep me at a distance. Don't try to fix us. Do your work and keep hating me. Protect yourself."

"Or what?" I stepped away from him, jerking my hand free from his hypnotic touch.

"I might bite." He clicked his teeth on the final syllable. "Consider that a warning."

He nodded a farewell and disappeared out the door, leaving me to wonder if I should heed his advice or if he was trying to get under my skin. My gut had told me to stay away from him since the moment we met, but I couldn't deny my body had other ideas.

An hour later, I decided to give up. There was no way I could choose between the amazing pieces in here, especially with my head still spinning over Smith's warning. Dropping onto one of the plush chairs, I waited for Harriet, who'd insisted on bringing in a selection of accessories. The trill ring of my mobile shattered the temporary silence I'd been granted in her absence. I fished it from my purse, groaning when a picture of my mother flashed across the screen.

"Hello, Mum," I answered, knowing I couldn't dodge her any longer. Avoiding my mother was like trying to stay dry under water—completely impossible.

"Where are you at?" she asked suspiciously. "I hear music."

"A strip club. I got a new job."

"Don't be vulgar. It's not that kind of music." Her voice carried the weight of years of disappointment in it.

I sighed. "I'm at Harrods, Mother."

"Is that in our budget?" she asked. Budget had become my mother's favorite word since the death of my father.

"It's in my budget."

"Do not take that tone with me," she warned, and suddenly I was ten years old again. "I called because I heard about your new job. You hadn't mentioned it."

So much for keeping that a secret. I considered asking who had ratted me out, but she'd always been protective of her sources. I could only imagine she had an entire network of spies in the London area dedicated to the task of tracking and reporting my every move. "I just started, and honestly, I'm not sure it's going to work out."

"Not with that attitude."

Harriet bustled into the room, holding up a few different belts. I never thought I'd be happy to see her. "Mum, I need to go. The shopgirl is here."

"Come to the estate this weekend. We should discuss how this impacts Stuart Hall," she ordered, revealing the real reason she'd bothered to ring me in the first place.

"I think I have to work." That probably wasn't a lie. Over the last couple of days I'd gotten the impression that Smith expected me at his beck and call at all hours.

"What kind of job is this?" She didn't bother to hide the distaste in her voice. Considering she'd never held a position outside of wife and estate manager, it didn't surprise me. Even if it stung a little.

"I already told you: stripper."

"Belle!" Admonishment rang in her voice.

"Sorry, Mum, gotta go!" I hit the button to end the call and turned the ringer off, thankful she didn't have the number to the phone Smith had given me.

Yet.

Undoubtedly she would before the month was out. I smiled weakly at Harriet. "I'm not actually a stripper."

"I knew you were joking." But something in her voice told me she suspected I must be in some type of unsavory business. Perhaps she's misread today's dress-up session. "I've arranged to have your items delivered to your flat this afternoon. Will you be there to sign for it?"

"I won't be, but my aunt can sign for a delivery."

"Perfect. Have you decided?" she asked.

"Harriet, this has been the most tiring day of my life, and it's not even one in the afternoon. Choose for me. Everything is lovely. I'm certain it will be fine."

She raised her overly plucked eyebrow dubiously. "I'll see to it then."

Something told me that was going to be the last easy decision I made for a while.

CHAPTER EIGHT

Tonight was a test—an important one. Not only for my associates, but for me as well. No matter how much I liked Belle, if she couldn't be docile for one evening, I couldn't justify keeping her around. I'd given her enough slack as it was. It was obvious she was going to continue to ask question and push the limits. The issue was that I enjoyed it when she did.

She appeared at the building's entrance as soon as the Veyron parked. Determined to set the right tone for the evening, I climbed out of the car, rounding it to open the door for her. I stopped with my fingers on the handle.

I hadn't approved this dress. I would never approve this dress for an appearance outside my bedroom floor.

Silky white fabric clung to her exquisite body, fluttering down her legs, draping low between her breasts. Despite the gown's off-the-shoulder sleeves, there was nothing remotely reserved about this dress. It poured over her like creamy milk, highlighting the curves of her breasts and hips. Pert nipples poked through the thin fabric, and I knew with absolute certainty she didn't have a stitch on underneath. Her hair was tucked into a small knot at the nape of her neck. Other than dark lashes and red lips, she wore no makeup. She didn't have to. She was a walking wet dream.

Belle accepted my hand as I helped her into the passenger side of the Veyron, flinching slightly as I slammed the door shut behind her.

I was too pissed for words the entire way to the Carlton. I shifted hard, punching the paddles behind the steering wheel furiously as we zipped in and out of traffic. Belle held her tongue, but I got the sense she was enjoying having provoked me more than ever before. Why on earth had I told her to continue doing so?

Because you want a reason to punish her. There was no denying that was truth as my dick stiffened in my trousers. I wanted her over my knee with her smooth alabaster ass presented for my palm. But that was a desire I needed to keep in check. Our lifestyles were incompatible in more ways than one.

My cock hadn't come to the same conclusion by the time we pulled up to the valet stand. Getting out of the car, I buttoned my suit jacket, knowing it wouldn't remotely cover my bulge if anyone was looking.

"My message told you to wear something modest," I hissed in her ear as she pushed herself out of the car.

"You should have seen the other dress I considered." She smiled serenely at the valet, ignoring me. I passed the key fob to him, catching his sleeve before he could turn away.

"I know, I know," he said with an unimpressed groan. "Your car is worth more than my salary."

"That car is worth more than your life," I corrected him. I didn't bother to measure his response. I didn't care, so long as he knew where he stood in the pecking order.

"Somebody's concerned about the size of his dick tonight," Belle muttered as I held open the door for her.

Placing one hand on the small of her back, I guided her inside before leaning down to her ear. "That is one thing I never worry about, beautiful."

And Christ, she was as beautiful as her name advertised tonight. The dress was revealing—too revealing, given the company we were keeping this evening—but it skimmed softly down her body, rippling over her toned thighs with each step she took. Upright, the neckline was less risqué. I just had to make sure no men stood over her this evening, which meant marking her as my own. The fact that she was my assistant might have been a boundary to the rest of our party until she showed up looking like forbidden fruit.

The silky fabric felt like nothing under my palm. My hand was warm, but she stiffened the moment I made contact before relaxing into my touch. Her reaction pleased me a bit too much.

"Anything else?" she asked under her breath. "Should I only speak when spoken to?"

"If you're going to behave like a child then I suppose so."

The maître d' bent toward the back of her chair, but I stepped in front of him and pulled it out. Belle didn't speak as I greeted the others already present. She nodded and shook hands as I introduced a half dozen people to her. When I finally took my seat beside her, I reached for my napkin and came up empty-handed. Belle dangled it in the air between us. Turning I took it, temporarily mesmerized by the radiance of her smile. No one would guess that we'd spent the last twenty minutes arguing with one another or that we'd fought all morning. As I'd suspected, she knew exactly how to maneuver this situation.

For the next half hour, I made small talk with the rest of the table while Belle gossiped politely with the other escorts. A hush swept down the table as the final guests arrived. Belle's eyes flickered to mine as a few of the others stood in greeting, but I shook my head. There was no need for us to do so.

Hammond paused at my seat as he made his way to the end of the table.

"Smith," he said, shaking my hand.

I raised an eyebrow at the jovial greeting. It had been four days since I last saw him. Longer than usual but hardly a record. Then I realized his attention wasn't directed at me. Hammond's smile was focused over my shoulder.

I stood, pushing my chair back so that I could block him from getting too good of a view. But Hammond merely dropped an arm around my shoulder and drew me close.

"Goddamn, that's a pretty piece of ass you've brought this evening," he whispered.

"Hammond, this is my new assistant," I said in a stiff voice.

Belle held out her hand, splaying her polished fingernails in a gesture as timeless as femininity. Hammond caught it, but instead of shaking it, he bent to kiss it. The bastard's gaze traveled down with him. Judging from the intrigued look he shot me, he'd gotten enough of a glimpse.

Fuck.

I cleared my throat, and he relinquished his hold of her. Sitting quickly, I replaced the napkin on my lap and then slung an arm over the back of her chair. Her eyes darted to the side, but she didn't question me.

Dinner arrived in courses, Hammond having a penchant for ceremony. When they served the salad, Belle's hand bumped mine as she picked up her fork. She jerked it swiftly away, but we had both felt the subtle shot like an unexpected jolt from a power outlet. We spent the whole meal speaking to everyone but each other. As my conversation died down, I began to eavesdrop on hers.

"I'm certain we've met," she said to the woman on the opposite side of the table. "If only I could place you."

Georgia Kincaid shrugged, a demure smile pinned to her face. "I'd remember you."

Demure and Georgia were mutually exclusive concepts. She knew exactly where she had met Belle, and she wasn't going to remind her. That meant it had been business, and any business involving Hammond's right-hand girl was bound to be dirty. Georgia's eyes flashed to mine, narrowing into catlike slits for a moment while Belle handed her glass to the waiter. I shifted my chair over so that my shoulder brushed against Belle's. She froze, her hand poised in midair, before she regained her composure.

Every touch between us this evening had been innocent, and yet none of them had. Each graze of our skin was accidental. Unplanned. Uncomplicated.

At least, it should have been.

I restrained myself from pushing closer to her, from making more extensive contact. I'd invited her into the lion's den, and she'd shown up looking like a piece of meat. It was my duty.

But it was a problem I was unfamiliar with. I had no doubt Hammond had fucked my assistants in the past. Hell, Georgia probably had as well. It was a nonissue unless their loyalty to me was compromised. But the thought of either of them laying a finger on Belle drove me to move even closer until we were no longer sharing unavoidable bumps of the hand or legs. Under the table I swept my knee along the side of her thigh, my eyes trained on the naked flesh of her shoulders. The goose bumps that surged over her skin enthralled me.

I stayed that way, my leg pressed to hers, and began a new conversation with Hammond regarding an investigation into his jewelry store's payroll. We spoke in a code long established between the two of us. I was so absorbed in the discussion that I nearly startled when I felt a hand squeeze my knee.

I glanced over at Belle, who shot me a pointed look.

Final warning.

Moving my leg away from her, I noticed Hammond studying us intently. All my attempts to claim her had only brought more attention to her.

"Belle, how old are you?" he asked.

"Twenty-four." Her smile was dazzling.

"About the age of my daughter." He reached over and took Georgia's hand, but instead of a quick, fatherly squeeze, he clasped it. Georgia placed her free hand over his and held it there.

"I had no idea you were related." Belle somehow managed to sound polite even though her eyes shone with dismay.

"There's not much of a resemblance," he said seriously.

I sighed, shaking my head. "Georgia is adopted."

"Oh!" Belle looked somewhat relieved, but not entirely.

"I have a large adopted family," Hammond explained. "I was raised to believe it was one's civic responsibility to help those who needed it."

"And Georgia needed it?" Belle asked, a sharp current running under her words. Her innocent expression hid it, but I hoped no one else could read her as well as I could.

"Georgia came to me when she was fifteen. Bad home life. She's worked for me ever since." Hammond tipped his wine glass slightly at the lovely brunette.

"She worked for you? But she's your daughter."

"Hammond believes in helping oneself," I interrupted, concerned at where this line of questioning might lead. "He simply gave many of us a leg up."

"Us?" Belle repeated, glancing from Georgia to me.

"At one time even Smith needed help," Hammond said good-naturedly. "Although you'd never know it now. Is he as stubborn with you as he is with me?"

"I imagine more so," she said dryly.

"Some things never change," Georgia added, her mouth coming to rest in a perfect pout.

Or rather a suggestive pout. Belle stiffened but kept the smile on her face.

"You'll have to excuse them. Those two grew up together." Hammond's words should have sounded like the equivalent of an affectionate ruffle of the hair. But, like Hammond himself, they came out twisted. Wrong. A perversion of what a normal man might mean.

I couldn't explain to Belle that Hammond was exactly that. A perversion. There had been no possibility of keeping her away from him. Some ties ran too deeply. The kind of ties that bound and gagged and suffocated more when you tried to fight them.

"Wait!" Georgia exclaimed, her hand flying to her chest. "I do know you!"

I gritted my jaw, bracing myself for whatever new move she was making.

"We have mutual friends," she continued.

"We do?" Belle countered, no longer trying to mask her disbelief.

"Alexander and Clara." The names gushed from Georgia's mouth. It was obvious that she had been waiting to reveal this all evening.

"Alexander and Clara? Um, how do you know them?" Each syllable was carefully chosen. Belle had begun to see the eggshells lining her path.

"Hammond is a jeweler," I interjected. This time when I moved my chair closer to hers, she didn't shrink away.

"I made Clara's ring," Hammond said.

"That was Alexander's mother's ring." Belle was testing him just as much as he was testing her.

"I made it for his mother. As well as Alexander's wedding ring and the one for young Edward's friend."

"Fiancé," Belle corrected him coldly.

"Of course, I go back with Alexander almost as long as I do with Smith." Georgia rested her chin on her hand. So far she'd barely shown her true colors to Belle. She'd been friendly and gracious, but underneath it all she dripped venom.

Judging from how Belle shifted in her chair, my assistant saw through her facade nearly as well as I did.

Georgia knew it, too. Now that there was no reason to hide her fangs, she struck. "You were engaged to Philip Abernathy. Such a shame. What a cad. Already engaged to that awful Pepper Lockwood."

The intake of air beside me was audible. Belle's hand flew to her stomach. "I hadn't heard that news."

"It's a rumor, of course." Georgia made quote marks in the air. "But Father designed the ring. I expect they'll announce it in the papers any day."

A poisoned silence fell over our end of the table before Belle pushed her chair back so quickly it nearly toppled over.

"Thank you for a lovely evening," she sputtered. "Please excuse me, I'm afraid I'm rather tired."

"Not at all." Hammond's grin showed too many of his crooked

teeth. "Do drop into the shop some time. I'd like to get to know you better."

Belle's face turned green, and I half expected her to vomit on him. Before I was on my feet, she had hurried out of the private dining room.

"You can retract your claws now, Georgia," I said to her coldly.

"However did you find her, Smith?" She plucked at the tines of her fork. "Such a lovely, simple creature."

"Stay away, sis." I nodded tersely to Hammond, not trusting myself to say anything else.

Belle was waiting on the curb outside the Carlton with her arm extended out to hail a cab.

I pushed my valet ticket into the attendant's hand as I passed him. "Bring it around immediately."

There was a murmur from the small line waiting for their cars, but the man jogged off to bring around the Veyron.

"I'm going home," Belle called as I came closer. "Alone."

"Fine." I caught her upper arm and dragged her away from the side of the street. "But I'm taking you."

"What about your family?" She didn't bother to hide her disgust any longer.

"You don't choose your family, Bellc."

"It sounds as if you chose them."

"No, I didn't." I glared at her, daring her to press me further.

The Veyron roared to the curb, and the attendant jumped out of it. I handed him a hundred pound note as I opened her door. She got in without a fight but as I shut the door, she said in a low voice. "How can I already know you better than I knew him?"

The statement settled heavy on my chest. She didn't know me. Not really. She knew nothing of my past. Little of my work. She knew how I took my coffee, and she'd seen me naked. That shouldn't have been enough for her to feel that way.

And yet as we took off, I had the most peculiar sensation that she was right. We didn't know all the minute details of our past lives, but she already knew what buttons to push. She could already anticipate my responses. She could give as good as she took. I couldn't say that about most women.

I couldn't tell her that she could never know more than that—that she wouldn't want to.

"I've been called out of town for a few days. I'll be back this weekend." I tapped the paddle shifters, and the Veyron revved into third as we merged effortlessly onto the motorway.

Belle continued to gaze out the window, but her throat slid as she swallowed the news. Without thinking, I shifted the car into automatic drive and reached for her hand, hoping to draw her thoughts away from the past. Her head swiveled, revealing wide eyes framed by wet lashes. She looked at our hands, loosely clasped together, and then to me. Our eyes met, and past the tears, I saw confusion overtake the sadness.

The same turmoil seethed within me. Apprehension. Anger. Denial. But most of all: need. God, I wanted to take her to bed and show her what it was like to be possessed. Kiss away the tears trickling down her face and replace her fear with mind-numbing bliss.

She drew her hand back slightly, a signal that she'd made her choice.

Denial.

It was the safest option. But it was quickly becoming the least viable one. I had my own choice to make.

I tightened my grip, crushing her delicate fingers inescapably. She had made her move. I had made mine. This time she didn't pull away. We drove in silence to her flat, my hand clenching hers possessively. There was no turning back now.

I pulled the Veyron up to the curb, wanting to turn it off and take her upstairs. My body already coveted my new possession. I wanted to strip her down, rip off her panties, and show her what it meant now that she was mine.

But tonight wasn't the time.

"I'll be back by Friday," I told her in a low voice.

"Friday," she echoed.

Abandoning the wheel, I caught her head in my hands, turning her face up to mine. The tears had evaporated, replaced by a hunger that burned so fiercely that she moaned when we made eye contact. I caressed my palm down her cheek and captured her chin so she couldn't look away.

Those eyes. That mouth. The way her body angled itself toward mine. Every inch of her needed to be fucked. My thumb brushed over her bottom lip, and her mouth opened instinctively.

So receptive.

"Can you behave while I'm gone?" I asked sternly. My balls tightened at the thought of what I would do to her if she didn't.

"Yes, Sir," she breathed, her petulant nickname for me taking on a new, and much more welcome, meaning.

I smeared her lipstick with the pad of my thumb, enjoying the way she gasped and held her breath—as if her life depended on my touch "I have to get to the jet now. Go inside. Tonight I want you to dream about me and what I'm going to do to you when I return."

Her teeth bit down on the end of my finger. I slapped the side of her cheek softly until she released it.

"Friday," she whispered it like an incantation.

"No one touches you until I do, beautiful. Not even yourself." It wasn't a promise or a date. It was an order.

Belle wriggled in her seat, but for once she didn't challenge me. I released her, pulling away and breaking all contact. She opened her mouth to speak, changed her mind, and popped the handle on her car door. She slid out of the seat gracefully, considering how low the car was to the road and how high her heels were. She'd almost exited when my hand lashed out and caught hers. She turned hopefully back to me.

"What was in your past no longer matters," I informed her in a soft voice. "Now that I'm here, no one will hurt you, Belle. I won't allow it."

And if they tried, I'd kill them.

CHAPTER NINE

"No news?" I called over the frenetic pulse of Brimstone's sound system. The club was packed, making it as hot as the hellfire that decorated the walls. I wiped beads of sweat off my forehead, remembering guiltily that it had been my idea to stick to the main level where we could easily dance.

David gave me a thumbs down as he pushed through the crowd. Edward followed behind him, a cluster of shots held high over his head.

"I just want to know before *Us Weekly*," Lola grumbled at my side. Since Clara had officially gone on bedrest earlier this week, gwe'd all spent the last few days obsessively checking our mobiles for updates on the baby. The crisis, which the doctors assured all of us was completely normal, had provided a welcome distraction from Smith's absence.

Or rather Smith in general.

My belly tightened as I thought about him. I'd expected him home today, but still no word. It was beginning to feel like my life was measured out in texts and voicemails. I grabbed a shot from Edward and downed it. Now I could pretend the warmth spreading through my core was from booze rather than the conflicting emotions tumbling through me.

"Clara rang to tell me she requires a photo of you dancing, and I quote, with a man. Don't shoot the messenger!" Edward held up his hands, but the smirk spreading over his charming face undermined the effect.

"Not bloody likely!" Lola cried, coming to my defense. "She'll have to accept one of her best friend and her sister."

Lola took a shot, slammed the glass down on the table, and tugged me out onto the dance floor. Clara's baby sister had turned out to be wildly different than I'd expected. Any occasion I'd spent with her, either Clara or their mother, Madeline, had also been present. As she began to grind against a guy on the dance floor, motioning for me to join her, I realized it took a lot less to loosen her up than the other women in her family. Five minutes ago, I'd been casually picking her brain about up and coming grassroots publicity campaigns. She'd been focused, driven, and completely brilliant with her thoughts. Then she flipped a switch and turned into a party girl.

I had to admit I found myself liking her more.

She reached out, wagging her fingers for me to come closer. I giggled, the effects of the vodka already setting in, and pressed against her. The guy dancing behind her slid his hands from Lola's waist to her hips, then they disappeared. Lola pushed me gently forward and peeled herself off of him, shaking her head in annoyance. It was too dark to see his face in the club, but the man held out his arms.

Lola laughed as she hooked an arm around my neck and we pushed our way further into the crowd. I'd had my reservations about wearing a minidress in London's fickle autumn weather, but now I was grateful I had taken the chance. I lost track of time as Lola and I danced with each other, obliging various men who wanted to join in—until they became handsy. My black dress clung to my slick skin as the DJ morphed the music from a fast, electronic rhythm to a haunting, deep pulse. It was slower—languid almost—and it vibrated through my flesh into my bones. My head fell back as I let it undulate through me.

A pair of familiar arms circled my waist, and I relaxed against Edward. The perks of having a gay best friend included, but weren't limited to, always having a dance partner and always having a dance partner who wasn't trying to get his hand up your skirt.

The record merged seamlessly into a Lana Del Ray mix and I dropped lower, circling my hips against Edward. His strong arms supported my gyrations, but the closeness of his body was only making me warmer. I pushed my hair off the back of my neck and held it in a loose bun as we continued to move to the beat.

A third hand gripped my shoulder, and my eyes flew open to find Smith glaring possessively down at me. In his suit, he stuck out from the rest of the crowd. Then again he would have stuck out anywhere. But his tailored three piece was where the professional look ended. His hair was mussed across the top matching the wild look glinting in his eyes despite the club's dim lighting.

"Excuse me, mate." Edward shoved his hand off of me.

I snapped out of my shock and darted between them just as Smith's hand clenched into a fist. Placing my palms on each of their athletic chests, I turned to Edward and mouthed, "It's cool."

His eyes narrowed, but he stepped away. He tilted his head in acquiescence to Smith and shot me a look that said I'd be hearing about this later.

Smith's hand closed over mine, and he pulled me out of the mass of squirming bodies and toward the back door. Locking my knees, I forced him to halt in his tracks.

"Come. Now."

A quiver of anticipation snaked across my skin, but I shook my head. "I need to tell my friends I'm leaving."

I had meant to tell him to fuck off. I'd planned to. Now all I could think about was following wherever he led.

"They'll figure it out." He tugged on my hand, but I yanked it away from him again.

"They'll worry." I didn't wait for any more of his orders. Pivoting around, I made my way back to our table with Smith following behind me. He paused leaving some distance between himself and my friends.

"I take it that's Smith," Edward said, distaste coating his words. He studied him for a moment then frowned. "God, that man's dick must be a heat-seeking missile."

Lola bounced up to the table, dripping with sweat. She looked from me to Edward and back again. "What's going on?"

"Have you heard the one that starts 'two alpha males enter a bar?'" I bit out.

"Sounds like a one-hander!" She wiggled her middle finger suggestively. Her gaze traveled a few feet past me. "Speaking of killing kittens..."

"Meet Belle's alpha du jour." Edward nodded toward Smith.

Lola grabbed my arm and shook it. "Why are you not having sex with him right now?"

"Because we're in public." I removed her hand gently from me and patted it. "I'm getting out of here."

"Getting off, you mean." David made a kissy face next to Edward who swatted him on the shoulder.

"Don't encourage this behavior," he warned him.

"You've been praying she'll get laid for months and now you want to cock block her," David said in exasperation. "Not cool."

Edward looked over my shoulder. "I wanted her to get laid. Not make up for all the lost time in one night."

"How do you know—"

"Honey, I might be gay, but I'm still a male."

"Then I should get going. I have plans for the rest of the night." I stuck my tongue out at him as David passed me my wallet.

Displeasure radiated from Smith as I approached. I stopped short and crossed my arms over my chest. I wasn't going anywhere with him until he cooled off.

"You need to get out of here," he informed me.

"Maybe you need to leave," I said haughtily. He'd told me that he liked it when I provoked. Considering it annoyed me when he gave orders, I'd have no problem giving him exactly what he wanted.

A low rumble vibrated from his throat. He'd actually growled. I did my best to look unaffected as I drenched my knickers. So much for holding on to my dignity. Smith lunged forward, catching me around the waist and crushing me against him. "Come. With. Me."

The club faded away. There was only us. Only the heat scorching through me where our bodies met. Only the air he breathed. Only him. I blinked and nodded. There was no point in trying to break the spell. I didn't want him to relinquish me back to the swarming crowd. I wanted him to carry me away and choose my fate.

Smith let go, seizing my hand as he turned around and led me toward the rear entrance. As we neared the door, a bouncer moved to the side.

"Mr. Price." He tipped his head and opened the back door.

An evening breeze sang along my damp skin, instantly cooling me down. I raised my face toward the stars and inhaled the fresh air greedily.

The Veyron was parked in the back alley, guarded by another member of the Brimstone security team. He took his leave without a word.

"Come here often?" I asked, watching the man disappear into the building.

"The owner is a client." He opened my car door, my hand still locked in his tight grip.

Maybe it was the fresh air, or finally being free from the noisy, packed dance floor, but the events of the evening began to click into place. "How did you know I was here?"

"That doesn't matter." His tone was thick with warning. "I've been trying to reach you for hours."

"A phone doesn't really fit in this dress. I left it at home." I shrugged.

It got the reaction I had expected.

Smith grabbed my hips and backed me into the brick wall behind us. "Your ass doesn't fit in that dress."

"You don't like it?"

"It's not a dress. It's a bandage."

"Actually it's a bandage dress." I bucked my hips against him, brushing across his stiffening cock. "Does it make you hard when I talk back?"

In a flash, he pinned my arms above my head. His face slanted over mine, hovering dangerously close before his mouth trailed along my jaw. "I told you to behave."

His teeth nipped my earlobe.

"I did," I moaned.

His mouth moved lower until his teeth sank into my shoulder. Hard.

"I saw another man touching you," he roared. "He had his hands all over you in this pathetic strip you call a dress."

I groaned, partially because he had gotten the wrong impression and partially because his lips were on my collarbone. "Edward? He's as gay as a maypole."

"He was touching what is mine!" Smith exploded, slamming my body against the wall with the weight of his. There was no insinuation—no subtlety—to the act. He ground lewdly against my belly, digging his cock into the soft flesh.

"Yours?" I repeated breathlessly. "I don't belong to anyone."

"That's where you're wrong, beautiful." He pulled back, and we both went still as we regarded one another. The line was in front of us. We'd tiptoed around it. We had teetered on the edge. But we hadn't crossed it. Not yet.

Smith groaned, his eyes snapping shut for a brief moment, before he leapt over it.

His mouth collided with mine, mashing against my lips so forcefully that I tasted blood. I didn't know if it was mine or his. I didn't care. I only wanted more. More of his taste. More of his tongue. More.

I was completely under his control. My lips moved in sync with his. My mouth parted for his forceful tongue. He would take me when and how we wanted, but he would take me.

"Is this what you want, beautiful?" he asked as he licked the edge of my teeth. "Do you want me in your mouth? Where else do you want me?"

Here. There. Everywhere. My synapses fired rapidly, overwhelmed by the sensations crowding through my body wherever our skin met. I moaned, squirming closer to him. There was no chance of me processing words. I could only show him what I wanted.

"You're going to have to be clearer," he murmured against my mouth. "When I take you to bed, there will be no yes or no. You will belong to me. Now tell me, are you ready to be mine?"

He drew back and waited.

I struggled to tell him what I needed to say. In the end, it was five simple words.

"Shut up and fuck me."

CHAPTER TEN

We made it as far as the garage.

Smith threw the Veyron into park and was out of his seat and at my door before I'd unbuckled. I accepted his hand, my legs wobbling as I pushed out of the car. The combination of excessive speeding and lust had left me shaky.

His arm hooked around my waist. Propelling me against the car, his lips crashed into mine. He tasted like bourbon and sex. My hand tangled in his hair, holding him to me. He was intoxicating, and I needed a fix only he could give me. I'd spent so long denying him—denying myself. Now I was ready to let go and shed my inhibitions and my clothes. The window was cool against my heated skin, and my other arm clutched the frame of the car. My fingers slid over the sleek metal, and I moaned into Smith's mouth.

He captured my tongue, sucking it into his mouth until I felt the sharp edge of his teeth.

He had promised to bite.

My body fought to get closer to his. There were too many clothes. Not enough skin. Smith drew away and spun me around, pushing me until my body molded to the curves of the car.

"Let me show you why I object to this dress," he murmured into my ear as he pushed his leg between my thighs and nudged them open. "See how easy your pussy is to access?"

I tried to nod, but my cheek was smashed to the top of the car, my breath fogging across the metal.

He grabbed a fistful of my hair and wrenched my head back. "I can't hear you, beautiful."

"Yes," I gasped.

"Yes what?" He yanked harder, forcing my neck to arch uncomfortably.

A warm gush of arousal coated my sex as I whimpered, "Yes, Sir."

"Good girl." He lowered my head gently, stroking the side of my face. Then he trailed kisses down the curve of my neck. "I'm going to claim your pussy with my mouth now, and I want you to stay right here like this. Do not move."

A desperate sob escaped my lips, and he pressed his mouth against mine as his hands wrenched my skirt up to my waist. "I know you want to give your body to me. No one's ever protected you before—treasured you, have they?"

My eyes closed as I shook my head.

"But that's what you need, isn't it?" He tucked a strand of hair behind my ear while he stroked his knee along my swollen mound.

I wet my lips as my eyes opened and found his. I didn't have to say yes. He knew.

"I'm going to take care of you, beautiful," he promised. "I'm going to make you feel so fucking good."

His fingers slid under the bands of my thong and twisted. They snapped hard, stinging across my hips as he ripped away my underwear. The lace grazed across my seam and I bit my cheek to restrain from jerking away. He tossed them to the garage floor. "I've thought about tasting you since the moment we met. Open wide for me, so I can."

I gripped the car as tightly as I could, tottering on my heels as I wriggled my legs open farther. Smith's hands ran down my body as he knelt between my splayed thighs. The tip of his finger traced my seam, sending a jolt of electricity sizzling through my swollen sex.

"You're so goddamn wet for me. Ripe and ready." His low voice raked over my skin. He pushed deeper, stretching me open as he thumb circled over my engorged clit. But instead of leaning into me, his arm hooked around my hips and yanked me down, forcing my knees to bend just enough that I was squatting over him. One more quick jerk, and he'd pulled me to his mouth. His tongue lashed out, stroking along my sensitive slit.

For all intents and purposes, I was sitting on his face, clinging to a Bugatti. The realization lit a fire that crackled down my nerves, setting my body aflame. My thighs burned with the effort of staying upright, but it only heightened my awareness. Pleasure curled inside me, winding tight as Smith sucked my greedy clit. When he flicked it with his tongue, I cried out, nearly losing my balance. I crushed myself to the car as Smith caught my hips to steady me.

"I won't let you fall," he assured me, his voice thick with desire, "but you're going to let go and come on my tongue."

I groaned, shaking my head, but he paid no attention. Or he didn't care. I couldn't hold myself up much longer—couldn't handle the overwhelming sensations taking over my body. Smith nipped my clit and I fractured. The feverish strain occupying my body morphed into ecstasy as he sucked it between his teeth. My arms fell away as I plummeted, pleasure echoing across my limbs.

But I didn't hit the ground. Smith's strong arms bracketed me. His tongue anchored me. I slumped against the car, numb, but he didn't stop ravaging me with his mouth. My thighs tried to shut against his persistence, but they proved too weak. He slowed his machinations, stroking gingerly along my pulsing cunt until I felt my muscles contract.

Impossible.

There was no time to filter more through my oxygen-drenched brain before my limbs spasmed as he coaxed me to another mind-blowing orgasm.

This time when my climax subsided, my muscles betrayed me entirely. But before I could stumble, Smith swept me into his arms and pinned me to the car, cradling my body against his. I was lost for words. He'd fucked them all right out of my head.

Brushing his thumb over my lower lip, he pulled it down until my jaw fell open. "Now I want to see your sexy mouth in action."

I reached down, fumbling for his zipper, but he shook his head. Smith kept his arm around me as he led me around to the driver's side of the car. "I'm not sure what makes you more hot—me or my car?"

My mouth opened in protest, but he pressed it shut with his index finger.

"I don't care what turns you on as long as it belongs to me, beautiful." There was a click, and the door swung open. "I want your knees on my driver's seat. Show me how beautiful your cunt is when it's naked and quivering in my car."

I stumbled back, grabbing onto the doorframe as I twisted around and climbed into the bucket seat. The steady pulse between my legs grew more demanding as my skin slid over the buttery leather.

"My most priceless possession and my most expensive one," he said, his words taking on a husky tone as he pressed his palm to my sex.

I didn't clarify which was which. I should mind that he thought of me as his possession, but I couldn't bring myself to. I only wanted to be claimed by him. Owned over and over. My mind had stopped processing anything outside of him, his touch, and wanting to please him.

Behind me, I heard the swish of a zipper. Angling my neck, I watched as he withdrew his cock. I'd seen it before but not like this. It jetted from his groin, majestically flanked by a heavy set of balls. I'd known he was endowed, but seeing it now, fully erect, thrilled—and terrified—me.

"No need to be scared." Smith seemed to sense what I was thinking. "I won't take you until you're ready."

I pressed my lips shyly to my shoulder. It wasn't like he was my first. Far from it. But it was clear he was in a different league than my past lovers. I wasn't even sure he was playing the same game.

"Don't hide your mouth," he ordered. "I want to see it in action. I told you I wasn't sure if you were fucking me or my Bugatti. Show me what that sweet mouth can do to my car."

Maybe it was because I was on display. Maybe the two orgasms he'd already given me had fried my brain. Maybe I'd held out for so long that I no longer knew the difference between what I wanted and what he wanted. But instinct took over. I moved farther onto the seat, crawling closer to the steering wheel, until my tongue touched the soft leather. It tasted expensive, like luxury and sin. Shifting my eyes over so that he was in my sight, I dragged my tongue along the circumference. The warm natural musk of the leather mingled with faint traces of salt from Smith's hand. Angling my head, I ran it over the stitched interior of the wheel, savoring each bump.

Out of the corner of my eye, I saw Smith's hand close tightly over his shaft. I moaned as he began to stroke himself off. I was torn between wishing it was my hand and wanting to continue my performance for him.

Creeping up the steering wheel, I brought my lips to the dashboard, taking time to kiss each button.

"That's it, beautiful. Show me how dirty you are." The hand on my ass pressed hard, increasing the pulsating rhythm of my clit from a faint tick to a drum solo. His reaction spurred me on and I dropped lower, lifting my ass into the air as I pressed my mouth to the center console. The shiny chrome left a metallic taste on my tongue. The car—like us—was the perfect union of opposites, both luxuriously rich and undeniably modern at the same time. I drew my tongue up the metal of the gear shifter, circling the tip of it around the knob before popping my lips over it and swallowing it deep.

Smith released a groan behind me. "I can't wait any longer, but I'll be gentle."

The warm crest of his cock nudged against my entrance, and I bit down onto the leather knob in anticipation. He waited a moment, allowing me to adjust—or, at least, prepare myself. Then he began to push inside. My folds, still swollen with blood, ached as they stretched to accommodate his considerable girth. God, his shaft was impossibly thick. I drew back, abandoning my vulgar exhibition so that I could catch my breath as he buried himself deep inside of me.

This is what I'd been fighting. Pleasure. Indescribable pleasure.

"I'm going to fuck you hard, Belle," he growled.

My breath caught and I waited. When he didn't begin, I pushed my hips back, trying to take his dick deeper.

"Not yet." He petted my back as he continued with shallow, leisurely pumps. He was taking his time with me even though I kept trying to race forward ahead of him. When suddenly he withdrew, he left a hollow craving in his wake. "I want to see you when I come."

I manoeuvred onto my back as he pulled a condom from his pocket. He ripped open the foil with his teeth, stroking himself as he pushed the condom over his tip and rolled it down. "If you aren't on birth control, you will be by next week." Another command. "I want to see my cum dripping from that pretty pink pussy."

I nodded, my teeth sinking into my lip as I tried to resist the urge to jump him. I considered telling him I was on birth control, but I couldn't wait any longer to have him back inside me. Smith was running things tonight. I could only imagine what would happen if I tried to take the reins. When he'd finished, he extended a hand. I placed mine in his tentatively, and he pulled me to my feet. But as soon as my shoes touched the floor, he scooped me up, holding me against the car and over his shaft.

"When you're ready, beautiful."

My hips immediately dropped lower, taking him to the root. I might be sore in the morning, but for the moment, I was going to savor all eight delicious inches of him. Smith didn't miss a beat. Wrapping his arms around me, he cupped my ass and carried me to the front of the Veyron. Laying me gently over the bonnet so as not to break physical contact, he flashed me a wicked grin. "I just lived out one of my adolescent fantasies."

"Me, too." I hooked my thumbs over the straps of my dress and shoved it down to expose my breasts. My nipples beaded in the cool air. "Let's see what we can do about the rest of them."

His mouth closed over the pert furl before I'd finished the

thought. Squeezing my breast, he retreated for a second before plunging his mouth over the other nipple. God, I hoped he had good insurance, because there was going to be a dent from where he'd fucked me so relentlessly into the hood. My back arced off the car and he seized me, using my body as leverage to pound deeper. Harder.

He didn't give me an orgasm, he captured it. Claiming my pleasure as if it was his own, and this time as I splintered around him, there was no light. No sound. No fireworks. He'd wrecked me entirely, and I came with a scream that shattered the air surrounding us. Smith's face tensed, his jaw contracting, as his arm snaked up and held my neck.

"Look at me," he ordered, his pace never faltering as he shifted me in his arms.

I tried to open my eyes, but they no longer seemed to work. My head felt heavy, my brain drenched with too much oxygen. When it lolled to the side, he forced it back up.

"Look at me." This time an angry edge glinted from the command. His fingers fastened around the back of my neck and my eyes flew open as the pressure increased. "This is it, beautiful. I'm about to come, and when I do, this pussy will belong to me. You will belong to me. You can still say no. Tell me to go fuck myself if you want. This is your only chance."

His mouth smothered mine for a brief, heated instant.

"Once I come, there's no turning back for either of us," he warned, his green eyes sure and steady. They didn't waver even as he thrust tirelessly. "Choose now and never look back."

Even if I could think, I didn't have to. I'd made my decision the moment he held my hand in this car. I might have made it the first time I saw him.

I wound my fingers in his hair and brought his mouth to mine, sealing my choice with a kiss, as he took what was his.

CHAPTER ELEVEN

She felt good in my arms.

I'd fucked women recently, but putting your dick in an available slot wasn't complicated. This was complicated. This was different.

I'd wanted her from the moment I saw her, but I hadn't anticipated what would happen when I finally had her. The last few days away from her had been a blur, stuck in Paris, conducting a deposition with a hard-on. I guessed there were worse places to have a perpetual erection than France.

"You made me crazy when I couldn't reach you earlier." She was in need of a far less gentle reprimand, but this time I'd let it slide with a tongue-lashing. My expectations, while firm, were new to her.

"I didn't know when you were coming back."

She tucked her head under my chin, close enough that I caught the scent of lilac in her blonde locks.

"You didn't have your phone." If I stuck to the facts, I could be stern. It was best to set a boundary for myself until personal limits could be discussed.

"No pockets," she mumbled dreamily, cuddling closer to my chest as I pushed the button for the lift.

"Planning on going to bed?" I asked dryly.

She stifled a yawn, shaking her head.

I backed into the lift, hitting the second floor button with my elbow. Tilting her chin up with my little finger, I continued, "If you'd had your phone, I could have reached you earlier. I could have been fucking you for hours. But you didn't have it, did you?"

"No," she whispered.

"You were unavailable at my convenience. Now I'm going to be forced to keep you awake for hours."

Her blue eyes rounded as she grew more alert.

"I haven't had my fill of you yet. Neither of us are sleeping until I do."

"You're saying I won't go to sleep until you're satisfied?"

"No, beautiful," I corrected her gently. "I'm saying neither of us are going to sleep until we're satisfied. I spent the last few days plotting what I was going to do to you. We're just getting started."

I didn't offer her another option. I'd given her a choice in the garage. Hell, I had been offering her outs since her interview. She'd given herself to me. That would be the last decision she made this evening.

"I understand." Her lips split into a tentative smile.

I raised my eyebrow. "Do you?"

She lifted her soft fingers to my cheek, hesitating until I shifted my face against her palm. Holding her hand there, she met my gaze. I saw questions in her eyes. There was fear and confusion, but also hunger. "Yes, Sir."

Her whispered response told me what I needed to know. She understood, on some level, what she was getting into. Although I would need to take it slowly with her.

But for now, I would take her to bed.

Sunlight crept over her peaceful face. Her blonde hair fanned out, haloing her head, and making her look even more the part of an angel. She shifted in her sleep, curling a hand under her cheek.

What was she doing to me?

Some broken things could never be fixed. I knew that. I'd witnessed it over and over again. I had watched as the cracks of time and heartbreak destroyed people. It was too much of a burden to bear—to try to pick up the pieces and heal. I'd always believed it was safer to shield your wounds and arm yourself against future attacks.

But last night I had laid awake and counted her breaths, catalogued each of her movements. The serenity she found in her sleep radiated from her. I could almost feel it seeping through my skin.

I told myself that sleeping next to her left me unguarded. Vulnerable. But the truth was that I didn't want to close my eyes.

Belle's lips began to move although she was still asleep. I propped myself up on my elbow, torn between waking her and hoping she would settle back to sleep. Instead she flipped onto her back, her body stiffening. Tossing her head against the pillow, a small cry escaped her lips.

The anguish of that sound wrapped itself around my heart and squeezed. She was mine to protect, even in dreams.

Laying a hand against the side of her face, I caressed her skin, calling her away from the nightmare and back to me. Her eyes fluttered open, filled with terror. They darted over to me, fear turning into confusion.

"I've got you, beautiful."

Relief washed over her gorgeous face at the sound of my voice. The pressure in my chest relented, and I leaned over her, pressing a kiss to her forehead. She relaxed against the pillow, making no move to pull the covers over her body or draw away from me.

Her reaction felt dangerously like trust.

"Are you watching me sleep, creep?" she murmured sleepily.

"You were having a nightmare." My protective impulse urged me to take her in my arms and lock her away. Instead I brushed hair from her face. "Does that happen often?"

"Isn't one bad dream enough?" She rolled toward me, pushing her face against my palm.

She was avoiding the question...but why?

I had no right to push it further. Instead I slid an arm under her torso and drew her close. She curled into a ball, and we fell into a dark, dreamless sleep together.

CHAPTER TWELVE

She was gone when I awoke. A mixture of anger and panic rose in my chest, but I pushed it away. There was no reason to believe she had left—unless she'd finally figured out that she'd wandered into the wolf's den. Unlocking my mobile, I checked the garage security cam. Her car was still parked there. I fell back against my pillow.

Belle Stuart was going to be a handful.

When she was naked and writhing for it, she'd do anything I asked. That much I knew. The rest of the time she was a wild card.

If only I was attracted to more predictable women.

Swinging my feet over the side of the bed, I spotted her dress wadded on the floor. That made me grin. She obviously hadn't gone far. I tossed on a pair of boxer briefs and went on the hunt. When I found her, I'd show her what she missed by crawling out of bed early.

A quick search of the kitchen and living room yielded nothing. She hadn't gone to the bedroom I showed her. I stopped and stared at the door across from hers.

There was no reason to check in there. I'd warned her about the consequences.

I finally found her gliding along the bottom of my pool.

Stark fucking naked.

I watched her move effortlessly, water rippling across her curves and her blonde hair billowing behind her. It wasn't a terrible way to spend a Saturday morning.

When she pushed her upper body up and over the side, she shot me a wicked grin. I held out a towel.

"I'm not quite done here. Why don't you join me?" She pushed onto her back, allowing her perfect tits to float to the surface. It was an enticing offer.

"I don't swim," I called out.

She giggled. "Then why do you have a pool?"

"So pretty girls will get naked and go for a dip." I squatted closer to the edge so I could get a better view of the rest of her.

"Why don't you come in and show me what you do to those girls?" she suggested, batting her eyelashes.

"Why don't you come out?" I countered.

"Because I'm the one that's naked." She dove back under the water, giving me a view of her ass.

It was almost enough to convince me to jump in. Instead I stood my ground. When her head broke through the glassy surface of the water, I crooked my finger and beckoned her back to me. "I need room to achieve all the ways I'm going to fuck you."

Her arms swept over the surface. "There's plenty of room here."

Fine. If that was how she wanted to play it. I turned and headed toward the door, dropping my shorts on the way out.

Belle was in the hall before the lift arrived. Water trailed over her body and her hair snaked down her neck, dripping wet. Her lips were purple, but she showed no other signs of being cold. She sashayed past me as the lift doors opened. "Going up?"

"I was thinking about going down." Prowling in, I pounced on her, pushing her arms over her head. Her wet body sent droplets of water cascading down the mirrored surface. "Turn around, beautiful."

She obliged, bending so that her ass became an unmistakable

target. Christ, the things I was going to do to her. But for now I wanted to try something else. I knew it would elicit a reaction.

I stroked my palm over her perfectly round rear and then smacked it hard enough to leave the imprint of my hand. Five unmistakable red lines on her fair skin.

Belle yelped, but she didn't pull away or turn around. She kept herself ready for whatever I decided to do to her next.

"I warned you to get out of the pool," I said in a husky voice, stroking the mark I'd left on her ass cheek.

"You asked me to," she purred.

"Never mistake my commands for a request, beautiful. Or there will be consequences."

"What do you mean by—" Her question was cut short by a stinging slap to the other side. "Oh!"

"Starting to get the picture?" I asked in a rough voice. "I wanted to fuck you, and you played coy. This is what happens when you don't listen."

She curled up on the balls of her feet. I couldn't tell if she was bracing for the next blow or hoping for it. I also didn't care.

"Your body has been responding to me since the moment we met, begging me to tame it." Hooking an arm around her, I wrenched her to me and pressed my cock against her stinging backside. "Do you want to be tamed?"

She mumbled something, her ability to speak reduced to unintelligible whimpers. I thrust my arm up her body and wrapped my hand around her neck. "Do you want to be tamed?"

"Yes, Sir."

"Very good," I murmured my approval in her ear as I pushed my knee against her bare sex. The moisture I felt there had nothing to do with the pool. "Did I make you wet when I spanked you?"

She bobbed her head as best she could with my fingers clenching her neck.

"I'll teach you how to please me, beautiful, but for now, if you ask nicely, I'll fuck you." I pushed my dick harder into the fleshy mound of her rear.

"Please fuck me," she choked out.

I waited. She knew what I wanted without me having to remind her. But she said nothing. Disappointing. I'd counted on her instinct to submit to me to kick in.

I felt the slide of her throat as she swallowed, and then she whispered, "Please fuck me, Sir."

That was the missing piece. I wanted her to beg for it, and someday she would. For now a polite entreaty would do the trick. Reaching down, I grasped my cock in my free hand, guiding it to her sopping slit. "I don't have a rubber."

"Don't care," she gasped, widening her stance to give me better access.

The warm head of my cock skimmed along her slit as I coated myself with her arousal. "I received your medical report in the profile I ran on you. Clean and still on birth control despite your claims that you had sworn off men. If you have an objection to continuing without condoms, I would state it now."

When she remained silent, I continued, "Why stay on the pill? Was it because you wanted to fuck me the first time we met?"

She sucked in a breath, unable to answer me. She had wanted me the first time we'd met. She'd told herself she wouldn't let her guard down, but she hadn't stopped taking her pills. She'd known all along that we would wind up here. It was inevitable. That a man like me could never be completely denied.

"I need to see this," I groaned and released my hold on her. With both hands, I spread her cheeks open and watched as the tip of my dick breached her perfect cunt. The pink tissue stretched over it as I sank inside her. I pulled out slowly, marveling at how her sex rippled over my shaft. "I could do this all day. I love watching your greedy pussy take my cock."

"Please," she cried as I continued my slow assault.

My fingers slid to her hips as I rammed into her with quick, deep strokes. "I want to see my cum dripping from inside you."

"Oh god," she called in a strangled voice. "Fill me with it!"

It was a request I was more than happy to oblige. As the first hot spurt of my seed lashed inside her, she came. She tightened over me, her body beginning to shake from the force of her climax. The warm constriction of her pussy milked more, squeezing jet after jet and draining me entirely.

We collapsed together against the wall of the lift, my dick still pulsing within her.

"Don't move," I ordered. Withdrawing slowly, I watched as cream dripped from her quivering cunt. "You're so lovely with my cum leaking from you."

Belle didn't move or speak. She simply stayed smashed against the wall until I drew her away from it on wobbly legs.

"Can you feel it?" I asked.

I wanted her to tell me that she loved it—that she was every bit as filthy and lewd as I'd hoped she would be. She nodded, a numb expression frozen on her face.

"It's hot," she whispered.

"Touch it."

She slid a trembling hand down, parting her folds with her fingers.

"That's it, beautiful," I coaxed, placing my hand over hers and smearing the thick liquid across her swollen sex.

Her head fell back as I helped her caress her overwhelmed pussy.

"I want to watch you come again," I growled, adding pressure to her hand.

She bit her lip as her hips began to buck against our fingers.

"Let go!" I demanded.

A guttural cry ripped from her chest as she exploded. When the tremors started to fade, she fell silent, her mouth still opened in a perfect O. Angling down, I took a kiss and then another until I felt myself begin to stiffen again.

"Are you ready for me to show you now?" I asked again. "Are you ready to be tamed and at my mercy? I assure you that you'll enjoy every moment."

She brushed her mouth against mine, then bit into my lower lip, tugging it gently between her teeth. "I'm ready to please you."

I crushed myself against her as I felt for the control panel. I didn't care where the lift took us.

I was only ready to begin.

Belle crawled across the bed and dropped onto the mussed-up sheets. Before last night, it had been a long time since I took a woman to my bed. I'd preferred hotels simply for the sake of discouraging any unwanted attachments. Belle looked like she belonged here, as though she already owned the place. That should bother me more than it did.

Crossing to my closet, I opened a small box that had been left undisturbed for years. I knew exactly what I needed from it.

I returned to the bedroom, holding it in my hand. She raised a curious eyebrow when she saw the long red feather attached to a leather wrapped wand. I'd always appreciated the juxtaposition. With one end I could provide a woman's flesh with the faintest hint of pleasure, with the other I could turn her backside red. I could only hope Belle would appreciate both sides it had to offer.

"Roll over on your belly," I instructed as I took a seat on the edge of the bed. I grabbed a pillow and wedged it under her head. She watched me as I caressed the silky plume with my fingers. "Do you understand what I mean when I say submission?"

"I have an idea," she said dryly.

"You've been submitting to me since last night," I explained. "What went through your mind when I told you to bend over or when I instructed you to fuck my car?"

"I wanted to please you," she whispered. Her breathing came in short, shallow pants now. She wanted it as much as I wanted to give it to her.

"Submission is about control. My control over your body. I enjoy possessing you nearly as much as I enjoy giving you pleasure. Have I given you pleasure?"

She nodded, the cheek pressed against the downy pillow growing pink.

"Now for some people it's about pain," I explained, smacking the leather end against my hand.

"Is that what it's about for you?" There was fear in her voice now.

I brushed a reassuring finger down her cheek. "For me, it's about pleasure. There is a fine line that exists between the two. When I spanked you in the elevator, it made you wet. Why?"

"It excited me." The fear had been replaced by embarrassment, and she hid her face.

"Don't do that," I ordered. "Look at me. I don't want to hurt you. I want to make you feel alive. You were excited because of how it made you feel."

"Free," she said.

"And owned at the same time. When people say opposites attract, I think they're really talking about sex. When you give control over to someone else, it allows you a freedom to experience total bliss. If I strike you with this end, it will sting. The other end will soothe. By combining the two opposites, the sensations overcome you. They liberate you so that all your body can understand is pleasure." I drew the feather along the curve of her spine, watching as her body tensed from the sensation. "Last night I warned you that once I took you, I would claim all of you. Do you still consent to giving yourself—your body, your power—over to me?"

For the moment I would continue to ask until I was positive I had her trained.

She licked her lips before replying softly. "Yes."

"Taming you isn't about changing you. It's about teaching your body to restrain itself until I command it otherwise. Only I can free you, and you can only be freed by allowing me that control." The tip of the feather tickled across her still glowing backside. "Right now you want to respond to this. Push it away or beg for more. I decide when it stops, just as I decide when there will be more."

I shifted farther onto the bed until I was kneeling beside her. "Get up on all fours."

She pushed up on her hands and knees as I stroked her back with my hand.

"I haven't told you how perfect your body is–smooth and soft. I pictured what you looked like naked the first time I saw you, but my imagination failed me. The reality is so much sweeter." I took the feather and placed it against her bare shoulder. "You'll feel this moving over you, but you aren't to budge. Can you do that? Simply respond 'yes, sir' when I ask a question, unless you want me to stop."

"Yes, Sir," she murmured. Her hips wriggled a little as she spoke, but I stopped them with a quick smack.

"Don't move. I'm training you now, showing you how to be tame so that you can please me. That's what you wish to do, right?"

"Yes, Sir," she answered more quickly.

Trailing the feather along her shoulders and up the back of her neck, I watched for a sign of movement. When she stayed still, I continued, drawing it lower until it caressed between her shoulder blades. I ran it down the curve of her spine, pleased to see she could control herself.

"I want you to open your legs for me." I moved the feather lower until it brushed her ass. Belle pushed her knees to the side. "Wider."

Her sex was swollen from our recent lovemaking, still engorged with desire. I placed the plume against it, running it quickly back and forth until I was positive she could feel the delicate fibers through the sensations crowding through her body. Belle's thighs began to shake, but she held herself motionless.

"Right now, you want more. I decide when you'll have it. I decide when you'll orgasm. Do you want to come now?" I asked, continuing my gentle assault of her pussy.

"Yes, Sir," she moaned. I could hear the strain in her voice.

"Not yet. There's so many things I want to show you," I told her in a soothing voice. "How good it will feel to crawl to me and ask for my cock. How well I'll treat you when your body obeys me. Sometimes though, I'll want to take you to the edge. Right now, it must feel like torture, having this soft feather whispering promises on your skin, but if I do this"—I flipped it over in my palm and smacked the leather end across her folds—"it makes you want it even more."

I continued to do this, brushing the soft tip over her fevered flesh and then slapping the other end roughly until her mound had plumped even more. A trickle of arousal seeped through her seam, but she remained in place.

"You're learning your lesson well. I am very pleased with you." Bending down, I traced my tongue along her wet slit. I could feel her fighting to remain still, and I pulled back. "I wanted a taste, beautiful. I know it's hard. I don't expect you to learn it all at once."

Dropping the feather tickler on the bed, I scooped her up and turned her into me. Her legs spread, but she stopped herself before she slid onto my cock.

"Is this what you want?" I asked, pushing my shaft toward her aching entrance.

"Yes, Sir," she breathed.

"Then get on me, beautiful. I want to watch you ride my cock."

She lowered herself slowly, impaling her body on my shaft. I rocked into her until I was buried so deeply that she froze in my arms.

"Are you sore?"

She nodded.

"Then let's go slow and make it last." I cradled her back as she leaned away from me and began to circle her hips. "But you should know, I'm not nearly finished with you."

"Promise?" she whimpered as her breathing sped up.

"Yes," I reassured her, rolling my groin against her. "Now fuck me, baby. I want to hear you scream."

CHAPTER THIRTEEN

A change of scenery and clothing seemed the best way to start Monday morning. I dropped a note onto Smith's nightstand telling him to make his own coffee, and I'd see him at his office at eight. Then I headed across town, thankful that I was getting a head start before the streets turned into parking lots filled with morning traffic.

It took me all of two seconds to pluck the tailored black dress that Smith had seen me try on at Harrods from my closet. A sentimental gesture, perhaps. But then again, if my experience with men had taught me anything, it was that he probably wouldn't even notice.

Then again, Smith wasn't most men.

I had time for a quick shower but little time for additional primping. Thankfully, this weekend's nonstop cardio session seemed to have given me a permanent after-sex glow. A coat of mascara and a swipe of nude lipstick and I was all but ready for the day.

Coming out of the bedroom, I jumped, temporarily surprised to see Jane waiting for me in the kitchen. Her unstyled platinum hair stuck up even more than usual. That and the loose fuchsia kimono she wore belied that she'd just gotten up. She smiled at me as she took a kettle off the hob and poured water into two waiting cups.

"You look refreshed," Jane said, passing me a warm cup of tea.

I stirred in some sugar and milk, studiously avoiding her eyes, and shrugged. "I didn't have to work much."

"Apparently you didn't have to sleep either," she said in a knowing voice. There was a point hidden under that statement. I was expected to spill as to my whereabouts for the past few days.

But what had happened between Smith and me was too new for me to share. It might have meant nothing. Just a case of two consenting adults finally giving in to their more carnal natures. Still, I'd never been with anyone like that. Raw. Unfiltered. Up for anything he suggested. It had been like tuning into a private frequency. I knew what he wanted from me and I did it. No questions asked.

I sipped my tea slowly to avoid burning my tongue and considered how I felt about all of it.

"You're overthinking things," Jane informed me, breaking through the wall of thoughts I'd constructed in a matter of seconds.

My eyes flickered to hers. I had no doubt that Jane would think nothing of my sexual escapades. I'd been treated to the dulcet sounds of some of hers over the last few months. She could help me understand how to feel about the shifting dynamic between him and me.

"Maybe I am," I admitted. This weekend was still ours. It belonged to Smith and me. I didn't want to share him, not even the memories he'd given me. It was a possessive streak I didn't realize I had.

I abandoned the cup and leaned over to kiss her on the cheek. "Why are you up so early anyway? I've never seen you out of bed before ten."

"My flatmate finally came home. I thought I'd better say hello before she disappeared again." Jane pursed her lips. She'd checked me, but I wasn't about to give up my cards.

"Did you worry?" I asked apologetically. That hadn't been my intention.

"Not at all. I received your text." She waved off my concern before turning a piercing stare on me. "So you aren't going to give me any of the juicy details, huh?"

A sly smile crept over my face. I couldn't hold it back.

Jane merely laughed, winking as if I'd just given her all the dirt. "I think that's detail enough."

THERE WERE TERMS FOR WHAT I'D DONE WITH SMITH. ONES I'D only read about in books. None of my past lovers had a penchant for dominance, which might have been why I never suspected I would be so open to it. Now I felt myself hungering for his hands on my body in ways no man had ever touched me. The slaps. The fingers around my neck. The desire to hold myself on edge and be restrained. It was all new to me, and I found myself wondering what it said about me. Part of me worried that it was seriously fucked up to crave his control, but the stronger half of me didn't care.

When I finally arrived, breathless, at work. I waltzed past Doris and went straight to Smith. He'd said I belonged to him now and I was eager to be back in his possession.

If I'd expected an affectionate greeting when I reached the office, I would have been disappointed. But because I was still growing accustomed to Smith's mercurial moods I'd prepared myself. Still his cold reception hurt.

"You weren't there when I woke up." He didn't bother to look up at me. His tone was so cold that I half expected ice crystals to form in the air.

But they only fired me up. I'd given my body to him but not every waking moment of my life. Perhaps allowing him so much authority over me in bed had given him the wrong idea about where we stood. No matter how much I'd enjoyed our weekend, I was still the same girl he'd hired a couple of weeks ago. Mostly. "I left a note. I needed to go home and change."

Smith continued tapping a message into his mobile. He frowned slightly but said nothing more to me.

Was he really that pissed off to wake up alone? "I'm not sure what I did wrong. I needed to change. I was under the impression that clothing-optional weekends ended before Monday morning, but maybe you need to send an office memo."

His lips twitched but he didn't smile. A few moments later, he dropped his phone on the desk and finally shifted his focus to me. "I'll see that a few items are delivered to my house."

Sheesh, down boy. How had he managed to go from dismissive to giving me a dresser drawer so quickly? It was enough to drive a girl to drink.

"I don't think that's necessary. I have my own place"

"On the contrary." Smith leaned back in his chair and steepled his fingers. "You have a room at my house that you may have occasion to use. You should have some things there. It's unnecessary for you to drive halfway across London to pick up fresh clothes."

His purely pragmatic response left a funny taste in my mouth. I crossed my arms over my chest and glared at him. "Would you prefer if I use that room?"

"Clearly, I prefer you naked in my bed. But since you clearly want to establish boundaries, I merely pointed out a practical solution where both our needs can be met." Smith grabbed a stack of folders and stood. With one hand, he buttoned his suit jacket before he strode out of the door of his office.

I could hear him instructing Doris on what to do with the files, but I didn't care. Maybe I was being just as hot and cold as he was. But he had to see how ridiculous it was to expect a woman to go to work in the dress she'd been clubbing in the Friday before.

"There's also the issue," he continued as he reappeared in the doorframe, "that occasionally we might want to go somewhere that requires you be dressed on these, what did you call them? Clothing-optional weekends. But if you'd prefer to go all the way home with no knickers, so be it." He paused, mid-stride and took my hand. "And since I didn't get to say it this morning. Good morning, beautiful."

He pressed his lips to my knuckles, trying to charm his way out of this discussion. That was not about to happen. Smith needed to understand that regardless of how much he paid me, he couldn't expect to cage me entirely and that there were certain things I wouldn't budge on.

"I tend to always wear knickers in public," I said, not bothering to hide the caustic note in my voice.

"Not around me." He sank back into his seat, a devilish grin carving over his face. "I want your pussy bare, and if I find anything covering it, I'll just rip it off."

"I hope your clothing allowance will cover new undergarments." I refused to play into his game. At least, I wanted to believe I could refuse. But somehow I found I'd taken a few steps closer to him.

So much for willpower.

"It doesn't seem like you'll need many." His index finger rested thoughtfully over his lips.

Fire burned in my core. All he had to do was look at me and I was ready. It was going to be hard to stand my ground on any issues if his mere presence turned me into a puddle of arousal.

Smith had been in control since the moment he showed up at Brimstone. Maybe he needed a taste of his own medicine.

"But when you aren't around," I whimpered, prowling closer to him, "I'm not certain I'll be able to control myself."

Smith raised one eyebrow as I leaned down on his desk, giving him a full view of my rack.

"I'd be disappointed in you if you couldn't," he responded in a serene tone, but I caught a blood vessel twitching in the side of his neck.

"What would happen if I didn't? If I lost control?" I sauntered around the desk and pushed myself up on its top. Crossing my legs, I gave him my most dazzling smile.

"I'd advise you to never let that happen." His hands dropped to the arms of his chair, and he clutched them, angling his upper body closer to me. The space between us was growing smaller by the second. "Or I would punish you."

"Punish?" I repeated, more than a little shocked to hear such an archaic term from his lips despite our foreplay over the weekend. "Would you spank me again?"

"For starters. Then I'd make you suck my cock until you were so wet, you were begging for it to be inside you. But you know what happens to bad girls, beautiful."

"Enlighten me." I drew the words out, allowing them to linger on my tongue far longer than necessary.

"When you disobey me, I can't give you what you want." He gripped the thick bulge in his trousers, stroking down the hard length of his cock for emphasis. "I can't give you this."

I wasn't about to give in so easily, even though the thought of him denying me pleasure set my heart racing. "Good thing I have a battery-operated boyfriend."

"That would be a very naughty thing to do. And you wouldn't need this then, would you?" he prompted as he unfastened his belt. "Except we both know that you can play with all the toys you want, and they'll never make you come like I will. Do you remember what it was like? How you screamed?"

My ass squirmed higher on the desk. I tried to make it look purposeful, but the truth was that I was losing my control of this situation and I was losing it quickly. There was only one thing for it.

Gripping the edge of the desk with my palms, I pushed myself off and immediately dropped to my knees. Scooting between his legs, I stroked the back of my hand along his hot length.

There was one sure-fire way to regain the upper hand over a man. My fingers deftly unbuttoned his fly, but before I could pull down his zipper, the phone on his desk rang. Smith's hand shot out and caught my wrist as his other picked up the receiver.

I leaned down and pressed my mouth to the bulge in his pants, but he moved his chair away. With a flick of his chin, he mouthed, "Get up."

I yanked my hand free and continued to work on his pants, but he stood, nearly knocking me over in the process.

"No, I'm available to discuss the clause now. We all need this merger to go through as smoothly as possible," he said into the phone as he took a step away from me.

The message was loud and clear. My advances were unwanted. I scrambled to my feet, embarrassment flushing across my cheeks as I tugged down my skirt. Smith leaned over and scribbled something on a piece of paper.

At least if he was going to be a dick, he was going to explain himself. But when he handed me the note, there was only one word scribbled on it.

Coffee.

Motherfucker. That was the note I wanted to pass back to him. Instead I crumpled up the piece of paper and marched out of his office, slamming the door behind me.

By the time I'd gotten through the line at the coffee shop on the corner, I'd considered a hundred different ways to murder him. Poisoning his espresso seemed the easiest and most poetic, but it was definitely the fastest way to get caught. Although I thought a police officer might let me off when he heard my reasoning.

Smith had refused my blowjob.

That was obviously grounds for some type of extreme reaction.

Stopping at the corner newsstand, I grabbed a copy of Trend magazine and began to page through it. If I wasn't going to poison him, I was going to make damn sure that his coffee was cold before it hit his lips.

Revenge was best served cold, right?

An article on the perfect little black dress caught my eye and I flipped to it. The pages were stuck together, changing the article headline to "Bless."

I smiled at the thought. Any girl would agree that the right black dress was definitely a blessing.

Meanwhile, I ignored the shrill ring of my text notification at first but finally dug my phone out of my purse when it sounded for the second time. But there were no messages. Wrong phone. Digging my personal mobile out of the bottom of my purse, I nearly dropped it when I saw the note from Edward.

EDWARD: We have contractions! Get to the hospital.

I turned, stuffing the magazine into my purse and nearly spilling the coffee in the process.

"Miss! Miss!" The newsstand's owner gestured wildly to my purse.

"Oh, here!" I passed him the coffee and dug out a five-pound note. Tossing it to him, I took off down the street before he could hand me the change.

I was nearly to the carpark when my mobile began to ring with an incoming call. It took me a moment to realize it wasn't the one in my hand. I pulled my work mobile out. Smith's name flashed across the screen. I took one look at it and hit decline.

Then I turned it off altogether.

CHAPTER FOURTEEN

Norris, Alexander's personal security guard and oldest friend, met me in the parking garage, ushering me past the swarms of well-wishers and paparazzi that had shown up for the blessed event. As far as I knew, only three people were on the guest list. Me, Edward, and Alexander.

And the baby, of course.

All the frustration and embarrassment I'd felt when I left Smith's office had vanished, leaving only excitement that I was about to meet my new, if unofficial, niece. Half of the Royal Protective Services were parked at various entrances to St. Mary's. I could hardly blame Alexander after the year he'd had. But despite the massive available security, he was a mess when he met me at the door.

"How is she doing?" I tried to peek around him, but Alexander caught my arm.

"She's having a rough time. I finally convinced her to have some pain medication."

I squeezed his shoulder in support. "You should be in there. Edward and I will wait out here."

"Actually, she's pretty put out with me at the moment."

"So you want me to go in and remind her that you hung the moon?" I guessed.

He smirked, but the grin quickly fell from his handsome face. "She didn't take my joke about being her lord and master all that well five minutes ago."

"She must be in a lot of pain." I didn't bother to remind him that he had gotten her into this mess in the first place.

"Look, she coped with this pregnancy for far too long without my support. I'm going back in there in ten minutes whether she wants me to or not."

"I'm fairly certain that as the ruling King of England, you can go anywhere you want."

"I didn't think she'd like it if I reminded her of that either."

"Give me a few minutes." I ducked inside before he could keep me there any longer. Alexander had become the center of Clara's world, but she was the center of his universe. I didn't always appreciate feeling like I was in the middle of that, but I also couldn't deny that he made her happy. No matter how frustrated she was with him, there was no way she was this without him at her side.

"Thank God. The testosterone level in the room was beginning to make me ill," Clara announced when I entered. She held her hand out to me just as the monitor at her bedside spiked. Clara let out a strangled cry, her hand still extended, and her other clutching her swollen belly.

I rushed to her side and took her outstretched hand, wondering if the contraction was as painful as the death grip she had on my fingers. "Breathe."

She shot me a warning look.

"Or don't," I said flatly. "But I don't think not doing it will help."

Clara exhaled forcefully and dropped back against the bed.

"I think you broke some of my fingers," I informed her, trying to wiggle feeling back into them.

"Sorry," she said sheepishly.

"No problem." I passed her a cup of ice chips from the table next to her bed. My experience with childbirth was limited to what I had seen in movies. As far as I knew, women screamed, cursed, and sucked on cubes of ice. There were more bizarre rites of passage but not many, in my opinion. "Now why has Alexander been banished."

"Because I'm going to take this"—she held up her IV line—"and strangle him with it. He seems to have forgotten which one of us is birthing this baby."

"What does the doctor say?" I switched the topic away from her husband quickly.

"I'm not dilating fast enough. They gave me some useless pain pill, and now they're monitoring the baby. Oh and a nurse told me half of the damn country is outside waiting for me to push her out."

"Keep things in perspective," I said soothingly. "A couple hundred of years ago and they would have all gotten to be in here watching you."

"That might be the only thing that's changed for the better," Clara muttered, catching her breath as another contraction hit her. "Distract me."

"I slept with Smith." I blurted out the first thing that came to mind. So much for keeping the news to myself.

"I know," Clara cried. When she went limp again, she gave me a weak smile.

"News travels fast."

"Edward said you two practically shagged on the dance floor at Brimstone," she said breathlessly

"Edward is a cad."

"He also said Smith almost punched him." Clara threw me a pointed look

"Yes, Edward and I were dancing too suggestively. Smith must be the only person in England who hasn't heard the prince is gay."

"I am?" Alexander's deep voice called as he appeared in the doorway. "Then how did we get into this predicament?"

The effect of his presence on Clara was immediate. Despite her big talk about being tired of his over-protectiveness, her whole face changed when he entered. It lit up the room. Even when she was annoyed with him, he still had that effect on her.

It had been one of the first warning flags to me that Philip and I might not be the right fit. I'd chosen to ignore it at the time. Now I wondered how I'd ever been able to. Maybe because I'd been so desperate to find someone who loved me even a fraction of the amount that Alexander loved Clara.

A nurse followed Alexander into the room and shooed me out. "I need to check her progress. You can come back in a minute."

"I'll go find Edward." I squeezed Clara's hand, but when I went to release it, she gripped it tighter.

"I'm not sure I can do this," she whispered.

"That makes one of us, because I know you can." I gave her a quick kiss on the cheek and turned on Alexander.

"Try not to piss her off."

"I think I missed that boat nine months ago," he muttered.

I pushed him toward her. In my experience, neither of them could stay mad at each other for very long.

The halls of St. Mary's were empty. The entire Lindo Wing had been cleared out with limited access to staff and visitors. My phone chirped, and I caught a message from Lola.

LOLA: Madeline is threatening parental divorce if she's not admitted.

BELLE: Do you want me to speak with Clara? She might let her in.

LOLA: Definitely not. There's not enough pain meds in the world to get Clara through that. I've got her under control. But let me know what's going on in there.

I promised her I would and then continued my search for Edward. Rounding a corner, I caught sight of him in a lounge. His fiancé David grinned at me as I entered with my hands planted on my hips.

"Are you hiding?" I accused them.

"Nappies. Bottles. I'm game for any of it," Edward explained, "but I was in there for ten minutes and that was more than enough."

"He just told me he was glad neither of us could give birth," David told me.

"Not going in with the surrogate?" I asked.

They both responded at the same time.

"Maybe."

"We're not having kids."

I put my hands up in surrender. Apparently I was starting fights all over London today.

"What do you mean we aren't?" David demanded.

"Have you seen how screwed up my family is?"

David crossed his arms and grinned as he shook his head. "If I recall correctly Alexander said the same thing about children."

"Thankfully, you can't get knocked up," Edward bit out.

"This is not the last time we're discussing this," David warned as he stood up. He gave me a quick hug before he headed toward the door, calling over his shoulder. "Talk some sense into His Highness."

"Apparently that is my official job title for the day: *She Who Talks Sense Into the Monarchy*." I grimaced. "Exactly how have I wound up being best friends with half the royal family? The lot of you is completely cocked up."

"How's it going?" Edward asked. He patted the now empty seat next to me.

"I think it would be going better if my life made any sense," I admitted. "I'm not sure how I'm supposed to offer advice when I'm busy making all the wrong choices myself."

"Things didn't go well with Smith?" Edward guessed, wrapping an arm around me.

I shook my head, leaning into him. "Things went too well with Smith."

"I wish I had your problems," Edward teased.

"I'll trade you," I offered. "I think David and I would have beautiful babies."

"Keep your hands off my man," Edward said in mock-warning. "Besides, it looked like you snagged one of your own the other night."

"I thought I had." At least, I could go into this with Edward without giving him all the dirty details. Normally I might have tried to talk with Clara, who knew a thing or two about getting involved with a complicated man, but she had other things to worry about at the moment. "I don't know. He's so demanding."

"In the bedroom?" Edward asked, his eyes glimmering mischievously.

"Everywhere." I didn't add that no part of me minded his compulsive attention to detail between the sheets.

"Well, I learned how hard that can be watching the couple of the hour." Edward paused, rubbing his chin thoughtfully. "I think you have to decide if you see a future with him."

"I don't know him well enough," I admitted. "But I wouldn't mind spending a couple of weeks in his bed."

"Then make that boundary clear. Look, Belle"—Edward leaned forward and squeezed my knee—"we both know you can be a little resistant to the idea of a relationship."

I snorted. "Can you blame me?"

"Not one bit, but don't get so caught up in keeping things safe that you stop taking chances. Take it from a guy who made his boyfriend pretend to be just friends for years."

"Yeah, you might not be the best person to give relationship advice now that I think about it," I teased.

"I went legit!"

We were both laughing when David popped his head in.

"They're taking Clara into surgery."

I was on my feet in an instant. "Is everything okay?"

"The baby is showing signs of distress."

He didn't have to say any more before we were all booking it back toward her room. We arrived just in time to see them wheeling her out into the hall.

"Belle!" she called my name frantically.

I rushed over to her.

"If anything happens—"

"Nothing is going to happen," Alexander interrupted her.

"If anything happens," she continued, tears sparkling in her eyes "take her shopping. She's going to have a fantastic dad. I want to make sure she has some girl time, though."

I swallowed back my own tears that threatened to spill down my cheeks. I didn't need to encourage her by showing her I was scared. "We'll take her shopping. Who do you think taught you how to dress? Or have you already forgotten?"

"Sir," the doctor interrupted, "we need to get her down the hall."

Alexander's and my eyes locked and then he was running along her side, hands clasped. His mouth was moving, but even though I couldn't hear what he was saying, I could imagine.

Life might not be counted in moments, but that was only because in times like this, moments seemed to stretch into hours. Edward and I took turns pacing by the entrance to the surgical room. No one had told us how long it might take.

"She's going to be fine," David assured both of us as he rubbed Edward's shoulder. My friend caught his hands and held them tightly.

We'd lost so much already this year. It seemed that every moment of joy was overshadowed by tragedy and horror. My called-off engagement. The attack at the wedding that had resulted in Edward's father's death. The car accident. It seemed that fate kept trying to take Clara from all of us.

She might have grown tired of Alexander's obsession regarding her safety over the last few weeks, but personally I was glad he was in there now. I'm pretty sure death himself couldn't have gotten past him to get to her.

Behind us, a door opened and we all spun around, hoping to finally have some news. But instead of a doctor, Smith stood there with his tie loosened and his hair disheveled.

"How the hell did you get in here?" I demanded. I didn't want him here. Not now. Not while I was feeling vulnerable and certainly not after how he'd dismissed me earlier today.

He held up a bag. “I brought you some food.”

I crossed to him, my arms clamped tightly over my chest. “That doesn’t explain how you got in here.”

“I represent a few of the physicians here,” he explained. “I called in a favor.”

“You should have saved it, because I don’t want you here.”

“Too bad,” he said dismissively. He shifted his focus to Edward. “They told me she’s been in surgery for about a half hour?”

“Yeah.” Edward’s eyes narrowed. Smith’s memory might be short, but Edward clearly wasn’t over their showdown at Brimstone.

“There’ll be news soon. It takes a while to get everything sewn back up.”

My stomach lurched at the thought. I hated that my best friend was in there and I couldn’t be. Then again, clearly I didn’t have the constitution to be at her side.

I grabbed Smith by the arm and dragged him into the corner. Everyone had enough to worry about without adding our bickering to the list.

“How did you know where I was? This is the second time you’ve mysteriously shown up where I’m at.” He’d found me at Brimstone as well. Either he really could read my mind, or I should probably be considering a restraining order.

“Your aunt told me where you were on Friday,” he explained, tugging his sleeve loose from my grasp and smoothing it back out. “And today? Well, it might have been harder to figure out if every media outlet wasn’t reporting that your best friend is currently pushing out the country’s next monarch.”

“Thanks for the food, but I’m not hungry.” I started to turn away but he stepped closer, rooting me to the spot.

“That was an important phone call earlier,” he explained. “I wasn’t going to be able to concentrate with your lips around my cock.”

“I promise to never bother you in that way again.”

He tilted his head. “Like it or not, you do work for me, Belle. Sometimes I have to handle things privately.”

"You told me I would be there for everything," I reminded him. "But the truth is you haven't shown me one thing about yourself. I know nothing about you, Smith."

"It takes time to know someone." But his eyes lied.

"Yeah, it does, but you have to show them the truth," I reminded him softly.

Smith leaned closer until his lips brushed my ear. "Have you shown me everything yet, beautiful?"

I jerked away. He'd hit a nerve I didn't want plucked today. Or ever. Some memories were best left in the past. What I couldn't get over was that he was purposefully keeping certain elements of his business from me. I could understand client privilege, but he wouldn't answer a simple question about what type of law he specialized in. Now he was trying to twist my words. Just like a lawyer. "I've had enough experience with men that turn things back around on me. I'm not interested in that game, Mr. Price."

"I'll leave this here." He set the bag of take-away on a nearby chair. Inclining his head politely toward Edward and David, he turned to go. "Take a few days off, Miss Stuart. Spend time with your friend. I'm sure she needs you more than I do."

I wasn't sure what stung more: that he'd dismissed me or that he'd let me win.

"Wanker," I screamed as the door closed behind him.

"That is the second time someone has yelled that at me today. So much for commanding respect," Alexander said behind me.

I spun around, not realizing my little scene had drawn more of a crowd. But all my fury evaporated when I saw a tiny pink bundle in his arms.

"Elizabeth, meet your Auntie," Alexander cooed, bringing her over to me. "She has a very dirty mouth."

I nudged him the ribs. "You're one to talk, Daddy. How's Clara?"

"Resting," he said, his eyes never leaving his daughter. "Both of them are perfect."

The look on his face said it all. His world had just gotten a little larger. He had more power and money than most of us could ever dream of, but all that mattered to him was the tiny baby girl in his arms and her mother down the hall.

My heart constricted. That was love. As I took Elizabeth carefully from him, I experienced my own awakening.

I did know what love was. I'd seen it. I felt it now toward the people in this room. Maybe that was as much as some people got in a lifetime, and really, wasn't that enough?

I glanced back at Alexander and saw the pure joy written across his face.

Not everyone could have happily-ever-afters. Clara and Alexander deserved theirs. I'd just make certain my little godbaby didn't fall victim to the idea of fairytales.

"Once upon a time, there was a beautiful princess," I whispered, giving her soft, pink forehead a kiss, "and she could do anything she wanted without a man..."

CHAPTER FIFTEEN

Spending the week holding the new addition to my life did wonders for my soul, but it did little to allay the ache of absence I felt elsewhere. Smith had sent food and flowers, but he hadn't shown himself again at the hospital. I'd been grateful for that. It had given me the time I needed to realize the mistake I had made by letting him into my life—or at least into my panties.

By Friday, Clara was back home, adjusting to her new life as a mother, and I had to face my boss.

Boss, I reminded myself. That was where our relationship began, and that's where it needed to end. If I couldn't control my feelings about Smith, I would have to walk away. The income I'd get from a few weeks pay would be enough to get my business off the ground floor, and if working for him meant continuing to put my heart in jeopardy, then I would find another way to get it started.

His face registered no emotion when I strode up to his desk and handed him a cup of black coffee on Friday morning. He looked good—too good—and I silently cursed him for wearing a navy pinstripe suit that fit his athletic body like a glove. His hair was neatly combed back, and I longed to reach out to muss it up. I'd seen what he looked like after my hands had held onto it for traction as he fucked me. Part of me missed it. I missed the primal, raw beast that had taken over my world. But Smith was a wolf hiding in a tailored three-piece suit, so why was I so determined to offer myself as his next meal?

"I'll pick up your suits from the cleaners this afternoon. I've arranged for the penthouse at the Plaza when you go to New York next month." I continued to rattle off the list of things I'd taken care of or would by the afternoon.

"Can you have Doris file these for me?" He passed me a large stack of folders.

I hadn't known what to expect when I returned today. I'd expected to want him. Part of me had wondered if I would fall into his arms. I hadn't expected the distant professionalism he was exhibiting now. Not after he'd spent a small fortune delivering food and gifts to the hospital.

"Is there something else?" he asked, tapping his chin with his index finger impatiently.

It was like nothing had happened between us. But if Smith thought he could just ignore what we'd done and the lines we'd crossed, he had another think coming.

"Let's get one thing straight," I hissed, clutching the pile of folders in my arms tightly. Air stung my index finger, and I realized I'd given myself a paper cut, but the sharp, if insignificant, discomfort was only a reminder that men equaled pain. "I hate you."

Smith leaned back in his leather chair and crossed his arms behind his head, regarding me with an arrogant smirk. "Do you always let people you hate fuck you, Belle?"

What I wouldn't give to wipe that smug grin off his face, but doing so would put me in dangerous proximity to his lips. Unfortunately, I didn't trust my body to not betray me, especially since it knew the mind-blowing orgasms he was capable of giving me. "Hate-fuck is exactly the right term," I said, purposefully mishearing him. "I hated every minute of it."

There was a pause after the words fell from my lips. The office was entirely quiet, neither of us moving. Neither of us breathing. It was a dangerous silence. The kind that followed a lie. The moments seemed to slow until Smith's hand swung out, sweeping across the paperwork on his desk and sending his lamp flying across the room. He was on his feet before I had processed his reaction. This time when his fingers lashed out, they caught the waist of my skirt as he yanked me against him, knocking the folders to the floor.

"Don't lie," he warned me. "Don't fucking lie to me."

"I do hate you," I breathed, even as the words hitched in my throat. Could he hear my heart pounding? It felt as if it was going to burst from my chest. My body was strung out on the strange cocktail of hate, lust, and hope.

Smith pushed me down, so that I was seated on top of his desk. His phone began to ring, but I barely registered it as he reached under my skirt and yanked off my thong.

This was where I was supposed to say no. Hit him. Scream. But I realized then that I didn't want any of that. I didn't want to deny him. I only needed him to show me he still wanted me after our fight earlier this week.

And now that he had, I could see how stupid the fight had been. I'd been petulant. He'd been condescending. We both needed to make amends and this was the perfect way to do it.

He didn't miss a beat as he clicked the speaker button on his office phone. His eyes were trained on me and the intensity of his gaze sent my shallow breaths into full-blown pants. Stepping between my legs, he urged my thighs open wider as he reached for the scarf tied loosely around my neck. Bringing it to my lips, he held it there until my mouth parted as willingly as my legs. I bit down on the knot, grateful to have something to stifle the gasps I knew were coming.

"Hammond," he said in a clipped tone, his hand sliding under my skirt. "I was under the impression we were speaking over dinner tonight."

He traced along my seam, his feather-light touch sending a pool of moisture gushing to welcome him. My eyelids clenched shut as I waited, spread in invitation, for him to fuck me however he saw fit. All I cared about was that he filled this desperate ache building in my core. But his other hand curved around my neck and squeezed, forcing my eyes to fly open. My startled gaze met his. There was no question who was in charge here, so when he withdrew his hand, he mouthed, "Eyes open."

"I merely wanted to discuss our plans," Hammond answered. "Is this a bad time?"

Thanks to the knot blocking my mouth I couldn't yell yes, but Smith merely smiled wickedly at me and shook his head. "It's the perfect time."

Smith pushed a finger between my wet folds and circled my engorged nub, drawing a smothered moan from my lips.

Oh god, I wanted him inside me. I wanted this torturous game of foreplay that had coloured our time together to end. I wanted to be fucked, and Smith knew it, which is why he continued his teasing strokes along my pussy. I was a trapped animal, cornered by a predator I had no hope of escaping, because I didn't want to be freed. I wanted to be devoured.

"I want this meeting to be between the two of us," Hammond informed him. "Leave your toy at home."

I was dimly aware of the fact that I was the one being uninvited, but I didn't care. I couldn't care about it at the moment. Not with Smith's fingers working their clever magic on my clit. The man was infuriating. He was a connoisseur of the slow burn, and I was learning quickly that he didn't mind taking his time when it came to pleasure. What he didn't seem to understand was that sometimes a girl needed a quick, rough shag.

"Miss Stuart is my assistant. She comes when and where I tell her to." His eyes landed on mine, and the implication was clear. He wasn't speaking to Hammond now. He was instructing me. I wasn't getting off until he said I could.

"This is a private affair. I assure you that you will have no need for her," Hammond argued, growing agitated but still trying to stay cool. I recognized the sound of it because it was exactly how I felt.

"I always have a need for her." Smith's finger plunged inside me, followed by a second one. He rolled and kneaded, coaxing me closer and closer to the brink. I held on through sheer force of will, not allowing myself to fall over the edge. My hands clutched the edge of his desk frantically, searching for an anchor as his touch set me adrift at sea. The water was calm, but the current warned of oncoming waves—the kind that would push me under and hold me there.

Hammond's tone switched from businesslike to snakelike instantly. "Need I remind you that she's connected to some very important people."

Smith shifted forward, pressing his weight against my body as the pad of his thumb settled over my clit again. A shudder wracked my body, and my legs coiled around his waist. His breath was hot on my face, his lips inches from mine. I longed to kiss him—to close the gap that always stretched between us. Between his words and the magnetic pull of his body, it seemed possible. But it wasn't, especially given the scarf wedged between my teeth. No, another kiss was dangerous in more ways than one. Kisses were expectations, and I didn't dare expect anything from Smith Price.

He was sending me mixed messages: controlling me, controlling my body. Protecting me while pushing me away. Keeping me close even as he shut me out. And maybe I was reading this one wrong, too. Maybe what he was trying to tell me was lost in translation, twisted by the heady pleasure he was ravaging on me. Smith leaned down and brushed his lips briefly over my forehead as he increased the pressure of his hand between my legs. "And now she's connected to me."

It was in his voice—the command to let go—and I plunged headfirst into his storm. Pleasure battered me, tightening across my limbs until my skin felt as though it would snap from the pressure, and then...release. I climaxed in bursts, clutching the desk while my legs snapped shut like a sprung trap around his body. The fingers inside me, the hand continuing its tireless siege, were my anchors. My whole being centered around him and the pleasure he could give me.

Or refuse me.

I could hear the voice on the other line, but it had faded, lost in the rush of blood and pheromones coursing through me as I endured each crest and crash. Smith murmured something I couldn't comprehend and hit the button on the receiver. In one swift motion, he tugged the scarf from my mouth, freeing my final few gasps of pleasures. He held the loose scarf by the knot and drew me forward. There was no resisting his pull, not while he had me—for all intents and purposes—collared. And certainly not while I was still throbbing with the memory of his touch.

The orgasm had only succeeded in making me crave him more. All the rational reasons to stay away from him—to keep myself emotionally detached—vanished as he pulled me roughly to his lips, still gripping the scarf. He'd released me, but he still had me caged. And with each day, the possibility of escape—the possibility of leaving him—grew more incomprehensible. Couldn't he see that he didn't need to trap me? To control me? That I was becoming his?

That I already was his?

Our lips crashed together, and I lost myself in him. Resisting him was like holding my breath and this kiss was the gasp following its release. I wanted to swallow him, consume him, let him infect my blood—and god, I hoped he felt the same way.

He pulled back slightly, his mouth still grazing mine, and tightened his hold on the scarf until there was no slack left. My hips squirmed forward to seek contact with him. The orgasm had been mind-blowing but not altogether satisfying. His closeness coupled with the spots where we touched only made me want more.

"You liked it when I played with you, beautiful." His teeth nipped at my lower lip, sending a shock of desire jolting through me. "You're such a good girl. Always doing as I say. Feel how hard that makes me."

I pried my fingers from the edge of the desk and gripped the erection tenting his slacks. He was firm and hot, and I involuntarily caressed the hard length, imagining how it would feel inside me. Smith groaned and pressed closer as he unfastened his pants with his free hand.

"I'm going to take you, Belle," he growled, "and I won't be gentle. I'm going to fuck you hard."

I opened my mouth to welcome the scarf, knowing I'd need it to muffle my screams, but he shook his head.

"I want to hear you while my cock is inside you. No holding back or I'll punish you."

"Punish me?" I repeated, half fearfully and half hopefully.

"You like that, don't you?" he asked as he shoved down his boxer briefs, allowing me full view of his generous length.

I grew wetter at the sight and at the thought of what a real punishment from Smith might entail.

"It depends," I hedged.

"I've spanked you before."

A blush crept over my cheeks and I nodded. "Only playfully though."

"This won't be playful," he said in a low voice as my fingers closed over his shaft. He rocked against my grip, stroking himself with my clenched fist. "It will burn and sting and I won't stop until your ass matches your pretty pink cheeks. You won't be able to sit down without remembering my hands."

Oh my god. I refrained from turning over and presenting my buttocks to him. I wanted to know what it would feel like to be completely possessed by him, knowing any true pain I experienced at his hands would be matched by pleasure. I needed his hands on me—violently, passionately, any way I could have them.

His eyes hooded thoughtfully as if he could hear what I was thinking. "Not yet. You haven't earned a punishment."

"What have I earned?" I asked in a breathless voice.

"This." He rocked against my hand, sending his hot velvet shaft against my palm. He grabbed my hip, digging his nails into my tender flesh and urging me roughly around. My scarf slid loosely around my neck, still gripped by Smith. His palm spread across my back, and he shoved me down, flattening my breasts against the cold, smooth surface.

"Spread your legs and show me your pussy," he ordered.

My legs parted willingly. I'd been with other men, but none of them had ever produced such instant, wanton reactions in me. I couldn't refuse his demand, even though I felt a tingle of self-consciousness as I put myself on display.

"I've told you about how I wanted to fuck you the day we met," he reminded me as he nudged open my folds. He paused there, torturing me with a patience I didn't share. "I wanted to twist those pretty pearls around your neck like this"—he tugged the scarf sharply—"and watch your red lips gasp for air while I screwed you. I wanted to know if I could turn a good girl bad. You've proven to me that I can, haven't you?"

He already knew the answer. He already knew how to undermine my self-control. All he had to do was ask and I was his. My screams. My body. My pleasure. It had all belonged to him since the first time he took me in his sights.

"Put your hands behind your back. I'm in control."

I did as I was told, crossing my wrists over my tailbone and tilted my head so that my cheek rested on the desk. I could see him out of the corner of my eye, still in his suit, his tie still knotted at his throat.

"I'm going to fuck you hard, beautiful." His cock slid a fraction of an inch inside me, stretching my hole until I'd been reduced to a consuming ache at my core. "You're going to walk around the rest of the day full of me, and you're going to feel it. Do you want that?"

I nodded, my teeth instinctively finding my bottom lip.

Smith jerked the scarf, raising my head from the desk. "Answer me when I ask a question. Properly."

"Yes, Sir," I breathed as my heart raced, already anticipating what was about to happen.

"Oh, beautiful"—he pushed me gently back down to the desk—"I love it when you call me by my proper name. It reminds me that you're a lady even when you're being a slut. It tells me you know who you belong to and what I expect. Your behavior deserves a reward, so ask me for what you want."

I licked my lips, my eyes closing in expectation. "I want you to fuck me, Sir."

My response was met with a stinging slap across my ass.

"Ask," he repeated.

"Please, will you fuck me, Sir?" I squealed as the heat of his rebuke spread through my bottom.

"Yes, beautiful, I will." He thrust his length roughly until he was pounding deep inside me. His hold on the scarf tightened, lifting my head until I was staring blindly at the ceiling, too lost in the rhythmic strokes to see anything but stars. His other hand left my hip and closed over my wrists. Smith tugged them back, raising me higher so that my breasts bounced against the cold wood. He plunged in and out, alternating between slow thrusts and violent ones that lifted my feet from the floor. As his pace quickened, so did my breathing until I could no longer hold back my cries. They spilled from my lips in anguished sobs.

It was too much. The control. The way he dominated every inch of my body and mind. It was everything I'd ever wanted and never knew I needed.

Smith drove deep, impossibly deep, and buried himself against my soft cervix. Circling his hips, he pushed the small of my back with my pinned wrists and manoeuvred my body so that my clit pressed against the crisp wooden edge of his desk. It dug into the pulsing bud. Then he began to screw me again with deliberate precision, grinding it as I swelled over his punishing cock. My mind went blank except for the vibrations of pleasure that burst from my core and rippled through my body. There was only his cock. Only him.

"Come," he ordered gruffly. His voice strained from the nearness of his own climax. "I want to hear it. I want everyone in this building to hear it and know that you belong to me now."

As if to prove his point, his body crushed against mine, impaling me on his cock. My head snapped back, allowing his lips access to my neck as a scream ripped through my throat. I cracked along with the howl, ecstasy spilling through me and igniting the nerves that ran like fault lines across my flesh.

Smith growled, his teeth sinking into the curve of my neck, as the first hot jets lashed against the battered entrance of my womb. His hand released my wrists, allowing me to catch myself as I fell forward. And then the fullness of his cock vanished, replaced by the last spurt of his seed onto my tailbone.

The sensation of him lingered inside me. Before him I'd never allowed a man to come anywhere but my mouth. Now I wished Smith would mark me every day. He stepped back and I felt his eyes surveying his prize, but I was too blissed out to move. Not that my legs would be steady enough to hold me anyway. His fingers skimmed across my swollen seam, spreading me open so that the evidence of his climax leaked down my sex.

"Do you feel that, beautiful?" he asked in a husky tone. "Your pussy is full of me. Who do you belong to?"

"You, Sir," I mumbled, the production of complete thoughts still proving difficult.

Smith slid an arm under my torso and drew me up. I turned into him, nuzzling my face against his suit jacket and breathing in his spicy cologne. He pushed my skirt down and pulled me closer, tipping my chin up so that our eyes met. The hunger that had shone from his eyes was sated, and he kissed me softly.

"The car will pick you up at seven."

I blinked, trying to clear the fuzziness in my head. "I thought I wasn't invited."

"Your place is at my side. I've missed having you there this week, and I won't be without you this evening." There was no mistaking the finality of his words, and I wasn't about to argue. Not when it was exactly what I'd longed to hear. "Be ready by seven."

"I'm always ready for you." I flushed as I spoke. There would be no mistaking what I meant either.

"Talk like that will get you bent back over this desk, beautiful," he said gruffly, "and we both have work to do."

He released me and I looked away, suddenly overcome with shyness. There was still so much I didn't know about Smith—so much I didn't understand about him and his job—and yet I'd given myself to him fully. He rested a hand on the small of my back and I could sense that he wanted to reassure me. Neither of us spoke as I buttoned my blouse, but when I was finished he leaned in, his mouth brushing my ear.

"It's a formal dinner. Wear stockings, and heels tall enough that I can fuck you when I need to, but leave your pussy bare," he ordered.

My breath hitched and my mouth went dry, but I forced myself to respond. "Yes, Sir."

"I want you to come home with me tonight," he continued, and his cool eyes studied me as he spoke. He pushed a lock of hair out of my face. "Cancel your plans for the weekend, you're going to be rather tied up."

A spasm of excitement shot through my core, but I did my best not to show him how aroused the thought of another weekend in his bed made me. As much as I lusted for his body, I needed to maintain some control of our relationship. I might turn into a reckless addict when he touched me, but I wanted the balance of power to remain equitable the rest of the time.

"I'll do my best to clear my calendar." I wouldn't promise him more that that, even if I knew there was no way I could resist his request.

"Clear it, beautiful. I plan to spend the entire weekend making you come and I'm not taking no for an answer."

His head slanted, crushing his mouth to mine, and I melted into him. In the end, I didn't say yes. There was no other choice.

Who was I kidding? This wasn't equitable. Not even a little. I was falling for Smith Price. Hard and fast.

I just hoped wherever I landed, I wouldn't find myself there alone.

CHAPTER SIXTEEN

London traffic turned into a nightmare midday, so despite the fact that Smith had left the Veyron keys sitting on the reception desk—an act I took as an invitation—I decided to hit the pavement to finish out my to-do list. I made a mental note to thank Smith for keeping all of his personal and business needs in a relatively compact geographic area. But heading out on foot meant that I had considerably less time to deal with things before tonight's dinner plans.

I hoped this evening ran as hot as this morning had. Smith and I seemed to be stuck on a perpetual roller coaster, vacillating between on and off, hate and affection, hot and cold. When we were apart, I couldn't decide if I actually liked him, but when we were together, I needed him.

I always wanted him.

"Belle!"

I froze on the spot. There was no way I'd just heard his voice, but turning, I discovered I was wrong.

Philip stood on the walk in front of the law office and ran a hand through his floppy blond hair. He looked like the same lanky Harris Tweed ad. Although his hairline might be receding. With any luck, he'd wind up bald before his thirtieth birthday. Karma had a lot on her plate, but it appeared she had my back on this one.

"I'm sure you weren't expecting to see me," he said awkwardly.

"No, it's more like you're the last person that I wanted to see," I said coldly, before tacking on, "ever."

I had no idea what he was doing here. I'd spotted him at Clara's wedding before things had gone wrong. Retrospectively, I had considered it yet another bad omen. I'd managed to avoid him ever since.

Now he was standing in front of me. I waited for my heart to leap, waited for any sign that I still had feelings for him. Mercifully, there were none. All I felt was a pit opening up in my stomach. There were very few times in my life when I'd wished the earth would swallow me up. This was definitely one of them.

"I know things ended poorly between us."

I threw my head back and laughed at his choice of words. It felt liberating.

"I heard about you and Pepper. Congratulations." My voice took on a snide tone. "I hope you won't mind if I don't send a gift."

"Belle," he began, but I held a hand up.

"There's really nothing left for us to say to one another. I have errands to run." I walked away, ready to leave Philip behind—and all the baggage that came with him.

"I heard about your new job working for Smith Price," he called, stopping me in my tracks.

"It's going well." I shrugged as I turned back. So this was what we were reduced to—small talk about jobs. What was next? The weather? For the first time, I realized just how little we'd had to say to each other over the years. Maybe it was meeting Smith, but now I saw Philip for the bore he was. I'd spent the last few months believing he deserved a bitch like Pepper Lockwood. Now I realized she was getting hers as well. She had to put up with him for eternity.

"He represents a lot of bad people," Philip warned me.

Philip hated Alexander as well. In fact, he condescended to most people he knew, including me. But coming out of the woodwork to lecture me about my boss was the final straw.

"Don't you dare!" I exploded. "Don't come around here and pretend like you have something of value to add to my life. Your opinion no longer matters. It never should have in the first place."

Philip took a step closer to me, and the knot in my stomach tightened. "I care about you, Belle. I still love you. When I heard you were working for him, I had to say something."

"You lost the right to say anything when you cheated on me. And don't talk about loving me. You don't lie to the people you love." It wasn't an accusation. It was the truth, and we both knew it.

"Do you think he's being honest with you?" he probed. "Has he told you the crimes his clients commit? Who he's in bed with?"

I blushed scarlet at his choice of words, and Philip fell silent.

"I see," he said after a long moment. "You're in bed with him."

"That's none of your concern."

"He helps murderers go free, Belle. His father was involved in organized crime. I'm sure he hasn't told you what happened to him."

My blood turned to ice in my veins. His father was dead. I hadn't asked for details. Maybe I should have. "He isn't the only person with a dead father. That doesn't make him a criminal."

"Some people can have terrible fathers and come out unscathed. Smith Price isn't one of those people." His voice was low with warning, but all I could hear was the word terrible.

"My father wasn't a bad man." My lip began to quiver. Despite everything Philip had put me through, he had never once intuited that he judged my dad. Now I knew otherwise. "No wonder you decided to trade up. I guess you do care about who you're linked to. I would have thought you had better taste than Pepper."

"It's more complicated than that, Belle. I was trying to end things with Pepper. You were the one I wanted to be with, and I'll never forgive myself for hurting you."

The excuses began to flow. I'd unleashed a flood of apologies that I didn't need or want.

"And now you're engaged to her," I reminded him.

"She told me she was pregnant," he said flatly.

"Then I guess more congratulations are in order." Acid rose in my throat, and I fought the overwhelming urge to vomit. At least he was close enough I could do it on him.

"She's not," he continued. "She's trying to trap me."

"Oh c'mon, Pip." I purposefully used the childhood nickname he hated, savoring how it felt on my tongue. "One blonde or the other. What's it to you as long as someone's willing to hang off your arm and pretend you're interesting?"

"I deserve that. But I know which blonde I want on my arm. I meant it when I asked you to spend the rest of your life with me. I don't care about your father or what happened in the past. We can get through anything now." He moved so close to me that I could smell the familiar scent of his aftershave.

"Why are you here? Because if you think I'm going to fall into your arms, I'd suggest you walk away before I cut off your balls."

"You weren't innocent either. I knew about Jonathan, and I didn't say anything. It really doesn't matter to me," he added quickly.

"It matters to me!" I cried. "I don't want a husband who's always looking for someone more spectacular."

"There's no one more spectacular than you," he said in a solemn tone, and then before I could process what was happening, I was in his arms. His lips sought mine, making contact. For a split second I melted into his familiar embrace. But almost instantly, my body rebelled, rejecting his touch. I realized I didn't belong to him anymore before I managed to push him away.

"When I said it was over. I meant it. I've never done second chances." I wiped the back of my hand over my mouth, smearing lipstick across it.

"That's no way to live life," he advised. "Sooner or later, you'll have to give someone a second chance."

"Later then, because that second chance will never be wasted on you." I spat the words. "I could have wasted my life with you in a loveless marriage in exchange for money and mediocre orgasms. You know what I realized since we've been apart? I never loved you. I loved the idea of a husband. I'll never make that mistake again. Life is too short to waste it on people who don't even know you."

"I know you," he pressed. "I know you like milk and two sugars in your tea. I know you prefer Kate-style Louboutins and that you secretly wanted to major in fashion but your mother wouldn't let you."

"That's not knowing me. When I have a nightmare, what is it about? What song instantly makes me happy? If I could have dinner with one person, who would it be? Answer those questions," I challenged him. When he didn't respond, I continued, "You can't because you don't know me at all. You want someone that never existed. That girl—that façade—is gone."

"You were never a façade with me."

"That you didn't even realize it proves my point." I shouldered my purse, shaking my head. "Have a nice life, Philip."

"Who was it?" he asked before I could go. "The person you would have dinner with. Do you even know?"

I knew exactly who it would be, but Philip didn't deserve an answer. He didn't deserve anything from me, especially not my time. I walked away, leaving him with the memory of a girl he used to know and nothing more.

My flat seemed deserted when I finally made it there with a pile of dry cleaning and my mail. Considering how much time I'd spent away from home between Smith and the baby, I'd half-expected to discover Aunt Jane had brought home a new lover. Her soft spot for artists and musicians meant that more often than not we had someone staying on our couch.

Jane stumbled into the kitchen with a sleep mask perched on her forehead. "Look what the cat dragged home!"

"I've been at the hospital with Clara and the baby."

"How is she doing?" Jane asked, her forehead wrinkling in concern.

"She's well. Alexander is over the moon, even if he's trying to act like a tough guy. They headed home this morning, so I'm back to work." I gave Jane a brief squeeze before I headed into my room. Tonight was an important date on two counts. Firstly, I had to find an appropriate dress to wear. Smith was potentially about to piss off one of his biggest clients, simply to prove I'd been wrong about the dynamic between him and Hammond.

"And getting laid," Jane guessed, following me into my bedroom.

"And that," I admitted.

Jane dropped onto my bed. "How are things going with your new conquest?"

My aunt had always had a way with words. "Conquest? I thought the woman was the conquest."

"Not Stuart women," she said, her mouth twisting into a wry smile. "Girls like us don't wait around to be caught. We take charge. We write the rules to the game."

"Maybe so." I didn't feel that way about Smith. He was definitely conquering me, but I hadn't exactly been easy prey. "To be honest, I'm not really certain who is capturing who anymore."

"When it comes to love, that's the best way to play it." Jane winked.

Sheepishly, I grabbed my leopard weekender and began to toss a few must-haves in it. My favorite face cream, a new toothbrush and razor. I hesitated when I opened my underwear drawer. If Smith had been serious earlier, I ran the risk of him destroying all my frilly, lacy thongs. I threw them in the bag anyway. He could afford to buy me more.

"Going away for the weekend?"

"No, I'll be here in London." I zipped the bag shut and shifted my attention to my closet and what to wear this evening. "And I'll have my mobile on."

"I wouldn't dream of interrupting your plans." She laid a hand over my packed bag. "I know you're pretending to be busy, love. What's really on your mind?"

I plucked a velvet gown from my closet. "It's September. Can I wear velvet yet?"

Jane shook her head no, and I hung it back up. I stared at the rack for another five minutes before I realized that the reason that I was seeing no options was because I wasn't really looking. My head was stuck on Jane's question. I spun around and pressed myself against the door frame. "Philip came to see me today."

"I didn't see that coming," Jane admitted.

"Neither did I. It wasn't a welcome visit," I assured her.

"Good. Don't be that girl who goes back to a cheater. They never really change."

"Do you think that's true?" My thoughts drifted from Philip to what he had said about Smith. I knew he was keeping things from me, but it wasn't as if he knew my life story yet either. He hadn't answered my questions about the law he represented or how he had more money than ninety-nine percent of Londoners. I didn't want to believe what Philip had said, but if it was true, could I live with that? Especially if Jane was right and people didn't change?

"Oh, people grow up," she continued thoughtfully, "and where true love is present, there's always evolution. A good man will grow with you, walk beside you. That's not to say he'll be a saint."

I smiled at that. Sainthood wasn't one of my requisites for lovers.

"But when a man is out trying on different vaginas, that's not what happens."

"Have you ever considered writing a book?" I asked her, sighing as I went back to picking out my evening wear.

"I'm not sure people are interested in what an old woman has to say about love." She waved off the suggestion. "Particularly one who's left a string of broken hearts in her wake."

"I'm interested," I informed her. "I would be lost without you."

"In that case, spill. You've been holding out on me."

"I just...he's so..."

"Enough said." Jane patted me on the shoulder and swept toward the door. "Don't be scared to give someone a chance because someone's hurt you before. Just be smart enough to stay away from the ones who have."

CHAPTER SEVENTEEN

I expected to be a third wheel at dinner, and instead I was a fourth. Hammond smiled coldly as we entered the private dinning room at La Rue. He rose, buttoning his blazer, and waited as Smith pulled out my chair. I took a seat, unfolding my napkin, and pinned a smile to my face. It was harder than expected, given that I was seated across from Georgia Kincaid. She didn't bother trying to look pleased to see me. Her dark hair was swept to the side, cascading over her shoulder. Her slinky red shift was more revealing than mine. The fitted grey dress I'd chosen revealed only my bare shoulders. It was clear she was a woman who drew power from her sexuality. I wasn't opposed to using such methods myself, but I had little doubt that my mere presence was statement enough regarding my influence over this situation. Georgia's eyes flickered to Smith. Their gazes met and something passed between them unspoken. I hadn't figured out their relationship yet, but I knew I didn't like it.

"It's so nice to have you with us, Miss Stuart," Hammond remarked as he sat back down.

Considering that I'd been present for his phone call with Smith earlier this afternoon, I understood that wasn't the case. "Thank you for inviting me."

Hors d'oeuvres arrived along with a selection of white and red wine. I brushed a piece of lint off the linen tablecloth, wondering if the whole evening would consist of us pleasantly lying to each other, or if they'd actually discuss whatever business Hammond wished to speak about with Smith.

A warm hand dropped onto my bare knee. My own found it instinctively. For a brief second, I wondered if that was too much, considering the newness of our relationship. Smith knitted his fingers through mine, our hands clasped under the table. It felt strange and wonderful—and far too promising.

"I assume you've had a chance to review the contracts," Hammond said as he speared escargot onto his fork. He brought the buttery morsel up to his mouth and left it hovering there.

Smith nodded as he set his wineglass down. "I have. It seems things are in order. Are there specifics that concern you?"

"There are, but I suppose they can wait. No reason to mix business and pleasure." His teeth clicked against the tines of the fork as he sucked the snail off it.

"I was under the impression this was a business dinner," I said in a soft but unwavering voice. I wasn't interested in double entendres this evening. He had wanted to see Smith for a reason.

"I would never dream of discussing something so boring in the presence of a lady," Hammond responded.

My eyes flashed to Georgia, but she seemed nonplussed by his use of the singular. In the few times I had met her, lady hadn't been a descriptor I'd applied to her. Still, it was another none-too-subtle reminder of my unwanted presence.

"Don't worry." I shrugged, tapping my fingers on the stem of my glass. "I'm certain it will go over my head. I'm not a lawyer."

Just a woman. I kept that thought to myself.

Hammond tilted his head as if to say well-played. He turned his attention back to Smith. "There are certain exclusions I want to see drawn in before I'll sign the papers. My control over my shares needs to be airtight."

"Understood," Smith said.

This was what he needed to talk to Smith about alone? From the way Hammond had spoken on the phone, I'd expected something much worse. Considering his attitude toward my arrival, I'd imagined he needed help covering up a murder.

"There's also the issue of the nondisclosure clause," Georgia added.

Apparently she was more than a pretty face. That didn't surprise me one bit. Everything about her rubbed me the wrong way. I could tell she wasn't someone to underestimate.

"It's been dealt with," Smith said in a clipped tone. "The final documents should be ready by Monday."

Hammond shook his head slowly. "I want them by tomorrow."

"That's simply not possible." Smith leaned back in his chair, withdrawing his hand from my grasp so that he could cross his arms behind his head. "I won't be available this weekend."

"I pay you to be available at all times." Hammond leaned forward, placing his palms on the tabletop.

"I will be available for emergencies, of course. But I doubt a simple realty deal qualifies as an emergency."

The atmosphere in the room crackled with testosterone as the two men stared at one another. Neither looked prepared to back down.

"Boys, let's not be combative," Georgia suggested in a sugary voice. It was enough to make me nauseous.

But I took a cue from her. "I'll have Doris pencil in the changes for your review and fax them over. I assume you have no issue sending them to my email if they're simple contracts."

Every head at the table swiveled toward me. Georgia's expression had changed from practised disinterest to decidedly intrigued, whereas Hammond looked constipated. I couldn't bring myself to look at Smith. There had been a clear line in the sand, and I had crossed it.

"My job is to make Smith's life easier. I'm certain we can find a solution that doesn't infringe on his personal time." I drew my mobile out of my purse and waited to see if Hammond would call my bluff.

"A lawyer doesn't have personal time, Miss Stuart." Hammond laughed as he spoke, but I knew it wasn't a joke. His dark eyes glittered with unrepressed malice. This was a warning.

"I can place a call to Richard. He should be able to review simple changes over the weekend," Smith offered. "If you don't mind someone else executing the contract."

Hammond's jaw tensed, and he took a moment before he spoke. "I suppose Monday will be acceptable."

"Excellent." Smith shifted in his seat and grabbed his fork. "Did you order the duck?"

Nothing had really been discussed. No important or confidential information exchanged, but still my pulse had rocketed into a frenzy. Pushing back my chair, I excused myself to the powder room. Smith glanced up at me but didn't move.

"I'll go with you." Georgia stood to join me. "Us girls should stick together."

Somehow having her with me didn't seem like it would be strength in numbers. I smiled graciously and paused for her to join me. I gripped my clutch tightly as we walked silently to the loo. Inside I ducked into a stall and sank down onto the toilet. I didn't have to go. I'd only come here to collect myself and sort through what had just happened.

"How long have you worked for Smith?" Georgia called through the door.

"Not long." Short answers seemed to be the best course. Giving up on my quiet time, I stood and flushed before joining her at the vanity.

"You appear to have a handle on him," she continued as she reapplied her lipstick in slow, precise strokes.

"Not even a little." Maybe a little casual girl talk would smooth the path between us. I tucked a loose strand of hair behind my ear and began checking my own makeup. "He's difficult to read."

"He is," she allowed. Spinning around, she settled against the marble counter and glared at me. "And how long have you been fucking him?"

I froze, returning her stare in the mirror. "Excuse me?"

"Smith knows better than to bring the hired help to a private meeting." Georgia arched an eyebrow in challenge.

"He prefers I attend all his dinners," I informed her. Smith had been quite clear on that when I took the job, but I had the sinking suspicion that his professional life wasn't nearly the open book he'd insinuated it was. "I'm simply doing my job."

"How interesting," Georgia purred. She moved closer to me, lowering her voice as she sneered. "I didn't know Smith employed whores. He's never needed to before."

"I'm sure your cunt has always been freely available," I hissed, officially losing my cool.

"Careful, princess, or I won't be so friendly in the future."

I snorted and grabbed my powder from my bag. Georgia wanted to make me squirm and that wasn't going to happen. I pressed the sponge to my nose, ignoring her.

"I know all about you," she continued. "Hammond is very particular about the people his associates employ. I haven't decided if you're as big of a gold digger as your friend, Clara. It would be hard to top that. But seeing as you're already sleeping with Smith, I imagine you'll give her a run for her money. Although you must have hated to lose out on your own crown."

"Clara must love you," I said flatly. "I'm already hoping you'll be my bridesmaid."

"Smith isn't the type that gets married. So if you're hoping he's going to ride in on a white horse and carry you away, I suggest you wake the fuck up." She planted her hands on her hips and waited for her last attack to hit.

"Your determination to rattle me is truly pathetic." I turned to face her. We'd see which one of us could be rattled. It wasn't going to be me.

"It's adorable how tough you think you are. Call me when you realize who he really is."

"He must be really good in bed," I said, feigning ignorance on the subject, "because you're clearly not over him."

"Smith and I have never been together. We grew up together. He's a brother to me, and any bitch who thinks she'll come between that is going to land herself in a rather large pile of shit." Georgia snapped the lid of her lipstick with a loud click and dropped it into her purse. "You know nothing about him."

"I will," I promised her.

"Allow me to offer your first insight." She pushed past me, purposefully knocking her hip into me as she crossed to the door. "He's the jealous type."

That I could have guessed, but I kept my face blank. She'd have to let me in on something more interesting if she thought I'd get upset.

"He wouldn't take kindly to finding out his flavor of the week is whoring around with her ex-fiancé."

From the corner of my eye, I spotted myself in the mirror. Face white. Mouth slack. So much for not letting her get to me.

"I pop by the office frequently. You might want to have your little sexcapades elsewhere. Unless you're hoping Smith will beat him to a pulp."

"My personal life is none of your business," I said through gritted teeth.

"That is where you're wrong. Hammond might not like to mix business with pleasure, but that's my primary job description. I collect sins."

"That sounds like a waste of time."

"I've found it to be quite lucrative." She tugged open the door and paused. "Your sins are in my files. Keep that in mind."

She left and I fumbled for the counter. I knew a thing or two about sins. So far I'd been outrunning mine. Now they were about to catch up with me.

When I returned to the table, Smith stood and caught me by the arm. "Our business is concluded."

Apparently the private dinner wasn't going to include the main course. After what had happened in the loo, I was disappointed to cut the evening short. Between the cat and mouse game and the threats, my stomach was tied in knots. Hammond accompanied us to the exit. Taking my hand, he pressed his thin lips to it.

"Always a pleasure. Until we meet again."

I, for one, wouldn't mind if some time elapsed between now and then. Drawing my hand back, I forced a smile. Where was soap when you needed it?

Smith gave a curt nod and guided me out the revolving door. As it spun shut behind us, he grabbed my hand and strode toward the valet, dragging me behind him. He shoved his ticket into the attendant's hand along with another hundred pound note.

"I assume I don't have to tell you which car."

"No, sir," the boy said as he took off for the lot.

As soon as he was gone, Smith rounded on me, pulling me roughly against him. "You didn't correct him," he growled.

My mind went blank. Him? Had Georgia gotten to him in the few minutes before I'd returned from the powder room? I wasn't certain how to explain. I shouldn't have to, but judging from the possessive heat rolling off of him, he didn't feel the same way.

Any other man wouldn't believe he had a claim on me. Any other man I might have told to sod off. Why did Smith already have such a hold on me? Warning bells rang out in my head. This was exactly what I'd been trying to avoid. Now, not only was I jumping into the deep end, I found myself yearning to. The lines between us were blurred. I didn't know when I was crossing one, and I didn't know what the consequences would be when I did. All I knew was that I wanted to bend them. Break them. Just like part of me wanted him to break me.

"I'm sorry," I said softly. There were no other words that felt appropriate. I didn't owe him an explanation, and I wanted his punishment—wanted his hands to take control of my body.

"You don't need to apologize because he called me sir," Smith said, gripping my hips forcefully. "That title belongs to your lips."

It took me a moment to register that he was talking about the valet, not Philip. I breathed out, relieved and disappointed at the same time.

I wrapped an arm around his neck, drawing his mouth toward mine. "And what belongs on your lips?"

"This." He swept a kiss over my mouth. His hands drifted up, skimming quickly over my breasts. Despite the brief contact, my nipples beaded in expectation. The small flame of desire that had been stifled by my anxiety blazed into an inferno. "These. Your pussy. All of you belongs on my lips, beautiful."

The rest of my fear melted away in the heat that small word inspired. Until him, fantasy and reality had been separate worlds, lying far from one another. Now they both centered on him.

He leaned in, moving his mouth to my ear. But he didn't kiss me. "What did Georgia say to you?"

"Nothing that mattered." And none of it did matter. Not anymore. Not with him so close to me.

"Stay away from her," he advised. "She doesn't play by the same rules."

"And you do?" I asked, my focus shifting from foreplay to business.

"No, I don't," he confessed. "Does that scare you?"

"Yes," I whispered. If I wanted the truth out of him, I had to be honest myself.

"Good. You should be scared of me. Don't ever forget that, beautiful." He nipped my earlobe with his teeth for emphasis.

Breathing him in, I pressed an index finger to his chin and shook my head. "She told me you were the jealous type."

"I own many things. Most of them are replaceable. But occasionally, I obtain a priceless piece. Do you understand, beautiful?

I shook my head slowly no. The shades of it were there, but not the complete picture.

"You are priceless to me, so yes, I would be very jealous should someone try to come between us. I would hate to hear Georgia was trying to be that person."

The implication was clear. "She was warning me," I admitted as the Veyron zoomed to the curb.

Smith didn't move toward his car, his green eyes trained on me instead. I could lose myself in those eyes. It was a dangerous proposition. I'd been led astray before by a man. I was determined not to allow that to happen again. I'd pushed him away but there had been a moment when I opened myself to the possibility. However fleeting it was, I'd allowed another man to touch me. It was only made worse by the fact that I'd sworn never to speak to that man again.

"She saw my ex kiss me in front of your office."

Smith moved then, catching my upper arm and hauling me to the waiting car without a word. His whole body was rigid. I sensed his barely contained fury seething within him, and I wasn't the only one. The people wandering past us stopped and whispered.

I knew I should pull away. Yell. Scream. Put a stop to this now before it got out of control. But I put up no fight when he opened my door. I sank into the passenger seat without a struggle. It wasn't reasonable. It wasn't smart.

And I didn't care.

CHAPTER EIGHTEEN

Smith didn't speak the entire ride. By the time he parked the Veyron in his garage, I regretted my decision to come with him. The fascination I'd felt in front of the restaurant had evaporated, leaving only trepidation. He'd spoken of punishment and submission before. I'd never really considered what that might entail.

He exited the car without a word and walked to the lift, leaving me to scramble after him.

That was your chance. He hadn't asked me to come with him. He hadn't demanded I follow him. And I still had. I paused a few steps from him. He stood with his back to me, and I considered my options. I could walk out now. Or I could see where this led. I'd enjoyed his teasing slaps and smacks. I'd wanted more.

But how much?

I closed the gap between us and followed him into the lift. Smith pushed the button for the second floor. We were headed straight to the bedroom. The ache of expectation built in my core, filtering slowly through the rest of my body, until I was practically humming with need. When the doors zipped open, Smith placed his arm across the threshold and waited for me to exit. I stepped into the hallway.

"Bedroom."

One word. It surged through me. Squaring my shoulders I marched inside his room, stopping just past the doorway.

"Strip."

My eyes locked with his, but he looked away immediately. What I had seen in those deep emerald orbs chilled me. Reaching under my arm, I tugged down the zipper of my gown, still watching him. Still hoping he would turn back to me. He didn't. My dress puddled to the floor, and I stepped out of it, wearing only a nude silk bustier and stockings. I'd left my knickers at home as he requested, but he didn't acknowledge that.

"Everything."

It took me a few moments of fumbling to unhook all the tiny fasteners by myself. Smith's gaze had returned to me—or at least my body. There was no affection in his face. He was vacant—a void. There was no way to read him, because there was nothing to read. When I'd pulled off my last stocking, I stood exposed before him.

Smith circled around me, studiously avoiding my eyes as he inspected me. Then he uttered one final word, "Flawless."

I blushed under his scrutiny, both pleased at the praise and nervous about what came next.

He snapped his fingers. "Kneel before me."

I dropped before him, one knee at a time.

"I'm attracted to a fiery woman. Some men aren't. They like their women quiet. Docile. But a woman with a sharp tongue—a defiant woman—that's what gets my attention. You've had my attention since the moment we met, Belle." He paused and ran a single finger along the curve of my shoulder. Then he stepped in front of me, putting me eye level with the unmistakable bulge in his trousers.

I barely resisted the urge to snap open his fly and take him in my mouth. He wanted a defiant woman and I could be just that, but something held me to the spot. Curiosity, I suppose. I was curious what he wanted to do to me. Even more curious if I would let him.

"Perhaps what happened today was innocent, but I'm going to need you to prove that to me. I'm a man who prefers evidence to hearsay. Call it a hazard of my profession. Proof is much more convincing than words." He peeled off his suit coat and loosened his tie. When he unbuttoned his top button, a small moan slipped from my mouth. Smith tapped my cheek with the side of his hand, reminding me to be silent. "Your body responds to my requests even when you don't. I've learned how to read it by watching you since that first day. It will tell me everything I need to know. Do you understand?"

I nodded, my eyes flickering up to stare at him. My hands longed to reach for him. I wanted to touch him almost as much as I wanted him to touch me.

"But more importantly, do you consent?" he continued in a low voice. "You are free to leave at any time. You are free to tell me to stop. I won't prevent you from leaving. The things I'm going to do to you might feel demeaning. They're supposed to. But if I'm correct, you will enjoy them. Just as I'll enjoy bridling your defiance and seeing where your loyalty lies. Do you have any questions?"

"How will you know that I'm not performing?"

"You're clinging to your bravado, beautiful." A note of affection colored his tone, but it quickly shifted back to domineering. "No one performs that well. I'm going to strip you bare and make you squirm until your mind ceases to function except to follow my commands."

My body burned, my knees stinging against the marble floor and the rest of me aching from want. "I consent."

"Very good. Stay."

I didn't budge, but I felt him moving away from me. The room seemed to darken without his presence, and I resisted the urge to turn around and look for him. I understood the expectations of me even if they were difficult to follow. My body relaxed instantly at the sound of his footsteps but tensed again when I heard the soft clink of a chain.

Out of the corner of my eye, I spotted him drop into the chair by the window.

"Come to me, beautiful."

His request washed over me. I felt wanted. Alive. I pressed my palm to the floor and began to push myself to my feet.

"Crawl." The word lingered on his tongue.

Instantly I shifted forward, placing my other hand on the floor. The hardness of it registered faintly in the back of my mind, but my only conscious thought was of him. Each shuffle of my knees, each clap of my palm against marble took me closer. Smith lounged back, his chin propped against his hand. Two fingers pressed thoughtfully to his mouth as he watched my progress. When I got to his feet, I dropped back onto my heels and placed one hand onto the chair cushion, carefully avoiding touching his thighs.

"You may come closer," he said in a gentle voice.

I pressed my cheek against his knee and breathed him in. His woody cologne flooded my nostrils and the warmth of our small contact seemed to both feed and quell the fire raging inside me. Closing my eyes, I understood the truth.

There was only him.

The heat of his fingertips trailed over my collarbone. His scorching touch was followed by cool, smooth leather. It wrapped around my neck tightly enough that I inhaled sharply. Fingers swept under the strap, reassuring me that I could breathe.

"Turn around and hold up your hair."

I looked to him then. Smith paused and cupped my cheek. "You're doing so well, beautiful. Now turn around."

I did as I was told. Resisting the urge to touch the leather fastened around my neck, I moved to face away from him and lifted my hair, exposing the nape of my neck. The sharp, distinct click of metal sent goose bumps rippling across my skin.

"Hands and knees," Smith instructed.

A cold metal chain snaked down my back as I lowered myself on all fours. A tiny voice inside me dissented to this and the rest of me—my muscles, my senses, my thoughts, my very soul—hushed it. My arousal surged so plentifully that I felt it trickle down my seam and drip to the floor beneath me. A shudder wracked my body, a trembling promise of things to come.

"That made you wet," Smith murmured, dipping a finger between my weeping folds. He lightly brushed it, releasing more fluid. "I leashed you and you nearly came. I took you over, took away your decisions, took away your freedom. And soaking your pussy with want is your response, beautiful. Do you know why?"

I searched for a no, but all I could force past my lips was a whimper.

"You've even given up your voice. Everything you are centers around me and what I will allow you. My finger." He pushed inside my sopping hole and hooked his finger to massage my g-spot.

"My mouth." Warm, soft lips swept over my swollen sex.

"The hand that holds your tether." He gave a tug, forcing my head back. "I took away everything and how do you feel?"

Liberated. It wasn't the word that flashed through my head so much as the concept itself. I felt light, as if a burden I'd carried my whole life had lifted from my back. I nearly believed I could float away. But the chain that had freed me anchored me to Smith.

"You've given me something precious." Smith stood and moved to the front of me. Dipping down, he caught my face, granting me the first peek of the gold lead he'd attached to my collar. He drew me up by the chin, and I effortlessly returned to a kneeling position. Reverence smoldered across his beautiful face, light glimmering from his eyes. "Trust."

The realization crashed through me. I trusted him. I gave him the one thing I'd sworn never to give a man again, and I didn't even know why. We'd known each other such a short amount of time. I'd never been the type that believed in soul mates or love at first sight. But right here, right now, I'd handed him control. He could do with me as he pleased, and I wanted him to.

"But now I need to know if I can trust you."

The pleasant exhilaration his last insight had given me vanished. It wasn't that I feared him. It was that I was scared of what I was about to reveal to him—and myself.

"Hold this." He pushed the leash against my mouth, and my lips parted, instinctively taking it between my teeth. Smith rubbed a hand over the thick outline of his dick. "You're so pretty with your mouth dripping gold chain."

He lifted his foot up to me, and I tugged off his shoe, repeating the action with the other until his feet were bare.

With deft fingers, he unfastened his belt and dropped it. Its buckle clattered on the floor next to me. The sound gave me an idea. I held out my hands, crossing them at the wrists. I would give him more. More of what pleased him. More of my trust. Smith was looking to make a judgment about me. I would make his decision easier.

"Please, Sir," I pushed the words past the chain in my mouth.

"You want those bound, too?" he guessed, bending over to pick it back up. "Hands behind your back."

I crossed them behind me, and Smith leaned over me, pressing his groin against my face as he looped the belt around my wrists. When he straightened again, he unbuttoned his trousers and pushed his pants and boxers off to reveal his erect cock. Moisture glistened on its crown, beckoning me to lick across its tip. I'd yet to have my mouth on him, but his fingers closed over it.

He smacked his shaft against my cheek, knocking the chain from my teeth. "Do you want this in your mouth?"

"Yes, Sir," I squeaked, not daring to act on the impulse.

"In your pussy? Between your tits?" he continued. "How about up your ass?"

I licked my lips and nodded.

"Now this is important, beautiful. I know other men have fucked you. I wish that wasn't the case. That somehow I'd found you sooner, because I want to own all of your pleasure. Since I can't, I'm going to have to spend a lot of time fucking their memory right out of your pretty little head. When I'm finished, your body will only remember me." He tipped my chin higher with his index finger. "Men have had your pussy, and judging from the way you licked your lips just now, they've had your mouth. Has one come on your tits before?"

I shook my head no. The Oxford boys I'd been with tended toward traditional sexual activities, like missionary position.

Smith leaned down, his face angling toward mine until our lips were nearly touching. "Has one been in your ass?"

"No," I breathed. I couldn't stop myself from squirming a little.

"Not tonight, beautiful," he reassured me with a gentle kiss. "Those things can wait until you're ready. You've saved them for me after all. I want to take my time when it finally comes. Now suck my cock."

Smith took hold of the leash again and stepped back, forcing me to move awkwardly to keep myself upright. It was more difficult than I'd imagined with my hands secured behind me. As I neared him, he drew the leash tighter until I was at eye level with his erection. He left little slack in the chain, and the message was clear: this was where I belonged. This was my pillar. Smith. His cock was simply the nucleus of his masculinity. Forceful. Strong. Unyielding.

I wrapped my lips over the tip and he groaned. I had what he wanted. Willingness. Resilience. Release. Part of me wished I could use my hands. I needed him to climax. I was eager to taste him and desperate to please him. Smith grabbed a handful of my hair, urging me lower.

"I'm going to come in your mouth and wash away Philip's presence," he growled, tightening his grip on my hair until my scalp sung with pain. "You forgot who you belonged to today. That was an error that I can forgive, because you've proven you know now. But tonight I need to mark you with my teeth, with my palm, and most of all, I need to fill you with me."

He wanted to claim me—brand me—as his. Warmth spread through my chest, and I hollowed my cheeks, sucking furiously, determined to aid his mission.

Frantic.

Smith sensed this and pulled away. "Slowly. We have all night, beautiful. Don't wear yourself out, because you aren't going to get much sleep."

This time when he offered himself to me, my mouth sank slowly down as I savored his smooth, rigid shaft, curling my tongue around it languidly.

"That's better," he rasped. His hips rolled in circles against my mouth, urging himself farther. I relaxed, taking him deep in my throat.

It was a new experience. Smith didn't want quick shags or blowjobs. He wanted pleasure, the kind one could only find in a continual exchange of power. I was on my knees, but as his breathing sped up, I knew I was the one in control. When the first hot spurts shot down my throat, I finally understood.

We were claiming each other.

Smith groaned, bucking hard against my mouth as he came. I took it all, only releasing him when he finally guided my head away with a gentle touch. Reaching down, he dragged me to my feet. With a few swift movements, my hands were free. The chain dangled between my breasts, and he stared at me for a moment, his emerald eyes distant with thought. Then he scooped me off my feet and threw me over his shoulder. I'd barely processed the change in circumstances before he tossed me on the bed. Smith sank down on the ground and hooked an arm around my thigh, wrenching me to the edge of the bed while his other hand collected my leash. He yanked the chain down and inserted it along my seam. Moving it back and forth, he tortured my tender clit. My hands grabbed for the sheets, bracing for when he finally granted me relief. After a few minutes, he drew the chain away and plunged his tongue into my crease. I cried out, feeling the first emissaries of pleasure bolting through me. But Smith knew how to make it last. He licked and sucked me to the edge and then backed off, concentrating on another area until I came to the brink again. He settled over my clit and flicked it with his tongue until my body tensed, then he pulled away.

I was torn between crying and screaming, but I didn't have the strength for either. Instead I whimpered, hoping he would take pity on me. Every nerve at my core was enflamed. A gust of wind would have sent me over the line. But I suspected Smith would never allow that to happen.

"Hush, beautiful," he ordered, undoing the collar around my neck as I writhed. "I'm going to give you what you need, and then you're going to milk me with your perfect cunt."

His cock nudged against my cleft, and I flowered open for him. Smith slid in with one powerful thrust, severing the ties that held me captive. I arched against him from the force of my climax, and he caught me in his arms, holding me up, as he continued to pound into me.

"You feel so tight," he whispered as he chased his own orgasm. "God, beautiful, your pussy is going to bleed me dry."

I was limp in his arms, boneless and soporific, but I clung to him, kissing his neck, brushing my lips across the stubble on his chin. My attentions drew his mouth to mine. We collided together, fighting to crush closer. Our tongues tangled, and I sucked his into my mouth. I didn't merely want to be owned by him. I wanted him to fill me. I wanted nothing at all to separate us.

Smith lowered my body to the bed, never breaking our connection. My hunger shifted from hopeful to inevitable as he rocked inside me with deep, precise strokes. I cried out against his mouth as tremors quaked through me. Smith's mouth opened wider, swallowing the sounds of pleasure that belonged to him.

When we finally collapsed onto the bed, Smith gathered me in his arms and tucked me against his body. We lay like that for a long time. My fingertips grazed his shyly. The world seemed as new as the bud of a relationship we'd nurtured to this point. Smith caught my hand and brought it to his mouth before withdrawing from me. I held back a sigh, but my disappointment was short-lived when he lowered himself and laid his head on my hip. He brushed his fingers over my sex before pressing his palm to it.

"I want to own this. What do I have to give you? I'll buy you anything. Your own Bugatti? Diamonds? Name your price."

He just had. "You. A Price is my price. Smith Price. That's all you have to give me, and I'm yours."

"An intriguing proposition," he said, his mouth curving into a teasing smirk. "May I counter-bid?"

"No." My denial was firm. Irreversible. This was an all or nothing relationship, and we both knew it.

"I was merely going to suggest a trial basis," he whispered, his attitude no longer joking. "You may think I'm equal compensation now, but we both know that between this gorgeous body and wicked mind, you're worth a premium."

I brushed his hair back from his forehead, shaking my own. "Your body is beautiful."

"The ugliness is inside," he said in a low voice. "When you finally see it—"

"Don't show it to me," I murmured.

"I wish it were that easy." His hands slid under my back as he coiled himself around me.

"It is. This is a fresh start."

"I've never been very good at starting over," he warned me.

"Neither have I." It was one thing I'd never admitted to myself before. "We'll hold each other to it."

"Belle, my tastes..." He trailed off. After a pause, he continued in a strangled voice. "I don't take a woman to bed. I take all of her. I've only shown you a sample of what I'll do to you. If that scares you, leave now. I'll let you go."

But we both knew that was an impossibility. "I've never done anything like that, but I liked it. I—I wanted more."

My cheeks flushed with my confession.

"Oh, beautiful, I'm going to give you as much as you can handle." He bit playfully into the curve of my hip, continuing lower until his tongue skimmed along my bikini line. "And then I'm going to give you more."

I wanted to ask him to promise me, but experience had shown me promises were as easily broken as they were made. A hunch told me he'd also learned this the hard way. Smith didn't offer me a placation. In the end, he crept back over me, and as our bodies joined together, we sought out the answers to questions we hadn't dared asked—the only way we knew how.

CHAPTER NINETEEN

The room was cloaked in darkness when I rolled over, my body searching for hers. Coming up empty, I stroked my frustrated cock for a moment. I couldn't believe she was already out of bed after I'd practically fucked her into a coma last night. I found her writing at the kitchen island, wearing nothing but a button down, which displayed her toned legs. Her hair was slightly tangled, and she still glowed from last night. I allowed myself a moment to drink her in. She glanced up from her paper and grinned. I'd been caught ogling her, but I couldn't care less. The slight movement had revealed a navy necktie knotted loosely around the upturned collar of my shirt. Her fingers wrapped around it, and she pretended to adjust it.

Holy fuck.

"I wasn't sure if we were starting today with work," she purred. "I thought I better dress formally."

"We'll never work again if you continue wearing that," I informed her. Rubbing sleep from my eyes, I opened the refrigerator and fumbled for a few light breakfast items. Despite how little sleep I'd actually gotten, I felt refreshed in a way that only hours spent making a gorgeous woman come could. Pulling a carton of strawberries out, I eyed Belle, who hadn't stopped scribbling in her notebook. "Writing down the details, beautiful? I doubt you're going to forget a moment."

"Then he placed his finger...'" she trailed away, shaking her head.

"How long did you let me sleep?" I asked, realizing it was nearly noon.

"A couple of hours." Her pen swept over the paper as she spoke.

I couldn't see what she was drawing. "A little bit bigger, beautiful."

"Actually, I'm working on something unrelated to your cock."

"That's unfortunate."

"Narcissist." She dazzled me with a wry smile.

"Looks like that make me want to eat you for breakfast," I warned her, sliding a knife from the block.

Belle sighed but didn't drop her pen. "My body cannot handle another orgasm before food. It might actually kill me. You drained every drop of energy I had last night."

"Noted." I went to work popping the stems off the berries.

She returned to her note-taking, making me even more intrigued. If she had been as famished as she claimed, why hadn't she grabbed a bite when she came down here? Especially if she'd been in the kitchen for hours. I shifted the cutting board closer to where she sat and peeked across the counter. There was only one word on the page, although it was sketched out over and over. One with swirls. Another thin and modern. And a half dozen other iterations.

Bless.

Her palm flattened, obscuring the page, and I glanced up to discover her eyes wide with embarrassment.

"It's nothing," she said, quickly shutting the notebook.

"It looks like a logo," I guessed. That or she had gotten some serious compulsion issues past me.

She kept her hand over the book, neither confirming nor denying my suspicion. I sensed her hesitation to tell me any more. Best to drop it.

"I want to start my own website," she blurted out. "Company, really."

"You've never mentioned that before." I supposed it was natural that she hadn't until now, but some part of me wished I'd already known. I'd had to catch her in the act of working on her idea. Now telling me about it was less discussion and more confession.

Belle's eyes flickered away, her expression changing from guilty to haughty. She tugged a hair band off her wrist and twisted her golden hair into a messy knot. "You don't exactly like to talk about work-related issues."

Ah. This again. "Technically you work for me now, so isn't everything work-related?"

She lifted an eyebrow, as if waiting for me to explain how last night was work-related. Laughing, I tilted my head in surrender. "I suppose we've clearly crossed the professional and personal life boundary."

"I think we obliterated it actually."

"Speaking of." I prowled closer to her and pressed my lips to the space under her ear. She melted against me before pulling away. "Maybe we should obliterate it further."

"Eat. Food." She emphasized each word with a laugh.

"Okay. I shall make you a meal almost as delicious as you on one condition."

"Which is?

I let her question hang in the air a moment, knowing she assumed my condition would be wicked. I finally answered. "I prep and you tell me about your company."

"Technically, I don't have a company," she hedged.

"Beautiful, I love it when you play hard to get, but I don't like it when you underestimate yourself." I held a strawberry out to her, savoring how she caught it with her teeth. "That was a sample of what I can offer you. Now tell me about Bless."

She licked juice off her lips, nearly distracting me from my mission.

"C'mon, beautiful. I have other ways of getting it out of you." Part of me hoped this led to coaxing it out of her. "I promise once my tongue is on your cunt, you'll tell me anything I want to know."

"You are so full of yourself, Price." But her throat slid on my name, her mind obviously thinking about the other name she had for me.

"I know you'd like it if I fucked it out of you, but you also want this." I brandished another berry.

She swiped it from me with a grimace and flipped open the notebook to another page that featured a hand-drawn graph. "Bless is 'black dress' combined. You've heard the term 'little black dress,' right?"

"I think so," I said dryly.

She tossed the stem of her strawberry at me. "The idea is basically couture clothing for rent. A customer can sign up for a monthly plan and then put items into a wardrobe. We send them out. They send them back. Voila!"

"So it's a subscription service." I scooped up the berry pieces and dropped them into a bowl.

"Yes."

"Aren't there other companies that do that?" I asked. If I was going to be remotely helpful at getting this idea off the ground, I would have to ask every question that came into my head just like an investor. I hoped her answer proved she was prepared for the task.

"Yes, but," she continued swiftly, "none of them focus on couture and designer clothing."

"Is there a reason for that?"

"Because the clothes are ungodly expensive, which means you need lots of capital and insurance for the stock," she admitted. "Most of these other companies offer subscriptions based on number of items out at a time."

I crossed to the fridge and pulled out a bottle of heavy cream. "How will Bless be different?"

"God, you are a lawyer," she teased but immediately grew serious. "Tier-based subscriptions. Designer clothing pricing already falls into tiers. There's a difference between buying Michael Kors and Versace. There should be a difference when you rent them, too."

"It sounds like you have this all worked out." There were a

million more things to consider, but only time and persistence were going to get her from concept to company. I poured the cream onto the berries.

Belle peeked into the bowl, her eyes lighting up. But she didn't steal it, instead she popped onto her feet and opened the cabinet. My shirt lifted along with her arms as she reached for the beans, revealing the curve of her butt cheek. "Coffee?"

I moved behind her, grabbing her around the waist and pushing my stiffening cock against her ass. "I think if you're going to wear that, we should avoid anything that could burn you. I can't guarantee not to spill if I catch another glimpse of your pussy."

"You promised me food," she reminded me even as she turned and buried her face against my chest.

My hand instinctively reached up to stroke her hair and pull her closer. She fit here—in my arms. The curves of her body molded seamlessly against me, as though God had created her just for me. But that was impossible. God didn't owe me any favors, and he certainly had nothing to reward me for. Perhaps I was her punishment, although there was no crime she could commit to deserve me.

Or maybe she was my salvation. I pressed my lips to her forehead.

"What are you doing to me, Belle Stuart? You're changing me—rewiring me," I murmured.

Belle tipped her face up, revealing eyes full of her questions that, at the same time, offered me answers.

"I need to feed you," I said in a soft voice.

"I'm not hungry anymore...not for that."

But despite the invitation, I couldn't see past my duty. When I'd taken her, I'd chosen her. I'd placed her under my care and protection. But for the first time, I truly comprehended what that meant. Sliding my arms down, I cupped her ass and lifted her. Belle's legs wrapped tightly around mine, but even the tempting heat of her pussy against my waist couldn't divert me. Carrying her across the kitchen, I lowered her onto the island.

Her eyes closed as she opened her mouth expectantly, but instead of my lips, I pushed a strawberry past her teeth. She moaned as she sucked it free from my fingers and swallowed.

"You're making me jealous, beautiful." I ignored how my balls tightened as her tongue swept traces of cream from her bottom lip. Her teeth tugged gently on the same lip before she opened her mouth wider.

This time when I brought it to her mouth, I held it back, waiting until the cream pooling on its tip dribbled down her neck and onto her collarbone. A spot landed on the tie around her neck.

"Better take that off," I suggested, feeding her another bite while my free hand unknotted the silk necktie.

Belle peeked down at the stain on my three hundred pound tie. "I hope it isn't ruined."

"Fuck the tie," I growled, wrenching it off of her. I brought a handful of berries to her, smashing them across her lips, savoring the way the juicy cream poured over her chin. It only made me realize how good she would look with other things dripping from her mouth. Belle grabbed my fingers and sucked them into her mouth, licking the remnants of her breakfast from them.

"Aren't you hungry?" she asked.

"Such a simple question from such a sinful mouth." I was famished actually. There was no point to trying to salvage the shirt she'd chosen, so rather than mess with unbuttoning it, I gripped the placket and yanked. Buttons scattered across the granite as the shirt slipped over her shoulders, revealing her pert breasts.

"The housekeeper is going to wonder what you were up to...oh!" Belle lost her train of thought as my tongue lapped up her neck and then forced its way into her mouth. She met my hungry kiss voraciously, weaving her fingers into my hair and dragging me closer.

When I pulled back, we were both breathless. "I'm not done eating yet."

Picking up the bowl, I spilled the remainder across her tits. Without hesitation, I bent to lick it off of her. My arms bracketed her back as my tongue sucked cream from the stiff tips of her nipples. Nothing had ever tasted so good. Cream pooled in her belly button, and I dragged the puddle down, tracking it to the swollen apex of her cunt. Slipping two fingers into her wet slit, I spread her open, allowing it to stream across her sex, coating the delectable pink bud as it ran down.

I wanted to suck it clean. I wanted to pull her clit between my teeth until she screamed for the release only I could grant her. But I needed her to beg. I derived my self-control from the promise that patience would yield her breathless and supple. If I had to adjust my whole life around this new compulsion I felt about her, then I would remind her that her existence centered around me from now on.

Keeping my touch feather light, I circled around the nub with the tip of my tongue. Belle's head fell back, and my arm braced her more tightly as a tormented cry burst from her. My lips twitched at the sound.

"That's right, beautiful," I grunted into her swollen sex. She writhed against the movement of my lips, but I drew away. Only far enough to prevent her from locking onto a source of friction. Dipping my tongue into her cleft, I flicked it, appreciating the faint contractions already beginning in her channel. She was close, but I wasn't nearly finished with her.

Abandoning her pussy, I returned to her breasts, closing my mouth over her nipple and sucking the soft tissue into my mouth. In a flash, Belle tucked up her knees and planted her feet on the edge of the counter as she sought relief between her legs.

"Get back down there." She barely forced the words past her breathless pants.

I couldn't have that. I tapped her chin lightly in warning, and her clenched eyes flew open. "I don't take commands."

"I'm sorry," she breathed. "Please get back down there, Sir."

"Not even if you command me nicely," I said, wrenching her hips forward so that her knees smashed against her breasts. I crushed my body against hers. "Do it again, and I'll have you on your knees, sucking me off, and then you'll spend the rest of the day with a bare, needy cunt. Do you know what happens then? No chairs. No sitting.

No friction. All you'll do is wait until I allow you pleasure again. Now what do you want to ask me, beautiful?"

"Please may I come, Sir?" she shrieked as I circled my hips against her tortured sex. Her whimpers wracked through her as I held her trembling body.

"That's a proper request," I said, knowing praise would soothe her.

Her wild eyes met mine, and another plea fell from her lips. "Please kiss me. Oh God, kiss me, Smith."

My mouth collided with hers. She hadn't asked. She hadn't begged. Still the desperation in the request plucked a string in my heart I'd thought was out of tune. Instead the note rang through me, vibrating at a pitch I'd forgotten. Her heels dug into my sides and pushed down my boxers, freeing my cock. In one smooth motion, I lifted her ass and slid inside her.

A strangled cry—half pleasure, half agony—ripped through her. I smothered her anguish with another kiss. Her hand slipped from my hair down to the nape of my neck as she clung to me. I straightened up, refusing to break the kiss, and her legs encircled my waist. Keeping one hand on the small of her back, I held her steady as she lifted her ass up and then plunged it back down.

I wanted to whisper dirty things in her ear and watch as her body reacted but not as much as I wanted my lips on hers. My tongue forced itself deeper into her open mouth. Every fibre of my being longed to fill her. My cock. My mouth. It wasn't enough. I needed more than her body. I coveted her soul.

Sensing her muscles tense, I thrust harder, hammering her toward devastation. She fell apart in my arms, crumbling into a wreckage of sobs and screams that exhorted my own climax. I cracked open at the core, erupting inside her until all that was left was a tangle of sweaty limbs. I held her there, unwilling to extricate my body from hers.

Because I no longer knew where I ended and she began.

CHAPTER TWENTY

I'd never considered having two sinks in my master bath an asset until this morning, but as Belle poked through the drawer looking for a spare toothbrush, the space felt like it had been made for the two of us. The white tiles on the walls and floor reflected the light from the windows, making the room as light and airy as her presence made me feel.

I grabbed my shaving brush and lathered my face before I slid open my straight razor. The method took a precision that I appreciated. One wrong move and I'd cut the hell out of myself. Belle paused and watched me intently.

"That looks dangerous," she commented as I rinsed the blade so I could continue.

"I prefer a close shave," I told her, flipping the straight razor closed and holding it out to her.

She took it cautiously and smiled shyly. "I rather like when you have a little stubble."

"Why is that?" I moved closer until our bodies lightly brushed one another's.

"What did you call it earlier? Friction?" There was a playful tone to her words. She'd become giddy at the memory of our kitchen encounter. If I had it my way, she'd look at every room in this house and feel the same exhilaration.

"It grows fast, beautiful," I promised her. "I'll show you just how fast tomorrow morning. But for now, finish this for me."

"Me?" She tried to push the razor back into my hands. "I don't know the first thing about how to use that. What if I miss and slit your throat?"

"Then I will die a happy man." I took her arm and guided her to the toilet. Sinking onto its lid, I tilted my face to expose the area still covered in shave soap. "Just like this."

I opened the razor and placed her fingers in the correct positions, noting that her hand was trembling. "Don't be scared. I'm not."

"You aren't the one wielding an eighteenth century street weapon." She sighed and held the blade closer to my face.

Turning her wrist so that it was at the proper angle, I guided her hand down, enjoying the slight tug as the blade swept over my skin.

"Your turn," I told her.

She moved the razor over and hesitated before pressing it gently against my face and repeating the motion I'd shown her.

"And I'm still alive," I teased her softly.

"Careful, Price," she warned me. "I'm still the one with the sharp object."

I lifted my chin, exposing the much more delicate skin of my neck. The wrong angle or a moment of panic and that would be the end of her shaving career. "Let the razor guide you," I advised.

She approached the task with more confidence this time, drawing the blade swiftly down until it was finished. I started to stand, but her hand pressed on my shoulder. "Wait. I missed a spot over here."

I turned my face, allowing her access. The blade glided over the curve of my jawline smoothly until it caught, sending a sharp twinge of pain ringing through my flesh. Belle startled away from me as apologies spilled from her lips. "I'm so sorry. Oh my God, you're bleeding."

"It's nothing. I've cut myself before." The sting had already dulled.

"But I haven't cut you," she whispered. Leaning down, she brushed a kiss over the wound. I watched her, mesmerized, as she licked the small smear of my blood from her lips.

Taking the straight razor from her, I snapped it closed and threw it into the sink. I reached for her, but she bounced away, breaking the hypnotic spell of the act.

"Uh-uh." She wagged her index finger in my direction. "I have a lunch date with your favorite person."

"Oh?"

"Edward, so I need to get in the shower." There was a mixture of finality and challenge in her tone.

"He's important to you," I surmised, which meant I needed to get a hold on my feelings about her being around other men. "We should have dinner with him."

"Are you going to hit him?" she asked in a dry voice.

I shrugged noncommittally and grinned. "Only if he deserves it."

"We could invite his fiancé, so you feel less threatened." Belle's eyes glinted with amusement. "But before we do any of that, I need to shower!"

I sprang to my feet and pounced on her. Backing her into the wall, I trailed a string of kisses along her jaw. "We'll both get in the shower," I suggested. "I'll wash you."

"The point of a shower is to come out cleaner." But she giggled, and I knew it was a done deal.

Stepping away from her, I held up my hands in surrender. "Get in the shower. I'll put on some music."

"Music, huh?" She scurried over and turned on the water.

"Music soothes my savage side. It's your best chance at controlling me if you're going to be naked and wet within a ten mile radius." Unlocking my phone, I accessed the house's sound system and chose a playlist. A few seconds later, a bluesy rhythm filled the air as Mick Jagger began to croon.

"The Stones?" she asked. "I pegged you as more of a classical listener."

"Beautiful, this is classical. I grew up with the Stones."

"God, for a second I thought you were going to tell me you're their lawyer."

"I'm not. " I winked at her. "But I know their lawyers."

"Of course you do." She brushed her lips over my shoulder. It was a relatively chaste kiss, but that didn't matter to my dick.

I swatted her ass, shooing her under the water. "Get in before I change my mind about joining you."

Returning to the sink, I splashed cool water on my face to rinse away any remaining residue. I fully intended to behave myself, but the reflection of Belle in the mirror gave me other ideas. She twisted under the shower stream, tilting her head back so the water washed down her hair. Steam had begun to fog the room when I slid open the glass door and joined her.

"I thought this was my shower," she called, blinking water from her eyes.

"It's a double shower. You're not the only one who needs to get cleaned up." I smirked as I switched on the set of shower heads on the opposite side. Leaning back into the warm stream, I reached for my dick and began to pump it with my fist. My eyes hooded lustily as I watched her soap up her tits.

"Are you enjoying yourself?" she called, lathering the flat plane of her stomach. Her fingers dipped between her legs, washing her pussy a bit too thoroughly.

"Are you?" I asked, massaging my balls as I continued to stroke myself off.

She shrugged and turned her back to me, rubbing lather over her round ass. I was definitely enjoying the show, but it seemed some audience participation was in order. I hooked my right arm around her waist and pulled her against me, guiding my cock to her slippery entrance. Pushing the crown barely inside her, I paused.

"Isn't it better to get dirty now when cleanup is so easy?" I said in a gruff voice, pistoning deeper into her channel.

She leaned into me, allowing my left arm to snake between her breasts. I shoved my cock fully into her, lifting her feet from the ground as she cried out.

"This is admittedly a bit slippery," I whispered in her ear.

She took the cue as I lowered her to the balls of her feet and bent forward, pressing her palms to the tiled shower wall.

"I can't decide which view I prefer," I said in a husky voice. "Your gorgeous cunt stretched over my cock or the look on your face when you come." I slid inside her, relishing how the velvet smooth walls of her pussy squeezed my shaft. It was good, but I needed more. Withdrawing, I spun her around and pinned her against the wall. In a swift motion, I'd hoisted her against the tile and thrust back inside her. Her arms splayed across the wall as I continued my relentless assault. In the background, a new song began to play, and I matched the tempo as water spilled across us.

"Tell me what you want," I growled, pounding roughly into her.

Her arm lashed out and grabbed my face. "You. I want you."

"Fuck, beautiful. I'm yours." We crashed into one another, our bodies sliding in frantic unison as we searched for release together. When her hold on me tightened, I captured her mouth, sucking the sounds of her climax into me. I felt her pleasure flooding through my veins as I unleashed my own, emptying myself into her tight cunt.

I helped her gently to her feet, keeping a hold on her so she wouldn't slip. She blinked at me, still lost in a haze of bliss, as I found the bar of soap. Reaching between her thighs, I ran it along her folds, washing away the cum spilling from her. She clung to me as I rinsed the lather off. I didn't release her as we stepped out of the shower. Wrapping a thick towel around her, I rubbed it roughly across her skin until it glowed pink.

I took her hand to help her into the bedroom, but she shook her head. "I think I can walk."

"I won't be satisfied until you can't," I warned her.

She disappeared through the door, swaying her ass saucily the whole way.

"Are you sure you have to meet Edward?" I called in to her. "If you stay here, I can make it worth your while."

The thought I'd be without her, even for a short period, made me want to bend her over the sink and fuck her until she begged to stay. I'd endured our separation this week, sensing that she needed space. Now that she no longer required that, it was difficult to give her any.

Pausing in the doorway, I watched as she unwadded her gown from last night and studied it.

"I wasn't planning to do the walk of shame," she admitted with a grin. "And no knickers to boot."

"I'd prefer you wear knickers when you go to lunch with another man, even a gay man." I crossed to my closet and flipped on the light. "Come here, beautiful."

"I don't think I can fit in your shorts," she said dryly, but the sarcasm faded from her voice as she spotted the dress in my hands.

"I had a few things delivered here," I explained, stepping aside to display a rack of clothing selected by her stylist at Harrods. "Shoes are over there."

Her feet belonged in Louboutins, and I'd made certain she would have no shortage at her disposal. A dozen pairs in varying styles from sky-high to demure lined the shelf. She pranced over to them, trailing her fingers over the leather.

"I only forgave you yesterday afternoon." She rounded on me. "When did you order these?"

"Tuesday."

"You're awfully sure of yourself." Her eyes narrowed, and I sensed she was struggling between annoyance and delight.

"I hoped you would come back." I went to her and ran my knuckles down her jawline. "And if you didn't, I was going to drag you back here."

"Has anyone ever told you that you're a bit of a cave man?" she said, her lips twitching with a suppressed smile.

"Beautiful, I'd be a happy man if I only had to fuck and eat," I admitted, angling my face to bite her shoulder.

"I think you also had to hunt and find shelter," she said, pushing me away and grabbing a pair of heels.

"I already have the biggest cave, and"—I grabbed my dick—"the best tool."

"Later, you can show me how to use it, but now I'm getting dressed!" She swiped the closest garment and dashed out.

When I'd finally picked out a casual pair of trousers and a tailored button down, I emerged after her. She was slipping a heel on, bent in a graceful position that was the very definition of sensual femininity. She straightened up and shot me a warning look.

"I'm going to dry my hair," she informed.

I grabbed her as she tried to pass me and kissed her. "Come back to my bed tonight."

"Wild horses," she whispered. I released her, smiling at the reference. I couldn't be dragged away either.

My mobile buzzed on the nightstand, and I realized that wasn't quite true.

"This is Price," I answered. My light mood vanished like clouds stealing across the sun. I listened intently as my mind started sorting through options.

By the time, Belle reappeared in the room, I was fully dressed. "I need to go into the office. I'll drop you off."

"Is anything wrong?" she asked, grabbing her purse.

Only everything.

I kissed her forehead. "No. Everything is perfect."

CHAPTER TWENTY-ONE

Smith insisted on driving me to my lunch date with Edward. He coasted through the streets of London, blaring the Rolling Stones. When we reached the restaurant, he put the Bugatti in park and leaned in for a kiss.

"Behave yourself," he advised me.

"I think you prefer it when I'm bad." I left him with that thought as the valet opened the door for me. I swayed my ass saucily as I climbed out, knowing he was paying attention. In the bedroom, he held all the power. Outside of it was a different story. A fact I was prepared to show him at every possible convenience. The uniformed man looked distinctly disappointed that he wasn't going to be parking the sports car.

Considering Smith hadn't relented on letting me drive it, I understood his pain.

The dining room was crowded with the afternoon crowd, popping in to grab an early tea or a late lunch, but I spotted Edward's friendly face from across the room.

Edward set down his menu and rose to greet me as I neared him. Grabbing both of my hands, he studied me for a moment. "You're glowing," he accused. "Tell me that's a new skincare regime."

"No." I smacked him in the shoulder as I sat down. "I spent the night with Smith."

I reached for my glass of water, shrugging like this was no big deal. Edward tipped his glasses to the end of his nose and shook his head like a disappointed schoolmistress.

"I can't help it if I have needs."

"Needs which you denied for months," Edward reminded me as he perused his menu. "Then you picked the biggest todger out of the bunch and shagged him."

"I think Philip qualifies as the biggest todger." In fact, I knew he did. "Especially after yesterday."

Edward opened his mouth to beg the story out of me as the waitress appeared. I took my time ordering, having recently discovered the impact of being forced to wait for satisfaction. By the time she hurried off with her notepad, he was drumming all ten fingers on the table.

"Story. Now," he demanded.

"It's not much of a story." I pressed my index finger to the tine of my fork until a prickle of pain shot across the tip.

"Don't be coy with me, woman," he warned me. "I have access to people that can find out."

I snorted at this, trying to imagine sweet Prince Edward pulling such a corrupt move. He wasn't the type. His brother, on the other hand, would already have someone following me. "But then you wouldn't get all the good details like how I felt and what went through my head."

"What?" he pressed. "Why were things going through your head?" He pushed his glasses higher on his nose, looking as if he might explode any moment.

This really was kind of fun, but since I was still sorting through my own tangled emotions about the last twenty-four hours, I supposed I needed to come clean, particularly if I wanted his insight. Or, at the very least, a sympathetic ear.

"Philip showed up outside Smith's office yesterday."

Edward groaned and leaned back in his chair, scanning the room as if every patron in the establishment would simultaneously groan along with him. “I bet that went over well.”

“Smith didn’t see him,” I clarified. “Not that it mattered.”

“Oh?” His voice peaked on the word.

“Let’s see. The abridged version is that he made a mistake, and he wishes he could take it back, but Pepper lied to him.”

“How shocking,” Edward said in a dry voice. “I swear those two deserve each other.”

“I couldn’t agree more. Then he kissed me, and I felt nothing.”

“He kissed you?” Edward repeated.

“Apparently I’m very desirable all of a sudden.” I wanted to tell him more. About the kiss. About Georgia’s threat and Smith’s reaction. But something held me back.

“You’ve always been desirable.” The reaction reminded me of Smith.

“Smith does that, too,” I said without thinking. “Gets on my case when I’m being hard on myself.”

“I’ll admit I like him a little more hearing that,” Edward said, somewhat grudgingly.

“Me too. I think I might be getting in over my head,” I admitted. “Our relationship is moving so quickly that I feel like I need to grab something and hang on.”

“Sounds like you’re falling in love.”

I scoffed at this, shaking my head. It was way too soon for that, but my chest tightened a little as I considered it. “That would be terrible, considering my best friend hates him.”

“Maybe he’ll win over Clara,” Edward teased. “But in all seriousness, if you care about him, he must have some redeeming qualities.”

“He wants you and David to have dinner with us,” I told him, waiting to gauge his reaction.

“Sounds like he’s falling in love, too. Or at least he wants to be a significant part of your life.”

“Maybe.” It was all I could commit to for now. Although I suspected Edward was right. “I made the mistake of believing a man wanted that before.”

"Philip was a prat. He never deserved you."

I raised my water goblet in toast to this. "That is definitely true."

Our food arrived a few moments later, and conversation shifted to talk of wedding plans.

"When are you going to set a date?" I'd been prodding him about this for months, adopting the philosophy that if pressure could turn a lump of coal into a diamond then I could exert enough force to see that Edward finally made it down the aisle.

"If only UK law applied to everyone equally."

I speared a Brussels sprout on my fork and waved it around. "Correct me if I'm wrong but isn't Alexander the one who grants permission in this case?"

"Yes," Edward said with some hesitation.

"Than I don't see what the problem is. He's going to say yes." I had no doubt about that. Both Alexander and Clara seemed as anxious as I was to see the two happily married.

"It's more about the court of public opinion." He held up a hand to stop me from interrupting him. "I know this is modern times, and there's been very little backlash. If it was my father's decision, it would obviously be a no-go."

"But it's not, so why are you waffling?" I abandoned my food altogether and stared him down.

"David went from being my secret to being in the public eye so quickly that I'm not certain he knows what he's getting into. You've seen what happened to Clara in the last year," Edward reminded me. "I don't want to put him through that."

"You should have considered it before you popped the question, because that man is already picking out baby names." I'd seen how David's eyes had lit up when he held Elizabeth in the hospital. He was ready to be settled with a family of his own. "And Clara was the victim of a psycho and bad luck."

"Alexander thinks there's more to it than that." Edward's voice lowered conspiratorially. "He's been investigating what happened at the wedding."

My blood turned to ice. "I thought he dropped that."

"This is Alexander we're talking about. Clara is his world. Come on, Belle, there's no way Daniel could have acted alone, and until we have answers, all of our lives are on hold."

"Does Clara know about any of this?" My thoughts, which had been muddled for most of the morning, now came into precise focus. My best friend was home with her newborn baby while the people who'd tried to hurt her were still loose. "Or it possible Alexander's just being overly paranoid?"

"Not this time," Edward said in a grim voice. "Without knowing who was behind it, I can't risk another royal wedding."

"Elope," I advised. "Give David his wedding, and stay off the radar of whoever is behind this."

"I think David would like that idea even less than having to wait. You've seen his wedding planner."

I had, in fact, contributed to the bulky binder of ideas David had been storing since the proposal.

"Take it from someone who knows both of you. David wants to marry you. He won't care how, and if that means giving up a dream wedding, he won't even blink." I continued, admitting something that I hadn't had the courage to before, "I wanted the dream. The dress. The party. The exotic honeymoon. I was so blinded by the perfect wedding and what I thought would be the perfect life that I didn't realize I'd chosen the wrong man."

"Speaking of the wrong man," Edward murmured, his gaze shifting past me. I followed his line of sight in time to see Philip and Pepper sitting down a few tables over.

It was as if I was looking into a carnival mirror. A year ago it might have been me being seated with Philip. Now the leggy blonde at his side looked like a sexed-up version of myself. Pepper was dressed in an ivory top with a black tulle skirt that was too short to be in good taste. Whereas I'd cut my hair, she'd kept hers long, styling it into the long waves I knew Philip preferred. Philip nodded noncommittally as she told him something, her hands gesticulating wildly as she spoke. The diamond on her left ring finger caught the light, sending dazzling sparkles shining off of her.

I had to admit that I enjoyed knowing that he was looking for an out.

"Don't you own that outfit?" Edward asked, sounding as unimpressed as I felt.

"You're confusing the skirt and the man," I said dryly. Although, in all fairness, I'd never owned either of them.

"I guess the engagement is official." Edward kept his tone even, obviously not wanting to add salt to the wound.

"He admitted as much to me yesterday. I told him he was getting what he deserved." I swiveled back in my seat, pressing a hand to my nauseated stomach.

Edward's eyebrows knitted together, creasing his smooth forehead. "You okay?"

"Yeah. I just feel like I have some unfinished business there." I knew I did. I'd spent the last half of a year wedging open the door for Philip to return. Yesterday I'd shut it, but now I needed to lock it permanently.

Edward shifted the conversation back to lighter topics, but even though I tried to relax, I could feel the two of them at my back. When I caught Pepper heading to the loo out of the corner of my eye, I stood.

"Excuse me a moment." I didn't wait for him to object. He had to have seen her get up, given that he was facing their table, but if he was going to stop me, I didn't give him the chance.

Pausing at the door, I said a silent prayer that no one else was in there and pushed it open. Walking to the sinks, I dug my lipstick out of my purse and applied it, scanning the mirror until I saw her heels in one of the stalls. I took a deep breath and waited. My stomach flipped over when I heard the toilet flush.

Now would be a very good time to run. I ignored the little voice warning me away. I wasn't running any more. Not from this anyway.

Pepper emerged from the stall, smoothing down her puffy skirt and froze when she caught sight of me. I smiled wickedly into the mirror and pivoted around to face her.

"Imagine running into you here." I dropped the tube of lipstick back into my purse and glared at her.

She crossed to the far end of the sink and turned on the tap. "If you're planning to break my nose again, I should warn you that this time Philip won't be able to talk me out of a lawsuit."

"I'm not, but seeing as I have my own lawyer now, it would be an interesting case." If anything, I didn't want to break her nose, I wanted to break her neck. Not because of what she'd done by wrecking my engagement but because of the havoc she'd inflicted on the people I cared about. She needed to be taught a lesson. The trouble was that I'd tried to teach her that lesson on multiple occasions, including the time when I slugged her. Some bitches never learn.

"That will come in handy when I break your nose, I suppose." She talked a big game, but I saw her hands shaking.

"Lovely ring." I couldn't help but notice it was much smaller than the one Philip had given to me. I supposed when you gambled and lost, you don't place as much money on the next bet.

"We're getting married this winter," she informed me, her voice taking on the catty tone she'd perfected through years of terror.

"I can see that. Cold-blooded people normally prefer chilly weather. Less jarring," I added.

This was going exactly as I'd imagined it would, but not how I had hoped. I'd gotten in my shots, now it was time to say what I came in for.

"Actually, I followed you in here for a reason," I began.

She picked up a paper towel from the basket and dried her hands. "Of course, you followed me. I don't know how to spell it out to you, but Philip belongs to me now. Please refrain from stalking me over it."

"Just like King Albert belonged to you? Or Alexander? You've certainly owned a string of men. At least this one is pretending you have a future with him." Damn it, I'd fallen right back into her petty trap. Squaring my shoulders, I refocused on my purpose for being here. "I wanted to thank you. If I hadn't caught you with Philip, I'd probably be married to the wanker right now—and I'm guessing you know how boring that would be."

"He never would have married you," she said, bypassing my jab at her fiancé. "You never would have married him."

"Then I guess I would have been thanking you either way," I said serenely. "The thing is that, until recently, I didn't know what a little man Philip was in every way. Now that I've experienced a real man, I know how deeply unsatisfied Philip made me."

"Perhaps the fault lay in you. I don't have the same problem." She tossed her hair over her shoulder and took a tentative step toward the door.

She might not have learned not to provoke me, but she clearly feared being in proximity to me. I tallied that as a victory.

"There was one other thing." This is where I was going to lower the bomb I hadn't intended on dropping. "Since technically you did me a favor by ridding me of Philip's dead weight, I think I should return the kindness. Do you know where he was yesterday morning?"

Pepper's jaw tensed but she shrugged. "I don't have to keep tabs on him. He's completely loyal to me."

"Then you'd be surprised to hear he came to see me at work. He told me about your engagement and about how you lied about being pregnant."

"I didn't lie," she snapped, blinking away sudden tears. "I lost the baby."

As much as I hated Pepper Lockwood, my heart sank for her. Maybe a child would have forced her to grow up and see life outside of her own needs. "I am sorry to hear that. But you should know that he asked me to come back to him."

"Liar!" she shrieked.

I barely had time to duck before the basket of paper towels whizzed over my head. "And then he kissed me."

I was grateful that there was nothing else she could throw within reach. As soon as my words sank in, she straightened up and shot me a nasty look.

"You can lie all you want, Belle. I'm marrying Philip and you can't stop me."

"You have my blessing," I told her. "I've felt for a long time that you two are truly meant to be. I only hope you don't destroy everyone that gets in your path."

"Then might I advise you to stay clear of me." She ran past me and vanished out the door, leaving the truth hanging in the air behind her.

When I rejoined Edward at the table, he gave me an interested look.

"Whatever you said to her did the trick, because they left in a hurry," he informed me.

"I said what I needed to say." I left it at that. Edward knew all the details. He didn't need me to fill in the gaps.

"Well, half the restaurant heard what you said to her, because she was screaming it at him. It was quite the floorshow. I almost applauded." A smirk carved across his mouth, and he lifted his glass this time.

I tapped mine against it, appreciating the celebratory clink. Placing it back on the table, I smiled.

"Do you want dessert or was that sweet enough for you?" he asked.

"More than sweet enough," I confirmed, "but let's get dessert anyway."

EDWARD KISSED MY CHEEK AS WE EXITED THE RESTAURANT, then hastily looked around. "Thank God, Smith isn't here."

"I told him there was nothing to worry about," I said as I shouldered my purse, feeling the vibration of an incoming text message. As Edward headed the opposite direction, I pulled my mobile out.

SMITH: All afternoon i've been thinking about your brown sugar.

I smiled at the lewd reference to this morning's unorthodox breakfast and our musical shower.

BELLE: Don't start me up or you won't be getting any work done this afternoon.

I kept the phone in my hand as I headed toward the Tube. Smith might not like the idea of me taking public transit, but it would be ridiculous to hail a cab to get all the way to my flat. Before I could make it underground, another message arrived.

SMITH: Have a little sympathy for the devil and come into the office.

I shook my head. The man was insatiable, a trait I found I really appreciated. Dashing off one more text, I hit send before descending into the station.

BELLE: I promise later there will be satisfaction.

As I swiped my Oyster card, I realized I'd lost my connection and shoved the phone back into my purse. There was something soothing about taking the Tube, and I settled into my seat, studying the other passengers. Mums trying to keep their toddlers from toppling over when the car banked hard. Tourists trying to decipher an Underground map before they missed their stop. Teens listening to music, completely oblivious to the world around them. And a couple shamelessly making out in the corner.

That was something I couldn't imagine doing with Smith. Considering how far he'd already taken me, I hadn't thought there was a limit. Still, just seeing the pair go at it made me smile.

Bollocks. Edward was right. I was falling for Smith. That or I'd swallowed a load of butterflies. It seemed that overnight I'd become one of those girls walking around with her thoughts in the clouds and a goofy smile pinned to her face—and I couldn't care less. The lights overhead flickered momentarily as we shot through a tunnel, casting a shadow over my happiness.

There were things I didn't know about Smith. We hadn't spoken of our pasts, although I guessed he knew a lot more about me given how carefully he had screened my application. I shouldn't be so easily consumed by him. Not until he started opening up, but considering how he made me feel, did it even matter?

I was still pondering this question two connections later when the overhead speaker called my stop. As soon as I was out, I checked my phone.

SMITH: Let's spend the night together.

Apparently, the Stones had a song appropriate for every occasion. All of my doubts evaporated at the thought of his hands on my body. I had a million questions for him, but I couldn't expect them all to be answered at once. Maybe his newly discovered playfulness was the first step in letting me get closer to him.

But I couldn't help toying with him now.

BELLE: You can't always get what you want.

That would get him riled up. In fact, I'd never met a man who so easily got what he wanted, especially from me.

Another message appeared on my phone, not from Smith. An address. Apparently someone had their numbers mixed up. I slid away the notification as another text arrived from him. I could almost hear his voice as I read it.

SMITH: Gimme shelter.

The song immediately began to play in all its raw, brutal power. That he'd chosen that one sucked the air from me. It was the crux of the problem. A wall separated us still, and I wanted nothing more than to tear it down brick by brick. I knew then that I would give him shelter. I would give him anything he asked. I only wanted to know what a man like him needed protection from.

I couldn't continue the game. No response felt appropriate. The only thing I could offer him was myself. I had to hope that would be enough.

It felt good to be home. My flat had been my safe space for the last few months, protecting me from the threats of the real world outside. Jane had opened her door when I needed it most, and even now with life starting to finally look up, returning here felt like the solace I needed from the changes taking hold over me.

I threw my keys down next to a stack of yesterday's mail and called out for my aunt. The voice that answered made me shudder.

"We're in here."

My mother's voice.

Steeling myself, I forced a smile and walked into the living area. Some children look like their mothers, but once again I was struck by how different we were. I looked much more like my father, which was perhaps the reason my mother's lips pursed as I came into view. I was an unwelcome reminder of the life that she had lost.

Her eyes were as dark as the raven hair pinned elegantly up on her head. It had begun to gray at the temples since the last time I saw her, but I kept this thought to myself. As always, she was impeccably dressed in a rose dress suit and pearls. We both liked expensive clothing. That was as similar as we got.

Mother scanned me, not bothering to hide her disapproval of my dress and its revealing neckline, but she didn't say anything.

Our relationship was built on what we left unsaid.

"I didn't know you were coming to town," I said, leaning in for the obligatory cheek kiss. She accepted it without returning it.

"You wouldn't commit to a meeting time," she reminded me, "or tell me anything about this new job. My aunt hasn't been forthcoming either."

Jane smiled pleasantly at her and poured hot water into a chipped teacup. She held it out to her.

Mum took it, grimacing as she spotted its imperfection, and turned the irregular side away from her. I hated her for that.

"I've been very busy." I dropped into an overstuffed armchair and crossed my legs, knowing that it drove her crazy.

Ladies cross their ankles. I heard her voice correcting me in my mind. Most of my memories of my childhood included useful tidbits such as that. If she had any idea how unladylike I'd become, she would probably faint.

"What is on your neck?" she asked, leaning forward to zero in on whatever she had spotted.

My hand flew to my throat, but it was too late. I hadn't actually checked myself for marks. Now I had no idea what she was referring to. Bite mark? Bruise? Hickey? They all seemed pretty likely.

Jane swooped to my rescue. "It looks like her seat belt must have rubbed her the wrong way."

"Seat belt?" Curiosity colored my mother's words. "I didn't know they used seat belts on the Tube."

"Belle has her own car now," Jane said.

I glared at her. So much for saving me. Jane shrugged, as if to say 'let's put our cards on the table.'

"Your own car?" my mother repeated in a strangled voice.

It didn't matter that the family estate's garage housed a dozen luxury automobiles that we couldn't afford. All she heard was that I had betrayed her.

"It's not mine," I fibbed. "It's for work. I only use it to run errands."

I'd already decided if I ever left my job, I wouldn't keep the car, which made it a perk of my position and nothing more. I left out that it was a Mercedes.

"What is this job anyway?" she snapped. "And before you get smart with me, I didn't appreciate your off-color remarks the first time."

"I'm not a stripper," I reassured her. Well, not really. I didn't know if there was a term for a woman who shagged her boss. "I work for a lawyer as his personal assistant."

"At least it's nothing important." She leaned over and placed her teacup on the table in front of her. She might have just thrown it at me for all intents and purposes.

It amazed me that after all this time she could still hurt me with her words. Of course, I'd never developed a thick skin so much as I had a smart mouth. My sarcasm bothered her more anyway.

"Belle is quite happy with her new position." Jane rose to my defense, glowering at her. There was nothing like seeing my aunt's feathers ruffled.

"Unless it pays the mortgage then it's not important," Mum

explained. She looked to me as if I would volunteer to write her a check.

My salary could pay many of the estate's expenses, but it would leave me with very little to get back on my feet. Since I'd left for school, the ties that bound me to my childhood had frayed. In the last year, they'd broken entirely. Still, guilt tugged at me.

"Just enough for rent," I lied.

Jane bit back a smile across from me, barely hiding it before my mother turned on her. "It's disgraceful that you would charge your own niece rent."

"London is very expensive." Jane blinked as if this was reason enough. Neither of us were about to tell her that I hadn't written Jane a check since I'd moved into her spare room.

"I came with good news." Despite this announcement, my mother sounded anything but happy. She twisted the strand of pearls around her neck.

"Please share," Jane finally prompted when it was clear she was waiting for us to show a respectful amount of interest.

"We've been approached to rent the estate to the BBC for that period drama the Americans like so well."

"Wexford Hall?" I offered, frowning.

"Yes, they were unable to reach a deal with the Abernathys. Apparently, Philip was quite demanding in his negotiations and suggested they contact me about using our home for future filming." Mother's pointed look could pierce flesh.

"He wasn't doing us a favor." I got right to the heart of the matter.

"Don't kid yourself, Belle." She dismissed my response with a wave of the hand. "It was clearly a peace offering. Philip wants to make amends with you."

"Philip is engaged to the woman he cheated on me with." Only my mother would walk into my own home and suggest I take back the asshole.

"He's very unhappy. He feels he made a mistake."

I froze for a moment as I processed what she was telling me.

Clutching the arms of the chair so I wouldn't fly out, I leveled my gaze with hers. "Please tell me you've become a psychic."

"He came to see me earlier this week. I gave him my blessing to approach you." It was clear from her tone that she saw no issue with this.

"He's engaged!" Maybe if I said it louder, she'd finally hear me.

"Men make mistakes. Lord knows your father made plenty."

"Father didn't sleep with other women. He was loyal." The rage simmering inside me began to boil over.

"Yes, but he made mistakes. However, the estate was always his top priority. How would he feel to hear you were shunning a chance to protect it from ruin?"

That was my mother. It was up to me. It always had been. Staff needn't be trimmed. Cars couldn't be sold. Considering the BBC offer was the first concession she'd ever made regarding her lifestyle. "His loyalty to that estate—to you—killed him."

"He killed himself," she said coldly.

My hand clapped over my mouth as an unwanted mirror swam into my head.

Dangling, lifeless feet. Daddy was being silly and he wouldn't stop. I got on a chair and tugged his leg, but he still wouldn't come down.

Screams. Screams from her mouth.

And then I hit the floor hard. I curled into a ball. Mummy didn't even care that she'd knocked me off.

She just kept screaming.

Screaming and pulling on him.

Tears filled my eyes as I covered my ears.

Jane's arm wrapped around my shoulders as I tried to claw my way back to the present. When I found myself back in my flat, the tears belonged to me and not the five year-old girl in my memory.

"Get out," Jane said, pointing toward the door.

"We have business to discuss," my mother said, ignoring her. "Thanks to your father's poor business acumen, all decisions regarding the financial state of the estate must be approved by my daughter."

"You don't have a daughter," I croaked past the rawness creeping up my throat.

"How I wished that was the truth. A son would have been useful. He would care about his family. Instead I was stuck with you," she snarled.

The barb didn't stick. I'd known she felt this way my whole life. "Do whatever you want with it. Because if you leave it to me, I'll burn the fucking place down."

"Language!" she reprimanded me.

"You obviously didn't hear me," Jane roared. "Get out of my house, Ann!"

She stood, tugging down her tailored jacket and cast a hateful glare at me. "I'll send the BBC contract for you to peruse. Either sign it or take Philip back, but standing by and ruining what I've rebuilt is not an option."

Her final words were still ringing in my ears when the door slammed closed behind her. It was a joke really. In the last nineteen years, she'd rebuilt nothing.

Certainly not me.

CHAPTER TWENTY-TWO

The contracts were in my inbox when I arrived at the office three hours ago, and I was still staring at them. One stroke of the pen would sever a tie that had bound me far too long to past mistakes—mistakes not of my making. But it would also introduce scrutiny. The decision to withdraw my inherited stakes in my father's nightclub shouldn't raise any eyebrows, but it would. I'd set the wheels in motion months ago, hoping to dissolve my interest quietly. There had been nothing to risk then.

Now that had changed.

My extended family could offer Belle protection. That was never a question. The question was what it would cost me—and her. And that protection was absolute until my partners deemed either of us a threat. Whether or not I chose to sign the papers decided the man I'd become. For a fleeting moment, I considered if my father had faced a similar dilemma.

The door to my office creaked open, and Belle poked her head through the gap.

"Am I disturbing important lawyering?" she asked, but her cheerful smile didn't reach her eyes.

I pushed back my chair and patted my knee. "You are always welcome to disturb me, beautiful."

She hurried over to me and settled onto my lap. She was as stunning as when I'd dropped her off this morning, polished and radiant, except for the red rims around her eyes. Tipping her chin so she faced me, I studied her anxiously. "What happened?"

"Nothing. I'm tired." It was a lie, but a well-meaning one. It wasn't the dishonesty of someone ashamed of wrongdoing. I'd spent enough time around guilty people and criminals to know. This was the lie of someone guarding herself. She had been hurt. I stiffened in my seat, attempting to remain calm. It would wound her more to force the issue, even though doing nothing to the offender left me feeling murderous. Then it occurred to me that I might be the assailant. Perhaps I'd pushed her too far yesterday evening.

"Maybe we should take it easy tonight," I suggested. "Grab takeaway and watch a movie on the sofa."

"You have a sofa and a television?" she said in mock surprise.

Her mood was shifting, and I pulled her into me, determined to lighten it entirely. "I'll admit I don't often use them."

"Too busy bedding women?" she guessed, nuzzling under my chin.

"Do I detect some jealousy?" I had, and I liked it. "Usually I'm stuck at work at night. Lately, I've had a reason to go home though."

"A quiet night sounds nice," she finally said, "as long as it ends with a good shag." She shifted, straddling her legs over my lap and bunching her skirt in the process.

My fingers dug into her hips, holding her there. "That I can promise you, beautiful."

"I took my knickers off before I came in, so I'd be bare and ready for you," she whispered, grinding her pussy against my trousers. The raw eroticism was at odds with the sweet flutter of her lashes. She was chaos, charming one moment and wanton the next. Knowing her was the most exquisite turmoil I'd ever experienced.

A knock at the door startled us apart. Belle shot me a questioning look. I couldn't blame her. It was a Saturday afternoon. We should be the only ones here. There were only four people who had keys to the front door. I didn't have to guess who was visiting.

"Hammond," I informed her. "We had some business to discuss."

Another lie so close to the truth that the edges of it blurred. He would be here to talk business, but I wasn't expecting him. His presence indicated news had moved more swiftly through the grapevine than I had predicted. I'd hoped to confront this next week. Now Belle would be here to witness the fallout.

"Come in," I called out, bracing myself for the fast approaching storm.

"I should go," she murmured, and I did my best not to look relieved. There were things she would learn about me in time, but it was too soon to unveil the ugly underbelly of my life. Not while she could still run.

Belle smoothed down her dress swiftly, regaining her composure before Hammond strode through the door.

"The lovely Miss Stuart." Hammond spread his hands in greeting. "Can I pour you a drink? Smith keeps the good stuff socked away for me."

Picking up her purse, she fluttered her lashes sweetly at him. "I was just on my way out. Next time."

Next time. My hands balled into fists at the thought. Every time she was in the room with him, I swore there would never be a next time.

"I'll see you at your place?" Belle spoke to me, but her eyes were glued on Hammond as though he was a snake that might strike at any moment.

I'd always liked smart women.

"It may be a few hours." I glanced to Hammond, who confirmed this with a wink. I wanted to kiss her but not in front of him. It would only be ammunition, and frankly, I didn't want to share her even for a moment with him. God knows even the most innocent action could be perverted to suit Hammond's twisted desires. Belle disappeared out the office door with a faint farewell, but despite her graceful exit, I sensed her need to flee.

Hammond lit a cigar as the office door clicked closed. Thick puffs of spicy smoke wafted through the room, and my mind flashed to my father sitting in this office. Both the memory and my current visitor were unwelcome.

"I'm told you're pulling out of Velvet." He didn't waste time. No, time was money to a man like him, and he'd never let you borrow one red second of it.

I dropped onto the sofa and slung an arm over its low back, releasing a heavy sigh but none of the exhaustion that had brought it on. "Where did you hear that?"

"Does it matter?" He took the chair opposite of me and assumed the same position. He'd always loved the imitation game. Although he seemed to have forgotten that he'd taught it to me. Mimic your opponent. If they act casual, be casual. If they lie, lie as well. When they ask questions, ask another.

"I suppose not. It's not a secret." I crossed my leg and watched as he did the same.

"Then why not come to me?" What he was really asking was whether or not everything was on the up and up.

"Honestly, I didn't think you'd care. It was my father's hobby, not mine." Hobby was a kind word for it. Obsession would have been more appropriate. Aberration still more correct.

Hammond stroked his jaw, his eyes and thoughts distant. Mentioning my father always had that effect on him. The memory of the man was enough to send us both spiraling back through time. "You can't cut your father's legacy from your life, Smith."

"I can try," I said through clenched teeth.

"You might as well slit your own throat then and drain his blood from your veins. It would be just as practical." Hammond's words took on the stern, fatherly tone that I loathed. I'd found it soothing once. That had been my first mistake.

"I'm a silent partner. Georgia can handle Velvet without me. I haven't even stepped foot—"

"That's not what matters. Velvet is an important thread linking you to this family."

He called them threads, but they were chains. We each wore them, some more willingly than others. Hammond's extended family was linked through his many entrepreneurial endeavors. By the time one realized the true nature of the business, they were bound too tight to escape. Velvet was a chain I needed to break.

"I have more than enough threads connecting me. Need I remind you that my name is on every contract you sign." This wasn't a hand I wanted to play. Not with Hammond who rarely saw past sentiment and instinct. Facts never interested him. It was an important thing to keep in mind.

"And you have the protection of your profession. One that I gave you."

"That's funny," I said lightly. "I seem to recall the Law Society granting me that profession after a few years of school."

"This isn't a lark." Hammond jumped to his feet and I rose, reversing his imitation game back on him. "You will maintain your ownership share in Velvet, and if I continue to hear more disquieting rumors—"

"And who are you hearing these rumors from? I know you've never had a taste for legality, but I'm partial to having access to all the evidence." There was a rat amongst my inner circle. The news didn't shake me. I paid my people well enough, but I never expected their loyalty. I learned a long time ago that loyalty was a whimsical notion that had disappeared along with chivalry. Occasionally I got glimpses of both but never long enough to believe they existed. But I couldn't allow the betrayal to go unrecognized. It would only feed Hammond's paranoid nature.

"You think I don't own your people? Doris. Garrison. Mrs. Andrews. Everyone can be bought for a price. They just can't be bought by a Price. Your father made the mistake of learning that lesson the expensive way." Hammond blew smoke in my direction and glanced toward the door Belle had exited through. "Someday, I'll own her, too. Sooner or later, everyone needs something from me. And the delicious part is that you won't even know when I buy her off. She'll come home and suck your dick and play house just like—"

His rant was prematurely cut off by the hands around his throat.

My hands.

"All I have to do is squeeze," I warned him.

"Then you're both dead, but it won't be quick and clean this time," he wheezed, his cheeks reddening. His cigar dropped to the floor. "My heirs will see to that. You'll be there to see it, too. All that bright red blood on her pretty pale skin. She'll be alive. She'll be begging you. And there won't be a goddamn thing you can do."

"How do I know you won't order it as soon as you leave?" I demanded, wringing his wiry neck harder. Shoving my shoulder into his chest, I pinned him against the wall.

"You don't," he admitted with a gasp. "Guess you'll be a gambler after all."

I pictured it: his eyes bulging out of his head, his doughy flesh shifting from red to purple. And I could almost imagine the feeling of freedom that would accompany his final moment—a relief I'd never known.

But that freedom would be short-lived.

My hands dropped to my sides. Hammond inched away, rubbing his neck.

"I'm glad you came to your senses, boy."

"I'm not your boy," I snarled.

"Your father would be disappointed in how little respect you show your elders." Hammond crushed the smoldering tip of his cigar with the toe of his oxford, leaving a black hole in the Oriental rug.

"I think he'd be more disappointed that he was dead before he could destroy every last person he claimed to love." I turned my back on Hammond. I couldn't afford to let him see any more. Not while I was so raw. Now while I was so out of control. I would slip again and there would be consequences.

"Your mother lived a perfectly lovely life after his death." Hammond fastened the button of his blazer, shaking his head in disgust.

She'd been a shell of a person since that day, and we both knew why.

"Yeah, thankfully, someone took care of her." I pulled the stopper on the Macallan I kept for clients and poured myself a drink.

"Drinking this early?"

I wanted to tell him to shove his fatherly tone up his ass. He hadn't earned it. No one in my life earned the right to call themselves a father. I gulped it down and poured another. "I'm in business for myself. I'm calling it an early day"

"That's where you're wrong, son." Hammond placed a heavy hand on my shoulder. "You're in business for me."

I bit back a laugh. If only he knew the truth, but then again, he'd refuse to believe it.

Hammond paused in the doorway, his hand on the knob. "I'm going to forget this ever happened. For your father's sake. But don't ever pull that shit again."

I gave him a terse nod then swallowed my second Scotch. As soon as he was gone, I grabbed the bottle.

I'd had a plan. One that required patience. But more importantly: no attachments. Now all that had gone to hell. Because of her.

There were two ways to keep her out of Hammond's sights: never let her out of mine or make her a nonissue. One was more foolproof than the other. It was also the one I wasn't certain I could live with.

I'd have to drink until I could. What did they say about the road to hell? Who fucking cared. I was already on it.

My father was buried in a graveyard next to eighteenth century poets. Hammond had pulled one final string, obtaining the plot for him—a nod to my father's love of books. On the few occasions that I'd ventured here, I'd wandered through the ivy-clad tombstones wondering if it assuaged his guilt. Tonight I knew it couldn't.

A statue of justice with her blindfolded eyes and scales stood guard over his grave. Considering his love of literature, my father would certainly appreciate the irony. I stared at her unseeing eyes. She had been a popular image in university law classes. Most of my classmates had believed she actually existed. I might have once, too, but I didn't remember being that naive.

Humphrey Price. Beloved Father and Husband. Protector of God's Justice.

I laughed, filling the quiet cemetery with the hollow sound. It echoed across the stones. Drawing the nearly empty bottle of Scotch from my coat pocket, I dropped to the grass in front of his marker. I raised it to him.

"I suppose we finally have something to talk about. Where should we start?" I paused as if he might respond. "No ideas? Well, there's woman troubles. You had your share of those. Although based on your marriage, you might not be qualified to offer me guidance there. We could discuss the law. Judging from the rather ostentatious display erected in your honor, you might have more insight into that topic, especially given the clientele we share."

I took a swig out of the bottle. "Oh, hell."

I chugged the rest and tossed the empty bottle on his plot.

"You would have loved that, but then again you loved anything with a higher proof content than your legal cases, right? I have to ask you. Did Hammond spin you gold in exchange for my soul? Is that how the story goes?" Hatred churned through my blood, slowly raising it toward the boiling point.

"I guess I'll be seeing you soon. For now, allow me to leave you with a token of appreciation for everything you did for me in life." Pushing myself to my feet, I stared down. He was down there, rotting, his flesh food for worms. He didn't belong here next to men of talent and character. His place was in hell. I could only hope he burned there now. Unzipping my fly, I whipped out my dick and pissed on his name. It was the closest thing to solace that I would ever offer him.

CHAPTER TWENTY-THREE

I'd meant to go straight to Smith's house, but Hammond's appearance sent me in another direction. Before I'd fully comprehended what I was doing, I'd found myself in Chelsea. The address that had been sent to my mobile wasn't visible from the street. If it had been anywhere else, I might have reconsidered exploring, but this was Chelsea. Still when I found the purple door tucked carefully off a quiet side street, I paused.

I had no idea who had sent me the text message. Or why. Not that I had enemies to speak of. I sincerely doubted Pepper Lockwood would go to this much trouble to return a broken nose. No, I hadn't come this far to turn back now. I tried the handle but it was locked. Searching for a knocker or doorbell, I came up short. I was about to give up when the door buzzed and clicked open. No one met me at the entrance. The hallway was dimly lit, but the walls had a lustrous sheen that drew my hands to them.

Velvet.

In the distance, a faint rhythm pounded. It was a bit early for a nightclub to get going, even for a Saturday, but instinct told me this was no ordinary club. I pushed myself forward, trailing my fingers along the plush wall coverings. The simple wrap dress I'd thrown on in my rush to get ready this morning wasn't really dance floor material. Hopefully, the early bar crowd wouldn't notice. When I rounded the corner, I knew that they would.

I clamped my mouth shut, sucking back the gasp that tried to get out, but I couldn't keep my cheeks from heating.

The fuchsia-haired bartender scanned me up and down from across the room while I tried not to look directly at her rubber waist cincher or the pierced nipples it boosted into display. I flashed her a smile, wondering whether I should turn tail and run or play it cool. Clearly the text had been sent to the wrong mobile number. I gripped my purse tightly, preparing to make as dignified an exit as possible when a couple in the corner caught my eye. The woman was wearing a collar tethered to a leash. Memories of last night poured into my head. I had been that girl yesterday. I hoped to be her again tonight.

Maybe I wasn't as out of place as I'd feared.

Gathering my courage and ignoring my nerves, I walked up to the bar. "Gin and tonic."

The bartender's eyes narrowed, but she grabbed a bottle of Nolet's and poured the drink. Apparently this place catered to the kinky and the wealthy. I took a sip of my cocktail, my eyes glued to the couple on the couch. The woman knelt at his feet while he spoke to another man seated across from them. Both men were fully clothed, but the only thing she wore was the collar. Would I do that if it were Smith holding my leash? The question aroused me, and I considered shooting him the address in a text, but then I would have to explain how I had wound up here. And I didn't have a good answer.

As I watched, the other man stood and approached the couple. The woman's head fell forward to hide her tears, and her lover brushed a hand over her cheek. I touched my own, knowing exactly what that caress felt like. Then he handed the other man her leash. Her head stayed down as she crawled away with him. The two headed down a corridor, and my stomach turned over.

He had given her to someone else, and she had gone willingly, despite her sadness.

Throwing down my credit card, I called for my tab.

"It's on the house," the bartender said, pushing it back to me.

"I'll pay." I practically spat the words. I didn't want to owe this place anything. Not when it was clear what was expected of women like me.

Like me.

Oh God, what had I gotten myself into?

But Smith would never.

She shrugged and started pouring another drink. "That's expensive shit. I'd rather you paid, too, particularly if you're going to waste it. But it's not up to me."

"Who is it up to?" I pressed, looking around me. I'd been sent here, admitted in, and now someone was paying for my drink. It was clear this was no longer a coincidence.

"It's up to me," a woman's voice informed me.

I spun on my stool, shocked, even after recognizing her voice.

Georgia Kincaid stood there, lips pressed tightly together. She closed her eyes for a moment before motioning that I should follow her.

"You aren't supposed to be here," she hissed as we headed down the dark corridor the man had taken the woman down.

"Whatever." I halted in my tracks, refusing to follow her any farther. "You're telling me that you didn't send me this text?" I waved my mobile at her.

"That's exactly what I'm telling you," she said in a cold voice. Her bony fingers closed over my upper arm, and she yanked me through a blue door. "What are you doing here?"

"I already told you. I got a text." I was beginning to lose my patience with Georgia. I hadn't had much to begin with. "What is this place?"

"Even you aren't that dense." Georgia shut the door and pressed herself against it. It was easier to see her in the better lighting, and my jaw dropped. She was wearing a black lace bustier and not much else. Leather straps corseted her trim waist and matched the cuffs she wore on her wrists.

I didn't know if she was going to kill me or flog me.

"A sex club. Lovely. I knew I was overdressed." I spun around in the room, hoping to see a sign marked 'this way out.'

"Don't get all prudish on me now. You can't be too uptight if you're fucking Smith." Georgia sauntered past me and dropped onto a red velvet divan.

I ignored her and focused on what I really needed to be concerned about. "Why would someone send me here?"

"Maybe they want to spank your bony ass," Georgia said dryly. Her arm curled under her head as she leaned back, exposing the tops of her nipples over the frilly strapless top of her corset.

"I'm going to need you to try to not be a twat for one minute," I snapped. Few things made me uncomfortable in my skin, now I was in a place that made it crawl, with a person I despised. I wanted answers and then I wanted out. Immediately.

"And I need to think." She glowered at me as she stood up and started pacing the room. "Let me see your mobile."

"No way in hell." I wasn't about to give her access to the private line Smith had given me.

"Chill, princess. Show me the text." She moved beside me, looking over my shoulder at the screen. Her breast brushed my upper arm and I jumped away. "Please calm down. I'm not trying to have my way with you."

"I'm sorry. This place is a bit overwhelming." An apology was in order, even if I loathed her. I had no reason to suspect she wasn't trying to help me, and it was pretty obvious that she hadn't been the one to send me here.

"Velvet," she said, tapping the mobile to pull up the message's detailed report.

"What?" I asked in confusion.

"This place is called Velvet," she said matter-of-factly, then switched focus to the task at hand."There's nothing here to say who sent this to you. Do you always blindly go to places at the request of anonymous callers?"

I could tell exactly what she thought about that. "This is a private line. Only one person has the number."

"Smith?" she guessed, and I nodded. "But that message wasn't from him."

"How was I supposed to know?" I'd meant to ask him at the office until we were interrupted by Hammond's appearance. Then I'd forgotten.

"Because Smith would never send you here." Georgia paused to let this sink in. She planted her hands on her hips. "You'll have to tell him you came."

"Why would he never send me here?" I asked in a small voice, completely bypassing her advice. Up until this moment, I'd been ready to leave here and never speak of it again. Now I was being told that I couldn't.

"That's for him to tell you," she said, tacking on, "when he's ready. But tell him yourself that you came."

"And if I don't?"

"He's going to find out," she warned me. "It's up to you whom he hears it from. I suggest it comes from your lips. Since you're fucking him, I'm certain he's shown you a taste of his preferences. You're not ready for real punishment yet."

I tilted my chin up and stared her in the eye. "How do you know?"

"Because you were sitting down," she said in measured syllables.

My knees buckled, and I fought to stay on my feet. I had to look away from her. My gaze zeroed in on an innocuous abstract painting on the wall behind her. I focused on the strokes of black and white until I regained control over myself. "I'll tell him," I said finally. "But answer one question for me."

Georgia crossed her arms over her chest. "I can't promise you I will."

"Has he been here?" I barely got the question past my dry tongue.

"Yes." She held up her hand as my mouth opened again. "That's all I'll tell you, and I only told you because you already knew. It's up to Smith what else he chooses to share with you. But remember this, you don't know what secrets he keeps behind closed doors. Now I'm escorting you out of here."

I didn't put up a fight as she led me back to the side door. Georgia stepped onto the street beside me, despite her daring ensemble.

"Get rid of that phone," she said quickly. "Tell Smith, and in the future, don't be so fucking stupid."

"I went to a club," I retorted, feeling braver outside Velvet's walls.

A grim smile twisted across her lips. "No, you didn't. You walked into the lions' den."

CHAPTER TWENTY-FOUR

The gates to Clarence House were always open for me. Except for when they weren't. As dismal rain drizzled from the autumn sky, I explained for the tenth time who I was to the guard, who was obviously new.

"It will be on your computer," I explained.

"Miss, you might be correct, but the royal family has been quite clear that they don't wish to be disturbed." He backed up a step as he informed me of this.

My eyes narrowed. He should be afraid of me. I had half a mind to climb the gate. By the time he figured out the phone system to call reinforcements, I would be long gone. Of course after the day I'd had, I would probably be arrested. Edward would love getting the call to bail me out.

Edward.

"I assume Edward is allowed in?" I asked him.

His eyebrows knit in confusion under his beret. "Prince Edward?"

"No, that vampire from the movies," I snapped. "Of course, Prince Edward."

"Well, yes-s-s," he stammered. A bead of sweat appeared on his forehead, but I knew he couldn't wipe it off in front of me.

"Can you call him?" I asked sweetly, attempting to ratchet down my bitchiness.

"I could, but—"

"Either call him or find Norris, but do not make me call Clara's mobile and wake up the baby!" Apparently remaining calm was a futile endeavor.

"Yes, Miss. I mean, Ma'am. I mean, Sir."

I shook my head. "You're heading in the wrong direction there, soldier."

"I'm not a soldier, I'm a—"

I held up a hand, incapable of listening to his correction. "Just call him."

I watched through the guard stand's window as he fumbled with the phone and eventually got someone on the line. A minute later, he came back and handed me my I.D. "I'm sorry for the confusion, Miss Stuart. We've tightened security."

"And you just started?" I guessed.

The confused look I'd come to expect crossed his face. There was no point trying to help him through it. The kid was a lost cause. I waltzed up to the front entrance, marveling at the grandeur of Alexander and Clara's temporary home. Soon they would be forced to make a move to one even larger, but for reasons known only to them and a few others, they'd stubbornly chosen to remain here for the time being.

The guard at the door opened it for me and I stepped inside. Despite its spacious interior and the priceless antiques and art that filled each room, it had a cozy, casual feel. At least relative to most palaces. That was why they had wanted to bring their baby home to this place. Here they could focus on building their family instead of ruling a monarchy.

Alexander met me at the top of the stairs. "Edward texted me. I'm sorry for the trouble."

"I figured you might not want mobiles going off with a newborn." I brushed beads of rain from my hair.

"That was thoughtful." He sounded grateful for my caution. I supposed half of the world wanted to get a glimpse of Elizabeth or a statement from the new parents.

The thoughtful Belle had disappeared when she crossed the threshold. "Of course. Now I need to see my best friend, and I don't care if she's resting. I really am sorry, but this is an emergency."

"And if I refuse?" he teased.

"I'll remind you that not only did I know her first, but I convinced her to sleep with you."

"You learn something new every day," he said with amusement. "I suppose I owe you one."

"You owe me several," I informed him as he guided me down the hall. "How is she?"

"Breathtaking." His voice was filled with the same awe that always accompanied his thoughts on his wife. "She's never looked lovelier."

When I walked into the nursery, Clara glanced up and gave me a small smile. Elizabeth was in her arms, sleeping peacefully. Clara's dark hair cascaded over her shoulder, and her skin glowed against the creamy backdrop of the nursery walls. The whole image reminded me of a portrait of the Madonna with child.

"I can wait," I whispered, realizing how insignificant my own needs were right now.

"No, you're fine," she said softly. "I should put her down, but I can't help wanting to hold her. Come here. She looks like an angel."

I tiptoed over, not wanting to wake her, and peered over Clara's shoulder. The baby's cheeks were rosy, and as I watched, she let out a tiny sigh and smiled in her sleep.

"She's perfect," I murmured.

"I have to agree with you," Alexander said from the doorway. His powerful form filled the doorframe as he guarded his wife and daughter. He crossed over to us and leaned down to take the sleeping bundle from her arms. "I've got her. You two go talk."

I nodded my appreciation to him. Clara struggled to her feet, and I reached out to help her up.

"This is going to be a long recovery," she said with a sigh as we headed across the corridor to her bedroom. A fire had been lit, and we hunkered down into the two cozy chairs stationed beside it.

Pulling my knees into my chest, I searched for where to begin.

"Male trouble?" Clara guessed, flipping on a lamp next to her.

"Is it that obvious?" Earlier today I'd been so certain my relationship with Smith was heading in a positive direction. Now I wasn't.

"I recognize the face you're making. I believe I made it several times over the last year." She screwed up her face into a cross between a frown and a grimace.

"I hope I don't actually look like that," I said in a flat voice, but I couldn't help but laugh.

"You look much prettier when you pout," she promised me. "I'm still all swollen from last week's blessed event."

"I think motherhood suits you. Alexander told me you'd never looked lovelier, and he was right."

Clara's expression shifted, a smile lighting across her face at the mere mention of her husband.

"Watching you fall in love with Alexander showed me how messy love can be, but also that it's worth fighting for," I told her. It had been messy with me and Smith from the start. After today things were bound to get worse. "What I don't know is why you chose to fight at all?"

She exhaled deeply, and I could tell she was choosing her response carefully. "This isn't going to sound very helpful, but I don't think I ever really had a choice. Being with him was inevitable. I actually tried to fight loving him and I couldn't. That was exhausting. When I decided I wanted to be with him, it wasn't any less difficult. It was simply easier to fight for us than against us."

"I think I understand." I did understand. Since I'd met Smith, I had tried to keep him at a distance. Even after I'd given myself to him, I had pushed him away. And still we kept returning to one another. "Does it feel a bit like addiction?"

"This is serious," Clara said, shifting forward. She winced and grabbed her stomach.

I dropped to the floor in front of her. "Are you okay?"

"Yes." She waved off my concern and leaned back again. "I'm still recovering, remember? Now stop trying to change the subject."

I stuck my tongue out at her and scrambled back into my seat. "Believe me, I want to talk about this. I can't seem to sort it out on my own. It's like my head is a jumble."

"You're falling in love," she said in a gentle voice, "and that is scary for you, especially after Philip."

"I never loved Philip," I admitted to her.

"I suspected that, but that doesn't mean your relationship with him didn't affect your life. You may not have loved him, but you trusted him and you gave your loyalty to him."

"And then he royally screwed me," I finished for her, tacking on a sheepish, "No offense, Your Majesty."

"You are never allowed to call me that," she informed me. Her eyes went distant for a moment as a wry grin spread over her face. "Look how much has changed for us since we left Oxford. I'm married and you're shagging your boss."

"Plus you becoming the Queen of England," I added dryly. Neither of us had seen any of this coming, which is why it made the rocky terrain more treacherous to navigate, especially since we were increasingly doing it alone. Or rather, with someone else at our sides. It felt good to be here with her now. It was as close to normal as either of us were getting. "You know I always have your back, right?"

"I count on it," she said. "Back to this whole falling in love business."

I groaned. So much for our moment. "I don't know if I'm in love with him."

"That's the thing about the fall. You don't really feel it until you hit the ground."

"And up until then?" I asked. Since admitting I hadn't loved Philip, I realized I'd never been in love before. All of this was new to me, and it was a change that wasn't entirely welcome given today's revelations.

"You feel exhilarated—like you're flying. There's moments of panic, of course, but then you let go again."

"And when you hit bottom?" I asked.

"Just hope he's already waiting to catch you." Her words were bittersweet, almost wistful.

"Like Alexander caught you?"

She shook her head, pursing her lips ruefully. "I'm pretty sure I caught him."

"Only you would be strong enough to," I told her. I moved to the arm of her chair and sank down beside her, hugging her close to me.

"It's worth it," she continued.

"What is?" I murmured.

"The fall. The hard landing. If you know it's the right person."

There was a time when I would have asked her how I knew I was choosing correctly. I didn't need to tonight.

CHAPTER TWENTY-FIVE

Night had fallen, but I hadn't moved. I belonged here among the moss and ghosts—a shadow of a man adrift in the space between life and death.

The soft crunch of footsteps on grass came near, and I startled out of my malaise. Knocking over the empty bottle, I hurried to my feet to face the intruder. At this time of night, it was either a sentimental tourist wanting to commune with the dead artists buried all around me or someone who knew where to look for me. In either case, I wasn't interested in company.

"God, I can smell you from here." Georgia came into view, waving a hand over her nose. She was dressed in leather pants so tight that I imagined she'd had them sewn on and a matching motorcycle jacket. She'd obviously come here from the club. "How much did you drink?"

"Not enough," I said, kicking the bottle at my feet. "I'd offer you some, but Dad and I drank all of it."

"You are drunk if you think your dad is here. Newsflash: he's worm food." She dropped to the grass, folding her legs beneath her. Apparently she thought she was invited to my private party.

"You're comforting as always." I sat back down beside her. I could ask her to leave, but expecting a favor out of Georgia was like believing in life after death. Utterly pointless.

"I had no idea you still came here." She gazed past me at the tombstone and let out a long sigh.

"I haven't been here in years."

"Why tonight?" she asked, fixing me with a penetrating stare that would leave lesser men fumbling for words.

She'd never had that effect on me. "The better question is why are you here? Or rather, how did you know I would be?"

No part of me believed Georgia had simply stumbled into the graveyard and happened upon me. She was seeking me out, which was never a good sign, particularly since we'd chosen to limit our contact with one another.

"You're not nearly as mysterious as you think you are. Hammond mentioned he visited you at the office."

"Did he mention I nearly choked him?" I asked her, wishing I hadn't finished the bottle of Scotch so quickly.

"It might have come up," she said wryly. "And since my father reminds you of yours, I played a hunch."

"You're good at that." Too damn good. It was unnerving how easily she got into other people's heads, especially when it was my head. It was what made her good at her job and better at her hobby. Not that there was much difference between the two. Either way, she was screwing somebody.

"I didn't come here to discuss dear old dad."

"I didn't think you had." At least she had found somewhere relatively safe to talk. The only witnesses to our meeting had lost the ability to tell tales long ago.

"Your charming new plaything showed up at Velvet today."

The boozy haze enveloping me evaporated instantly, and I was back on my feet, looking for something to hit besides marble grave markers. "How the fuck did that happen?"

"A third party sent her the address—on your private mobile."

Goddammit, Hammond hadn't been lying when he'd told me he'd gotten to my people. "I'll have to fire my staff."

"Including your assistant?" Georgia pressed.

"I doubt she sent the message to herself," I said coolly as I mentally calculated severance pay.

"You know it's the right move. She needs to be cut loose, Smith." The cattiness she'd exhibited toward Belle was absent from this proclamation. Georgia was being rational and undeniably smart. I couldn't feign security concerns with Hammond if I kept her on.

"It's more complicated than that."

"Don't tell me that you didn't see this coming. Or were you too blinded by your erection to think straight?"

"Fuck you, Georgia," I growled.

"We swore no attachments. Not even with each other. I believe your words were 'we have to be calculating.'" Her tone dared me to challenge this fact, but I couldn't.

"We're not the type to get attached." Which is why I hadn't seen Belle coming.

"She was chosen to fulfill an objective," she continued. "Now that's been blown to hell. There are other avenues for us to pursue."

"We can pursue them without me abandoning her. If anything, her continued presence is a smoke screen. Her connections haven't escaped Hammond's notice. If he suspects—"

"Jesus, do you hear yourself?" she interjected, shaking her head and sending dark locks blowing in the breeze. "She'll be a target. Is that what you want?"

"It's a smart plan," I hedged.

"You'd risk her life? She must be nothing more than one sweet piece of ass. That's cold, even for you."

"I learned from the best." I couldn't look at her. The truth was that I had learned ruthlessness from someone else. Georgia had merely honed my capacity for it.

"Destroy her then." Georgia shrugged and pushed up to her feet. Brushing off the back of her pants, she continued, "It's no skin off my back, but we both know you can't handle more blood on your hands."

"I thought I was cold."

"You are, but you're also not a murderer. It's the one sin you've avoided."

It didn't feel that way though. I'd never stolen someone's final breath or stopped a heart, but I'd been stupid. People had died. Although technically, she was correct, and I hated her more for it. "Unlike some."

"I was born for sin. It's in my DNA," she said with a scoff, unwounded by my barb. "So take my advice. Let her go."

"Why should I?" I demanded. It wasn't like Georgia to get sentimental. Getting in her way simply meant getting knocked down.

"Because you care about her," she said in a soft voice, "and if you're still capable of that, maybe there's still hope."

For the rest of us. She left it unsaid but it was there, hanging in the air between us.

"Don't hope for absolution," I warned her. "God abandoned us long ago."

CHAPTER TWENTY-SIX

I took the lift down to the lowest level, stripping off my dress in the corridor and kicking off my heels. I needed to think, clear my head. Today's revelations had settled over my chest, leaving me gasping for air. I pushed open the door and walked to the edge of the pool. Without thinking, I dove in, instantly freeing myself of my own weight. I stroked across the bottom, only emerging to suck in a breath and disappear once more below the glassy surface.

Smith's past didn't belong to me. I couldn't hold him accountable for the life he'd lived before we met. But I no longer understood how I fit into it. Our relationship had evolved rapidly into a compulsion. The mere fact that I was here now was proof of that, and it forced me to ask what I actually needed from this.

I knew what I wanted. His body. His soul.

Him.

Every part of me craved more. He'd consumed me, but what happened on the other side of this affair? If I walked away now, it would destroy me. How much worse would it be in a week or a month? Or a year? I could only dream of holding onto him that long. I floated to the top, keeping my face under water until my lungs burned from the effort. I was searching for proof that I was alive outside of his existence. My arms drifted to my sides and I let it all slip away. The fear. The anger. Until all that remained was desire. It had to be enough.

I was dimly aware of a surge of water. The sound of a splash. I lifted my head, sputtering and sucking in air as two arms coiled around me, drawing me higher out of the water.

"Belle!" Smith shouted, slapping the side of my face. There was no playfulness. Only a thwap that stung across my cheekbone.

Thrashing in his arms, I broke free and dove away, swimming as fast as I could, but he was on me. This time when he caught me, he hauled me around and crushed me to his chest. I blinked against the burn of the chlorine and gathered my strength to fight him off again. My palm collided with his chest, catching on wet fabric. Startled, I looked down to discover he was fully clothed. My eyes flashed to the edge of the pool where only his shoes rested.

"What the hell are you doing?" I screamed.

"Oh God." He grasped the nape of my neck and forced me to him. My body reacted immediately, ceasing to struggle against his hold on me. I dissolved into his arms, tears mixing with water until I no longer knew if I was crying or drowning.

It was how I always felt around him.

"I saw you in the water," he choked out. "I thought..."

I saw it through his eyes then. My body floating on the surface, weightless and still. The image flashed to my father's feet.

And then I knew. No matter what I did. No matter how far I pushed it. He had brought me to life, breathing essence into my being with his kiss—with his touch.

"You promised me things," I accused, losing what precious little control I had over my emotions in a torrent of sorrow and betrayal. "You promised to protect me, but you never told me why I needed protection."

"I know." He brushed water from my cheeks, hushing me with gentle sounds until I'd calmed. "I heard what happened today—where you went. I'm sorry you had to see that."

"Because it was your dirty little secret or because it's what you have planned for me?" I bit out, smacking his hard chest until my hands ached.

"You don't belong there. I never wanted you to see that place."

It wasn't enough. I wasn't certain whatever could be. "But those are the things you want to do to me. The things you've already done! Which is it? Which piece of your life is the lie: me or the club?"

"Some choices we don't make for ourselves. That place, my life—my profession—was my birthright from the day I was born. I didn't ask for any of it. I didn't want it. I can't expect you to understand. I don't ask you to."

But I did understand. I'd spent my own life torn between the reality of my family's name and what I wanted for myself. I'd never been able to see either without the other. It had directed me, perverting my fate long before I understood the nature of my inheritance. My mother had taught me to value luxury and material goods because that was how she filled the void inside her. It was how I'd filled my own until Smith came into my life.

I couldn't shake the feeling that I was trading one vice for another.

"I do know. I understand, but that doesn't solve anything," I whispered, afraid of what I was really saying.

"No, it doesn't," he agreed. "I'm not certain I'm capable of being normal. I've been fucked up too long to know. But you make me want to search for it, and when I saw you in the pool, that feeling slipped away. I'm not losing it again." He grabbed my face roughly. "I'm not losing you."

"What if you don't have a choice?" The question tore through me.

"When I pulled you out of the water, I knew I had a choice. That we always have a choice. There's no assurance that they're easy ones, but we do have them. All those people that told me I didn't and forced my hand—all those people that did the same to you—they were lying to us, beautiful. We can choose the direction we travel. The only thing left to decide is if we do it together."

I wanted to believe it was that easy, but I knew it wasn't. "What about choosing to be honest with each other?"

"That's something we can do—in time. There are things I can't tell you about my life. Ugly things. You've seen my darkness. You've let it touch you. But I don't want that for you. I don't want you to spend your life looking over your shoulder," he said in a low voice. "But I also can't bear the idea of turning you away."

"Then don't," I pleaded, burying my face against his neck. "Let me in here."

I placed my hand on his chest, measuring the hard, steady beat of his heart.

"You're already there, beautiful. Isn't that enough?"

It was tempting to believe it could be. "No. You claimed me, Smith. Chose to protect me. I want the same. I need to claim you as much as I need to protect you."

"No one can protect me." The words were hollow, so unlike the confidence that usually oozed off of him.

But despite his rejection of the idea, I saw the truth. He'd opened himself to me. He was vulnerable. Exposed. Could the rest come with time?

"The reality is that you don't need my protection. You're strong. You choose to face the storm when others fly away from it." He kissed the tears from my cheeks and smiled sadly.

"So have you," I informed him, choking on the raw ache in my throat.

"Birds of a feather," he whispered. "Stay with me. I know you have no reason to wait for answers. I'm asking you to take a chance. Fly into the storm with me."

He urged my legs around him and pressed his forehead to mine, never breaking eye contact.

"I'll shelter you," he promised.

My answer was there, hiding in his tumultuous gaze. He never guarded the secrets there. Not from me. I didn't know their names or crimes. I could only accept that with time I would.

So I corrected him. "We'll shelter each other."

CHAPTER TWENTY-SEVEN

I stood in the hallway, staring at the crack of light under the door. A wail shattered the air around me, freezing me to the spot. I forced my hand to reach for the knob, but no matter how much I stretched, I couldn't reach it. With each scream coming from the other side, my panic rose. I lunged forward and fell.

Fell.

Fell.

I jerked awake, still panting as I sat up in the bed. Smith lay beside me, sprawled on his stomach with the sheet tangled between his legs. I considered shaking him awake, but before I could, my dream returned to me. I'd seen that door before.

You have no idea what he keeps behind closed doors.

Georgia's words at the club.

I didn't think as I slid silently from the bed. Grabbing a blanket from the end of the bed, I wrapped myself in it and padded into the hallway. The lift dinged as it arrived, and I tensed as the insignificant sound echoed in the silent house. Inside I pushed the button for the third floor. I hadn't ever made it back there after Smith had shown me the room he'd set aside for me. Perhaps if I had, my curiosity would have gotten the better of me before now. The doors slid open, revealing a dark hall, but as I stepped into the corridor, a series of automatic lights illuminated. One by one they blinked on. The final light switched on between the two doors at the end of the hallway.

My footsteps fell heavily as I slowly walked forward. I had no idea what I would find. Most of me screamed to turn back and flee to the safety of Smith's bed, but I continued, propelled by an unseen force. It seemed to drive me. I paused when I reached my destination, my eyes flashing between the open door that had been given to me and the one that remained closed directly across from it. When my hand reached toward it, my fingers closed over the knob. It turned effortlessly.

The door had been closed, but not locked.

A slant of moonlight fell in a streak across the room, but it wasn't enough to see by. Sweeping my hand across the wall, I found the switch. Only one bulb flipped on but it was enough.

Everything about the space was eerily similar to the room Smith had shown me. The one I was permitted to be in. But as my eyes adjusted to the light, it came into clearer focus. Heavy dust coated the furniture and cobwebs hung from the ceiling. The bed was unmade, sheets wadded into a ball at the foot and the comforter hanging half off the mattress. A half dozen pillows were scattered across it as though someone had simply gotten up for the day and left it.

Smith had a housekeeper. A woman I'd never met. But I knew from the pristine condition of the rest of his house that she was diligent, which meant this room had been left in this state purposefully. I wandered to the desk where mail waited in a neat stack. Dust billowed around me as I picked up a letter and blew it off to read the address. It wasn't a surprise that it was posted to this house, but my heart skipped when I saw it was addressed to a woman. Margot Pleasant.

If this had been her room, why would she leave it like this?

I searched through the pile of unopened envelopes, hoping for a clue. Nothing was out of the ordinary except their condition.

Turning away, I continued my search, stumbling over a heel on my way. I leaned down and picked it up. It was about my size. Tossing it into the corner to avoid tripping over it again, I stopped at a vanity. Bottles of perfumes and tubes of lipstick littered its top, covered in so much dust that I couldn't read their names or brands. I looked up and froze. My face stared back at me. Not once, but a hundred times. Small slivers of my mouth and eyes and nose reflected in the shattered glass.

I yanked open the drawer of the vanity, discovering more cosmetics and nothing else.

I spun around, zeroing in on my next target. A large cedar chest under the window.

Who was this woman? Nothing in this macabre museum of her life gave me any answers. I would have to keep digging.

Opening the lid carefully, I peered inside the trunk. A thin, reedy cane rested at the bottom next to a pair of handcuffs and rope. The rest of the items were harder to make sense of. There were clamps and tubes attached to chains and hoses. Rummaging through it, my hand closed over a dildo. I dropped it immediately. One woman's treasure...

My throat constricted as I backed away from the chest. Smith hadn't wanted me in here for a reason, one that was becoming increasingly more obvious. The tightness found my stomach. I should leave, but I couldn't stop looking. Not until I was certain.

God, I hoped I was wrong.

The closet door loomed in the far wall, beckoning me toward it. Steeling myself, I headed straight for it and pushed the open door. When I switched on the overhead light, a row of dresses greeted me. Beautiful gowns and simple shifts. Shoes and more shoes. And next to all of it, a selection of suits, tailored to a specific man.

Tears swam into my eyes as I caught a familiar wool sleeve in my hand. They were all black. It was the only difference from the ones he wore now.

This wasn't her room. It was their room.

"She kept her name," Smith said behind me.

Whipping around, I found him standing in the room behind me, holding the letter I'd cleaned off. His hair was tousled, and he wore a fresh layer of stubble, but nothing else. The brutal masculinity of his naked body stirred a familiar ravenousness in my core. I closed my eyes and tried to shake the feeling from my body, but his presence was too powerful. When I reopened them, he'd moved closer to me, making his magnetic pull even harder to resist.

"It was a blow to the ego at first, but after time it made sense," he continued. His voice was distant, caught in the past.

"Margot." Saying her name out loud made her feel more real. I wanted to take it back, wishing I'd never spoken it in the first place. "Did you love her?"

It was the most important question, and the one that should matter least.

"I loved her more than she loved me," he admitted, his eyes returning to me. "We were young and stupid and filthy rich. I'd had the world handed to me without asking for the bill. I never imagined the price would be so high."

I swiped at the liquid threatening to spill down my cheeks, embarrassed to be jealous even though it seemed certain I had a right to be.

"Where is she?" I asked although I dreaded his answer.

"Dead." The word was flat. Emotionless. A statement of fact and nothing more.

"I need to go." I shoved past him, but he caught me by the arm.

"You need to understand!"

"Understand what?" I exploded. "That you keep a shrine to your dead wife? Who, by the way, you've never mentioned. Or maybe understand that she's dead? Tell me what you want me to understand."

It was clear he didn't have an answer to that.

"What do you expect me to do? Hold you? Drop to my knees and suck you off so that you'll feel better?" I yanked away from him and sat down on the edge of the bed. "Maybe you could fuck me and pretend I'm her."

Rage blazed in his eyes as he hauled me off the bed, throwing me over his shoulder. "I don't want you to be her."

"Put me down!" I demanded.

"No. Not until you calm down."

"My apologies," I hissed. "Please put me down, Sir."

"Don't do that," he warned me as he carried me kicking and screaming toward the lift. "Do not sully our relationship."

"Oh, it's fucking sullied." I whacked his shoulder blade with my palm, only managing to hurt my own hand.

We got off on the second floor. I'd stopped trying to fight him. Now my plan was to run the moment he released me. He couldn't keep a hold on me forever.

"I'm going to set you down," he explained when we entered his bedroom. "And you're going to want to run. Swear you won't."

"Or what?" I dared him.

"I'll tie you up and fuck you until you don't have enough strength to leave."

"You wouldn't." But deep down, I knew he would, and even worse, I knew I would enjoy it.

I wasn't about to give him that satisfaction.

"Fine. I swear."

As he lowered me to the floor, he whispered. "Remember that I'm not only stronger, I'm faster, beautiful."

"Don't call me that." I crossed my arms over my chest. He could try to talk his way out of this all he wanted, but there was no backpedaling. He'd crossed a line.

"The day she died," he began, "I shut that door. Then I went to the cabinet and got my father's gun."

Despite my attempt to remain remote, my mouth fell open. An overwhelming longing to take his hand flooded through me, but I held my ground, even if I was listening.

"Things were a mess between us. I suspected she was seeing someone else. She was as hotheaded as I am. It made for interesting fights."

Another grotesque similarity between the two of us. I gulped, attempting to swallow this revelation.

"It was rainy. A car hit her. She and the other driver died on impact."

"I've heard this story before," I said softly, "but it had a different ending."

"An accident. Nothing more. At least, that was how I saw it. I blamed myself. She had gone away to cool down after a fight."

"An accident is hardly your fault." I couldn't believe I was comforting him.

"No one ever bothered to tell me that. By then, my father was gone. My mother had checked out on me a few years later. I had this house and an important job, catering to my late father's clientele. I wanted one person in my life to be real, I closed the door and accepted the lies." He paused and looked me directly in the eye until I turned my face away. "Do you know why I don't go into the pool? My father drowned there."

"An accident." The word slipped off my tongue, but this time it left a bitter taste in my mouth.

"Hammond told me I was born under an unlucky star." His jaw twitched, and before I could stop myself, I ran my hand along it. Smith caught it and held it to his face.

"Am I just a replacement?" I whispered the question.

Smith's eyes closed. "No. You're the original."

"I saw the toys. I've been inside Velvet." I shook my head. "I'm not sure I belong in your world."

"You're wrong, beautiful. That isn't my world."

"But why do you..." I trailed away, unable to ask the question.

"I was introduced to kink at a young age. Hammond makes certain of that. He started screwing Georgia when she was fourteen. Most of his business centers around sex, and she is the shining jewel of his empire. He molded her to a very exacting standard. You see, everyone has to have vice. I had too many. The only one that stuck was dominance. I'd love to blame him for that, but it's on me. I'm built that way."

"Me, too," I admitted, my voice trembling. "You tamed me."

"No, beautiful. I just was lucky enough to see you wanted a leash."

I forced myself to ignore the hunger gnawing at my core. Giving in to it wouldn't solve anything. "Why hide it from me?"

"If no one can see your scars, why show them?"

The answer splintered across my heart. It was easier to pretend—to project the semblance of a normal life. "I've gone through the motions since I was child. Always following the path chosen for me. I don't want to do that anymore."

"Birds of a feather," he repeated his earlier sentiment. "Neither do I."

"Then why continue representing him? He's a pedophile."

"I can't explain that to you."

Two steps forward. One step back. "Like hell you can't!"

"You have to trust me." He laced his fingers through mine and brought my hand to his lips. "I never intended for this to happen between us, and now I have to think for both of us."

My eyes narrowed into slits. "I can think for myself."

"I want you to think about yourself," he corrected me gently. "On Monday, I'm firing everyone that works for me, including you."

"And I thought we were getting somewhere." I tried to pull away from him, but he tightened his grip.

"You're going to work on Bless. I've already funded your business account."

"No!" I shrieked. "I didn't ask you to do that."

"It's not a hand-out. I've drawn up paperwork fully vesting an anonymous party in the company. Me. I recently sold my interest in Velvet, and I need to invest that money somewhere."

"It sounds like a hand-out," I grumbled.

"I need you to stay busy, especially since we'll be spending less time together." The note of apology in his voice did nothing to soothe the misery that accompanied this revelation.

"Because you'll be focused on hiring another staff," I said flatly.

"Amongst other things. I don't want you to know any more than that."

"Why?"

"It wasn't a coincidence that I hired you. You were handpicked for the position for me. I didn't know why until later," he admitted, "by then it was too late."

I stared at him, completely flabbergasted. "To fire me?"

"To let you go." He dragged me roughly into his arms. "You should have walked out of that office that day. I should have thrown you out. Now it's too late for both of us."

As his words sank in, I knew he was right. I'd come back to him again and again, ignoring the warning signs, and I would continue to.

"Will I see you?" I murmured into his chest.

"Yes." I heard the smile in his voice. "You can't keep me away. We just have to be careful."

"Until when?"

He pressed his lips into my hair and remained motionless for a long time before answering. "I wish I knew."

I didn't say anything. I'd gone numb, unable to process all the information.

"However," he said, his words strained, "if you choose to leave tonight. Or in the morning. I will understand. I won't promise not to come after you, but I'll try to respect your wishes. Regardless, the business account will be waiting for you."

"I don't want your money. I want you."

"You have me, beautiful." His head angled down and he kissed me. "All of me, even my bank account. Deal with it."

"I can be defiant," I reminded him, smiling grudgingly despite the ache building inside me.

"Channel that into Bless, and no one will be able to stop you."

"And until Monday?"

By picking me up, he answered my question, and he carried me back to bed. Dropping me onto it, he eyed me as a knowing smirk twisted across his lips. "Until then I'm going to make you come until you can't remember your own name—or any of this. Just you and me."

I crawled forward and beckoned him closer with my finger. When he was within reach, I ran my tongue over the ridges of his abs. "I bet I can make you forget your name first."

"As long as you don't forget it, beautiful." He grabbed my shoulders and threw me back on the mattress. Pouncing on top of me, he pinned me to the spot and lowered his mouth to my belly.

I wouldn't. That was my choice—to stand in the wind and withstand the rain even as the first ominous clouds appeared on our horizon. Smith's hand shot out and grabbed mine as he moved between my thighs. We would face the coming storm together.

COVET ME

CHAPTER ONE

It finally happened. After weeks of tireless searching, I was here. I hadn't expected much from outside the building, but inside I'd discovered more than four walls and some windows. The studio was airy, and despite the chill that had crept through London as autumn moved ever closer to winter, a warm light flooded through the room highlighting all the space had to offer. I had found my own little corner of London, tucked snugly in Chelsea. This was where I would take the next step in my life.

Of course, everything from the walls to the shelves lining them needed a fresh coat of white paint. Maybe ivory. I also had a fair bit of furniture to obtain, given the space was entirely empty. But none of that bothered me. It had potential–and the right price tag.

"What do you think?" Julian, my inhumanly patient realtor, asked. I'd been a challenge for a man who normally sold business fronts to multi-billion dollar corporations. But he had been a saint, showing me half of the available commercial properties in Central London, and his persistence had paid off.

"It's perfect," I murmured, my mind already imagining where office tables and garment racks would fit.

"The owner will want a twelve month term," he began to rattle off the particulars but none of it mattered. This was where the next phase of my life started. My fledgling idea was quickly becoming a real business: Bless. In a few months I'd have the space packed with desks and dresses. It all felt like a surreal dream.

An incoming call startled me from my fantasy, the familiar ringtone a reminder that I already had more than most women would dream of. I shot Julian an apologetic smile as I dug it out, but he waved it, having grown use to these interruptions in the last week.

"Hey, beautiful." Smith's gravelly voice sent goosebumps rippling over my skin. If any man could bring me to orgasm with words alone, it was this man. Thank god, I'd never told him that or he'd call me on the hour.

It was bad enough that just hearing him resulted in soaked panties. Then again that might have been the result of a week without physical contact. After he'd fired me as his personal assistant, we hadn't risked seeing each other more than a few times a week at first. It had been seven days—our longest successful streak at keeping our hands off each other—as of this morning. Judging from my body's reaction, it was time to break that record.

"I found it," I whispered into the phone. I didn't need to say more than that. Despite the distance we'd kept with one another for the past few weeks, I had no doubt he'd been keeping tabs on me. Still I couldn't tell him more. There was no reason to believe my new private line had been compromised, but there was also no reason to assume it hadn't. "Bless has a home."

"We should celebrate." The suggestiveness in his tone was far from subtle, and I hooked my one leg behind the other to soothe the ache growing rapidly between my thighs.

"Oh yeah?" As usual, he'd reduced me to simple sentences. When it came to Smith Price, I preferred to let him make the plans for both of us because his plans usually resulted in hours of agonizing, glorious, wild sex. I had a million things to worry about at the moment, but pleasure wasn't one of them. Not tonight, at least.

"Somewhere private—just the two of us. I'll text you the address."

"Yes, Sir," I breathed, not caring that Julian could overhear the conversation. My words were as much a promise of what tonight would bring as his invitation had been.

The line went dead and I was brought back to earth. Turning, I caught a knowing smirk on Julian's face as he checked his mobile.

"Whoever your mystery man is, I want to meet him." Julian slid the phone back in his breast pocket.

I raised an eyebrow and shook my head. "Why? So you can steal him?"

"Maybe we can share," he suggested in a teasing tone.

"This is one toy I definitely don't share." It came out more defensive than I'd intended, but I couldn't be blamed for my reaction. Smith was mine, and coping with our precarious situation had only made me more possessive of him.

Julian waved a pedicured hand. "As long as he feels the same way. "

Of that, I had no doubt.

"Let's go back to the office and start the paperwork," he said, switching topics.

Now that was something I could be talked into.

THE ADDRESS SMITH HAD SENT ME GAVE ME NO IDEA WHAT TO expect but when I arrived on a cozy, quiet street in Holland Park, I was a bit surprised. I'd anticipated a hotel not something so *residential*. A quick peek at my phone revealed that I was definitely in the right place. Grabbing my bag from the passenger seat, I slid out of the Mercedes, locking it twice despite the quaint neighborhood. The car, an overly lavish gift from my boyfriend, had become a second home over the last few weeks. I loved it almost as much as I loved the man who gave it to me.

I froze in my tracks, overwhelmed by the peculiar sensation that overcame me as I considered the fact that I loved him. Our relationship had endured its fair share of bumps in its short history already, and I couldn't quite be certain that love wasn't going to be a major road block. Neither of us had said it. It had been implied, and perhaps I was being stubborn but I wasn't going to be the first one to pop the l-word. Maybe I was simply scared. Smith was still a mystery to me in so many ways, and the last man I'd thought I'd loved had proven my judgment wasn't the best when it came to men.

But Smith Price wasn't any man. He was something more—something primal and commanding. He stole my breath away and decided when I could have it back.

Get a handle on yourself! Shouldering my purse, I shook off my apprehension, writing it off as cold feet. It had been nearly two weeks since I'd seen him. That was enough to make any woman doubt herself, but I wasn't that girl. Not anymore.

Still I gripped the railing a little too tightly as I climbed the steps to the house. The night air brushed across my naked sex, reminding me exactly why I was here. My panties, per Smith's preference, had come off in the car and been shoved into my bag. I felt exposed and powerful at the same time. Things might be strained between us but I had exactly what he wanted.

Before I reached the top step, the door swung open, revealing *exactly what I wanted.* My knees buckled slightly at I drank in Smith in his charcoal, grey three piece suit. It was unjustifiable that the sight of any human being could have such an effect of me. I'd be lucky to make it inside before I was on my knees in front of him.

Smith's handsome face was blank as he welcomed me in, but I spotted the amused glint in his green eyes and the slight twitch of his lips that proved he was holding back a smile. I'd fallen for that cocky smirk as hard as I'd fallen for him. It had been my undoing when we met. Now knowing it was there, hiding behind his calculated stare, made me wet.

"Hello, beautiful." He took my bag and threw it on the ground, not waiting for my greeting before he'd scooped me up and carried me past the foyer. My arms coiled around his neck, inviting his lips to find mine. But he had more self-control than I did. His mouth pressed to my forehead before he deposited me on a leather sofa.

"Like it?" he asked.

I blinked, momentarily dazzled by his presence, and forced myself to look around the cozy room. Paintings that clearly fell into the priceless category hung along the walls and a fire crackled in the ornate fireplace. It looked much more like his law office than his own home, and I shot him a questioning look as I replied, "I do."

"One of my investments," he explained as he unbuttoned his jacket. He didn't take it off, which pleased me. I had plans for him tonight that included that suit.

I was so absorbed in my own fantasies that it took me a minute to realize he'd said something else. "Sorry?"

Smith's head cocked to the side, and he sighed as he ran a hand over his head, ruffling his dark blond hair. "I can see that you need a little pleasure before business."

"Yes, Sir."

The simple statement ignited a fire in his eyes that burned so fiercely that I bit down on my lip to keep from moaning. I'd given him the nickname in a moment of petulance. It had stuck when I discovered how demanding he was behind closed doors—and how eager I was to please him.

Smith leaned down, placing his palms on the arm of the sofa as he shook his head. "We play by my rules. Do you need a reminder?"

That sounded very much like a threat and a promise all rolled into one. He'd been known to dish out a playful spanking when I teased him or played coy, but I'd yet to bear the full brunt of what I knew he was capable of delivering. The thought might have scared me before, but as the days passed without his hands on my body, I found myself desperate for his touch.

"You want it that bad, huh?" he said, employing his uncanny knack for guessing exactly what was on my mind. "Don't try to force my hand, Belle, or I'll make you wait for a punishment even longer than I'll make you wait for an orgasm."

I glowered back at him, unwilling to show that his warning had deflated me. Instead I pushed myself up and crossed my legs, taking care that he got a glimpse of what I *wasn't* wearing under my skirt. "So you bought this place?"

"A few years ago." He made no sign that he'd noticed my lack of underwear. Disappointing. "I meant to sell it."

"Didn't get around to it?" I asked dryly. Only Smith was capable of sitting on a prime piece of London real estate for so long without making a move. Another symptom of his maddening self-control. His bank account allowed for it, while the rest of us were stuck sharing flats.

"I have other ideas now." But he didn't elaborate further. His eyes cooled as his thoughts went elsewhere.

I took a deep breath and waited for him to return to me. When he didn't, I took a chance. "I missed you."

It was a simple statement, but emotion colored my voice. Instantly, I wished I could take it back. I'd promised him I could be strong when he'd revealed the precarious nature of our situation. Melancholy sentiments had no place in our arrangement. For the most part, I'd been too busy focusing on my sudden entrepreneurial reality to worry about our relationship. At least in the waking hours. It was harder when I finally dragged myself to my bed—alone. Now that he was in front of me, the ache that had occupied those restless nights was swiftly overtaking my resolution.

But instead of reprimanding me, he sank down beside me and pulled me onto his lap. "Beautiful."

His pet name for me calmed the longing that had suddenly swept through my body. Although it didn't entirely soothe me.

"I spent all afternoon planning what I am going to do to you," he murmured as his index finger tipped my chin up to meet his gaze.

"And?" I prompted hopefully.

His mouth twisted as he winked. "I think you'll approve. But I thought we could talk for a bit. I'm told normal couples discuss their day before they get naked."

Couple. It seemed like too casual a term for the bond he and I had already formed. And normal? That definitely didn't apply to us. Still, there was a certain appeal to the concept.

"Normal couples don't have to sneak around," I reminded him. So much for trying things his way.

"Normal couples," he responded tightly, "don't have homicidal bosses."

There was that. Our separation hadn't been by choice, a fact that I wished I could forget. Smith's ties to his employer were far from average. He was caught in a tangled web of treachery that I'd only narrowly avoided being trapped in myself. Thanks to him, there had been no sign that Hammond, the man pulling the strings that kept Smith tethered to the past, had any further interest in me. That would change if he knew things weren't over between the two of us.

"Tell me about Bless," he commanded, obviously ready for a change in topic.

There was so much to tell him, even though so little had actually been accomplished. "I found a studio in Chelsea within my budget."

"Budget shouldn't be in your vocabulary." His forehead creased as he spoke, but I cut him off before he could force me to take more money.

"I'm starting a business. Of course, I need to consider my finances, and besides that, it's exactly what I was looking for. If it had been too much I would have told you," I lied. I had absolutely no intention of taking any more of his funds without actually needing them.

"What's mine is yours."

"Is that so?" I asked playfully, toying with his belt buckle. It was increasingly clear to me that we both needed to loosen up, and I had a pretty good idea of how we could to that.

My response earned me my first genuine smile. "Are we calling it quits on the small talk?"

"We could chat about the weather, but honestly, you aren't the only one with plans tonight."

"Think you're going to top me, beautiful?" He ran a finger across my lower lip and my mouth opened instinctively.

Now that would be impossible, especially given how much I craved his authority. I pressed my thighs tightly together, afraid to leave a damp spot on his wool trousers. "I wouldn't dream of it."

"Good girl." I felt his fingers close over my skirt. Pulling it down, he wrenched the garment off and tossed it away. "I was going to suggest we have a bite to eat, but there's only one thing I want for dinner."

So much for protecting his suit pants. I bit my lower lip, spreading my legs in welcome.

"I want to see the whole menu first," he whispered into my ear as he unbuttoned my blouse with the slow attention to detail that drove me crazy. His fingertips grazed slowly over each section of newly exposed skin. Then they skimmed across the lace cups of my bra before he unhooked it. It fell away, and in one fluid motion, he lifted me into his arms and stood. "I think you'll find the upper floor much more interesting."

He nibbled at my neck as we ascended the staircase. By the time we reached the bedroom, I was breathless with anticipation. Smith deposited me onto the bed and took a step back, surveying his prize as he began to undress. He took his time with this as well. Smith was the type of man who might push a woman against a wall, shove her panties aside, and fuck her, fully clothed. But when he took a woman to bed—when he took me to bed—that urgency was replaced by a deliberation that sent shivers across my skin.

Shrugging off his jacket, he folded it in half and laid it over a chair in the corner. He repeated the action with his tie, then his shirt. Each garment given the utmost care. It was the world's slowest—and sexiest—striptease. Because Smith didn't reserve that treatment for his expensive suits alone. Every inch of my body would be shown the same attention.

Besides, when his shorts dropped to the floor I got my first glimpse of what was on my menu, and god, I wanted a taste. Scrambling onto my hands and knees, I crawled to the foot of the bed, mouth open. Smith prowled forward, the curves and ridges of his muscular body haloed in moonlight. He stopped a foot short of me, giving me a closer look at what I wanted while keeping it out of reach.

"Ask."

My whole body was asking, but that wasn't what he meant. At first I'd found Smith's dominant nature intimidating. Now I found it liberating, and after the week I'd had, I wanted nothing more than to lose myself entirely to his domination. "Please, Sir."

"Roll over," he instructed as he came closer.

I turned onto my back, instinctively hanging my head over the edge of the bed so that he could guide the crown of his cock to my lips.

"Have you been touching yourself?"

I did my best to shake my head 'no' but I was way too focused on wrapping my mouth around his luscious organ.

"But you wanted to," he guessed. He paused to groan as I swallowed his shaft. "I know how hungry your pussy is. It's almost as insatiable as your greedy little mouth. It must have been hard to deny your needs, beautiful. You may touch yourself now."

Reaching back, I gripped his root for leverage, my free hand delving willingly between my folds. Nothing got me hotter than being on display for him, except maybe being splayed out under his possessive eyes with his dick in my mouth. My body trembled when my fingertip found my swollen clit. I circled it, rolling my hips against the welcome pressure. Truthfully, I had no desire to touch myself when I was apart from him, knowing it could never satisfy my craving. Only he could do that.

"Fuck me, beautiful. Your mouth feels good," Smith rasped, his eyes hooded as he watched me.

God, I loved putting on a show for him. Nothing had ever made me feel more alive—more irresistible—than when those eyes were on me. I existed for these moments.

He pulled away from me and leaned down so that his face was inches from mine. His arm snaked down, gripping my wrist and bringing my arousal-coated fingers to his lips. "I need to taste that."

Smith sucked each finger leisurely, turning the pulse at my core into a sharp, insistent stab of want. My legs dropped open on the bed as I began to squirm, restraining myself from pulling him down on top of me. He dropped his hold on my hand, his mouth still clamped over my middle finger, and hooked his arms under my shoulders. Finally releasing me, he flipped me onto my stomach and climbed into the bed. I didn't dare move as he positioned himself behind me. I knew better than to interrupt him when he was taking the reins. His hands dug into my hips as he wrenched my spread thighs over his lap. I was facedown on the mattress, my hands clenching the linens for strength.

"I've missed this." He stroked his palm across my buttocks and down to the quivering mound between my legs, sending a jolt of electricity charging through the sensitive spot. "I can feel how much you want to be spanked. Did you miss my palm on your ass?"

"Yes, Sir," I moaned against the fabric. And I had. It made me feel filthy how much I'd missed it. The first slap hit the right cheek lightly, and I bit down on the comforter, afraid I would come just from the contact. Heat blossomed across the tender skin, and Smith caressed it lovingly.

"More?" he prompted.

I nodded, my teeth still clenched.

"Ask me for what you want."

My mouth fell open, the plea falling wantonly from my lips. "Please spank me."

"Happily."

The next thwack was harder, jarring me so forcefully my legs tried to clamp shut against Smith's waist. I just needed a little friction. But Smith was far too skilled to allow that. Instead I endured a series of smacks ranging from playful to punishing. When he finally stopped, my ass stung from the erotic assault. My mind was blank, capable only of processing the hot, pulsating sensation spreading through my behind. Smith didn't say anything as he yanked my body another few inches back and inserted his cock inch-by-glorious-inch in my throbbing entrance. His hands stayed on my waist, keeping me still as my body acclimated to his girth.

"You're so wet and so tight. Are you ready to come for me?"

I choked out a yes. *Oh God, yes. Yes. Yes. Yes.* It was the only word that held any meaning, and I screamed it as he thrust inside me, liberating the climax that he'd built in my core. He hammered relentlessly so that with each violent stroke another wave of pleasure seized hold of me. I clawed at the bed, trying to hold on to the feeling. I never wanted it to stop. I never wanted him to free me. But as the spasms quieted, he withdrew and guided me carefully onto my back before pushing back inside.

"Look at me," he demanded in a gruff voice. "I want you to see what you do to me, Belle."

I forced my drooping eyes open as he rocked slowly. Smith's thumb found my clit, and I watched as his shaft disappeared inside my body.

It was the hottest thing I'd ever seen. Smith towering between my spread legs, the root of his shaft visible between the pink folds of my flesh.

My muscles tensed, already readying themselves for the next unstoppable onslaught.

"Fuck, beautiful!" he grunted as I felt the first unmistakable jet shoot against my velvet channel.

I lost myself with him, my legs wrapping around his waist to urge him faster as we unraveled together. When he finally stilled, he gathered me in his arms, sealing his mouth over mine. Our limbs tangled together as the kiss deepened. This was where I belonged. This was the man I belonged to. Breaking apart, we collapsed, still knit around each other. His hand cupped the side of my face, drawing me back to his lips and the promise of much more to come.

CHAPTER TWO

Despite the crowd at CoCo's the next afternoon, I felt more relaxed than ever. It was amazing what a night of orgasmic bliss could do for a girl. From the corner of the restaurant, Lola waved me over to the table, grinning widely. The smile vanished from her face as a waiter appeared at the table to take our drink orders. The lanky server looked a bit too pleased to have two women in his section. He squatted beside the table, but before he could get a word out, Lola cut him off.

"Bourbons. West's please," she instructed him, dismissing him without a second glance in his direction. When he disappeared toward the bar, she shot me an annoyed look. "He's been hovering like a puppy since I sat down."

"That bad?" I asked with a laugh as I hooked my bag over the back of my chair.

"Worse. He needs to reconsider his tactics if he thinks he's going to be picking up more than my signed bill." Lola shrugged good-naturedly and tapped her phone on, switching to business mode. "Now let's chat about where you're at with publicity."

One of the reasons I'd approached Lola to tackle this issue was due to her ability to get down to business. Today was obviously going to be no exception. The trouble was that I didn't really know where to start. Unfolding my napkin and placing it on my lap to buy time, I tried to think. "Honestly, I just secured a business front. I still haven't received the logo comps and we haven't begun to buy inventory yet."

Not to mention the fact that most of my ideas were mere scribbles in a notebook at this phase.

"Have you written a business plan?" she asked as she swiftly typed a note on her mobile.

"Um, not exactly. Not an official one. I have a lot of notes." Smith had pushed me on this as well, but he'd also been more than happy to distract me from completing the task.

"That's your second order of business then. Before you jump into it, I need a one page summary pitching the idea and explaining the subscription tiers and how much you anticipate charging."

I raised an eyebrow at her. "I thought you were consulting."

Lola tilted her head. In this thoughtful position, she looked more like her sister, Clara, than usual. "About that..."

I braced myself as she paused. If she backed out now, I was screwed. I barely had time to shower every day. There was no time to find another publicist willing to strategize this early in the game.

"I want in," she said, surprising me. "This is my last year at university. Next semester I need a job. Know anyone that might hire me?"

There was no ignoring the implication in her question. "You want to actually work for me?"

So far the reactions to my unexpected foray into business had been a mixed bag. Most of my friends were enthusiastic but only mildly interested. My mother had almost had a heart attack. And Smith? I still wasn't certain. He'd fronted the expenses, but he'd also been looking for a way to get me out of Hammond's sights. Funding my company might have simply been a calculated move.

"Unless you don't want me." Lola took a sip of water, her expression totally unreadable.

"No!" I said too loudly, cringing when a few other patrons turned to stare at me. I lowered my voice and leaned over the table. "I definitely want you. I think I've got the right idea for the business side of things, but I'm not a PR expert. It's just...I can't really pay you. *Yet.*"

Or maybe ever. I silenced the voice. It was too early to give up.

"I figured." Her response was nonchalant. She tucked a dark strand of hair behind her ear. "Look, I don't really need money. What I do need is something I can get excited about. My father has been breathing down my neck to partner with him on some new start-up, but for many reasons, I don't want to go that direction. So since I don't have to worry about money, I want to build something of my own. I could even contribute additional finances."

"Finances aren't an issue," I reassured her as my cheeks heated.

"Then let's get started," she suggested as the waiter reappeared with the bourbons.

"We have a business name and a studio space, are we ready to get started?"

She smirked at this, running her finger along the rim of her glass. "We have an idea. Let's start selling it. I want to approach the high-end magazines by week's end to do features on you and the business. Publications create content months in advance. We'll want the press when we're up and running, not months after we launch."

Things were moving fast. A week ago I had an idea, now I had a partner, a storefront, and more on my plate than I'd bargained for. It was beyond exciting, but underneath the initial thrill, there was a fair amount of anxiety. "It's okay to be scared, right?"

"Yes. If your life doesn't scare you a little, you probably aren't living," she said without hesitation, raising her glass. "To partners."

"I hope you're right." I touched my drink to hers and shook my head. She had no idea how much my life scared me sometimes. "To terrifying new possibilities."

By the time we'd finished a short strategy meeting, I found myself anxious to get back to the office. The blissful calm that I'd experienced since leaving Smith this morning had been replaced by a frantic desire to focus. In two days, I'd managed to secure an office and a business partner. Digging my phone out, I bypassed checking my overrun inbox and tapped out a message to Edward.

BELLE: Bless has two things to celebrate this week!

EDWARD: I knew you could do it, babe! Drinks on Saturday? I want to hear all about it.

BELLE: You're on.

EDWARD: I'll text you the details in a few.

Before I could drop my mobile back into my purse, an incoming call buzzed from an unknown number. I stared at the screen, torn over answering. I knew I should let it go to voicemail given the circumstances, but I couldn't ignore the fact that I was a businesswoman now. The call could be important. In the end, curiosity won out over patience.

"Hello?" I answered.

"Have you reviewed the documents I messengered to your flat?"

My eyes closed involuntarily at the sound of my mother's voice. "Did you block your caller ID?"

"I can't get you to answer my calls, and those documents are of a time-sensitive nature," she said, sounding far from apologetic about deceiving me.

I'd been avoiding her calls for weeks, along with the unopened envelope that had arrived after our last disastrous visit. She'd made it clear then that I was nothing more than a signature to her.

"I also heard you're going through with this foolish website business," she continued swiftly. No doubt she had a lot of complaints to lodge before I ended the call. "Where did the capital for that come from? Did your aunt finance it?"

"Aunt Jane hasn't given me a penny." *Just emotional support, I added to myself.*

"It would have been a far wiser course of action to focus your energy on our estate."

My estate, the unwanted birthright I'd received when my father died, was the last thing I wanted to think about. Once I'd been willing to marry well to keep it afloat. Now I didn't care if it sank, or my mother along with it.

"I assume you have everything under control," I responded coolly. She'd never asked me for my opinion on how we might deal with the estate's debts. Instead she'd simply harassed me to find a way to maintain her aristocratic lifestyle.

"The producers want to start shooting the show this Christmas," she said, her tone taking on a level of exasperation somewhere between panic attack and meltdown.

"I'll review it when I have time." In truth, if it meant getting her off my back, I'd sign the entire grounds over to the BBC immediately. But I suspected it was going to be more complicated than that, and I didn't want to spend what little time I had with my personal legal counsel talking through contracts.

"I would hate to have to take further action," she threatened.

I stopped in my tracks, accidentally causing a couple to knock into me on the pavement. Mouthing an apology, I darted to the front of a shop. "Care to explain what that means?"

"If you have a company, you have assets," she said in a smooth voice. "The estate is in your name, which means I can transfer its debts to you."

"If you do that," I said between gritted teeth, "pack your bags."

"I can't believe you would throw the woman who gave birth to you out on the street!"

"That is one debt that's been paid, and I definitely don't owe you for anything else," I hissed, quickly adding, "I'll review the contracts."

I hung up, fury vibrating through me. Pressing my back to the glass window, I stared out at the midday crowds while I forced myself to breathe. Smith would never allow her to ruin Bless, but I couldn't ask him for help without coming clean about the depth of my estate's financial crisis. I'd sign the papers and with them grant her and it a few more years of life support until I could finally pull the plug on them both.

CHAPTER THREE

Tugging at the bill of my baseball cap, I glanced casually down the street. I'd had worse ideas in my life but not many. But after my recent rendezvous with Belle, I found myself too distracted at work to accomplish much. Her recent absence felt more acute than it had in weeks, as though I'd opened a fresh wound and had to restart the healing process. Except I didn't want to. Instead, her absence festered and stung, leaving me desperate to claw at the itch.

I approved of her choice in location, her building situated in a quiet pocket of the neighborhood where she would be tucked away safely. Maybe it would help soothe the possessive curiosity that ate away at me all hours of the day. I knew where she lived. Now I needed to see where she worked. I'd reined in my desire to have her followed, settling instead for the satisfaction of knowing her car was LoJacked. Too much interference on my part would undermine the front we'd contrived. But it wasn't easy having my heart walking around outside my body.

The knob welcomed me in, a fact I noted with displeasure. She should be more careful. I opened the door and poked my head into the studio. She was at her desk, her usually neat hair piled into a sexy tangle on the top of her head. The loose black t-shirt she wore draped over her pert breasts. She'd never shown up in my office dressed this casually. I'd have remembered yanking her jeans around her ankles if she had. Her lack of makeup, save for her bright, crimson lipstick, only made her look sexier. This was Belle behind closed doors. This was Belle on a night in. This was the Belle I coveted—the natural, untamed version she hid under couture dresses and high heels. It was the part of her she kept to herself—the part I wanted to claim as my own.

"You should really lock this," I announced as I quietly entered.

She jumped, her hand fluttering to her chest, at the unexpected interruption. Confusion flashed in her pale blue eyes as she took in my similarly dressed down appearance before her sinful lips twisted into a wicked smile.

"Jeans and ball cap? Is it casual Friday?" she asked, dropping her pencil on the desk.

"Wednesday, but I took the afternoon off." I closed the door, making certain it locked behind me.

She leaned forward, affording me a better view down her shirt. "What's in the bag?"

If she wasn't more careful about putting her tits on display, she'd never find out. "I brought my girlfriend lunch."

"You are committed to this normal bit," she said.

I'm committed to you, beautiful.

I kept the thought to myself, uncertain where it came from and what exactly it meant. Also because it sounded a bit too much like a fucking greeting card. I dropped to the floor and folded my legs underneath me. "Have you eaten?"

She shook her head and joined me as I pulled containers out and handed her one.

"What do you think?" she asked, waving her spoon at the space surrounding us before digging into her curry.

I looked closer, uninterested in eating myself. "Lots of potential."

"It's a blank space," she admitted.

But I understand what she saw in the studio. It was large enough to accommodate a start-up inventory. Eventually she would need a bigger home base for Bless, but for now it would keep her busy—a distraction I was counting on.

We discussed plans over chicken tikka masala, but I hardly noticed the food. All I could see was how her face lit up as she shared her vision for the empire she was creating. She'd come in to my life deceptively, a pawn in an agenda she knew little about. Now that I'd made her part of my life for real, I would do everything in my power to help her achieve her dreams.

"Care to give me the grand tour?" I asked when we'd piled the leftovers back in the sack. Standing, I held out my hand, drawing her up to her feet and into my arms.

"There's not much to show you." Her voice took on the breathless tone that always made me hard. "The loo's through that door. My desk is right here. That's all."

"Show me what it's going to be," I encouraged her, doing my best to ignore the steady throb of my cock.

Taking my hand, she led me over to the shelves. "This is where the packing and shipping materials will be. Over there"—she pointed to the adjacent wall—"we'll have the clothing racks. I'm still working out the best system for organizing them."

I glanced over at the rickety table she was using as her desk. "And that's where your desk will be."

"That's where my desk is." She frowned a little as she surveyed it.

I made a mental note to purchase one and have it delivered.

"You're plotting," she accused me. "I have everything I need and enough money to get a base inventory ordered. A desk isn't on the priority list."

"You need a new desk," I said dryly. "One for an executive."

"Are you insulting mine? It holds my computer. It's the right height. It's yet to fall apart." She continued to rattle off a list of all its benefits before I pressed my index finger to her mouth.

"Beautiful, there's one problem with it."

She narrowed her eyes and drew back. "Which is?"

"I can't fuck you on that one," I said in a gruff voice, grabbing her hips and yanking her back. Show and tell was over. "I've been dreaming about nailing this hot CEO on her power desk."

"I guess you'll have to settle for the floor."

I raised an eyebrow, taking her chin in my hand. "You don't belong on the floor...unless you're on your knees."

"I'll write that down." The slight tremble in her voice undermined her barb. It was my favorite form of foreplay, watching as she shifted from bold and confident to panting and desperate.

Trailing the back of my hand over her cheek, I murmured, "I'm so fucking proud of you."

"I haven't done anything yet," she whispered, an uncharacteristically shy edge running through her words.

"Don't do that," I ordered. "Don't doubt yourself, because there's nothing to doubt."

She tilted her face against my hand, her eyes closing. "I needed to hear that."

"I'm going to tell you every day," I promised her. I would find a way to, even if it was nothing more than a text. My business was built on the bones of my father. Everything about my life was the result of my own broken soul. Belle's career would never be that way. It would be honest and empowering and daring—just like her.

"I miss you," she said in a low voice that sliced through me.

"I know, beautiful." Cupping her jaw, I angled my mouth to meet hers and brushed a kiss over her lips. "This won't last forever."

"What if I want it to?" Her eyelashes fluttered down as she spoke.

"This separation won't last. We"—I corrected her—"are forever."

Christ. So much for not giving her too much hope. I shouldn't have told her that, not when I couldn't stand behind those words, even if I meant them.

"How can you be sure?" Her voice was so small, as fragile and lovely as she was.

She was asking a lot of me today, more than I was able to give her. I could only show her by sating her thirst for reassurance in a more primal language—one I knew she understood. Slipping my hands to her waist, I unzipped her jeans and dipped my hand into her panties.

Holy fuck, she was soaked. I'd been correct. This was exactly the consolation she needed.

"Does it make you wet to know I own you?" I asked as my lips swept down her throat. "To know I've claimed you as mine?

"Forever?"

"Forever, beautiful," I repeated as I pushed her jeans to the floor. "You belong to me."

She watched transfixed as I freed my cock from my pants. I loved when she looked at me like that—apprehensive and fervent, as if it was the first time. Lifting her by the ass, I carried her to the wall. She wiggled in my arms, pushing her hot, moist pussy in invitation against my shaft. It slid slickly across my tip and my restraint slipped. I slammed her against the plaster, sending dust scattering over our heads.

"Is that what you need?" I asked, grinding against her swollen mound. She shuddered as she nodded, bucking furiously in a frantic ploy for more contact. Her fingers gripped my shirt as she urged me closer, her shapely legs coiling around my waist. "This is why I have to tie you up, beautiful. You can't fucking control yourself, can you?"

She bit her lip, but it didn't hide her smirk. The woman could give as good as she got. She knew exactly what buttons to push.

"You want to play coy?" I rolled my groin, so that she couldn't get enough leverage. Pinning her with my hips, I wrenched her arms over her head and continued to circle her engorged clit mercilessly until I could feel it throbbing against the head of my dick.

"Bad girls have to wait for it," I warned as I bit her collarbone. Bending lower, I captured the peak of her breast in my teeth and began to suck the tip through the soft cotton of her t-shirt. She arched against me, fighting my hold on her wrists, but I held her steady. "Bad girls need to be taught lessons like *patience*."

A low, throaty cry escaped her mouth as I moved on to her next tit. My dick jolted at the sound, growing so hard that it physically hurt. Fuck, that was the cost of patience. I was starving for her, turning inside out with want. I wanted to push inside her sweet cunt and destroy her like she threatened to destroy my self-control. But if it meant I could torture this beautiful, perfect woman until she was begging for release, I could subsist on her squeals and moans. Each sound she made was more delicious than the last.

"Please," she sobbed. Dropping her lips, she continued to plead, but her whispered entreaties were lost on me. This was becoming a lesson in temperance for both of us.

"*Shh*, beautiful. I'm going to make you come–*hard*–when I'm ready for you to."

I was always ready for her to come, but this time I needed to watch—needed to see my dick marking what was mine. Dropping her hands, I guided her back to her feet as she scrabbled at the wall so as not to fall. Her shirt clung to her belly, giving me a better view of her soft, creamy thighs pressed together so tightly that only the barest hint of her delicate pink folds was visible. Quivering. Raw. It was fucked up to get off on making her wait and I gave not one fuck. Gripping her hip, I spun her around and pushed her gently to the wall. Belle melted into it, arms splayed, sticking her ass out to me like an offering.

I hooked my arm under her left leg and pinned her knee against the plaster. I shoved inside her, giving her no time to acclimate as I began to drive my cock deep, the force of my thrusts lifting her entirely off her other foot.

"Oh God, I'm yours," she cried out. "Yours."

"Yes, you are," I crooned, my hand sliding from her hip to clutch her neck. I buried my mouth against her ear, relishing her soft gasps as I squeezed. "I'm going to fuck your pussy raw so that you remember that."

She tensed around me, clamping down in quick, violent surges—and then she fell away, coming with such force that the pulse of her channel milked my own climax from me. I stayed inside her watching as my climax leaked around my root, our bodies still notched together. When I finally withdrew, it spilled down her seam and she dashed toward the loo to clean up.

I tucked my dick back in my pants. Satisfied but not altogether sated. She reappeared, darting around me to reach her pants, but I snagged them before she could. My mind already preoccupied with the other spots in her office that needed to be christened.

"I won't get any work done today without those." She planted her hands on her narrow hips.

"Consider it repayment for all the times you kept me distracted at the office." I dangled them just out of reach.

"You hired me...and fired me."

"And now I have a perpetual erection at work," I admitted. "Maybe I should come and work for you. Of course, my office has much sturdier furniture."

She licked her lips, no doubt remembering the things I'd done to her on my desk.

I smirked and tossed her the pants. "That's why you need a real desk."

CHAPTER FOUR

"What does it mean that we've chosen a quiet little spot for Saturday night drinks?" I asked as I slid onto the stool beside Edward's. The pub he'd chosen was off the beaten path, far away from the usual hot spots we frequented on the weekends. Apart from a few regulars who took up residence at their tables as if they were holding court, the place was empty. After the busy week I'd had, I was more than happy with his choice.

"I suppose that we're in danger of becoming adults." He pecked my cheek in welcome and grabbed my hands to study my ensemble. "You even look like an adult."

I batted his hand away as I adjusted the skirt of my dress underneath me. Since he'd texted me to meet him here, I'd opted for a simple navy sheath, leather jacket and boots. "Are you saying you don't approve? Because you're wearing jeans. I didn't even know you owned jeans."

"No. Only that we are in danger of being old," he teased, a bemused grin lighting across his boyish face. "I suppose our dancing days are behind us."

"Next stop the retirement village, but first a drink."

Edward passed me a pint with a laugh. I took the beer, clinking it against his.

"So I was told we needed to celebrate," he prompted.

I quickly filled him in on the developments of the last week. Edward played the best friend perfectly, exclaiming gleefully at the right moments.

"And how are you feeling about all of this?" he asked.

Edward had kept his questions to a minimum since I had surprised him and Clara with the news that I was starting my own business. If he had any concerns over where my capital was coming from, he hadn't expressed them. He also hadn't questioned my sanity. He'd left that part to me.

"Overwhelmed," I admitted, "but in a good way."

It was nice to talk about it with someone who didn't want to bounce strategy ideas. One of the reasons I'd left Lola off the invitation list for the evening. And while Smith was certainly interested, we both had a tendency to get easily distracted by other activities.

"Well, if you need any dashing models, I am available." He struck a ridiculous pose that sent us both into a fit of giggles.

"Sadly, we're focusing entirely on female lines at the moment."

"My offer stands," he said in a serious tone.

Swatting him on the shoulder, I decided it was time to change the subject. "So wedding bells?"

"My reprieve was short." He downed the rest of his drink and shook his head. "I'm afraid you can leave the betting pool open. We haven't set a date."

"You can't avoid it forever." I'd seen how massive his fiance David's wedding planning notebook had gotten in the last few weeks. Edward was working on borrowed time.

"Soon," he promised.

"Ugh, I hate when men do that!" I snapped. "And I bet David does as well."

"Why would you say that?" he countered, motioning for another round from the bartender. "Are you having romantic troubles?"

"Don't try to turn this around on me," I warned him.

"All's fair. You've been avoiding the subject nearly as long as I've been avoiding the aisle."

"That's not even remotely true," I said flatly. "I got fired a few weeks ago. How long have you been engaged?"

"Nope," he stopped me. "I changed the subject. You got fired, but have you ceased all duties involving Smith Price?"

"God, no wonder you're avoiding the altar if you think of it as a duty!"

"I knew it!" he exclaimed, shaking a finger in my direction. "Did he fire you because he couldn't get any work done around you?"

The arrival of the next round saved me from having to answer the question. It wasn't that I wanted to keep things from Edward, but the status of my relationship needed to remain on the hush-hush.

"You know I could really use a second set of eyes on these logos I just got."

"You really are all business." Edward bumped my shoulder. "Show them to me."

"I guess Lola isn't the only workaholic." But even as I spoke, I pulled my phone from my jacket pocket.

If Edward had an opinion on that, he didn't say anything. He had plenty of thoughts on the logo, however. An hour later, we'd settled on combining the modern style of one with the graphic of another.

"It's perfect," I said, visualizing what the revised logo was going to look like as a text flashed across the top of my mobile. Tapping it, I read through Smith's message twice. It didn't make any sense, but before I could respond, another one appeared. There was no mistaking the picture attached. I recognized the lush velvet corridor immediately.

He wanted me to meet at Velvet. The club he'd sold. The place he'd asked me to stay away from.

I swallowed hard, trying to digest his request as I checked to make sure the message was actually from him. It had come from his number. He had to have a good reason for inviting me, but everything about it felt wrong. A flutter of panic tumbled through my belly as I considered what it would be like to walk back through that door.

"What's wrong?" Edward said, studying my face.

"Nothing." I forced myself to sound cheerful as I pocketed my mobile. "Apparently I have a date."

"David will be thrilled to have me home early. He got the new issue of*Modern Wedding*."

I tried to smile, but my mouth had stopped working; instead my heart raced as we said our goodbyes. When I finally slid into the Mercedes, I pulled my mobile back out, praying I would find another message informing me that this was all some ill-conceived joke. But there was nothing waiting for me, which meant if I wanted answers, there was only one place to go. Buckling up, I braced myself for the ride ahead.

CHAPTER FIVE

"I thought I was the one with the twisted sense of humor," Georgia said as she entered her office and found me staring at the security feed for Velvet's outer door.

"There's nothing funny about this." I didn't take my eyes from the screen. Part of me still hoped Belle would make another choice. But she hadn't called me. She hadn't questioned my message. And that meant she was on her way.

"What exactly is your plan?" Georgia asked. "I know she hates this place, but I've seen it in her big doe eyes. She likes it rough. What if she shows up expecting you to tie her up?"

"Belle has no interest in anything this place has to offer." She'd made that clear after her first—and only—visit here. It was a sentiment we shared. The only thing I found more sickening than finding myself back inside the club was knowing that I had lured Belle here as well.

Georgia moved next to me, adjusting the ties of her revealing corset and leaving me eye level with her exposed tits. "If you aren't willing to give her a good whipping, I would be happy to."

She fingered the petite cat-o-nine tails sitting on her desk for emphasis.

"No one touches her," I growled.

"You're adorable when you're acting like a caveman." Georgia smirked and picked up the whip. "Need to let out some of that pent-up hostility?"

We hadn't scened together in years. It disgusted me now to recall how far she pushed me to go each time. Georgia wasn't truly happy until she was nearly broken. With most people she put on a brave face. She'd only ever begged me to hurt her more. Between that and the absolute lack of sexual chemistry between us, it had always been a one-sided experience.

Hammond had ruined my life, but he'd twisted her into a creature incapable of feeling anything outside of pain.

"I'm not interested." I pushed the proffered whip away.

Her coy grin vanished into haughtiness. She could see that I pitied her.

"Submission isn't about sex," she spit out at me. "Or have you forgotten that?"

I hadn't. I knew exactly how it worked. "I'm not in the lifestyle, Georgia. Not anymore."

"Bloody hell, you aren't," she challenged me. "I saw how she watched the members the night she came here. You've collared her."

"You can't collar Belle." The idea was laughable. Collaring a submissive and leashing a wanton woman were two very different things. Belle responded to kink. She welcomed it, but that went no further than sex—for either of us.

"Well, aren't you the enlightened, sensitive male." Georgia screwed her delicate features into a grimace.

It didn't matter what she thought. The truth was that it would be much easier if I could count on Belle to be obedient, but I didn't want her that way. Yes, I wanted to collar her and tie her up and fuck her until she couldn't walk. But in the morning I wanted to hear everything that came out of her smart, sexy mouth.

"That's where you screwed up," Georgia said as if she was psychic. "You let it get emotional."

I stood, tired of watching the security feed. "It should also be emotional, G. That's why you're screwed up."

Leaving her to chew on that, I made my way to the bar and ordered a Scotch from the club's newest bartender.

"You giving a demonstration tonight?" Ariel asked.

I smiled tightly and shook my head. "I'm sitting out tonight."

"That's too bad." She leaned over the bar top conspiratorially. "I've heard about you. I was hoping to see you in action."

"I can't imagine what you've heard, because this isn't really my scene anymore." I swallowed the rest of my drink and ordered another.

"People say you're cold. Ruthless. That you push your subject to the edge, but that no one ever safes out."

I didn't like to remember that part of myself. Taking a swig of my refill, I realized that if I was going to accomplish the task I'd been given, it might be my only choice. I had a decision to make. I needed this to be a clean break. I needed her to never want to look at me again. It was the only way to ensure Hammond would lose interest in her. Setting down my tumbler, I unbuttoned my shirt.

"Are there any subs here tonight?" I asked Ariel.

"That would be me," Georgia called from the doorway. "The rest are collared and their Masters aren't sharing."

I slid my shirt off, annoyed that she was my only option. But if I had to choose between taking a trip down fucking memory lane with her and Belle's safety, I knew where I stood.

"Any preferences?" I asked her.

"The prayer stool."

Of course, it was always at the top of her list. That was Georgia. She sought absolution through pain and found salvation in sin. "I'm using the cane."

"Dom's choice." But I could tell she was satisfied.

We crossed in silence to the corner of the room where the stool waited. Georgia knelt down, folding her hands in front of her.

"Is the pageantry necessary?" I asked as I lifted her skirt to reveal her bare ass.

"It is for me. I know exactly what you're doing," she whispered, "but if I'm going to put on a show, it's going to be a good one. By the way, your pet is here."

I paused for a moment, resisting the urge to turn and look for Belle. Instead of giving in, I reached forward and took the cane from a hook on the wall. It felt strange to have the reedy instrument in my palm. I hadn't used one in years and then it had been playful. Georgia didn't want a game and Belle needed to be scared.

It sliced through the air and cracked across Georgia's ass cheeks, immediately leaving an angry red streak on her pale skin. She barely reacted, maintaining her blasphemous position. She lasted three more stripes before her knees buckled and she had to grip the leather armrest.

"Enough?" I asked in a harsh voice. A kind Dom would soothe her injuries with a gentle touch, but I wasn't a good Dom and Georgia was far more depraved than a typical sub.

She shook her head.

I struck her three more times before I saw tears leak from the corner of her eyes. Dropping the cane, I tugged her skirt back into place and helped her stand. Before I could leave her, Georgia threw her arms around me and kissed my cheek, whispering in my ear. "Thank you for not holding back."

I peeled her back, revulsion and concern warring inside me. In some ways, she was my only friend. The only person who truly knew who I was and what I was capable of. It made me feel responsible for her well-being. But Georgia didn't want to be helped. Whatever balance her life needed, I would never give it to her.

Turning away from the corner and wishing I could leave this part of my past there, I found myself staring into Belle's tear-filled eyes.

I'd expected her to come. I'd known she would and that she would witness this. But knowing hadn't prepared me for the look on her face like she didn't know who I was.

She was the one person I wanted to know me, and I had to end things like this.

I walked toward her, picking up my shirt on the way. This

needed to be done publicly. It was the only way to be certain Hammond would hear of it. But doing that meant forcing her to endure the humiliation of my actions.

"You came," I said as I slipped my shirt back on and began to button it.

"I thought you were crazy," she whispered, "asking me to come here. But now I see that isn't the case at all. You're only cruel."

She pivoted away from me, and I caught her arm.

Get it together, Price. Stopping her wasn't part of the plan.

"I needed to blow off some steam," I lied. "I didn't think you'd be up for it."

"Is that what you want?" she asked in horror. "What happened to it being about pleasure?"

"It can't always be about that." I shrugged, unable to meet her eyes.

To my surprise, she kicked off her heels and reached for the zipper on her dress. "Is this what you need, Smith? You want me to get naked, so you can beat me and prove what a big man you are?"

I smacked her hand away. That was not how I wanted this to play out. Regardless of what she thought, she belonged to me and I wasn't going to share her with anyone. I certainly wasn't going to push tonight any further. There was no need. I sensed her pain, feeling it as acutely as if I had been the one under the cane. The scene had done the trick.

But Belle wasn't the type of woman to run away crying. She would punish me first.

"C'mon," she mocked. "Take out your stick and let's go."

"I don't want this with you."

That stopped her in her tracks. Her hand fell limply to her side, her lip beginning to quiver. "What do you want with me?"

"Nothing." It hurt worse because it was the truth and a lie. I wanted her to leave. I wanted her to run. Just as much as I wanted to give all of myself to her.

A single tear escaped down her cheek, and she wiped it angrily away. "That can be arranged."

But she didn't make a move to leave.

I wanted to ask her if she was okay. I wanted to walk her to her car. I wanted to take her home and make love to her until she forgot what she had seen. Instead I forced a glowering look on my face. "Well? What are you waiting for?"

"Nothing. Absolutely nothing."

Snatching her shoes from the floor, she dashed back toward the velvet-lined corridor that led outside. My eyes followed her progress, my body fighting me to go after her. Rather, I walked slowly back to the private office, feeling Ariel's shocked eyes on me.

I didn't watch as she left the club, even though Georgia had turned Velvet's security cameras on her. Letting her go had been difficult, but seeing her actually do it might prove impossible.

"It was the right choice." Georgia's sharp voice interrupted my thoughts.

"But is it one I can live with?" I said softly. My animosity toward her had fled the club along with Belle. "Don't answer that."

"Hammond suspects you two are involved. Your penchant for disappearing hasn't gone unnoticed. Neither will tonight's events. It's the best move you can make."

I rounded on her, my hands clenching into fists. "This isn't a game."

"It is a game," she shot back, "to Hammond at least. You can't get away with not playing. Not if you want to take her off the board."

She was right, and I hated it. I'd hoped we could ride out the storm longer, so Belle knew exactly where she stood. But warning her of what to expect would only have undermined the effectiveness of my strategy.

"What are you going to do now?"

"I need to call our partners." I forced myself to focus on the next rational move.

"There's no need to involve them." Georgia perched on her desk and crossed her arms over her voluptuous chest.

"Who the hell do you think forced this course of action?" I had my mobile out before she could respond.

Georgia huffed and slid off the desk. “Don’t put too much stock in their ability to protect her.”

“What choice do I have?” I asked gruffly as she walked out of the room.

“Smith.” The voice on the other end sounded surprised to hear from me.

“Let’s cut the bullshit,” I said, skipping through the obligatory pleasantries. He didn’t need me kissing his ass.

“I didn’t expect to hear from you directly.”

I bet he didn’t. “Look, it’s done. I cut her loose.”

“You’ve made a wise choice.”

“I don’t give a damn what you think of my choice. She’s still of interest to Hammond. There’s no one I can trust to keep tabs on her.”

“And you want me to?” he guessed.

“No one would second-guess your motivations,” I reminded him.

“It’s done. Is there anything else?”

“Yes, consider speaking with me before you pull something like this again.” I was losing my cool now. What did it matter if another ally wanted me dead when I was already on someone else’s hit list?

“You work for me.” The friendly tone evaporated from his voice.

“I don’t work for anyone.” I hung up before he could respond. I’d gotten what I needed from him, and even if I found his tactics questionable, I trusted his word. That wasn’t something that was easy for me, but I didn’t have a choice. Not where Belle was concerned. He’d watch out for her and his resources were unparalleled. He was the best chance I stood at keeping her from Hammond’s grasp.

“You know how to make friends,” Georgia remarked, lowering herself carefully into a chair.

“Do you want some water or something?” I asked out of obligation. I didn’t have to imagine the condition she was already in.

“Let’s not pretend that was anything more than a calculated move,” she said with a snort. “You did what you had to do.”

I had, and I was the one who had to live with it.

CHAPTER SIX

Life became an endless cycle. Go to work, obsess over launch, go home, obsess over launch, sleep. Rinse. Lather. Repeat. After a week I'd managed to get myself into a comfortable, mind-numbing rhythm that allotted almost no time to think about Smith. Almost.

Anger was swiftly shifting to sadness. Because despite the jam-packed schedule I'd been keeping, I was still aware of the fact that he hadn't called. Not to explain himself. Not to apologize. The lack of communication only confirmed my biggest fear: I meant nothing to him. I had only been another toy in his collection. Ignoring the piles of to-do lists cluttering my desk, I shot off an email to my brother, the only other lawyer I knew, to discuss my options. My fledgling business was tangled up with a man that I never wanted to see again.

Lola sashayed into the office a minute later with an oversized white leather tote hooked in the crook of her elbow and her arms brimming over with a stack of fashion magazines. She dropped it all onto one of the empty shelves littering the room. Stepping back, she surveyed the space, sizing it up after being absent for most of the week attending her last semester of classes. As usual she looked like she'd stepped from one of the pages of those fashion magazines, outfitted in a chic, loose tan sweater with a Burberry scarf knotted loosely at her neck. She'd paired skinny jeans with leather riding boots to complete the classic look that gave her the air of a woman much more sophisticated and worldly than your average twenty-two-year-old.

My mobile rang and I snatched it up. When I saw it wasn't Smith, I told myself that my lightning fast answering reflex had nothing to do with hope. I held no hope that there were any emotional ties binding me to him, which was why I should have been glad to see my brother's name on the screen.

Lola raised her eyebrows, no doubt responding to my frantic movements, and I smiled, holding up a finger to give me a moment to take the call.

"I just read your email," John said as soon as I answered. I pictured him in his leather desk chair facing his office window, which afforded a stunning view from one of the top floors of the Gherkin. "Can you pop by the office this afternoon for a few minutes?"

"Yes," I responded automatically. I wanted this dealt with as soon as possible. "How's two?"

"Perfect. I'll let security know to send you straight up."

We hung up without saying goodbye. As far as I could tell, pleasantries and affectionate farewells were reserved for siblings who had actually grown up in the same household.

Setting a reminder on my phone, I turned my attention back to sorting through the various contacts I needed to reach out to. Bless still had no inventory and procuring clothing was going to be as vital as securing clients. When I began scribbling a list down from the computer screen, Lola cleared her throat softly.

"So do you want to tell me what's wrong?" she asked, dropping onto a stool by my makeshift desk.

I glanced up, fingers freezing over the keyboard, and blinked. Did I? I'd managed to avoid Edward's check-in calls for the better part of the weekend, and Clara was lost in baby land, which meant I hadn't actually talked about the break-up with anyone. But confessing the situation would mean sharing the backstory and that was complicated.

"I'm behind," I answered instead. That was true, at least. I was just busy. So busy I hadn't even said hello to her.

"*You're a machine*, and not in a good way. It's like working with robot Belle around here." Lola folded her arms over her chest, shaking her sleek dark hair. "Something is up."

"Yeah, we're supposed to be launching this company in two months," I snapped, "and I don't have inventory or a website or a marketing plan."

"But you have a partner," Lola reminded me. "Stop trying to do it all yourself and let me tackle the website and marketing."

I relaxed back in my seat and nodded. She had a point. "I had a boyfriend. Now I don't."

It was all she really needed to know. All any woman ever needed to know, and judging by the way her pink lips pressed into a grim line, she didn't need to hear more. "I get it, but don't switch into survival mode. So the cad is out of the picture, you still have a lot of people who have your back, and I'm one of them. You aren't doing this all by yourself."

"Wow, for a minute, I could have sworn Clara was here," I teased.

Lola straightened up and smirked, tossing her hair back over a slender shoulder. "*We are sisters*, even if she has much better taste in men."

"It sounds as if I'm not the only one with man trouble," I noted. It wasn't surprising exactly. There were too many Philips in the world and not enough Alexanders.

"Not trouble exactly. I'm just not interested. I'm either supposed to be impressed by the size of their portfolio or the size of their ego. Apparently they didn't get the memo that size only matters when it comes to one thing."

"And then there's the fact that Clara married the King of England," I added.

"It does put life into rather harsh perspective," Lola agreed with a laugh. "Mother doesn't understand why I haven't snagged my own world leader. Of course, she doesn't know that the last time I was forward with a man, he came out of the closet five minutes later. Obviously I need to focus on my career."

"You did Edward a favor," I told her, smiling at the memory. "But I'm with you. Who needs a man to take over the world?"

"That, I'll drink to." She picked up an empty Starbucks cup and tossed it into the rubbish bin.

"Sadly, we haven't stocked the office bar yet," I said dryly.

"An oversight which will be remedied shortly. For now, I'm taking you to lunch." She held up a hand when I opened my mouth to protest. "A *business* lunch. Divide and conquer. That's how we're going to do this."

I grabbed my bag and followed her out the door, locking it behind us. She was right. I couldn't do this alone, and if I was going to pay Smith's investment back and finally be free, a battle strategy was definitely in order.

A FEW HOURS LATER, I MADE MY WAY ACROSS TOWN, MY MIND spinning with all of Lola's ideas. I was so preoccupied that I nearly walked past the security checkpoint at the entrance of my brother's building.

"Miss?" A uniformed guard stopped me and gestured toward my purse.

"Oops." I unzipped it and held it out for his inspection.

He peeked in with a flashlight. "Are you carrying a mobile phone? We need to check that."

"Um, probably." I rifled around and came up empty. "I must have left it at the office."

"Do you have an appointment?" he asked dubiously.

He thinks you're a flake. What professional showed up for a meeting without a mobile? I seriously needed to get my act together if I was going to evolve into a business mogul. I dug out my wallet and showed him my ID. "I do. Annabelle Stuart. I'm meeting with John Stuart."

"Head on up," he said after checking his list, adding, "you do know your way?"

"I'll be fine," I reassured him, taking off for the lift. Due to the mortifying security check, it was nearly two and I didn't have a mobile to let my brother know that I'd be late. It was exactly two when I reached his floor and tore up to the reception desk.

"I'm here for John Stuart," I told the girl behind the desk in a breathless voice.

"Mr. Stuart is expecting you." She gestured to the left. John's law firm was the exact opposite of Smith's small private practice. Nearly a dozen lawyers practiced here, filling the roles of solicitors and barristers alike.

"Belle." He rose politely as I entered, bowing slightly and tugging at the cuffs of his Harris Tweed jacket. Everything from his thinning hair to his clothing choices and odd adherence to decorum made him appear much older than thirty-two.

I never knew what to do around him. Shake his hand. Curtsy. In all fairness, he'd never been anything but unfailingly kind to me, despite the awkward favoritism our father had shown me. No doubt owing to my mother's interference.

"How are you?" he asked, once again proving himself the essence of civilized formality.

"Busy," I admitted, not sure if I could handle a round of small talk. "You?"

"I've also been quite busy."

We sat for a moment in awkward silence before he glanced at his computer screen. "I was quite surprised to hear you were starting a business. It doesn't seem like something your mother would approve of."

"She doesn't," I said flatly. I didn't miss the way his eyes tightened as he spoke of her. My mother had always made her disapproval of my choices known in private. She'd been publicly vocal about her disapproval of John's existence. Wicked stepmother indeed.

"I can empathize with the position you find yourself in then." His tone had softened. We both understood how it felt to be unwanted. Although, in comparison, he'd had it much worse. After his mother had died, my father had remarried. His new wife, my *loving* mother, had immediately shipped John off to boarding school, and he had stayed there until university. "It should make Christmas quite interesting."

"I propose we let Ann enjoy her estate by herself this Christmas," I suggested. It was the first year I'd be single, and while Philip had never been much emotional support, he'd been a distraction at least. I had no interest in spending the day being analyzed and found wanting.

"It is *your* estate," John reminded me in a clipped tone. "Perhaps *you*could un-invite *her*."

"Do you recall the end of Jane Eyre? I wouldn't put it past her to try to roast us both alive." The joke lightened the mood a bit but didn't fully erase the implication of his words. John had inherited my father's title as his only son, a right granted to him by British law, but I'd wound up inheriting the family estate. I had no doubt my mother had forced our father to disregard John in all other ways as well.

"So is your mother this unwanted investor?" John asked.

"Thankfully no." I shook my head, actually laughing at the thought. If my mother had any money, she wouldn't give it to me. "But unfortunately I have, or rather had, a personal relationship with the current investor."

"And now you don't," John guessed, but he didn't press for details. It was probably obvious from the red flushing across my cheeks what kind of relationship it had been. "This isn't normally my area of expertise. I don't work directly with clients any more since I became one of the firm's barristers."

"Oh," I said in a small voice. My legal problems were about to get a lot more expensive if John was unable to handle the issue.

"I am able to handle litigation," he clarified. "I generally don't though, so you might want to seek a second opinion because you might not like mine."

"Fair enough." I braced myself for his response, breath caught in my throat.

"As an investor, he has little claim on your actual business. He may choose to divest and force repayment, but from what you told me in your email, his interest is entirely financial. He shouldn't interfere. If you feel that you want him out, I'd repay the investment and be certain he's not written into any legal documents as a shareholder moving forward."

It wasn't the worst news he could have given, but it wasn't exactly what I wanted to hear. I suppose I'd hoped John could offer some sort of miraculous solution that hadn't occurred to me. But Smith was part of my life until I could buy him out.

"You're disappointed," John noted.

I dismissed his concern with a wave of my hand. "It's a feeling I'm used to."

Our eyes met, and for the first time in many years, I saw the same painful memories I'd carried reflected in someone else's eyes. We'd never spoken of our father's death. It was the ghost that no one spoke of in my family.

"A word of advice?" John offered. "Not as your lawyer, but as a... brother. Move on. Don't feel guilty for taking what has been given to you and don't apologize."

"No apologies," I repeated.

John's gaze faded into the distance as he reiterated, "None."

CHAPTER SEVEN

Andrew's office was everything mine was not. Perched on one of the highest floors of his building, it loomed over the city's financial district. To be honest, the whole thing reeked of a sort of masculine inferiority syndrome. Why else erect something that looked like a towering dick in the middle of London than if you couldn't get yours up?

"I've reviewed the documents and I see no issue with proceeding," he informed me as he reappeared. One of my oldest friends from law school, the years—and corporate law—hadn't been kind to him. It showed in the lines creasing his forehead.

Perhaps I would be similarly worn down if I'd pursued a more traditional practice. Although it hardly seemed fair that life had been so hard on him when I was the one entangled with criminals.

"Then everything is in order?" I asked, ready to be done with this business.

"Legally," Andrew agreed. He gestured for me to take a seat before crossing the room to pour two Scotches. "Personally, I would be a bit more concerned."

I took the drink he offered me without responding. I knew exactly what the personal stakes were, and I'd already made sacrifices to ensure whatever chaos ensued from finalizing the sale of my holdings in Velvet would be restricted to me. But Andrew was a decent man. He'd advised me on difficult cases before, which is why I'd entrusted him to handle this one swiftly and privately.

"Hammond isn't likely to roll over on this, Smith." He took a long sip and shook his head. The implication was clear. He couldn't understand what I was thinking. Of course, he'd also never been as mixed up with a client as I was with my boss.

I swirled the amber liquid in the bottom of the glass as I considered how to respond. I trusted Andrew as far as I trusted any professional acquaintance. "I don't expect him to. But there is a personal reason that I want out of the club. A couple, actually."

It didn't take a genius to guess that I wanted free from the sordid enterprises Hammond had built throughout London. It probably also didn't take much to piece together that my father had been a victim of Hammond's organized crime empire and that the odds were I would suffer a similar fate. Most of my associates had figured that out long before I did. What might be harder to comprehend was why I was purposefully drawing attention to myself now.

"I'm still retained by Hammond," I finished.

"But are you in his good graces?" Andrew asked. He placed his empty glass on the side table and leaned forward. "You have to know this is suicide."

I did know that. The clock had been ticking since last spring when I'd found myself in the precarious position of choosing sides. "I wish I could explain myself. Doing this with the club will hardly matter, but it's important for me to sever ties with Velvet."

"She must be something." He rubbed his chin with a sigh.

So he had guessed. While most might assume I wanted out of the twisted birthright my father had left me, Andrew saw through me. "Tell me. Is it obvious because you know me or because I've lost my touch?"

"Lucky guess," he assured me. "You are as unreadable as ever, my friend."

I wanted to breath a sigh of relief, but instead I tipped my head, smiling tightly.

"This will bring attention to her as well." His forehead creased as his tone grew serious.

"I've taken measures." He didn't need to know more than that. While he might be trustworthy, I'd learned a few things from my unlikely partnership with Georgia. People could be bought. People could be sold out. And people, especially men, had a tendency to spill secrets when they got a chance to put their dicks in a warm, welcoming pussy.

"You're smart, even if this a particularly stupid move. I certainly hope there won't be fall-out."

There would be. The only choice I had was to be outside of the blast radius—a feat which I already knew was impossible. But keeping Belle far from the danger was something I could control. No matter the cost.

"You've considered that if he makes a move, it might not be a physical attack. Your entire career is in his hands. There's more ways to kill a man than to put a bullet through his head."

"I'm prepared for that as well." There were no more reassurances I could offer him. Even if I had been willing to lay out my entire plan on the spot, it would risk too many others in the process. "I wish I could be upfront with you. Your concern is touching."

"You're a good man. I simply want the best for you." He held out his hand, and I shook it firmly.

That wasn't a sentiment I was accustomed to hearing. If Andrew knew me better—if he knew the things I'd done—the thought would never have occurred to him. But there was a small comfort to be taken from his words. I could never hope to absolve myself of the sins of my past but trying had to count for something.

Andrew patted my shoulder as I left his office. I'd thought that some of my burden would be lifted when I relinquished my claim to Velvet, but instead it felt heavier than ever before. The move had come at a price, and while I'd been willing to pay it, I still felt its sting.

Stepping inside the lift, I toyed with the mobile in my pocket. There was only one person I wanted to call to share this news with, and she was absolutely off-limits. That was the missing piece. The reason that finally snipping a thread that linked me to Hammond hadn't been the victory I'd expected. No doubt Belle would have shot off a smart-ass remark that redirected my attention from the inevitable consequences of my actions to thoughts of spending the evening taming her attitude. My cock stiffened a little at the fantasy. No amount of rationale could convince him that I'd made the right move.

The lift came to a stop on the next floor, and this time when the doors opened, I blinked, wondering if my imagination had finally gotten the better of me. It was going to be a long ride down the remaining flights if my daydreams were becoming so vivid.

But judging from the way she froze on the spot, confusion turning into pain, she wasn't an illusion. Belle paused, as if considering her next move, before she walked in and took up the farthest possible spot in the compartment. Her gaze remained trained on the buttons as we began to descend once more.

Of all the lifts in London, she walks into mine.

Her perfume lingered in the air, and it took a considerable amount of effort to restrain myself. My dick was having none of it, having grown rock hard at the sight of her. The burden I'd felt entering the lift seemed to lift and deposit itself directly onto my chest. How did you tell a woman that you hurt her to protect her?

I wanted to shove her against the wall, hitch up her skirt, and claim what was mine. Because Belle Stuart was mine. I'd let her walk away, but I hadn't let her go. She wouldn't stop me. That much I was sure of her. She might be managing to pretend I didn't exist, but I could see it in her body language. In the way she rubbed her calf nervously against her shin. In the slight tap of her fingers on the metal rail that ran along the perimeter of the space. In the sharp intake of breath that came every few seconds.

She was as aware of my presence as I was of hers. Her body

responding to the memories I'd given it. If I lifted her skirt and shoved my hand between her legs, she'd be as wet as I was hard.

Just one taste. One stolen kiss. One bite to her pale shoulder. One hand wrapped around her slender throat. One more moment.

But giving in would undo everything I'd worked for, and it would make the pain I'd caused her worthless. She had more value than that. I owed her more respect than to toy with her.

When we reached the lobby, I exited without a word. It was easier that way.

For her at least.

CHAPTER EIGHT

Lola descended on me as soon as I made it back to the office, her obvious excitement distracting me from my run-in with Smith. I was barely through the door before she had me cornered. She twisted her hands, bouncing on her heels. The girl was practically vibrating. Sidling past her, I dropped my bag on the floor and sank into my chair.

"Well?" I prompted, concerned that she might explode if I didn't give her some attention. The last thing I needed was to have to repaint. Closing my eyes, I tried to focus on her and not my heart-breaking encounter in the lift.

"I didn't want to say anything before because I figured it was a long shot. But then I got a call, and oh my god, Belle! This is it!" she gushed.

I opened one eye and stared at her, wondering if I'd missed something vital in what she'd just told me. "Forgive me, but what is it?"

"*Trend*!" she exclaimed, glaring at me like I should know this.

Despite the nonsensical stream of information spewing from her, this got my attention. I sat up, both eyes open, and waited.

"Abigail Summers's assistant just phoned me. They love the idea behind Bless and want to do an exclusive editorial."

"*Trend*?" I repeated. Now I understood why Lola was barely coherent. *Trend* was the most widely recognized fashion magazine in the world and had been for nearly fifty years. As a start-up, we wouldn't have been able to afford an ad on their website. A magazine editorial was beyond my wildest fantasies. "Oh my god!"

Tears spilled down my cheeks even as I began to laugh. It was full-blown hysteria. Here we were sitting in an empty office space. No website. No inventory. No customers. And somehow we'd managed to land an opportunity half of the fashion world would kill for.

"How did this happen?" I finally managed.

"A professor I'm working with this year used to be editorial staff," Lola explained. "She gave me the contact info and told me Abigail was looking to spotlight up-and-coming female entrepreneurs. It's part of a whole girl power theme they're focused on this year."

"I can't believe this." And I couldn't. It was as if the universe had taken pity on me and dropped a gift in my lap.

"The only catch is that you need to be in New York by Tuesday," Lola said.

My smile evaporated. "Wait, what?"

"The story is as much about you as it is about Bless." Lola shrugged her shoulders as if this made perfect sense.

Except that it didn't. In the fashion world, I was a nobody. My greatest contribution to that world so far was a couple of maxed-out credit cards spent during irresponsible shopping sprees. "What about you? You should take the interview."

Lola's background at university, not to mention her legacy as the daughter of two self-made millionaires, made her the perfect candidate for a major magazine piece.

"I have school," she reminded me. "Plus, Bless is your company."

"It's our company," I corrected her.

"You're generous," she said. "It will be someday when I've fulfilled my end of the deal. That much I can promise you. But this is still your baby. You had the vision. Besides you have a great story. Abigail loved it. Jilted by her fiancé, a bride-to-be ditches the no-good jerk and starts the next big thing in modern fashion merchandizing."

"When you put it like that, it does sound exciting. Except look around, Bless is pretty much still an idea." Nothing confirmed the validity of this more than the barren space surrounding us.

"In today's market, ideas are currency—and currency is still money," Lola informed me.

"You're taking very different classes than I did in school," I said with a smirk.

"Look, you are going to New York, and you're going to prove what a badass you truly are. No second-guessing yourself now. You're going to blow Abigail Summers away." Lola tilted her head, daring me to challenge her.

"It's not like I'll actually meet with Abigail," I said. I needed to align my enthusiasm with Lola's. This was an amazing chance. But keeping a level head also seemed a necessity.

"No, you will," she corrected me, flying into another frenzied announcement. "The whole thing is like a conversation between the two of you. The magazine spotlights the business while the interview is more of a mentoring session."

I lost the ability to speak. There was no way I was prepared for this. I'd spent the last week gathering the basic info. I'd rented an office. I had an elevator pitch. None of that was enough to impress someone with Abigail's reputation.

Lola's eyes narrowed. "Why do you look like I just gave you a death sentence?"

"I'm not certain you didn't."

"*Trend* is taking care of most of the travel arrangements. I'll handle the rest." She snapped into decision-making mode. "I'll also draw up a bunch of talking points you can use to discuss the brand and our plans. But don't forget, she wants to mentor. Massage her ego a little and get her feedback."

She had a point. If all else failed, flattery would get me through.

"While you're gone, I'll finalize the website plans with the web designer and start reaching out to the designers," she continued.

"Now this is important. Do you have stuff to wear? It has to be this season!"

I could tell by the way she looked me over as she said this that my choice of outfit today had worried her. I wore a classic ivory blouse and navy pencil skirt. There was nothing sexy or exciting about it, but I had owned it for three years and it still worked. It wasn't the height of current fashion, however.

"I have clothes." I swallowed hard on my own words. I had clothes given to me by Smith. My wardrobe not only had some current pieces, it had all of them. Without a doubt, they would impress Abigail Summers. I just had to bring myself to wear them. I'd shoved them in the back of my closet and studiously avoided them since that night at Velvet. Now I would be forced to take a huge leap forward in my career with the burden of my obligation to Smith weighing me down. John's words from earlier in the afternoon echoed in my mind.

No guilt. I was going to have that tattooed on my forearm.

"You gain a day heading to the U.S., but you're going to be exhausted, so you leave on Monday."

"Fuck, fuck, fuck," I said under my breath, mentally running through the list of things I needed to have done before I took off. Manicure, at the very least. Maybe a wax. My hair had gotten longer due to being distracted by Smith and then the business. There was no way to get into the hairdresser on time.

"Relax," Lola instructed me. "You have the whole weekend to get everything done. And try to take a minute and be happy. Don't get too caught up in your to-do list that you miss out on the amazing."

I lunged for her, wrapping her in a tight hug. "Thank you!"

"Thank you for trusting me to be part of this." She squeezed back. "I've got things here. Oh, and I'm going to call the landlord and have him change the lock. I watched you lock the door earlier and it popped right open when I got back from our lunch. I think it's broken."

"Was anything missing?" I asked with a frown.

"No. I checked," she reassured me. "Your phone was sitting right out on the desk. Thank god this is a quiet neighborhood."

"Speaking of, I need to get to my neighborhood and to my closet."

Lola pecked me on the cheek, and I rushed toward the door.

"Hey," she called after me, "you deserve this."

Hell yes, I did. Nobody was going to hold me back anymore. Not even myself.

THE SENSUAL, UPBEAT RHYTHM OF SAMBA MUSIC FILLED MY flat by the time I arrived there with freshly manicured hands. I couldn't resist swaying my hips as I made my way into the small living room I shared with my aunt. Jane grinned wildly as I joined her, holding out her hands. I took them nervously, allowing her to lead me into a few steps until I tripped onto the rug. Jane snorted as I stumbled and fell onto the sofa. She continued moving with the beat, her silk house robe swirling wildly around her. When the song ended, she plopped down beside me.

"I'm also afraid to tell you that it's Friday evening." Jane pursed her lips knowingly. "I wouldn't want you to go back to the office."

Jane hadn't pressed me when I came home a week ago crying. She hadn't needed an explanation at all. And she'd managed to keep her mouth shut about the insane number of hours I'd been spending on Bless. Apparently that grace period was over, but I didn't care. I'd spent the last two hours allowing myself to celebrate the biggest achievement in my very short career's history.

I pulled the latest copy of Trend from my tote bag and threw it in her lap.

"Ever read this?" I asked. Now that I was the one brimming over with the news, I wondered how Lola had been able to remain so composed.

"Not for years." Jane paged through it, stopping occasionally to scan an article. "I haven't exactly followed fashion trends for the past twenty years. It's very liberating."

I rolled my eyes at her insinuation. Jane supported my idea even if she didn't quite understand its appeal. "It's my job to follow them," I reminded her. "Anyway, they want to feature Bless."

"That's wonderful!" Jane cried, dragging me into a hug. When I pulled back, tears sparkled in her eyes.

"Don't do that," I warned her, already feeling wet heat prickling in my own. "Or I'll cry."

"You've worked so hard and you've picked yourself back up. I couldn't be prouder."

A lump formed in my throat, and no matter how hard I swallowed, it didn't budge. I'd spent most of my life searching for my mother's approval. Jane had filled that void for me. Making her proud meant more than anything.

"I leave for New York on Monday."

"This just keeps getting better." Jane's eyes twinkled, but this time it wasn't the glisten of tears. It was mischief. "The city that never sleeps. What fun."

"Business," I corrected her. "It will probably be a few meetings and some room service."

"That won't do." Jane shook her platinum head. "And you'll never get away with it anyway. It's impossible to go to New York without it getting under your skin. It's so alive there, it's infectious."

"I'll use protection," I said flatly. There had been a time when visiting the city had been on my bucket list. Knowing I was going there alone, and for a business trip, sucked some of the flavor out of the opportunity. And more importantly, the trip was about Bless. Now wasn't the time to be distracted by romanticizing the city. Not when I needed to be laser-focused on the task at hand.

"Before you leave the country," Jane said, her tone taking on a seriousness that meant I was about to get an earful about something, "call Edward. That boy is beside himself. He's so worried about you that he stopped by here last night."

"I will," I promised sheepishly.

Jane's penetrating gaze saw right through me. "He's not going to rub it in. He cares about you."

"I just wanted to pretend nothing was wrong," I admitted in a low voice.

"No, you wanted to avoid what was wrong." Jane knitted her soft, papery fingers through mine.

I nodded, knowing she'd nailed it. "I should call him."

"Sooner rather than later," she suggested.

"Sooner," I echoed. It was time to stop avoiding what I'd been through and focus my energy on what I had in front of me. My friends. My business. And a trip to New York City.

CHAPTER NINE

Monday morning found me with bags packed, waiting for a car service outside my flat. With any luck, Heathrow would be calm enough that I would have time to grab a cup of tea before my flight, but I wasn't counting on it. The driver was already five minutes late, and with each second that passed, I thought of something new to worry about. Did I have my passport? A check of my bag confirmed I did. Had I packed a toothbrush? They probably had those in New York if I'd forgotten. Was I going crazy? Yes. Definitely yes. When the car finally pulled to the curb, I snatched up my luggage as the window rolled down, revealing a familiar face.

"Your drivers have arrived," Edward called jovially.

"My drivers are late," I scolded him, not feeling even remotely upset. He'd been over the moon when I'd finally called him. He hadn't even mentioned Smith. Undoubtedly Lola had kept the rest of our tight-knit group abreast that there was trouble in paradise.

"Do you know how hard it is to get His Royal Highness out of bed?" Lola yelled from the driver's seat as I slung my bag inside the back and slid in. I'd opted for a comfortable knit dress that still looked professional. I had no idea who would be meeting me at JFK

International, but I wasn't taking any chances. I'd even worn stockings.

"In my defense, I had no idea there were two six o'clocks," Edward said, shifting so his arm was casually resting on the armrest between the seats.

"Try looking at a clock," Lola suggested as she merged onto the motorway.

The good-natured bickering continued between the two of them, nearly lulling me back to sleep.

"You have your flight information, right?" Lola asked.

I shook the cobwebs out of my head. "I have what you sent me."

"A driver will meet you at the baggage claim and get you to your hotel. Abigail's assistant is supposed to send that info this afternoon, so check your email when you land." Lola rattled off a half-dozen other instructions and I smiled and nodded. It was all information I already knew, but I appreciated how earnest she was about this trip.

"I can't believe I can't get either of you to come with me." I'd tried. Lola had been clear it was impossible, but Edward's refusal had been more puzzling. "Too busy with matters of state? Couldn't ensure you'd have a security team available?"

Edward peeked back at me, shaking his head, and gave me the side eye. "There was no time to arrange a proper welcoming parade. A prince must have his standards."

"You are so full of yourself." Lola smacked his shoulder, her eyes never leaving the road.

"Of course, I am. I'm royalty," he shot back.

"Tell her the real reason," Lola demanded haughtily.

"I knew something was up." I pointed a finger at him. "You. Tell. Now."

"If you must know..." he trailed away.

"I must," I pressed. It wasn't like Edward to be so secretive. It was actually a good thing that he didn't have the same responsibilities as his brother. I wasn't entirely certain he could be trusted with classified information.

"David and I are meeting with Alexander," he admitted in a quiet voice.

"Finally!" I threw my hands up in the air. "I don't know why you've held out so long."

"He's not going to say no," Lola added, echoing the opinion I'd expressed to Edward at least a dozen times since he'd proposed to his boyfriend.

"It is slightly more complicated than cold feet," Edward said flatly.

My eyes narrowed. Edward had come out publicly almost a year ago and proposed to his longtime boyfriend a few months later. Despite pressure from Clara, David, and myself, he'd been dragging his feet on setting a date for months. "They might not be cold, but they're certainly slow."

"So explain it to us," Lola said.

"I can't." This time his refusal was straightforward and firm. Judging from the way Lola's head jolted in surprise, we were both taken back.

"What do you mean?" I said with a laugh. We'd never shared the more sordid details of our love lives. I really didn't think he wanted to hear about Smith's penchant for dominance. But neither of us had ever shied away from analyzing even the most mundane aspects of our relationship statuses.

"I mean, I can't." Edward ran a hand through his curly hair and slouched back into his seat, turning his gaze to stare out the window. "Please don't ask more."

Maybe I was wrong about his ability to keep secrets. Although I couldn't fathom what he was hiding from us now.

"Fine. Can I ask who your maid of honor is going to be?" I said, shifting the topic to clear the heavy tension in the cabin. "I have an idea if you need suggestions."

"I was thinking we might elope," Edward said. "How are you with the beach?"

"I'm good with that." Reaching forward, I put a hand on his

shoulder. I wouldn't force him to tell me more, but I still wanted him to know that I was here for him. He took it and held it for the rest of the ride. We chattered about cakes and honeymoon locations, each of us avoiding the questions that had been left unanswered.

But as we pulled up to the drop-off lane at Heathrow, I couldn't help but wonder when relationships had gotten so complicated. There was a time when Clara and I kept nothing from one another. These days we barely had time to talk, and she'd never been terribly forthcoming about her private relationship with Alexander. Now Edward was shutting me out. It didn't diminish my love for either of them, but it did hurt, especially given how closed-off Smith had been about his personal life outside our relationship.

Uh-uh. My conscience interrupted me before I could descend into the spiral of self-doubt any further.

Edward popped out of the car and gave me a swift kiss on the cheek. We both did our best to ignore the number of travelers who stopped to snap a pic. It was one of the liabilities of being best friends with him.

"Tomorrow morning, they'll be reporting that you've gone straight," I whispered to him. I could see the tabloid covers now. Given the whirlwind I'd been privy to in the last year and a half, I could probably write headlines for them.

"Once you go gay, you never stray," he teased, passing me my bag from the backseat. "David will get a good laugh out of them."

Lola rolled her window down and blew me a kiss. "See you in a few days."

"I'll call you," I promised her.

"You better. See if you can get Abigail to take a selfie with you for our social media feeds."

I agreed, even though there was no way in hell I was going to embarrass myself by asking for that. Abigail Summers didn't strike me as the selfie type.

Inside the airport doors, I groaned when I saw the security line and found myself cursing Edward for not coming along once more.

There would be no way I'd have to wait in that line with him at my side. Hauling my bag over to the ticketing counter, I handed my passport over to check my bag.

"Miss Stuart," she chirped, "how many bags will you be checking today?"

"Just one." I'd managed to cram it full of six pairs of shoes and a dozen more dresses.

"Very good. Here's your boarding pass. Since you're flying in first class, you can use the fast track security lane to the left."

I glanced down at my ticket in surprise. Apparently, *Trend* didn't mess around. "Thank you!"

My trip was already off to a great start. After bypassing most of the line, I not only had time for a cup of tea but a croissant as well in the airline's private lounge. Scanning through *The Telegraph,* I spotted familiar faces on the society page. Apparently Pepper Lockwood wasn't going to heed my warning and kick Philip to the curb. I stuffed the last flaky bite of pastry in my mouth and drained my tea. Those two deserved each other. I was certain it would be a long and painful union for the both of them. Smith had cured me of any lasting bitterness over Philip's betrayal. Or maybe he'd just replaced my bitterness over that break-up with bitterness over our own relationship ending.

The few times I'd flown overseas to visit a friend in Los Angeles, I'd been forced to do so in economy, which wasn't terrible on an international flight. Until I was seated in first class international. I was pretty sure I could ask for a kidney transplant and receive one. I opted to stretch across my seat like it was a luxurious divan while flight attendants brought hot towels and champagne. Lunch and breakfast were served on respectable bone china. Given that I was about to spend the next five years or so building a business, I wasn't getting used to the treatment. Every dime would have to go right back into Bless to make it the success I envisioned.

But I was going to bloody well enjoy it now.

I'd brought my laptop, but after an hour spent reviewing the talking points Lola had prepared—which I had memorized before take-off—I abandoned the computer in favor of a smutty novel I'd grabbed from the airport bookstore. But reading about sex with a broken heart turned out to be a bad idea.

"Do you want this?" I asked the flight attendant as she delivered a refill on my champagne. I'd better slow down or I'd pass out before I could even claim I was jet lagged.

She glanced at the cover and shook her head, leaning down to whisper, "I already read that series. What did you think?"

"Not my cup of tea." It was best to leave it there. The champagne I'd consumed threatened to take over and spill the emotional tale.

"It is a little kinky." She bit her lips, blushing as she said it.

Poor thing. I could guess that her experience with kinky ended in those pages. I kept the opinion to myself and shoved it in the magazine holder.

The way I saw it, after my failed literary attempt and the disastrous exchange with the flight attendant, I could give in to the champagne and cry. Or I could use it to my advantage and fall asleep.

Neither option felt very empowering, but at least if I slept, I wouldn't have to ask for tissues.

A few hours later, I was gently shaken awake by the kind woman. She handed me back my book to store for landing. Looking out the window, I caught sight of the Statue of Liberty, which looked disappointingly small from this height. It was my first trip to the east coast of America, and if there was one reason I was happy to be going alone, it was so I could be an awful tourist without judgment.

JFK proved slightly less civilized than Heathrow. I shot off a text to Lola as soon as I was through customs.

BELLE: I thought there was going to be a cavity search. Americans take their airports very seriously.

There was no response and no email with the information she'd promised me, but there was a man holding a sign with my name on it in baggage claim. Underneath was scrawled Bless.

Bless was real. Today was the proof. I was across the pond on a business trip. For a split second, I wished Smith could be here to see that. The thought squeezed my heart, and I quickly dismissed it.

"I'm Annabelle Stuart," I told the man with the sign.

"Welcome to New York," he said in an accent I'd only heard on television. "Are you here for business or pleasure?"

"Business," I responded as he led me to the baggage carousel. I no longer mixed the two.

CHAPTER TEN

As the car hurtled through the narrow lanes, the driver honking impatiently, I tried to take in the city for the first time. The streets of New York were as crowded as I'd imagined they would be. Everywhere there was chaotic blend of colors and people, all rushing toward the next item on their daily schedule. It made my head hurt. London was by no means a quiet metropolis, but this was something entirely different. Life in all its wild vitality pulsed from every direction.

We flew past a park full of activity. Even leisure time felt rushed here. Sinking against my seat, I closed my eyes and took a deep breath. So the city intimidated me. Big deal. I wasn't exactly a wallflower. I was accustomed to high-pressure situations. I'd been the maid of honor at the most infamous wedding in history after all. Tension fueled my passion, and I would work that to my advantage.

A few minutes later, the car slowed to a merciful stop, and I peeked back out the window to find the bustling entrance to one of the largest, and grandest, hotels I'd ever seen.

"Are you certain we're in the right place?" I asked the driver, allowing my confusion to show. *Trend* had been the one to arrange my accommodations, but I had a hard time believing they set up relatively green entrepreneurs in such lavish quarters.

"My sheet says to deliver you to the Plaza," he informed me. "This is it."

"Okay," I managed, but the words were barely out of my mouth before he was out of the car. He circled to the back as a bellman opened my door and offered me his hand.

The kindly gentleman seemed unfazed by the fact that my mouth was hanging open. "Welcome to the Plaza, Miss."

"Thank you." I took his hand and clamped my mouth shut. I deserved to be here. At least that was how I was going to have to sell this to myself.

That was harder when I walked through the doors. Marble floors morphed into marble columns, leading to a sweeping staircase. Clusters of richly upholstered chairs perched on plush rugs dotted the lobby, and a massive crystal chandelier scattered light across the wide space. A bellhop wheeled a cart with my baggage past me, and I followed him to the hotel desk.

"Checking in?" the woman behind it asked in a pert voice. She studied me for a moment before her eyes softened. I had the feeling I'd just passed a test.

"Annabelle Stuart." I handed her my passport and unzipped my wallet to retrieve my credit card.

"Oh yes, Miss Stuart." Her tone completely changed as she checked the computer screen. "We have you in the Hardenbergh Terrace Suite on the Penthouse level."

I bit the inside of my cheek, not wanting to sound like an idiot by asking another person if they were mistaken. Maybe I wasn't the only Annabelle Stuart arriving in New York today.

"It's on the twentieth floor. Your key card will grant you access. Please keep it with you at all times. The Plaza values the privacy of its guests, so security may ask to see it on occasion. Geoffrey, your personal butler, is available to you twenty-four hours a day should you require assistance."

I held out my credit card, suddenly more afraid to have her run it.

It carried a limit that probably didn't cover the entrance fee to a place like this. To my relief, she waved it away.

"Everything has been taken care of. Geoffrey will show you to your suite." She beckoned across the lobby, and a man came forward dressed in a long tailcoat and white gloves. He looked as though he'd just stepped from the pages of an old novel.

"Miss Stuart." He tipped his head politely and lifted my bags from the trolley while I checked for an earpiece. Both the receptionist and the butler acted as if they'd been waiting all day for my arrival, and while I was positive I was about to make a splash in the business world, I hadn't done it yet.

As he led me toward the private lift off the lobby, I considered pinching myself. Maybe I was dreaming. Of course, I wouldn't put it past Lola to name drop to secure me above-average accommodations. But while I might be close personal friends with the British Monarchy, I was no princess. Something wasn't adding up.

It wasn't until the butler pressed the button for the twentieth floor that the pieces started to form a sickening picture. As the floor numbers lit up in swift succession, carrying me toward the top of the Plaza, my stomach dropped out. Suspicion turned into nauseating certainty as the lift doors slid open to my floor.

"I'm at your service during your stay," Geoffrey reminded me as he swept a key card over the lock. I mumbled something unintelligible in response. "Pardon?"

But Geoffrey wasn't getting clarification today. As I stepped into the suite, my eyes landed on the room's other occupant—the last person I wanted to see.

And the person I wanted to see more than anyone in the world.

Smith towered before me, a brutal pillar of masculinity, mercilessly clothed in a perfectly tailored suit. His strong jaw tensed slightly as our gazes met, his green irises flashing with possessiveness as he took me in. I knew the secrets he shielded behind those eyes as well as I knew the perfectly hewn body hidden under his clothes. His hands curled into fists as though he was trying to keep himself away from me. That desire was entirely mutual.

"Mr. Price," Geoffrey greeted him as he stepped in behind me. "Should I deliver these to the master bedroom or the guest room?"

Smith's face went blank as if Geoffrey had begun to speak in a foreign language. The message was obvious. A man like Smith Price didn't invite blondes to his suite to sleep in the guest room. The composed butler shifted uncomfortably on his heels.

"Leave them by the door," Smith instructed, holding out a wad of bills. "I'll see to Miss Stuart from here."

The words had an unwanted effect on me. My mouth went dry, my heart speeding up to a frenzy as I felt the magnetic tug of Smith's presence. It took every ounce of restraint I had to stay put and wait for the door to close behind me.

"I hope these accommodations are to your standards," Smith said stiffly.

So we were down to small talk. Of course we were. He'd gotten me into a hotel room in a strange city under false pretenses. I imagined he'd be bringing up the weather next. Anything to avoid the fact that he'd damn near kidnapped me. Or that he'd avoided me the last time we saw each other. Or that the last time we'd spoken it had been after watching him take a cane to Georgia Kincaid.

"My best friend lives in a palace. You're going to have to try harder to impress me," I snapped back.

"New city. Same attitude," he said dryly.

"Don't start with me," I warned him. "Answers now."

"I rearranged my travel to coincide with yours." He spoke as if this answered any of the questions I might have.

"Let's see. That doesn't tell me how you knew I would be in New York or how you hijacked me at the airport. Or most importantly, why you'd even bother?" I bit out. "We're over, remember? Or are you having a bout of amnesia? You're not my controlling, overprotective boyfriend anymore. You decided you'd rather play with another toy."

It hurt to say that out loud. I'd been avoiding the reality of my situation since I'd left him at Velvet, saying only what I needed to silence the people in my life smart enough to guess things hadn't ended with Smith when he'd fired me from my job as his personal assistant.

"I never stopped being controlling or overprotective." He took a step closer. "Or your boyfriend."

"Then we're definitely interpreting the events of the last time we spoke to each other differently." I backed up, eager to maintain a safe distance from him. "Or is this just part of your game?"

"You're not a pawn to me, beautiful, but yes, this is part of a game."

"Then let me be clear: I'm not playing." If I moved quickly, I could grab my bags, but there was no way I'd make it into the lift before he reached me.

"I don't want you to."

"Then walk away again," I dared him. "Or better yet, let me leave now. You had no problem pushing me away before."

"There are people who want to hurt you, Belle, and as hard as it is for me to stay away from you, I will walk away before that happens."

"How can you say that?" I demanded. "What kind of life do you think I'll have without you in it?"

The thought was nearly too much to bear. I'd gotten through the last week through compartmentalizing. I'd tucked Smith and the memories we'd shared into boxes and tried to ignore their existence. But deep down, I knew the only reason I'd been able to do so was because I hadn't believed things were truly over. Now that I was forced to face the fact that they might be, I could barely breathe. I couldn't process what he had done to me or why, but deep down I'd suspected there was a reason for his actions.

A low rumble emanated from his chest at being challenged. Smith's hand shot out and clutched my upper arm, his nails digging into the tender skin as he shook me. "I don't give a damn about that. All that matters is that you're breathing. That I know no matter where we are and how much distance separates us that air is passing through those beautiful lips." He dropped his hold on me and took a step back, turning to face the window that looked out over Central

Park. "You're strong, Belle. You are going to create a global empire. Someday you'll forget all about me."

"Is this why you brought me here?" I whispered, my voice brittle with the emotions building in me. "To break my heart again? Because I have news for you, there's nothing left to break. It's shattered—dust. Nothing will ever fix it."

Smith's eyes closed as he shook his head. His hand dropped to his side, breaking the electric connection sizzling between us. "I never wanted this for you. I tried to stay away."

"And you came for me anyway. Or am I just a line item to check off? Was it easier to export me across the Atlantic to do this?" It was a good thing we were in a suite the size of a house because I'd gone from whispering to screaming. The questions scratched my throat as I flung the accusations at him. The pain felt good—real—unlike the surreal nightmare that had trapped me.

"I don't know why you're here," he admitted, "or why I'm here. When I found out you were coming—"

"How did you find that out?" I interjected, crossing my arms as if they could afford me some amount of protection from what was happening.

"I have my sources."

The calmness of his answer made me want to chuck a lamp at him. "Sources? You mean *secrets*."

"Yes!" He rounded on me, stepping so close that the heat of his breath brushed over my face. One more inch and there would be no space left between us. "My secrets protect you. This is killing me. It would be easier to put a gun to my own head than walk away, but who will be there to protect you then?"

"I can protect myself," I said in a measured tone, forcing myself to ignore his closeness, even as a tight ache spread over my skin. One touch. I needed it. I needed one split second of contact to remember as I faced a lifetime of denial.

Which was why I kept myself frozen in place. Giving in wouldn't sate me. It would only make it harder.

"That's where you're wrong." Smith's head fell back as he drew a ragged breath. "Why did I fall in love with you?"

The world skidded to a stop, time slowing to a standstill as his words sunk in. I was still processing when he caught my waist and pulled me violently against him. His lips took even as they gave, reminding me that I belonged to him as he surrendered. All conscious thought fled me as I tangled my fingers in his hair and held him to me. The fear vanished, but the anger remained and I bit into his lip until I tasted blood. Smith groaned, sweeping me off his feet as he smashed his mouth harder to mine and carried me toward the stairs. I had no idea where they led and I didn't care so long as I didn't have to let him go. I drew back, panting, when we reached the top step.

"You're mine," I breathed.

His eyebrows ratcheted up at my possessiveness, but a smile carved across his chiseled face. "In perpetuity."

"That sounds binding," I murmured, a giddy wave of hopeful fear overwhelming me. A moment ago, he'd tried to say goodbye to me. Now I was in his arms. I had no idea what came next.

"As your lawyer, I can assure you there is no escape clause." He pressed his forehead against me. "I can't stay away from you."

"Then don't," I suggested gently.

"I will protect you. You've given me your body, and I'll protect it with my own," he vowed.

"And what about my heart?" I placed a hand on his firm chest. "You carry it with you. Protect it?"

"With every breath I have left on this earth."

I wiggled from his grasp, landing lightly on the balls of my feet as he steadied me. Smoothing his necktie down, I inhaled deeply and released the fear and anger lingering in my core. My fingers closed over the silk, and I tugged gently on it as I led him through the door into a massive bedroom. Smith watched as I reached behind me and drew the zipper of my dress down, allowing the garment to flutter to the floor. I stood before him in my lacy garter and stockings. His jaw tightened as he loosened his tie, sending a pang of anticipation rolling across my exposed skin. My nipples hardened into points, struggling against the lace holding them captive. Smith tossed the tie to the floor and adjusted his erection as his face darkened with the dominance that consumed me.

"Show me," I commanded him, emboldened by his swift, physical reaction. "Show me you belong to me."

His eyes flashed, but he didn't protest. This wasn't how the game was played. Instead he crossed to me, stripping off his shirt and abandoning it. I braced for his hands—for the rough and unyielding brutality with which he always took me, but he dropped to his knees before me. His hands crossed in supplication before him.

He was giving me control. I bit my lip as he carefully plucked the satin gripping my stockings until my garter no longer held them, then he hooked his fingers around the band of my panties and drew them slowly to my feet. He waited as I stepped out of them and widened my stance, granting him access to my sex. Smith's mouth brushed over the smooth skin of my belly, trailing lower until his mouth closed hungrily over my pussy. He didn't use his hands, rather he planted them on the floor as the warm, moist tip of his tongue flicked along my seam, spreading me open. He worshipped me like this, on his hands and knees, his tongue stroking patiently until the first moan spilled from my mouth. He forced his tongue into my hole, circling my swollen entrance until my legs began to shake. I grabbed his hair to keep myself upright as he clamped his teeth gently over my clit and began to suck, urging the first trembling spasms of climax from me. But he didn't relinquish his position, instead he swirled his tongue languidly over my captured bud, freeing me from the agony of want to the numbing bliss of pleasure.

My knees buckled, and he held me upright without changing position. I wanted to collapse against him, needing the familiarity of his arms around me. Smith, however, appeared intent on a different means of comfort. He looked up to me, eyes burning, and waited for my next instruction. My fingers loosened my hold on his hair, but I didn't release him. Pulling softly, I guided him to his feet, still lost for words, and pointed to the bench at the foot of the bed before letting him go. He went to it and sat without a word.

"Take off your pants," I finally managed, my tone lacking the authority usually present in his demands, but he did as he was told anyway.

I studied him for a moment, my eyes lingering over the brutal lines of his arms and legs before they lighted upon the cock jutting up against the flat plane of his abdomen. My mouth watered at the sight, and I had to stop myself from crawling to him in offering. I was in charge, and I wasn't likely to get that opportunity again for while. Reaching behind me, I unhooked my bra and let it fall away. My stockings had rolled down slightly, but I didn't adjust them as I sauntered toward Smith, shamelessly swaying my ass.

"How does it feel to give me control?" I purred, tipping his chin up with my index finger.

"Different," he admitted with a smirk.

I tapped his cheek with my palm. "You're not the only one who can dole out punishments."

Smith crossed his hands behind his head and leaned back, giving me better access to his cock. "Punish away."

"I don't know if I'm punishing you or rewarding you," I said, playfully slapping his shaft.

"Keep doing it and I'll let you know," he advised.

But I had other plans for him. Straddling his lap, I dropped lower until my sex hovered teasingly over his crown. I rocked back and forth, lightly sweeping my slick seam over him. Smith's eyes closed as he groaned.

"A man only has so much patience, beautiful."

"I know you have better control than that," I said in a low voice even as I lowered farther, allowing his crest to breach my folds.

"I wouldn't count on it," he said gruffly. "I'm about a second away from flipping you over and spanking your petulant ass for being coy."

"I see. Is this what you want?" I nudged myself against his tip until he was barely inside me.

"Beautiful." His voice was thick with warning.

Now or never, I thought, knowing he wasn't joking about punishing me. There would be time for that later. The realization coiled through me, tightening across my muscles as I sank down, swallowing his shaft to the root. A slow grin spread across his face.

"That's it," he coaxed.

"How do you like being topped?" I murmured, brushing my lips over his.

"I could almost get used to it." He didn't move as I continued to roll my hips, seeking the perfect balance between depth and friction. He was so deep that it almost hurt—in the best possible way. I didn't ever want to get used to this delicious pain. I wanted to feel it each and every time we made love.

"Say it," I panted as I continued to writhe on his lap.

Smith's fingers found my nipples, pinching and toying with them until my breasts plumped, growing heavy with arousal. "Say what, beautiful? That your body was made for fucking? Or that I want you on my cock every day for the rest of my life?"

A strangled cry escaped me as I shook my head. I was so close—too close. All I needed to be pushed over the edge were three little words. The ones that I'd longed to hear since things had grown so complicated between us. He was everything I never knew I needed, and while that terrified me, I couldn't imagine a day without him either.

"I know," he soothed, wrapping an arm around my waist and drawing me closer. I melted into him as his hips began to thrust. He plunged into me with the precision of a man who understood exactly where a woman wanted to go and also how to get her there. "I know what you need to hear. I love you. Telling you is something I'm going to do every single day, beautiful."

"Oh God, I love you." I forced the words out as tingles turned into a wildfire, spreading white-hot through my limbs as his words burned across my heart. They'd branded me as his, imprinting across me like the molten tip of a knife. I was free and claimed. Liberated and bound. Smith Price owned me entirely.

Soft gasps turned to shuddering cries as I clung to him, wanting him deeper. I needed to be full of him, and as my taut muscles uncoiled around him, I moved harder and faster, lifting my ass and pushing back down even as my own climax diminished into subtle aftershocks that vibrated through my heavy sex. Smith grunted, jerking me down harder as he came, his eyes locking with me. The look we shared was raw and unguarded, each of us lowering our defenses.

His actions—his words—could kill me. I'd opened myself to him, exposed my weaknesses. But he'd shown me his as well. He'd taken my heart and transplanted it with his own.

Apart we were unguarded—defenseless to the outside world.

Together we were invincible.

CHAPTER ELEVEN

Belle slid onto the bed, collapsing into a boneless heap across the downy comforter. I studied her for a moment, trying to process what we'd both committed to. I'd brought her here out of selfishness, convinced I would be able to keep the situation under my control, but as always, she'd effectively destroyed my self-restraint on arrival.

That's what you wanted all along.

Now she was back in my bed. I'd almost managed to sell myself the lie that I could give her up. She looked up at me with her wary, cornflower blue eyes, and I knew she guessed what I was thinking. Reassurance was in order for both of us before we wound up shouting again. Sinking onto the bed, I beckoned for her to come closer. Whatever dominant streak had possessed her earlier was gone now, and she pushed herself swiftly into my waiting arms.

"This is where you belong," I murmured as I kissed the top of her head, drinking in her comforting scent. I wouldn't deny that fact any longer.

"I never forgot that." The accusation was back in her voice. Whatever bliss I'd given her during our lovemaking session hadn't lasted.

"You have questions." I stated it as a fact. We'd given in to our emotions as soon as we saw one another. Now we needed to grapple with the larger issues that threatened to tear us apart.

"Only about a million." Her eyes flickered up to mine, and she stared me down.

"Ask and I will do my best to answer."

"Was the break-up staged?"

God, the woman could be a lawyer. She certainly knew how to go for the throat.

"Yes," I admitted. Her body tensed beside me, but I pulled her closer.

"By whom?"

There was that killer instinct again. Apparently she was going to let the fact that it involved Georgia Kincaid slide. For now. "I work for Hammond, but I also work for someone else."

"No shit, Sherlock," she retorted. "I figured that out a while ago."

But she hadn't figured out whom I worked for, or she wouldn't be asking me for that information now.

"Belle, I said I would do my best to answer, but I also need to protect you. That information is dangerous."

"You don't trust me." Her face fell as she spoke, and I resisted the urge to spill all of my secrets.

"I trust you, but I also love you. I have to weigh the possible consequences of you knowing too much."

"Fine," she huffed. "Was all of this a set-up? Do I even have a meeting tomorrow?"

"I'm a silent partner in Bless. I don't interfere. Your meeting with Abigail Summers is your business."

"And yours, too, it seems." This response was slightly less sarcastic. Progress. "Did you arrange for the meeting?"

I stared quizzically at her. It wasn't like her to show such a lack of confidence. She'd gone about starting Bless with the tenacity that had drawn me to her. Of course, I'd recently fucked with her perception of the world. The idea that I'd undermined her in any way left a bitter taste in my mouth. "You did that."

She relaxed a bit at this revelation.

"Beautiful, I gave you some money. That's where my contribution ended."

"Good." She snuggled against me, obviously pleased. "Speaking of money, how the hell does a lawyer afford a Bugatti and house the size of Harrods and a suite at the Plaza?"

I knew this question had preoccupied her for some time, and it wasn't the first time she'd hinted at wanting answers. More than once, she'd made offhand remarks about my wealth. "From my father. It's not a subject I like to discuss. I'm paid very well for solving questionable legal matters for my clients. But my wealth came from my father's life insurance policy. He left it all to me."

"How much was..." she trailed off, her eyes widening at her own rudeness.

"Ten million," I answered before she could feel too guilty.

"But, your house. Your car."

"It doesn't add up," I finished for her. "The house belonged to my family. My father purchased it not long after we moved from Scotland when he first started working for Hammond. It was an adventure to me at the time. It wasn't until I was an adult that I questioned exactly how he afforded it. Inflation hasn't risen that much." My joke fell flat in the tension hanging between us. "Now I know he must have done something truly heinous to receive such a reward from Hammond."

"Why do you keep it?" she asked softly as she placed her palm on my chest.

I clasped it tightly and shook my head. "I don't know. In a way it's a necessary reminder of what he's done to me and my family. To my parents. To Margot."

She tensed at the mention of my ex-wife.

"It reminds me of what I need to do," I said in reassurance, "not of her. The estate is like a chain around my neck. I can't free myself from it."

"Maybe you could take it off?"

"We both know it's not that simple." Belle carried a similar burden with her family estate.

"You're right. But even if you owned the house. That's not exactly an obscene amount of money."

"Are you saying that I'm worth an obscene amount of money?" I teased.

This time my light-hearted comment had the intended effect. "You are priceless."

She jerked up and smacked me quickly on the lips.

"You're getting us confused again." I brushed her hair back and felt my adoration for her multiply once more. "I was too young to take my inheritance, and as luck would have it, Hammond was the executor in charge of the funds."

"You call that lucky?"

"Not all luck is *good* luck. He invested it for me. God knows how much seedy information he used, but he turned it into a hundred million pounds before I was nineteen."

"A hundred million?" Belle repeated in shock. "And he just gave it to you?"

"Technically, it was mine, but yes. He did. It was play money to him. If he'd lost it all, it wouldn't have mattered. That he made that much didn't matter either. Although it did have the effect of winning me over. Suddenly, I owed him. So when he suggested I take up law at the university, I didn't refuse. It never even occurred to me that I had a choice."

"That's something I understand, too." The melancholy trace of obligation colored her words. "And by the time you started working for him, he owned you."

"You've heard this story before," I murmured, drawing her into my lap.

She blinked, her full lashes fluttering innocently over wise eyes. "Some parts were left out."

"I didn't like those chapters." I swallowed and looked away from her.

Belle's soft hand guided my face back to hers. "No good story lacks conflict. It made you the man you are."

"And what kind of man am I?"

She didn't shrink away at the harsh undercurrent in my voice.

"The kind of man I love," she answered simply.

"I am truly sorry for that."

This time her slap wasn't playful, and my hand shot out and caught her wrist in a tight squeeze. She pulled back, but I didn't relinquish control.

"Don't speak about the man I love that way," she ordered me.

"I don't take orders from you." But despite myself, I smiled. How this woman managed to turn my world upside down every time I was with her was beyond me. The fact that I liked it was even harder to grasp.

"This time you do," she said resolutely.

For a split second, I considered flipping her over and reminding her exactly who was in charge. Instead I shrugged. "Noted."

"That's all?" she countered. "You're not going to spank me?"

"Oh beautiful, I'm going to spank you. Hard. But I'm going to make you wait for it, because I think that's exactly what you want." She squirmed a little, rousing the attention of my cock, which had grown bored of the round of twenty questions. "I have other things in mind first."

"Oh yeah?"

I'd successfully steered her away from the unpleasant topics that had consumed the last hour of our lives.

"Lay across the bed. Feet over the side," I instructed her as I scooped her off my lap and deposited her back onto the sheets. Belle wiggled into place, and my gaze raked over the sight of her long legs still covered in silk stockings and the lace garter resting snugly across her belly. Reaching down, I unhooked it and drew it away before I shredded the hosiery from her.

"Those were expensive," she informed me.

"You really do want a spanking," I said gruffly, stroking my cock with my free hand as I appreciated my work. "I'll buy you more. But for now..."

I wadded the ruined stockings in my hand and held them to her mouth. She shot me a murderous look before she allowed me to stuff them in.

"You can't get yourself in more trouble if you can't talk, beautiful." I stroked my index finger along the plump curve of her lower lip. "Now stay."

My balls tightened as she held still. She was annoyed with me. That was clear. But she couldn't deny me either. The woman really was the perfect bottom. Submissive to a fault when I stripped her down and fiery as hell the rest of the time. Walking to the closet, I stopped and retrieved my tie from the floor. Then I pulled another one from a hanger. The two ties I'd asked her to choose between on her first day on the job. I'd given her a choice that day. She wasn't getting one now.

Returning to the bed, I lifted her leg, guiding her to bend it at the knee. Belle raised an eyebrow, but thanks to the makeshift gag, she couldn't question me as I took her wrist and brought it to her calf. I looped the silk tie tightly, binding her arm to her ankle, and ignored the muffled protest. Apparently, her obedience was a little out of practice.

"If you want me to stop, nod." I waited. But despite the frustrated look on her face, she stayed still and lifted the other leg. "That's what I thought."

I repeated the action. Stepping back, I surveyed my work, admiring the way the bindings put her cunt on display. In a few minutes, her muscles would begin to ache, but I had no doubt that she'd grow wetter with each passing second.

"I'll be right back." I swallowed a laugh as she shook her head and fought against my handiwork. "No."

Picking up the other stocking, I lifted her head and wrapped it around her mouth to prevent her from spitting out the gag. "Do you still want this?"

She stopped fighting and relaxed.

"Then be patient," I said before striding out of the room. I had what I needed already, but I took my time gathering it. Right now, she was probably trying to wriggle free, but only so she could pounce on me. The longer I waited, the more primed she would be. And I'd told her I had plans for her. In the end, my own impatience won out. Belle was still in the bed. She'd managed to scoot herself to the edge.

"Not the best idea," I told her as I set the champagne bucket and towel on the nightstand. "I don't want you bruising your ass before I get a chance to." Drawing out a cube, I held it over her chest, the heat of my hand sending droplets of icy water trickling over her breasts. Her nipples pebbled into beacons of want instantly, and I couldn't resist the urge to take them in my mouth. I sucked each one until I heard her moaning into the gag. Dropping the ice cube onto her navel, I straightened up and watched as it melted into a puddle on her belly before I took another from the bucket. I allowed this one to drip along her engorged sex, the water mixing with the slick proof of her arousal. Belle's eyes rolled back at the sensation, and I moved the remainder of the cube down, bringing it to the tight pucker on display. Her eyes flew open when it made contact, and this time she cried out. The sound made me want to shove my dick inside her, but I refrained, enjoying the little game too much for it to end so soon.

Belle loved being tied up. She got wet when I collared her. But nothing made her body respond more than promises, and I had a few to deliver.

"I'm going to fuck this," I told her, pushing the ice against the quivering hole. "And you are going to beg me to never stop."

She rocked against my hand, urging more contact, even as she looked like she was about to cry.

"It's okay," I soothed her. "I know you want it, beautiful, and I'll give it to you, but not tonight. You have no idea how much I want to right now, but you aren't ready. We're going to work on that. Is that okay?"

She nodded and I smiled. The ice was completely gone now, and

I took another and placed it at the apex of her seam. "Don't move. If that ice falls, I'll have to stop."

Her body tensed, doing her best to comply as it slowly leaked down her slit. I drew my thumb across her pussy, coating it in the slippery arousal spilling from her and began to circle the tight entrance of her ass. "I love your ass. I want to fuck it and paddle it and worship it. You want that too, don't you?"

A choked sob escaped from her as she nodded again.

"Baby steps." I pushed against the snug rim until I was stroking her inside. "I can see your clit pulsing. It must be so hard to stay still, but you're doing so well. I love watching you fight your urges to give me control. It makes me so fucking hard." I pushed deeper and twisted to allow my other fingers to play with her cunt. Sliding my index finger into her weeping pussy, I found her g-spot and began to knead.

"You're going to come so hard for me in a minute, baby, and I want you to let go. You have no control, and I want to see you surrender to that. Can you do that?"

She didn't respond, but I felt her tightening around me. Quickly slipping another finger inside, I moved faster until I was fucking her relentlessly with my hand. Her thighs shook, and she arched up, fighting for balance that her bindings wouldn't afford. I pressed my other hand to her belly, anchoring her to the mattress as she transformed into a convulsing, sobbing wreck before my eyes. Her muscles gave way, too tired to fight any longer and the orgasm ripped through her, sending a gush of warm arousal onto my hand as she came. Then she went utterly still, save for the muscles quivering from the effort that came with being tied up. I withdrew from her slowly, savoring the way she continued to pulse against my fingers. Wiping off my hand with the towel, I then swept it gingerly over her sensitive pussy. Her head flopped from side to side to let me know it was too much, too soon.

"You're such a good girl," I murmured as I undid the ties and rubbed the indentations left on her flesh. "Good girls get to come like that. Are you going to continue to be good for me, beautiful?"

I took off the gag, and she breathed a yes, licking her dry lips.

"Wait right here." I stepped back and she shook her head. I *tsked*softly. "I'm going to draw you a bubble bath, and then I'm going to carry you to it. It might be a while before you can stand on your own two feet again."

"Yes, Sir," she whimpered as she lolled across the bed.

Fifteen minutes later, I scooped her limp body up and placed her in the bath. Belle relaxed into the water, her nipples grazing across the glassy surface. I corked the champagne I'd rescued from the bucket as she soaked. She jolted at the pop, but her eyes remained closed.

"Open your mouth, beautiful," I coaxed, sitting on the edge of the tub.

She obliged, her lips parting to reveal her white teeth. Slowly I drizzled champagne over her full lips, allowing it to trickle over her chin. It spilled across her collarbone, turning into a stream that ran between her perfect breasts.

"Seems like a waste of Dom Perignon," she murmured past the bubbles foaming over her tongue.

"I told you I was giving you a bubble bath." I emptied the bottle. I'd order another later. Another the night after that. I wanted to pamper her, treat her like the queen she was.

"Care to join me?" she asked shyly.

"That can be arranged."

Belle scooted forward, allowing me to slip in behind her. She melted against me as my arms coiled tightly around her torso, drawing her close. From now on, I wasn't letting her go.

"I wish it could always be like this." She sighed, releasing the wish as quickly as she'd stated it.

"Tonight it will be," I whispered in her ear.

"And tomorrow?" she pressed. "Can we pretend that this is our life?"

I heard what she was really asking: could we pretend the outside world didn't matter? I wanted to tell her we could—to promise the nightmare was over. But I'd lied to her before, and I was tired of it.

"Tonight it is."

"And tomorrow?" she asked again.

"Yes," I said, meaning it. Wanting it. "And every day it's in my power."

It wasn't enough. Not for either of us. But for one night, it could be.

CHAPTER TWELVE

The outfit was all wrong. The neckline was too low, dipping to the valley between my breasts. The skirt was too long. It fit me perfectly, as had every piece that had arrived courtesy of Smith's shopping excursion to Harrods, but it still wasn't right.

It wasn't sexy or daring or *enough.* I stared into the full-length mirror in the bathroom, trying to get a handle on exactly what was wrong. Given my company's title, a little black dress was exactly what I needed to wear to this afternoon's interview. But in New York, everyone wore them. I needed to stand out without drawing attention, and I had no idea how to do it.

"So much for becoming a fashion mogul," I muttered at my reflection.

"You're already a fashion icon," Smith said. He came up behind me and wrapped his arms around my waist. "Now what is the problem?"

"It's missing something. I have to impress this editor." Just getting an interview wasn't going to ensure a coveted spot in her magazine. The thought set off a new wave of self-doubt. There were people who would kill to have this opportunity, and I was going to cock it up.

Those people would have no problem walking into the *Trend* offices and wowing everyone with their poise.

God, if I couldn't nail a magazine article, how would I succeed in business?

"You are going to impress her." Smith spoke with an assurance that was typically male, but I shook my head.

"I have tried on every piece I brought."

"Wait here." His arms slipped away, and he disappeared back to the bedroom. When he returned, he held a pair of Louboutins. "These landed you your last job."

I took them, studying the leopard print. They were amongst my favorites, but I couldn't help worrying the print was cliché. I was definitely overthinking things now.

Smith seemed to sense my reluctance. Dropping to one knee, he reached for the shoes. Then he reverently slid them onto my feet. "You walked in to my office in these shoes, and I knew right then and there, you were different. Here was this gorgeous woman. She was polished and professional. I wanted to fuck you on the spot."

"I'm not sure that's what I should be going for," I said dryly.

"That was my response," he said as he stood and took my shoulders. Spinning me around, his eyes met mine in the mirror. "I responded that way because I knew you were a woman who knew what she wanted."

"I wanted a job," I murmured.

"And you got it."

I'd also received him in the bargain. Maybe he was on to something. I studied myself more closely. The black dress, which had felt ordinary moments before, had transformed with Smith's addition. Suddenly I wasn't average. I was bold and commanding. I straightened up, a smile creeping across my face.

"These must be lucky," I said at last.

"That's not it." He shook his head and pulled me against his hard body. "They're simply a representation of who you are. Sexy, sophisticated. A woman that doesn't have to try to draw the attention of everyone in the room."

"You're pretty good at this," I teased. "Do you want a job?"

"I don't think I could handle working under you, beautiful. I'm far too fond of being on top."

Of me. Of the world. Of everything he touched. A tingle danced down my spine. I'd gotten his attention and somehow I'd kept it.

"It's time you stop second-guessing yourself and you start listening to the truth," he continued.

"Are you going to go all alpha on me outside the bedroom?"

"If that's what it takes," he warned me lightly. "But I'm not going to have to, because you already know all of this. You just have to believe it."

I dropped my head to his shoulder. "Now I know why I fell in love with you."

"Were you doubtful before?" He grinned wickedly, pressing his lips to a spot behind my ear.

"I've had my moments." I turned into him, tipping my chin to drink in his handsome face. When we were together like this, it was easier to see how it had happened despite how hard I'd fought to keep him at a distance. I had questioned why I fell in love with him. Hell, I'd worried about my sanity. But since the moment I'd realized I'd fallen, I'd known I loved him. Now, how and why didn't seem important. Not so long as we could stick together.

"You are going to have them eating out of your hand," he promised me.

"How do you know that?"

"Because you've had me eating of your hand since the day we met," he explained. Then he sealed his confession with a lingering kiss that left no room for doubt.

THE EDITORIAL OFFICE OF *TREND* WAS HOUSED IN A BUILDING every bit as imposing as the bustling streets of New York. My eyes traveled up, trying to take in the full glory that was home to the oldest and most important fashion magazine in the world. As if on cue, my mobile buzzed.

"Are you there?" Lola asked when I answered.

I cradled the phone closely, pressing my index finger to my other ear to block the street noise. "I'm here. Remind me why you aren't?"

"Because I have to finish this bloody portfolio. Remember, talk like we're already a huge success," she advised.

"That would be easier if we had so much as a website," I muttered, my stomach flipping over as I stared at the revolving door in front of me.

"It went live two hours ago."

"What?" I squealed. "Are you some type of witch?"

"That's bitch," she corrected me. "We're open by invitation only. Now go in there and wow Abigail Summers."

We hung up, and I strode into the lobby of Dwyer Publishing. If I had the time, I probably would have been intimidated by the polished marble floors and or the oversized screens displaying recent magazine covers. But a freak out was not on the schedule. Instead I headed toward a the lifts.

"Floor?" An attendant asked as I stepped inside.

"Twenty-five."

"Very good." He pushed the button and then returned to a practiced position.

I stared at the old man and his pressed uniform, wondering how long he'd done this job. He'd probably delivered many a hopeful fashionista to that floor. I had half a mind to bombard him with questions.

"You'll do fine," he said kindly as the lift shuddered to a stop.

I managed a nervous smile. The doors slid open and I came face to face with a pretty redhead. Light freckles dusted her porcelain complexion, and, perhaps knowing basic black would only wash her out, she wore a brilliant, emerald green shirt dress.

She stuck her hand out. "Katherine Harper. Abigail's assistant. Can I just say we're so excited about the Bless concept?"

"Th-thank you," I stammered.

"Can I get you anything? A coffee? Water?" She paused, screwing up her face in an effort to recall more options. "Oh, tea?"

"I'm fine," I assured her. Given the way I was shaking, I'd probably spill it all over myself.

"Are you ready to go straight into the interview or would you like a moment?" She continued leading me through the maze of cubicles toward a large corner office.

"I'm ready." That was a lie, but I pasted my smile on.

Katherine waved as we passed a desk. "That's Nolan. He's our international editor. We've borrowed him from France for a few weeks."

Nolan tipped his head, not bothering to look up from his tablet.

"He thinks we're all crass and overweight," she whispered when we were out of earshot.

Judging from that acknowledgment, I'd sensed he had the typical French attitude toward Americans. At least I didn't have to interview with him.

Katherine seemed immune to his attitude, however. She'd dismissed him as easily as he had dismissed her. "We're so eager to hear all about Bless and where you came up with the concept."

Was this what it was like to be wined and dined—in the business sense?

Katherine froze in her tracks and spun around. Her overly cheerful demeanor was replaced by a conspiratorial whisper. "This is pretty overwhelming, isn't it? The first time I walked in here, I thought I was going to throw up."

"I still might," I admitted with a grateful smile.

"Look, Belle, you have a great idea. When I read your partner's pitch, I was sold, and trust me, there are a lot of women who need this service, myself included. Do you know how hard it is to afford to keep up with my own job? I have to come to work in the latest pieces." Her voice continued to lower as she spoke. I could tell it wasn't something she shared lightly. I'd only been in New York for a day, and I already felt like I couldn't keep up with it.

I took a deep, steadying breath. I was here for a reason. The business plan I'd finished over the weekend was solid. Lola's publicity and marketing plan was incredible. We even had the money to fund our launch. Standing in front of me was our first target customer, and she was already sold. Things were in place. "Thanks. I needed to hear that."

"Believe me, my credit cards thank you." She squared her shoulders, her eyes widening in excitement. "Ready?"

"Yes." This time I meant it.

Considering the powerhouse impression I had of Abigail Summers, I was surprised to come face to face with a petite brunette whose hair was piled messily on top of her head. A pair of Versace reading glasses perched on her long nose. Only someone as powerful as the editor of *Trend* could command respect without doing her hair in the morning. She glanced up from her desk long enough to appraise me disinterestedly before turning her attention back to her file.

"This one." She held out a piece of paper, and Katherine scurried to grab it.

"Your appointment is here," Katherine interjected as her boss continued to sort through papers.

"Is she?" she asked, her voice flat as her gaze fixed on me. "Thank God, you're here. Call the doctor, I think I need a new prescription."

Apparently she was a little sarcastic and a lot bitchy. Katherine's eyes darted from me to the desk and back again, softening apologetically at the edges. Annoyance stirred in my chest. I'd dealt with plenty of people like Abigail before. I'd even worked for a man just like her, and if my experience with Smith had taught me anything, it was that people like that only responded to strength.

"Belle Stuart." I stepped toward her desk and stuck out my hand. "It's a pleasure to meet you, Abigail."

So much for staying safely in ass-kissing territory. Arrogance appreciated flattery, but it respected confidence, and respect yielded more between two parties. At least that was what I told myself.

I could also have just totally screwed myself.

Abigail snatched her reading glasses off and tossed them on her desk, rubbing her temple before gesturing for me to take a seat. "Kat, grab us some coffee."

Maybe I'd made the right call, although I decided against telling her that I preferred tea.

"Belle, is it?" Abigail said as soon as her assistant had left the room. "Tell me why you're here again."

I knew exactly why I was here. I'd been going over my talking points for days. Lola had grilled me over them before I'd flown out. The fact that she had no idea why I was in her office was what was tough to swallow.

My eyes locked with hers, and I paused to consider my answer, and that's when I saw it. A slight flicker glinting ominously. Her face was otherwise unreadable. But that was all the information I needed. She knew why I was here.

"Your magazine wants to do an editorial on my start-up," I said in a sugary tone. There was no need to call her on her deception. Abigail Summers was either testing me or punishing me. Either way, I had a good feeling of where I stood with her.

"Let's cut to the chase, shall we?" She folded her hands on her desk and waited for me to respond. I nodded. "We're both busy women, so I see no reason to pretend otherwise. I told Katherine she could do these little pieces because she's concerned about the magazine's image. Or rather, my image. I don't really give a fuck what people think about me."

"I find that refreshing," I said sincerely.

"Then I hope you won't be offended when I tell you that I don't care about a start-up company unless they're cloning Michael Fassbender. No offense."

My eyebrows raised as I pressed my mouth into a thin line. Oh, I was offended. Mostly because her message was pretty clear. "So *Trend* isn't doing a series on female entrepreneurs?"

"It is," Abigail said, "but I'm not. Frankly, this meeting is a waste of my energy."

"Frankly," I said as I stood back up and smiled down at her, "I feel the same way. I'll show myself out."

Katherine met me at the doorway. "Is everything okay?"

"The interview is over," I told her, "and I was leaving."

She sucked in a breath as she shook her head. "I'll be handling the interview personally. I just wanted you to meet my editor."

Too little. Too late. I'd met her brilliant editor, and I was smart enough to know that I'd been dragged into some type of internal power struggle. I dealt with enough of that in my personal life.

"Belle," Abigail called, "I'm sure you're a bright woman with vision and promise but *Trend* isn't about spotlighting potential. It's a showcase."

I should let it go. The best course of action was to nod and walk away. There was very little potential for fall-out in that scenario. But it was pretty clear there was very little possibility that *Trend* was going to be featuring my company. "A showcase whose subscription sales are down over twenty percent in the last year. Your magazine has also cut print runs to less than half of what they were five years ago even though digital magazines only account for 10% of your sales. Not to mention that you're actively courting advertisers for the first time in twenty years, because they're no longer coming to you. Showcase whatever you want. You're the editor. But take it from someone whose business is in the growth stage, you need to worry a little less about your traditions and a little more about your relevance."

Her face remained impassive as I dumped this on her. Abigail picked up her glasses and slipped them back on. "Enjoy your time in New York."

I'd been dismissed. It wasn't the first time, but it was the time that carried the most heartbreak. I'd invested my dream in today, and it had all been a sham. Bless still felt vulnerable to me, as if one wrong move would kill the whole deal.

And I'd just made the wrong fucking move.

I didn't bother to return Abigail's pleasantry; instead I walked out, leaving a dazed Katherine behind me. I'd just passed Nolan's cubicle, wondering if being a wanker was a prerequisite to work here, when she caught up with me.

"I'm so, so sorry," she said breathlessly. "I have no idea what that was about."

I spun around, trying to keep my frustration in check. Katherine had been kind to me from minute one. This wasn't her fault. But since she was the only one around, she was going to bear my rage. "It was about control. She's in control of this magazine."

And you're not, I added silently. I had no idea what was going on between Katherine and her boss, but I had a pretty good idea that neither of them particularly liked one another. It was obvious that Abigail didn't care for her or her ideas.

"She was the one who okayed the idea." A defensive current ran through Katherine's words. "She specifically chose you."

"And she unchose me." I felt a little calmer now. "Katherine, don't worry about it. I'm not interested in being a pity piece. In a few years, she won't be able to ignore me or my company, but I'll be more than happy to ignore her."

Katherine's lips twitched, but she kept the smile off her face. "I'd appreciate that."

"Something told me that you might." The down button on the lift dinged as its doors slid open. "Good luck."

"I'd say the same to you, but I don't think you're going to need it. Not with your attitude."

"Thank you," I said as I stepped inside. "For your words earlier and for the chance to come here."

"I'm not certain you should be thanking me for that." She laughed but it sounded hollow.

I held the door open with my arm. "No, you showed me earlier that I belong here. I belong in your magazine."

"I wish it was my magazine."

"It was your idea to reinvent its image, and it's a good one," I assured her. "But I think right now we're both in the wrong place. I'm going to take this lift and get back to where I'm supposed to be."

"If only I knew where I was supposed to go." Her tone grew wistful.

"You'll figure it out, and when you do, give me a call. The world needs us promising women to stick together."

Katherine leaned in and pecked me on the cheek. "You're right. Now if you'll excuse me, I have to stay here and do my time."

As the lift carried me to the lobby, I considered what Abigail had said. By the time I reached the ground floor, all my anxiety had vanished. This terrifying, life-changing meeting had been nothing but a blip. So *Trend*wouldn't be catapulting my company into super stardom? I could do that on my own.

I dialed Lola, worried that she'd finally fallen asleep, but she answered immediately. "How did it go?"

"Abigail Summers told me that *Trend* wasn't interested in potential, so I rattled off those figures you gave me on the magazine's subscription issues."

"And then what?" Lola was breathless on the other end.

"She told me to enjoy my trip and went back to work." I glided through the revolving door and found myself back in front of the Dwyer building. This time it didn't feel so imposing.

"You scared the most successful woman in fashion." Lola paused. "You're on your way."

"So you aren't mad?" I asked with relief.

"Not at all. There was no way we could launch in that publication timeframe. We aren't ready!"

I froze in my tracks. "Then why am I here?"

"I wanted to scare the future most successful woman in fashion," she teased. "I sent you because now you've faced your biggest rejection. How do you feel?"

"Like proving her wrong," I answered automatically.

"And you're going to."

Yes, yes, I was.

CHAPTER THIRTEEN

The room was utterly still, its furnishings and lighting carefully chosen to blanch color from the room. Walking into the old, and very off Broadway, theatre had the effect of stepping into a vintage postcard. The whole place belonged to a different place and time, even the actors who quietly made their way onto the stage as an antique grandfather clock struck the hour. The two actors unrobed and began to dance in a slow, haunting rhythm. Their movements mirrored one another's and as they're hands finally met, they arched backwards writhing as the song's tempo sped up. But despite how their bodies smashed against one another, they remained separate—two forces of motion colliding but never combining. It was a fight for control.

They had no audience save one beautiful older woman. The lurkers would arrive at dusk for their vicarious thrills.

The Looking Glass was a macabre floorshow, a spectacle of sensual burlesque that managed to unnerve and incite at the same time. I approached the woman watching silently at the bar. She didn't look up as I came nearer, didn't demand to know how I'd managed to get into the closed theatre. Her eyes remained glued to the conflict on stage, her auburn hair cascading down her shoulder and blocking me from studying her once familiar face.

"Mistress Alice," I greeted her in a low voice. That was what she was known by here—the moniker she'd given herself when she concocted her theatre of dreams—but that wasn't her real name. Very few people in New York knew that. In fact, I currently might have been the only one.

She didn't look to me, although her lips curved into a slight smile. "You're on the wrong continent."

"But am I in the wrong place?" We'd seen each other through the years on my occasional trips to the States for business or pleasure. This was the second time she was my business.

"I doubt that, Smith." She stood, her silk robe fluttering gracefully closed over her long legs and gestured toward the rear corridor.

Age had made her lovelier and distance had made her softer. The lines of her elegant face had sharpened even as her smile had grown kinder. She'd only had to put an ocean between her past and herself. It hadn't been a desperate choice. It had been a calculated one.

"How is Georgia?" she asked as she softly closed the door to her private dressing room.

I swallowed. Of course that would be the first person she asked about. "She's well." I didn't elaborate further at this point. "How are you, Samantha?"

"Business is thriving." It wasn't an answer.

I raised an eyebrow.

"I'm lonely," she admitted. "My children insist on staying in London and my lovers tire quickly."

It was a more direct answer than I'd expected, but then again, Samantha had never felt the need to engage in the perverse mind games her husband was so fond of.

"And Hammond?" she asked dutifully.

"Complicated." I chose the word carefully. She was, in point of law, still married to him. Although she'd put an ocean between them nearly ten years ago.

"Everything with my husband is complicated." Her voice was

brittle, coated in regret and self-recrimination. "And you and your sister still work for him?"

"Yes, we do." Now we were coming to the point. Samantha had always considered Georgia and I her adopted children, and in reality, she'd been the nearest thing to a mother I'd had for a very long time. Even as my own mother faded from this earth, she was there. She'd tried to protect us when she realized that the intentions of her husband were far from paternally motivated. But, in the end, she'd ran as we all did. She'd been the only one to ever successfully do it.

Her eyes snapped shut and when they opened they flashed. "She should have stayed."

"I shouldn't have taken her back." It was the closest I'd ever come to apologizing for my naivety.

"You were young." Samantha dismissed my confession. "God knows what Hammond told you was happening to her here."

He had sold me lies and I had swallowed them, choosing to believe that I was the hero sent to deliver my helpless sister from the dangerous chameleon that had deceived us all. I'd flown to New York and lured her home, delivering her into the hands of the true predator.

"In so many ways I broke her as much as he did," I said softly, recalling how readily she'd sank to her knees at Velvet before the cane.

"She's not broken. It would be a mistake to ignore the obvious fact that she is naturally submissive," Samantha advised. "Despite that, his actions were unforgivable."

"You took her for a reason and it never occurred to me to consider that."

"Have you ever considered that she wanted to go back?" Samantha asked in a soft voice that highlighted the trace of Scottish burr that we both shared.

Yes. I had come to understand that Georgia had chosen to return to England and to Hammond's bed. Just as she had chosen to continue this charade. But with age had come a rationality that had saved her, in part, from herself. There was an intentionality to her decisions that had been absent then. "She was too young to make that choice."

"But now she's made another?" Samantha guessed. "Or have you come to see my show and play?"

"Both, I suppose. If you have tickets available."

"For you and?" She trailed away, the question hanging in the air between us.

"A woman."

"That I suspected," she said dryly.

"And yet you asked," I countered. "My girlfriend is with me on this trip."

"She must be important to bring her here—or perhaps she is understanding?"

"We'll come for the show." My message was clear. Belle could appreciate Samantha's delicate, provocative theatre, but I wasn't about to descend with her to Wonderland, not after what had happened with Velvet.

"It's a pity that you two don't see eye to eye on such matters."

I hadn't come to explain the intricacies of my sex life with her. "I'm afraid there's a bit more to it than that."

"You'll bring her then. I'd like to meet the woman who captured your interest so entirely."

"Perhaps." Given what we had to discuss it was possible her invitation would be rescinded. Time and distance might undermine the sense of betrayal she'd once felt. She had remained married to Hammond through the years.

"I suppose there's no sense avoiding this business any longer." Her arm stretched toward a weathered side table for a crystal decanter. Samantha poured us each a drink.

"You still have a penchant for gin." I set my glass to the side.

"I see you don't."

The truth was I didn't have the stomach for drinking today. "There's been some developments at home."

Samantha downed her drink in one long swig. "And you're here to do what exactly? Drag me home or warn me to stay put?"

"I'm here as a courtesy."

"To whom?" she asked.

"To you." This was my calculated risk. Telling Samantha was a gamble, because her loyalty to Hammond was questionable. To my knowledge the two hadn't spoken for years but they also hadn't divorced.

"I have a feeling I'm going to need another drink." She filled her glass again but she didn't gulp it down. Instead she caressed the rim with her index finger, her eyes staring straight through me to a place beyond this room.

"Hammond is under investigation." The trick to cluing her in was to only give herself enough warning to prepare her own affairs.

"Does he know this?"

It was the one question I'd hoped she wouldn't ask. If I lied and said he did, I ran the risk of her innocently revealing it to him. If I told her the truth, I gave her the rope to hang me.

Samantha's head tilted so that her gaze refocused on me. "You don't have to answer that."

My silence already had, and my hesitation had told her something else.

"I don't blame you," she said after a few moments of heavy silence. "He's done unforgivable things...."

"But?" I sensed the qualification without her making the excuse for him.

"No but." She smiled wanly and took a drink. It slid down her throat with an audible gulp. "As his lawyer you know we're still married. What happens if...if he's arrested? Am I in danger?"

"There's no longer an *if*, Samantha. The arrest is coming."

She didn't ask how I knew that. She'd already guessed I had a role in what was to come. "Will I be extradited?"

"That's highly unlikely."

"But not impossible." She didn't wait for me to answer. "It's no matter. My affairs have been separate from his for years."

"That was a judicious move," I reassured her. It was entirely possible that she would be sought out by the courts, but more than likely as a witness against her husband's crimes. That she had fled the country so many years before indicated that she too feared his reach. But giving the mounting evidence we'd collected and turned over to the authorities, her testimony was mostly unnecessary.

There was little more I could do to reassure her. I'd accomplished what I came to do. "I should be going. I'm certain you have things to attend to before this evening's performance."

"I appreciate you coming here to warn me," Samantha said as she walked me leisurely toward the door. "It's best not be caught off-guard by hearing it from the paper, I suppose."

"You did your best to protect us. You tried to help Georgia." I lowered my voice. "You genuinely cared when so few people did."

Samantha took my chin in her papery hand and studied me before sighing. "But did I do enough?"

"You did more than anyone else." I wrapped my arms around her lithe frame and hugged her tightly. She had tried and although I'd once blamed her for abandoning us. I understood now. Some choices were between life and death. Living with Hammond—living with his toxic deceit—was a slow death. I couldn't begrudge her flight from that agony.

"Bring this woman to my show." Samantha's eyes narrowed into slits as she poked a finger into my chest. This time it was an order. "I'd like to meet her and perhaps you'll show her other things as well."

I clenched my jaw, trying to hold back what could be misinterpreted as an insult. "She struggled with Velvet."

"Velvet has its own ghosts," she said wisely. "You're unmatched there. You have too much history with that place."

She was right. There could never be a true exchange of power there. Not while I clung so tightly to my control whenever I entered its door.

"I'll consider it," I reiterated, still unwilling to commit.

"Don't hide who you are from her, Smith." The sharp edge of warning ran through her words.

"She's seen the beast inside me." I spoke so softly I wasn't certain she could hear me.

"There is no beast," Samantha admonished, ruffling my hair. "Only a man."

I wanted to believe her, but she saw me through a mother's eyes, and although she had some sense of the depths of my depravity, our relationship had never crossed the lines that Hammond's had with Georgia. "If only that were true."

"All humans are creatures subject to our basest needs."

I didn't bother to correct her again. I'd given Belle a choice. I'd hinted at who I was. I'd given her a taste. She'd chosen to stay with me. She'd also chosen to walk away. The woman was subject to nothing. She was the one in control. That made her the only light shining in the darkness of my world.

It made her the only one capable of saving my soul.

CHAPTER FOURTEEN

I wandered the streets for a few hours as I contemplated my next move. Decisions had to be made. When I finally returned to the hotel, I nearly stumbled on the leopard print heels that had been left in the entry. She'd made it as far as the suite's dining room table. I watched her from the doorway, not wanting to disturb her as she worked. The purple glow of twilight lit across her fair features, turning her porcelain complexion rosy. Belle was always lovely, but today haloed in the late afternoon light she looked like an angel—a fucking brilliant, sexy as sin angel. Her brows knitted together as she typed furiously. Withdrawing my mobile I snapped a photo of the unguarded moment. The shutter sound broke her concentration and she glanced up, a smile spreading slowly across her face.

"I hope you got my good side," she muttered in mock annoyance.

I laughed as I selected the picture and set it as my mobile background. "They're all good sides."

"You're too easy on me." She leaned back in her seat, revealing more notes strewn around her.

That was because being with her was easy. It hadn't always been. Not when we had been caught up in trying to deny our attraction to one another. Since we'd given in the outside world had gotten more complicated but us—the us that existed in private—was simple.

"How was your meeting?" I crossed to her and began to knead her shoulders. Belle shifted back, allowing me a glimpse of her pale, creamy throat.

She sighed before answering in a tired voice, "Terrible."

"Oh?" I had to restrain myself from loosing my temper. The idea that things had gone poorly—that she was upset—lit a slow, simmering rage at my core.

"It doesn't matter." Her hand caught mine and squeezed, instantly soothing the fury building inside me. "I don't know what I expected, but the editor was a bitch."

I made a mental note to look into this editor. "I'm sorry."

It was the most comfort I could offer at the moment.

"I'm over it. Really," she said when I shot her a dubious look.

"Dinner?" I said. I didn't believe for one second that she'd written off whatever had transpired this afternoon. Perhaps a little wine would ease the story out of her.

She bit her lip, glancing quickly to her laptop. "I have a few more emails to return."

"Isn't the lawyer supposed to be the workaholic?"

"I know, right?" She pulled gently out of my grasp. "Give me an hour?"

"That will be perfect, beautiful." I pressed a kiss to her forehead before excusing myself to attend my own business. An hour would also give me time to prepare for the evening.

Georgia didn't answer her private line, not shocking given the time difference between London and New York. No doubt she was preoccupied with matters at the club. I'd seen to most of my other affairs before I'd left which gave me to time to arrange dinner. An hour later, I pried Belle from her work and led her onto the suite's private terrace with my hands clapped over her eyes. Only a pink sliver of sunset remained over the horizon. The city was covered in a dusky haze that sketched buildings into shapes and the trees of Central Park into bare limbs against the twinkling lights of distant skyscrapers. Autumn in New York was a magical time, when the bustling city contracted in preparation for winter.

I released her when we reached the table that Geoffrey had set up in the middle of the patio. A half dozen candles illuminated the simple spread of pasta I'd asked him to procure from Garazzo's, one of the few establishments that had survived since the first time I'd visited the ever-changing metropolis. There was a certain elegant rustic quality to classic Italian home cooking, and Belle's gasp of delight rewarded the effort I'd put into arranging the dinner.

I pulled out the chair, my hand remaining on its back until her napkin was tucked into her lap.

"This looks amazing," she said, ladling a massive helping of pasta onto her plate. "I just realized I skipped lunch."

"So your meeting was terrible but you still felt the need to work all afternoon?" I couldn't quite figure out if she was working through disappointment or trying to keep herself busy to avoid feeling it.

"It was," she admitted. She swirled her fork around the noodles and took a large bite.

"I'd like to hear about it."

She paused as if to consider my request before she related the events of her interview with Abigail Summers. When she finished I was barely controlling the seething anger about to boil over.

"You're mad," she noted when she finally finished.

"It was disrespectful," I said in a low voice. I could think of a few more choice terms to describe Summers's behavior but I kept them to myself. I

"Yes," she said, "but Abigail Summers gets to be disrespectful. Honestly, I'm over it."

"You?" I repeated pointedly.

"Apparently," she said, dropping her napkin onto the table and creeping over to my lap, "I deal quite well with rejection these days."

"Don't look at me, beautiful. I'm not about to test your theory." My arms circled around her trim waist. "I only want you closer."

We stayed like that under a black painted sky. The noise of the city dying away until the only sound I processed was her faint breathy inhalations.

"Up here you can almost see the stars." She gazed into the darkness, searching for their glittering presence. "It was one of my favorite things about my family's estate."

She spoke of her family home as if it was already lost. I knew otherwise, although I'd chosen not to get involved until she asked me —or the situation became dire.

"I hardly remember the stars," I admitted.

"We should go somewhere quiet where they aren't hidden by the city," she murmured.

"Of course, beautiful."

"I want it to be like this forever," she whispered. "Just us."

Us. The subject had been on my mind perpetually since she had arrived in my suite yesterday. If I was being honest I'd thinking about us since long before then. Here, high above the chaotic city, we seemed possible once more. I hadn't been able to figure out how to make it work in London. I had forced her to face me so that I could explain. My orchestrated betrayal had burrowed like a deeply imbedded thorn, and I'd been certain that the only way to remove it was to tell her the truth. Or as much of it as I dared to share. "We could if we stayed here, beautiful."

She laughed lightly but the bell-like sound ceased when her eyes met mine. "You're serious?"

"Why wouldn't I be?" I asked her. "You're the only thing tying me to London and now you're here."

Belle tilted her gorgeous face up to stare at me. I already knew here answer. "I have a life in London."

"I know. I wan't serious," I said dismissively.

"You were serious," she said, her voice growing softer as she continued, "I wish I could be, too, but I have Clara and the new baby. My aunt. Edward."

I had to remind myself that the ties that bound her to London weren't the shackles that held me captive. Belle had people that she loved, something that I didn't, holding her there. Each name she spoke was a reminder that I wasn't her entire world.

"You look jealous," she accused.

"You can't blame me for wanting you all to myself." She could, in fact. It was selfish and short-sided. Those people had made her who she was, transforming her into the woman I loved, and if I could, I would take her away from all of them. Samantha had been wrong. I was a beast, a primitive creature that knew nothing beyond my own wants. And right now, I would trap Belle if I could. Back her into a corner. Scare her into staying. And not an ounce of me felt guilty for that.

"You're going to have to learn to share," she teased, trailing her index finger across my palm.

"I don't share, beautiful," I reminded her. "You belong to me."

This silenced her. When she finally spoke, her words came out in halting and half-formed. "I do. But...Smith, I want....more."

"More that me?" I swallowed hard on this revelation.

"Yes, and no," she tacked on swiftly. "If I have to choose, I'll choose you. Every time. At any cost. I just wish it wasn't the case."

"I do, too, beautiful."

This time I spotted the slide of her throat. "Then we'll move to New York. It would be good for Bless."

She was willing to give it all up. Uproot her existence and fore sake all others. It was what I needed to know. "No," I said firmly. "Birds of a feather, remember?"

"I don't want to go home if its going to be dangerous for you," she murmured, finally giving words to the fear that had driven her to such a desperate agreement.

How could I tell her that I wanted to keep her here for that reason? That returning to London together was akin to painting a bullseye on her back? "I don't want to give you up."

The thoughtless words slipped from my mouth and lodged between us.

"What happened to facing the storm together?"

I turned away from her, searching for her answer in the dark, moonless night. She grabbed my face, her nails digging into my jaw.

"Don't you dare." A hysterical edge seeped into her voice. "You were right. I can live without you, but I don't want to. I am strong, but I'm stronger with you. We're stronger."

But we aren't invincible. I kept the thought to myself. "I'm stronger with you, too."

And yet, she was my greatest weakness. She had made me vulnerable. If Hammond made a move, if he placed stock in suspicion, it was no longer a simple matter of killing me.

"Then don't ever say that again." She blinked and tears cascaded down her face. "Don't ever fucking saying that."

I swiped them away with the pad of my thumb. "I won't."

"Sometimes you can be such a bloody wanker," she said with a sniffle.

"And still you love me," I teased.

"No one ever accused me of having good judgment." Her lips curled at the corners.

This was how I wanted to spend this time with her. Trials awaited us in London and, sooner than I would like, we would have to face them. "We only have a few days. Let's enjoy them. Pretend that we're on a holiday and we have nothing but a blissful, simple life ahead of us full of sex and success and..."

"And?" she prompted, willingly joining me in my game. "What else do we have in this ideal life?"

I brushed a finger along her chin. "I don't know. If we're playing pretend, I suppose we could have anything we wanted."

"If only." Belle's eyes fluttered down, her cheeks darkening.

"If only what?" I pressed. "What do you want, beautiful? Let me give it to you. Maybe not today or tomorrow. But someday. Let's keep ourselves focused on someday."

"I don't know. It's...silly. I don't even know what I was thinking exactly."

I understood. Belle was a woman—an ambitious woman—but

that didn't mean she'd given up on more domestic pursuits. "A ring?" I guessed.

"Someday," she repeated softly. "I know it's a long way off. I'm not ready either. I just..."

"What else?" I asked, ignoring her insecurity. "A baby?"

Her eyes widened. "You don't...um..."

"I don't seem the type. I know, but I'll let you in on a secret. People change, beautiful." I kissed her softly. "You changed me."

Never mind that all of this was a fantasy. For a moment I needed to pretend it was possible, because she deserved that much. If she was willing to give up everything for me, I wanted her to know that I would do everything in my power to give her a full life.

"Are you saying you want a baby?" she asked, her eyes narrowing suspiciously. "Or are you trying to get in my knickers?"

"I'm always trying to get in your knickers." I slid a hand down her belly and pushed it between her thighs. "A baby is a while off, but I wouldn't mind the practice."

"How generous of you." The dryness of the comment was undercut by her sharp intake of breath as I rubbed her sex through her dress's silky fabric.

"I can be *very generous*." My thumb began to circle, using the material for added friction. "Even when you're fully clothed, I can't keep my fucking hands off you. It feels good, doesn't it? Having your panties scratching over your clit? Are they wet yet, beautiful?"

I already knew the answer. Her dress had grown damp as I continued to manipulate her pussy through her clothes.

"Yes," she moaned.

"I can feel it." I captured her mouth and kissed her deeply. When I broke away, she was trembling. "We should get you out of these clothes."

Hooking an arm around her, I guided her onto her feet. My fingers found the zipper hidden under her arm and I slid it down slowly as I continued to kiss her. "You're mine, aren't you?" I asked. "Do you want me to claim you for all of New York to see?"

We were far too high up to risk casual sightings from the street, and the seclusion of our suite's terrace afforded a great deal of privacy. I had no desire to share Belle or her body with anyone else. Still there was no way to discount any voyeurism.

Her breath sped up and she bit her lip before nodding.

"You're so dirty." I continued to strip her until she standing naked in the crisp, evening air. Her nipple were sharp points, and although she shivered, she didn't complain of the cold. "It's cold, isn't it? But you want it so bad that you don't care. Get on your knees."

Belle lowered herself one leg at a time. Her wide eyes remained expectant as she stared up at me. I backed away from her, unfastening my belt and then my trousers. By the time I reached the terrace railing, I was stroking myself off with one hand. With the other I beckoned her to come to me. There was no hesitation as she dropped onto her hands and crawled obediently to my feet. She rocked back onto her heels until she was kneeling before me.

I brushed my thumb over her lip, smearing her red lipstick over her mouth, my other hand still on my cock. Pushing the tip of my thumb past her lips, I smiled approvingly as began to suck it. "Do you know why crawled to me, beautiful?"

She nodded but didn't answer, too intent on the finger she had between her lips. I pulled it away and waited for a response.

"Because I'm yours," she whispered. The dark fringe of lashes fluttered innocently over her large, blue eyes as she answered. She felt the truth of us–understood the primal, irrevocable connection that we had formed. It was an undeniable as our need to breath. It was as captivating as my obsession with her.

"Always," I promised her.

She leaned forward, pressing her mouth to the bulge of my dick. I felt the heat of the kiss through the fabric of my pants and my balls tightened. The way she kept her eyes glued to mine as she worshipped it made my cock throb. It was hard to patient with her offering her body but I didn't want to move. Not while she waited for permission, looking so fucking gorgeous on her knees.

God, I loved this woman. It would be a mistake to think she wasn't the one who was actually in control. She had me, quite literally at the moment, by the balls. I fisted her hair and jerked her head back no longer able to deny myself. Her tongue licked across her lower lip as I pulled my dick out.

"You may," I told her, knowing she waiting for me to instruct her even as I knew what she really wanted.

Belle's tongue lashed out, sweeping along the length of my shaft as she drew her lips to my crown. She swirled the tip languidly before she swallowed me to the root and began to suck.

"That feels so fucking good," I grunted, tightening my grip on her hair. "I love having my cock in your hot, greedy mouth."

But there were things I loved more and right now they were on display for me. The petite buds of her nipples, the generous curve of her ass. I'd never say not having her on her knees but right now I needed to possess her. I wanted my hands on her body, holding her steady as I took her. I pulled her away by the hair, her lips popping loudly as I broke the suction.

"Up," I commanded, grabbing her under the arm and hauling her to her feet. She liked it rough and I fucking loved to comply. Pushing her forward against the rail, I slid my belt free and wrapped it around her wrists before hooking it over the rail and fastening it.

I left her like that, tied to the railing, naked and trembling in the night air as I rolled up my sleeves. It was quite the sight: the most perfect woman in the world, stripped and bound, against the New York skyline.

"Are you sure you don't want to move to New York, beautiful?" I murmured against her ear. "I don't know were else I can find a view like this."

Her hips wriggled back, searching for contact and I smacked her ass lightly. Tonight was on my terms.

"I'll take that as a no." I fondled the soft mound between her thighs as I spoke until she was whimpering and shaking. "By the time I'm done with you, you might reconsider."

Then I slid deep inside her and gave her something to think about.

CHAPTER FIFTEEN

The pain shot through me and I twisted, trying to escape it. I cried out, but no sound issued from my throat. I wanted it to stop. I wanted him to stop, but we were well past that point.

The cane cracked down against my tender flesh and I collapsed. This time it hurt so badly that my breath hitched. My legs burned with the effort of fighting as the ropes bit into my wrists. Smith circled me and I gazed, pleadingly, up at him. But he either didn't notice or he didn't care. He was someone else—someone I didn't know. Where was the man who loved me? Why had he been replaced by this monster?

I sat bolt upright in bed, my skin slick with sweat. Smith fumbled for the light on the nightstand as I gasped for air.

"What's wrong?" he asked, reaching to soothe me.

I scrambled away, glaring at him. His look said it all. I'd been replaced by a wild creature, my only thought to protect myself.

"It was a dream," he said in a low voice. "A nightmare."

A dream. None of it was real, even though I could swear I felt the sting of where I'd been struck. I wrapped my arms around my chest, hugging my body as I began to rock.

"Beautiful, you had a nightmare," he repeated. This time the truth sank through the fog of sleep clouding my consciousness.

We sat in silence for a few minutes as I gradually came back to the here and now.

"Do you want to tell me?" He spoke gently, and I collapsed at the kindness in his voice. He was still here. He was still Smith. My Smith.

"You...you were beating me," I choked out. "Beating me with a cane."

His lips pressed into a thin line, a vein twitching at the side of his jaw. We both knew what had prompted the dream. It was a subject we had avoided speaking of, but there was no possibility that we could ever fully ignore it. I understood that now. This time when he reached for me, I didn't attempt to escape. Instead I let him pull me against his body. He murmured soothing praise in my ear as he stroked my back. Even then I couldn't let it go.

"Why?" I pushed the question past dry lips. "Why did you do that? Why did you choose her?"

"Because I wanted you to walk away and never look back." His confession was harsh only due to the truth it contained.

I knew that was the reason he'd put me through that scene. But regardless of his intentions, I couldn't dismiss the pain it had caused me to see him striking Georgia in Velvet. Or the betrayal that clung to the memory.

"Why her?" I repeated.

"Because she was willing and because I knew it would hurt you."

I jerked away from him, not bothering to hide the horror I felt.

"Do you still want a submissive?" I demanded. "Someone you can beat? Will you ever be happy with me if I can't give you that? If I won't?"

"I don't want that," he said in a firm tone that left no room for questioning. "I didn't want to put you through that to begin with, and it's certainly not the life I want. Or the life I've chosen. I chose you, beautiful."

"That night you chose her." I spit the accusation at him. "You still like it, don't you? Dominating a helpless woman?"

"No! I don't. That's my past. It's not my future."

"If it's what you needed," I continued, ignoring his answer, "take me there. Tie me up. Whip me. Choose me."

"I already chose you, and I don't need to do those things to you. I want our relationship to be out of pleasure. I want to make you come and make you laugh. I want you to be happy." But the flatness of his response suggested he understood that it was far more complicated than that.

"You asked me to go there. You hurt me and then you came back for me!"

"My hand was forced. You know what I'm trying to accomplish."

"No! I don't!" I exploded. All he'd given me were partial explanations, enough to soothe but not enough to appease the gnawing uncertainty that came with my self-doubt. I felt ashamed for offering my body to abuse at the same time that my desperation grew to manic levels. "Take me there."

"Absolutely not."

His denial stung, and I shook my head. "Not there. You came to New York for a reason. There's a club here surely. Tell me I'm wrong."

He hesitated and I knew immediately that I'd trapped him.

"Where?" I pressed. I stumbled out of bed and began pulling items from the closet. "What do you wear to a BDSM club? Or do I go naked?"

"Come to bed."

But I wasn't giving in this time.

"Take me there. Show me." My voice softened. I couldn't be kept from this part of his life—this element of his past—any longer. "I want all of you. I won't settle for less."

Smith's expression was unreadable as he appraised me. Finally, he spoke. "Wear a dress. Nothing expensive."

"Panties?" I began to tremble as I pulled a simple black shift from a hanger.

"Yes. I'm not putting you on display." He held up a hand when I opened my mouth to protest. "I'll show you why I came to New York.

I'll take you to who I went to see, but it ends there. If you fight me on this, I'll put you a flight in the morning."

"You can't dictate my life, Price."

He flinched at my use of his surname, but I was well past caring. It was time to face our demons and try to survive them. I couldn't live with the possibility that we couldn't. I had to prove to myself otherwise.

From the street there was nothing special about the building the cab driver delivered us to. It was past midnight, and there wasn't a soul in sight. The cabbie looked nervously at the spot. "You sure this is the place?"

"Yeah, we're good." Smith tossed a tip in his direction, which effectively silenced his concerns.

Smith didn't reach for my hand as we walked to the door. Unlike Velvet, it opened immediately and the sound of smooth, dreamy music floated toward us. I stepped in behind him and stopped. This wasn't a club, it was some type of late-night theatre. On the stage, a group of scantily-clad dancers performed a sensual number. Two men pushed and pulled, tugging at the woman in between them. She collapsed in one's arms only to have him toss her in the air. The other man caught her, even as her hair grazed the hard wooden floor beneath them.

There were only a handful of people in the audience. No doubt the show was drawing to a close. Turning on my heel, I shot Smith a withering glare, but he looked past me.

"Mistress," he said in a greeting, and I spun around to face an elegant woman dressed in a sweeping, floor-length gown that glistened ruby in the dim, atmospheric light. She was in her mid-forties, her hair cascading gracefully over a bare shoulder.

"You've joined us, and I see you've brought your friend." Her thinly plucked eyebrow curved into a question mark.

"Belle, meet—"

"Samantha," she interjected. "My clients call me Alice, but you're not a client."

It was an explanation of sorts, but I found myself struggling to process what I was experiencing. So this was the woman who Smith had come to see. Judging from the Scottish accent that coated her words, she was someone from his past.

"Welcome to The Looking Glass. It's a pet project." She motioned for us to follow her to the bar. Catching the bartender's eye, she held up three fingers. A moment later, three petite glasses sat before us.

"Absinthe." She lifted one and handed it to me. "It makes the impossible probable."

I swallowed it in one gulp, nearly gagging on its unapologetically licorice flavor.

"She wanted to meet you," he explained, not bothering to take the drink she offered him.

Samantha studied me for a moment with sharp eyes. "I think she came for more than that."

"I came for answers," I said. If no one was going to start talking, I was going to start asking. "Like who the hell you are and why he had to come so far to talk to you?"

"She is a fiery one." Samantha spoke to him as if I wasn't there.

"You have no idea," I warned her.

"You came for answers, but you also came for release," she guessed. "From the secrets that are burdening you and the fear that accompanies them."

It was like talking to a goddamn sphinx. If I'd hoped she'd be more forthcoming than my mysterious boyfriend, I supposed I would be disappointed. But nothing surprised me anymore, not when it came to the complicated, thorny relationship I had with Smith.

"Samantha is Hammond's wife."

I'd been wrong. He could still shock me.

"I left him years ago," she said in elaboration. "Smith keeps me apprised of what's going on at home."

"And what did he tell you?" I asked. "Probably more than he told me."

"That a shift in the wind is coming."

More riddles.

"He came to warn me," she continued, waving a hand dismissively as though it was nothing out of the ordinary. "And you came for Wonderland."

"Does this bitch come with a decoder ring?" I snapped, but she only laughed.

"I can see why you aren't taking her as a submissive."

Damn right, he wasn't. I was too busy seething to actually say it out loud.

"You'll take her there and show her. It's the only way to soothe her." Her instructions were clear, and it left little doubt in my mind that Hammond's wife had been as deeply entrenched in London's seamy, sexual underbelly as her husband.

"We'll take a look." His meaning was clear.

But that didn't mean I was going to abide by his wishes.

"You know the way," she told him. Then she leaned closer and whispered in my ear, "Fall down the rabbit hole and open your mind."

My skin crawled from the heat of her breath, but as soon as she said it, she vanished back into the theatre.

"Show me," I commanded. Tonight I was calling the shots, and he was going to have to deal with it. Smith motioned toward a corridor and I strode forward. There was no place for fear here, but my blood still pounded erratically in my veins. I'd asked to come here, and now I would face the thing that scared me the most.

The fear that I couldn't be what he needed.

A door painted in gem tones waited at the end of the hall, and Smith opened it for me. There were more people inside than had been in the audience. Apparently, Samantha had the same penchant for covering her sins as her husband. A few heads turned in our direction, but no one spoke as we passed through the richly decorated lounge. On the far side of the room, a large mirror reflected back the scene before me. A naked couple sat on the couch, and at their feet a woman bound in red rope held the end of a leash in her teeth. After my experience at Velvet, I didn't find this shocking, but it made me queasy. This was the world Smith had once inhabited. It was the world he might still want to be part of, and I wasn't certain I could exist there with him.

Smith bypassed the seating area and went to another door. He paused, as if steeling himself, and opened it. I followed him inside, surprised to find it empty. I startled as a lock clicked into place behind us. I turned my attention back to the only furniture in the room: a strange X that loomed in front of a large window. Peering through the glass, I realized I was looking at the lounge. The mirror I had seen had been a trick. I waved at the people on the sofa, but they stared past me, unseeing.

"They can't see us," Smith said as he removed his jacket. "If we're going to do this, it will be on my terms."

I opened my mouth to protest, but he silenced me with a raised hand.

"I'm not sharing you. I'm not putting you on display," he informed me in a gruff voice. "And I'm not torturing you, but I will show you what I want to do to you."

His words shivered through me and I nodded.

"Take your clothes off."

I rushed to peel the dress over my head. It took several attempts given that my hands were now shaking as badly as the rest of me.

"I'm not going to hurt you," he reassured me. "And as soon as you ask, this stops. Say the word red and it's all over."

I could do that. I could do this. I trusted him.

Didn't I?

Smith took my hand and guided me toward the cross. "Put your arms up."

I placed my arms against the wooden planks.

"I'm going to fasten you to this," he explained. "And then I'm going to punish you for doubting me."

I gulped against the lump that formed immediately in my throat.

Smith buckled a leather restraint over each wrist. Then he bent down. I struggled to see him, but then I felt another leather strap fastening over my ankle. I was spread before him, naked and bound. I'd asked him to do this, and now I needed to trust that I could live with whatever came next. He stood next to me and slowly unbuttoned his shirt before stripping it off. The sight of him, bare from the waist up, made my sex throb. But this wasn't about pleasure. That's not why I was here.

I was here to be punished.

I wished I could say that the thought scared me more than it excited me, but it didn't. I hung my head in humiliation. This was how badly I wanted him—how much I needed to be part of his world.

"You're stunning," he said. "Your fear makes you more beautiful, and your trust makes you irresistible. I'm so fucking hard right now. I want to fuck you until you beg forgiveness, but that's not what you want is it?"

I tried to nod but I couldn't. Smith's hand caught the back of my neck. "Answer me."

"No."

"What do you want?"

"To be punished," I answered in a small voice.

"Good girl." Smith released me and moved across the room, out of my line of sight. When he returned, I heard the slight slap of something against his palm. A moment later, cool leather brushed along my backside. "Breathe, beautiful."

I forced myself to even as panic swelled in my chest. Then he struck. I flinched but only as a reflex. The tails of the whip barely smacked along my skin. They spread like teasing tendrils over my ass. I felt my flesh warm, but it didn't hurt. Instead the pulse growing between my legs ratcheted up.

"You're already getting wet," he commented. "I can see it. This isn't going to hurt, but you're going to wish it would. Because then you wouldn't have to feel the ache of your cunt with each strike."

I moaned as he lashed me again. The heat radiating through my rear was pleasant, but it wasn't the pleasure I craved. I squirmed against my restraints, my thighs trying to press together for relief.

Smith clicked his tongue. "Only I can grant you release. That's what you want, isn't it?"

I choked out a yes.

"Then ask me to whip you again. This time I won't stop."

"Please, Sir." The request fell from my lips as naturally as a breath.

He complied, swinging the whip in fast, successive motions that stole every thought from my mind. All that existed was the want building in my core, and each time he struck, I willed the tails of the whip to smack against the swelling need at my center. But he knew what he was doing. He would deny me pleasure until he determined I deserved it. My teeth bit against the soft flesh of my bottom lip as I struggled to keep my pleasure in check. He'd pushed me to the edge, and I had to cling to it, knowing he would be displeased if I allowed myself to lose control. But it grew harder as he continued, until the pleas began to spill from my mouth. Wanton. Urgent.

The whip flapped to the floor, and I heard the merciful click as his belt unbuckled. Smith placed a palm over my sex lightly. If I could move, I would have pressed into it and shattered at the contact.

"You're dripping." There was lusty approval in his voice now. He reached up and quickly unfastened each hand. I gripped the wooden cross for support as he undid my ankles and helped me down. "Against the window. You're going to look out at those people you fear while I fuck you, and then you're going to know that this—that what happens here—is between us and only us. It always will be."

He guided me to the glass, and I flattened against it as he wrenched my hips back. The head of his cock nuzzled against my sensitive seam, and I braced myself, knowing I wouldn't be able to control myself when he finally breached my entrance.

"You're going to scream when you come," he instructed in a husky voice. "And you're going to thank me for fucking you—for making you mine."

He paused, the tip of his penis positioned against me, and then he plunged inside. I cracked open, pleasure flooding through me as my cries poured out. Through the window, nothing changed. No one moved. No one looked up at me. I didn't exist to them. I only existed here in the presence of the man who had claimed me as his own.

"That's right. This is what you need. I know that, beautiful." He continued to thrust tirelessly as I quaked around him. And as my spasms calmed, I cried in gratitude.

"Thank you. Thank you. Thank you." I said it because it was the only thought I was capable of. He'd given me what I needed. He'd centered me even as he stretched me thin and taut. This was what I needed. He was what I needed, and I would never stop marveling at that.

When his pace finally slowed, he lingered inside me. Brushing a strand of hair from my mouth, his lips moved against my ear. "This is what I want—to give you everything you need. Everything you deserve. Nothing else matters."

He gathered me in his arms and held me for a long time, whispering how much he loved me. And I believed him. The realization settled deep inside me, taking root in my bones, as unshakable as the love I felt for him.

CHAPTER SIXTEEN

The bed jolted underneath me, and I opened one eye to Belle's smiling face. Hoisting my body up, I lounged drowsily against the headboard. She was already dressed for the day in a soft cashmere sweater that made her eyes look nearly gray in the morning light. If she was feeling any lingering doubt about last night's activities, it didn't show. I cupped her chin for a moment and studied her.

"Morning, beautiful," I yawned. The only better way to wake up was when she was still in bed naked with me, but opening my eyes to her smile was a very close second.

"We're going on an adventure," she announced as she crossed her legs under her, revealing a pair of jeans and suede boots. Apparently I'd slept through a shower and who knew what else.

I bit back a laugh at her infectious enthusiasm. "I thought we went on an adventure last night."

"*Not* that kind of adventure," she clarified, raising her eyebrows before winking at me. "We've spent enough time inside this week."

I didn't miss the suggestive way she said inside.

Inside her? Inside our hotel room? Inside a dungeon? As far as I was concerned, inside was geographical perfection. But it would be unfair to prevent her from spending any time in the city, especially since she'd never been here before. I stretched my arms and reached for her, but she wiggled out of my grasp. "You have me at a disadvantage. I'm not even dressed."

"Uh-uh." She clicked her tongue against the roof of her mouth as she shook her head in refusal. "We leave soon and I haven't seen anything. You're going to have to spend a few hours keeping your hands to yourself, Price."

"Really?" I called her bluff. I lifted the bed sheet and peaked underneath. "Don't be offended, mate. She still likes you."

She swatted my hand away, and I dropped the sheet, taking advantage of the opportunity to catch her. Pulling her into my arms, I shifted so she could feel my erection pressing against her ass.

"I haven't seen anything touristy," she said, nuzzling against my neck. "Take me out, and you can be as handsy as you want tonight."

I had her exactly where I wanted her, and she was negotiating. After spending yesterday with her at whip's length, all I wanted was to spend the day in bed making certain she received hours of pleasure. "If my girl wants to go out, I suppose I need to put this away and get dressed."

"I do want to go out." Her teeth nipped at her lower lip as she struggled with her own battle of want versus need. "But it would be a shame to waste this."

Her hand slipped under the sheet and found my shaft. That was the kind of conservation effort I could get behind. I flipped her on her back and climbed on top of her before she could change her mind. I'd been wrong—this was the perfect way to start the day.

Nearly bare tree limbs tangled together over us as we made our way into Central Park, their leaves crunching under our feet as we walked hand-in-hand through the green space. Winter was drawing closer, and the chill of the air nipped at our exposed faces. We'd both bundled up for the outing. Belle had managed to find her sweater after our morning lovemaking, but she'd settled for a skirt and tights after we realized her pants were missing in action.

They were under the bed, but I wasn't above playing dumb if it meant I got to spend the day looking at her shapely thighs.

"There's a zoo here somewhere," she said to me, "and a pond and oh!"

She stopped in her tracks to stare at a man painted white from head to toe. He stood motionless, a small box at his feet. Digging into my pocket, I dropped a few dollars into it and the man began to move, blinking and shifting as if confused to find himself coming to life. Belle watched in rapt attention, delight drawing her lips into a radiant smile. After a few minutes, the performance artist settled into a new position, crouching low with his chin resting on his hands.

"I hope he finds a new audience soon," I said we continued along the pavement.

"He will." Belle beamed as her grip on my hand tightened.

There was a magic in the air that seemed to hover all around us. It felt palpable, as if we could catch it if we were patient enough. Maybe it was the peacefulness that seemed to exist here despite the city teeming with life that lay outside its boundaries. Or perhaps it was simply the company I found myself in.

We happened upon the pond by accident and paused there to watch two boys raise sailboats across it. Belle clapped and cheered next to me before she traipsed over to the cart selling the boats and bought two for us.

"Care for some friendly competition?" she asked, bending to place her boat onto the water.

I moved behind her to block the view of her ass. Gripping her hips, I squeezed. "I don't like to lose."

"Neither do I," she warned, her eyes flashing mischievously as she released her boat.

"Cheater!"

"It's not my fault you're so easily distracted." She shook her behind as I rushed to get my own boat on the pond. In the end, she trounced me so soundly that I knew I couldn't have won even without her head start. That wasn't going to stop me from giving her shit about it for the rest of the day.

"You are shameless," I told her as we walked to the other side to grab the boats. We passed them to a family sitting nearby.

"I can't help winning." She shot me a haughty look.

"Shameless. Competitive," I muttered under my breath. "You're such a Price already."

Belle inhaled sharply at my words, but before I could judge her reaction, she tugged away from me and pointed to the arched entrance of the zoo. She had reacted though. Just as she'd reacted the other night on the terrace as if my suggestions both frightened and thrilled her. They had the same effect on me if I was being honest, but for vastly different reasons.

I paid the admission, and we spent the next few hours wandering through the compact animal sanctuary, enjoying each other's reactions as much as the animals. Near the primate exhibit, a chimpanzee tossed an apple to me and motioned for me to eat it. I took a bite and tossed it back.

"I'm pretty sure that's against zoo rules," Belle said dryly as we continued on before it became a game of catch.

"Animals and I understand each other," I said, wrapping an arm around her waist and drawing her closer. She melted into me, laughing."

"Sometimes I think you belong in a cage," she admitted.

"You're probably onto something, beautiful." I leaned over to whisper, "Later I'll show you how primitive I can be."

Belle shook her head, a giggle bursting from her even as her eyes darted toward a small girl and her mother. Longing flashed across her face, but she smiled widely as the child passed us. It confirmed what I'd suspected. Belle was every bit as interested in starting a family as she was a business. It seemed like a long shot that I had more to do with that than a biological clock, but then again, she hadn't even been interested in dating when we first met.

"What are you thinking about?" she asked, drawing me from my thoughts.

"That I'm hungry," I lied. I wasn't about to share these insights with her, not when she wasn't conscious of them herself. Instead we found a cart selling hot dogs and ordered two. Settling onto a park bench, we ate them, discussing the strange ways Americans dressed their food.

"They can't put all of that on one of these." Belle shook her head as I recounted the hot dog I ordered once in Chicago.

I raised a hand. "I swear."

She opened her mouth for further questioning as a ball of color tumbled over at our feet. Belle reacted immediately, helping the small child to his feet as his mother rushed down the path. The boy had begun to cry, and Belle soothed him in a quiet voice as she brushed debris from the knees of his pants.

"Thank you," his mother said in a flustered voice when she finally reached us. She took his hand and led him away. "You've got to stop running away, Gabe!"

Belle sat back down and watched as the pair made their way to the zoo. There was no mistaking the look on her face. Longing. She wanted a family. She wanted a child.

God, I wanted to give it to her. I wanted everything with this kind, beautiful woman who seemed to inherently understand how to live a full life. I wanted her to teach me how to do the same. I never thought it was possible that I could be a good man. With her, it seemed possible. She made me believe I was more than the sum of my past mistakes.

I'd entertained the thought of more before now but only to gauge how she reacted to the idea of commitment. This was different. It was as if I'd spent my whole life waiting for this moment, and now that it was here, everything that came before it seemed to fall away. I hadn't even known it was waiting for me.

"Are you done?" I wiped a bit of mustard from the corner of her mouth.

Belle eyed me curiously. She hadn't missed the husky undertone that colored my voice. I couldn't pretend as if every bit of me wasn't pulsing with this revelation.

She crumpled her napkin and tossed it into the rubbish bin. When she turned back toward me, I captured her mouth, pouring the promises I wanted to make into the kiss. Her soft hand caught the back of my neck and held me there.

I felt it. I knew she did, too.

We didn't have to talk about it. It was as real—as tangible—as the touch of our bodies. It was also as complicated and tangled as our limbs were becoming as we gave into one another fully. We were only a man and a woman, committing to the basic, urgent call of our biology. I wanted to take her right there and then, but I restrained myself.

"Take me to bed," Belle panted when we finally extricated our tongues from one another long enough to speak.

Neither of us spoke as we dashed back toward the Plaza. Overhead a sudden rumble announced rain moments before the first drops splattered on our cheeks. The deluge was as quick and unexpected as the revelation I'd just experienced. By the time we reached the hotel, we were both so drenched that no one thought anything as we ran toward the lift. It was the perfect alibi.

I couldn't wait for twenty flights. My fingers slipped under the band of Belle's sweater, and I peeled the soaked garment over her head. Wrenching the straps of her bra over her shoulders, I freed her breasts, my mouth closing over her tender nipple as we rocketed up the lift. Her hands splayed against the mirrored glass as I bit and sucked. Reaching under her skirt, I tore at her tights, ripping the seam that covered her pussy just as the lift doors slid open.

There could have been an entire cadre of Japanese businessmen standing there and we wouldn't have noticed. Scooping her into my arms, I carried her toward the suite, unable to keep my mouth off her. Off her lips. Off her skin. She was perfection incarnate—a goddess and a temptress rolled into one. At the same time, she was so much more than that. I could spend my whole life studying the dictionary and never discover all the terms to describe how wild and sensual and fucking brilliant she was.

"I need to be inside of you," I groaned as we slammed against the door. Belle fumbled to undo my pants as I let us inside. We nearly fell, but I caught her against the door. Shoving her panties to the side, I pushed into her slick cunt. It would take nothing to push me over the edge. I wanted to fill her. I wanted to watch her face as I emptied my cock inside her. But Belle's head fell back as she began to moan.

"S-s-so good," she crooned before crying out in pleasure. "Fuck me, Smith. I want to feel it."

Oh, she was going to feel it. She'd still be feeling it tomorrow, and if I had my say, she'd be feeling it next week.

More dirty words fell from her lips before I crushed our mouths together. She didn't need to ask. I was never going to stop. I was never going to give her up. When she finally tightened around me, I braced her against the wall and hammered us both to a shattering conclusion. But as Belle slumped against me, I didn't withdraw from her. Instead, I cupped her ass, urging her legs around me. Carrying her up the stairs, I laid her in our bed and slowly undressed us both.

Despite my powerful climax, my erection hadn't flagged. She made no protest as I crept over and slid inside her. I could only comprehend this. Her nails digging into my back—scratching across my skin. The brush of her soft breasts against my chest. The slow circle of her hips against the thrusts of my groin.

"You're mine," I growled, pushing onto the palms of my hands so that I could rock deeper into her channel.

I dared to look into her eyes, dared to hope that I would find the same fervent wonder I felt there. Instead I saw fear. I shifted my weight and lifted a hand to her cheek. I wanted to wipe it away—erase the anxiety and doubt that tainted our relationship. But I knew it wasn't as simple as that. All I could do was offer her reassurance that she was wanted.

That she was loved.

Because my God, I loved this woman, and if I had to spend every day proving it to her, I would.

"Forever." I pushed the word out between breaths. "Mine forever."

And longer.

I didn't want her body or her heart. I wanted her soul. I wanted everything down to her last breath.

A tear glinted from the corner of her eye and I kissed it away. She smiled shyly and arched into me, offering me her lips. I took them—captured her kisses, shared her breath—as I took all of her and made her my own.

CHAPTER SEVENTEEN

The next few days passed in a blur as we tried to jam as much into the remainder of our time here. Sex and museums and shows and sex and shopping and sex. We'd given in to the fantasy of what our lives could be like—and it felt good. Wicked and selfish and fucking amazing. Our impending return to London meant sharing Smith with others, most of whom I neither liked nor trusted. It also meant working out how to mesh our lives together. For the most part, we'd avoided speaking of what would happen when we reached Heathrow. We'd be together. We'd agreed on that. The rest we'd have to sort out.

But when our final night in the city arrived, a heavy pressure built in my chest. It clawed through my breast, searching for an escape, which I was pretty certain would come in the form of hysterical crying or hyperventilating or looking up immigration requirements. Here it had been easy to ignore the trouble waiting for us in London. Smith seemed equally anxious. He spent the morning on his mobile, pacing the length of the terrace as he made calls.

It wasn't how I wanted to spend our last hours here, but I knew he was worried. He'd tried to protect me from his associates before.

Now he was planning to take my hand and walk with me into the lion's den. At noon, I peeked outside and found him, sitting quietly.

"Is everything arranged?" I asked as I dropped onto his lap.

Smith's arms coiled around me, and he nodded even as his eyes remained distant. "Mostly. There are a few last minute issues."

"There always are." But my response didn't soothe him. Smith wasn't here with me—not really. His thoughts—his concerns—were elsewhere. As much as I wanted to draw his attention back to me, I understood what was going on. Since I'd discovered the nature of his involvement with his employer, I'd been concerned for his safety. How much worse was that feeling for him?

"I'm sorry, beautiful. I have to take care of a few things." He planted a kiss on my forehead. "How about dinner? I'll arrange reservations for seven."

"Okay," I said slowly, "but that gives me a lot of time to go shopping."

This earned me a grin, but it faded too quickly. "Take my card. I added you to my accounts."

"I have my own money," I protested.

"Belle"—Smith grabbed my chin and forced me to meet his gaze —"we have money. Get used to it."

I didn't argue with him further. Instead I decided if he was going to insist that I make a dent in his bank account then I would go shopping for him. Not that the man needed clothes. That didn't stop me from purchasing a variety of new ties, which was admittedly a bit selfish on my part considering how I hoped he'd use them. As I passed the men's jewelry counter at Saks, I stopped in my tracks.

"Can I see those?" I asked, jabbing at the glass.

"Lovely taste," the associate remarked as she removed the gold feather cufflinks from the display and passed one to me. "Unique but elegant."

But my thoughts were caught in the past, recalling the gentle, exciting introduction I'd had to Smith's sexuality at the touch of a feather. I swallowed, wishing I was with him now. "I'll take them."

I tried not to feel guilty as I passed her his credit card. As much as

I wanted to buy them from my own money, I knew that wouldn't merely deplete my account but it would probably carve a giant sinkhole in it as well. I resisted the urge to chicken out as she handed me the card slip, and a few minutes later, I'd tucked the carefully wrapped package into my purse.

Although I probably had more time to kill, it seemed like a good idea to stop now. But when I checked my mobile, it was only four in the afternoon.

Research. I wouldn't buy anything, I thought as I headed to women's fashion. But it was part of my job to be on top of the market. It occurred to me that I probably should have spent more time in New York working on that. But an hour of research was better than nothing. I was already going home without an interview. Neither Lola nor Katherine had been in touch with more news.

The spring lines were beginning to filter onto the racks, but many of the pieces I happened upon were the same. Since there was no rush to launch at breakneck speed, we needed to be purchasing the lines as they came out. I pulled out my mobile and shot off a text to Lola. It was the middle of the night in London, but I didn't want to forget to strategize that with her. It was already five, so if I headed back now, I'd have time to get ready before the car arrived. After a day denying myself, squeezing in a bubble bath seemed like a good compromise.

I had nearly reached the escalator when a mannequin caught my eye. There was no fighting it. I had to see the price tag. I had to touch the fabric. The sleeves were barely capped, and although the neckline didn't so much as reveal the collarbone, there was a classic sexiness that was impossible to deny. It was something more than a little black dress. Perhaps owing to the full skirt that draped gracefully to the floor in the back but that swept up in a slight angle to fall midcalf.

"You should buy it," a familiar voice advised me as I studied the gown.

I pivoted to find Katherine Harper behind me. "Peer pressure, huh?"

"That's not just a dress, that's a statement." She paused as we admired it.

"I'm not sure I have an occasion for something like this. It might be a bit much to wear to dinner with my boyfriend."

"The occasion is wearing it," Kat said with a laugh, tucking a scarlet strand behind her ear. "Wear that and something magical will happen."

"You should work here." She already had me sold.

"I might apply after the week I had." She chewed on her lip nervously. "I'm so sorry again about what happened."

"Don't worry about it," I stopped her. "If I let every bitch who spoke cruelly to me stop me, I would never have gotten here in the first place."

"Sounds like you have some perspective on this."

"You should meet my mother."

"Look I'm working on Abigail. I don't know what crawled up her ass"—Kat's hand flew to her mouth. "Sorry! I just mean she's been a little hostile lately. In a month she'll be pitching me a female entrepreneur story. I'll keep you up to date."

"Thank you." It was easier to say that than to tell her not to bother. Abigail Summers had burned a bridge with me. Life was way too short to deal with thundercunts.

Katherine continued to chat with me while I had the sales associate ring up the dress. I was almost to the hotel when Smith texted me.

SMITH: Ran out on some business. Car will pick you up at seven.

So much for the miraculous qualities of the gown. If I was lucky, he would be there on time. I chose not to be upset though. We were both here on business. If I made myself up and sat alone at the dining table, there was always wine.

Every once in a while a woman puts on a piece of clothing or a pair of shoes and *magic*. I'd seen that magic on Clara's face when she stepped into her wedding gown. I'd felt it when I put on my first pair of Louboutins. It sounded ridiculous, and it wasn't something I could explain exactly. Except that some clothing was transformative. As I zipped up the black dress, I felt that magic settle over me.

I didn't bother to look in the mirror as I slipped on a pair of simple black heels. It didn't matter how I looked. Not in this dress. It was how I felt. I was a princess on the way to the ball. I was Audrey Hepburn catching every man's attention in the room. I was Belle Stuart, and I was fabulous. As I entered the lobby, the heads swiveling to watch my progress told me I was right. A bellman ran to open the door as I approached and I smiled at him.

"You look lovely this evening," he complimented me as I swept past him. "Do you need a car?"

"I have one picking me up at seven." I glanced around, looking for a private sedan.

"Ah, Miss Stuart?" he guessed.

I nodded and he pointed to a long, sleek limousine idling at the curb. The driver jumped out and ran to open the door. I accepted his help getting in, wishing Smith was here with me. Leave it to him to spoil me even when he wasn't around to enjoy it. I didn't ask where we were going. Instead I looked out the window. We cut through Central Park, and my mind drifted to the day we had spent there. Something had shifted that afternoon. Smith had shown me a vulnerability that was uncharacteristic. Making love had been raw and passionate, and most notably, not kinky. And yet it was the sexiest night of my life. There'd been no distance between us—no exchange of power. And although I enjoyed it when he got rough or ordered me around in bed, that night had been about connection.

Like the weekend before he fired me. Like the last weekend we'd spent openly as a couple before we pretended to break up—and before we'd actually broken up. I pressed my hand to my stomach as it lurched. Tonight was our last night together in New York. We were supposed to go home to London as a couple, but Smith had made it clear that he would always choose my safety over our happiness.

He was going to try to end things between us. And I wasn't going to let him.

Not this time.

My safety wouldn't matter if I couldn't stay away from him, and nothing was going to separate us again.

Except an ocean, a little voice interjected. Smith had expressed his interest in staying in New York. It wasn't something I wanted to do. But he'd spent the last few days saying goodbye to me. The more I recalled the time we'd spent together, the love we made, the more obvious it became. He wanted to show me he loved me—prove it—before he left me again.

I swallowed against the tears building in my throat. Why would he fix me if he was only going to break me again?

Because he does love you, the voice said. It was a rational reason. Perhaps if he could prove his love then it would be easier to know he was making a decision to protect me. But love wasn't rational or patient or easily dismissed. Love consumed and changed. Love took two people and joined their hearts. Distance, death—nothing could separate them. And if life ripped those hearts apart, there was no way to ever heal, too many pieces were missing.

I refused to let the tears fall, just as I refused to let him walk away. If there was danger we would face it together.

There were no other options.

I repeated this silently, willing the words to take shape so I could cling to them for strength, as the limousine slowed to a stop in front of a spectacular glass cube. A large blue sphere glowed inside the nearly dark building.

"Excuse me," I called to the driver. "Do we have the right address?"

But he was already out of the car and opening my door. "The Rose Space Center. That's where I was directed. I'll wait here for you."

I was going to have a chat with Smith about his strange desire to reroute me mid-trip. I somehow doubted there was much food inside. I took the driver's hand and stepped out of the car. "It doesn't look open."

As if on cue, a security guard appeared, stepping toward the entrance. "Miss."

I was so flustered that I realized I left my clutch when I reached him. For a second I considered going back for it, but curiosity won out. The interior was dimly lit, giving shape to a variety of exhibits that were closed for the evening. The guard entered behind me, and I turned to him with hands spread.

"Follow those," he advised, tipping his head to the ground.

I followed his gaze to discover two rows of candles. Their flames flickering into a path. I walked slowly, slightly concerned that my skirt might knock one over. I was so focused that I stopped in surprise when I reached a doorway. It was so dark that I couldn't see inside. I gripped the frame and stepped cautiously through. As my heel touched the floor, a million glittering lights lit up the space. I stared up in wonder as the night sky appeared before me. A star soared into blackness in the distance. I was so mesmerized that I didn't hear Smith approach until he took both of my hands. Opening my mouth, I found myself speechless.

"I found the stars for you," he said in a low voice that was rich with husky emotion.

"It's beautiful." It was the most I could manage to say. He'd stolen all my words just as he'd stolen my heart.

"You're beautiful." He held out my arms and studied me. Here we were under the most dazzling display of stars I'd ever seen, and Smith couldn't look away from me. "Every day I wondered what I did to deserve finding you. Every day I question why I get to keep you."

"Smith," I began but he shook his head and I fell silent.

"We're going back to London tomorrow."

This was it. I swayed shakily on my feet, and he caught me around the waist. "Don't," I pleaded. "Don't leave me again. I won't let you."

"I'm not leaving you," he promised softly. The faint starlight shadowed half of his face, etching the rest in brutal, magnificent lines. "Never again."

His words freed the tears I'd kept confined during my ride here. He brushed them from my cheeks as they began to fall.

"Hold out your palm," he instructed me in a gentle voice.

I turned my trembling hand over and waited.

"I'm not getting on one knee. I'm not asking. This isn't an engagement ring." Even in the darkness, the band he placed in my palm glinted with fire, the diamonds catching the light of the stars overhead.

"I don't understand," I admitted as I stared at the ring.

"It's our future. It's our life. That's a wedding band, Belle. It's in your hands now—along with my heart and everything else I have to give you." He closed my fingers over the band. "You're what I want. You're the only thing I've ever wanted. I've been waiting for you my whole life. Now my life is yours."

I barely processed it as he kissed me, and when he backed away, he didn't press me to speak.

"It's up to you. There's the door. There's the ring."

"Smith, I..." But I didn't know how my own sentence ended.

"Our lives are complicated. This isn't."

I opened my hand and picked up the ring. It felt complicated—and heavy—and a million other emotions that didn't have words.

But he was right, this was up to me.

CHAPTER EIGHTEEN

"I'll have a gin and tonic."

Belle raised her eyebrow as if she disapproved of my choice of beverage. "Tea."

The flight attendant moved on, scribbling down our order.

"A little early to start drinking," Belle commented when the attendant was out of earshot.

"Time does not exist in a straight line, especially on an airplane." I glared at the console dividing our seats. "I've never been jealous of the economy cabin before."

"I think you can make it seven hours without touching me." But she moved her hand to rest where I could hold it.

"At least I don't have to completely keep my hands off you." I studied her as she relaxed back into her seat. "You should get some sleep."

"That's not what you said last night," she said with a wink.

"Last night I was trying to convince you to see things my way." I glanced down to her naked ring finger. "I see you aren't wearing it."

"Smith." She paused, her pale eyes searching my face. "I just need a little time before..."

"The ring doesn't matter." I lifted her hand and kissed the spot where it should rest. "It's an object. Nothing more."

She belonged to me, and I belonged to her. I needed to focus on that.

Belle closed her eyes, our hands still clasped. "I don't think I'm ready."

My chest tightened at her words, and I pressed my lips together. It wasn't what I wanted to hear, but she had every right to express her opinion. "I'll have to prove you wrong."

"I meant I don't think I'm ready to go back to London," she clarified, not bothering to smother the exasperation she felt. "Although I do love when you prove me wrong."

"It doesn't sound like it, beautiful," I teased. "Don't hold it against me. Providing evidence to the contrary is my job."

"You aren't my lawyer," she reminded me, propping open one eyelid.

"Consider me a witness for the defense."

"Are you defending yourself?" she asked.

"I've gotten quite good at it over the years."

The light banter had proved my case. I needed to move her attention away from the trouble brewing at home. After staying up all night, showing her exactly what I had to offer as part of my proposition, she needed rest. "Sleep," I repeated.

"Why does that sound like a threat?" She yawned as she spoke, frowning when she realized I was right.

"Because it is a threat," I told her. "Once I have you home, you won't be sleeping much. Last night was only a preview of what's to come. There won't be a divider between us forever."

"I might have to take a separate bedroom. Maybe you were onto something at your old house," she said, referencing the private quarters I'd given her. She hadn't once slept in them.

"Our house. Our bed." I liked the sound of it, and from the way she grinned sleepily, she did as well, even if she was going to be a little shit about it. No ring, but she had agreed to move in. Not that it had even been up for negotiation. I needed to be assured of her safety at all times. I assumed we had two days—a week at the most—before news of our domestic arrangement reached Hammond. That would give me enough time to hire a private security detail and a driver. That hadn't been a part of the discussion either, and I knew when I finally revealed the expectations, she wasn't going to be happy.

She'd have to learn to live with it—and me.

"You're so demanding." Another yawn. "Caveman."

"Later I'll throw you over my shoulder and show you how primitive I can be. But for now, sleep."

Her eyelids drifted down, and a few minutes later, her breathing took on a steady rhythm. The flight attendant returned, and I sent back Belle's cup after accepting my own. Sipping the cocktail, I memorized the peaceful, dreamy expression she wore, etching the curve of her cheekbones and the dent of her lip. I stored the image deep inside me where I kept all my memories of her. It was a place that couldn't be touched—that couldn't be stolen from me. No matter what happened, I would have those moments until I drew my last breath.

Abandoning my drink, I absentmindedly rubbed my own bare finger. I'd once thought wearing a wedding band was worse than being collared. I'd watched acquaintances and colleagues accept the shackles and then proceed to spend the years complaining about their restraints. Most of the people I knew who married wound up divorced. I had no doubt that Margot and I had been on the way there ourselves when she died. I'd already spoken to a lawyer, the same one who'd drawn up our prenuptial agreement.

I'd made a mistake marrying my first wife. I'd been young and blinded by her dazzling smile. But I'd protected myself.

There would be no need for that with Belle, which was why I'd walked into Tiffany and purchased the diamond band that she'd relegated to her carry-on. I'd made my decision. Now I just had to convince her that I hadn't lost my mind. My thoughts returned to the night before. She was lucky there was a divider or I'd start working on my case immediately.

Suddenly London felt even farther away. I groaned and spread a blanket over my lap. Sleep felt like a very good idea. She needed rest, and I needed to escape the erection that was bound to last more than four hours. Belle sighed in her sleep, her lips turning up at the corners, as if she'd heard my thoughts in her dream.

"Sweet dreams, beautiful," I muttered as I adjusted my cock and closed my eyes, reminding myself that I could, in fact, keep my hands off her for seven hours.

Even if I didn't want to.

CHAPTER NINETEEN

Heathrow was a zoo when we finally made our way through customs and headed to get our luggage. I took each step slowly, dreading what lay before me. I hadn't mentioned to Smith that I'd failed to tell my friends that I didn't need a ride from the airport. Instead I held his hand, leaching whatever strength I could in preparation for the inevitable confrontation waiting for me.

I spotted Edward's curly hair before we'd reached the bottom of the escalator. He was dressed casually in a pair of jeans and a long t-shirt. No doubt in an attempt to blend into the crowd. Not that he could if he wanted. More than a few people were whispering excitedly as they passed him by, but he didn't seem to notice. My stomach lurched as his eyes scanned the crowd, searching for me, and I silently cursed Lola for not being the one to come inside to retrieve me. Edward's gaze landed on me as we stepped off, and his welcoming smile vanished immediately when he saw I wasn't alone. It was too late to disappear into the crowd. I'd been spotted, and from the looks of it, there was no way I was escaping an explanation for the sudden reappearance of my ex-lover.

Where was a firing squad when you needed it? I'd much rather be facing one of those than the disappointment plastered across Edward's face.

Edward glared at me as we made our way toward him at the baggage claim. He caught me in a hug as soon as we reached him, muttering, "Most people bring home a t-shirt as a souvenir."

"Watch it," I warned him. I knew there was no way to avoid this fight. I'd known it when I purposefully chose not to cancel his plans to pick me up.

Edward straightened up, puffing his chest a little as he stuck out his hand. Smith accepted, shaking it. The gesture was courteous on both parts, but it was far from friendly. The two had a long way to go.

"If you two are done beating your chests, can we get the luggage?" I darted away, leaving them to continue their show of masculinity.

Smith followed me, grabbing my hand and spinning me toward him. I didn't have time to process anything but the firmness of his lips on mine as he captured my mouth in a deep, possessive kiss. A self-respecting girl would have pushed him away, but I melted into him instead. When he pulled back, he shook his head. I'd hear about this later.

Two fights in my future, and I'd only just hit solid ground.

"I suppose you'll be riding with him," Smith said, glancing over his shoulder. Edward glowered back.

"Yes." This wasn't up for debate, but he didn't fight me on it.

Smith retrieved our bags, but he didn't pass mine along. "I'll take this to the house. See you there tonight."

I winced as I nodded. There was no way Edward was going to miss that.

He grudgingly handed me off to my best friend with another kiss goodbye and made his way toward the car park.

Edward said nothing as we left. When we reached the pavement, Lola waved to us from the driver's seat of her car. She frowned, tipping up her sunglasses as I climbed in beside her.

"Did they lose your bags?" she asked.

"Nope. Bags are safe," Edward answered for me. "Her mind is another story."

"Should we go then?" Lola sounded as confused as I felt.

"Yes," I said with a sigh.

She popped her glasses down and hit her turn signal as she made her way into the airport traffic. Lola didn't require further explanation, but I knew I wasn't getting out of this that easily.

I pinched the bridge of my nose and braced myself, but Edward remained silent. I'd completely sidelined him. I knew that, but I didn't deserve the silent treatment. This was hardly the first time anyone in our close-knit group of friends had made up with an ex. I'd expected reproof, but it didn't make it any easier to bear, especially with Edward sitting like a giant, seething lump of disapproval behind me.

"Are you going to yell at me or what?" I finally snapped when I couldn't stand it any longer.

"For what?" he asked. "I have no bloody clue what just happened."

"Is this about the bags?" Lola's eyes darted to me and I shook my head.

"This is about Belle getting off the plane with Smith Price," Edward informed her.

"What?" Lola exclaimed, squealing in excitement.

"No! We aren't happy about this," Edward interjected, flopping against the back seat.

"We aren't?" she asked. Looking over at me, she repeated herself, "We aren't?"

"He isn't," I explained. "I'm...confused."

"Did you go mad? Price treated you like shit. He hurt you! So badly that you wouldn't even talk about it. How the hell did you even run into him? Aren't there millions of people in New York?"

Lola bit her lip as if she was holding something back. Edward couldn't see the gesture from his seat, but I caught it. She shot me a guilty look over the rim of her glasses.

"I told him she was going," she admitted in a quiet voice.

"Do you mind pulling over?" Edward asked. "I don't think either of you are sane enough to operate a moving vehicle."

"Oh, sod off. She's an adult."

"That's questionable," he muttered.

"You told him I was going to New York?" I asked her.

"It was more like I bragged about it," she said, tapping the steering wheel nervously. "I caught him slinking around outside the office."

"You what?" This was news to me. "You might have mentioned that."

"Well, I didn't know why he was there, so I told him you were busy getting ready to head to New York for an important interview. Look, I thought I was doing you a favor. No man likes to hear that their ex is moving on."

She had done me a favor, even if Edward was glaring murderously at her.

"Thank you," I said sincerely. "We spent some time together and talked."

"And then you shagged each other, and he managed to convince you to come crawling back."

That stung. Edward had no clue how complicated things were between us. But now, more than ever, I needed his support.

"I'm in love with him," I announced. "And if you don't like it, you can suck a big one."

It came out more immature than it had sounded in my head. Next to me, Lola began to shake before she dissolved into giggles.

"Noted," she said between laughs.

"I just don't want to see you get hurt." Edward appeared unmoved by my proclamation.

I swiveled in my seat and met his gaze. "I don't need your approval, but I'd like it anyway. Your opinion means a lot to me. I know Smith can be a little hard to get a handle on."

"Impossible, you mean." He exhaled and then smiled. "I want

you to be happy. I just hope he doesn't cock things up. Promise me that you'll take things slowly."

Now didn't seem like a good time to mention the diamond wedding band burning a hole in my purse. I hadn't been sure what to expect when my friends found out that Smith was back in my life. Thankfully they had no clue how precarious our situation truly was. I'd keep that—and Smith's unorthodox proposal—to myself for the time being.

"I will," I lied.

"So when he said he'd see you at home..." Edward trailed off, leaving me scrambling for an answer.

In the end, I went with the truth. I'd have to keep enough from him in the coming months as it was. "I'm moving in with him."

"We have very different ideas of what taking it slowly means," he said flatly.

"I never moved in with Philip. I'm not making the same mistake with Smith." It was a pitiful excuse, and judging from Edward's tight-lipped reaction, he thought so, too.

"I heard from several designers," Lola said, switching the subject. I shot her a grateful smile.

"Which ones?"

She rattled off a list, but my thoughts were elsewhere. Tomorrow I needed to focus on Bless, but right now I was still reeling from all the changes I'd brought home with me. Smith had seen this coming when he asked me to uproot my life. That's why he'd left the decision, quite literally, in my hands. I was the one who had to live with the consequences. The only comfort was that I'd be doing it with him by my side.

Jet lag was the perfect excuse to escape the uncomfortable tension that permeated the car, and as soon as I was in my flat, I dropped my bags. Drooping against the door, I tried to fight how deflated I already felt. Edward's disapproval agitated me. I didn't like being on the outs with a friend, especially over a man.

Especially since that man was going nowhere.

But there was nothing for it, and Smith expected me across town. After sleeping on the plane, I was wide-awake and somehow still exhausted. Tomorrow I had to get my butt in gear. Tonight I had to sort through the events of the last twenty-four hours.

My gaze traveled through the flat's open floor plan. This flat, and another just like it, had been my home for the last year and a half. But the sense of comfort I usually found when returning through its doors was absent, replaced by restlessness. I didn't belong here anymore, but did I belong at Smith's? Both options felt like little more than shelter at this point.

"I thought I heard you." My aunt swept into the room in a pair of silk pajamas. "You look tired."

"I am and I'm not," I told her as she reached for a bottle of wine. "None for me."

"I'll drink a glass in your honor then," she said dryly. "Dare I ask about the trip?"

"I wouldn't know where to start." I slid onto a chair, propping my elbows up at the table.

"How was the interview?" she asked as she poured herself a drink and joined me.

I snorted. How was it possible that the least interesting aspect of my business trip was the actual business? "It was a no go. The editor proved to be a first-rate bitch."

"At least you have experience dealing with that type."

"Speaking of Mum, has she called you?" I already knew the answer.

"Daily." Jane's lips pursed in distaste.

"I'm sorry. I'll deal with her tomorrow." Add that to the list of chores I was dreading. I still hadn't bothered to look at the paperwork she'd sent over regarding the estate. I'd meant to call my brother and have him review the documents. Instead I'd wound up across the Atlantic. It seemed I was turning avoiding my mother into an art.

"It doesn't matter. What else do I have to do? Frederick locked himself in the studio to finish his latest opus."

Despite the chaos I found myself in, I smiled. Listening to Jane discuss her conquests was the best distraction in the world, but even her wild stories couldn't completely deter me from thinking about my own romantic entanglements.

"You've been married. Why?" I blurted the question out of nowhere.

Jane sat her glass slowly on the table. "I take it there's a reason for this question."

My cheeks burned but I managed to nod.

"I have, and I haven't." She shook her head and sighed. "I've had husbands, Belle, but I've never really been married. That sounds crazy, doesn't it?"

"Yes," I admitted, laughing with her.

"Men have asked me to marry them, and I've complied. Some died. Some left. But I never truly felt married to any of them."

"I guess that explains why some days you're an old maid and others you're a divorcée." Jane's twisted idea of lovers had always amused me, even though it also confused the hell out of me.

"Some days I'm more one than the other." She tapped her glass. "I'm guessing you want to know why."

I did want to know, because right now I needed to understand—understand why some people got married and others didn't. And why some marriages lasted a lifetime and others failed. I was grasping for answers I wasn't certain existed, but I was more than willing to listen to anyone that would talk about it.

"I loved a man once. If that sounds like the start of a sad story, it is."

"What happened to him?" I asked her in a quiet voice.

"Life. Pride. Fear. It's much easier to pretend to make a commitment you don't really intend on keeping than it is to face the prospect of giving everything you are to one person. That takes trust."

"And you didn't trust him?"

"I didn't trust myself," she clarified, running a hand over her platinum hair. "And by the time I did, it was too late. He married someone else."

"Do you still miss him?"

"Every day. I regret it. Lovers distract me, but no one has ever filled the void his absence left in my life. Maybe that's why I said yes whenever a man asked me to marry him. I was scared that I might look back on that relationship with the same regret."

"So if you could, would you change it?"

"I'm an old, wealthy woman who's seen more of the world than most. The politically correct thing to say would be no. But yes, if I could go back, I would change things." She shrugged, her eyes growing distant. "Perhaps I would have regretted that course of action. I'll never know and I guess that's what eats at me."

She settled against her chair, her gaze zeroing in on me. "Now tell me why you asked."

"Because I'm afraid." I swallowed hard on my confession. It was difficult to admit that I was scared of what I wanted most in the world —precisely *because* I wanted it.

"Then take my advice, love. Do what scares you. It's what keeps you alive. It's far better to live with the regret of a relationship that doesn't work out than to live with the pain of loss." Reaching across the table, she took my hand in hers. "I'm guessing you have a lot more to tell me about New York."

"Yes," I whispered. But I wasn't ready to share yet. Not until I'd come to grips with my own decision.

"When you want to tell me, I'll listen." She didn't pressure me for more information.

Tears smarted in my eyes, and I gripped her hand fiercely. "Thank you."

"If I have to live my mistakes, at least you can learn from them." She squeezed my hand before releasing it. "Now do you want a glass of wine?"

"No, there's someone I need to see."

"I thought there might be," she said wisely. "Don't be afraid to trust your heart, Belle. It's your compass, let it guide you."

I nodded, even as my world spun around me. How was I supposed to follow my heart's direction when I couldn't be still enough to know where it pointed? The only thing I knew was that right now it was pointing me to a house in Holland Park. I couldn't see further than that, but journeys began with a single step. I was ready to take the first one.

CHAPTER TWENTY

It was the first time we'd met in person, but I took no stock in this changing the nature of our arrangement. The only thing that had brought me to him was my own desire to escape my tangled past, and a sense of obligation to the people Hammond had destroyed. I couldn't be certain which was more important to me. Not anymore.

He didn't offer me a drink as I took the seat opposite him. I didn't even warrant a handshake. There had never been a time for pleasantries in our relationship and today would prove no exception.

"My expectations were made clear." It was an icy welcome, but the one I had expected after I'd received his message this morning.

Undoubtedly, news of my sudden appearance at the airport with Belle had already filtered up to him. That was the consequence of allowing her friends to see us together. Considering she arrived at my house—our house, I corrected myself—with packed bags the night before, it was better to face the repercussions now.

I gripped the arms of my chair, but restraint when it came to this subject wasn't my strong suit. I bristled at the thought of explaining my choices to him. "I'm the one who has to live with my decisions."

"But you aren't the only one who will live with the consequences," Alexander growled, transforming from cold and impassive to ferocious instantly. It was a trait well suited to a king, but not one that I particularly admired. His shoulders squared in challenge. We were matched in size. But that was where our similarities ended. We each viewed ourselves as in control of the board and the other as a mere pawn.

"I agreed to participate in this witch hunt," I reminded him in a low voice. If he was going to choose dominance, I would show him that control was a key element of that path. A fact that he'd never understood in our long and sordid history. I'd watched him rise and fall and then ascend the throne. I respected that journey, but I also saw the truth behind his own willful determination. "I didn't seek her out. She was sent to me."

"And when you realized why, you continued to use her," he accused me, his blue eyes flashing. "You were instructed to discontinue your relationship with Belle Stuart."

I leaned forward, placing my palms on his desk. "I'm Scottish. We've never been very good at taking orders from a king."

"You should have considered that before you came to me seeking absolution."

"I came to you because you sought out the information I had, and in doing so, I broke every tenant of my profession." Now I was seething. If I didn't manage to calm myself, I'd regret more than my words.

Alexander glowered at me. His disgust with my actions was as evident as his concern for Belle's safety. It was the only reason I hadn't shown him just how little I cared for his overbearing directives. I loosened the knot of my tie and forced myself to sit back. The more distance I kept between the two of us, the better.

For his safety.

"I can't assign added security to her if you two continue to see each other openly." He said it as a warning, but the reminder was unnecessary.

"I'm aware of that. I assure you" I clenched my fists, cracking my knuckles to release the tension building within me. "Her safety will remain my concern."

"Has it ever concerned you?" Alexander folded his arms behind his head and swiveled in his chair to face his window.

I hoped he found comfort in the views of his garden. "You've lived a life of privilege. You've never wanted for protection. I don't expect you to understand that, outside the walls of a palace, the world doesn't bow to other men's whims."

"You think my desire to ensure her safety is a whim?" He didn't bother to turn back to face me. In his mind, I was no more important than any other servant. "You're so much colder than I thought, and I've always considered you heartless."

I was out of my seat before the last word left his lips. My hands slammed down on the table, but Alexander didn't move. "I think that you have no idea what you're doing or this would be over by now. I gave you everything you needed to prosecute him for his crimes months ago. You've had him in check, but you've made no move."

"We aren't playing chess, Smith. And I'd remind you that I am the King. I'm the one who must decide if a threat is removable."

"Then what's stopping you? Hammond is expendable. The threat dies with him. The only people he's ever groomed to replace him have betrayed him."

Alexander turned then, his face a stony mask as he regarded me hovering over him. "You'll excuse me for not entirely trusting a man capable of such deception."

"I had nothing to do with the attack." This wasn't the first time that I'd stated this fact, and I had a feeling it wouldn't be the last. Not while he clung to his paranoia. It was clear no amount of evidence would convince him that Hammond was the only person he needed to worry about. "You know he's the head of the monster. Cut him off and the rest will die."

"I don't want to cut him off." He spoke through gritted teeth. "I want him to suffer. I want him to know fear."

"Then I'm not the one risking anyone's life." I stepped back and shook my head, my contempt now matching his. "You have the power to bring this to an end, and yet you refuse to stop it."

"He murdered my father."

"Let's not pretend that your obsession stems from a need for filial retribution. We're beyond that. This is insanity."

I'd had enough—enough of the cat and mouse game. Alexander had made me a target. Now he was effectively making Belle one as well.

"You're right," he said, surprising me. "This has very little to do with my father. In the event that my personal role in Hammond's fate is ever revealed that's how the story will be spun. Who could blame a man for seeking his father's murderer? Who could judge a man that assassinated an assassin? It's a matter of national security."

"But it's more than that to you," I pressed.

"It is much more personal than that," Alexander hissed. "You provided me with the evidence that Hammond aided Daniel on the day of my wedding. I was never the target that day. Nor was my father. For reasons that are still unclear to me, Hammond wanted him to kill my wife. I suppose that part of me does want retribution for my father's assassination, since he was the one who prevented her murder."

"That is something I can understand." And I did. The thought of Belle becoming another victim was impossible to bear. But it didn't remove his culpability for not bringing the man to justice.

"That surprises me." He folded his hands in his lap and regarded me with a calculated gaze, as though he might be able to see through me and my intentions.

"I don't care if you doubt my empathy for your situation, but I won't continue to sit back and allow you to do nothing." Or was that what he was playing at? If he waited, one of us would be forced to take action ourselves. Why should a king do his own dirty work?

"I told you I wanted him to suffer. Not because of my father or what he did to me, but because I know beyond a shadow of a doubt that he's made three attempts on Clara's life. He fueled Daniel's perverse delusions. Not once but twice. And when that didn't accomplish his ends, he sent someone on a suicide mission to run her off the road. I want to know why, and then I want to flay him alive."

"And that's worth continuing to risk her life? You're as heartless as I am." I spoke flatly, understanding now that no amount of reason would breach the mad spite the man clung to.

His fingers steepled, pressing together so tightly that the tips turned white. "Says the man risking the life of a woman he claims to care for."

"I love Belle. I don't take the danger she's in lightly. It would behoove you to show the same concern for Clara."

"Clara is my wife," he shot back. "And as such she is my concern."

"And Belle is my wife," I exploded, "so she is also very much my concern. My only concern."

Alexander fell silent, studying me as if to ascertain the validity of my claim.

"We were married in New York," I continued in a cold voice. "I will not live without her. Not for king and not for country."

"That complicates matters."

It was the understatement of the century. "Tell me something I don't know."

"You will protect her." He released a deep breath as he rubbed his temple. "And I can do very little to help you in that regard. Hammond will find out, of course."

"I assumed as much, but I also assumed we were much closer to ending this."

"Now we'll have to be."

The atmosphere in the room shifted as two opposing forces melded into something unfamiliar. No longer were we two men grappling for authority against one another. For the first time since we'd begun this quest, I felt allied to the man sitting before me.

I dropped back into the chair facing him. "I never intended to force your hand."

"Perhaps you should have. I underestimated your commitment to her."

"In your position, miscalculation can be a dangerous weakness." He needed to be reminded that his duty wasn't to his own petty vengeance, but to the people he claimed to love. I wouldn't apologize for being the one to make him see that. I wouldn't apologize for anything I had to do to ensure my wife was safe.

"We have days then." Alexander reached for his mobile and shot off a text. "You took precautions to contain this information."

"Yes." Belle and I had agreed to keep our marriage secret even from our closest friends. Not that I had anyone to share the joyful news with. Only her. But if it was a hardship for her to deceive those she loved, she hadn't fought me. I suspected she was still processing her decision.

"He'll still find out. You should be prepared for that. I told you that I didn't understand why he persists in coming after Clara. My only theory is that he does so in an attempt to get to me." Alexander shook his head, as if it were impossible to understand the man's motivations. "Had I known the first time she was attacked that there was more to what had happened, I would have gone to any lengths to protect her, even if it meant giving her up."

"And yet you didn't," I pointed out.

"When I understood the true nature of the situation, she was already carrying my child."

I stared him down. No man that loved as possessively as him could actually walk away. "And if she hadn't been?"

"I don't waste my time pondering that. She is my life. I chose her."

"Then choose to do what it takes to protect her." This time, I was the one giving the order. His obsession had to end, and swiftly. For all our sakes.

"I will."

It was as solemn a vow as I had made to Belle. It left no room for doubt in my mind.

Standing, I stretched out my hand and Alexander took it, sealing our mutual understanding. Relief washed through me. The life that I dreamed of—for her—was finally within my grasp.

I turned to leave, but as soon as I reached the door, I came face to face with the object of Alexander's mania. Clara stood outside his office, her arms wrapped protectively around her waist. She glanced up at me with searching eyes. But I didn't have the answers she sought. I didn't know this woman, but I knew what she meant to him —what she meant to my wife. So I inclined my head. It wasn't a gesture of deference but one of concern. Alexander had kept this from her. That much was clear from her pale, sickly expression. I wished I could do more or offer her some comfort, but that was his job now. I didn't dare come between her and Alexander, even momentarily.

It was time for each of us to face our fears. Ignorance was no longer an option, nor was inaction. I could only hope she was as strong as the woman I'd fallen in love with, but despite how little I knew of her, I'd watched her grace in the face of public pressure and tragedy. Alexander had been wrong to hide the truth. He would have to deal with the fallout.

We all would.

CHAPTER TWENTY-ONE

I would never get through all of these emails. Apparently every person I'd reached out to in the last month had chosen to respond to me while I was in New York. Lola had failed to mention that we hadn't heard from some designers, we'd heard from nearly all of them. I couldn't help wishing that I'd spent more time working and less time in bed with Smith during our brief overseas holiday.

"You are a strong, capable woman," I said out loud, simply because I needed to hear it, even if I didn't quite believe it. Maybe it would be easier to sell myself on the idea once I was on top of things again.

By noon I was considering throwing my laptop across the room when my phone vibrated.

CLARA: I'm stopping by. Okay?

I responded that it was more than okay and waited with my eyes glued to the door lest I reconsider my decision not to smash my computer against the wall.

Clara arrived with a sagging diaper bag, cradling a pink bundle. I swiped Elizabeth from her arms immediately, cuddling my godbaby closely. Elizabeth curled her legs up and nuzzled into my shoulder.

She was so tiny and delicate still. I could hold her for hours and never grow tired. Instinctively I began to rock her.

"Careful or she'll spit up on your shirt," Clara advised, hovering nearby.

"That's okay," I cooed, kissing her velvety forehead. "Auntie Belle doesn't mind."

Clara held out a burp cloth, her eyebrow arching as I took it and maneuvered it under Elizabeth's head.

"What?" I asked as I continued to sway with the baby.

"You have baby fever," she accused.

My mouth fell open. Of all the ridiculous accusations, that had to be the worst. Business fever? Yes. An unrelenting passion for shoes? Obviously. Completely punch-drunk in love? That was undeniable. "Would you prefer I didn't want to hold her?"

"No." Clara shook her head and held out her arms. "But I'll take her back now."

My eyes narrowed and I turned away from her outstretched hands. "You get her all the time, and I've been away for the last week."

"I think that proves my point." Clara's tone couldn't be drier if she shoved a bag of cotton balls in her mouth. "And speaking of your trip, tell me about it."

I turned back to her, studying her suspiciously. She wanted to hear about more than my trip to Central Park or my interview. On the surface, her blue eyes were as glassy as the surface of the ocean on a windless day, but underneath that facade of calm, the waters churned. I knew her too well not to see that.

"There's not much to tell." I hated lying to her. I hated the way the deceit clawed through me, scratching at my stomach and squeezing my heart. I'd done it before, keeping Alexander's letters hidden to protect her from more heartbreak. But I didn't have a selfless excuse now. Even if I had my reasons.

And judging from the pain flashing across her pale features, she already knew much more than she was supposed to.

I took a deep breath and made a judgment call. "I'm back with Smith."

Clara nodded, but I didn't miss the slide of her throat. She knew more than that.

Christ, how much did she know and why?

"This morning, I overheard a rather odd argument. I was walking by Alexander's office, and he had a visitor."

I felt the blood drain from my face, and I took a step back until I felt my desk chair bump the back of my thigh. I definitely needed to be sitting down for this one, especially if I was going to be holding a baby.

"My husband was talking to a man I've never actually met," she continued, her voice breaking as she spoke. "And they were fighting. About what happened the day of our wedding. Stop me if you already know all of this."

"Clara, I don't...I didn't..." I couldn't process what she was telling me. "You have to believe me that I didn't know anything about this."

"Nothing?" she demanded, swiping furiously at the moisture pooling in her eyes. "Because that man knows you, and from the sound of it, he knows you intimately."

"Not nothing," I admitted. I wouldn't feign ignorance. She had never met Smith, but she knew enough to guess it was him in Alexander's study. A numbness spread through me as her words sunk in. Smith and Alexander. It was unfathomable.

Smith had been involved with this since long before we met, which meant the two had known each other longer that I'd known him. And suddenly all the half truths he'd told me began to click together, forming a realization I wished I could ignore. I had been sent to Smith—to get to Alexander and Clara. And the times he'd pushed me away hadn't only been to protect me, it had been to protect them as well.

Elizabeth began to whimper in my arms. I rubbed circles on her back, wishing for a moment that I were the one being held. I longed to be innocent and blameless—only capable of need—because now I couldn't differentiate between needing and wanting.

"Start being honest with me and quickly." Clara's sternness took me aback.

I'd never seen her like this. She was scared, that was something I was familiar with, but she was also fearless. Whatever information I had to give her, she could handle it. My best friend hadn't always been that way.

"Smith. I don't know where to begin." I hesitated, searching her face for some sign that she didn't hate me, but coming up empty-handed. "He's been working to bring a man named Hammond to justice."

"Hammond?" she repeated in breathless horror. "The jeweler?"

"He's a little more than that," I told her flatly. I really wished Lola had gotten around to setting up the office bar that we had discussed.

This time it was Clara's turn to sink shakily into a seat. "I don't understand."

"Honestly, neither do I." I could only hope she saw how earnestly I meant that.

"What else?"

I had a feeling that she had heard a lot more outside that office door. It hurt that our relationship had been reduced to a test. I didn't know what she had already found out, which meant the only way I could hope to pass her examination was to tell her everything I did know.

"I didn't know he was working with Alexander." It seemed important to get that fact on the table right away. "I had absolutely no clue that they even knew each other.

"Wait, that's not entirely true," I stopped myself. "An acquaintance of Smith's said she knew you both. It didn't occur to me that it might be important until now."

"Who?" Clara asked in a hollow voice.

"Georgia Kincaid."

Her face blanched. She didn't have to say a word. She knew Georgia as well as I did, which wasn't to say all that well. But we both knew the most vital information regarding her. I wanted to ask her how she knew, but considering the way she clutched her chair as if she was barely staying upright, I thought better of it.

"I guess you've met her." The joke did nothing to lighten the mood.

"Alexander hired her to keep an eye on me after Daniel got into our house. Obviously she did a fantastic job keeping tabs on him since he managed to get through security on our wedding day."

"I can't say that I like her."

"But none of that explains why any of this is happening." Clara chewed on her fingernails as she spoke.

Standing, I brought Elizabeth back to Clara to occupy her hands. She took her daughter and held her close, pressing her face against the baby's petite head. When she looked back up, tears streaked down her face.

"It's going to be okay," I whispered, wishing I believed it.

"Is it? Because none of this feels okay. Alexander would barely talk to me when I confronted him." A sob punctuated her words. "And now I find out that you're keeping things from me as well."

"I didn't want to." I knelt by her side, placing my hand on her knee. "I didn't know you were involved. If I had..."

"What?" she demanded. "You would have told me? Excuse me if I don't buy that."

I sat back on my heels, stung by her accusation. "I didn't want to worry you when I found out that Smith was involved with these people."

"And what about the fact that you married him?" she shot back. "Were you worried about telling me that, too?"

My mouth fell open. So that was what she'd been holding back. I searched for an excuse, a reason that would account for how terrible the revelation made me feel, but I came up empty-handed. "We haven't told anyone," I said meekly.

"My invitation must have been lost in the mail." She looked away from me, her thick hair cascading over her shoulder like a dark curtain falling between us.

"Believe me, you didn't miss much. The butler at our hotel

married us in our suite." A vice grip squeezed my heart at the memory that I'd kept secret since that night. Sharing it put me in an impossible position. God, I wanted to tell her the details and giggle and marvel that I was married. But the circumstances surrounding our union made that impossible. Perhaps that was why the ring was still tucked into a box in my purse.

"I'm not anyone. My best friend. My husband. You've all been lying to me, and I don't know how I'm supposed to feel about that."

"We were trying to protect you." That much was true. That much I understood. Clara had endured more fear and pain in the last year than I could even imagine. I hadn't wanted to add more weight to her shoulders.

"By lying to me. The people I love don't trust me enough to support them."

"Would you have supported me?" I blurted out. "Because I'm not even sure that I made the right call."

"Then why did you do it? Why did you marry him if you knew the kind of man he was?"

Anger burst through me, setting my blood on fire. "Because I'm the only one who knows what kind of man he truly is."

"Edward told me he hurt you," Clara said in a flat voice. In her arms, Elizabeth stirred and I watched as Clara lowered her to nurse.

This was what was supposed to be preoccupying her now: caring for her child. The joy she should have felt had been stripped from her, and I didn't know how to give it back to her.

"Smith tried to break things off." She deserved an explanation, and if anyone could understand the complicated nature of falling in love with a powerful man, she could. "Now I know why."

"So you knew the danger and you chose him anyway?" Clara sucked in a breath. "Belle, I won't lie. I'm angry with you, but I'm also terrified for you."

"Do you think I'm not scared? Because I am. But I'm more scared of losing him—and losing you. Right now all I want to do is escort you back home and lock you away."

"You sound like Alexander." Her nostrils flared and I wondered just how much of a tongue-lashing he had received this morning. "I had to sneak out just to come here."

"You didn't," I exclaimed. Popping onto my feet, I grabbed my mobile from my desk.

"Don't you dare text him."

I paused, torn between the duty I felt to each of them. It was foolish to let her run around without protection, but I hated the idea of betraying what fragile trust might still exist between us.

"I love you too much to let you put yourself in more danger, and you love her too much"—I pointed at Elizabeth, who was still suckling contentedly—"to risk her."

Clara's eyes narrowed, and I knew then what it was to choose the safety of someone you loved over their happiness.

"I'm sorry." But I could tell my apology meant very little to her.

"Use mine," she said before I could continue the message. "Call Norris. He'll come for me, and then you won't have to deal with Alexander."

I raised an eyebrow. "I can deal with Alexander."

"I can't," she said softly. "I love him. I love you. But right now I want to be alone. Norris will understand that."

I decided not to argue with her. Alexander's personal bodyguard had always been capable of maintaining a much cooler head when it came to Clara, and I knew he wouldn't allow anyone to harm her. Digging her mobile out of her diaper bag, I dialed his number and explained the situation.

Neither of us spoke as we waited for him to arrive, and when he finally came to retrieve her, Clara didn't spare a glance in my direction. No goodbye. No hug.

I'd told Smith I had a life to return to in London. Now it seemed I didn't.

CHAPTER TWENTY-TWO

I stayed at the studio, not ready to face Smith but not able to work. As evening approached, I realized I'd done nothing but stare at my computer's screensaver for the last few hours. Grudgingly I forced myself to stand and gather my things. My eyes landed on a pale pink blanket strung over the back of my chair. Clara had left it.

Whatever stability my hours of numbness had given me dissolved. They were my family—Elizabeth and Clara and Edward. I'd lost sight of that, and now I'd done what might prove to be irreparable damage to my relationships with them. I picked up the blanket and held it to my chest, closing my eyes and wishing to be set free. For all of us to be free.

But wishes were for fairy tales, and I had no hope that the universe had any interest in sending me a miracle.

I folded Elizabeth's blanket and stuck it in my purse before I locked up and walked to my parked car at the end of the street. I'd return the blanket tomorrow, and I'd apologize to Clara—and then somehow we'd find a way to move forward. Because I wasn't about to lose my best friend.

The Mercedes's lights blinked as I hit the unlock button. At least at this time of night there would be no traffic. After Clara's visit, I wanted answers only Smith could give me. I'd known he was deeply entrenched in a plot to bring Hammond down, but the fact that he was working with Alexander still stunned me. As had Clara's confrontation regarding my spontaneous marriage.

I'd agreed to keep that a secret, and it shredded me to know that she'd found out before I could tell her. Before she'd even had a chance to meet him.

Clearly I was losing my mind. And that left me feeling uprooted. Smith was my anchor, but was he dragging me down? It stung to admit I might have made a mistake. Mostly because I hadn't even had time to come to grips with the sudden change in my life.

Opening the door, I moved to drop my bag on the passenger seat when I realized I wasn't alone.

Hands grabbed me from behind before I could process this fact. I kicked out, trying to free myself. But the hold on me tightened. The man shoved me against the side of the car, knocking the wind from my lungs.

I couldn't breathe, which meant I couldn't fight.

Fingers closed over my hair, jerking my head back.

"Such a fancy car for such a pretty lady."

My stomach roiled, and I choked against the bile that rose in my throat as I struggled to find my own voice.

Scream, a voice deep within me commanded. I opened my mouth, and his hand clamped over it, catching the cry for help before it could take flight.

"No, no, beautiful," he chastised me. "None of that now. Why don't we go for a ride?"

Beautiful. Hearing that from this strange voice, so intent on humiliating me and probably much worse, spurred something inside me. That wasn't his word. He had no right to call me that. Just as his hands had no bloody right to my body. Whatever fear locked me into place shifted, and I threw my elbow back. I knew with absolute certainty that I had to stay out of that car. The jab caught him in the ribs, and he lost his grip on me, giving me just enough time to twist away.

But not enough time to run.

He caught the back of my shirt and I tripped, crashing to the pavement in a heap, my ankles twisting underneath me. Pain shot through my leg, but I forced it away. Scrabbling forward, my nails raked against the concrete as I attempted to regain my footing.

The man hauled me back, and I heard the nauseating rip of fabric as my blouse tore at the shoulder. I wriggled, hoping that I could shrug it off. Right now it was the only thing holding me captive. But my attacker was too quick. A heavy weight pinned me to the ground, and my chest constricted as I fought to breathe under the massive burden.

"You aren't going anywhere," the cold voice informed me. His hands snaked underneath me, feeling along my body. My stomach. My breasts.

Another wrench, and I felt the cool night air on my skin as my shirt fell open, exposing my bare back. His knee pressed into my tailbone as his hands continued to wander down.

This wasn't happening.

I wouldn't let it. The scream I'd sought broke past my lips, rupturing the quiet night.

"Shut up, bitch," he snarled.

But I wasn't about to do that. I continued to howl. Someone would hear. Someone had to.

The sickening sound of my zipper stole my cries, and I writhed, my hands splayed out and searching for salvation from the rough cement. My fingers brushed something cold and metallic, and I grabbed my keys, hitting every button in the process and setting off the car alarm.

"You shouldn't have done that," the man yelled, tearing them from my hands. But it was too late. The Mercedes wailed for help as he frantically tried to shut off the alarm.

And then silence.

The street was still empty. No one had heard, and now he had my keys. Gathering every ounce of my strength, I bucked against his hold, knocking him off me. I rolled, and before he could jump back on top of me, I swung the heel of my shoe directly into his stomach, narrowly missing his groin.

The miscalculation cost me. Rather than dropping him, the strike only made him more infuriated. His hands closed over my throat. The sharp edge of a key pressed into my skin. My legs continued to kick, but I made no contact.

"You're a stupid little girl." Spit splattered over my face, and my head fell to the side, afraid of being so close to this man's mouth and the hatred spewing from it.

He grabbed my chin and yanked my face back to his, his other hand still clasped tightly around my neck. His fingers spread up, covering my mouth and then he plunged them inside, wrenching my jaw open. I bit down, but I couldn't get the momentum I needed. He laughed as he held me there.

Trembles wracked my body.

"I just wanted your car, you stupid bitch." His knee smashed into my stomach, and I arched up, gasping for air I couldn't find. "Now maybe I'll take something else."

I collapsed under him, panting, as tears pricked my eyes. I stared up at him, my willpower deserting me. I pled silently with the stranger, even as I memorized the crook in his nose and the long scar that ran along his temple.

If I stopped fighting, what would happen? Right now it seemed like my only choice. I made peace with the fact that I wasn't walking away unscathed, but I decided then and there that I would walk away. I remained still, bracing myself for whatever came next.

"That's right," he crooned. "You want it, don't you? You're hot for it. Can't let anyone know that a classy lady like you likes to be fucked, can you? Got to put up a little fight. But I got what you need, baby."

My body spasmed, and I choked on the vomit I could no longer hold back. The man dropped his hold on me, and my head rolled to the side as I coughed up bile.

"Dirty bitch," he screamed. His hand grabbed my hip, his weight shifting as he flipped me onto my stomach and yanked up my skirt. "This is a much better view. I bet you like it everywhere."

A fingertip hooked around the strip of my thong, and I began to shake. Inside I screamed but the sound was trapped. I was frozen in place, completely at the mercy of evil.

And then I heard the sirens. I didn't know if they were coming for me, but they were there and the sound gave me the power to cry out.

"Fuck." The hand disappeared, but he didn't get off of me.

I knew then that we were both calculating the same thing: how much longer?

"You got lucky this time," he hissed, flattening his body against mine so he could hiss in my ear. "But don't worry. I'll find you, baby, and finish you off. I know how bad you need it."

His groin circled my ass as I began to sob.

"I hate when a woman cries." His hand closed over the back of my head, seizing my hair. He pulled back and captured my mouth, his tongue darting between my lips. This time I bit. Hard. Iron flooded over my tongue just as my face smashed against the pavement. Pain seared through my temple, but before I could process what had happened, he'd slammed me down again.

I knew then that I was going to die. Through the agony, Smith's face flashed in my thoughts. I didn't want him to blame himself. I didn't want it to end like this, but as my neck snapped back and concrete rushed to meet me once more, I knew there was no stopping the darkness.

CHAPTER TWENTY-THREE

My heart pounded as I bypassed the check-in desk at the hospital's emergency entrance, striding instead toward a nurse's station when I reached St. Mary's.

"Belle Stuart," I barked at the nurse sitting behind the counter.

She glared at me and pointed to a chair. "Only immediate family is allowed in to see her. The doctor is with her now."

"I am her family." Impatience seethed through me. I didn't have time for this woman or her petty rules. I needed to find my wife. I needed to see her. If no one was going to tell me where she was, I would find her myself. I slammed open a door marked Authorized Entry Only with a small thank you tacked onto the bottom. Trust the British to be polite in every circumstance. That was one trait I hadn't been born with. I had too much of my mother's blood in me.

"Sir!" the nurse called behind me, but I was already down the corridor, my eyes darting into every open door.

I could feel myself getting closer, but with each step I took that didn't bring me to Belle, the furious panic building inside me swelled. I hated hospitals. I hated the stench of sterile death that permeated their halls. I hated the cold, impersonal interiors created to give you nothing to cling to when you were given the worst news.

This was the only time I'd stepped foot in one since Margot had died. The doctor's platitudes floated to mind as my brain prepared itself to relive that day. Only this time it would be worse.

It occurred to me that I was on the eighth floor, high enough to ensure I wouldn't survive if I could find an open window. My unease grew, and I began to open the closed doors, not bothering to shut them. Angry protests filled the air as I ravaged my way down the hospital wing.

And then she was there. Eyes closed, monitor softly beeping.

A pair of hands closed over my shoulders, hauling me away from her room, but I jerked away.

"Sir, you need to come with us," a security guard advised me, one hand on the baton hooked on his belt. Another stood silently a few feet behind him.

"That's my wife," I informed him through gritted teeth. "I was told immediate family was allowed in."

"They are," he responded calmly, "but we need to check your identification first, and frankly, it's up to the hospital if they want to press charges."

I tugged my suit jacket down, willing myself to regain my composure. "Call Dr. Roget and tell him Smith Price is visiting a patient. He'll vouch for me."

"We can do that in the lobby." The guard gestured for me to follow him outside, but I didn't budge.

"You can also tell Dr. Roget that I'll be donating a generous sum to the children's wing in gratitude for the care my wife receives. I know they need to hire a new oncologist."

The guard inhaled deeply, and I could tell he was weighing his options. A man who took his job seriously would drag me to the curb. A good man wouldn't be able to ignore the offer I'd just extended.

"Stay with him," he ordered his companion before turning back to me and leveling a finger at my chest. "I hope your story checks out, because I will personally see that the only hospital room you visit is your own."

I didn't bother to respond to his threat. Because I didn't give a damn. My story would check out, and Roget would get his money. It felt kinder than blackmailing him with the details of his relationship with a certain mutual acquaintance. Although I'd bring Georgia into the picture if it became necessary. I grabbed Belle's chart from the end of her bed as I went to her side. It was easier to read the status of her injuries than it was to look at her. Contusion to the right eye. Hairline fracture to her right cheekbone. Ten stitches to the temple.

Inconclusive evidence of sexual assault.

My knees buckled, and I dropped to the ground. I didn't believe in God, but I prayed then as I pressed my head against the mattress. I prayed for forgiveness that I didn't deserve. I prayed for her eyes to open. Not to absolve me—I didn't want her to—but so that I could look into them and find the strength to leave her.

Because if I didn't, I was going to kill her. It wouldn't be my hands that did the deed, but her blood would be on them all the same. I'd been selfish. There was no denying it now, each beat of her heart on the monitor reminding me that she'd almost taken her last breath tonight.

"Mr. Price," a clipped voice greeted me, and I lifted my head to see a young doctor enter the room. She rounded the bed and collected the clipboard. "I'm Dr. Grant. Your wife is going to be fine. We gave her a little sedative to help her sleep. I can see you've already reviewed her condition."

"Has she been conscious yet?"

"She woke up in the ambulance and stayed awake for most of the procedures. She was cognizant enough to ask us to call you."

A few minutes ago, I would have been throwing that in the nurse's face. Now I only cared about one thing.

"The chart says there was inconclusive evidence of..." I trailed away, unable to say the words.

"Most of her clothing was still intact when emergency crews reached her."

"What does that mean?" I choked out, my hands balling into fists.

"Her underwear was still on," Dr. Grant said softly, "but we did find evidence that she had recently had sex. I know this is a very personal question, but when was the last time you engaged in sexual relations with your wife?"

"This morning," I answered immediately, "and twice last night."

Dr. Grant blinked in surprise and glanced down at the chart. I got the feeling she found my answer impressive, but I didn't give a shit. "It's very possible then that the DNA we recovered was yours."

I didn't want to consider that it might not be.

"When will she wake up?" I asked. I had to see her eyes flutter open one more time. I had to tell her that I loved her. Just as I had to believe she would understand why I could no longer put her in this kind of danger.

But there was one more thing I had to know. "Did you catch him?"

"No." She shook her head sadly. "It appears to be a random carjacking gone bad. Her purse was recovered from the scene. I'm sure the police will catch up with him."

I gave her a grim smile. "I'm going to stay with her."

She didn't deny the request, which was smart because it wasn't one.

Random. That was one word that definitely didn't apply to this case. A carjacker didn't attack a woman and leave her purse. This was targeted and purposeful, which meant Hammond had found out about us much sooner than I had hoped.

Forcing myself to stand, I dragged a chair next to her bed and sank down into it as I dialed a number on my mobile. The time for retribution was at hand.

I woke to a hand brushing across my forehead. Lifting my head to discover I'd fallen asleep in the worst possible position, my eyes met hers. Belle's face was swollen, a purple rim circling her eye, and she was still the most breathtaking thing I'd ever seen.

"Hey, beautiful," I murmured as I sat up and took her hand.

"Do I want to ask for a mirror?" She licked her lips as she spoke.

I shook my head. "No need. You look gorgeous."

"Liar," she accused with a faint smile that didn't reach her tired eyes.

"Do you remember what happened?" I asked her, steeling myself for her answer.

"Some asshat tried to steal my car, and I was stubborn about it."

I swallowed and forced myself to ask the question I didn't really want answered. "Did he...did he rape you?"

"No." She winced as she tried to sit up. I sprung to my feet to help her, part of my burden lifting from my shoulders. It didn't make any of this okay, but I couldn't help but be relieved.

"The hospital wasn't sure," I explained.

"He made it pretty clear he was thinking about it." Her eyes darted nervously to meet mine. "Would it have mattered if he had?"

"It would have mattered in how quickly I'm going to end his life." There was no point in pretending otherwise. Hammond was at the heart of this, but whatever goon he'd sent to handle his dirty work would find himself paying the price as well.

"Smith." But the plea in her voice was lost on me.

"Don't worry about that right now," I said in a soothing voice. Leaning down, I brushed my lips gingerly over her forehead.

"It's not your fault," she whispered.

But we both knew that wasn't true.

"Belle, I can't allow this to continue." My words came out in halting fragments, each one more difficult than the last.

Tears welled in her giant blue eyes but they didn't spill over. "Sorry, Price. I made my choice. You're stuck with me."

"Not if it means—"

"I know our wedding was a bit unorthodox," she interrupted me, "but I'm pretty sure we got to the vows and all that stuff about death and parting, sickness and health."

"You can't ask me to ignore this," I said, more harshly than I'd intended.

But she didn't shrink away. Instead she sat up and glared at me. "No, I can't. But you're my husband, so you're going to have to deal with it."

I closed my eyes, trying to bite back the smile tugging up the corners of my mouth. "Are you ever going to listen to me?"

"You like it when I provoke you," she reminded me.

I couldn't deny that was true.

"I couldn't live with myself if something happened to you, beautiful."

"And I wouldn't want to live with myself if I ran away. I guess we'll have to learn to live with each other."

It was reckless to listen to her—reckless to give in to what my heart wanted. But when the doctor came in a few hours later, I was still there. I had put her in this position, and I couldn't desert her now, not while she was so vulnerable—not while I was still breathing.

I'd claimed her as my own. She was mine to protect, and maybe it was foolish to covet her after tonight's events, but she belonged to me and no one was going to take her away until they dragged me to hell.

CHAPTER TWENTY-FOUR

As the Bugatti pulled to the curb outside the Westminster Royal I turned to Smith in surprise. We'd stopped by my flat for a few things, narrowly avoiding Jane who was out on an errand. When we had left, I'd expected to return to one of his houses. Not that I had anything against luxury hotels, but I was beginning to think his paranoia was getting the best of him.

"First, no purse. No identification. No mobile." I sighed deeply. "And now a hotel?"

"It's best to be on the safe side." He didn't meet my eyes as he said this. He'd avoided looking at me since we left the hospital. He'd even turned away while I changed in the bedroom of my flat.

"The police said this was an isolated incident." I repeated their words, wishing I believed it. It was better for Smith if I, at least, pretended I did.

He didn't respond; instead I followed him inside. The penthouse suite was every bit as lavish as one would expect from a five-star hotel. Even though it occupied an entire floor that overlooked the Thames, it reminded me of the suite we'd shared in New York. How was it possible we were only there a few days ago?

"You should get some rest," Smith called as he took my bag to the bedroom. "Or eat something. We can order in."

He was treating me like a patient, which only reminded me of what had happened. It wasn't as if the constant stabbing pain that occupied half of my face wasn't memento enough.

"I slept at the hospital." I paused, my eyes finding the floor. "I can't face another nightmare."

Smith reacted almost instinctively, taking me into his arms. He was careful to turn my body so that he didn't touch any of the swelling. "I'm here now, beautiful. Let's watch a movie."

He didn't want me. Not like this. Any other time, he would have taken me to bed and claimed me. The fact only made me feel worse, but I forced a smile.

Smith arranged the suite's sofa so that I could stretch out next to him. We settled in, his arm draped carefully over me as he flipped through channels. Finally he found an old black and white classic playing late on a BBC channel. But I wasn't interested in the drama on-screen, not while my whole life was in turmoil.

I was in a strange place under the influence of a cocktail of drugs that seemed intent on luring me back to the nightmarish realm of my memories.

"I've never seen this," I announced, wanting his attention on me.

"Seriously? We're going to have to educate you in Humphrey Bogart then." He stared down at me with a look of such pure love that my heart constricted, feeling as if it might explode.

He still loved me, despite what had happened. But another man's hands had been on my body tonight, sullying the bond that I shared with Smith, and no matter how hard I tried to escape that, it clawed at me. I felt raw. Vulnerable. I didn't want to sleep, and I didn't want to be awake. I couldn't face this, and he seemed content to pretend nothing was wrong.

But everything *was* wrong, terribly so. I clamped a hand over my mouth and then scrambled up to the bathroom. I sank down in front of the toilet, positive that I was going to vomit. My stomach heaved, but nothing came out except desperate gasps and dry, choking sounds. Smith rushed in and knelt at my side, gathering my hair.

"Are you sick?"

I shook my head. I wasn't, not physically at least. That this was all in my head made it harder to bear. The heaves of my chest turned to sobs that racked through me.

"I'm sorry." But my tears cracked my voice, making it hard to speak.

"You have nothing to be sorry for." He released my hair and dropped to sit next to me. "Nothing."

"Then why are you so scared to touch me?" I was being hysterical. I knew that, but I couldn't control how I felt any more than I could take back what had happened.

"Do you think that I don't want to?" he asked. "I'm afraid I'll hurt you or..."

"Or?" I prompted. I needed to know how that sentence ended, needed to know that his every thought wasn't caught up in how to extricate himself from the mess we were both in.

"I want nothing more than to make love to you right now," he said in a hushed voice, brushing a finger down my forearm. "Not fuck. Not dominate. I just want to feel myself inside of you, but that's not how this works."

"Why not?" I challenged, growing angry at the idea that we were both denying what we needed.

"Because it's my job to take care of you, and I've already fucked that up enough."

I couldn't stand the anguish pooling in his green eyes.

"I need you to show me I'm still yours. That you still want me."

He stood and my heart splintered along the fissures that had barely healed from the last time he had broken it. Someday there would be no heart left at all, only scar tissue. But tonight, my heart could still feel and the agony Smith inspired was far more acute than any physical pain I'd endured.

But then he bent down and lifted me to my feet before scooping me into his arms. He carried me slowly into the bedroom, whispering the vows he'd said to me only nights before. Laying me carefully across the bed, he stripped off his clothing until he was bare. His cock bobbed as he approached me and hooked his fingers over the waistband of my pants. He drew them off in one fluid motion.

"In the hospital, when I saw you there, and you were breathing, do you know what happened?" he asked as he palmed his dick. "I got hard. I wanted you so badly that I had to hide my erection with a pillow. You know why, beautiful? Because I always want you. Because your very breath is mine, and it hadn't been taken away from me. I needed to stay away from you—needed to not touch you—because I couldn't bear to make you suffer."

"Don't stay away," I cried, my hands struggling to slide off my panties. "I need to know you still want me."

"This time when I say we have to do this on my terms"—he lifted my leg and bent to kiss the softness of my inner thigh—"it's not because I want to dominate you, it's because I won't be able to forgive myself if I cause you pain."

Our relationship had always been about pain commingling with pleasure. It was what had brought us together, and now that intimacy had been robbed from us. More than anything, I wanted to pretend nothing was wrong. I wanted to crawl to the edge of the bed and take his cock into my mouth, but I knew he wouldn't allow it. And his control over this situation was the only remnant of what we had shared only this morning.

"I want to see you," he rasped. He leaned over me, hovering to keep his weight off me. I wanted to pull him down and force him to release the primal masculinity he kept from me now, but I remained still. Smith ran his fingers down the neckline of my camisole, his eyes pinned to my face. "I want to be careful, so I hope you aren't attached to this."

He pinched the fabric in both hands and stretched until the threads gave way. He had no way of knowing that another man had ripped my blouse from me tonight, just as he had no way of knowing that simple act done with the utmost care and concern had erased that memory, replacing it with an image of love. He opened it gently, freeing my breasts to the air and then slowly slid the tattered remnants away.

His fingers danced over my skin, dodging the bruises left behind by the attack, and then he began to kiss me. Smith's mouth moved lower, his lips and tongue flickering across my skin with a light touch that reminded of the tip of a feather. Tonight there would be no playful whips and smacks though, but there would be want. Want that consumed me like a flame blazing into a fire. Want that vanquished any fear I felt.

There was no fear at Smith's hand. No trepidation. He'd taken my body and given me his very soul in return.

"I'm going to make you feel good, beautiful," he whispered, his breath tickling over my abdomen. "I'm going to take all the pain away for as long and as often as I can."

My head fell back against the sheets as he dipped his tongue between my thighs. He licked along my seam with a reverent patience that drew the attention of my nerves until all sensation in my body was centered there. He kissed the plumping flesh of my mound, sucking the whole of it fervently into his mouth. A low moan emanated from his chest, and I bucked against the vibration it sent trembling through my skin.

Oh god, this man. This sinful, cocky, broken, perfect man was going to make me come without ever breaching my folds.

He drew back as soon as my abdomen tensed and hooked his arms under my thighs, yanking my legs over his shoulders. His hands slid down to cup my ass, holding me in the air as he kissed my tortured pussy.

"I'm not through with you yet. I only wanted to make sure I had your undivided attention."

That sounded a lot like a promise. I grabbed the sheets and held on.

"I love burying my face in your ripe cunt, tasting your sweetness on my tongue. I just had to stop and admire how pretty you look with your legs around my neck and your pussy plumped and ready for me. I'm going to take good care of you both. Forever, beautiful."

He kept his eyes on me as he lowered his mouth to fuck me. I watched, white light creeping into the edges of my vision, as his tongue parted my slit. The tip of it flicked across my clit until I was gasping and pleading. But he wasn't ready to let me go yet. He flattened his tongue, stroking the length of my sex languidly. I writhed beneath him, nearly vaulting out of his grip. Digging his fingers into my hips, he rocked me back and forth against his tireless tongue.

"Please, please, please." The word fell from my mouth with each sweep of his tongue over my clit.

He paused just long enough for my want to throb painfully through my core, and then his mouth clamped greedily over my engorged nub.

My back arched off the bed as I ground myself against his mouth. There was nothing but him and the pleasure he poured through me. My anchor. My release.

When he finally lowered me to the bed, I sagged bonelessly, my legs sliding from his shoulders and my climax still pulsing at my core.

"You got so fucking wet when you came." He groaned as he nudged the head of his cock against my slick entrance. "I'm going to be tasting you for weeks."

I bit my lip shyly, my eyes drooping as I prepared myself for more.

More and never enough. That seemed like a pretty solid foundation to build a future on.

"I can feel your cunt squeezing my tip. Does it want more?"

"Yes, Sir," I panted.

"No, not tonight. Tonight you're my wife—*my partner*."

"Your equal?" I teased.

"You're always that." Smith licked his lower lip. "I only hope I'm yours."

He was in every way. I wanted to tell him that. I wanted to press my body to his and feel this man who belonged so entirely to me, and I to him. But before I could find the strength to move, he slid inside me, effectively destroying any possibility of me moving. Not when he was piercing me to the core. Not with him rooted fully inside me.

We began a slow, sensual rhythm. Neither of us rushing as we lingered in the sensation of our union. He filled me, and I consumed him until we were one body, melding and morphing into a perfect symphony. Our tempo increased gradually as we rocked together, but then Smith stopped and withdrew.

I missed him immediately, longing for the completeness only he could grant me.

He moved farther up the bed, propping his back against the headboard. "I need to hold you."

I rolled to my stomach and crawled to his lap.

"Slowly," he urged as I lowered myself, one hand guiding his shaft home. I cried out at the deepness, my ass circling the delicious fullness stretching me as I settled onto him. "That's it, beautiful. »

Strong arms coiled around my torso, his warm palms flattening against my shoulder blades. He cradled me to him as he began to roll his groin against me. I clutched his chest for leverage as he sought the perfect angle. He shifted, the friction of his movement urging my seam wider so that my clit raked across the coarse patch of hair at his root. My head tipped forward, and I barely noticed the smart of pain as my forehead pressed into his shoulder.

"I want to be inside of you every day for the rest of my life. I wish I was strong enough to give you up, but I'm not," he said gruffly into my ear.

"You promised me forever," I whimpered, as my hips sought to drive him deeper inside me. There was no escape. I wouldn't allow it.

"And I'll give it to you. Forever," he repeated, plunging harder until I was nearly bouncing. His arm dropped from my back, and he took my hand, pressing my palm to the center of his chest. "Yours. All of me. It's all yours. My future. My heart. My very life."

I closed my eyes and concentrated on his rapid, but constant, heartbeat. My own life hadn't begun until the day I met him, and someday when he was gone, it would draw to a close. I'd spend every moment until then fighting for him.

We'd made a decision together, and we'd said a vow. But now we had faced that which would attempt to rip us apart, and we were still here.

"I love you, Smith Price." My mouth closed over his, skimming his lips lightly.

His groin constricted beneath me, and we rode toward our forever together, sharing soft kisses as we fought to get closer, preparing for the battle we faced outside these walls. When he finally slowed, his mouth curved into a cocky grin.

"You look pleased with yourself," I noted, even as I sagged against him. He had a right to look pleased. On the list of the world's top orgasms, that one had blown them all away.

"I was just thinking that I love you, Belle Price."

I tilted my head back to scowl playfully at him, even as a happy peacefulness descended over me.

"You should have objected before you said *I do*, beautiful." His index finger tipped my chin up, and he placed a cautious kiss on my bruised lips.

"Can I file some type of negotiated contract?" The truth was that I wanted his name as much as I wanted him. My own surname held nothing but sad memories. It was my father's name, not mine, and if I had to choose a man's name, Smith's was the one I wanted.

"I doubt your lawyer will advise that," he said dryly.

I huffed in mock exasperation. "Belle Price it is, I suppose."

"On that note"—he deposited me onto the bed and swung his legs over the side—"I'll be right back."

I slumped against the pillows, languid contentment taking residence in my limbs. I was blinking sleepily by the time he returned.

"I took the liberty of stealing this from your purse." He slipped back into bed, my wedding band pinched between his thumb and forefinger. "Because it belongs with you."

Smith captured my hand and gently urged the ring onto my finger. I stared at it, trying to process how much my feelings had evolved about wearing it. The circle of flawless diamonds set into gold no longer felt heavy. It no longer dazzled. It simply felt right. It was as timeless as our love. No beginning. No end. Just forever.

"If you'd prefer a different one..." he began.

But I shook my head and leaned forward to kiss him hard on the mouth. I blanched as my cheek bumped his accidentally, but I swallowed down the pain before he could spot it. "Don't you dare try to take this ring off my finger."

"Good, you can pick out my ring." He slid an arm around my back, and we lay there staring at the new addition to my finger.

I glanced at him in surprise.

"What?" He shrugged. "I belong to you, beautiful. If you don't want me to—"

"Oh, you are wearing one," I informed him.

"I like it when you're jealous," he teased, knitting our fingers together.

"I just want everyone to know you're mine," I whispered, "so they know how lucky I am."

"That makes two of us. Now get some rest, Mrs. Price," he ordered, tugging the covers over me.

"What about Ms. Price?" I countered.

"As long as you're a Price," he murmured as he reached up to dim the lights.

"Forever." My eyes closed as I fell into a dreamless sleep.

CHAPTER TWENTY-FIVE

Purple. It was the only word filtering through the haze of painkillers clouding my brain. I lifted my hand and gingerly touched my swollen cheek. The woman in the mirror flinched as pain shot through me. No wonder Smith had been so hesitant to touch me. I looked like hell. No amount of makeup was covering this up, and trying to smooth foundation over the bruise seemed like a pretty bad idea.

Smith appeared behind me, watching my reaction in the mirror. His strong hands gripped my upper arms, and I closed my eyes, savoring the touch.

"Give it time," he commanded in a low voice. "I'm going to arrange for a nurse to stay with you today."

I spun around, shaking my head. "No, don't do that."

The thought of being alone with a stranger was too much to bear.

"I can't leave you like this, beautiful." He raised a hand to brush back my hair, taking care to avoid my wounds. I saw the horror in his eyes and, behind it, an emotion that stole my breath.

"Then don't leave me." I bit my lip in an attempt at seduction and immediately regretted it as a searing throb rocketed through my temple.

Smith reacted instantly in concern, but I pushed him away. I couldn't stomach his pity any more than I could the reality of what had happened. The police had found my car, but not the man who had attacked me. That fact, combined with the soporific effects of my pain medicine, had my emotions at maximum capacity.

I swallowed against the tears that seemed perpetually lodged in my throat. "I'll call my aunt."

"Are you sure?" Smith's eyes softened, as if to remind me that the fury he couldn't hide was in no way directed at me.

"Yes."

He waited while I made the call from the hotel phone, perhaps suspecting I hadn't planned to at all. When I hung up with Jane, he brushed a kiss over my lips.

"I love you."

I caught his hand, clutching it desperately.

"I'm coming back." He spoke solemnly, and I relaxed my hold, allowing him to gently pull away.

I wanted to tell him not to go. Or ask when he was returning. But some part of me that hadn't been shattered in yesterday's attack resisted. I wasn't that girl. I didn't want to be. I couldn't permit it to change me.

As soon as he was gone, I took another pain pill, swallowing it down with a gulp of wine. If I was going to spend all day pent up in a hotel room, I didn't want the option of thinking.

But even as a languid stupor descended over me, my brain continued to reel, replaying the attack on a constant loop. Smith hadn't told me that I had been targeted, a decision I saw as calculated. However, I knew it had been. Coincidence was bumping into a friend at a restaurant. Being beat up when your husband worked for the city's resident crime syndicate wasn't.

I froze when I heard a knock at the door and braced myself for Jane's reaction. If she had thought it strange that I'd given her the room number of a hotel, she hadn't said anything. But she wasn't anticipating this. I took a peek before I opened the door.

Jane's mouth went slack, and I had to drag her inside, locking the door swiftly behind us.

"Who did this?" she demanded, her voice thundering through the quiet room.

"My car was stolen." There was so much more to the story than that, but I wasn't certain I had the strength to tell it.

And then the questions began. Had the person been caught? Why was I at a hotel? Where was this boyfriend of mine anyway?

"He went out to handle things," I said, hoping the answer implied he was doing something simple like checking in with the police.

Jane guided me to the sofa and sat me down, worry creasing the lines on her elegant face. "Belle, are you in trouble? Is this is something else?"

I clenched my eyes shut, but it couldn't stop my tears. "I can't talk about it."

"Did he do this?" she asked in a low voice that sounded positively homicidal.

"No," I said firmly.

"But he knows who did." She didn't wait for my response before she was picking up her purse. "I'm taking you home."

"No!" I leapt up. I couldn't imagine what would happen if Smith returned to find me gone. I was already sick over whatever had drawn him away from here this morning. If I disappeared, he would go straight to Hammond.

"What are you hiding from?"

Everyone. No one. I didn't know how to answer.

"I'm safe here." That's all she needed to know.

"And Smith?"

"He's dealing with it." I couldn't tell her more than that, not while everything was so screwed up. I already wished I hadn't asked her to come. Too many people in my life were already caught up in this nightmare.

Jane's gaze drifted to my hand. Her mouth pressed into a thin line but she didn't say anything about the band of diamonds sparkling on my ring finger.

Another thing I would have to explain when the time was right. For now I was grateful that she seemed keen to ignore it.

I patted the spot next to me, and Jane sank back down, still holding her purse. A large manila envelope stuck out of the top of it.

"What's that?" I asked, eying it as my blood turned to ice.

"Nothing." She twisted the bag away from me, but I reached out and snatched it.

It was addressed to me. Tearing it open despite her protests, I withdrew a stack of legal documents. If I had thought things couldn't get any worse, I was wrong. I scanned through them, not understanding half of what they said but getting the gist.

My mother was moving forward with the legal action she'd threatened, and she'd made her case not only against me but also against my ownership stake in Bless. I stared at them for a long minute, saying nothing, and then I began to laugh. It racked my body, making my face throb, but I couldn't stop.

Jane yanked them out of my hand and studied them for a moment before tossing them across the room.

"Sod her," she announced, taking my hand.

Gradually my laughter subsided as I faced the reality that confronted me. I was being attacked on all sides, and I didn't know which direction to start throwing punches.

CHAPTER TWENTY-SIX

My fingers drummed impatiently against my mug. The coffee in it was cold and had been for at least half an hour. I'd left Belle at the hotel over an hour ago. Withdrawing my mobile, I checked her message again. I was in the right place at the right time, but there was no Georgia. The longer I waited, the more exposed I made myself. I took out my wallet and tossed a few pounds on the table for wasting the waiter's time.

I wanted to believe she had forgotten, but as I started the Bugatti, my thoughts turned to more sinister explanations. Without thinking, I began to cut through traffic, heading back to a place where I'd vowed never to return. I arrived in record time, mostly due to breaking the speed limit at every opportunity. The street was deserted, which wasn't unusual given the time of day. Only the most hardcore of Velvet's clientele would be here at this hour, I thought, which gave me no pleasure.

Punching in the security code, I entered the familiar corridor that led straight into a past I'd wanted to leave behind me. Sultry music drifted through the air, a relatively tasteful choice for once. As I entered, I found the space entirely empty save for Ariel, Velvet's newest and most faithful barmaid.

She looked up from the bottles she was arranging, her expression quickly shifting from casual interest to surprise.

"Is Georgia here?" I asked as I started toward her office.

"Nope." Ariel glanced around, as if to make sure before turning back to stare at me. "She called in for the week. Some excuse. Hammond arranged for a temporary manager."

"Is he here?"

She shook her head, to my relief. The last thing I needed was one of Hammond's errand boys rushing back to inform him of my presence.

"I'll admit I didn't expect to see you back here," Ariel said a bit too conversationally.

I paused, studying her for a moment. Her pink hair was gelled into a Mohawk, and unlike the last time we'd met, she was wearing a t-shirt and jeans. She wasn't actually here to tend bar, which meant Velvet wasn't open.

Velvet never closed.

I relaxed my face into a smile and slid onto a barstool. I could be charming when necessary, but it was a lot fucking harder when every impulse in my body wanted to leap over the counter and throttle her.

"What are you doing here anyway?" I asked, fingering the edge of a napkin. "This place is dead."

Her eyes darted over her shoulder, but she continued to pull liquor from the cabinets to replenish her stock. Finally she turned around, bracing her palms against the edge of the wood and shrugged. "Inventory. We had a busy weekend. I don't like to get caught unprepared."

"I can respect that. Neither do I." I kept my tone conversational, but there was no ignoring the threats hidden beneath our words.

Ariel's pierced lip curled up, and she leaned lower so that her t-shirt flapped open to reveal her tits. "Why? You interested in doing something else?"

This was why I'd discounted her before. It was obvious she was hot for what went on in the club. She'd practically begged me to do a scene the last time I'd come here. That she'd been treated to a display of my dominance only sealed her interest. Her voyeurism had blinded to me to her true intentions, but it had also undercut her purpose.

It was a dangerous thing taking on a job when you couldn't control your desires. It had always undermined Georgia's power. Ariel appeared to suffer from the same lack of self-restraint.

I undid my cufflink, tossing it on the bar, and rolled up one sleeve. Ariel's tongue darted between her lips as I repeated the action on the other side to reveal my forearms. It was my signature move. The one that I had become known for amongst those in the lifestyle. Her eyes hooded as I stood up and analyzed her.

She was lacking in every way. Too eager. Too fresh. She'd watched but she'd never participated. Hammond must have seen something in her that I was missing. But then again, he liked the malleable type—women he could mold into whatever his black soul desired.

Ariel fidgeted in front of me, her fingers twisting together under my penetrating gaze.

That's right. I might have lost my desire for anonymous submission, but I hadn't lost my touch. There had been a time when I could walk into this room, pick out any woman I saw, and she'd be on her knees. Ariel was about to prove I still had that ability.

"I assume that's an offer." I slid off my tie and popped my top collar button. But that was where I stopped. My body belonged to Belle, and this bitch wasn't getting anything more than a hand around her throat. "Serpent Room, now."

It was easy to slip into the role of Dom, a fact that I took little comfort in as I walked toward the aptly named private room. It had always been my least favorite due to its gaudy use of snakeskin leather as its primary decor, but it was where this snake belonged. Ariel entered behind me and I pointed up. She scurried to the center of the room, lifting her arms to the row of shackles that hung overhead.

This was going to be far too easy.

"Do you want me to undress?" she asked hopefully.

Fuck no.

"Did I tell you to speak?" I growled.

She fell silent, and I went to work binding her wrists to the inescapable restraints.

"This is what you wanted," I accused, circling around her. "So much so that you're willing to feed yourself to the wolf."

"Yes, Sir," she panted.

I slapped her. "You don't get to call me that."

Her eyes fell even as her legs wiggled apart.

That isn't where this is going. I kept the thought to myself as I rounded on her restrained body. Her breathing sped up as I took a step closer. But rather than stripping her, I wrapped my arm over her shoulder and closed my fingers around her neck.

"You're going to answer some questions now."

The effect of my words was immediate. Ariel jerked against the shackles, trying desperately to free herself.

"It's too late for that. You wanted to be dominated, and I'm going to do just that. You're going to tell me every fucking thing I want to know." I squeezed her throat to emphasize that I was the one in control.

"No!"

My grip tightened, cutting off her air supply. "You're new at this, aren't you? No need to answer. I can't believe Hammond trusted you to do this job. That's why you came to work here, isn't it?"

I loosened my hold on her, and she gulped for air but didn't speak.

"I don't think you understand," I snarled, sliding my hand up to her jaw and capturing it. I leaned into her, my mouth pressed close to her ear as she tried to writhe away from me. "Desperate men lose control. I'm not desperate, but you have no idea how far I'm willing to go for answers. That was a simple question, so answer it. Did he send you here?"

"Yes," she bit out.

"That wasn't so hard, was it?" I seized her hair with my other hand. "Have you been feeding him information on Georgia?"

She didn't answer, and I jerked her head back, yanking her hair at the roots.

"Yes!" she screamed.

I held her there. Now we were getting somewhere.

"And me?"

This time she whimpered. "Yes."

"How did he know where to find my wife?" It was a foregone conclusion that he'd discovered the truth about Belle, and I didn't have any more time to waste on ferreting out the answers I needed. Not after the attack. It wasn't going to be an isolated incident, and I wanted to know his next move.

"He's tracking her," she answered in a soft voice.

"How?" I demanded, forcing myself to ignore the fear that stirred inside me.

"Your mobiles. It was harder for him to get to your wife's, but then the stupid bitch left it in her office and went out to lunch. He's tracking all of you." She laughed at this, and I froze. I wanted to strangle her. I wanted her to gasp for her last breath, but I wasn't through with her yet.

"Georgia?" I asked.

"That's been taken care of."

I threw her head forward, ignoring her as she called after me. She deserved to die, but when Hammond realized she had betrayed him, he'd take care of that. I'd been finished doing his dirty work for too long to take care of her now.

Belle was safe for the moment. I'd made certain her mobile had made it home with the rest of her personal belongings before we left the hospital. But Georgia. I dialed her mobile again, but it went to voicemail.

"How would he do it?" I muttered to myself, leaving Velvet behind. The image of my father floating lifelessly in the pool swam to mind. His death had been ruled an accident.

It's unfortunate what can happen when one's left alone.

That's what Hammond had said to my mother at the funeral.

I didn't think, I just reacted. Georgia's flat was around the corner, and I didn't bother to look as I threw the Bugatti into drive and sped toward it.

An eerie silence greeted me as I entered her flat. She hadn't changed the locks in years, which was convenient for me but deadly for her. I flipped on the lights and began to search. Rushing into her bedroom, I caught sight of something just beyond the bed.

A hand.

I rounded the bed and dropped to my knees beside her into a pool of blood. Her eyelids fluttered as my hands went to the wound in her abdomen. There was too much blood. It spurted past my palms as I tried to apply pressure. She was pale even in the darkness, her lips turning a sickly shade of blue.

"Smith?" Her voice was faint—confused—as she fought to open her eyes.

"It's okay." But it wasn't. I let go of her and pulled my mobile out of my pocket. It slipped from my bloody hands, and I fumbled to retrieve it. Dialing 9-9-9, I yanked a sheet from her bed and wound it into a tight ball. Holding it to her wounds, I pulled her body with my free arm into my lap. Her dark hair pooled around her.

"He knows." Crimson spilled from her lips as her words bubbled out.

"I know. Hold on. Help is coming." I needed her to stay awake, but I was afraid to allow her to continue talking.

She tried to shake her head but lacked the strength. "He knows where she is."

"She's safe," I said as I shushed her. "She isn't at home."

"Smith!" Georgia swallowed against the frothy blood that came with the exclamation. "The man who came here..." She gasped, her face screwing up as she searched for her voice through the pain. "He made a call. He's going to the Westminster Royal."

The world stopped around me, realization colliding with horror. I had no idea how he had found her. No idea how long he had known. No idea what I would discover when I reached her. Fear seized my chest in an icy grip. I looked down at Georgia and whispered, "I'm sorry."

There was no choice between staying and going. No choice between these two women who occupied such vastly different corners of my life. One was my past. The other my future. And yet I was tethered to this spot.

"Go." Georgia's command was no more than a breathy whisper, but I felt the thread tying us to one another snap. This had been our choice all along—a sacrifice we were both willing to make to be free.

I left her there, her life seeping out onto the carpet, knowing soon she would finally be liberated.

CHAPTER TWENTY-SEVEN

The Bugatti roared as I pushed the gas pedal to the floorboard, dodging in and out of traffic in a desperate attempt to get on the A3212. I kept my thoughts focused on the road. Turn. Merge. Being present was the only thing that kept me from drowning in my past or fearing for my future.

A car veered across the motorway, narrowly missing me as it tried to avoid the scene of an accident. I slammed on my brakes as the cars in front of me slowed to allow emergency crews to reach the scene.

I hit the steering wheel. "*This* is a fucking emergency!"

Reality screeched toward me as I came to a full stop. In gridlock there was no way to keep my thoughts from drifting to what had just happened. And the reality of the situation came to life in front of me.

Georgia's blood.

It was smeared over the wheel. On my hands. I rubbed the wheel with my sleeve, but there was no way to wipe my hands.

It had been a sick joke for years: calling her my sister. A jibe we were all too fond of hurling at one another. But as a lump formed in my throat, I knew she was the closest thing I'd had to living family for most of my life. I had spent that time questioning her motives and being judgmental of her choices, but it was only now that I knew I had loved her. Maybe that was what it was like to have a sibling. Constant annoyance. Misunderstanding. Realizing what they meant to you far too late.

Hammond would answer for what he had done to her.

But the thought of her murder only made me more aware of the danger that Belle faced now.

Somehow, they knew where she was. It was entirely likely that they'd been following me this whole time, but I couldn't be certain. Ariel said they were tracking our mobiles, which meant it didn't matter that I'd left hers at her flat when I'd had mine with me the whole time.

I dialed her number anyway and waited until it went to voicemail.

Hitting the voice activation button, I asked for the Westminster Royal.

"Price. The penthouse," I ordered as soon as the front desk answered.

"I'm sorry," a cheerful girl chirped. "We have a 'do not disturb' request for that guest."

"No shit," I snapped, "I placed that request. I'm trying to reach my wife. It's an emergency."

"I'm sorry, sir. I can take a message if—"

I hung up on her. Why the fuck had I put that "do not disturb" instruction up? Because I'd stupidly thought she was safe, and now there was no way to warn her. I could call the police, but I had no doubt that my response time was more efficient than theirs. I tried her number one more time. God, I wanted to scream at her voicemail message.

I threw my mobile onto the passenger seat when she didn't answer. I had just pulled off the motorway when it began to ring.

"Belle?" I answered in a clipped tone. "You need to get out of there."

"This isn't Belle." Hammond's familiar voice crawled under my skin "Although it looks as if you're on your way to see her now. I'm sure she'll appreciate a romantic surprise more than getting a call ahead of time. She doesn't expect you to return to the hotel for hours after all. I'm told newlyweds are particularly sentimental. Perhaps you should pick her up some mums on the way."

I didn't miss the reference to funeral flowers. "Hammond, when I get my hands on you—"

"What, Smith? What will you do to me? You have had the opportunity to take me out for months and yet you never take it. Your father. Margot. You never sought retribution then." He paused, and for a moment, I thought the call had dropped. "Of course, perhaps this foolish witch hunt you've gotten caught up with is your own petty attempt."

"It's over," I warned him. "You know who's been investigating you."

"Yes, I do," Hammond said, sounding nonplussed. "Albert was investigating me as well. I think he had about as much evidence as either you or his son do now."

"Why?" He wanted to brag, and I wanted to keep him talking. If he was on the line with me, he couldn't be hurting her. "Why go after Clara? Why Belle?"

"I suppose I'm a bit of a romantic. I love a tragic love story. Did Samantha tell you that when you visited her?"

My blood ran cold, and I gripped the wheel, my knuckles turning white. I could see Westminster Royal ahead, but it wasn't close enough. "You spoke to Samantha?"

"Of course. Do you honestly think she escaped to New York and started over? I really thought you were smarter than that. If I'd known you weren't, I wouldn't have bothered putting you through law school. Samantha is, shall we say, indebted to me. You can understand that."

I didn't care to hear more about Samantha's betrayal. Not when so much was on the line. "You haven't answered my question."

"Oh, yes, why prey on your sweet, young wives? Honestly, Clara was simply a means to an end. I wanted Albert out of the picture and, boy, was her ex-boyfriend a crackpot. After his own attempts failed, he was so grateful to have my help. He only wanted to keep her from Alexander. We had several opportunities really, but it was so poetic to have it happen at the wedding—and no one doubted for a minute why he'd done it. They assumed it was the efforts of a mad man, and the King simply got in the way. Nothing covers up one sin like another scandal."

"Alexander guessed. He knew there was more to it." I took pride in that now, in my fragile camaraderie with a man who had the ability to see through to the evil at the heart of such actions.

"Of course, he did, but that hardly mattered since he hesitated to make a move. Too much information. Who could he trust? He couldn't take action. But you knew that, didn't you? When you went to him and begged for him to finally see this thing through to the end. It was how I found out that you'd gotten married. That stung, son. I shouldn't have heard it from someone else."

"I'm not your son," I growled.

"I would have sent my congratulations earlier," he continued, ignoring me, "but I didn't have your current address. My present is being delivered now."

"If you touch one hair on her head—"

"I wouldn't dream of touching her. Belle is a lovely girl. Our mutual friend was quite put out that he didn't get to spend enough quality time with her the other evening."

"Stop this," I demanded. "You can have me. No struggle. I'll come to you. Alexander won't have me as a witness. Just leave her be."

"And call off Jake's fun? He's been looking forward to seeing you again. Give him my regards."

Then the line went dead.

CHAPTER TWENTY-EIGHT

I sat up in bed, rubbing my eyes out of habit. White-hot pain pierced my temple. I blinked back the tears that flooded to my bruised eye. This was going to take some getting used to.

"How are you feeling?" Jane asked, her eyes crinkling in concern when I finally reached the parlor.

"Fine," I lied. I might feel better when Smith was back, and when I could finally leave here. I'd chosen sleep rather than obsessing over his return.

Jane got to her feet, examining me as she came closer. "Do you want another pain pill?"

I shook my head, but the sudden motion loosed a new wave of pain, and I flinched.

"I think you better have one, love."

I didn't put up a fight as she went for my prescription bottle and a glass of water.

"Have you eaten anything today?" she asked as I swallowed the pill.

"No," I admitted sheepishly. "I haven't really eaten anything since last night. My stomach is bothering me."

"Of course, it is." She frowned. "That's an opiate. You shouldn't take it on an empty stomach."

I sighed. As usual, she was probably right. "I guess we could order room service."

"Or there's that curry place around the corner?" she offered. "We could get some fresh air."

It was a calculated suggestion. Jane was still trying to suss out what was going on. I didn't want to tell her that Smith would lose his shit if he found out I'd left the hotel. Instead I pointed to my face. "I'm not quite ready to debut this in daylight hours."

"I suppose that makes sense." But there was doubt in her voice. "I'll only be a few minutes."

"I'll be fine." So far Jane had been more of a babysitter than a nurse. Sitting on the sofa while I napped and plying me with pain pills when I woke. And questioning me at every opportunity.

"Okay, it's just a jaunt. I almost forgot." She pulled my mobile out of her bag. "You left this at home. Best you have it."

"Thank you." Contact with the world outside seemed like a pretty novel concept at this point. I frowned when I saw a missed call from Smith. No doubt he was freaking out that I didn't answer.

"I'll be right back."

I locked the door behind Jane and immediately called him back, but the phone went to voicemail. Checking the time stamp, I realized he'd only called a few minutes before. He was probably already trying to call me again.

I tugged at my pajamas. They clung to me, sticky with the sweat of nightmares. A bath seemed like a pretty good idea. If Smith was going to have to encounter this mug when he got back, the rest of me could be presentable. It would be good to feel human again. Plus, I'd never gotten a chance to clean up after last night's lovemaking.

That was the trouble with all these meds. I couldn't quite function normally. They made me move in slow motion. I blinked, drowsily, as the latest dose began to take effect. For a second, I considered if it was smart to take a bath, but Jane would be back momentarily, and who ever drowned in a tub?

I opened the music app on my mobile and found my Rolling Stones playlist. Listening to the music Smith loved soothed me. I turned up the volume and dropped it on the unmade bed.

I turned the tap on, waiting for the water to get hot as I slipped out of my pajamas and into a hotel robe, then studied myself in the mirror. The bruise had begun to turn black, yellowing around the edges. Since there was nothing they could do about the hairline fraction other than wait, I was stuck with the swelling until it healed. Thank God I didn't have any business meetings scheduled.

I let my hair down, noting how far past my shoulders it already was. Maybe when my parole was up, I could see a stylist. I'd have to keep the fringe to hide the gruesome scar the stitches would leave.

Focus on what you can change, I told myself. I could deal with the scars left on my body, the rest would take time.

Walking over to the tub, I dipped my finger in to check the temperature.

Perfect. Relief was at hand.

My fingers closed over the knot of my robe, but before I could tug it loose, my ringtone interrupted the music.

Dashing back for it, I made it halfway across the room when a shape hurtled toward me. I barely had time to brace myself before I slammed into the wall. The ringtone ended, and my mobile began to play "Give Me Shelter."

Falling to the floor, I scrambled backwards, dragging myself by my hands toward the bathroom. I reached the door before the assailant did, kicking it shut with my foot. Jumping up, I turned the lock and searched the room frantically. The door shook on its hinges as the man bashed against it repeatedly.

I spotted a window above the toilet and ran for it. Balancing precariously on the toilet lid, I tried to pry the window open. It was nailed shut. Looking around, I grabbed a towel, wrapped it around my hand and ducked as I put my first through the glass. It shattered, shards skimming across my face and clattering to the floor. I pushed aside the remaining glass with the towel and pulled myself up. I stuck my head out, noting with dismay that it was almost a dead drop from the eighth floor. But there was a small ledge below that felt a whole lot safer than sticking around here. I wriggled farther through the opening, catching my shoulder on a large shard. It sliced through my skin, but I barely felt it.

And then I heard the door fly open. I moved faster, deciding then and there that I'd rather fall to my fate than stay here to be murdered. I had my hips nearly out of the window when hands closed over my ankles. I screamed as loudly as I could, hoping it would carry over the traffic to the tourists below.

He hauled me back inside, slamming me to the tile and kicking me hard in the ribs. I curled into a ball. There didn't seem to be any other option but to take it and hope.

"Miss me?" he asked, and I froze at the familiar voice.

"Our date ended so suddenly the other night. I tried to call and apologize, but you haven't been answering your phone, Belle. So I thought I'd stop by and see how you're doing." He jerked me up by the hair, dragging me to my feet to face him. I hadn't seen much of him in the dark, but I saw now that he was about Smith's age. Good-looking. Except for the homicidal mania glinting in his eyes.

"Wow, that is beautiful." He gripped my face roughly and I screamed. A wicked smirk twitched on his lips. "Do you mind if I take a picture of my handiwork? I so rarely get a good before shot. There's a really lovely sense of movement when someone's still alive. It's just not the same after I've already killed them."

I said the only word that came to mind. "Please."

"Please?" he laughed. "Do you have any idea the man you married or what he's capable of? Sorry, baby, this is eye for an eye. I'd love for you to tell him hello, but unfortunately, you'll be in no condition to deliver the message."

He dropped his hold on my face, curled his fist and punched me in the stomach. My mouth gaped, searching for air. I was still gasping when he shoved me into the bathtub. Fluid shot down my throat, burning my lungs. My hands flew wildly, splashing against the porcelain, searching for a grip.

And then he let me go.

CHAPTER TWENTY-NINE

The Rolling Stones greeted me as I walked into the suite. I called Belle's name but all I heard was a violent splash. I skidded into the bathroom as Jake plunged her face back into the water, holding her head under. I raced toward him, springing mid-step and tackling him. Belle arched out of the tub, spluttering as she collapsed to the floor.

"Go!" I yelled just as Jake knocked me off my feet.

Metal glinted as he lunged toward me, and my hand shot out, catching his wrist. We struggled as Belle shook a few yards from us, still trying to catch her breath.

Christ, she might need CPR, and I was in no position to give it.

I swung my knees up, managing to catch him in the ribs and throw him to the side. I rolled on top of him, forcing his wrist and the knife over his head.

"You son of a bitch," I spit at him.

"You knew this was coming, Price." He struggled to speak as we both fought to keep the knife in our control. "You've known for years."

"I had nothing to do with her death." But it didn't matter what I told him, and I was well past willing to negotiate with this piece of shit.

"Margot would be here now—"

"If it weren't for Hammond," I screamed. "How do you still not understand that?"

Of course Hammond had chosen him for this. A man with a vendetta was harder to fight. Good thing I had one of my own.

"She was going to leave you," he panted under me, "and you couldn't take it. Couldn't admit that she didn't love you."

"I don't care who she was fucking. We were both fucking anything that moved. She was still my wife. I would never have hurt her."

"Even though she was going to expose you for what you really were and take all your money?"

Glass ground into the tile as I heard Belle's palms sliding over the floor, but to my horror, she sounded as if she was coming closer instead of running.

Jake smiled, his eyes darting over my shoulder. "And now I'm going to take her away from you. That's what you deserve."

I took a deep breath, braced myself and head-butted him. His nose crunched on impact, but I shook off the momentary daze.

Jake lolled back, stunned, which gave me enough time to snatch away the knife. I backed away from him slowly as I got to my feet, keeping the weapon in front of me.

"Are you okay, beautiful?" I called, not daring to take my eyes off Jake. He'd clamped his hand over his nose, but he wasn't down for the count.

"I'm fine," she answered in a breathless voice.

"I want you to go. Walk out of here and go down to the front desk. Tell them to call the police."

"I'm not leaving you here," she cried.

"For once, do as I say," I ordered. We were nowhere near out of danger and wouldn't be until I got her out of this room. Then I could take care of this once and for all.

"Have you told her?" Jake asked with bloodstained teeth. "About your first wife?"

"I know," Belle called petulantly over my shoulder.

"Then you know why this is going to happen. If I don't do it, someone else will. We live by a code. Eye for an eye. Retribution."

"How biblical of you," she shot back.

How was it possible that I could love her and want to strangle her at the same time? I shot a warning glare over my shoulder.

"Go," I repeated in a low voice.

"Not a chance."

"You seem like a nice girl. Spirited," Jake called as he struggled to his feet. Abandoning his bloody nose, he began to brush glass off his clothes. "I think Margot would have liked her. What do you think, Price?"

"Don't move," I warned him.

"I bet she's wild, too. Let's have a little fun for old times' sake. You can watch. She was so hot for it the other night, but I bet you already knew that." Jake took a step closer. "Did you forget how to share? We always shared. That's the problem with adults. We forget our manners. What did you say the first time you shared Margot? 'Careful, she bites.' Christ, you had to ride that bitch from behind if you didn't want stitches."

Belle inhaled sharply at this revelation.

"That was a long time ago, Jake. We were kids, just like you said, and I grew up." I said it more for her benefit than his.

"It's a pity. It seems like you grew up when you cut those brake lines in her car. That was a very selfish thing to do."

"I had nothing to do with that." I didn't know why we were still arguing, except that I hadn't gotten Belle out of the suite yet.

"I've been thinking. Since you're going to get to see Margot first, give her my love. Although I doubt she's hanging around saving you a seat. But then there's a special spot in hell for you."

Suddenly, he ran at me. My hand lashed out, knocking Belle toward the wall seconds before he launched into me. We stumbled backwards, flipping over and landing in a heap at the foot of the bed.

Jake didn't move. Pushing his body off me, he fell over, the knife sticking out of his chest.

Belle clawed against the doorframe, rising, eyes wide with horror as she took in the scene.

"Come here," I said softly.

She looked apprehensively at his body, still clinging to the door. I forced myself to stand, ignoring the sharp pinch in my side as I went to her.

"Oh my God." She clapped a hand over her mouth as she took in my blood-stained clothes.

"Not mine," I reassured her. She'd been in no condition to realize they were bloodied when I arrived, and right now I didn't have the time to explain. "I need you to leave. Go to Alexander and Clara. You'll be safe with them."

As safe as she would be anywhere.

She shook her head frantically. "I won't leave you."

"Don't be stubborn. For once, I'm *not* in the mood to be provoked." I forced a smile. "Go and call the police from the front desk and then call Clara."

She looked to the mobile still playing music on the bed.

"Don't use that one," I said in a flat voice. "You have their numbers?"

She nodded. "Smith...you need a witness."

"They'll take me in for questioning, beautiful. It's clearly a case of self-defense." Tears pooled in her eyes, but I took her hand. "I'm a lawyer, remember?"

"I don't want to leave you," she whispered.

"I know." I brushed a kiss over her lips. "But we both know that's not Hammond lying there. I need to know you're safe. As soon as they release me, I'll come to you."

She didn't question that logic, even though she was smart enough to know I wouldn't be joining her any time soon.

"I love you," she said softly.

"I love you, too." I trailed a finger down her throat longingly. "Birds of a feather, right? You're a helluva fighter."

"I'll fight for you," she promised.

I closed my eyes and pushed her away, the implication clear. She kept a hold of my hand, and I heard a choked sob as our fingers slipped apart. Then she was gone.

I dropped to the floor, holding my side. I pulled out my mobile and dialed a number from memory. "I want to report a murder."

CAPTURE
ME

CHAPTER ONE

The music stopped playing as my call ended. My mobile slipped to the floor, and I slumped against the wall. Opening my suit jacket, my fingers fumbled on the buttons of my shirt until I reached the last one. Lifting the sticky, blood-soaked layers, I groaned.

Fuck, that was deep. Stitches were in my future.

"You're going to need a lot more than that," I called over to Jake. He didn't answer. Probably because he was dead.

See you in hell.

He'd had it coming. Jake had been responsible for the brutal attack on my wife yesterday. Then he'd returned to finish the job, but I'd stopped him—permanently. It didn't matter that he was acting on the behest of my crooked ex-employer. He'd decided his own fate when he got mixed up with Hammond.

So had I.

But one more dead man also meant one less witness in the coming case against Hammond. With Georgia gone, that didn't leave many options. We had emails and a few recorded tapes of meetings, but Alexander wasn't convinced it would be enough. After tonight—

after his attacks on Belle—I would do everything in my power to bring him to justice. Even if justice came by my own hands.

I'd been a lawyer long enough to know the courts were skewed in favor of those with power or deep pockets. Hammond had spent his life amassing both, and then he'd used it to systematically target those he deemed threats.

He'd clearly placed me on that list.

I stared at the destruction around me as I waited for the police to arrive. Broken glass. Tumbled furniture. Splintered door. Dead body. It was either a murder scene or a *really* good party.

Of course, I had to trash the most expensive hotel room in London. This was going to eat up more than the damage deposit, which meant my credit card bill was going to be hell next month.

You're losing it, Price.

I knew it. I could feel it. But even as my thoughts scattered around me, I couldn't collect them. Blood puddled on the floor, and I watched, fascinated, as it dripped in slow motion from my torso.

My mobile rang, displaying Hammond's number, and I slid my thumb across the *accept* button. "Price 1. Jake 0," I announced. "I can't believe you used Margot to rile him up. That was low."

"All's fair."

I wedged my mobile against my shoulder. It was getting too heavy to hold. "In that case, I should inform you that Jake is going to need a skilled undertaker."

Hammond chuckled. "He really was no match for you. Did you think I'd let him kill you?"

"What about my wife?" I squeezed my eyes shut and reopened them, trying to make the room come back into focus.

"I don't care about her," Hammond growled. "This is between you and me."

"Then leave her out of it."

"This is war, son."

"Who's winning?" I asked. I knew the latest score, but the rest was becoming a bit hazy.

"Well, any moment now you'll be arrested for Jake's murder. That puts me up one." Hammond cackled on the other end.

I didn't. It wasn't a very funny joke. "I don't get a point for Jake?"

"We're only scoring the big game. After you're in jail, that only leaves three more to mark off my list, and you conveniently sent your wife right to the other two targets. I can't decide if I should strike tonight while they're all together, or wait until you've stunk up your cell for a bit. It would be fun to read about the arrest of an insane murderer claiming a plot against the British Monarchy."

"Yes, except the British Monarchy is on my side." I blinked as the door flickered in and out of existence. I tilted my head, trying to see where it went.

"For now. But do you think you're the only one feeding information to the palace? Alexander doesn't put all his eggs in one basket. When he receives evidence that you were working for me the whole time, he won't be keen to clear your name. You won't be able to help any of them behind bars."

"Interesting twist, but no one will buy it."

"I'm a very convincing storyteller, Smith. Enjoy your time with Detective Spade. He's been so looking forward to meeting you."

The line went dead, and my hand dropped to the ground. It was getting harder to think, and so dark. Did Belle turn out the lights as she left?

Belle.

Her beautiful face floated through the haze occupying my brain. It was as if she were standing in front of me. Porcelain skin, framed by loose blonde waves, and a haughty smirk that made my own lips twitch.

Belle.

Whatever his plans were to frame me, she was the loose end that he couldn't leave untied. No matter what evidence Alexander had against me, she would never believe it. Which meant that she was next on Hammond's hit list. It was the reason she'd been on it in the first place.

I forced myself to my feet. Damn my chivalry for calling the cops.

I really had to do something about this guilty conscience. I groped for my phone, slipping it into my pocket as I shuffled to the door and fell against it. Blood smeared across the polished white trim behind me.

DNA. *DNA everywhere.*

Christ, I might as well just leave a trail of breadcrumbs behind me.

I snatched a pillow off the sofa as I passed it, ripping off the cover and pressing it to my wound. It would need attention, but for now the most I could do was stop my blood from leading right to me. But it was no use. It splattered at my feet as I stumbled down the corridor. I clutched my jacket closed as I entered the lift. The couple next to me continued to talk even as the first drop of blood hit the floor of the compartment. I wasn't making it out of here. Reaching forward, I ran numb fingers over the buttons, lighting up as many floors as possible.

I got off as soon as the doors slid open. I lurched out, my knees buckling as my eyes landed on a janitorial closet. Lunging for the knob, I twisted as my world went black.

CHAPTER TWO

I stepped into the lobby of the Westminster Royal in a bloodstained satin robe. Obviously, I knew how to make an entrance. Crossing swiftly to the front desk, I leaned against the counter to steady my shaky legs. The woman working froze as she took in my battered appearance. I'd stunned her into silence.

"I'd like to speak to the manager," I said in a lowered voice. I didn't want this to be a scene. We were alive. The rest could be sorted out as privately as possible.

Relief fluttered across her face. No doubt she was thrilled to pass me off to someone else.

And that pissed me off.

Part of me wanted her to care about the traumatized woman in front of her. Shouldn't she ask if I was okay? But answering that would be easier if someone hadn't just been murdered, even if it had been self-defense.

It was too much to process. That was the real reason I was angry. I was here, but my mind was trapped in the hotel room I'd left behind.

My eyes flickered up to catch the shocked expressions on the faces of guests as they passed me. Smith had brought me to our suite through the private lift reserved for important guests, saving me the embarrassment of gawking strangers. I must look the sight—beaten to hell from my first encounter with Jake and now covered in fresh cuts. I pulled my robe more tightly closed and heard a tinkle as shattered glass fell from the folds of the fabric to the marble floor.

And I was worried about drawing attention to myself.

What in the bloody hell are you doing here? I had no idea. Smith was upstairs, waiting for the authorities next to a dead body. I should be at his side. My husband might be paranoid about the possibility of Hammond coming to finish the job, but, honestly, there was no way he was going to walk into a crime scene. He was far too smart for that. Hell, even his hired help wouldn't dare.

And Smith was far too smart to think there was a real threat, which meant I'd been sent away purposefully. Slivers of ice shot up my back at the realization. There were a lot of rational explanations for why he would send me away, but our relationship didn't exactly function in the realm of rationality.

Safe from immediate danger, my head was clearing more each second.

The woman I'd spoken to had cornered a well-dressed man. They were far away enough that I couldn't hear them, but I didn't miss the glares they threw in my direction, the looks a curious mixture of concern and annoyance.

It seemed they wanted to avoid drama as well.

Then again it was possible they knew exactly what was going on. Jake had gotten into our hotel room somehow. Had an employee of the Westminster Royal given him access?

Hammond could buy friends anywhere, and I suspected he kept more than a few people in his back pocket for occasions such as this.

I needed to get out of here. Smith had told me to call the police, but was he really going to sit and wait for them to arrive?

I'd been sent away because he was hiding something.

Without thinking, I dashed toward the lift, darting in front of a couple. I muttered an apology as I jumped into the compartment and jabbed the button to close the doors before they could react.

Enough people had seen me in my current state. I didn't need to awkwardly ride the lift with any more. At least the penthouse was on a private floor. If the police hadn't arrived yet, no one had discovered the scene either.

But when the lift doors opened, I froze. A trail of blood spatter led to the open door of the suite. Someone had been bleeding when they left, and I knew it wasn't me. At least, not this badly. Either Jake hadn't died or...

I didn't want to consider either possibility.

Rushing toward the open door, I ran into the room and nearly stumbled over the lifeless body of my attacker.

He was dead. That might have been a relief if it weren't for the bloody passage I'd just navigated. If Jake was dead, this blood led to Smith.

Think.

Acting purely out of fear wasn't going to help the situation. With trembling fingers I slipped off my robe, trying to ignore the dead body in the room. Tremors wracked my body, making it a struggle to pull on the clothes I'd left laid out on my bed earlier. Running around in bloody silk seemed like a bad idea, and it was a problem I could fix.

I took a steadying breath as I gathered my hair into a ponytail. I needed to be in control of myself, if nothing else.

Stuffing the robe into my bag, I surveyed the space for any more personal belongings.

We'd brought very little with us. Smith's idea. It was as if he'd suspected what would happen. But the most damning evidence couldn't be shoved into a tote, and I didn't have time to clean it up.

Satisfied that I'd gathered all my belongings, I pivoted slowly toward the hallway. This time I noted the smear of blood on the doorframe. I wanted to believe it was Jake's blood on his hands, but he would have had to bathe in it to produce the trail he'd left in his wake.

Smith was bleeding, and he was bleeding profusely.

He might need an ambulance, but if that was why he'd sent me to call the police, why had he left? A normal person would call for help regardless, but in that moment all I could think of was finding my husband.

What was I supposed to tell medics anyway? That he had been injured and had gotten lost on his way to call the authorities. Smith was a fugitive. He knew that, and the police would know it as well. Even if right now he was wounded, I was going to kill him.

If he's not dead already.

The thought chilled me, but I pushed it from my mind and walked swiftly to the bank of lifts at the end of the hall. There was no way to know which one he took. Only that, judging from the blood spatter, he had headed down to the main floors rather than taking the private lift to the parking garage. I had no clue why.

The trouble was that there was no way to figure out which one he took. Studying the wall, I spotted a smudge of blood on the buttons, and then I had an idea. Peering closer, I found another smear of blood near the frame of the rightmost lift. He'd gotten on that one. Closing my eyes, I centered myself and focused on my need to find him. Then I pushed the button to call for the lift. It took five minutes and several confused passengers before the one I wanted arrived. By the time it did, I was relieved to discover it was empty. The trouble was that half of the buttons on the interior control panel had blood on them.

Think, Belle.

I pressed each one, praying I would find him quickly. I needed to see him—touch him. He was the one real, tangible element of this living nightmare we were trapped in. I *had* to find him. Surely, he would have gotten off sooner rather than later. The lift doors slid open two floors down to reveal more blood. I followed it, steeling myself for what I might find at the other end. But it only led to a janitorial closet. I opened the door before I could chicken out. The hall light slanted across the dark cupboard and fell over Smith's crumpled body.

Circling my fingers around his wrist, I checked for a pulse and choked back a sob when I felt the faint thrum. It was slight, but it was there.

Now if I had any idea what to do.

Judging from the heat pricking my eyes, my body voted *cry*. But thankfully my bitchy, crisis-management side kicked in and saved me.

Sliding my arms around his torso, I attempted to lift him. He was too heavy. Damn all those sexy muscles. I swiped away an escaped tear and collapsed to the floor beside him.

"Wake up!" I demanded. "I know you're a stubborn arse, but I need you to listen to me for once."

I wiped angrily at the tears that were now dribbling freely down my cheeks. "We said forever, and I'm going to need you to make good on that, Price."

I waited for a response. I begged for one.

Smith didn't move, save for the shallow heave of his chest as his breath grew ragged. I needed help and I had no idea how to get it.

Pushing his weight off of me, I knelt in the dark and began to pat him down. And then my palm made contact with smooth, cool glass. His mobile.

One person I knew would come—no questions asked. At least not right away.

I dialed the number without a second thought, drawing the door closed and enveloping us in darkness. I settled against the warmth of my husband as the phone began to ring.

A FAINT RAP ON THE DOOR WOKE ME, STARTLING ME FROM A dreamless sleep. It was either salvation or damnation knocking, but either way it had to be opened. Time was running out. I pushed it open with my foot, blinking against the relative brightness of the hall until a familiar—and welcome—face came into view.

Edward's face betrayed no emotion as he took in the sight at his feet. He pushed his tortoiseshell glasses up on the bridge of his nose, and shook his curly-haired head. "You shouldn't party so hard."

Neither of us found the joke funny. Nothing so small could dispel the tension clouding the air between us.

"Thank you." There would be questions later. Hard questions.

Questions I didn't want to answer. Right now, though, all that mattered was that he had come.

"I assume you have a plan."

Not really. Plans were for people capable of movement. Of action. Of thought. Up until a minute ago, I hadn't been certain that I would escape this spot. But now I needed to have some idea of what to do. I swiped on his mobile and found his contact list. It was a long shot—and not one I was fond of taking, but Georgia might be able to help. Before I scrolled to the G's, another name caught my eye.

"There's a number in his phone for a Dr. Roget," I told Edward. "If we make it out of here, I'm calling it."

"Not much of a plan," he commented.

I didn't bother to tell him that Plan B involved Georgia Kincaid. Instead I shot him a look of warning. "Right now, my plan is to survive the next five minutes, and when we accomplish that, we'll focus on surviving the next ten."

"We could call Alexander," he suggested.

"No!" It was harsh, but it was gut reaction. Alexander might be able to help us—he'd gotten us into this mess, after all—but instinct told me to keep tonight's events as far from Clara and her daughter as possible. It was bad enough that I'd dragged Edward into the fray.

"As you wish."

I held out my hand. "Help me up."

Edward didn't press for an explanation. He just reached down and hauled me to my feet, but as soon as I stepped into the light, his fingers tightened around my wrist.

"What the hell happened, Belle?"

He hadn't seen me yet. I had hoped he wouldn't until after my injuries were healed.

"It's not important." I shook my head. "Smith's wounds are serious. He needs to be our focus."

Edward didn't move. "Did he do this to you?"

"God, no," I said in surprise. "He saved me."

Edward didn't push for more information as he lifted Smith over his shoulder. "Okay, so we have an unconscious man. You looking like you just went ten rounds. I guess we take the lift to the lobby?"

"Your sarcasm is unnecessary." But he had a point. Edward was hardly inconspicuous when he wasn't carrying a body. Waltzing through the front door wasn't an option.

I snapped my fingers as it hit me. "The Bugatti. He left it in the private garage."

"Lead the way."

Taking the lift was out of the question. I couldn't risk that the police were already here. Heading for the stairs up, I braced myself for the prospect of entering my hotel room again—of seeing Jake again. But when I opened the door from the stairwell, I immediately threw myself back into it. Police were already swarming the scene. And I knew it wouldn't take them long until they discovered the trail of blood and began to investigate it.

Smith had acted out of self-defense. That—not to mention his alliance with Alexander— would be enough to save him from prosecution. I wasn't in the least concerned with him going to jail. But with Hammond alive, nowhere in London was safe—not even a jail cell. The best course of action was to stay off Hammond's radar entirely, which meant only trusting myself.

"Now what?" Edward demanded, shifting Smith's weight. "Not to worry you, but they'll be shutting this whole place down pretty quickly. We need to leave now."

"The stairs."

He didn't complain as he carried Smith toward the sub-level of the hotel. When we reached the final landing, I closed my eyes and turned the doorknob.

Edward muttered something that sounded like "miracle" under his breath as it swung open.

"There it is," I yelled, pointing to Smith's one-of-a-kind sports car.

His eyebrow shot up when he spotted it.

"It's a two-seater," he pointed out.

"You drive."

Edward propped Smith into the passenger seat and I climbed

into my husband's lap. In the dark I couldn't see his wound. Now I didn't want to look. But I slid my hands to the hot, sticky bloodstain and applied pressure. My medical experience was limited to common sense and what I'd seen in the movies.

I wasn't certain either would help him now.

"Where are we going?" Edward asked as he threw the car in reverse and screeched toward the exit.

Hopefully, Dr. Roget was a friend—a good friend.

A tired voice answered on the second ring. "Price?"

"This is his wife," I said in a rush, ignoring the pang of guilt that surged through me as Edward shot me an incredulous look. "I don't know if it's a mistake to call you, but Smith needs help. *Discreet* help."

I was either making the right call or leading us into a trap, but I didn't have many options.

"Can you make it to St. Mary's?"

"Yes, but..." I hesitated. I'd wanted to avoid a hospital and all the prying questions that would come with it.

"There's an oncology clinic connected to the east wing. It's closed for the evening; I'll meet you there."

"Thank you," I breathed, but he'd already hung up.

I repeated the instructions to Edward word for word. He nodded quietly, not bothering to speak even as his jaw tensed. The car sped up as we zoomed toward our destination and an uncertain fate. He had questions, and probably more than a few harsh words for me.

I couldn't bear to think about the answers he'd want eventually. Instead I focused on the fact that Smith's blood was still warm on my skin, which meant he was still alive.

For now.

CHAPTER THREE

As promised, the oncology clinic at St. Mary's was dim when we arrived. Cast in shadows, it was nondescript. Another boring, anonymous building closed for the night. A tingling dashed across my skin, raising goose pimples. Somehow the sheer genericness of the scene made what we were doing more terrifying. I glanced nervously at Edward as he parked the Bugatti near the entrance. The light of a single street lamp filtered weakly into the car, casting his curly head in a faint halo.

The look suited him. It took more than a fair bit of loyalty to drag a soon-to-be murder suspect across town, especially considering he didn't care for Smith. In that moment, I wouldn't have been surprised to discover he was hiding a pair of wings.

"Are you sure about this?" he asked, peering through the car's tinted windows at the eerily silent building.

"Yes." But I wasn't. Not really. If Smith was conscious, he would probably tell me I was making a mistake trusting Dr. Roget, but that was the whole problem. He wasn't awake, and with each passing second the reality of his injuries grew grimmer. I had no choice but to make a decision, and I'd decided it was worth the risk.

Edward exhaled heavily, giving me a terse nod before he

climbed out of the driver's seat. Coming around the car, he helped me out. I was careful to avoid getting any more blood on his clothes, which instantly seemed stupid given he was already covered in it. But the more stains he wore home, the more questions there would be, and right now it was best to keep others out of the situation.

His eyes narrowed as he took in Smith's sallow coloring, but he didn't say anything. What could he say? That this was serious? That it might be too late? Those thoughts had already crossed my mind. Thank god, my best friend knew me well enough to know that. I didn't think I could handle hearing the truth spoken out loud. Not yet.

Edward lifted Smith's body out of the car, then turned on me. "If this proves to be a mistake—"

"It isn't," I reassured him—as much as myself.

"If it is," he continued, ignoring me, "then you get the hell out."

"Edward, I'm not—"

This time he interrupted me. "I'm not debating this with you. It's what Smith would want."

I jerked in surprise. He was right. Smith would want me to run. My best friend and my husband didn't generally see eye to eye. It felt strange for Edward to channel him now, and it only served as a reminder that Smith wasn't capable of delivering the warning himself.

And although I detested being told what to do, I couldn't divorce the demand from the men behind it. Tonight I needed to judge when to be headstrong and when to be smart, especially if I was going to keep all of us safe.

"Fine," I agreed, leveling my gaze to his and staring him down, "as long as you run, too."

"And Smith?" Edward's tone was strained.

"He'd want both of us to get to safety."

"I'm not sure his concern extends to me," he said flatly.

I hadn't had the opportunity to catch Edward up on the truth about Smith's connection to our private circle. After tonight he deserved to know, but it would have to wait. "You might be surprised."

I left it at that.

Edward shot me a frustrated look as he tilted his head toward the entrance. "I'll follow you."

I took a deep breath and strode forward, stopping when I reached the glass doors. Pausing to gather my courage, I lifted my fist and rapped softly on the glass. The lobby was dark inside. Anyone could be waiting in there for me. My gaze darted to Smith and Edward, and I silently pled with the heavens that I wasn't leading them into a trap. Movement inside caught my attention, and I turned back toward the clinic to discover a man emerging from the darkened corridor.

My breath caught as I waited for him to unlock the door, but when he did, he frowned wearily at the sight of Smith. Waving his hand, he gestured for us to follow him inside. "Mrs. Price, I presume?"

"Yes." My mouth went dry as I answered him. I wasn't accustomed to being called by Smith's name. It was still too new, and it felt even more strange under these circumstances. Right now a normal newlywed was on her honeymoon, not rushing her husband in for clandestine medical treatment.

Roget led us into a room illuminated by harsh fluorescent light and pointed to an exam table covered in thin paper. Edward lowered Smith onto it gently and stepped away as Roget burst into action. I watched him as he worked, absently chewing my fingernails as I studied him. He was older, judging from the gray peppering the hair at his temples. The stress of his profession had worn a groove between his eyes that seemed to deepen as he continued to work. I had no doubt he was a doctor and that he took his professional responsibility to Smith seriously. But at the end of the day, even good men could be bought. A fact I was determined to keep front and center from now on.

"Will he be okay?" Edward asked, voicing the one question bouncing around in my head.

"Right now, I need to stabilize him," Roget barked over his shoulder, "and unless one of you is a nurse, I'd prefer to work without an audience. I'll let you know as soon as I have more information."

"I'm not leaving." I crossed my arms, realizing that I must look like a petulant child, but I didn't care.

"Mrs. Price, you asked for my help," Roget reminded me, not bothering to turn away from the line he was inserting in the crook of Smith's elbow.

"He's right, *Mrs. Price.*" Edward grabbed my arm and tugged me out of the room into the hallway.

I ignored his obvious dig at my marital status and twisted out of his grasp. "Do you trust him?"

"We don't have a choice, but you already know that." Edward stepped back, shaking his head. "It looks like we need to kill some time. How about a game of twenty questions?"

The reckoning had arrived, and given our current situation, I couldn't think of a single way to avoid it any longer. "Do you want to start or should I?"

"I'll start," he said with a hollow laugh, "if I can decide where to start."

"How about with the fact that I got married?" I offered in a quiet voice.

Edward wandered over to a line of chairs and sank into one. "I'll admit that I was hoping there was another explanation for that one."

"Like what?" I asked incredulously, taking the seat beside him.

"As far as I know, girlfriends aren't granted decision-making rights over their boyfriend's medical care."

"You're right. Maybe I should have lied." I slumped back, knocking my head lightly against the wall.

"That hurts almost as much as you not telling me in the first place. How? When?"

I closed my eyes and rubbed the bridge of my nose, in a losing attempt to delay the start of a stress headache. "In New York. Our butler married us in our hotel suite."

"That won't make the society pages." But the teasing edge that should have colored his words was absent.

"It killed me that you weren't there." I reached out and grabbed his hand, needing the contact. I had to know that despite this breach of trust we were still connected. "It still doesn't feel real."

"Who else knows?"

"Clara," I admitted with a sigh.

"I suppose that's fair."

I had known Clara for much longer than Edward, but that wasn't the reason she had heard the news before he did. "Actually, she heard through Alexander. I guess the danger of your best friend being married to one of the most powerful men in the world is that it's hard to keep secrets from him. He found out before she did."

"So basically you pissed off your best friends, hurt their feelings, married a guy we barely know, and are being chased by murderers. Am I caught up now?" This time, despite the dark tone, I caught a faint glimmer of amusement in his eyes.

I knocked my shoulder against his. "You've got the gist."

"And yet I have so many questions."

"So do I." It hurt to admit that even after learning so much more about Smith and his relationship to Hammond, new and damning information kept popping up. The man who had attacked me had been much more than a hired goon. His reason for wanting me dead had nothing to do with business. It had been deeply personal. How many more of Smith's old *friends* would pop up with similar agendas?

It wasn't something I wanted to burden Edward with, which meant the thought, like so many others, had to be carried by me alone.

"What else?" Edward prompted.

Apparently he had been serious when he proposed twenty questions. "Honestly, I wouldn't even know where to begin."

"How about with tonight?" he suggested. "What the hell happened? Half of that blood isn't his."

"No, it isn't." I gulped. I owed him at least this much information, but I wasn't certain I wanted to relive what had happened yet. "I was mugged yesterday. The guy beat me up."

"Christ, Belle." Edward wrapped an arm around my shoulders. I sensed the question lingering on his tongue.

"That's all," I reassured him. "He didn't..."

"Enough said."

I was grateful that he wasn't going to make me relive every harrowing detail from that experience—or face what might have happened if it hadn't been for the good Samaritan that called the police.

"It was pretty bad," I told him, feeling myself slip back into the darkness of that moment. I pressed closer to Edward, soaking in the warmth of his body.

"Why didn't you call me?" The chastisement was gentle, but there all the same.

"Smith was concerned that it was more than a mugging, so he checked us into the Westminster Royal and went to look into some things."

"He left you there?" Edward choked out.

"No! I called Aunt Jane." As soon as the words were out of my mouth, I froze.

Aunt Jane.

In the chaos, I'd forgotten to contact her. She would have gone back to the hotel, and...the thought was too horrible. I flapped my hand wildly before finally spitting out, "Mobile."

Edward dug into his pocket and produced his phone. He didn't say anything as I dialed her number and counted the rings.

She answered on the third one.

"It's me." I held back a sob and forced myself to sound as normal as possible.

"Thank God." In the background I could hear a cacophony of noise. "The whole hotel is locked down. They won't let me up to your room. They've evacuated everyone, but I can't find you."

My head drooped as I searched for words that would calm her without raising suspicion. There were none. "I'm not there."

"I can't say that I'm sorry to hear that." But even as she spoke, her voice ratcheted into a higher pitch. "Where are you?"

"I can't tell you," I said apologetically. Telling her would only endanger her, but it didn't make it any easier to keep the secret.

"I see." Jane was silent for a moment. "Are you safe? Is Edward with you?"

Of course, she would have his number programmed into her mobile. "He is, and I am."

"And Smith?"

"He's here." I couldn't bear to claim he was safe, not right now. "I can't tell you anything else, but please believe me, I will call you as soon as I can."

"I know, love. I'm here day or night."

I couldn't stand hearing the devastation in her voice. Aunt Jane understood, she always did, but I knew I had scared her. I could only hope her fear would be short-lived and that this would be resolved sooner rather than later. "I should go."

"Be safe."

I hung up, wondering if those would be the last words she ever spoke to me. If Hammond had anything to say about it, they would be.

When I looked up, Edward waited.

"How much do you know about Hammond and his relationship to your brother?"

His whole body went rigid as I spoke Hammond's name. He cleared his throat. "Enough."

Knowing anything about Hammond was too much for any person to bear, particularly because with each new piece of information learned, you realized how much more you *didn't* know. The man was an enigma. The only thing I didn't question about him was the fact that he was dangerous.

"We need to disappear," I whispered to Edward, "and I don't know how to make that happen."

"Alexander—"

I held up a hand to cut him off. As much as I loved my best friend and trusted her judgment, I needed her husband left out of this. "He can't know."

"He's after Hammond," Edward said as if this changed things.

"I know." I rubbed my forehead, searching for a delicate way to explain. "So was Smith."

"But then..." He trailed off as his confusion shifted into realization.

"Your brother is so obsessed he can't see straight. Until I know more—until I can talk to Smith, I need to disappear."

"I suppose I can't ask where you'll go," he said in a strained voice.

"I'll tell you if you have to know, but it might be best if you didn't." I didn't like the idea of Edward having to lie for me any more than necessary.

"I'll make a few calls."

I didn't get the chance to ask him who he would call before Dr. Roget appeared in the doorway.

"What are your blood types?"

"Um, A, I think." It sounded right.

"O negative."

Dr. Roget beckoned for Edward to join him.

"The joy of being a universal donor," he muttered, rolling up his sleeve as he went inside the room.

I entered behind them, my hand fluttering to my mouth to stifle a gasp at the sight of Smith hooked up to an oxygen mask and IVs.

"He needs a transfusion," the doctor explained, gesturing for Edward to take a chair next to the bed. "I can't risk going into the hospital for blood."

"Lucky that I'm here," Edward said through gritted teeth.

I shot him a grateful smile. A few minutes later, Edward's blood flowed through a tube into a collection bag.

"Now let's take a look at you," Dr. Roget suggested. "Perhaps somewhere more private."

My heartbeat sped up as I realized he wanted to take me into another room. Smith would be safe here with Edward, and the clinic was quiet. I'd only need to get off one scream if things went south. "Of course."

Edward's earlier warning echoed in my head. I braced myself as I stepped into the exam room across the hall behind Roget. But the doctor merely flipped on the lights.

"Your shoulder is bleeding," he noted.

I nodded numbly, admittedly surprised that this wasn't a trap. Had my world really been reduced to turning each stranger I met into an enemy? I tugged my shirt off my head, wincing as the fabric grazed over the wound I'd sustained trying to crawl out of my hotel window.

"Adrenaline," he explained.

I blinked and shook my head. "I'm sorry?"

"You've been functioning on adrenaline. It's kept you alive," he informed me. "That's why you forgot you were hurt."

"I was worried about Smith," I whispered.

"Understandable." He swabbed the cut with a wet cotton ball that transitioned from cold liquid to stinging heat on contact. "You should be worried."

"Is he going to make it?" I wasn't entirely sure I'd spoken the words, my voice was so small.

"He will. You acted quickly. Once the transfusion is complete, he'll be stable. For now."

"And later?"

"Unfortunately, you can't stay here." Roget smiled sadly. "As a doctor, it's not ideal to treat a patient and kick him out immediately, but there is simply no other way."

"I understand."

"Do you, Mrs. Price?" he asked pointedly. "I could make up an excuse and have him admitted within the hour, but he would be dead by tomorrow. Do you *truly* understand?"

"I do." The words scratched across my tongue. It was the second time I'd spoken those words this week. Each time they'd held a heavy meaning.

"I won't ask you anything else." He finished bandaging the cut and walked to the sink. "It's better I don't know."

"What will you tell them?"

"That Smith came to me for medical assistance, and I complied in accordance with my agreement with Hammond."

"You're going to play dumb," I sussed out.

His head bobbed. "I didn't attend to you when you came to the hospital, Mrs. Price. But I looked at your chart. You don't need to give me any more details."

He had already guessed. He knew Smith had gone from Hammond's golden child to number one on his list.

"The less your friend knows the better, especially given who he is."

I bit my lip to keep it from trembling. I'd known this was far from over. I'd hatched a plan. But the reality of enacting it was hurtling toward me with breakneck speed.

"When they come to ask, I'll mention Smith and his wife came." Roget wiped his hands on a towel and dropped it into a linen basket. "I should check on the donor's progress."

Edward would be left out of it. It was a small mercy, but one all the same. From tonight on I'd only have myself to rely on unless Smith woke up.

When he wakes up, I thought, willing myself to believe it.

CHAPTER FOUR

Each breath was a struggle and then it wasn't. But nothing could stop the barrage of nightmares that accompanied the heavy darkness oppressing my body.

Open your eyes.

I repeated the demand until my eyelids flickered open. Staring at white ceiling tiles, it took me a moment to realize I was breathing through an oxygen mask. I swiped against its sweaty rim, trying to push it away A million questions crowded in my mind and they all centered around one person:

Belle.

Propping myself up on my elbow, pain shot through me and knocked me back onto the table.

"I wouldn't try to get up," a cold voice advised me. "She'll be back in a second."

This time I ripped the mask off and swiveled toward the voice, ignoring the second hot stab of pain. Edward was a media darling, loved by the masses for his kindness and sweet nature. In a way, the prince was England's ultimate boy next door, but if the papers could see him now, they might take back the title.

He glared down at me, his face devoid of that infamous friendliness, and the message was clear: he was here for her. Not for me.

As if I gave a fuck. I'd dealt with the entitled attitude of his family long enough to know what they were really like. I'd tolerated them for the sole purpose of destroying Hammond. Now I'd have to tolerate them for new reasons, but I didn't have to like Edward. I was positive that the feeling was mutual.

"What the fuck are you doing here?" I asked in a scratchy voice before succumbing to a fit of coughing.

"You're welcome," he responded in a flat voice, holding up his arm to display the crimson tube taped to his flesh. "You need blood."

He didn't tell me more than that, but his presence here was enough to help me piece together some of my missing timeline. Although it didn't tell me where *here* was. Or where my wife had gone. I tried to push off the table again, but this time Edward caught me and held me back.

"Are you mental?" he demanded. "Can you stop trying to kill yourself for five bloody minutes?"

"Where is she?" I asked in a low voice.

"Your doctor is checking her out."

This time he couldn't keep me down. I swung my feet over the edge of the exam table as stars blossomed in my vision. Shaking my head, I tried to will away the wooziness.

"She's fine." Edward grabbed my shoulder. "I can't say the same about you."

"He's stubborn," Roget's baritone called from the doorway. "Smith, your lovely wife is here. Safe."

My gaze flashed over his shoulder, my heart beating against my rib cage like a trapped animal. I'd thought I'd sent her to safety, only to have Hammond dash that hope. It should have calmed me to know she hadn't gone to Clara and Alexander after my phone call, but the fact that she was here, unknowingly being treated by Hammond's personal physician, only made me more desperate to take her as far away from London as I could get her.

Belle peeked past Roget and then rushed to my side. Having her so close was enough to relax me, if only for a moment, and I collapsed down, exam paper crinkling under me.

"You need a transfusion." She fussed over me, brushing my hair from my forehead. Her eyes wouldn't meet mine, and when I finally reached up and tilted her chin, I found tears brimming on her lashes.

"Hey, beautiful," I said in a soft voice. There was no point in trying to reassure her. I'd fallen for a smart woman; it would be an insult to downplay what she had been through.

Or what was to come.

"You scared me, Price," she whispered. "I don't know if I should hit you or kiss you."

"As it so happens, I like it rough," I reminded her, stroking the back of my hand softly over her unbruised cheek.

Edward groaned, not even a meter away, and an embarrassed grin flitted over Belle's beautiful face. Even with her injuries, she was the most breathtaking woman in the world. She was classically beautiful with high cheekbones and delicate coloring, and she'd combined those features with the sensibility of an ingénue. Just thinking of her wearing sexpot red lipstick was usually enough to get me hard.

But none of that was what captured my attention and fueled my obsession. It had been her fire that undid me. Before her I'd had no interest in relationships, I had never considered that I could trust a woman again. Quite simply she'd lit a flame in me that I'd believed couldn't be reignited. She had given me a purpose beyond myself. She was my reason to live—and my reason to fight.

And she was in danger.

"I'd like to speak to Dr. Roget alone."

Belle's teeth sank into her lower lip as she studied me before she stood up and crossed her arms over her petite chest. "You sent me away once tonight, and look how that turned out."

"I'm only sending you to the hallway." I forced a smile. Belle huffed as she turned to leave.

Dr. Roget had finished removing Edward's line and was setting up the transfusion line. I shot Belle's best friend a meaningful look over her shoulder. He caught it and tipped his chin in recognition.

"There's an icebox down the hall," Roget instructed them. "He should have something sugary and sit down."

"Fine. C'mon." She slung an arm around his waist, and the two shared a smile so genuine that jealousy roared in my chest. Given that Edward was gay, I should have felt stupid. But I wanted that—a relationship that came easily. I wanted to make her feel lightened, not burdened. I wanted to make her smile, not cry. Tonight I'd failed to protect her. I was a failure as a husband.

The doctor tapped my skin for a vein, but I barely felt it. "How bad is it?"

"It could be worse," he said with a shrug, not bothering with a warning before he stuck me.

"How?" I asked dryly.

"You could be dead," he pointed out, "and in that scenario, she would be dead, too."

"Is that a threat?" I snarled, my hand lashing out to catch the cuff of his lab coat.

Roget calmly withdrew my fingers and continued to set up the IV. "We both took oaths in our professions, Smith. Mine has been easier to keep in many ways."

"Do no harm?" I asked with a laugh. He had done plenty of harm. We all had.

"My professional responsibility is to my patient. I am responsible for his health and his life. It doesn't matter who they are or the crimes they have committed. If the police bring in an injured criminal, it is my duty as a doctor to treat them."

"I've always wondered how you sleep at night," I muttered.

"I've often wondered the same thing about you," he said without missing a beat. "Your duty is also to your client."

"That's where we're different, Doctor. I know I'm scum."

"I know that as well." Roget settled onto a stool next to the table. "Hammond offered financial resources to the hospital that the state could not. I made a choice."

We all had made the same choice: to sell our soul. Hammond was the highest bidder in London. He always had been.

"I don't regret that," he continued. "I've saved countless lives through his donations."

"What about the lives he's taken?" I asked him.

"Regrettable." There was hesitation though.

At the end of the day, it was impossible to negate the red in our ledgers. No matter what we told ourselves, no matter what good we did.

"Georgia's dead," I informed him. "He killed her."

Roget's throat slid as he swallowed this information. "I'm sorry to hear that."

"He'll kill me, too—and Belle."

"Your wife is a smart woman, Smith. I've already advised her."

My eyes narrowed. "What game are we playing here?"

"No game, Smith. I didn't sit down to discuss ethics with you. I was trying to tell you that I haven't informed Hammond of your presence here this evening." Roget spread his hands as if offering me a present.

But we both knew it wasn't as simple as that. "He'll find out."

"When he does, I'll remind him that I was under orders to care for his family under any circumstances."

"I'm not his family. Not anymore."

He raised a bushy eyebrow. "I didn't know that. You simply showed up with your wife in need of medical attention. I sent you on your way, thinking nothing of it."

"It won't matter," I said with a sigh. "We won't even make it out of this city."

"I was surprised to see you'd made friends with people in such *lofty* situations. Perhaps you'll have more time than you think."

"Then you won't contact him at all?" I didn't hide my surprise at this possibility. Hammond wasn't known for jumping to rational conclusions. It was a gamble on Roget's part to keep this information from him.

"I told you that my responsibility is to my patients. Your well-being is my concern. As far as I know, Hammond will suffer no ill effects if you heal."

He would if I had anything to say about it. Roget's mouth pressed into a line, and he stood as if he suspected what I was thinking.

"I appreciate it." Despite Roget's professional claims, it was hard to be grateful to a man whose primary function in the world was keeping an evil man alive and healthy.

I listened to him, half-heartedly, as he told me things I already knew. I couldn't stay here. It would be dangerous for me to go to the hospital. I would have to leave when the transfusion was complete. I nodded at the appropriate times despite its uselessness. Roget would be the first person Hammond sought out when he learned the details of the night. We wouldn't have long before the next hellish onslaught was upon us.

"Can you ask Edward to come in?" I asked, interrupting him mid-sentence.

"Of course," he said in a pert voice.

Edward eyed me as he entered the room, the wariness of earlier returning to his features.

"I wanted to thank you," I told him. This time there was no question of my sincerity. At least, not on my end. "You were there for Belle when I couldn't be."

"It seems like you have a hard time being there for her," Edward pointed out. "Perhaps you aren't the man for the job."

Every instinct in my body wanted to tear him apart as he spoke, but I fought the urge. Clenching my fists, I forced myself to remain calm. "From now on, it is my sole responsibility."

"And what about your duty to others?" Edward cast a meaningful look down at me.

I wasn't interested in doublespeak anymore. "Tell your brother what I said. He's had enough information to hang Hammond for months. I'm out."

"He'll be sorry to hear that."

"But I suspect you aren't," I guessed. Up until now, I hadn't been sure if Edward was aware of his brother's private witch hunt.

"It is a son's duty to avenge his father. If you'll pardon the cliché, it's in our blood to believe that, but my true concern has always been with protecting Clara and Belle."

"And Alexander's is not?"

"He would die for Clara," Edward assured me. "I'm not certain he would make that sacrifice for Belle."

"He shouldn't," I said harshly. "That's my duty."

Edward looked away as he spoke quietly, "He told you to walk away from her."

"I've never been very good at taking orders," I reminded him, "which is why I doubt he'll mourn my loss."

"If anything happens to her—"

"Save your threat," I stopped him. "If anything happens to Belle, you won't have to seek me out. You won't have to kill me. I'll do it myself."

I extended my hand, and Edward took it, gripping it firmly in recognition of this understanding. I didn't care if he believed me. I trusted that he would seek me out if I didn't make good on my promise. But he wouldn't have to—I was a man of my word.

CHAPTER FIVE

Belle had fallen silent as soon as we left the clinic, and I was torn between forcing her to talk and being caught in my own thoughts. The farther we got from London, the darker the world grew outside the car windows. There were no street lamps illuminating the M4, and save for pockets of civilization tucked into the outskirts of London, night had painted the world black. Time lost all meaning as we drove speechlessly from the city we called home toward an unknown destination.

I suspected where she was taking me, but I'd understood why she had been hesitant to share her plans until we were safely outside the greater London area. There was no reason to believe we weren't safe, but I knew the same sense of foreboding I felt had settled into her bones. Somehow it felt better not to talk about what had happened—what was likely to come. At least, for now. In the cold, ink-black night, reality felt absent, as if we'd stumbled into limbo.

Emotionally, we had. It wasn't many marriages that tested the "'til death do us part" aspect so early on. I reached out and took Belle's hand, my face still turned to the anonymous world outside. It was enough to know she was here. She believed she was taking me to safety, but that was far from the truth.

I was removing her from danger.

My injuries had been the catalyst needed to motivate her to leave, and once I was certain she was safe, I would return to London and the unfinished business I'd left behind. Business that stood a pretty good chance of landing me behind bars or six feet under.

As we drove, a lilac sliver of dawn appeared on the horizon, brightening into a cheerful rose. I'd never hated the sunrise before, but this morning as it cast light across the unfamiliar landscape, I did. Belle's fingers tightened around my own as if she too feared what today might bring to our doorstep. Last night, we had survived. Before, a new day might have felt full of possibility, but now it only carried the prospect of new danger. In the night, we'd faded along with the world. The first streaks of sunlight bounced off the Bugatti's hood, exposing us. The dawn had caught up with us as it did all things.

We couldn't outrun time. Our only hope was to outrun the past.

A spray of glimmering light fragmented on the roof of the car, and I realized Belle was its source. The sun had caught the diamonds in her wedding band.

She was wearing it. Despite everything that had happened and despite how difficult the vows we'd made must feel to her now, she had finally put the damn ring on her finger. If I'd believed in a higher power, I might have seen it as a sign. Just as a new day appeared to taunt me, it had also reminded me that I had something worth fighting for. I'd joined this cause long before I met Belle Stuart—long before I'd understood why I felt compelled to.

Now I knew.

Every decision I'd made had brought me here to this moment, and while I wished the circumstances were less fucked up, I loved the outcome: her. Belle had come into my life for the worst possible reason, and somehow despite all the ugliness that surrounded our meeting, she'd given me something I thought was impossible. Love. Purpose.

Hope.

And even though I had a harder time holding on to the latter two gifts, the love was always there. And it was that love that kept leading me back to a place where I could believe again.

"You're quiet," she murmured.

That was the pot calling the kettle black. "You're a very focused driver. I didn't want to break your concentration."

"I'd like to see you try," she shot back, a grin tugging at her lips. But as quickly as the lightheartedness had appeared, it vanished.

"Pull over and I'll show you," I offered, trying to find it again. But there was no point. Moments of levity would be fleeting for the foreseeable future.

"How's your bandage?" she asked in a sharp voice, redirecting my attention to the trouble at hand.

I lifted my shirt and shook my head. "Nothing to worry about."

"Are you going to ask where we're going?" she prompted, her blue eyes flashing quizzically at me before returning to the road.

But I didn't need to ask. I'd seen the signs for Somerset several times in the last hour, and I knew exactly what we would find there.

"I could be kidnapping you," she continued dryly when I didn't respond.

"Beautiful, it's not a crime if I'd follow you anyway." I traced a figure eight on the back of her hand.

"I'm taking you home." The statement was confessional in nature, as if she expected penance in exchange for this revelation. Given her history with her family home, I couldn't exactly blame her.

"I know."

"I'm not sure we'll be escaping danger there."

"It will be better than being in London," I said.

She snorted, shaking her head. "You haven't met my mother."

"She gave birth to you, she can't be all bad." Although the fact that she'd sued her own daughter didn't support my theory. I needed to start putting on my game face now.

The look Belle shot me made me seriously doubt the validity of that statement.

"Stuart Hall is lovely during the holidays," she continued, but I couldn't help but notice that she had grown distant.

There were a million things to discuss before we arrived. We needed to have a plan of action. We needed to agree on a story to tell her mother. She needed to have my lawyer's information if I was arrested in connection to Jake's murder. All of that could wait though. Belle had faced my past, now I would help conquer hers. Because that was the only way we could look to the future together.

CHAPTER SIX

I imagined for some people coming home produced a warm feeling. Up until I met Smith, buying shoes was the closest I'd come to capturing that sensation. Home had never been my refuge. It had been the place I'd fled from as soon as my mother deemed me old enough to attend boarding school at the age of six—a year too late to retain my innocence. This place had stolen that from me. This house had whisked away my youth and demanded my blood and fear ever since. I wished I didn't blame my father for falling victim to it. As I'd grown older, I even understood to some extent. But I couldn't divorce what he had done with this place any more than I could pretend it hadn't happened. I had found his body, and even though it took me years to truly comprehend the permanency of death, the sight of his bloated, blue face had been glimpse enough.

"It's magnificent," Smith commented from the passenger seat.

I tried to see it through his eyes: the large brick expanse of the main house built in the seventeenth century; the manicured hedges that lined the circular drive that had once seen carriages and riders daily; and, of course, the grounds stretching past my line of sight to where the stables and various outbuildings still stood.

"Clara told me that it was like stepping into a Jane Austen novel," I told him.

He tipped his head in agreement. "It is."

My mother certainly fit the bill of the rude lady of the estate. I was sure good old Jane would have plenty to say about her.

I pulled the Bugatti to the front entrance and put it in park with a deep sigh. This wasn't exactly how I'd pictured bringing Smith to meet my mum. Although, in all fairness, I'd spent more time fantasizing about never speaking to her again. It hadn't crossed my mind that the two should be introduced.

"I'm assuming your mother doesn't know we're married," Smith guessed, his forehead wrinkling in concern as he studied my face.

"Unless you put an announcement in the paper, probably not." I didn't tell him that she had an uncanny ability to find out about my personal life. We had enough to worry about. I didn't need to stress over how much she knew about Smith and me.

"Your aunt wouldn't tell her?"

My chest constricted at the mention of Aunt Jane. I hadn't even told her I was married, although I had a feeling she had figured it out. "Definitely not."

I opened my mouth to clarify, but he stopped me.

"You don't have to explain. I know enough about the situation."

Like the fact that my mother was suing me for my business or that she'd forced my father to disown my half-brother. Smith might not have met her, but I was certain he already had an opinion.

A friendly, round face greeted me at the door. "Miss Belle!"

I shot Smith a warning look. I didn't want him to run around correcting anyone about my marital status yet. "Belinda!"

She caught me in a hug before I could explain my unexpected appearance.

"Aren't you the sight! Come in out of the cold," she commanded, waving us inside the massive entrance hall. I was careful to keep my back turned to the door behind me, focusing instead on the infectiously cheerful woman that had helped raised me. Belinda had been with our family for years, and I'd often suspected that she was my fairy godmother sent to protect me from my wicked mother. I could think of no other reason why the kind-hearted woman had stayed on the staff through both of my fathers marriages and his suicide.

"She's not expecting us," I warned her, my eyes darting to the staircase as if my mother might appear at any moment.

"Your mum is out on a ride. She went up to see the neighbors. Don't expect her back till afternoon." Belinda glanced around us looking for bags. Then she paused and studied us more closely. "What happened to you, child?"

My hand flew to the wounds on my face.

"Car accident," Smith lied smoothly, placing a reassuring hand on the small of my back. "I'm afraid we're both banged up. The doctor ordered rest, and I didn't trust Belle to get it in the city. I just started driving when she suggested we head here."

It was a perfectly rational explanation for how we looked, but what sold it was my husband's dazzling smile. I knew for a fact that he could charm the pants off a woman.

"Hopefully, my old clothes still fit." I couldn't imagine what I'd left behind between visits from university, but I knew there would be some things.

"Of course, they will, love." Belinda eyed me. "You still have your figure."

"But you..." I glanced at Smith, wondering if I could risk a trip to the nearest village.

"I'll pull some things from your father's closet," Belinda interrupted the thought.

I wanted to protest, but I didn't have many options. Not when all I wanted was to lock the door and hide.

By the time Belinda had brought us hot tea and a light breakfast, I'd forgotten my apprehension. She was what made this place a home. It was likely the reason my mother had been threatening to sack her for years.

But as my mother's shrill voice rang through the dining room, I remembered why it wasn't *my* home. "Who has parked that ostentatious vehicle in my drive?"

There was no point in trying to collect myself. That much I knew. Instead I raised my teacup, held it up in toast to Smith, and took a sip. I didn't bother to look up from it when she appeared in the doorway and stopped dead in her tracks.

She opened her mouth to speak but froze when she saw that I wasn't alone. Instead she held out one thin hand and beckoned for me to follow her.

"You refused my invitation to visit," she spat out as soon as we were out of eyesight. It was just like my mum to want to save face, if not ears.

"He can still hear us if you yell," I warned her, trying to maintain my calm.

"I don't know who that man is or why you think you can waltz in here and act like you own the place—"

"Because I own the place," I interrupted her, but she didn't stop talking.

"It is common courtesy to call before arriving at someone's home." My mother twisted her hands together as if wringing out a rag. I couldn't help but imagine doing the same to her neck.

"It's hardly a huge imposition on you," I pointed out, heat rising to my cheeks. "You have over thirty rooms here. I'm sure we can dust off the furniture in the south wing. You won't even notice we're here."

"That is hardly the point." She jabbed a finger at my chest. "I assume you received the papers I sent."

"You mean the papers you served me?" I shot back. So far she hadn't said a thing about my obvious injuries. She hadn't bothered to ask who Smith was or why we were here. She'd only focused on making it clear how unwanted we were in my family home—a home that I still owned.

"Let's not make this ugly," she said in a low voice.

"Afraid our *guest* might hear?" I said as loudly as possible.

"I have no idea who that man is."

I considered telling her he was my lawyer, simply to scare her. "Smith Price."

"Your former employer?" Of course, she knew who he was. "This is a delicate situation, Belle. I don't think you understand that."

"I think I do," I rebutted. "We wouldn't want people to know about our financial difficulties or that you're suing your own daughter for rights to her company. It's too late, Mother. You already made this ugly."

"If you had any hope of landing that man, you've seriously undermined the possibility," she hissed. "No man wants a woman who comes with financial baggage."

"Maybe you're wrong about that." Or maybe she was right. I hadn't exactly been forthcoming with Smith about the extent of my family estate's troubles. I hadn't wanted him to get involved before. I had been afraid he would take pity on me and attempt to bail me out. I'd never even considered the implications when I'd married him. In my mind, our lives were still separate in so many ways, but that wasn't the point of marriage—and it wasn't what I wanted with Smith. Given all that we'd been through, I couldn't imagine keeping anything from him. But perhaps hearing it shouted during a screaming match with my mother wasn't the appropriate way to go about opening up to him.

"Maybe," she muttered. "Perhaps he's simply after the house or the land."

I laughed hollowly. "He doesn't need our debt or our skeletons."

"You would be surprised what men will do for the chance at—"

"Pardon me." I whipped around to discover Smith's muscular shape filling the corridor behind us. "I couldn't help overhearing."

My mother glared at him, but he simply smirked back. It was the arrogant grin I'd once despised even though it made me weak in the knees. Now I loved it about him, especially when he leveled it at her.

"Perhaps I could," he admitted. "But I make it a point to be aware of all things concerning Belle. Naturally I wanted to be near her as she returned to her family estate."

"Naturally," my mother repeated in a dry tone. "Stalkers make it a point to know everything about a woman. Are you a stalker, Mr. Price?"

"Hardly." There was a glimmer of amusement in his eyes at the accusation.

"You'll forgive me if I tell you this is none of your business," my mother said coldly.

"Actually it is, seeing as I'm married to your daughter."

It was a miracle that in a house this old nothing burst into flames with the look she shot him. Her gaze continued to scorch as it turned on me. "Explain."

"When a man and a woman love each other very much," I began in a flat voice.

"Don't sass me, young lady."

Smith stepped between us. "Don't speak to my wife in that voice, ma'am."

She shrank back, a hand pressed to her chest. After a few minutes of silence, she straightened up. "Take the south wing."

It was a slap in the face to be sent to the far end of the house, considered shabby even for unimportant guests.

"We're preparing to film in the other wings," she explained when she saw my face.

"Including the north hall?"

"That hall is reserved for family," she said in a clipped tone. If there had been any doubt, I knew exactly where I stood with her now.

Belinda, utilizing her unparalleled eavesdropping skills, had listened in and beaten us to the guest wing before the awkward audience with my mother. Within minutes she'd fluffed and dusted, preparing the hall's largest suite for guests. I'd hidden in the room as a young child, knowing my mother wouldn't bother searching this part of the house. It was a small comfort that she was unlikely to check in on us now.

"Thank you," I told her sincerely.

She waved it off. "I imagine you two need to rest. Newlyweds are always so tired."

Smith turned just in time to see her wink at me. Apparently she'd caught that we were married. Regardless, I was happy to see her go. After the run-in with mother, I wanted to be alone.

"I see where you get your tenacity," Smith remarked as he settled onto the bed and kicked off his shoes.

I whirled around, pointing a shaky finger at him. "Take that back, Price."

"It's not an insult, beautiful."

My mouth fell open. Was he really comparing *me* with *her*?

"I only wish your father was here," he continued, "because I know that's where you got your heart."

I clamped my lips shut and raised my eyebrows, still offended.

"You look like her. You don't filter yourself, but beautiful, that's where the comparisons end."

I grudgingly sank onto the bed beside him, but I couldn't stay mad. I knew he was partially right, but not about my father. My memories of him were too fuzzy to have made an impact. "Jane was the one who really cared about me. I'd like to think I'm like her."

"I look forward to getting to know her better."

We stretched out on the bed, our arms pressed together. After the last two days, I didn't have energy for anything else.

"I'd like that, too." The words cracked over my dry tongue. Would we ever have that chance? It was impossible to say.

"Someday," he promised.

"How do you know?" I asked, staring at the ceiling. "How can you be sure we'll get through this?"

"Together. When you love someone you make it through the bad shit together. That's how love works. That's *why* love works." Smith turned his head to the side and brushed a kiss over my forehead. "Now sleep."

CHAPTER SEVEN

Sleep came in dreamless fits, and when I woke up, I discovered night had fallen again. We'd slept the whole day. Making my way to the bathroom in the dark, I fumbled for the light switch, momentarily startled to find myself at my mother's house. Almost instantly the last few days rushed back to me.

I stared into the mirror, but this time I didn't see the bruises or the cuts. All I saw was the exhaustion lining my face. I could feel it throbbing at my temples, the ache spreading across my skin until all that was left was the heavy weight of existence. I was alive, which was ostensibly a good thing—so why did I feel so burdened by every breath?

It was like those interviews you see on television after a natural disaster or a bombing. Half of the people are screaming with gratitude that they're safe, thanking god for it. The other half are still shell-shocked, too numb to understand what happened. I'd seen it a million times. I'd even witnessed it firsthand after the bloody events of Clara's wedding.

It was different to feel it. Or rather to not feel it.

. . .

When Smith had been in danger I was precise in my focus, attending to each moment as it came. I'd allowed myself a brief reprieve in bed with him, because I'd stupidly thought I could fuck away the pain and anger and fear I'd felt since we returned to London.

But now it was here, literally staring back at me, and I couldn't deny the truth any longer. The whole situation was a bloody mess. I had thought when I'd walked away from Jonathan that I'd chosen a new life for myself—a future of my own choosing. But had I only been kidding myself? Now I was back in the last place I wanted to be, facing not only the ghosts of my recent past, but those of my childhood. Death seemed to follow me. My father had been lured to a place so dark that he welcomed death. My best friend had gone to church on her wedding day, me at her side, and watched death attempt to steal her husband. A few nights ago, a stranger attempted to introduce me to death directly; I'd shaken death's hand and managed to live—only to watch the stranger die.

It all led to one painfully obvious conclusion: I was bad news.

I'd almost lost Smith last night. I'd felt his blood pulsing against the palm of my hand. It had been a miracle that he'd survived, and I doubted I'd be granted a second one.

My grip on the marble counter slipped, and I barely caught myself as I slumped to the floor. Apparently I was out to set a record for sudden, tearful breakdowns. But even though I swiped at them and took deep breaths, the tears kept coming. It seemed like I should have run out by now, but the events of the last week had tapped some emotional wellspring deep within me. There was a possibility I might never stop crying. All the emotion I'd held back, all the fear I'd nearly kept in check, had been released, and for the first time, I bore the full brunt of it. It choked me. It smothered me.

It felt as I'd been forced under water, life itself was drowning me, and the person who was supposed to be my life jacket was drowning alongside me.

Together. When you love someone you make it through the bad shit together. That's how love works. That's why *love works.*

Smith's words from earlier floated back to me. They gave me the strength to pull myself up and the courage to walk back into the darkness.

Smith stirred on the bed, and then his husky voice, still thick with sleep, broke the silence. "Good morning, beautiful."

"It's night," I said with a sniff.

"It's hard to think straight when I wake up to you." He rolled over and extended his hand.

I didn't need any further prompting. Dropping beside him, I molded my body against his. The darkness hid my tears, but he found them immediately, brushing them from my cheeks. Smith tilted my chin up, and as my eyes adjusted to the lack of light, he came into clearer focus. The first time I'd seen him, I'd nearly dropped my knickers. Now I learned to not bother wearing any entirely, but I'd also discovered that under his brutal beauty, behind his piercing green eyes, beneath that chiseled jawline, there was a masculinity so powerful it stole my breath away. Because Smith Price was a protective man as well as an honorable one. He wasn't afraid to fight, and he'd chosen to fight for me.

"I don't want you to cry," he murmured.

I swallowed and buried my face against his chest. "Can't help it."

"Maybe I need to find something else for you to do." His breath was hot against my ear. "Scream? Moan?"

"You aren't allowed to..." I couldn't even bring myself to say it. The idea that we couldn't have sex was almost unthinkable even when I didn't desperately need the intimacy. Smith's possessive nature made me feel secure, which I needed more than ever.

"Would it make you feel better to come, beautiful? Because, God knows I need to claim your tight little body. It's all I can think about." Past the sexy gruffness in his voice, I heard need that sent my core clenching in anticipation. "Do you need that, too?"

"But we—"

"I don't need my dick to fuck you. I don't need it to make you come. Besides that, are you questioning my control?"

A tremble rippled over my skin as I breathed, "No."

"I didn't think so." He released his hold on me and sat up in bed. "Turn on the light."

I scrambled onto my knees to flip on the bedside lamp.

"Too many clothes." He spoke each word distinctively, allowing the sentiment to settle over me.

I tugged my t-shirt, the lone item I was wearing, over my head, but I couldn't resist raising an eyebrow. "A t-shirt is too much now?"

"Anything that covers those perfect tits is too much." Relaxing against the pillows, he folded his arms behind his head.

I knelt beside him, my knees sinking into the mattress, and waited. Smith loved to put me on display and test my patience. Probably because I had none. We both knew that I'd be begging for it within minutes.

"On your back," he commanded in a low voice. "I want to see my perfect cunt."

A strangled moan slipped out as I lounged onto my elbows and spread my legs. I craved his possession—I needed it.

"That's right," he coaxed. "You know that's my body. I own it, don't I?"

"Yes," I whimpered, wondering when he would finally touch me, but not daring to ask.

"I'm so goddamn hard, beautiful. Do you remember the first night you gave yourself to me?"

He didn't wait for a response. We both knew that was an unforgettable evening. It had been the first time I had experienced his particular brand of dominance, something I never knew I wanted until he gave me my first taste.

"You fucked my car," he growled, his hand stroking the rigid length straining his boxers. "It was my most priceless possession before I found you. Now there's no comparison. Do you know why you're priceless?"

My throat ached at the raw sensuality in his tone, but I shook my head.

"I didn't have to buy you," he said. "You gave yourself to me."

I groaned, my hand sliding between my legs, unable to contain myself.

"Did I tell you that you could touch yourself?" he asked quietly.

I shook my head, fighting the urge to press my knees together to relieve the demanding pulse.

"You aren't going to touch yourself," he informed me. "You're going to fuck yourself for me—hard."

Smith's hand grasped my knee and held it. The heat of his skin on mine was enough to release a tiny quake of pleasure. I moved my hands lower, spreading my folds with one as I began to urgently knead my hungry clit.

"Show me how badly you want it, beautiful," he ordered, his voice deepening. "Fuck your hand."

I slipped my index finger in my hole, gasping as it tightened in response.

"More. That's not a request."

Biting my lip, I pushed another finger inside. My hips circled against the pressure building in my core, but I didn't dare come. I wanted to make it last. I wanted to push myself, because I knew it would please him.

"I've seen your pretty pink pussy stretched over my cock. I know how much it can take."

A third finger joined the party and I bucked against it.

"Do you fuck yourself like this?" he asked.

I shook my head, even though it was becoming harder to concentrate. If I wasn't careful, I'd lose control and then this delicious reprieve would be over far too soon. I doubted most women fingered themselves when they masturbated. On the off chance I'd ever need to pleasure myself again solo, I might have to add it to my repertoire.

"That's why you're scared," he teased gently as his palm caressed my inner thigh. "You're holding back, so I'm going to have to take over. Although I enjoyed your show."

I drew my hand back automatically, nearly coming as cool air hit the sensitized spot. Smith hooked an arm around my leg and dragged me closer, chuckling as I squirmed. His palm pressed me down to the bed. "Be a good girl and hold still."

I resisted the urge to scream at him. He'd proven he was more patient than I was. As much as he wanted to watch me orgasm, he could wait for it—and probably enjoy every damn second of agony. I didn't have that kind of self-control.

"You got yourself nice and wet for me." He stroked along the length of my slippery seam as he praised me. "I'm going to test you, beautiful, and it's going to hurt but then it's going to feel so good."

This was his way of asking permission. Smith didn't use a safe word. He didn't ask. He informed. I supposed that if I had an issue, I was meant to say something. I never had.

I never would.

Whatever he would give me, I would take with a *please*, a *thank you*, and an earth-shattering orgasm in between.

"You're going to be sore tomorrow," he promised as the first finger glided roughly inside me. "You need that, don't you? A reminder that everything is okay, and I'm going to make sure that you feel me with every step you take."

I cried out as he shoved another two fingers in my entrance. The sensitive tissue stretched as he plunged them in and out, but with each thrust, they slid in more smoothly.

"I'm not going to stop," he growled.

Tears smarted my eyes as a fourth finger worked its way in, but despite the tingle of fire, pain quickly began to shift into pleasure. The drops leaking down my cheeks were joined by a chorus of gasps and screams as Smith fucked me with his hand.

"Do you like that?" he muttered, his own breathing coming in pants as he watched me unfolding. He sat up, twisting his hand around and holding my belly to the bed. "What do you want, beautiful?"

"Fuck me," I sobbed. Own me. Control me. Ruin me.

The languid speed of his movement ratcheted up just enough to send my body shaking as my muscles coiled tightly and then his thumb nudged against the tight ring of my ass. It popped past the tight circle of nerves and pushed me over the edge.

I arched up, held down only by his hold on me, as my climax gushed violently over his palm. When I fell back, my muscles spasmed and I breathed in short staccato bursts, unable to catch my breath.

"That was so goddamn hot," Smith whispered as he released me. "You've never been that wet for me, beautiful. I'm going to need a taste."

My head flopped from side to side. There was no way I was capable of movement. It was entirely possible I would die in this position on this very bed—and it would be a brilliant way to go.

"Not how it works," he reprimanded me. "Get your ass off the bed. I want to taste your pussy."

I tapped into whatever reserve of energy my body clung to for emergencies and rolled onto my stomach. With shaky arms, I crawled up next to him.

"The doctor said I needed to rest for a few days," he reminded me with a cocky smirk, "so I'm going to need you to come a little closer."

His hands guided me onto my knees, drawing one over his upper chest until I was straddling him. Each hot exhale from his mouth sent a flutter dancing along my overwhelmed nerves, and then before I could process what he was thinking, he gripped my ass and slammed my sex over his face. His tongue swept along the wet folds as I heard the snap of elastic. Smith's groan vibrated through me and I fell forward, grabbing onto the headboard as he fucked me with his tongue. Despite the haze clouding my brain, I zeroed in on the distinctive slap of his hand roughly working his cock to the root.

He had his face buried in my cunt while he was getting himself off. It was too much—too hot. My hips began to circle his mouth, grinding against him, seeking release. He owned me, but I was claiming him—marking him as my own. Muffled grunts preceded the first jet of his seed hitting my bare ass. Just the sensation of its heat dribbling down my skin was enough to send me soaring. I came on his mouth, each wave of pleasure met with a spurt of his own.

Apparently, I wasn't the only one staking my claim tonight.

Smith carefully helped me off of him and then slowly got up. "Don't move."

I stayed upright, still clinging to the headboard as he circled the foot of the bed. "You look so lovely. It's giving me ideas of all the things I want to do that ass."

"Starting with cleaning it up?" I suggested, flashing a coy grin over my shoulder.

He laughed as he disappeared into the bathroom, leaving me to fantasize about what exactly he had in mind. But when he returned, he cleaned me up and drew me into his arms, his lips whispering promises across my skin as he lulled me to sleep in the security of his arms.

CHAPTER EIGHT

Stuart Hall grew less friendly as the days passed. By the end of the second week, my bruises and cuts were barely visible. But the other scars lingered, and with each new day spent under my mother's critical eye, I endured new wounds. Smith had taken over my father's study—the last place I wanted to spend time—so I had chosen to pursue a childhood passion: riding.

I'd made the mistake of using my mother's saddle early on, so she'd served a walnut torte at dinner that had nearly sent me into anaphylactic shock. Now I was careful to keep the opposite schedule of my mother, heading out in the early afternoon and returning to supper. I'd begun to think of it as the calm before the storm. A joke I might have shared with Smith if he hadn't made it his personal mission to spend every waking hour holed up on the computer.

The countryside around Somerset had suffered an early snowfall, and between that and the mist that clung to the ground near perpetually, this afternoon's ride had a dreamlike quality, which distracted me from the latest addition to my list of things to worry about. I'd avoided the woods on the far west edge of the property, opting to climb the rolling hills that lay between my family's estate and the neighboring Betford House. Today a plume of smoke rose from the chimney, surprising me. It had gone unused for many years, but either it had been sold or rented. Like many of us, the family had hung onto it long past the point of financial viability. I made a point to ask Belinda about its new inhabitants. As the sun peaked in the sky, fresh snow fell in downy tufts, clinging to my lashes.

"What do you think, Tuesday?" I leaned forward and brushed the snow from his mane before patting him. "Should we head back?"

Snowfall and fog could be a dangerous combination to an unskilled rider, and while I fancied myself pretty damn capable, it had been years since I had ridden on a regular basis. Urging Tuesday into a full gallop, we raced back toward the stables. His hooves kicked up the powdery snow along the way, leaving a fresh trail behind us. But soon snowflakes were falling so heavily that I couldn't see more than a few meters in front of me. When I saw the outline of the stables, I barely stopped before plowing directly into Smith.

He was wearing my father's long coat, his hands shoved into the pockets. I'd been too young when my father died to know if the coat had looked that way on him, but I doubted it. It was an industrial piece, meant to protect from the harshest of conditions and yet it cut in Smith's trim waist, highlighting his broad shoulders and well-hewn arms. But whether it was due to the distance I'd sensed from him or the disapproval written across his face, I wasn't interested in giving into my carnal desires.

Swinging myself off the horse, I grabbed his reins and led Tuesday past him. Inside it was warm, the space well insulated to protect the valuable animals my mother loved so. I'd long suspected she would rather have them sleep under her roof than her own daughter. Tugging off my cap and allowing my hair to tumble free, I mused that I'd be warm, at least.

"Dashing off into a blizzard." Smith's voice was low with rage.

Whipping around, I shrugged before returning to the saddle. "I spent holidays here. I've ridden in the snow plenty of times."

"That doesn't make it safe." He was fuming. There had been few times where I had seen my husband this upset. One of the last times I'd wound up in a leash and collar. I could only be so lucky this time.

His interest in the computer had long since replaced his interest in my body.

"I returned when it became hazardous." I brushed past him with the saddle. He caught my wrist on my way back.

"It's not simply the snow, beautiful. I didn't know where you were."

"If you paid any attention, you would know that I go riding at this time every day," I informed him in a cool voice.

His green eyes narrowed into slits. "We don't need to advertise that you've returned home, Belle."

So that was what this was about. Hammond. Everything came back to Hammond. Even after two weeks of security—two weeks of dealing with my irrational, hateful mother—it was still Hammond haunting us.

"Maybe I should go and cover my tracks. Hand me that broom," I said in a mocking voice.

"If you don't watch your tone, I'll swat you with it."

"I wouldn't if I were you," I warned him. "I might get attached. It will have been the most action I've seen in weeks."

"Are you finished?" he asked flatly.

Not even remotely. But I didn't trust myself to say any more. Maybe it was stupid to hold on to hope that this was a momentary blip. After all we had been through, and everything we'd recently given up, we were both bound to be stressed. It was what I told myself at least. I nodded, shooting him a grim smile, before turning on my heel and heading back to the main house.

Smith followed me, grabbing me by the arm and pulling me to him. "I know you like to provoke me."

"I thought you liked it, too." I tried to sound detached, but it was hard to remain unmoved when he brought up memories from the past.

"Your safety is more important than—"

"My happiness? My freedom?" It felt a little petulant to shout at him, but since I'd spent the last two weeks living under my mother's thumb, I was bound to regress a bit.

"Than your pride," he continued in a firm voice. "I don't like the idea of you out riding alone. Sooner or later someone is going to come looking for us here."

"We can't live in a locked room." I'd brought him here to recuperate and wait it out. Not to go into permanent hiding.

"Ask me to go with you," he suggested, brushing the melting remnants of a snowflake off my nose.

"You're busy," I pointed out, hoping he would open up to me about what he was doing.

"I'm never too busy for you."

It was reassuring to hear, even if it didn't answer any questions.

"Your lips are turning purple," he said, a warm smile carving across his face. "We should get you inside."

"Maybe you should warm them up first." The request was breathy and hopeful. It made me feel girlish to stand here in the midst of falling snow and ask a boy to kiss me, as though I'd been transported back to my youth. But this wasn't a childhood crush or my college fiancé. This was my husband, and the look he gave me wiped away any girly daydreams I had.

It smoldered into me, forcing me to forget that it was cold. There was only him and the silent magic of the snowy landscape around us. His hands braced my face, tilting it to that perfect angle, and when his mouth captured mine, the kiss heated more than my lips. My body responded as it had been conditioned to. It wanted pleasure, every bit of me ached for it, and that kiss promised it. Smith had taught my body what to expect when he claimed me, and now I needed for him to do so.

When we broke apart, breathless and wild-eyed, I stayed pressed to him.

"If we do it right here, what are the chances we get frostbite?" he asked.

"The stable's pretty warm," I suggested, tugging my lower lip into my teeth. Just the thought of him taking me there made me wet. If we didn't make a decision soon though, my trousers weren't going to be soaked, they were going to be frozen.

Smith pulled my lip free from my teeth, shaking his head. "If you're going to finally let me off bedrest, I want to take my time. I'm not sure a literal roll in the hay will do the trick."

"Then take me to bed, Mr. Price," I said silkily.

"My pleasure, Mrs. Price."

As he took my hand, the giddiness I'd felt overtook me and I started to run. He followed and by some miracle, we narrowly missed collapsing in a snow bank. I was dragging him toward the steps, when he stopped.

"Whose car is that?"

I shook my head, not recognizing the black Land Rover. "Everyone has one out here. It's a law, I think."

I gestured around us to the falling snow, but I knew it wouldn't make a difference. The spell was broken, even I felt the palpable terror in the air. It was unlike my mother to receive visitors during the winter months.

There's an explanation, I reasoned silently. Despite my protests, she'd continued to discuss contracts with the BBC. It seemed it didn't matter that I'd flatly refused to sign on the dotted line. "I wouldn't put it past her to call the television executives out here."

"Those are local plates," Smith said in a low voice.

Trust the lawyer to pick up on the most minute detail. But local plates meant local people. If it wasn't an executive down from London then it wasn't a hitman down from there either.

Smith gripped my hand firmly and led me inside. Neither of us spoke again until we reached the door, although I noted how his eyes darted cautiously around us.

He paused as he reached for the handle, then brushed a loose strand of hair from my face. "I love you, beautiful."

"Don't be dramatic," I whispered. "This isn't goodbye."

"Does anyone know when it is?"

I rolled my eyes, trying to appear nonchalant even as my heart began to beat rapidly. "Don't be philosophical either. We're going to go in there and discover my mom's hosting a bridge party—and then you're going to make good on your promise to take me to bed."

"As long as we don't get stuck playing bridge."

I didn't tell him that my mother had never played a card game in her life. As far as I knew, her social life consisted of trying to hack my social media accounts.

Belinda met us at the door, which I took to be a good sign.

"I was wondering if you'd ever bother to come in. Can't keep your hands off each other. I understand that, but try not to catch your death while you're snogging." She collected our wet coats and nodded toward the sitting room. "Mr. Jacobson stopped by."

"Jacobson?" Smith repeated casually.

"Our neighbor to the west. Great friend of your mother's. She plays bridge with his wife."

I should have already known hell had frozen over. I'd been watching snow blanket this house for the last few hours. At least the matter bore no further investigation.

Turning to say something to Smith, I caught him heading for the sitting room.

"Where are you going?" I whispered when I caught up to him.

"It's always wise to know your neighbors," he said in a meaningful tone.

My mother was pouring tea as we entered, and it was clear from the caustic glare she gave me that I was an unwanted addition to afternoon tea. The man across from her rose, smiling kindly, as he strode over to shake my hands.

"You must be Mary's daughter."

I held back a wince at his firm grip. "Annabelle. This is my husband, Smith Price."

Beside me Smith went rigid. I'd given our real names, but how was I supposed to lie in front of my mother? He'd been the one who'd insisted on checking things out.

"Oliver Jacobson," he continued. "I bought the house up the way."

Despite his smile, there was something rehearsed about his friendliness. I couldn't quite put my finger on it, but it rubbed me the wrong way. "Lovely. What do you do, Mr. Jacobson? Or are you renting your house to the BBC as well?"

I couldn't hold back the dig at my mother's get-rich-quick scheme.

"Nothing that thrilling, I'm sorry to say. I'm actually a member of the House of Commons."

So he was a politician. That explained a lot.

"It was nice to meet you," Smith interjected, "but I'm afraid my wife has been out in the elements too long. I really need to get these clothes off of her."

I bit back a moan at the thought.

"Of course! We must talk another time. I don't suppose you're a hunting man?"

"Not for many years," Smith said with a small smile.

"Then we must get you back in the field." Jacobson clapped his hand on Smith's shoulder. "I look forward to it."

"Hunting?" I repeated when we were out of earshot.

"The only trophy I'm interesting in bagging is your panties," he promised me.

"I'm not wearing any," I purred.

Smith stopped and grabbed my coat, pulling my body to his. "You went riding without knickers?"

I nodded, nuzzling against his jaw.

"You must be very, very cold."

I nodded again.

"Don't worry, beautiful. My palm is itching to warm your ass up."

We were interrupted by a soft cough. Spinning around, I discovered Belinda studying the floor.

"Yes?" Smith prompted, his voice strained.

"I'm so sorry, but Ms. Annabelle's delivery came from the village. She asked me to come find her when it arrived."

"Thank you, Belinda," I said, feeling the heat I'd felt at Smith's touch fade.

She shot me an apologetic smile before she disappeared down the corridor.

"As I was saying," Smith began, "we should really get you warmed up."

"You are still on bedrest. We need to behave," I reminded him. Denying him didn't come easily to me.

"I'll sit down while I spank you," he said dryly.

"Not tonight." I wriggled free from him. I had to be the strong one. There were too many complications now, and my mind was on the order waiting in my bedroom. Just knowing it was waiting for me was driving me crazy, and I couldn't risk him opening it.

Smith didn't stop me as I left him. Later he'd climb into bed beside me and soothe the savage ache building in my chest, even if he couldn't sate the need I had for his body. I had to believe we had more time in front of us.

I chose to.

CHAPTER NINE

There was a certain meditative quality to cleaning a rifle. My father had taught me years ago that the most important part of hunting was to know your weapon. He had been the one to show me how to disassemble each piece and thoroughly clean it. Each year he would take me to a private estate to shoot, which meant each year I had to take apart a new rifle, clean it, and reassemble. After his death, Hammond had continued the tradition until I left for preparatory school. As my education progressed to university, I lost interest in the annual hunting ritual.

But I hadn't forgotten the point of it.

Even after all these years, I went through the motions with the smooth precision that had been impressed upon me as a kid. Remove the stock and the scope. Disassemble the bolt. It was obvious that cleaning the rifle was completely unnecessary as I took it apart. Gunther took good care of the weapons that he housed on the premises. No doubt a profession he took pride in having been passed down, but I'd seen the understanding look in his eyes when I asked him for a bolt action rifle and the oil and rags necessary to clean it. He'd produced them all, handing me a tub of lanolin to weatherproof the casing.

"We adhere to tradition at Stuart Hall," he had explained. "I oil these rifles once a week, and never had one rust."

I accepted his traditional wax and a modern rifle. Another time I might have found the masculine ritual old-fashioned, but now I truly comprehended the point. A weapon was nothing to be taken lightly. Caring for it, knowing it—those were all aspects of earning the right to use it.

I'd handled other guns since university. Ones I hadn't bothered to sit down and respect. It was hard to consider that this was what my dad had been trying to teach me. Responsibility when granted great power.

Of course, if that had been the point, why in the hell had Hammond continued the charade for all those years? It certainly wasn't a sentiment that he shared.

A copper bullet remained in the chamber and I removed it, placing it on the table next to the rags. Turning back to my work, I caught the hint of my reflection in the reddish metal. The sight locked me into place—my own face distorted, barely recognizable, in the smooth casing.

The bullet was where the whole philosophy of power fell apart. I could know the gun, understand how it was put together, care for it. But at the end of the day, each bullet was new and unique in its own way. Each bullet was a decision. The rifle was my responsibility but the bullets were my choices.

Even as I thrust my bore brush into the barrel, I knew that no amount of cleaning could change what just one bullet could do. I'd shot more than a few fowl as a child. There had been no heaviness that accompanied those actions. I hadn't grappled with guilt as I cleaned my weapon after those hunts. It had been a simple matter of my place on the food chain.

But I wasn't preparing to track game now, which made the once-soothing action weigh on me. And the thing that burdened me the most was that there was no question in my mind if I would reassemble that rifle and load it.

I'd killed men before. In self-defense. Out of necessity. This would be the first time I did it in cold blood.

Jacobson's arrival had solidified my decision. Not that he was a threat. It was the ease with which he'd gotten into the house. Belle's mother had no reason to distrust a person who appeared at her door. A kindly neighbor was one thing, but I'd still been caught off-guard. I couldn't risk Hammond finding his way here. Striking first was the only way to ensure he wouldn't.

As I pieced together the rifle, I pieced together a plan. There would be no amnesty if I was caught. Not even Alexander could grant me reprieve from prosecution, but I'd happily rot in prison if it meant Belle would be safe. When I locked the last part in place, I stared at the bullet. There were boxes more for my use, and certainly I would need to practice using such a large weapon. My trigger finger had to be rusty.

So I didn't load it into the chamber. That was the one. I was saving it for Hammond. I'd looked at that single bullet and made a decision, but as I reached for it, a quiet cough startled me from my thoughts.

"I thought you would come to bed," she said softly.

It had disappointed her. How could I explain that I didn't know how to navigate this situation? I tried to show her, but she'd closed a door to me. It was in her eyes. She'd shut me out of some part of herself and I didn't want to force her to open up. At least, not yet. I could be a patient man when it suited my interest, and for the moment, I respected her right to feel confused. I wouldn't be able to respect it forever.

I shrugged my shoulders casually. There was no need to tell her the truth. She would only try to talk me out of it. "Jacobson mentioned hunting."

"I had no idea you were so fond of deer stalking," she commented in a wry voice, tiptoeing over to inspect my weapon.

"I used to hunt with my father."

She nodded, trailing a finger along the rifle's barrel. "Is it loaded?"

I picked up the bullet and shook my head. "I'll load it when I'm ready to use it."

She didn't need to know more than that. It was as close to the truth as I could offer her.

"There were always guns here growing up," she commented, her voice far away and lost in memory. "My father made it a point to tell me how dangerous they were."

"Do they scare you now?" I asked in a low voice.

She nodded and I felt my dick harden. It was an uncontrollable, if primitive, response. When she was in genuine danger, her safety was my only concern. But when I was in control and she showed fear, it was an entirely different story. She was secure. She could leave anytime. She could ask me to stop. Instead, when we were together, she confronted her fear and then she embraced it. I'd seen her tremble at the end of a whip, and it was a goddamn beautiful sight.

Right now there was no one in this world who could touch her, except for me. Maybe that was why I wanted to fuck her so badly.

I lifted the unloaded rifle, sliding my hand along its barrel. "And when I hold it? What do you feel then?"

"Scared," she murmured, her tongue darting over her lower lip, "and turned on."

"Have you held one before?"

She nodded, her eyes traveling in a continuous circuit from my face to the rifle.

"Have you fired one?"

She nodded again.

"Tell me the truth, beautiful. It scared you, but how did it make you feel when you shot it?"

"I like it," she breathed.

"Do you want to touch it now?" I held my hands out, moving the weapon closer to her.

Her hands lingered over the metal, and then slowly she guided the barrel to her chest. Seeing her with the gun pointed at her heart, even knowing it was unloaded, set off an internal alarm. But when I went to move it away, she held it firmly.

"I'm so wet right now." Her voice was barely a whimper. "You don't just control my pleasure, Smith. Right now it's all yours—my body, my life. I want it. I want you to control it."

I swallowed hard as she lowered herself to the floor and knelt before me.

"What do you want?" she begged. "Because I want to please you. I want to be your every fantasy."

God, she fucking was. I stared down at her wide eyes and full lips, her face tilted innocently up to mine. Lifting the muzzle, I trailed it along her chin. I didn't need a gun to get her to do anything I wanted. She'd already given me that gift. But that didn't mean I couldn't enjoy allowing my own darkness to take charge now.

"Suck my cock," I ordered her, not bothering to move the end of the rifle. Her fingers fumbled as she found my belt. "Slow down."

"Yes, Sir." She was always so eager to please, always eager to have me in her mouth. It made watching her lips wrap around it that much better. I felt my dick spring free as she tugged down my boxers.

I moved to set the rifle on the desk, but she shook her head. "Don't."

She was enjoying our little power play as much as I was. I rested the muzzle on her shoulder, freeing a hand, and grabbed her hair. Yanking her roughly to my groin, I pushed her mouth to my balls. She took them in her mouth for a minute before dragging her lips up my shaft.

"Is that what you need, beautiful?" I groaned as her tongue swirled over the tip. "You want me to force you, don't you? You don't want me to fuck your mouth. You want me to take it."

She moaned hungrily, nodding.

"Then suck it," I demanded.

Her eyes widened, but her mouth immediately closed over the crown. She moved lower, swallowing me to the root. Her delicate cheekbones were even more pronounced as she hollowed her cheeks as she sucked furiously. I'd unleashed a succubus, and I had no doubt she wouldn't be satisfied until she'd drained every last drop from me.

But then I wouldn't be satisfied.

"Get up." The command was thick on my tongue. Even though I wanted more than her mouth, it was never easy for a man to stop a blowjob in progress.

Belle pulled away, licking her lips.

"Pants off." This time my voice was hoarse. I needed to be inside her and I needed it now.

She scrambled to her feet and wiggled them off. In our time away from London and her waxer, fine blonde hair had begun to grow. It curled softly over her cunt. I made a mental note to demand she keep it that way.

I prodded her with the muzzle, motioning for her to bend over the desk. As she folded her perfect body, sticking her ass out to me in invitation, I moved the end of the rifle along her spine, sweeping it in a teasing stroke along her crack.

"You've been waiting for me to claim this," I said, "and now I'm going to, beautiful. I'm going to fuck your tight little ass. Ask me."

"Please fuck my ass. Please, Sir." Her voice was trembling as she begged. Her arms stretched out, grabbing the lip of the desk until her knuckles blanched white.

I was suddenly thankful for Stuart Hall tradition. Placing the rifle parallel with her, so that she was staring at it, I wiped my hands off on my pants and grabbed the jar of lanolin. Scooping some onto my index finger, I smeared it over my cock.

"This is going to hurt, but you asked for it," I warned her, rubbing the waxy cream over her tight pucker. "And once I start, I'm not going to stop."

"Please fuck me, Sir," she begged, dispelling any doubt I might have had at her interest.

I pushed my index finger inside her, moving it in and out until her ass was slick and welcoming. I wanted to fuck her hard—ride her ass until she was torn between screaming and fainting. Because I knew it would be the most intense orgasm of her life. But I didn't want to injure her.

Guiding the head of my cock, I prodded her taut entrance, helping her acclimate to the idea. As I slowly breached the tight bundle of nerves, she relaxed, blossoming open and allowing the tip to pop inside. She gasped in pain and I waited, savoring the small shifts in her movement as she adjusted to my transgressive organ.

"More," she finally whispered.

It took all the self-control I'd accumulated over years of topping not to give her exactly what she asked for. "I'm sorry?"

"Please give me more of your cock."

The plea held a note of fear.

I stroked a hand down her back. "You're completely mine now, beautiful. You've given me every piece of yourself. It makes me so proud to look down and see my cock in your ass, knowing that you chose me to take it."

She needed to hear the praise as much as she needed the time to continue to stretch and adjust to the new sensations. When I finally slid farther in, she cried out, arching up. This time I knew there was as much pleasure as fear mixing in her blood.

I swept her hair over her shoulder and leaned down to kiss the back of her neck. "Are you ready?"

"Yes, Sir." There was no moment of hesitation. Her voice was clear, colored with the lusty yearning that made her irresistible.

"I want you to come," I instructed her, "as many times as you want. As hard as you can. No holding back. No waiting for permission."

This time her assent came in the form of a desperate whimper.

I gripped each of her shoulders, rolling my groin and enjoying one last lingering moment before I kicked her legs wider, spreading her open so her clit rubbed against the edge of the desk. Then I drove into her. Hard. Holding her down I fucked her, slamming inside of her. Her ass swallowed me each time. It was as greedy as the pleas spilling from her lips. Beneath me Belle dissolved into a mewling, wild creature, crying out and clawing at the desk's surface. Her muscles contracted and released repeatedly, the force of the extended series of climaxes grabbing hold of my cock and milking it until I collapsed on top of her.

"You okay, beautiful?" I asked, brushing hair from her face.

She moaned, her eyes glassy with post-orgasmic bliss.

Helping her up, I pulled her onto my lap and wrapped my arms around her, murmuring an endless stream of praise until she came down from her high.

"You've been holding out on me, Price," she accused with a coy smile.

"I've been patient," I corrected her. I'd been dreaming of fucking her like that since the moment I'd laid eyes on her.

"Is it strange that it feels nice that we waited until we were married?"

"I appreciate you saving it for me," I teased. "How are you feeling?"

"Good, I think." She paused as if to assess. "I'll let you know tomorrow."

I carried her to bed then, ignoring the twinge of pain in my scar. I wasn't about to regret that recent physical activity.

"I'm going to use the loo." I kissed her forehead.

Belle had given me everything now. Physically we were closer than ever, which made it even more difficult to know we were still keeping secrets from one another.

I needed to tell her. She was strong enough to face what I needed to do. There was a possibility that she would try to talk me out of it, but she deserved to know that I was returning to London to end things with Hammond. Slipping back into the dim bedroom, I found her asleep, her face peaceful.

Innocent.

I wouldn't strip her of that. I wouldn't make her party to the choice I was making. I'd distance myself if it meant keeping blood off her hands. Belle was the one pure thing in my life and I wouldn't taint her.

CHAPTER TEN

When I woke the next morning, my wife wasn't in our bed, but there was note.

You earned a lie in.

My wife not only let me fuck her, she let me sleep in as a reward. I'd found the perfect woman.

By the time, I'd showered and dressed, I discovered I was hungry. But a snack wasn't going to sate my appetite. I would need Belle to do that. I found her in the foyer with our neighbor. He was obviously making himself at home.

"I apologize for dropping by unannounced." Jacobson pulled his cap off and smiled warmly at us.

My wife crossed her arms and returned the welcome, but there was a reserved tone to her greeting that I was certain only I picked up.

"It's a lovely surprise," Mary called, appearing in the entry. "Would you like a cup of tea? I can ask the maid to bring up a small luncheon."

I didn't miss her emphasis on luncheon. She'd obviously noted that I'd just woken up.

"I never partake in early meals." He patted the flat plane of his stomach. "It is how I've avoided my father's paunch."

Mary nodded as if this made perfect sense.

"To what do we owe the pleasure?" Belle interjected. This time her suspicion was more obvious, but if Jacobson noticed, he didn't comment.

"I was hoping to steal your husband," he admitted with a wink, as if this was a lark we were all in on.

Her smile cracked at the edges, growing brittle with impatience. Clearly, my wife had her qualms about Mr. Jacobson, something I made a mental note to discuss in private. For the moment, it was important to not draw attention to ourselves, which would be much more difficult if he had picked up on her paranoia.

"I'm afraid I'm a jealous woman. I generally don't share him, Mr. Jacobson," she simpered in a complete reversal of her previous attitude. At least she'd realized that she needed to contain her feelings in front of him.

"Understandable. Mary told me you're recently married." He held out his hand. "I didn't get a chance to congratulate you before."

I shook it, careful to tighten my grip just a little more than his.

"I was hoping I could convince you to go deer stalking. It's a bit impromptu, but I do find that spontaneity is the primary joy of country life."

"Indeed." I glanced at Belle, who raised an eyebrow but didn't make a move to stop me. "I'd be happy to. I've been cooped up a bit of late. Give me a moment?"

"Of course."

"Oliver," Mary moved closer to him and took his arm, "will you have a look at this letter I received from the local MP? I'm really not sure what to make of it."

Belle followed me as I headed toward her father's study. After her distraction, I'd left my rifle there the previous evening. Although as I stepped into the book-lined space, I felt a sort of kinship. The rifle belonged here, along with the strange trophies that peppered the room: a collection of fossils, a number of carved masks, and of course, the books. Although it might also have something to do with nailing my wife on the desk.

"You look like you belong in here," she noted in a quiet voice.

"A bit traditional for my taste," I remarked as I circled around the desk.

She pushed herself onto the top of it and brushed a hand over my shoulder. "Says the man with the bourbon and cigars in his office. Face it, Price. This place is gloriously unashamed of its masculinity—that's why you fit in here."

"Are you saying I should be ashamed?" I caught her lower lip with the pad of my thumb, relishing the moist heat of her breath on my hand.

"I'm saying you're glorious," she corrected me.

"If I didn't know better, I would think you were trying to get yourself fucked on this desk again, Mrs. Price."

"Unfortunately you've decided to go hunting."

Her lower lip pushed against my finger as she pouted. I shifted on my feet as my cock began to strain against my zipper. "I can stay if you've officially changed your position on the no fucking rule."

"Doctor's orders, not mine." She nipped the tip of my thumb and pulled away. "Last night was a moment of weakness. We probably shouldn't be so rough, and you should still be taking it easy. That's one reason you should stay. The other is that we know nothing about Jacobson."

"We can't live our whole lives in paranoia." I understood her concern. The truth was that if our situations were reversed, I'd be locking her in one of the estate's many rooms. But if I was going to have to keep my hands off her, I might as well get in some target practice.

Her eyes narrowed, no doubt sensing my hypocrisy. I'd never been able to pull one over on her. It was one of the reasons I worshipped her.

"Agreed, but we probably shouldn't wander around the woods with strangers holding loaded guns."

"When you put it like that, beautiful, I guess it's a good thing I'll have a gun as well." I chuckled softly at the annoyance on her gorgeous face.

"I don't like him," she said in a flat voice.

So we'd finally come to it. I had suspected as much from her chilly reception, but I didn't fully understand why.

"I'm an excellent judge of character," I reassured her.

"I don't doubt. What I doubt is your sense of self-preservation." She hooked an arm around my neck and drew me closer until our lips brushed softly. "You have questionable taste in friends."

Fair enough. "And impeccable taste in women."

I sealed my mouth over hers, capturing her lips and silencing her questions. For now.

Dry leaves crunched beneath our feet as we followed a foot-worn path through the woods. Jacobson looked as if he'd stepped out of a fucking nineteenth century painting in his tweed hunting jacket and tipped cap. I'd found a similar get-up in Belle's father's wardrobe, but I wasn't interested in playing the role of old money. It would certainly grant me no favor with Jacobson, whom I sensed was following a prescripted part himself.

"Mary said that you're a member of the House of Commons?" I asked, careful to keep my tone conversational.

"Yes." He grinned at me, bolstering his rifle higher on his shoulder and gestured to his clothes. "Don't let my wife's attempts at gentrifying me fool you, I am, unfortunately, very common."

"We share that then." I ducked under a low-hanging branch but straightened immediately when a sharp pang shot through my abdomen. The tree's bare limb scratched across my rifle's muzzle, and I winced at the horrible sound it made.

"Okay there?" he called out.

"Yes." I waved off his concern, resisting the urge to hunch over. "I'm still recovering from my accident. Every time I think I'm back to normal, I realize I can't bend over or lift something."

"Terrible luck. Was your wife hurt?"

He had to have seen the remnants of her injuries from the attack, but he was being a gentleman by feigning otherwise. "Not seriously."

"Word of advice. Never take a woman's pain lightly. They're so good at hiding it. Must come with the biology." He laughed lightly at the thought.

"Lesson learned the hard way?"

"I've been married for twenty-five years," he informed me. "I've learned most things about women the hard way. But listen to me scaring a newlywed. My apologies. Marriage is a splendid contract."

"Agreed." Despite all that had passed in the time since I had asked Belle to marry me, I'd yet to regret getting married. Not in the way most men did. I questioned my decision, wondering if the impetuous act had placed her in more danger. But I never questioned if I loved her. I never questioned that she was the woman I wanted to spend the rest of my life with, regardless of how short that life was. If we were blessed with twenty-five more years, I knew I would feel no differently then.

"I recall Mary mentioning her daughter was engaged, but if you'll forgive me, I thought it was to someone else."

Jacobson had been paying close attention for a man who had significant responsibility elsewhere.

"She was," I said, "but luckily for me, he showed his true nature."

"And you were there to scoop her up," Jacobson added. "You must be a very lucky man, Price."

I paused and stared at the back of his head. It was an innocent enough thing to say. No red-blooded man alive would see Belle and not consider me a lucky man. She was desire incarnate. Pure sex set on long legs.

No, it was something else entirely pricking at me, wanting me to acknowledge the underlying message in his words. The issue was that I had no clue what that message was relaying—or how I was meant to receive it. Given the precarious nature of our situation, I couldn't risk misreading him, which meant that despite his overt friendliness, I needed to keep him at arm's length. It was probably a mere hazard of my circumstances. Gaining my trust would be no easy task for anyone in the foreseeable future.

"I am," I said at last.

"And now you have an estate to run." He paused, his eyes darting around the woods. I waited until he shrugged as if to say 'not this time.'

"Any pointers?"

"I can hardly call Betford House an estate. House of Commons, remember? I wasn't born with a silver spoon in my mouth."

I nodded in agreement even as I filed the comment away for further consideration. But despite my intention of changing the subject, I found myself unable to disregard the obvious meaning behind his words. "Unlike some."

"Indeed. Nothing quite brings to light the disparity between the titled and the commoner so much as working in Parliament on the *lesser* side."

"The side that gets things done," I added, hoping to provoke him further. At the very least I could appreciate the irony of discussing the subject of class with him.

"Exactly. I can see you are a man of the people."

Who happens to be married to the best friend of half of the reigning monarchy.

"Yes, some of us have to earn our status," Jacobson continued, stopping by the gnarled trunk of a dead oak tree. "I bought my land, modest as it may seem to some, from one of those titled idiots. At least our government isn't issuing handouts to the elites anymore. He couldn't afford to keep his family estate when he was forced to provide his own income. It makes you wonder what other institutions might crumble if we stopped privileging birthright."

I had nothing to say to that. I'd been born with the proverbial silver spoon he'd spoken of. Even if my father had been from a working class family, I'd been handed my wealth. On the other hand, Belle had gone to university, worked, and started her own business despite the name she'd been born with. I wasn't about to share this analysis with my companion, however. I'd learned a long time ago that a lot could be learned from listening to a tangent.

"I'm being rude," Jacobson said suddenly. "Your wife has a title."

"Not as such. She's unable to inherit." Was he testing me? I gripped the butt of my rifle more tightly.

"Ah yes, sexist old practices. I do hope to see significant change in my political career."

"Meaning a woman can inherit a title or there are no titles left to inherit?"

"Touché, Mr. Price." His eyes flicked up to mine, something unreadable flashing through the warm brown orbs.

Before I could process the look, his rifle swung up, leveled directly at my head.

Well, beautiful, you were right. She always was. Unfortunately, the thought was far from comforting.

I didn't bother to speak or to argue. He'd have the shot off before I could raise my own weapon. All I could do was ignore the sudden racing of my heart. Belle would be smart enough to know what was going on when I didn't return. She could handle herself, and with me out of the picture, it was possible they might leave her alone. It was a lie I needed to believe.

His index finger waited on the trigger, as if to offer me a change to plead for my life or at least offer up one final, pointless plea for forgiveness. Then he squeezed. I heard the bullet split the air as it whizzed past my ear to an unseen target. I swung my gun off my shoulder just as Jacobson dropped the rifle and smiled proudly.

"Thanks, old sport. I think I got it." He walked around me, whistling congenially as I turned to stare after him.

Perhaps Belle had been right about the danger of going out with strangers with guns. I'd nearly killed a man while hunting.

"She's a beauty," he called from somewhere in the near distance.

Shouldering my rifle, I took a deep breath and tried to shake the sudden onslaught of nerves. I found Jacobson standing over a small doe.

"Give me a hand?"

I helped him heave the deer over his shoulders.

"Are you sure that's smart?" I asked.

"If anyone else is hunting in these woods, they'll have bigger problems than shooting me," Jacobson said in a dry voice.

We carried the deer back to Stuart Hall. After our earlier conversation, I'd hoped to see his home. Perhaps he was just an opinionated man, but I couldn't quite separate Belle's discomfort from our earlier conversation. It was far from a radical view to question England's desire to cling to its aristocratic roots. In a way, his open distaste for the titled and aristocratic class calmed me. He wouldn't have said any of those things if he knew too much about Belle or her connections. It wasn't in the British biology to be openly rude like that.

Gunther, the estate's gamekeeper, met us on the edge of the park in a small golf cart.

"I see you got yourself a prize, Mr. Jacobson."

"I did, Gunther. Would you be so kind?"

The ancient game warden was already loading it onto the cart as he asked. "Shall I send some venison to your house?"

"Yes. We'll have to freeze it since we'll be leaving soon for the city."

"I appreciate your stalking abilities, sir. I'm not as good with my trigger finger as I once was." Gunther clapped him over the shoulder.

"I've been helping to control the deer population," Jacobson explained to me as we continued toward the main house. "Mary refuses to open the estate to public hunting parties, and poor Gunther is not up to the task I'm afraid."

"That's very thoughtful of you." The man remained an enigma. He despised the titled class and here he was overseeing the Stuart's deer population.

"I enjoy the hunt. Too much time spent in chambers, I suppose. Shooting relieves the stress."

"Even when you come home empty-handed?" I asked.

"I never come home empty-handed, Mr. Price."

I glanced over at him without response, but his face betrayed nothing. It seemed I should take a closer look at Oliver Jacobson. We stood for a moment, regarding each other, and this time I was certain we were sizing one another up.

"Ready for lunch now?" I asked him. "Or some tea?"

My own hands were chilled to the bone from the cold dryness that had descended over Somerset this morning, but he shook his head.

"I think I'll get cleaned up," he said in a quiet voice. "I have blood on my hands after all."

"Of course." We didn't speak again as he climbed into his Land Rover and drove away from Stuart Hall, but one question remained even as he vanished from view.

Just how much blood was on his hands?

CHAPTER ELEVEN

With Smith out hunting on the grounds, I decided against my afternoon ride. There would be a certain poetic fuckery if after everything that had happened, I died in a hunting accident. That left little else for me to do except try to avoid my mother. That was generally possible given the sheer size of the estate, but today I bumped into her at every turn.

At noon, she appeared in the library—a room I'd never seen her step foot in—and announced that Belinda had tea laid out in the kitchen.

It was the friendliest my mother had been to me since our arrival. We'd spent most of our time keeping opposite schedules. Now she was seeking me out to make certain I ate.

"Thank you." I didn't entirely succeed at keeping the suspicion out of my voice.

"Not everything is a conspiracy, Annabelle." She sighed deeply, and for a split second, I saw myself in her, older and more tired, but I was there in the pale blonde hair and gentle blue eyes. "I do care if you eat. You're looking thin."

"I haven't been feeling well," I admitted.

"The accident?"

Amongst other things, I thought. Did she really expect me to talk about this with her? As a child, Belinda had cared for me when I was ill. She'd been the one who stayed up with me all night when I was sent home from boarding school with the chickenpox. I couldn't remember my mum bringing me so much as a cup of water. A few thoughtful words weren't likely to win me over now. "Yes."

It was the simplest answer. She still didn't know that there had been no accident, and since the news out of London had failed to mention my name, she hadn't suspected there was more to the story.

"If you change your mind." She waved as she disappeared down the corridor.

There was a real possibility that she was on drugs. It was one of the few explanations that made any sense.

All that I cared about was that she was back on schedule. I counted on my mother taking an afternoon nap each day so that I could use the telephone in her private salon. Smith usually holed himself back up in Father's study, which was mercifully across the house. One of the benefits of growing up here—and there were very few that I could think of—was that I knew exactly where to go to avoid other people.

I didn't like sneaking around behind his back, but it hardly seemed fair that he was in contact with people in London while I was cut off from my own life. Today he'd made it even easier by going out with Jacobson.

Dropping into her chair, I reached across her antique writing desk for the phone. I felt at home in this room, which was strange considering it belonged to my mum. Of course, since I'd spent much of my life actively deceiving her maybe it just came more naturally to sneak around here.

The first call I made was to Edward, but as was always the case, he didn't answer. Either he'd yet to figure out the strange number ringing him was me or he'd changed his number. I wasn't about to risk leaving a message either way. I should have grown accustomed to hearing his voice message, but my heart still fell into my stomach each time. I missed him, and more than ever I needed his particular brand of darkly humorous insight.

Being cooped up with my mother was doing serious damage to my sense of humor.

I considered calling Jane, but I didn't. She would know the number, and though she probably knew exactly where I had gone, I didn't want to risk confirming the fact.

But there was one person I could always count on to pick up.

"Lola Bishop," she chirped as she answered the phone.

"You still don't recognize this number?" I asked in a dry voice.

"I thought I was supposed to pretend I'd had no contact with you," she shot back. "See how good I am at it? Even you forget that's what I'm doing."

Lola had proven herself as a business partner and a friend, but in the last few weeks she'd come to be the person I could count on. She also had all the information I needed to keep myself from going crazy.

"Bad news? Good news?" she prompted.

"Good news." I didn't choose it because I was an optimist. Rather I always got it out of the way, because at the moment even the best news did little to cheer me up. There was just too much going on for me to pretend otherwise.

I listened as she shared the subscription growth rate. Somehow we'd already managed to double our paid subscribers in advance of our first official mailing. Lola had managed to gain a considerable amount of press despite the snub from *Trend*.

"When will you be back?"

She asked every time. I loved that she still thought I might answer her differently.

"I don't know. Please tell me there is more good news."

"Edward set a date," she informed me. "This spring."

I sucked in a breath and fought to sound excited when I asked for the exact date. I hadn't spoken to him in weeks. Would I miss his wedding as well?

"Did you talk to him?" I tried to sound casual as I asked but failed.

"Clara told me," Lola reassured me. "Edward's been missing in action lately."

The few times I'd managed to get a look at online tabloids had told me as much. I didn't know if he was lying low after the events at the Westminster Royal or if there was more to it.

"Speaking of, are you ready for the bad news?"

"Hit me." She had no way of knowing that she'd already delivered a devastating piece of information.

"The police announced they are no longer holding Smith Price."

"W-what?" I stammered. "They weren't holding him to begin with." My brain couldn't begin to process that statement.

"They claimed they had a suspect in custody in relation to the hotel murder," she continued, "but now they've released his name."

And claimed to have let him go. None of it was true. But it explained how we'd managed to stay here without incident for so long. Someone had lied to protect us, but our luck had run out.

If I'd thought I'd accepted the terror of my situation before, now I knew I hadn't. I'd been looking over my shoulder for weeks, but now just as I was beginning to relax, I learned that I'd been protected by a false claim. If Hammond had believed that Smith was in custody, he would be looking for him now.

"And there's a new envelope from the law office," she finished. "A bunch of various amendments to the original suit."

"Read them over," I instructed her. Dealing with my mother's lawsuit wasn't on the top of my priority list, but it wasn't going away on its own. It was laughable to consider that we were living in the same house and she was still having papers delivered to my office in London. However, I appreciated the distraction.

And the gold medal of passive-aggression goes to Mary Stuart.

I listened as she rattled off the particulars of the newest settlement proposals. So that was how she planned to use my presence here to her advantage. She'd smoke me out by offering to settle the case out of court. Given that I couldn't return to London, I didn't have many other options. Not that she knew that, but it seemed she had guessed.

That's why she'd been so artificially friendly this morning: she'd been gloating.

"It's mental," Lola announced when she reached the end. "I thought my mother was manipulative. Yours takes it to a professional level. What do you want me to do about it?"

"I assume John has seen these?"

"He sent them over," she confirmed.

"I don't suppose he had any suggestions." It was wishful thinking at its best.

"He only told me that you need to contact him. He can't make a move without your approval."

"Of course, he can't. He can't do anything without the approval of a woman in this family," I snapped. Guilt settled over me immediately. "That was bitchy."

"You have a right to be bitchy. This is a cocked up situation."

"You're too sweet," I told her. "I'll see if I can—"

The call cut short as Smith announced his presence by ripping the phone cord from the wall.

"Do you have any idea how stupid it is to call her?" he roared, tossing the ruined cord to the floor.

I shrank against the wall, shaking my head. There had been very few times that I had seen him this angry, and in most of those instances his fury was directed at someone else. I didn't particularly like being at the center of his rage. It radiated from him, rolling off his body in hot bursts of power that crackled in the air between us. But despite how formidable he looked, I wasn't going to back down.

"I have a life, Smith. Just because we left London..."

"We left London to ensure you kept living that life!"

"So I'm supposed to just sit here and wait while my business falls apart?" A tiny alarm went off in my head as I screamed. He had my best interests at heart. I knew that, but I couldn't seem to care. "We've been gone for weeks. No one knows where we are. Not even Lola."

"Don't you see that if anyone suspects that she knows where you are, you're putting her in danger? This is bigger than you missing your emails!" His words thundered around me, practically shaking the room.

I hadn't considered that I might be dragging her into this. Smith grew silent, his gaze fixed warily on me.

"I want my life back," I admitted to him in a small voice. I wanted to leave here. I wanted my friends. I wanted everything I had worked so hard to build.

I wanted normal.

We both knew there was no normal where it concerned us. I'd opted out of the possibility when I'd chosen to get involved with him. I hadn't known exactly what I was getting into then, but I'd had chances to walk away. Smith had given me outs and I'd refused each one.

"Did you know that they lied about having a suspect in custody?" I asked him.

His lips pressed into a thin line but he nodded.

"And do you know that they claim you were that suspect?" He didn't have to answer, and I didn't have to ask if he had heard about his own "release."

While I'd barely been allowed to check on my website, he had been keeping up with every bit of gossip in Britain.

"I'm going to return to London. I'll notify you when it's safe for you to follow." His voice was flat and the arrogant gleam that usually sparkled in his eyes had been extinguished.

He'd been defeated, and I'd been the one to do it.

"You can't go back." The thought made my head swim. "They'll kill you or..."

And then I understood what he was really planning. Smith had no intention of being our ambassador. His plan wasn't to scope the situation out back home.

"You can't," I whispered.

"There's only one way this ends."

"Not that way." I refused to accept it. All the frustration and fury I'd felt began to melt away, exposing the vulnerability at my core. "We do this together."

"I love how lies sound coming from your lips."

"I don't lie to you," I said in a soft voice. I'd kept secrets. I kept one now. But I never tried to deceive him—I never wanted to.

"I know, beautiful." He brushed his thumb over my lips. "You're lying to yourself."

"No." The heat of tears smarted my eyes and I blinked rapidly. "Together. We said a vow."

"A vow is only words."

My hands lashed out, shoving him backwards.

"Who's lying now?" I demanded. "You don't mean that, and fuck you for pretending otherwise."

He caught my wrist before I could push him again. Twisting my arm, he forced my body to his. "If you won't let me protect you, I will take whatever action I deem necessary to ensure your safety. You are my only concern."

I knew then how far he was willing to go—what he was willing to sacrifice. My breath caught in my throat as he pressed his forehead to mine.

"You are infuriating," he sighed.

The warm sweetness of his breath sent goose bumps rippling over my skin.

"Punish me." It was an offering. Not only to soothe the savageness I'd provoked in him, but to calm my own overwhelming anxiety. I needed him to take control. I needed to find the quiet, blank space I'd only found in the back of his hand.

"I won't punish you." He tipped my chin up and smiled sadly. "But I will free you if you wish."

"Free me." I breathed the entreaty.

"Go to the bedroom. Undress. Wait."

I didn't argue with him. I didn't care that we weren't alone in this house. I could think of only one thing: liberation.

And I knew it only came at his hands.

CHAPTER TWELVE

Smith took his sweet time coming back to me. Long enough that I considered touching myself just to see how he would react. I could almost imagine the look on his face if he came in to find me spread on the bed with my hand between my legs. It was a tempting proposition because it would piss him off.

And tonight I didn't want my husband. I didn't want a lover.

I wanted a brute.

I wanted all the primal, alpha male that he had to offer, and I knew from experience that he had a lot of that to offer me.

I'd been pushing his buttons for days, trying to hit the right one. After what had happened in London, he'd been different with me. Everything was a test, and I was terrified that I was somehow lacking. He'd seen me vulnerable and now he was constantly trying my fragility. Did he want me to break?

When he finally reappeared, I was still in the same spot with my hands folded in my lap.

Perhaps he wasn't testing me, after all. Maybe I was just testing myself.

"I had to go out to the stable," he explained as he produced a length of rough rope. He held it out for me to see. "Wild things can't always be tamed, beautiful. But they can be restrained."

I squirmed on the edge of the bed. There would be nothing as comfortable as a mattress in my future and I was grateful. I wanted to feel it. I wanted it to bite and sting and hurt. Because that pain would wipe away my fear and guilt and all the doubts that crippled me. In that moment I'd be able to forget my mistakes.

"You want me to be hard on you." He circled me. "I suppose it's a good thing no one else stays in this part of the house. You're going to scream and beg, and I'm not going to stop until you're writhing at my feet."

I swallowed even as my mouth went dry. "Yes, Sir."

He knew what I needed and why I needed it. Somehow he knew it even better than I did.

"Go to the fireplace," he ordered.

As soon as I was near the marble hearth, he motioned for me to turn around.

"Can you stand the heat, beautiful?"

The embers had died down, leaving only the smoldering remains of the fire the maid had lit the evening before when I retired to bed. The only fire I felt was the one kindling inside my core. It licked up my center and settled in my belly.

"Normally I would use something soft to do this." He slid the rope into a knot, yanking it across my skin. It scraped, burning a path in its wake. "But we don't have that luxury, and that's not really what you want, is it?"

I shook my head. It took all of my concentration not to back against him. I wanted to feel his body on mine—his heat, his flesh. But this wasn't about what I wanted. This was about what he wanted to give me.

To my surprise, the rope snaked around my torso and I looked down in fascination as he crossed it between my breasts. He'd captured them, forcing the bindings tightly enough that they plumped into swollen, painful globes, heavy from blood that had nowhere to go. My nipples hardened into severe points. One touch and I would be screaming. I wasn't sure if it would be from pain or from pleasure.

The idea made me wet.

"You're already excited, beautiful." He paused to run his hand over my pussy. "What a waste."

I bit my lip. He was going to make me wait for it, if he released me at all. We both knew he could take me to a place where thought gave way to sensation. In that space, there were no checklists or phone calls or worries, there was nothing but a visceral clarity of simply *being*.

"Hands."

I crossed my wrists, offering them to him. Smith separated my hands and he began to loop rope around one.

He paused and flipped my hair over my shoulder, leaning down to kiss behind my ear. "How flexible are you, beautiful?"

The question weakened me. I wanted to dissolve to the floor if only to allow him to shape me. To him I was clay to be used and formed to meet his needs. Smith's hand shot out and steadied me. Without meaning to, I'd begun to actually do it.

"It gets easier, doesn't it? Handing your body over to me. It comes so naturally to you—the need to please me." Reaching up, he caught my chin, wrenching my face up to meet his smoldering eyes. His thumb smeared my lower lip. I opened my mouth in welcome, but he shook his head. "Good girls get to suck."

He might not be punishing me, but he wasn't rewarding me either—and I loved it.

Dropping his hold on my face, his palm circled round to the small of my back. It only took a light touch to show me what he wanted. I folded over, blood rushing to my head as he urged me lower. When my fingers brushed the floor, he patted me in approval.

"You look so gorgeous with your ass in the air," he bent to whisper in my ear. "Put your palms flat on the floor, Belle. It will make it easier."

A tiny spark of conscious thought fired in my brain. *What easier?* But my body overrode it, complying instantly with his request. I slowly stretched until I was folded in half, both hands and feet on the Persian rug. He dropped to his knees and grabbed the rope tail at each of my wrists. The room was beginning to blur from the blood surging directly to my brain. I closed my eyes, searching for my center. Smith guided my legs wider.

"Part of me wants to keep you tied up all the time." A rope tightened around my ankle, pinning my wrist to my leg. Again on the other side. "That's a desire we share, isn't it? You want to be kept on display—available for my use. There's no need to deny it."

He stood and stroked a finger down my seam, gathering all the proof he needed that he was right on his fingertip. I groaned, overwhelmed by the blood surging to separate ends of my body. Sensation crowded the nerves, growing from a faint pulse to steady drumming.

The pressure of his hand disappeared. Metal clanged against the hearth's marble façade, and I stilled as the sharp end of a fireplace poker glided through the space between my knees. Smith tipped my chin up as far as my unnatural position would allow. He bent so that we were face to face as he stoked the dying fire behind me. "I don't want you to get cold."

I'd begun to tremble, but it had nothing to do with the temperature. The muscles straining to maintain my pose were partially responsible, the rest of the blame fell on me. Despite how easily I'd followed his instructions, holding still was proving harder and harder. But I had no other option. Not while there was a hot metal rod poking between my legs. Falling seemed like a pretty bad idea. The heat spreading over my backside reinforced my theory. I was rapidly growing hotter even as my limbs quivered from the stress of the bondage.

"Warm enough, beautiful?" His eyes pierced through mine. Smith wasn't challenging me, he was doing his part.

"Yes, Sir." I licked my lower lip, trying to wet my dry mouth.

"You're fighting it." He caressed my cheek. "Give in. I'm right here."

A reminder was all I needed. He was with me, which meant I was safe. Whatever fear I clung to was the result of a lifetime of self-preservation. My savior. My master. My partner. He was with me now, guiding me at my own pace to the quiet space I sought inside myself. Consciously accepting his presence meant embracing my burning muscles and trembling legs. Pain became my safety net, and when I let it consume me, it overtook me.

I was flesh quivering at his touch.

I was blood roaring under his palm.

I existed in the world he had created for me, and there I was free.

He moved to stand behind me, and my focus shifted along with him, my emotions massing around its axis. He was my certainty. Each of my breaths was nothing more than a revolution around him. A hand stroked the curve of my ass, dispersing the heat that had accumulated from the nearby flame. I closed my eyes, concentrating on the circular motion of his palm, already prepared as it paused before delivering a gentle smack. My heart began to beat with his hands as he spanked me in an alternating rhythm on both sides of my rear.

But this time, unlike the others, he didn't stop to rub away the angry heat from his assault. Instead he continued until I began to count my breaths.

In and out.

In and out.

When he finally paused, my cheeks stung and I was breathing rapidly.

"Better," he said.

I exhaled heavily, but he wasn't going to allow me to slip from the moment he had so expertly orchestrated. His hand slid lower, fondling my wet sex.

"Your cunt is so swollen, beautiful. I think it's jealous." He massaged me as he spoke, keeping his touch featherlight to prevent my climax. "This isn't about your pleasure. Not this time. You've felt ignored, so I'm going to pay attention—and I'm going to leave each inch of your body without any doubt that it's mine."

A sob of gratitude broke past my lips, and I swallowed it back, but not quickly enough.

He clicked his tongue on the roof of his mouth. "None of that.

I'm taking care of you. I have always taken care of you, and I always will. You need a reminder of that, beautiful."

His palm smacked my sensitive mound, and my mouth flew open in a soundless gasp.

"This is precious to me." He slapped it again. This time the force of it vibrated through my core. "Who owns this?"

"You do," I gasped.

He grabbed my hair and pressed his cheek to mine. "Who owns you?"

I struggled for words, barely managing to squeak, "You."

"I want you to think about that for a while." And then he was gone.

Seconds crawled by or maybe hours. Heat scorched my body, and I no longer knew if it was from the fire blazing behind me or from his attention to my bottom.

Or maybe it was just from him.

Maybe I was on fire because he wanted me to be. My brain began to process more details of my situation: the ache in my wrist, the strained feeling in my foot, the flicker of shadows around me. Slowly the world outside of us came into focus. Maintaining my position was becoming harder, but if I'd made it through his spanking, I could stay still a little longer.

I concentrated on my breathing, counting out each inhale and exhale. He had a point to prove, but I did as well.

I could handle anything he threw at me, and he needed to know that.

I had no idea how much time passed before he returned to the room. Droplets of water ran down his muscular calves, dripping to the floor. I drank in the sight, knowing that if I could find the strength to lift my head, I'd be treated to much more where that came from.

"I needed to shower," he explained, not sounding remotely apologetic for leaving me like this while he groomed himself. Smith squatted and kissed me softly, revealing more of his delicious body as he untied my left leg. Carefully taking my hand, he reached between my legs and hooked his arm under my leg. "Hold on."

It took more effort than I cared to admit to wrap my freed arm around his neck. With my other leg and arm still bound, he lifted me with a grunt, keeping my leg pinned to his waist. With a sure stride, he carried me the few steps to the wall. Lowering me on my one bound foot, he braced me gently to the wall, and hoisted my other leg higher.

He stroked my hair back with his left hand, encouraging my face to tilt up to him.

"Your eyes are still wild," he rasped, his own eyes hooding as he rocked his groin against my spread sex. "That's how I know that I'll never tame you. Your body is still restrained, but you're free."

I groaned as the tip of his cock pushed past my swollen seam, but he didn't enter me.

"I'm about to show you the value of patience," he said in a gruff voice. "I'm going to make you come so hard, beautiful, that you're going to understand why I kept you tied up. Because your legs and arms—they're going to be useless to you. I'm going to fuck your self-control right out of your tight little body, and then I'm going to fuck every thought from your pretty little head."

"Please," I begged.

"*Shh*," he hushed me, continuing to pet my head. "Be quiet so that I know you understand who's in charge."

I pressed my lips into a line, trying to barricade my whimpers and pleas. But even with my mouth clamped shut, tiny, desperate pants racked my body until I was heaving with my need for him. I'd finally learned the importance of shutting up.

"That's my good girl. I know it's hard, but you're doing so well." He reached to my bound breasts and brushed his thumb over my nipple.

I cried out in a strangled voice, pain and pleasure bursting through me.

"Fuck, beautiful. I want you so badly, but I need more of that."

I seriously considered stopping him, but before I could decide, he'd squatted to the ground, and his hand kept my free leg pinned to the wall as he caught my nipple in his teeth. I didn't even try to hold back my yelps as he sucked its furl deep in his mouth. Between the rope constricting them and the relentless, hungry heat of his mouth, pain pounded through my breasts, quickly shifting into violent pleasure.

His name spilled from my mouth. Probably because it was the only word I could remember at the moment.

"You make it so fucking hard to concentrate," he growled, rising back to his feet. He gripped my chin hard. "There's not enough of me. I want to taste all of you at once. Fill all of you. I'll just have to settle for my favorite sweet piece of you."

He shifted, wedging his cock at my entrance. His mouth slanted over mine, and his lips smashed into mine as he thrust so forcefully that weightlessness flipped my stomach over. If he noticed that neither of my feet were on the floor now, then he didn't care.

"Is that what you needed?" he coaxed as he rolled his hips in slow, deep strokes against me.

I could only groan, too lost to the fullness that had overtaken me.

"This is what I need," he moaned. "To be in your pussy. To feel it milking me. I want to feed you my cock every day, because I know you starve for it when I don't. I need to see your pussy dripping with me."

I did need it. I needed him so much that it was physically painful to be without him.

"Oh God, beautiful." His forehead pressed against mine as he continued to drive tirelessly inside me. "I want to feel you come."

It was all the prompting I needed. The first spasm hit low, a dull explosion rippling rapidly through my core. My muscles tensed in anticipation, and then my climax took over. Pleasure contracted every piece of me before shattering me to dust. I went limp even as small tremors continued to roll through me. Smith caught my sagging body, still hammering himself toward his own release.

A rumbling noise in his chest built into a howl as he unleashed himself deep within me, but he didn't stop. I could feel him spilling from me as he kept pounding me to another orgasm. This one stole my ability to see. All I could do was hold on.

"Need you so much, beautiful," he murmured between pants. "Need to fuck you. Need to feel you. Need you."

A fat drop of water rolled down my cheek, his words giving me strength enough to press closer to him. My arm tightened around his neck, and even though he was the one fucking me, I was the one holding him up. The world had tried to break us, but we'd discovered how to survive in each other's arms.

CHAPTER THIRTEEN

I rubbed Belle's rope burns with oil until I was satisfied that I'd seen to the minimal injuries I'd inflicted. She remained silent, watching me without comment. I'd taken her into subspace. It was what she had wanted—she'd needed to be freed from her own thoughts—but now I had to see that she returned back to the chaos of reality as gently as possible.

"Are you satisfied?" she whispered.

My forehead wrinkled as I capped the bottle. "I'm not sure what you mean."

"You wanted to punish me for disobeying you."

"Is that what you think this was about?" I asked her.

"You're always saying I need a spanking. This time I did something dangerous. I can see it in your face, you wish you didn't have to put up with me anymore." Her voice cracked as she spoke, and I heard tears forming in the fissures.

"This isn't about the danger, beautiful." I dropped my hand from her face and stepped away. "It's about how things have changed. I wish I could take back what happened to you—all of it. If I could give my own life to ensure you never met me and that you never suffered through what you did, I would in a second."

"How can you say that?" she asked in a breathless voice, but it was clear she didn't want an answer. Her mouth twisted, her teeth finally sinking in to her lower lip to contain whatever other thoughts she had on the subject.

There was no use tiptoeing around the facts though. "Because it's the truth. If you hadn't met me, you would be focused on Bless and spending time with your goddaughter instead of hiding. You probably would have found someone else by now."

"I'd probably be working as a secretary somewhere and eating a tub of ice cream every night," she shot back. Her arms curled around her torso and she hugged herself tightly, as if she could actually feel the loneliness.

Goddammit, Price. Why can't you ever say the right thing? The fact that I was so terrible at comforting her should be a sign that I was right, but I didn't mention that. "What I meant was that I know something has changed between us. I feel it. I don't know if you hate me or if you're scared of me. Or if you finally realized you made a mistake. After what I did to Jake, you've seen a side of me I wanted to leave behind, but we both know I never really will. You're pushing me to be harder with you. Rougher. You're seeking punishment, Belle, and you haven't done anything to deserve it."

"I thought you liked it."

"I do, beautiful. But you aren't my slave, you're my wife."

"You're right," she said softly, her chin beginning to quiver, "I am scared of you."

She could have stuck a knife through my chest and it would have been less painful than her confession. I'd known it was the case, but it didn't make it any easier to swallow. Belle was a strong woman—the strongest I'd ever known—and I'd stupidly believed she could handle this life and my lies. But there was a difference between being headstrong and being dumb. Trusting me would have been the latter. At least she finally saw that.

I bit down on the words of reassurance that wanted to escape. It would be too little too late—and besides that, could I even make good on whatever promises I made?

"But not for the reason you think," she continued. This time she spoke boldly, without a trace of the fear she claimed to feel. "You think that I don't know who you are, but I know you better than anyone. Because I know who you were and who you are now. I've seen the real you, Smith Price, and you can't fool me. You aren't the villain you fancy yourself to be. You are a good man who has faced impossible decisions."

"You saw me kill a man." I didn't want her to absolve me. Not anymore.

"I saw you save me," she whispered.

I couldn't stop myself from reaching for her. "Then why are you scared?"

"Because I've never given anyone this much of myself. One word and you'll break me. Without you, I don't know who I am."

"That doesn't make you weak," I told her, drawing her body to mine. "It makes you strong. I know because my love for you makes me invincible."

"You can still bleed, Price." She laid her palm on my chest, directly over my heart.

"But thanks to you, I've experienced paradise. Death can't take that away."

Her eyes closed, her lashes fluttering against tears. "I'm sorry. I just need a minute."

She rushed to the loo before I could stop her.

A vibration from my coat pocket kept me from following her. Right now, the last thing I needed was for her to find out that I'd been keeping a burner mobile with me. But I couldn't ignore that it was finally ringing. One person had the number. The only person I trusted Hammond didn't know about. Or Alexander. Or even Georgia. His instructions were to call me in the case of one of three events.

I barely caught it before it went to the voicemail box that I hadn't bothered to set up.

"Smith?"

I'd never been so glad to hear my lawyer's voice in my life. It should have given me pause about my profession to feel that way, come to think of it.

"Andrew, I assume you aren't calling because you miss me." I cupped the phone to my ear, swiveling around to check that the bathroom door was still shut. Until I knew exactly why he had called, I didn't want Belle to find out. I imagined him sitting in his lofty office looking out over London and the life I missed.

"Georgia woke up."

I released the breath I was holding. It wasn't the news I'd been hoping to hear, but it definitely fell into the good news category. "I didn't think she would."

"No one did, but haven't you always told me not to underestimate her?" Andrew reminded me.

It was a dangerous thing to turn your back on Georgia, and even more dangerous to discount her entirely. I should have known better. Now that she was awake, she'd be able to corroborate the events of that night, but she couldn't provide me with an alibi. Things were progressing rapidly. First I'd been named as a primary suspect in a false press release, now Georgia had pulled through.

"There's more." Andrew paused, as if to wait for my full attention.

"Go on," I prompted.

"Hammond has been indicted. They dragged him to..."

But I couldn't hear the rest of the particulars, I was still caught on the first detail. Indicted. Arrested.

"Because of Georgia?" I asked when I'd finally processed his revelation.

"I'm trying to find out now, but I've checked with a few people. It's safe for you to return to London."

"My name was in the papers this morning," I told him in a flat voice.

"Yes, you've been publicly cleared in the death of Jake Stanton."

"I had no idea I'd been publicly accused."

"Smith," Andrew said, sighing into the receiver, "you were very particular in your parameters regarding how and why I should contact you. I followed those instructions."

I pinched the bridge of my nose and nodded. I was taking out my confusion on him. "You're right. Thank you for letting me know."

"This is good news, right?"

I hung up rather than answering him.

It was good news, but it didn't feel real. I wanted to celebrate. I wanted to get in the car and return to my life, but all I could do was stare at the silent mobile in my hands. I'd waited for it to ring, and it finally had. For the first time in a very long time, what I did next was entirely up to me.

CHAPTER FOURTEEN

"You are being an insane bitch," I said to my reflection. I could see it. I could feel it, but I'd lost the ability to control it. Because things weren't bad enough already, I needed to add my own personal psychosis into the mix. There was nothing different about the woman staring back in the mirror. Since we'd been in Somerset, I hadn't bothered with make-up, and though I'd grown accustomed to it, I felt like a girl when I caught sight of myself.

Too often my hair was wind-blown from riding or pulled into a ponytail. My wardrobe had been confined to clothing I'd left behind the summer before university. It hadn't been long enough to declare any of it vintage, and none of it had come back in fashion. It was just old and poorly fitted. All of that had begun to slowly chip away my sense of self. There was no evidence of an empowered career woman here. Nope, just a girl forced to run home to her mother.

Smith was the only glue holding me to my former life. Without him, that version of me might vanish entirely. It was a reason to act crazy regarding every word that came out of his mouth, but it wasn't a *good* one. Somehow I'd fallen victim to the pitfalls of my sex.

"Get a grip and face it," I ordered myself, but I couldn't channel the sternness I saw in my own face. I felt more like crawling into the corner and crying.

He was planning something. That much was clear, and I fucking hated having to pull a trump card, but I wasn't above doing it. If Smith thought he was going to sneak off to London to deal with Hammond, he would have one mental basket case of a wife to answer to. Turning on the tap, I splashed cold water over my face.

It was time to stop skirting the trouble at hand. Smith was keeping a secret from me and I was keeping one from him. Time to come clean.

Yanking open the bedroom door, I froze. Smith was sitting, naked, at the foot of the bed. His bare body was generally enough to stop me in my tracks, but this time it was what he was holding.

A mobile.

A goddamn mobile.

I crossed my arms and glared at him. "What happened to going off the grid? Or did I imagine it when you ripped the phone cord *out of the wall* earlier?"

Apparently I wasn't the only one capable of fits of incensed irrationality. I had an excuse though.

"Belle," he began, but I held up my hand.

"Not done!" I snapped. "You have known everything going on in London, while I haven't even been able to call my best friends."

His head tilted to the side in challenge.

"Fine. While I wasn't *supposed* to call my best friends—and just so you know, I haven't called Clara. She probably thinks I'm dead. With any luck, I'll return to London with no business and no friends."

"Are you finished?" he asked after a moment.

"Not remotely." I was seething now, ready to bombard him with weeks of pent-up fear and frustration.

"You have a right to be upset."

I had the right and the capability. If only I had the right to be silent.

"Who were you calling?" I asked.

"No one." There was no doubting the sincerity of his tone. He might not have called someone, but there was a reason the phone was in his hand, and we both bloody well knew it.

"Don't lawyer me," I warned him.

"Coincidentally, it was my lawyer who called *me*."

If there were an Olympic event for literal interpretation, he'd be a medalist.

"Georgia's alive."

I stepped back, feeling for the wall before slumping against it. This was a good thing, so why did I want to cry? Probably because crazy Belle was jealous—*of a woman who had nearly died last month.*

It was time to adjust my priorities. Right fucking now.

"There's something I need to tell you." I couldn't wait any longer, probably because his news had my hackles up. I needed to claim him as my own, starting with making sure that he knew whom he belonged to.

"There's more," he continued, obviously deeming whatever information he had to share more urgent than mine.

Time for a reality check. "Smith, I—"

"I haven't spoken to my lawyer before tonight," he said, bypassing my interjection. "What you told me about being released as a suspect was news to me. Andrew had orders to call me only in the event of a major development."

And Georgia was a major development. Of course she was. Smith had grown up with her, although their adolescence was far from normal. The trouble was that I had seen the two of them together. I'd watched as he'd dominated her in their private club. She had enjoyed it. Smith was loyal to me—for now.

Everything was about to change. Would he run to her at the first opportunity he got?

"I know Georgia is very important to you." I tried to sound casual but the words quivered from me.

"I won't lie. I wanted her to be okay. She is important to me, but not in the way you think." He stood up and took a few strides toward me, pausing when he saw how I pressed against the wall to get away from him.

I would never get this out if he touched me. I couldn't help my reaction to physical contact with him, especially not at the moment. I'd been trying to broach the subject for a week and each time I'd wound up with some part of me wrapped around his cock instead.

"I don't want Georgia," he said in a firm voice. "I chose you. You know that."

I did, so why couldn't I believe it? Angry tears streaked down my cheeks as I began to shake.

"Belle, you've been through so much." He lowered his voice, taking another tentative step in my direction. "Maybe you should see a doctor in the village."

Oh what the hell.

"That's a probably a good idea," I sobbed, wiping my face with the back of my hand, "since I'm pregnant."

CHAPTER FIFTEEN

I collapsed to the floor.

I collapsed to the floor.

Fuck.

That definitely fell under the category of handling this poorly. There were things I needed to say to her—something I meant to tell her—and right now I couldn't find the words. Belle often left me speechless, but this was different.

Pregnant. Baby. *Father.*

Christ, Price, you aren't playing word association. I didn't dare to look up at her. Not yet. Not while she was crying, and I was on the floor and...she was talking to me again, but I couldn't hear.

Belle is pregnant. I repeated the statement over and over in my head. I was just getting used to the idea that she was my wife. Now she was going to have a baby—*we* were going to have a baby. A strange sensation bubbled inside me and then laughter burst from me.

"You're taking this well," she choked out.

I looked up at her then, a wide smile springing to my face. "We're having a baby?"

"Yes." Confusion temporarily suspended her tears. "Smith, I—"

Pushing to my feet, I took hold of her, cutting her off with a kiss. When we finally broke apart, she stared at me breathlessly. I cupped her chin and peered into her dazed eyes. "I thought I was the one delivering the good news tonight, but you topped me."

"It's usually the other way around," she said in an uncharacteristically shy voice.

She was different. Everything had changed in the best possible way. A door that had been shut to me for so long had finally opened.

"So you aren't mad?" she whispered.

"Mad? I'm over the moon, beautiful." I had never really thought about children until she came along, but even then the possibility had seemed a long way off.

"It's terrible timing." She tried to pull away, but I tightened my grip.

"Andrew called to tell me two things. You only heard part of the news," I said in a gentle voice, guiding her attention back to me. "They've arrested Hammond."

Belle blinked rapidly before squeaking, "Oh!"

And then we were both laughing. This was how newlyweds were supposed to feel: joyful. Even the happiness I'd felt saying "I do" in a suite at the New York Plaza couldn't match this, because that celebration had been colored by an unresolved situation. Now we were free to live as husband and wife. We could be normal. A baby wouldn't change that, it would just make it sweeter.

"I can't believe you're taking this so well," Belle said, snuggling into my chest. "I've been in a panic since I found out."

"I knew something was going on. I just thought you'd come to your senses and had decided to leave me."

She tugged back, her eyes flashing as she glared up at me. "Don't say things like that, even as a joke. It's not funny."

I bit back a joke about her hormones and kissed her forehead instead. The mystery of my wife's wildly uneven moods had been solved, but it hadn't been cured.

"I want to ask you a million questions, but for now I just want to hold you," I whispered. Leading her to the bed, I watched her as she climbed in, searching for signs of a change I'd missed. She looked exactly the same, and somehow even more beautiful. Lying down beside her, I gathered her against me and placed a hand over her bare abdomen. "You shouldn't have let me be so rough with you."

"The baby is about the size of a grain of rice, it's okay." Her fingers knitted through mine. "Besides that, I don't want things to change."

"They already have." Surely, she felt it, too.

"Fine, I don't want *that* to change."

I wasn't about to promise her anything on that account. If she had thought I was overbearing before, she hadn't seen the half of it.

STUART HALL'S KITCHEN WAS RELATIVELY CALM THE NEXT morning. I'd left Belle sleeping in our room, wanting to be certain she got plenty of rest. Belinda caught sight of me and scurried over, wiping flour off of her apron as she came.

"Short-staffed?" I asked, glancing around at the empty space.

"I am the staff," she informed me. "Mrs. Price keeps talking of hiring more staff, but she has no need. I can care for the lot of you."

Considering that when Belle and I departed the household would consist of Belinda, Gunther, and Belle's mother, I could see her point.

"I hate to add to your workload, but I want to make certain that Mrs. Price is brought breakfast in our room each morning."

"Mrs. Stuart frowns on serving food outside of the dining room or kitchen." Belinda twisted her fingers as she told me this.

"Let me make this easy on you," I said. "I'm not making a request. Mrs. Price will be brought breakfast each morning."

This wasn't a negotiation. Mary Stuart might run the household, but my wife owned the house.

"Of course, sir. Will she be wanting tea or coffee?"

"No coffee," I said firmly. "An herbal tea and fruit. Eggs. More than toast."

Belinda's forehead wrinkled as a knowing smile pulled on her lips. "The missus might not be able to stomach more than toast soon. If you'll pardon me saying so."

Of course it would be impossible to keep our little secret for long, but I hadn't quite been ready to share with others yet. I tugged at my cuffs, smiling tightly.

"It's not my business, and I won't be saying a thing," she assured me, "but I am an old woman, sir. It isn't hard to put two and two together. A package from the pharmacy and an overprotective husband. I'm only glad that she's found a man who will take care of her."

So was I. There had been a time when I wasn't certain that I could be that man, but that was no longer the case. I might not be perfect; however, I'd give her everything I had. Now that I was no longer a working attorney, my primary focus would be on her.

"What time would you like me to bring breakfast?" Belinda asked.

"Bring breakfast where?" Mary's harsh voice cut in.

Belinda looked up at me for instructions.

"I'll handle this," I told her, "and nine o'clock."

"Yes, sir. Excuse me, I need to speak to Gunther." She didn't wait around for the showdown. "I'll bring that up in a few minutes."

"Mr. Price, you might be under the impression that you have some authority in this house," Mary began.

"Interestingly, I was just thinking the same thing," I interrupted her.

Her eyes narrowed to pinpoints. "I am not running a charity."

"It's hardly charity to open a home to its owner," I reminded her. "Belle has avoided dealing with Stuart Hall, but I can promise you that I will not. I've allowed this situation to continue for far too long."

"That isn't your place," she retorted, but her voice cracked with uncertainty.

"Actually it is. Our lawyers will be in touch."

I left her standing, mouth hanging open, in the kitchen.

. . .

Belle was still in bed when I returned to our room, her blonde hair spread like a halo around her head. Creeping quietly into bed, I propped myself up on an elbow and marveled. I had known she was special the moment I saw her, and I'd spent the time since discovering just how much. The thought that she was carrying my child only proved everything I had suspected about her strength and courage. I wasn't thrilled that she'd kept it from me for even a short period of time, but I could understand her motivation.

All of that would change now. There was no more need for secrets or lies.

"Are you going to just stare at me, perv?" she murmured, her eyes still closed.

"I might."

"I can think of a few things that might be more fun." She peeked at me, her eyelids still heavy with sleep.

"I think you should see a doctor first. Hopefully your ass isn't too bruised."

"Don't get soft on me now, Price." But there was amusement in her voice. She pushed the sheet off, revealing her gorgeous body.

"You aren't playing fair," I noted, tracing the hollow between her breasts.

"I never do," she promised, shifting so that my fingers brushed her nipple. It hardened instantly, even from the light touch.

Every inch of me wanted to take it in my mouth and suck until she came. I wanted to watch her writhe and gasp, but I wasn't going to give in to the urge. "I'm a patient man."

"You're a control freak." She flopped onto her back with a sigh. "Are you cutting me off?"

"Only until we see a doctor."

"You're a sadist," she accused.

"And you are a masochist, beautiful." I leaned over and kissed her cheek. "We're a match made in heaven."

Despite her commitment to pouting, she smiled. "Birds of a feather."

CHAPTER SIXTEEN

After a week, it was hard to decide which I was more proud of: how well I was taking care of my wife or how much self-restraint I was showing. Keeping my hands off Belle was proving difficult. Every day, I studied her for any sign of change, but she looked the same. Still there was something about her. Maybe it was a flush to her cheeks or that she slept so deeply that she'd begun to snore. All I knew was that I was in a perpetual state of awe.

That, coupled with my determination to get the all clear from a midwife before we resumed our sex life, amused her. At first.

But that afternoon when she appeared in the doorframe of the study, I got the sense that her patience with me had run out.

She planted her hands on her hips in her best *do-not-even-try-to-fuck-with-me* stance. "I need to talk to you."

I settled into my chair and waited for her to unleash her fury.

"Not here," she snapped. "Privacy."

"Of course." I made it a point to remain calm. It seemed like one of us should. Things tended to get out of control when we both gave in to our emotions.

But when she led me toward our bedroom, I began to suspect her motives. Any doubt I had was laid to rest when she reached for the hem of her shirt and began to tug it off her head.

"Wait," I commanded, catching her hands and forcing her to drop it. "We're not doing it like this."

"Please tell me how we're doing it then," she seethed.

Judging from the almost painful rush of blood that flooded my groin, my cock was on her side. Belle getting angry had the unfortunate effect of making me hard. It always had.

Traitor.

"My mother is making my life hell because, in her words, you're acting like you run the place," she continued furiously. "Don't try to deny it. I've seen it. I even heard Belinda tell the grocery boy that the house had a new master."

I winced. Master sounded so antiquated in this situation.

"And do you have any clue how hot that is?" she demanded. "Telling my mother off and taking control? Do you know the only thing you aren't taking control of?"

I had a guess.

"Me!" She didn't bother to wait for my response.

"I've seen to it that you are fed. I spoke to Gunther today about keeping you off the horses. I'm running your property." I tilted my head in challenge. "It seems like I'm pretty well in control."

"You know what I mean."

I knew exactly what she meant, but I wasn't going to walk right into her trap. "Once you see the doctor—"

"The midwife said I didn't need to be seen until I'm eight weeks along," she reminded me. She crossed her arms and glared at me. "She also told me sex was perfectly fine."

"Did you mention that you like to be tied up and spanked when you're fucked?" I countered. I'd been involved in the scene long enough to know exactly how far I could take her without causing serious damage, but a pregnancy was new territory for me. Territory I wasn't entering without a little guidance.

"Of course, I didn't." Her lower lip trembled, and I realized that this was far from the good-natured tiff I thought we were having.

"Beautiful." I moved toward her, but she held up a hand.

"Smith Price, I am horny as hell, so unless you're going to come at me with your cock out, stay back. I am *so* not in the mood for a hug."

It took considerable effort not to smile at this. That was my wife—poised and well-educated, with the mouth of a sailor.

"Don't even think about laughing," she warned me.

Apparently I wasn't hiding my amusement as well as I thought. "I wouldn't dare."

"You would." She wagged a finger at me.

"Maybe you should spank me."

"Maybe I should get a vibrator," she shot back. "I mean if you're so disgusted with me now."

I was across the room before she could react, my hands closing around her shoulders. "You aren't going to goad me into taking you to bed, and no one speaks about my wife that way. Not even my wife."

"Please," she whispered. "You've spent so much time worried about feeding me and making sure I get enough sleep, but right now I need to feel close to you."

It didn't make any sense. I'd spent the last two weeks making certain she wanted for nothing, and somehow I'd still failed. "I guess my plans to finally be the man you deserve aren't working."

"Don't say that." She shook her head. "Maybe it's just the hormones. I should feel safe, but I don't. Something isn't right, and that might be in my head, but I need my husband."

"I'm right here," I promised her. Releasing my hold on her, I wrapped my arms around her delicate shoulders.

"But you aren't." Her tears came softly, and right then it didn't matter if she wasn't thinking clearly or if she was being emotional. An urge to protect her burned through my veins, drowning out the rationale I'd been feeding myself for the last week. Guarding her made no difference if she still felt fear. Every happy moment of our life together had been clouded with shadows; I wouldn't be the one to block the sun now.

"I am here. Forever," I promised her.

She opened her mouth, but my mouth was on hers before she

could protest. The kiss was unlike the cautious, brief displays of affection I'd given her since she told me she was pregnant. This one flirted with the boundaries I'd established for myself and then leapt over the line entirely. I didn't wait for her lips to part, I forced them open. She met my domination with equal hunger, smashing her mouth against mine until I felt teeth and tasted blood. It was as hot and messy as every moment I'd spent with her. In one word, it was perfect.

I broke away, leaving her breathless. "We do this my way."

"We always have."

Seeing her there, panting and wild, stretched my control until I could have sworn I felt it snap. We collided again. This time, I dipped lower, cupping her ass before hoisting her in one fluid motion. Her legs coiled around my waist as I carried her, our mouths still locked together, to the bed. Neither of us broke contact as I lowered her to the bed. My cock pushed painfully against my restrictive jeans, but I couldn't be bothered to undress us yet. Right now I needed to taste her. Belle squirmed under me, shifting her thighs to rub her groin against my erection. Even through the layers of denim between us, I felt her heat. I bucked against her, enjoying that as much as the friction.

The fact that she was still fully clothed was actually really working for me. Dipping my head, I found the peak of her right breast and bit down, sucking her covered nipple into my mouth. Even through her shirt and bra, it beaded.

Pushing up onto my palms, I hovered over her. "Hold still."

She stilled immediately. Obviously I wasn't going to get any resistance about doing this my way.

Dropping kisses down her abdomen, I stopped when I reached her waist and lingered for a moment. My fingers found the button of her jeans and I yanked it open. Hooking my thumbs along the waistband, I tugged. Belle got the idea and lifted her ass to help me as I slowly drew them off of her.

"Your panties are soaked." I brushed my palm along the cotton, and she trembled but managed not to move. "You seem to think you're the only one having a hard time with this? Let me make this clear to you. I've had a fucking erection since you told me. You have never been more beautiful to me. I spend all day wanting to find you and fuck you on the spot."

She groaned, bucking her hips up in invitation, but I pressed her gently back to the bed.

"Do you know how many times I've touched myself?" I asked her.

Her eyes widened as she shook her head.

"Zero. I'm waiting for you, beautiful. Because there is no one I want more. If I'm not buried inside you, I don't want to get off." I hadn't even been tempted. The idea of jacking off was almost unappetizing. "My orgasms belong to you just as much as yours belong to me."

"Please, Sir," she whimpered.

A familiar darkness swept over me, but I pushed it away. I wasn't here to dominate her. "Not now. Right now I'm your husband, and all I want is to hold you. I need to bury my cock inside you and feel you coming on me."

"Smith." She spoke my name as if I were her very breath. Her hands fisted into my shirt, and I helped as she pulled it over my head. Within a few seconds, we'd stripped down to nothing.

I slid my arms under her body and lifted her against me. Her legs fell open, and my cock nudged against her folds, settling into the welcoming cocoon of heat between her thighs. My mouth found hers, and we moved slowly, as languid as a dream. My shaft rubbed against her clit, gliding easily along her slippery sex until she was breathing heavily.

"This is what I need," I murmured against her neck. "Just to be with you, and only you."

The days where that would be the case were numbered. Why had I been denying her? This close to her, it seemed so silly.

"I need you inside me," she whispered, sucking in a breath as my tip brushed against her swollen clit.

"I need that, too, beautiful." Rocking back, I circled her pussy slowly until my crown slipped effortlessly inside. I sank into her, savoring each delicious inch of velvety softness. She was wet but so fucking tight that I almost came immediately. I had no doubt I was good for more than a few rounds, but I wasn't ready to give in yet.

"Oh God," she cried out in a breathy voice. "*Ohh*, fuck me."

But we weren't doing things her way. We were doing them my way. I didn't dare remind her of that. It would be impossible to take my time if I set off her wild side. I'd simply be holding on.

"You feel amazing," I praised her, circling my hips and taking care to maneuver until her pussy was spread open. I rocked inside her, each slow thrust bringing my groin into contact with her clit. "I want to watch you come on my dick. Take what you need from me. It's yours, beautiful."

She arched up as soon as the words left my lips, and I hooked my arm lower, supporting her as she began to slide and buck against me.

"That's right," I coaxed, feeling my balls tighten in preparation. "Show me how much you needed to fuck my cock."

I'd ceased moving entirely. Belle had taken over, driving down on me with reckless abandon. A frenzy possessed her as she rode me and as her movements grew more frantic, I grabbed her hips and slammed her against my cock in a tireless, swift rhythm until she shuddered violently, her arms flying up to grab my shoulders as she cried out. The sound of her orgasm spilling from her pushed me to the edge. I thrust until she was full of me.

We finally collapsed onto the bed, our limbs tangled together like wild vines. Belle grinned lazily at me as I stroked her hair, luring her to a well-deserved sleep.

"Regret that?" she asked, a note of apprehension in her voice.

"Making love to you? Never."

"Then don't hold out on me, Price. A girl has needs."

That was one need I'd be more than happy to meet.

CHAPTER SEVENTEEN

I was floating in my dream, my body buoyed carelessly on the surface of the water. Even though some part of my consciousness knew that I was asleep, I didn't mind. These were the dreams I could look forward to now. Calm, peaceful, liberated.

Just like me.

Dipping my head back, hair swirled around me like rays of light. I closed my eyes and allowed the peaceful sensation to wash over me. Then the first wave crested my body, the force of it pushing me under and shattering the glassy surface of the ocean. I kicked hard, thrusting my body up for air. I broke free of its hold, but while I gasped and sputtered from the unexpected assault, another wave rushed toward me.

I sat bolt upright, still panting. My hand dropped to my chest. My heart was pounding. I'd known I was dreaming, so why did I still feel on full alert?

A tiny surge of heat between my legs called my attention from the memory of the nightmare to the present. Throwing my legs over the side of the bed, I ran into the bathroom and dropped onto the toilet. I wanted to believe it was the remnants of our lovemaking, but

I knew this was different. It had a distinct familiarity that was unwelcome. It had happened to me before. I imagined it happened to every woman periodically. But this time, it wasn't a mere nuisance, it was terrifying.

I closed my eyes and said a prayer. I hadn't been raised to be religious, but once again I found myself calling on a god who owed me nothing. I had no relationship with him, but he was the only hope I had in that moment.

Folding the toilet paper into a tidy square, I reached between my legs and wiped.

Crimson.

Not a little blood—a lot of blood. The kind I might expect on the day my period was set to arrive.

But mine wasn't supposed to come for nearly nine more months. All the fear and uncertainty I'd felt since the moment I'd discovered I was pregnant faded into panic. I'd questioned if I could be a mother. If I was ready to become one. I'd driven myself crazy with anxiety. And now I knew two things:

I was ready.

And it was too late.

I wanted to believe it was from the sex. Women bled during pregnancy. Clara had at the beginning of hers, but in the deepest recesses of my being, I knew the truth. I couldn't hide from this. I couldn't lie to myself.

I didn't drop the bloodstained paper, instead I sat there and stared at it, trying to make sense of the violent shifts in my life. There was no point. This didn't make sense. This just was, and knowing that did nothing to squelch the rapidly growing ache in my center. So I stayed motionless and felt the one good thing Smith and I had ever done drain, drop by drop, from my body. With each passing second, a little piece of me died along with our child.

There were no tears. I'd cried too often lately. I hadn't saved any for this.

"Stupid bitch," I muttered to myself. "Cry."

Cry. Cry. Cry. I wanted the tears to come. I wanted to feel this, because what did it mean if I didn't? What kind of person would that make me? If I was this broken, I could never hope to be fixed.

I might have been there for hours. Or minutes. Time didn't hold a lot of meaning anymore. At some point, the cramps began. I'd wanted to feel this, but as my body contracted and pushed, emptying the future from my womb, I realized I didn't want to. Numbness was better. I would have traded every happy memory I had not to feel this now. The pain had stolen whatever shreds of self-deception I'd allowed myself. This wasn't a fluke. I wasn't being paranoid.

It was real.

When Smith finally appeared in the door, blinking sleep from his eyes, I didn't move.

"Beautiful?" He wasn't fully awake yet, but as he adjusted to the light, confusion swiftly turned to concern.

I was still holding the bloody paper.

He dropped in front of me and took it gently from my fingers, tossing it in the wastebin. Then his hands wrapped around mine, holding them firmly in his grip. He didn't speak. I'd married a smart man. I didn't want to hear placations. I didn't want to explain.

I just wanted him to be there.

I tried to look at him, but the sight of his handsome face, heavy with the weight of this, tore through me. Would it have been a boy? Would he have looked like his father? Some long-forgotten snippet from a biology class came to mind. Smith's green eyes would probably override the blue of mine.

Piece by piece, I was building an image in my mind. Green eyes. One dimple. He'd have dark hair like his father. In another version, a girl shared my fine blonde locks.

But the eyes were always the same.

That's why I couldn't look at Smith anymore. All I saw staring back was the painful reminder that I was quietly birthing death on a toilet.

I had no idea how long we stayed like that, but finally the

cramping dulled to a faint pulse. Drawing my hands from his, I turned my face away from him.

"Can I have a minute?"

He hesitated, and I wanted to scream. But there was no strength for it. In the end, he stood slowly, as if his limbs were stiff, and walked to the door. He shut it behind him, and I went about the necessary business of breaking my own heart.

I flushed the toilet and then I washed my hands, careful to keep my eyes on the floor. I didn't want to see the evidence of my loss, and I couldn't bear to look in the mirror. Because I wasn't sure whom I would see reflected back at me.

I wasn't the girl who went to bed last night. I was someone new, born of a pain that I felt physically, if in no other way, and I wasn't ready to face that stranger yet.

Opening the door, I discovered Smith. In his hands, he held a pair of knickers and a t-shirt. I took them wordlessly, wondering how long he had stood there. I should thank him, but it seemed pointless.

We were both doing what had to be done.

"I need something for the bleeding." I struggled to put it all together. I was talking out loud but not to him, walking myself through the necessary next steps.

But he responded anyway, rummaging through the loo's cabinets until he produced a dusty pink box.

I took the pads from him and shut the door. This wasn't for him to see. He didn't need to deal with this.

He was still there when I came back out. I tried to push past him, my only thought of climbing into the bed and pulling the covers over my head. If I closed my eyes, would I wake up?

"Do you need anything?" he asked in a soft voice.

What else was there to say? I needed nothing. I wanted nothing, except the blissful absence of conscious thought.

"Sleep."

He didn't press me further. Instead he followed me to the bed, but he didn't climb in beside me as I curled into a ball in its center.

Squeezing my eyes shut, I waited for sleep to find me, but before it did, I felt the soft comfort of blankets being tucked around my body. Then a hand pausing on my shoulder. It lingered for a moment. Then it was gone, and I was alone.

CHAPTER EIGHTEEN

She was so still as she slept that I found myself moving closer to check her breathing. My own mind refused to quiet. It whirled with the ways I could help her or the things I should say, but as dawn crept across the horizon, I realized they were all lacking. When she'd been in danger, I'd acted. I'd been able to do so without hesitation then. I'd acted out of an instinct that failed me now.

I couldn't protect her from this. Instead I sat on the edge of the bed and watched her sleep. Reaching out to touch her, I stopped midair and let my arm drop to the side. This was our life: celebration mixed with grief, tears mingling with joy. It was how it had always been for me, and now I'd fucked up her life, too.

When her eyes fluttered open, I was still there. It was the only support I could offer her.

"Take me to London." Her words were soft, floating in the air between us.

I could do that if nothing else.

Belle rolled over and closed her eyes, but her breathing didn't settle into the shallow pattern of sleep. She was cutting me out, and I couldn't blame her. But that didn't mean she wouldn't wake up with me by her side every morning, waiting until she was ready to cry or scream or talk.

For now, I would take her home.

CHAPTER NINETEEN

My mother met me at the door with a stack of contracts. Thrusting them into my hands, she tapped her foot. "I can't let you leave until you sign these."

"I've already told you—" I began.

"Let me make this clear to you. Belinda. Gunther. The people you actually care about here. Your decision affects all of them. I've made it easy for you." She held out a pen. "All you have to do is sign."

"I don't think you understand. I won't." I couldn't be any clearer on this. "I refuse to continue a relationship, even a business one, with Philip Abernathy."

"What have I done to deserve this?" She threw her hands in the air. "Why do you want to destroy me?"

"Maybe I have your flair for the dramatic," I said in a flat voice. "I have to go, Mum."

"You can't run away from your problems." Her voice held no maternal concern. This wasn't a mother giving her daughter advice. It was a bully delivering a warning.

"Believe me, I know."

Her nostrils flared as she studied me. "How old are you?"

There was a distinct possibility that she didn't know the answer, but I wasn't about to play into whatever she was setting me up for.

"You act as if you know about the world. You started a business. You snagged a husband. That hardly makes you an expert on life."

Heat seared through my palm as it smacked her face. I backed up a step when I realized what I'd done. But even though it had been wrong to hit her, she had been wrong as well.

"You have no idea what I know about the world," I choked out over the rage simmering into tears.

"Clearly, you don't know to respect your elders." She rubbed the bright red spot where I'd made contact.

"Nothing qualifies a person for respect. Not age or money or status. Respect is earned and you haven't earned mine." I spoke in a low voice so that she would have to strain to listen. I wanted her to pay attention. I wanted to know that she heard *every* word.

"Get out of my house," she hissed, her finger flying toward the door. "Collect your things and leave. Don't bother returning for Christmas, but I'd advise you to hold onto your lawyer. You're going to need him."

I didn't need to be told twice. I'd come here with nothing, and I would leave with nothing, except a brittle marriage and a broken heart. I had no interest in ever returning to Stuart Hall. All my adult life I'd felt uncomfortable and unwanted here, haunted by the memory of my father. Now it wasn't only the childhood I'd lost that lingered like a specter behind these walls, it was a future I wouldn't have. I'd found hope in this place and it had been stolen away.

Smith stepped through the front door, his gaze traveling worriedly over me. The concern hadn't left his eyes since he'd woken this morning.

"Did you say goodbye?" he asked.

Goodbye implied all the wrong feelings. Walking out that door, vowing not to return, that was my final farewell. But I couldn't explain this to him. He wanted to help me carry the weight of the things we couldn't change, but he couldn't bear this for me. This pain, this loss, this liberation, was my own. Each feeling so inextricably bound together that I couldn't untangle them. Maybe that was the reason the emotions carried guilt and shame with them.

"No," I told him. I wouldn't say goodbye. I would leave. Life had taught me that was the easier option.

CHAPTER TWENTY

We hadn't returned to my house in Kensington. Instead I'd taken us back to Holland Park, our brief residence before the attack and Jake's death. Now more than ever, we needed to be close to one another. I wanted to give her a home, because I didn't know how else to heal her. But so far it wasn't going according to plan. She had seen friends and I had cleaned out my law office. It was time to make a fresh start. I hoped that I would inside these walls.

"Where were you?" she demanded as soon as I was through the door.

I'd never expected to come home to her in an apron and pearls, but the jealousy and suspicion she'd hurled at me since our return to London was wearing on me.

"I am doing the best I can to catch up." I sank into the lounge chair by the fireplace, dropping my head into my hands. There was no way to make her see how hard I was trying, because right now she was far from rational. There was no chance I was going to call her out on being emotional though.

I didn't have a death wish.

"I went to the doctor today." She shrugged as if it was no big deal.

But it was to me. "I asked to come with you."

"You were busy."

She was angry. I could understand why, but it didn't make it any easier to bear the brunt of it. Although I'd continue to until I brought her back to me.

"I'm never too busy for you," I corrected her in a gentle voice. "What did she say?"

"I'm perfectly healthy. One in four pregnancies end in miscarriage. I've stopped bleeding so there's nothing more to do. We can start trying again as soon as we're ready," she rattled off the details of her appointment, her eyes distant.

It was the best possible news and exactly what she hadn't wanted to hear. Belle wanted a reason. I sensed it. She needed to blame someone or something, and without that concrete answer, she'd continue to blame herself.

"We can get a second consultation if you'd like." It was the best I could offer her.

"What's the point? You aren't interested and—"

"I'm interested. You are the only thing I'm interested in," I interrupted her.

"All you're doing is avoiding me," she accused, beginning to pace. "It's because things are boring now. You miss the excitement."

"Do you hear how crazy that sounds?" It was out of my mouth before I could think. But now that it was, I knew I had to stick by it. I had to find a way to break through to her.

"Crazy?" she repeated, her blue eyes blazing.

Or maybe not.

"You don't want to spend time with me. You leave all the time. You find me boring—or broken."

I wasn't certain what was worse—that my wife believed I no longer wanted her or that she felt broken. I didn't see her that way. I didn't treat her that way. I was no psychologist, but it wasn't too fucking hard to see a case of projecting at play. The trouble was that I had no goddamn clue how to prove she was wrong.

"Beautiful." I caught her around the waist and forced her to stop her frantic pacing. "I love you. I'm not going anywhere."

"Everyone leaves," she whispered. "Sooner or later. Your friends get married. Your lovers cheat. Your..."

"I'm right here, goddammit. I don't see you as broken. I see your strength."

Her eyes sought the floor, and I cupped her chin, drawing her gaze back to mine.

"I'm broken," she whispered.

"Then I will fix you," I promised.

We stared at each other. I could see myself reflected in the blue of her irises. It was the only way I wanted to exist—as a reflection of her.

As a part of her.

Which is why it killed me when she pushed me away.

"Let's face it. We barely know each other." She swallowed hard, turning away from me.

"That isn't true, beautiful."

"Really? Did you know that Lawrence Davies was my first kiss?" she countered shakily. "Or that when I was thirteen I wanted to be Billie Piper?"

"You're much prettier than Billie Piper," I said softly, but I knew I couldn't lighten the mood. It was time for a different approach. "I want you, even the shattered parts."

I moved toward her, grabbing her shirt. She resisted, but I pulled her to me anyway. She could fight me all she wanted, because I wasn't about to stop fighting for her. Catching her face in my hand, I forced her to look at me. "I love you. You can push me away and you can run scared, but I'm not going anywhere."

I kissed her unyielding lips, softening my own until she began to melt against me. Her body still understood what we meant to one another, even if her mind had fallen victim to doubt and self-recrimination.

"I need you," I said, pushing her roughly against the wall. My hand snaked up her shirt and I palmed her breast, catching her nipple between my fingers and tugging on it. Her head dropped back as a moan escaped from her. Despite the fury she clung to, she couldn't escape what she felt deep within her. Under the pain and anguish, she was mine. We both knew it.

"You can be mad, beautiful," I whispered, nipping at her ear. "And you can hit me and yell at me, but you may not doubt me. You may not doubt us. We're going to make it through this."

"What if we can't?" she murmured.

The pain in her voice stabbed at my own heart. I wanted to take it away—to carry her pain as my own.

"We can," I reassured her. "We can do anything we want."

Gripping her hair tightly, I jerked her head back until her lips were displayed as an offering. I pressed my mouth to hers, spreading it open with my tongue and capturing hers. The kiss was languid but possessive. I would woo her back slowly, taking my time to show every inch of her body that it belonged to me. Her body molded to mine instinctively. My hands brushed down her torso and hooked in her waistband, yanking down her skirt. It pooled at her feet, but I didn't allow her to step free of it. I knew how to set my wife free.

Twisting the elastic of her thong until it snapped, I slid the lacy remnants across her bare cunt. She'd begun to tremble. She'd kept her face tilted toward me, but her eyes had closed as she lost herself in the moment. Cupping her mound, I leaned closer, pressing my palm to her heat. "Whom does this belong to?"

"You," she breathed.

"That's right. I own this." I slipped my middle finger between her folds and found her clit. Massaging circles across it, I appreciated each gasp, each tremor running through her body. "I'm not stopping until you come, beautiful, but take your time."

I was desperate to free her, and as her hips began to buck against my hand, my cock stiffened. I wanted to take it out and fuck her until I'd wiped away all the pain, but I wouldn't until she asked for it.

Something she hadn't done since that night.

Her breathing grew more strangled, and the throaty sound made it even harder to keep my dick in my pants. Her pussy had grown slick on my fingers. This was it: the reset button. I should have pressed it days ago. Her knees buckled slightly, and I anchored her to the wall as the spasms began. They rolled through her. Belle's hands splayed against the wall, seeking leverage as she shook. Finally she launched herself forward, wrapping herself around me as she thrust desperately against my hand, riding out her orgasm.

After a few moments, her thighs squeezed, signaling that she had reached her limit.

"God, you're beautiful," I told her, dropping a kiss on her shoulder. "I want to take you to bed now."

She stilled in my arms, and I realized that I'd said the wrong thing. I'd sworn I wouldn't push her and here I was doing exactly that.

I'd never made that promise to her, but based on her reaction, she'd also assumed that I'd wait for her request—and I'd gone and cocked it all up.

"It's okay if you aren't ready." But it was too late. She'd already pulled free of me and I'd let her go.

"I probably won't ever be, so don't waste your time." She turned and ran toward the stairs.

"Belle!" I called after her, but she'd already slammed the door shut.

Closing my eyes, I slumped against the wall, searching for a solution I knew didn't exist. I couldn't help her while she pushed me away, which led me to one unbearable conclusion.

I couldn't help her.

But that didn't mean someone else couldn't.

Pulling my mobile from my pocket, I dialed the only person I believed could.

"She doesn't want me anymore." It slipped from my mouth by way of greeting. I barely heard the well-meaning refute on the other end. "She needs you."

I hung up without another word.

She could believe I didn't care, but it wouldn't stop me from trying to help her. And if she wouldn't talk, there were other issues to attend to. Matters of practical concern that I could see to. I wanted to believe dealing with them would distract me, but I wasn't an idiot.

Pausing at the foot of the stairs, I stared up. The silence of the house swallowed me, leaving me no choice but to walk out.

"You look like shit," Georgia commented as soon as I was through the door to her hospital room.

Georgia, despite her lack of make-up and her hospital gown, was radiant. Her thick, black hair only accentuated her pale, fragile skin. There were probably very few women in the world who looked better than her after a month in the hospital.

"It's good to see you, too." It *was* good to see her, but it didn't work with our relationship to admit it. We were only adoptive siblings after all. I hadn't wanted to go to the hospital when we got back to London, but after my fight with Belle, I couldn't think of anywhere else to go. The truth was that I had few true friends. Georgia wasn't always the warmest person, but she knew me better than anyone.

"Apparently it's harder to kill me than you'd think." She fumbled with a remote, pressing buttons until her bed tilted her up. "Not a big fan of this whole hospital thing."

"You have your own guards," I informed her. "You must be very important."

"Or a criminal," she said in a dry voice.

I dropped the pitiful bouquet of lilies I'd grabbed from a corner market on her bed stand. "They didn't seem so bad."

"I already fucked one," she said with a wave of her hand.

"And I worried that you were bored. Do the doctors supervise you at all?" I grabbed her chart and began to flip through it.

"That's private information," she said, leveling a glare at me.

"Save it for someone who hasn't seen you from every possible angle."

Still, there were remarks on the sheets that caught me off-guard.

Uterine scarring characteristic of multiple abortions.

Previous rape kit on file.

Scarring consistent with self-harm.

Then there was the information relating to the attack that had nearly killed her. I hooked the chart back to the bed and smiled like I hadn't just read all her secrets.

"Don't pretend, Price. You're terrible at it," she informed me. "You thought you knew the extent of my fuckedupedness."

"We both put on a pretty good front, but you and I both know that's something that no one else ever knows."

"Even your wife?" she asked pointedly.

"So you heard?" Apparently I could avoid Belle but not the subject of her.

"Good news travels fast. Gossip even faster. I'll admit I'm lumped into the latter category. I'd thought you had learned your lesson with Margot. So council, how do you plead? Guilty? Temporary insanity? Because right now I'm wondering what to try you with."

"Love." I rolled my eyes along with her. "I know. I know. We're supposed to be too cynical for that."

"I knew the first time I saw you two together."

It was an uncharacteristically sentimental remark for her. "Is that why you were so hard on her?"

"Of course. If she couldn't handle me, she definitely couldn't handle you." She flipped her dark hair over her shoulder and smirked.

"Belle is stronger than you think." I looked out the window, wondering if she was still locked in our bedroom. Did I just want her to be stronger? Or did I really believe that?

"Oh Christ, is this the part where we braid each other's hair and talk about our love lives? It's not really my forté."

Trust Georgia to keep things in perspective. "You should consider becoming a therapist. You have a real talent for soothing people."

"I already have a position lined up." She winked at me.

I didn't ask questions. I knew that whatever she was up to, I wanted no part of it. I'd detached myself from Velvet, the private BDSM club we'd owned, and now I was finally rid of our mutual employer. Georgia enjoyed some of the seedier roles she'd played in

Hammond's empire. I didn't judge her for that, but it was no longer where I belonged.

"It took you long enough to visit." She didn't hide the implication in her voice.

“Belle and I took an extended honeymoon in the country." There was no gentle way to say what I needed to tell her. We were skirting the truth. The person that had bound us together had been taken care of, but Georgia and I had been on different paths for a long time. Our relationship was dependent on a shared history that neither of us wanted to remember.

“But now it sounds like the honeymoon is over.” She sighed and grabbed a pudding cup from her bed tray.

“What happened to not caring about my love life?” I dropped into the chair in the corner, shaking my head.

“I care about you, wanker.” She pulled the foil off the cup and scooped some on her finger. “No spoon. I’m not allowed anything with an edge.”

She shrugged like this was no big deal. I pretended to let it slide, too.

She’d been deemed a suicide risk. Maybe we didn’t know each other as well as I thought. I’d always assumed Georgia’s lust for pain only extended to being dominated. I hadn’t considered she could be capable of harming herself.

“Maybe our relationships only work in times of crisis,” I said, returning to the previous subject.

Georgia snorted back a laugh. “That is such a male thing to say. Were you *in crisis* when you started fucking her?”

“That was different.”

“No, it’s not.” She shook her head, pushing herself higher up in bed to glare at me. “It’s the same. I won’t ask if you love her because, honestly, I don’t care and because I assume you must. Things got hard and now you want to bail.”

“I don’t want to bail,” I stopped her. She had the wrong idea.

“Sure you do. You’ve placed your loyalty with the wrong people before. Now you’re spooked. It’s natural.”

"I'm not the one who's spooked," I said in a strained voice. No part of me doubted Belle's loyalty to me. That was beyond question.

"Can you blame her? She's been through a lot."

I stared her down. Someone was keeping her very informed.

"I have my sources."

She had told me that she was fucking her guards. If she wanted information, she had no trouble securing it.

"Out with it," she demanded. "What happened?"

No one knew more secrets than Georgia. She collected them. In her line of expertise, they were currency. She could keep a secret, but she could also sell one. The thing was that mine wasn't worth anything to anyone but myself.

"She was pregnant."

"Past tense," Georgia noted, pain flashing across her face so quickly I wondered if I had imagined it. "I'm sorry."

It was amazing the effect those two small words had on me. Up until that moment, I had thought only of Belle's pain. I hadn't really felt my own. "I don't understand how I can miss someone I never met."

"Did you tell her that?" she asked in a gentle voice. It was a side of Georgia I had never seen.

I shook my head. "I've been so focused on trying to do whatever she asks."

"Trust me, she doesn't know what to ask for. She's grieving and she thinks she's alone."

"She's not," I muttered. What did I have to do to prove that to her?

"You know that and I know that, but believe me, she's not seeing things clearly right now. Bluntness is your friend."

"Speaking of being honest, I'm glad you aren't dead." Standing, I crossed to the bed and pecked her forehead, feeling a wave of fraternal affection.

"You and me both." She swatted me away. Georgia had never been one for public displays of affection. She'd much rather be publicly whipped than hugged. "Go home and talk to your wife."

"I'll let you know how it goes," I promised her. I'd come here because I needed to talk to someone who knew me, but as I left, I couldn't help but wonder if I knew her at all. Maybe my surrogate sister wasn't as badass as she let on.

"Don't make threats!" she called after me. She was going to keep putting on the show though.

Georgia was right. Belle and I needed to communicate if we were going to work through our issues. The circumstances surrounding our relationship had accelerated our courtship. We'd bypassed some important moments along the way, like how to depend on each other. We'd just assumed we could.

CHAPTER TWENTY-ONE

The spicy aroma of ginger and cinnamon drifted through the department store as I made my way through the hordes of holiday shoppers. Christmas had infiltrated every nook and cranny in the place, but the crowds milling about the ground floor of Harrods only annoyed me. It was Christmas Eve, and unlike me, they'd had weeks to do their holiday shopping. I had to cram mine into a day. It didn't help that I was feeling far from festive. There was a good possibility that everyone in my life was getting socks. I wasn't certain I had it in me to do more. Not this year.

It should have been the merriest time of the year for me. With Smith newly absolved of any wrongdoing in the death of Jake Stanton and Hammond locked up, I should finally be settling into married life.

But I just couldn't.

The doctor had assured me that my grief would lessen with time. I doubted it.

What did make me happy was that Edward had arranged for a private shopping experience on the fifth floor. While I didn't relish the idea of putting up with a simpering personal shopper, the less people I had to deal with, the better.

But as soon as a young brunette, whose name I'd already forgotten, showed me to the room, I stopped inside the door and gawked.

Edward jumped to his feet and rushed over to me. "I was beginning to think you were avoiding us. You've been back in London for days!"

"It's been seventy-two hours," I corrected him in an overly-harsh voice. He probably didn't deserve it. I knew he didn't, but it wasn't as if I'd been larking about since we returned.

The truth was that I had been avoiding him. I'd been avoiding everyone.

Edward stepped back and gave me an unimpressed look. He wasn't the type to put up with drama, despite how often it surrounded him. As a group, we'd managed to keep most of it from affecting our relationships with one another. It was the only reason any of us were still sane.

"You okay?" he whispered. "Smith called me a few days ago."

I sucked in a breath. How much had he shared with Edward? "I'm fine," I said dismissively. "I have a little PTSD."

"That's understandable. Everything is fine with you two though?" he continued.

My heart lurched, skipping a beat. I had no idea what Smith had told him, but the idea that my best friend was running a relationship check put me ill at ease.

"We're great," I lied.

"Good. I'd hate to have to kill him," Edward deadpanned.

I forced a grin at the bad joke. There were bigger problems to deal with now. It wasn't Edward's ignorant remark that had me on guard or the fact that I really would rather have been in bed, it was that our private shopping experience apparently included more than the two of us.

"I hope you don't mind that I came along," Clara said as she adjusted Elizabeth's swaddle on the couch. My godchild kicked it off immediately. "I think the days of swaddling are behind us. Farewell sleep."

"You could get a nanny," Edward suggested.

"Exactly who would Alexander trust around his princess?" she asked, snorting a bit.

"You two have a country to run." Edward took the squirmy, half-wrapped bundle from Clara. Offering her to me as I joined them on the couch.

I took her with trembling hands, terrified that I would drop her. It wasn't a fear that I'd had before. I'd never thought twice when I got the chance to hold her before we'd left for Somerset. Now that had changed. If they knew, neither of them would have dared to hand me that baby. But exactly how was I supposed to catch my best friends up on my emotional instability? That definitely didn't seem appropriate for a light-hearted holiday shopping excursion.

"*He* has a country to run," she corrected him. "I've got my hands full with that one."

"So I suppose the tabloid rumors that you're already pregnant again—"

"Are big, fat lies," she cut him off. "He'd love it, of course. I swear he's constantly talking about getting me pregnant again."

"Maybe you should make him get up with her more often."

"That's just it, he does. I swear he's up for every nappy change. I keep reminding him that he's one of the most powerful men in the world, he doesn't need to breed an empire." Clara laughed, turning toward me just in time to catch the first tear streak down my cheek. "Oh my God, what's wrong?"

They were on either side of me before I had time to react. I cradled Elizabeth closer, breathing in her sweet baby scent and searching for the right words. In the end, there were none, so I lied. "I missed her so much. She's gotten so much bigger."

All of it was true, but it wasn't the reason I was crying. Edward dropped an arm around my shoulder and hugged me closer. Clara gave me a slight smile, her eyes flashing to mine. I wasn't fooling her. Probably because she knew I was not the crying type. I was the one who held her while she cried. I'd barely cried when I left Philip. Of all the times my mother had shown up at university and belittled me in front of her, I hadn't cried.

"Sorry," I choked. "Smith had me up late. He's been celebrating for days."

"And yet none of us were invited to the party?" Edward said in mock dismay.

"It was a private party." It was becoming too easy to be dishonest with them. Since when had lying to the two of them become second nature?

It's self-preservation. The last thing I needed was another person pitying me. Smith already treated me as if I were broken.

"Speaking of, in honor of both of your infamous love lives, I arranged to start with the lingerie," Edward announced.

My stomach dropped out, but I forced a smile. It couldn't be any worse than shopping for other presents.

As if on cue, a salesgirl rolled a rack of filmy fabrics and lace into the room. Clara turned on Edward. "If I get pregnant, it's on you."

The two fell into a good-natured argument on the likelihood of Clara having two babies under two years of age and the effectiveness of birth control. By the time I'd half-heartedly ordered two negligées, I'd gone numb. The rest of my holiday shopping would have to wait.

"Is that the time?" I pretended to be shocked as I checked my mobile. "I'm due to meet Jane."

"But we've barely seen you," Clara said. She wasn't talking about today. She was talking about the last few months. I fumed as I said goodbye and gave Elizabeth a kiss. If anyone should understand how all-consuming love could be, it should be Clara.

So when she grabbed my hand and mouthed, "Call me," I could barely nod. I needed more time. I only wish I knew how much.

I DIDN'T HAVE AN APPOINTMENT TO MEET JANE, BUT THAT hardly mattered. My great aunt had played therapist to me and my friends for years, offering her particularly incisive insights into our personal lives based on her unique life experiences. Letting myself into the flat we'd shared not so long ago, I felt a rush of emotion. I closed my eyes and breathed in the scent of patchouli and black tea that hung thickly in the air. This was the closest place I had to home. I'd never felt welcome at Stuart Hall, my flats at university had a sort of transitory quality that prohibited them from feeling as such, and I hadn't lived in Holland Park long enough to call it home.

Jane flew around the corner holding a candlestick, which she dropped as soon she saw me. "You're going to give me a heart attack!"

But if I'd thought she was genuinely angry, her accompanying hug set me straight.

"I wasn't sure if my key would work," I admitted. After what had happened, I'd half-expected that I'd find the flat empty. Any address associated with me was sure to be a target.

"Clara saw to it that I had constant surveillance. I had to ask her to pull the boys from duty when I read that they'd arrested that man in connection with what happened at the hotel." Her face was grim as she spoke. "Was that the man that hurt you?"

"Yes and no." I shook my head and pulled away from her. "I really don't want to talk about it."

"What do you want to talk about?" she asked in a quiet voice. Her gaze flickered to the hand that bore my wedding band.

"Still married," I said with a bemused smile.

"You sound unconvinced." Jane had already begun to boil water for tea. If there were two things that she could be counted on for, it was tea and wine. Given that it wasn't noon yet, I was getting the former.

"It was hard." I didn't want to spill all my problems to her, despite her track record for helping me make sense of them. "I'm sorry I couldn't tell you where we went."

"I knew where you were," she scoffed.

"I suppose it wasn't hard to guess." All the time I'd spent protecting her had been a waste.

"That and your mother called right after you arrived, demanding to know when you had gotten married and how much your husband was worth."

"Mother of the year," I grumbled. It didn't surprise me that she only saw Smith as a new bank account, but it still stung. I guess being used by the people who were supposed to love you never stopped hurting.

Jane shrugged. She, like I, had given up on my mother long ago.

"It was better you didn't call. The papers have been full of information about the alleged conspiracy plot." She set a chipped cup and saucer in front of me.

I wanted to care enough to ask her about it or even pick up a paper at the corner store, but I didn't. Whatever information Hammond and his lawyers were feeding to the press would hardly be accurate. I'd lived the conspiracy, and I didn't need to endure it twice.

We lapsed into silence until Jane shook her head. "What's going on?"

I didn't know where to start or what to share. I wasn't even sure I could. My heart was still raw, and opening up might only make it worse.

"I love Smith," I began, "but I'm starting to realize how little we know about each other."

"You know you love him," she pointed out. "That's a solid start."

"And everyone in my life is mad that I married him. Maybe they're right and I made a rash decision." I kept trying to see it that way, but I couldn't. If anyone could put it into perspective, Jane could.

"I think sometimes that rash decisions are the best decisions. They're the ones you make on instinct, because you're in tune with your heart." Jane took my hand and squeezed. It was her signature move for good reason, because it always made me feel better. "You love him, and now you have to work out the rest. Do you want him in your life?"

"I do," I whispered.

"There's something else," she guessed. If the woman had a crystal ball, she'd be a damn successful psychic.

"I got...I mean, I was pregnant." It was easier to say than I'd thought. After days of working myself up over the secret, just admitting it had happened was a relief.

"Oh, love." Jane shifted and pulled me close.

"I don't even know why I'm so upset. It wasn't planned, and I'm so young. And well, *everything*." No tears came as I told her. It was as if I'd cried myself dry.

"Because you had a vision of a future, and it was stolen from you. That's hard for anyone." She rubbed her hand down my shoulder as she spoke. "How is Smith taking it?"

"Better," I said, tacking on, "I think."

"I have a feeling I know exactly why you're questioning your marriage." She pulled back and met my eyes. "You are both in mourning."

"I just feel angry and sad and helpless and guilty all at the same time. He was trying so hard to take care of me and I just kept pushing him. It's all my fault."

"I don't believe that," she said firmly, "and neither does Smith."

"How do you know that?" I asked.

"Because he loves you, too. Do you blame him?"

"No." But I hadn't exactly acted that way. I'd spent a considerable amount of time accusing him of small crimes since it had happened. "I've been cruel to him, because I'm angry with myself."

"And he's still there," Jane reminded me, "because he loves you. You didn't walk away from him when he was in trouble. He's not walking away now. I think, if nothing else, you two are willing to fight and that's going to make all the difference."

"What if it's too late?"

"For love? Never." There was no room for doubt in her voice. I had to just trust that she was right.

Smith didn't answer his mobile when I rang him. I couldn't face returning to an empty house. Not after I'd ripped open my heart to Jane. I needed to go someplace where I could feel like my old self. When I found myself in front of Bless's studio entrance, I knew I'd found my reprieve. As soon as I let myself in, I discovered how much had changed in my absence. The bones were still the same, but now the shelves were full. The racks of designer clothes I'd envisioned had become reality. On the far wall, Lola had hung a whiteboard counting the number of current subscribers.

671.

I dropped my purse on the floor, startling Lola who flew out of her seat. She'd allowed her dark hair to grow longer, making her look even more like her sister.

"Oh my God!"

I was being hugged before I could process any of this. "Is that right?"

Lola turned to where I pointed, a huge smile bursting over her face. "It is."

"I was hoping for like ten," I admitted. Hundreds of subscribers felt impossible. "You did it!"

"We did it," she corrected me. "This is your baby, I've just been playing nanny."

She was underselling her importance. Without her, none of this would have happened. Bless would have wound up defunct before I'd even launched.

"Let me look at you." She stepped back and studied me.

Considering that I'd thrown on a pair of leather skinny pants and a slouchy sweater, I doubted I looked the part. Lola, on the other hand, had paired tights with a simple, timeless wrap dress. There was a reason I'd begged her to be the public face of the company since she'd come on board.

"Not exactly CEO material, right?"

"Nonsense." She waved her hand, dismissing my self-doubt. "Your style is effortless. That's the hardest kind of look to achieve, which is excellent since the French office of *Trend* wants to profile you for next spring's issue."

I raised an eyebrow. My last big break with *Trend* had turned into a slaughter at the hands of the editor.

"You aren't working with Abigail Summers again," she assured me. "Believe me, I wasn't about to let you go to Paris without some assurances."

Paris. Could I go to Paris? Did I even want to?

"Don't even think of saying no."

"It's just...I think you should do it." That was the honest truth. As happy as I was to be back at Bless's helm, I wasn't certain I was ready to step into the public eye. Not after what had happened to me in the last few weeks.

"We will fight about this later. For now I have many important things for the boss to sign off on."

I listened as she rattled off information about the relationships we'd established with various brands. Unsurprisingly, a number of up and coming designers had jumped at the chance at supplying pieces at cost. A few of the older brands were being a bit pricklier. It was exactly what we'd suspected.

"I almost feel badly for taking such a discount," Lola commented as she showed me some of the newer designers' garments.

"We're not stepping on them to climb the fashion industry ladder," I reminded her. "We're taking them with us. Bless is going to build every designer it works with as much as we build our own business."

"You're such a guru," she teased.

That was an overstatement, but I'd encountered enough unscrupulous businessmen to know that I didn't want to operate that way.

"And John sent these over by messenger yesterday." She'd saved the bad news for last. Lola knew me too well. I wouldn't have been able to appreciate all the good news if we'd started off with the legal problems our company was facing.

But when I opened the manila envelope, it was a set of documents that I hadn't seen before. There was nothing about the lawsuit. Rather it was some type of consent to transfer my management of the estate. I could read through the legalese for hours and probably still not know what I was reading, or I could call John.

He answered on the second ring.

"John, what did you send me?" I asked the moment he said hello, bypassing the usual pleasantries.

"I was wondering when you would be back from your holiday."

There was no way John believed I'd gone on holiday to my family estate. For one thing, he knew me too well. For another, Smith's personal attorney worked in the same office, which we'd discovered by accident. But my older half-brother was nothing if not polite.

"I am," I said, "and I was looking at the papers you sent to the office yesterday. I guess I just don't know what they mean."

"It's the management transfer you asked for." There was a long pause.

"So I'm not in charge of the estate anymore?"

"I thought you would be pleased." Even over the phone, I heard his confusion.

"I am!" I said in a rush. "I just want to understand why. I don't want to get excited if she's going to drop this in my lap tomorrow."

There was a pause on the other end, then John cleared his throat. "I suppose I should have run all of this by you. I assumed when your husband dropped off the papers and we spoke that you had asked him to handle this business."

My hands reached for a chair and I rolled it to me. I had a feeling I shouldn't be standing when I heard this.

"The documents had your signatures," John continued.

"Of course." My buzzing brain was depriving me of any more useful statements. I had signed papers regarding the estate, adding Smith as a legal owner, but something told me I'd given him even more control.

"Your husband asked me to take over control of the estate until it could be transferred or sold."

A weight I'd never realized was on my chest lifted when he spoke. Tears formed immediately in my eyes and I tried to blink them away. Across the studio, Lola stopped in her tracks to stare at me. I waved her off and swiveled the chair to face the window so she wouldn't be privy to the spectacle I was making of myself.

"Belle?" John prompted. "If you didn't consent..."

"No," I said a bit too quickly. "I mean—no, I do consent. Things have been a little crazy here. I didn't realize Smith had settled it."

"It's odd. Your mother has threatened to sue for the estate or sell it for years, but that never felt like the right decision for you. I had no doubt when Mr. Price showed up that he had your best interests at heart. He seems like a good man."

"And you sound like a protective older brother," I teased softly.

"That brings up another point I would like to discuss with you." He stumbled as he spoke, and I braced myself for the bad news I'd been expecting when I took the call. "I'd like you to consider selling the estate to me."

"But..." I shook my head to clear it. "I never realized you wanted it."

"I didn't want to take it from you. I still won't, even though there is a legal case that it should be mine."

"That's news to me," I managed.

"Please don't think I'm threatening you," John said quickly. "I wouldn't dream of taking it away, but if you are considering selling it, I hope you will consider selling it to me. I know there's some debate as to whether I'm a Stuart."

"There's never been a question," I said in a firm voice. "Don't let one person make you doubt who you are. But I'm sorry, there's no way I can sell you the estate."

"I understand."

"Because you've always had as much of a right to it as I have," I added before he could get the wrong idea. "Maybe it's time for a Stuart with good intentions to take the helm."

"You're giving it to me?" I could hear his incredulity through the phone.

"Imagine how pissed off my mother will be." It probably didn't speak highly of me that I enjoyed that fact.

"I'm not going to kick her out."

He should.

"But I am in negotiations with the BBC."

I cringed, because even with my name removed from ownership of the estate, I didn't want Philip to see this as a peace offering. "I suppose that is your decision."

"Smith secured exclusive location rights for the next two series," he continued. "Philip Abernathy was being difficult and he saw an opportunity. He's turned over the rest of the process to me."

"So they aren't going to film at his house anymore." I couldn't help but smile.

"Only Stuart Hall," he confirmed.

"You really are the best."

"I could say the same for you," he said with a snort. "Given that an arrangement has been reached, although I'm waiting on contracts, Mary has agreed to drop the lawsuit."

"Are you a magician?" I asked, half serious.

"Nope, I'm a lawyer. Never underestimate my profession." He paused for a moment. "You married a smart man, Belle."

And a kind man and an under-appreciated man, I added silently. While I'd spent the last few days accusing my husband of not caring, he'd been working behind the scenes to free me from the burdens of my past. I wouldn't miss Stuart Hall. He understood that more than most, and he understood me more than anyone.

I thanked John and hung up. Rushing toward the door, I grabbed my purse off the floor.

"Leaving already?" Lola called.

"Yes, and you should too. It's Christmas Eve," I reminded her.

"Not all of us have a sexy hunk of man to drag under the mistletoe."

We'd have to work on that, I decided, but for now I needed to get home to the best gift I'd received all year long: the love of my life.

CHAPTER TWENTY-TWO

The small tree drooped under the weight of the dozen or so glass ornaments Smith had placed on its branches. This Christmas tree hadn't grown up before it was chopped down and hauled to market. It looked like something out of a sad children's book.

It was the most beautiful thing I'd ever seen.

"I waited too long," he said in a soft voice behind me.

I whirled around, coming face to face with my own Christmas miracle. His shirtsleeves were rolled up and he'd already abandoned his tie for the evening. He watched me hawkishly, no doubt wondering what extreme my mood would swing to this evening. But even as he studied me, his eyes were open and unguarded. I sucked in a breath as I took in the full force of those green eyes, remembering the day we met. He'd never tried to hide himself from me. Not really. Smith had hidden his past and his sins, but he'd always shown me exactly the man he was. It hadn't been the choices he had made up until this moment that defined him, but rather it was the absolute capability to make different ones. He had done bad things, but he was a good man. My confidence in that was as unshakable as my love for him.

And I'd spent the last few weeks making him doubt that.

"I'm sorry," I whispered.

He grinned, leaning into the doorframe. "For the tree?"

"For the pain," I said quietly.

"Oh, beautiful"—he reached out and trailed his index finger along the curve of my face—"it was worth the pain."

"All of it?" I nuzzled my cheek into the palm of his hand.

"Always and forever." There was a reverence in his tone that stole my breath.

I'd been too caught up in my own grief—my own agony—to see that he was hurting, too. He had been the strong one when I needed to be weak. He'd carried the burden of my responsibilities when I couldn't find the strength. I owed him more than I could ever give him in return, but I would start trying from this moment. I would choose joy over anger. Courage over fear. I would choose *him*.

"You're quiet again, beautiful." He spoke with an apprehensiveness that showed exactly how carefully he'd learned to tread around me.

I swallowed against the swelling ache in my throat. "I was thinking of how much I love you."

"What a coincidence, I was thinking how much I love you," he said with a smirk. God, how I had missed that arrogant grin.

"Oh yeah?" I cocked an eyebrow, hoping the light teasing would prevent me from turning into a blubbering, sentimental mess.

"Yes," he said, "and I was also imagining how you're going to look spread naked under that tree. It's the only hope it has for raising my holiday spirits."

I launched myself at him, nearly knocking him over as I smashed my lips against his.

"Hold on." He pulled back, laughing at my enthusiasm. "I have a present for you."

"So do I." I'd almost forgotten, too caught up in the moment. "Me first."

Despite today's earlier shopping experience, I'd stopped at

Harrods on my way home. Opening my purse, I found the box I'd nestled inside. I bit my lip nervously as I withdrew it.

"Are you going to give it to me?" Smith asked.

I held it out tentatively, a sudden and unexpected shyness overtaking me. He took the box and plucked off the red ribbon the salesgirl had tied around it. Inside he revealed a thick gold band. It was simple, its edges blunt and sharp. The ring was masculine without being ostentatious, powerful without showing off.

"I figured it was time." My words scratched across my dry tongue. "If you don't like it..."

"I don't like it," he said immediately, and my heart sank. "I love it."

He took it and slipped it onto his finger.

"Does this mean you still want to be married to me?" he asked softly.

I'd given him reason to doubt that. It wasn't something that I could take back, but I could prove to him that I hadn't made my commitment lightly, starting today.

"Would you consider putting up with me for the rest of our lives?" I asked him.

"I thought you would never ask." Leaning down, he kissed me hard on the lips. My body responded. I'd punished myself by denying my need for him for far too long. It was a mistake I planned to remedy as soon as possible, but Smith drew back. "Now it's my turn."

"I can't wait," I said breathlessly. Right now there was only one thing I was interested in unwrapping.

Smith peeled himself away and led me toward the tree and a single gift-wrapped package.

"I'm afraid it's not as lavish as yours," he said, holding it out to me.

It was rectangular in shape and lightweight. I turned it over in my hand, trying to puzzle out what was under the paper.

"It helps if you open it," he advised.

I smacked him playfully on the shoulder. "I'm taking my time. If you're going to force me to be patient then you have to be as well."

But I was actually dying to rip off that paper. I glanced at him, then the present.

"Go ahead," he prompted.

I tore into it with a glee I hadn't felt since I was a child. Somehow being with him made everything new again. I was no longer too grown-up for things like Christmas presents. Love had reopened doors I'd closed on myself.

Inside I found a copy of *Honey to the B*, Billie Piper's debut album. Her picture stared back at me from the cover, a knowing look on her face.

Smith didn't know everything about me, but he was listening.

"I just want you to know that I fully support you if you decide you want to revisit becoming a pop star." But despite the teasing words, his voice was thick.

"You've never heard me sing." My own voice cracked as I cradled the gift to my chest. It had probably cost him less than ten pounds, but it was priceless.

Smith cupped my face with his hands and gazed into my eyes.

"I want to know everything about you. I want you to know everything about me. All the stupid stuff we hide from everyone else—I don't want to hide that from you. I want you to share every moment of your life leading up to the moment we met, because I missed out by not being there. I can't even remember what life was like before we met. Somehow when I look back at my past, you're still there. You're part of me, and I can't see myself as anyone but that man who fell in love with you." He caught the first tear as it hit my cheek, brushing it away. "We aren't going to learn everything overnight, but that's why we have a lifetime, beautiful. We have forever."

Forever couldn't start soon enough.

"Make love to me," I whispered.

"Beautiful, you don't have to ask me twice." He stepped toward me, but I held up a hand.

There was no way I could wait for the bedroom. I'd been fantasizing about our reunion all afternoon. Just making it to Harrods to buy a ring had been an exercise in patience. "I've been imagining this all afternoon," I admitted. "Just knowing your hands would be on me again made me want to touch myself."

"You didn't dare though," he said, darkness clouding his eyes.

I shivered at his possessive tone. Shaking my head, I reached for the buttons on my coat. "I didn't," I promised him, "but I thought maybe you wouldn't mind opening two presents on Christmas Eve."

"What did you have in mind, beautiful?" He licked his lower lip as if he already knew the answer.

My sex went damp at the sight of his tongue. Oh God, I wanted that mouth on me.

"This," I murmured, tugging my coat open to reveal the French lace negligee I wore underneath it. It barely qualified as a scrap of fabric, leaving my entire body exposed. My nipples perked, pushing against the lace and the open air.

"Have you been walking around London wearing nothing but that under your coat?" A muscle tensed in his jaw as his gaze devoured me.

I squirmed under his piercing stare. He was either pissed off or turned on, but if I knew my husband, he was both. In my world, that was the perfect combination.

"I wanted to be ready for you," I murmured.

"And you are." He stalked closer, pushing my coat from my shoulders to the floor. "Such a pretty package. I can't wait for a taste of what's underneath this wrapping."

Smith's hands ran down my arms, raising goose bumps over my skin. When he reached my hands, he squeezed them for a split second before dropping them. His index finger circled the air, and I turned obediently.

"I can't decide which present is my favorite," he mused. He stroked the finger that wore my ring.

"It's a package deal," I assured him.

"Best Christmas ever." His mouth twisted into a wicked grin, a deviant glint shining in his eyes. "Turn around again."

I pivoted to face the wall, sucking in a breath as he lifted the lacy hem of my lingerie to my waist. His palm stroked across my rear, caressing it with soothing strokes. I groaned as he pushed his hand lower, urging my thighs to spread for him.

He leaned in, whispering gruffly in my ear, "That's it, beautiful. I want to admire my gift."

I waited, holding my breath, for him to touch me. Each moment that passed I wanted the rough touch of his fingers or the clever dance of his tongue on my clit, but Smith seemed content to look.

"Please," I said, finally releasing the air I'd been holding in my lungs.

"I've waited for this," he reminded me. "A connoisseur doesn't down a glass of wine all at once. He sips. He swirls. He tastes. I'm going to enjoy doing all those things to you, beautiful."

My hips wriggled as I fought the urge to press my thighs together for relief. The slightest pressure and I would come on the spot—and Smith had barely touched me. All I needed was his presence, because his words were foreplay enough to take me to the edge.

"I can see how wet you are," he continued, dropping a gentle kiss on my shoulder. I shuddered at the precious contact. "Your cunt is crying for me, isn't it?"

I whimpered as a warm gush of arousal coated my sex, confirming his claim.

"Answer me," he commanded.

"Yes, Sir," I answered in a strangled voice. It felt so good to say those words.

"That's better," he said in a quiet voice. "I know what you need, beautiful, and I'm going to give it to you—my tongue, my fingers, my cock. I'm going to fuck you for all the time we've lost. First, I want to watch you as you come."

He snapped his fingers, and I whipped around to see him pointing down. I zeroed in on the bulge straining against his trousers, and I didn't have to stop to think about what he expected or what I wanted. They were one and the same. My body responded, my knees buckling automatically as I dropped to kneel before him. My fingers didn't fumble as I unzipped his fly. His heavy cock fell into my hand, and I ran my fingers down its velvety marble as I became keenly aware of the steady, insistent pulse building in my clit.

I lowered my lips to its tip, but Smith stopped me.

"Undress me," he ordered me.

I shuffled on my knees, the rug burning against my skin as I moved. Drawing his pants down his firm, muscular legs, I waited for him to step out of them. Smith beckoned me to my feet and I licked my lips, glancing back at his dick hungrily.

"I want to watch you," he reminded me, "and I promise you'll have your chance."

There was no chance we'd be getting any sleep tonight. The thought was enough to satisfy me—for now. He wanted to watch me get off, but it seemed he didn't understand how hot it made me to watch him do the same.

As soon as I was on my feet, he brushed his thumb over my lip, pushing the pad of it into my mouth. "You're so hungry for my cock. I can see it, beautiful. But I know what you need, don't I?"

I nodded quickly as he unbuttoned his shirt leisurely. Each soft pop of a button drew a gasp from my mouth. The man could give lessons on sex appeal. Not that I was willing to share him.

Shrugging off his shirt to reveal the carved planes of his chest, he turned and walked to the club chair next to the fireplace. Taking a seat, he stroked the length of his cock. It rose up in invitation and I sauntered to him. This time I didn't hesitate or wait for instructions. He'd already told me what he wanted—*what he expected.*

I climbed into the chair, straddling him. Smith swept the tip of his dick across my swollen seam, lubricating it. It was a gesture I appreciated as I positioned myself over him. It was always easier for him to take me from behind or on top due to his sheer size. Dropping my hips, I lowered myself slowly, allowing my body to stretch over his girth. I cried out as I sank farther, swallowing him to the hilt.

I was full of him, and yet, I would never have my fill.

"Take it slowly," he warned me. "I don't want to hurt you."

But that wasn't a sentiment I shared. I'd already begun to roll my hips, savoring the delicious pain as his cock knocked against my womb. He was so deep that every inch of me vibrated with his presence.

"That's it, beautiful," he coaxed, guiding my hips in a rocking motion. "Show me how much you love riding your husband's cock."

His words ripped through me, coiling around my limbs and constricting for a split second before the pleasure filtering into my veins flooded through me. I threw my head back, bucking hard against the incredible pressure building, and screamed his name. My fingers clawed at his shoulders, seeking leverage, as the world shook around me. Or maybe I was the one shaking. It was impossible to tell. Smith took over, thrusting violently inside me until I felt the warmth of his climax.

When I finally dropped limply against him, he kissed me until the aftershocks of my orgasm had faded. "I could watch you all day."

Neither of us moved. We just lingered in the moment, still joined as one.

"I'm looking forward to seeing you come every day for the rest of my life," he said with a smirk.

I kissed it off his face, already feeling a familiar stirring in my belly. "We should have put that in the vows."

"An oversight," he agreed. "You'll just have to take my word for it. Will you?"

"I will," I whispered.

Smith's mouth found mine, our bodies already moving in unison as we sealed our promises to one another.

CHAPTER TWENTY-THREE

Belle's voice carried through the corridors as she shifted from humming to singing. She was back in the kitchen after a disastrous attempt to whip up a post-coital Christmas pudding late last night. I made a mental note to hire a professional chef before she burned down our house.

I thought I would never hear that sound again. Happiness. Walking to the kitchen, I paused in the doorway to admire her as she stirred a bowl full of questionable contents. No doubt I would be forced to eat that later, but for now the sight made me smile. If I'd been told yesterday I would be standing here now, I wouldn't have believed it. Maybe there was something to the idea of Christmas miracles.

The peaceful scene was interrupted by the vibration of my mobile. There was no one who had a reason to call me on Christmas Day, save for the woman standing a few meters from me. Whatever business had to be attended to I didn't want her to overhear. Not while her joy was still based in the fragile hope that better times were in store.

Striding back toward the study, I checked the screen. A surge of adrenaline rolled through me as I read the name flashing up at me.

This wasn't going to be a Happy Christmas call.

"I assume you aren't calling with best wishes," I said as soon as I accepted it.

"Unfortunately not." Alexander's tone was clipped. Neither of us wanted to be on the phone today, especially not with each other, which meant he must have really bad news.

"Whatever it is can wait," I stopped him. "You should be with your family."

"Believe me, I will be. But you're wrong. This can't wait. I just received word that Hammond's appeals have been granted."

My hand tightened over the mobile, afraid it would slip to the ground. It was taking a considerable amount of restraint not to throw the fucking thing across the room. What happened to the good old days when you could throw your enemies in the Tower of London? It certainly seemed that the tourist attraction might have a much better use. But this wasn't a laughing matter. This was life and death. "What happens now?"

"The House of Commons will commission a council to vote on the charge of treason. It's likely they'll overturn it, based on my impressions of the House ringleader. Apparently MP Jacobson doesn't find the evidence compelling."

"Jacobson?" I repeated.

"Do you know him?" Alexander's surprise was evident.

"He's Belle's neighbor. We went hunting."

"Maybe it's time you had another friendly jaunt with him," he suggested dryly.

There wasn't time for that. Jacobson hadn't been shy about his anti-Royalist sentiment. It didn't shock me to learn he wanted to see the whole case dismissed. I could try to change his mind, but experience had shown me that men with power weren't always malleable to outside opinions. I couldn't risk Hammond returning to his home and his sources. Even with an armed guard and surveillance, his connections could be enough to get his dirty work carried out.

"When are they releasing him?"

"They already did, Smith," he said in a measured tone. There was a long pause. "He was released into protective custody under Parliament's orders. I can't touch him. More than a few voices are disputing the treason charge. They aren't even treating him as if he's under house arrest. My sources tell me he left his cell without so much as an ankle bracelet."

Both of us were waiting for the other to respond. One of us had to have a plan of action. But I wasn't going to drag Alexander into mine. If he had one of his own, it was clear he shared the same sentiment.

It had only been a few days since I'd received a very different call. I'd celebrated the news of Hammond's arrest, only to have my heart ripped out. Sitting on the other side—knowing he was free—didn't grieve me. I'd been prepared to take charge of the situation before his arrest and I was still prepared to do so now.

Belle's gentle voice rose into a trilling soprano, loud enough that I could hear her all the way from the kitchen. The calm determination I'd felt morphed into a consuming obsession. Hammond had been released and the woman I loved, the woman he tried to have killed, was singing carols over the hob. Maybe my vendetta was as misplaced as her domesticity, but I wasn't going to wait to find out.

Darkness swirled around me, threatening to overcome me. It would always be that way. My life—my mistakes—were a storm waiting for the perfect conditions, and now they were here. The past had caught me in its cyclone and it would destroy everything in its path.

There might be time to get a security detail for her. But she would resent it. I resented it for her.

"Are you there?" Alexander's voice drew me back to the mobile.

"Sorry," I said, my mind still absent.

"I'm sending over one of my men."

"I hope you won't be offended if I refuse."

"I trust him with my life."

"You haven't always judged correctly on that front." The joke came out flat, because there was too much truth to it.

"I trust him with my daughter's life," Alexander said in a soft voice.

It was supposed to mean something, but I didn't have a child. That possibility had been stolen from me along with everything else. But I understood the value he placed on his wife and child. "I don't want her to know. It's Christmas."

"I understand."

Considering the secrets he'd kept from his own wife during the course of this investigation, I knew he empathized with my position.

"He'll be there soon, and I promise she won't think a thing of it."

At least there was no way he could deliver worse news. I hung up the call and wandered toward the kitchen. Belle had thrown on one of my undershirts. Her nipples poked through the thin fabric as she skated around the kitchen, gathering ingredients and grabbing spoons. She glanced up, a huge smile splitting across her face. It lit up the room.

All I wanted was to see that smile every day. I would have to settle for knowing that she was smiling, even if I couldn't be there to give her a reason to. I'd do whatever I had to in order to make that happen.

"Are you ready to taste test?"

"Sounds like a dangerous job." I wouldn't tell her, I decided as I grabbed a stool and took my place at the kitchen island. It was Christmas, and all I wanted was to see her happy today. I couldn't take it from her so quickly after she'd finally found it.

"This time I'm using a recipe from my secret arsenal."

"You have an arsenal of recipes?" I asked as incredulously as possible.

"Well, I have a friend who is a professional chef. She emailed me this and said it was foolproof. I'm not certain I believe her. It's a funny color." She waved her spatula as she spoke, showering me with batter and immediately dissolved into a fit of laughter as I wiped a spot off my nose.

"You missed some." She drew her thumb over my cheek, but before she could move away, I hooked an arm around her waist, drawing her between my legs.

"You have some on your face," I told her, trailing my lips down her jaw.

"I do, huh?" she asked breathlessly.

"Lots."

"You better clean me up." She wiggled her eyebrows saucily.

"My job is to get you dirty."

"If you insist." There was nothing innocent about the way she said it, but I knew differently. She was pure and true. I wouldn't allow anything to happen to her.

"Will that keep?" I asked her, emotion growing thick on my tongue.

"It should."

I doubted that, but I wouldn't be here to eat it. In a few hours' time, when it was ready to come out of the stove, she wouldn't care if it had turned out or not. By then she would know I was gone.

It was selfish to stay here with her now, but I needed to soak her in. There was no point in committing each part of her to memory. She was already there. I could close my eyes and summon her in my thoughts, each inch of her carved forever into my soul. Right now I needed to *feel* her.

The delicacy of her wrist in my hand.

How right it was when I had my arms around her waist.

The warmth of her slender body.

I needed to *experience* her one last time.

I searched for a way to tell her how I felt. *I love you* wasn't enough to convey how I felt about her. She had challenged me to be more than I thought I was capable of being. The change had been gradual, my sense of purpose evolving along with our relationship. Now I was inexorably bound to both. I couldn't walk away from my duty any more than I could stop loving her.

I'd promised her forever, but I'd lied. A future together was never mine to give her. I could only give her my love and the possibility of a life lived without danger. Removing Hammond was the first step in achieving that.

Removing myself was the second.

Dying for her seemed like a pretty good way to go in the grand scale of things. But that didn't make it any easier to walk away now.

"Uh-oh." She clicked her tongue on the roof of her mouth. "You're thinking."

"That's a crime, huh?" I swatted her on the ass playfully, trying to draw her attention away from my momentary lapse.

"With you it can be. Care to share, Price?"

"I was thinking about how much I loved you," I admitted.

"And?" she pushed.

"That was the general thesis. I love you. I worship you. Wondering how I can worship you more." All of it was true. I was just leaving bits out. Someday I wanted her to look back and remember my words, not my distance. If I only had an hour to give her, I needed it to last a lifetime.

"I have a few ideas." Her fingers slipped past my waistband to fondle my stiffening dick. Her hands were cold and I was hot, and everything about the moment—the love and the grief, the gift and the sacrifice—made me want to mold her body against mine. She tipped her face to mine, her eyes shining with hunger. As I stared into them, I wondered how much time I'd wasted on twisted scenarios when all I'd ever needed was her. She was my home. I'd fought that. I'd tried to contain her and my feelings with restraints and dominance, but the truth was that when I was inside her, she was my undoing. I'd spent so long trying to capture her in every way that I'd failed to see how she had captured me.

"Take me." The request fell sweetly from her lips.

"Forever, beautiful." My mouth angled over hers, and we collided, our bodies fighting to be closer together, as if we both sensed the inevitable. Each kiss was a tiny rebellion—each touch a moment of immortality. As I slipped inside her, rooted possessively to her center, she released a breathless battle cry, calling me to war.

CHAPTER TWENTY-FOUR

Christmas afternoon brought not only a renewed sense of peace but also Edward and his friend to the door. Smith answered, obstructing my view of our visitors. When he stepped aside, I gawked at the unfamiliar man at Edward's side. Maybe the holiday wasn't going to stay serene after all. But since I'd recently learned to wholeheartedly subscribe to the "guilty until proven innocent" philosophy, I opted to drag Edward into the house without accusation.

I peeked over his shoulder at the red-wrapped package. "Is that for me?"

"Of course not," he said, his mouth curving at my pretend dismay. "I brought this for Smith."

"Cad," I accused him. Reaching around his waist, I snatched the present from him.

"It's nothing spectacular. Considering I'd pretty much given you up for dead until a few days ago, I didn't do a lot of shopping."

I wagged a finger at him. "I fully expect that when I do die, you will bring presents to my grave, so don't make that mistake again."

"Like a shrine?" He shook his head, laughing. "Have you met Alexander's buddy, Brexton Miles?"

Brexton hadn't moved from the window. His hands were shoved in his pockets. He had a nonchalant air to him I didn't quite buy. It was pretty apparent that he was uncomfortable being here, which led to the obvious question: why had Edward brought him? And not David?

But even though I wasn't in the market I wasn't oblivious to Brexton's well-chiseled physique or the handsome face put on display by his shortly clipped hair. If I recalled correctly he had been in Afghanistan with Alexander, which made him a military man. So why was he here with Edward now?

My stomach rolled over. I had been gone for a long time. Edward had been reluctant to set a date and although his fiancé had scored minor victories on that matter, I'd suspected he was dragging his feet. Now my best friend was here with another man—a really, really hot man. I needed to get Edward alone for a major interrogation, but that was going to be easier said than done.

"I think so," I said hesitantly. "You were at the engagement party."

"And the wedding," Brexton called over, "but I don't think we officially met. I noticed you, of course."

There was a casual arrogance in his words that might have appealed to me before I met Smith. Now I could only hope it didn't appeal to Edward.

"Quiet neighborhood," Brexton remarked to Smith, turning his attention back to the street outside our home.

Smith abandoned his coffee and joined him, and soon the two of them were absorbed in small talk. Grabbing Edward's arms, I hauled him into the kitchen.

"It's not that kind of present," he teased. "You can open it in front of your husband. Of course, I suppose I owe you a really embarrassing hen party gift."

"I didn't have a hen party." I dropped the package on the counter and rounded on him.

"I wasn't the one who ran off and got married in New York

without telling anyone." He held up his hands in surrender. "I can throw you one now."

"I don't care about the hen party. I want to know what you're doing at my house on Christmas day—"

"Now I can't visit my best friend on Christmas?" He crossed his arms and glared at me over the rim of his glasses.

"You didn't let me finish," I snapped. He was not going to change the subject. "Why are you at my house with another man?"

His eyebrows knitted together as if he was having trouble processing my question. I could practically see the realization dawning on him. I wasn't asking him, I was accusing him.

"It's not like that, and I'm going to give you a pass for being paranoid because people have been trying to kill you lately." Judging from the flatness of his voice, he wasn't teasing me now.

"Then what is going on? What would you think if Smith showed up at your house with another hot blonde?"

"I'd wonder why Smith was at my house at all." Edward grabbed me by the shoulders and leaned down so that we were eye level. "David went to visit family for Christmas. His grandmother isn't all that keen on me."

"Homophobe," I muttered, instantly angry on his behalf.

"Actually, it's because she's Scottish. She wouldn't care if he was shagging half of Manchester United, but she doesn't want him marrying into the English royal family."

My own husband's Scottish heritage accounted for a similar sentiment. Thankfully he'd gotten over it quickly. The tension between them was bad enough. I don't know what I'd do if I couldn't be in the same house as both of them.

"And Brexton?" I prompted. "It's all well and good that David can't be here, but does he know—"

"That I'm spending the holidays with Alexander's army buddy, who is also a well-documented womanizer?" Edward pushed his glasses up, shooting me an incredulous look in the process. "He got the memo."

Taking a deep breath, I realized I was faced with two options. "I guess I can keep grilling you or I could open my present."

"Presents always win." He picked it up and shoved it into my hands.

Inside the small box was a petite coin purse emblazoned with the word "Mrs."

"Is this your blessing?" I asked, blinking rapidly in a failing attempt to keep tears at bay.

"I saw it and I thought of you, so I guess I must be used to the idea." He brushed his thumb over my cheek. "You're turning into a romantic on me."

"I have something in my eye." Turning away, I tucked it back in the box. There were no words to express what his acceptance meant to me, so instead I whirled around and launched myself into his arms.

Edward caught me. Hugging me tightly, he whispered, "Please give me a heads up in the future."

"I don't plan to get married again." There was no possibility of it actually. Smith was it. I'd mated for life. If we could survive the last few months, we could get through anything.

"So be it, but there's nothing else you want to tell me..." he prompted.

I dropped my head to the side and stared at him.

"What do Americans call them? Shotgun weddings? Am I going to be an uncle again?"

Of course that's what he would think. People didn't run off and get married without a damn good reason, especially to people they barely knew. I hadn't married Smith because I was pregnant. No, that had come later. It took all the strength I'd gathered in the last twenty-four restorative hours to keep my smile from slipping. "No baby."

Not yet.

It was the second time that little voice had piped up. I wanted to listen to it, believe that it had an insight into my future that I didn't, but the placing trust in my body after its betrayal was going to take a while.

"If we don't get back in there, they're going to start thinking we're having an affair," he pointed out. He'd gotten the hint and dropped the baby talk. Hopefully the next time the topic came up, we'd be having a very different conversation. "I can't believe you thought I was shagging Brex!"

"He's hot, sue me." I shrugged away as he playfully pushed me.

"I don't think it's appropriate for a married woman to talk that way."

I shook my head as we returned to the living room, whispering, "I'm married, not dead."

Brex had moved from the window to the sofa where he was casually texting. He might not be the threat I'd worried he was, but he was still very connected to my two best friends in the world. Edward caught sight of my face and shook his head.

"She's on the case," he warned Brexton.

"Am I being investigated?" he asked, flashing me a gorgeous smile.

Sorry, that's not going to work on me. "Yep. Rumor has it that you've taken a job at the palace. Now you're hanging around Edward. I just want to make sure you're legit."

He nodded as if this was perfectly reasonable, although I spotted a small smirk on his lips.

"Where's your family?" I asked. "Not spending Christmas with them?"

"I visited them this morning," he said without missing a beat, "at the cemetery."

My eyes darted to Edward, whose eyes were closed. He'd known I was going to make a fool of myself, and he'd done nothing to stop me. Lesson learned.

"I'm s-s-sorry," I stammered.

"I was a kid." He waved away my apology with the experience of a man who'd done it his whole life. "Whenever I'm in town, Poor Boy and his brother take pity on the orphan. Now that I'm living in London, they've decided I need a family for Christmas."

How was it possible for me to feel even smaller? First I'd accused

Edward of cheating, then I'd interrogated an orphan—was I going to start kicking puppies next?

"My dad's gone, too." And my mother might as well be. I kept the last part to myself.

"I hardly remember them," he admitted, pocketing his mobile. "I miss them, but it's more like I miss the memory of them, especially this time of year with all the families around."

"David wants to adopt," Edward informed us, "if you don't mind having two daddies."

"I'll take it under advisement."

"Smith's parents are gone as well. We're a rather sad bunch actually." I turned to look for my husband, but he was nowhere to be seen. "Speaking of, where did he disappear to?"

If I hadn't glanced to Brex in that moment I would have missed the look he shared with Edward. It was over in a split-second, but I'd caught it.

"What's going on?" I said in a low voice. My stomach clenched, flipping over as the tension grew between the three of us.

"Belle," Edward began, but I held up a hand.

"Think very carefully about what you're going to say," I warned him. I knew him too well. There was no way he could lie to me.

"I think he ran out to get you a present."

I pivoted around and stared at Brex. His composure held, which was how I knew he was lying. A guest would crack under that stare. They would stammer or laugh. There wasn't a single trace of guilt on his face.

"What exactly do you do at the palace?"

He held my gaze, and I saw the gears turning in his eyes. He wasn't sure how to spin this question.

"I will find out eventually, so if you're really a good friend of the royal family, then you should know that I'm not going anywhere and I'm going to guess you aren't either. I'll find out now or I'll find out later."

"I think you're overreacting," Edward interjected.

I ignored him entirely. I was far too smart to believe that.

"Where is he?"

"I didn't ask him where he was going." This time I believed Brexton, but that didn't mean I trusted him.

"There's been a development." Edward mouthed an apology to Brexton, who groaned as he sank back.

"I told him I shouldn't have taken you," he said. Brexton's friendly facade morphed into annoyance.

"Who?" I was running out of patience now.

"Alexander sent us over to check on things. He wanted to ensure your safety."

"And why would he want to do that now?" It didn't make any sense. The entire time we'd been in Somerset, I hadn't existed to the lot of them. Now they were sending over men to check up on me.

Edward glanced at Brexton. He was making a decision between us. After a few seconds, he turned to me. "Hammond was released on home arrest today. The House of Commons plans to overturn his indictment."

He could have punched me in the stomach and it would have shocked me less. "He's free?"

I'd frozen in place, afraid that I would turn around and discover him standing on the street outside my house.

"Not free. He's under guard at his house. And you are safe," Edward said. He moved toward me but I backed away.

"Explain to me how that is possible," I pleaded, looking from Edward to Brexton. "How does a man accused of assassinating a king walk away?"

I couldn't think of a technicality large enough to account for such a misjudgment on the part of the courts and Parliament.

"Hammond was hounded by the media his entire way home," Brexton responded. "Believe me, he's far from *free*."

"Well, I feel a lot safer knowing a bunch of reporters are keeping tabs on him," I said flatly. "I'm sure they'll get some good photos of him murdering me."

"No one is going to touch you," Edward said in a firm voice.

"And what about Smith?" They knew more about my husband's whereabouts than they were letting on.

"I was asked to monitor your safety," Brexton explained.

But Smith had gotten a free pass to leave. The fact didn't sit well with me.

"Just tell me where Smith is," I begged him, but I already knew where he was going. Hammond had been the barrier to our freedom before. I knew my husband well enough to know that he wouldn't allow him to become one again. Smith knew where to find Hammond, and I suspected Brexton did as well.

"It's better if you stay here and..."

But I'd already tuned out their well-meaning advice. Stay here and wait? Stay here and do nothing? That wasn't in my nature. Smith had gone to take care of the problem. I couldn't let him do it alone. We were too much alike.

Birds of a feather.

"Give me your keys." I stretched my hand out to Edward. He had them out of his pocket before Brexton pushed onto his feet. I snatched the car keys before things escalated.

"I can't let you leave," Brexton said.

I looked him up and down. "Do you have a gun?"

"No," he said. "I don't need one."

He was wrong about that. Smith had gone to Hammond because he believed he had no other choice. It was up to me to remind him that wasn't the case. No gun meant one thing to me. "Then you aren't stopping me."

CHAPTER TWENTY-FIVE

I took the Bugatti for sentimentality's sake. If I was going to murder someone, I figured I might as well do it in style. It would be one less joyride without the joy. The press would be camped out at his private residence, likely buying that Hammond was actually on house arrest. That wasn't a delusion I suffered from. He'd managed to be released before his treason indictment had been officially dropped. The press had bought the story the special council had concocted regarding a conspiracy. I hadn't. Mostly because I knew Hammond was guilty of every crime that had been listed against him and then some.

He had friends in powerful positions. I wouldn't find him at his home. That's where he'd want everyone to think he was. Instead, he'd go to a place he felt comfortable—the nondescript office he kept above his jewelry shop.

My key still worked in the lock. I didn't even bother removing it. I would leave it in the door. Tonight I would dispose of every remnant of my ties to Hammond.

I found him sitting in a chair looking out his office window at the street below. Christmas lights began to turn on as I stood there silently, watching him. The days were as short as the rest of his life.

"I was wondering when you would join me," he said, not bothering to turn to face me. "I thought perhaps you'd miss this Christmas given your marriage."

"I didn't bring any presents," I said dryly as he swiveled around. I took the chair opposite his. Right now the desk between us was his only protection.

"I know what you brought," he said in a thoughtful tone.

"You must have known this was coming after you tried to kill Georgia and me. How could you have expected us to overlook that?"

Hammond's fist smashed onto the table. "You honestly believe I would order either of you killed?"

"Perhaps it was the hitman you sent to my hotel that gave me that impression." I slid on a glove. There would be no mercy. Not for a man like him. "I'm afraid your argument is unconvincing. You might have considered your plea-bargaining skills before you pissed off your lead counsel."

"I don't care if you kill me."

That gave me pause, but I slipped on the second glove anyway.

He gestured to the other chair. "Care for a drink?"

"Forgive me if I don't trust you." I took the seat, tapping my leather-shod fingers.

"I've already told you I don't wish you dead, but if you need further proof, I'm drinking the Glenfiddich."

My mouth twisted into a knowing smirk. "Pour me a glass."

Hammond had bought the bottle when his doctor suggested he was showing early signs of Parkinson's. No diagnosis had materialized, but he kept the bottle anyway. He'd had it on a shelf for nearly seven years, thumbing his nose at death. But he'd taken it down tonight.

"There's something you don't understand about your situation," he explained. "I'm already a dead man."

"You will be soon," I promised as I took the rocks glass he offered me. I no longer had sympathy for him. The strings that once attached him to me no longer existed, which meant he could no longer pull them. I'd made my decision the moment I'd received word of his release.

"I know, but not at your hands, son. Don't burden yourself with my blood."

"I don't consider it a burden," I snarled. The Scotch splashed over the edge of my glass as I leaned toward him. "I consider it a privilege."

"You may not see it, but I've always protected you," he continued, "and I won't be able to any longer. Someone must always be ready to take the fall. My turn has come."

"I'm not interested in riddles." My patience with his games had evaporated long before I'd stopped playing. "You went after her. That is unforgivable."

"Loose ends must be tied. You know that better than anyone." He swigged from his glass, draining it to the very last drop. "You can find religion but you can't erase your sins."

"I'm no expert, but I think that's actually the whole point of faith." I had found something to believe in. I believed in *her*. It was through her love that I'd found absolution. I could never take back the crimes I had committed, but I could forgive myself for them. I had learned to worship her and I would fight for her, even give my life if necessary. It was such a simple decision when it came down to it. I'd chosen her in life and in death. I'd placed her life above my own because she had a light I couldn't bear to see extinguished from the world.

"There are circumstances out of my control," he admitted, pouring himself another drink. He held out the bottle, but I shook my head.

I'd allow him to get drunk. One small concession on my part. I didn't care if he suffered. It wasn't done out of mercy. His death was a means to an end. The safety of my wife. Nothing more. I didn't care about his role in King Albert's death or his attacks on Alexander and his family. I cared that a man as twisted and morally corrupt as him continued to breathe, continued to threaten Belle. It was an oversight

I meant to rectify. He needed to die, but I could let him finish his Scotch.

"I'm sorry about Margot." Apparently with each drink he took, Hammond planned to confess all his sins. I'd suspected she'd been unfaithful to me, even that she'd been a manipulation, but somehow having it confirmed brought an anger I thought I'd left behind.

"Did she ever love me?" I asked. It didn't matter. Not since I had found love with Belle, but I'd cared for Margot. The idea that it had all been a scheme weighed heavily on me.

"I couldn't tell you," he admitted.

I dropped my head, taking a deep breath. My whole life had been an unnatural progression of events orchestrated by this man. Even meeting Belle.

"You have to understand," he continued, his speech beginning to slur, "not all decisions are up to me. I can't control everything."

"That's not what you led me to believe my whole life," I snarled. My hand lashed out, knocking my glass over in the process. Good Scotch wasn't the only thing that would be spilled here tonight.

"Do you want the truth?" he asked. "I'll tell you as much as I can. Even now my loyalties lie with powers above me."

"Why cling to that when you know you'll draw your last breath tonight?"

"Call me old-fashioned." He poured more into his glass with a shaky hand. "Your father came to me looking for work. He knew what I did. He wanted the money, and like most good men, he believed himself above corruption. Like you, he assumed that he would be the mediator between the law and my crimes. At first that was all he was, but your father liked money, Smith."

I picked my glass up off the rug and poured a new drink for myself. "Tell me something I don't know."

My father had always cared more about money than me or my mother. He'd spent every moment at his employer's side. He'd left birthday parties and Christmas mornings to attend to Hammond's needs before mine. I'd always known where I stood in my father's priority list.

"Unfortunately, like all good men, he began to grow a conscience."

"And that isn't a problem that you've ever experienced personally?"

Hammond tilted his head. The barb stuck. "I've never been burdened with a conscience and having watched other men suffer from it, I can't say I'm sorry for it."

And yet he sat here apologizing to me for the injuries he'd inflicted upon my life. His morality was complicated but not altogether absent.

Stop it, I ordered myself. I refused to see things from his perspective.

"At first, more money soothed his anxieties," Hammond continued, "but I knew that wouldn't last long. In the end, I gave him a choice. Remove himself from the situation without a fight or lose everything he held dear."

"He can't possibly have chosen death," I scoffed. "He didn't care about anything but his house and his cars."

"He cared about you," Hammond corrected me, "and your mother. It was as simple as that. He could choose his death or yours. It was a relatively simple decision."

"And you want me to believe you didn't order Georgia and me killed?" The simmering anger I'd felt since my arrival erupted into a full boil. "Try again."

"I had no emotional attachment to your father," Hammond said flatly. "I respected him. I may have even liked him."

"I thought you were his best friend." Confusion was beginning to muddle my rage. My world had been turned upside down, and I didn't know if I wanted it righted. Was it better to believe my father had died a good man? A martyr? That in the end I had meant more to him than the life he'd always chosen over me? It wouldn't bring him back if I chose to believe Hammond's version of events, and there was a danger to trusting anything the man claimed. I'd learned that the hard way.

"He was the closest thing I've ever had to a friend. I can understand how that might be confusing. Men like me have many allies and many enemies. We don't have friends." Hammond's eyes turned glassy, lost in memories.

"Why Margot?" I demanded.

"I never wanted to murder another friend," Hammond said. "Somehow over the years, I'd grown to look at you as a son."

I laughed. "That I knew. What a fucked up father figure you were."

"Most young men would love to get a free pass to fuck and drink," he said.

"That's exactly why you've never been my father." When I was younger, I'd thought that was normal, but as I'd grown older, I began to see the situation for what it was: a perversion. Hammond had twisted me, just as he twisted Georgia, in an attempt to make puppets of us. "You made a mistake bringing us into the scene."

"Why is that, son?"

My hands clenched. I wasn't his son. I never had been. But after all these years, he still didn't see that. "BDSM is about power. The control of it. The gift of it. It taught me to use my power carefully. It taught Georgia the same. It taught us to distrust men like you."

"Since I discovered your betrayal, I've wondered where I went wrong. Thank you for telling me, even if it's too late to rectify."

"Thank you for fucking up," I said coldly. "You allowed me to see through you. It's the only reason I'm here tonight."

"To protect your wife?" he guessed. "There's no need. No one will touch you now."

"Not after I kill you." I felt no emotion as I said it, just a serene blankness.

"Unnecessary, but it may as well be you. Death seems kinder coming from a familiar face. That's why I'm here and not at home, you know. They want it this way. You didn't come of your own volition, Smith. You were moved into place. Don't you see that you're still a pawn in their game?"

He'd had most of the bottle now, which accounted for how little sense he was making. "It won't be kind, Hammond."

"I suppose it never is." He raised his glass. "A toast to our freedom."

But I didn't raise mine. I would have a drink with him, but there would be no celebration between the two of us. "You could have liberated yourself a long time ago."

"Don't be stupid. If you thought this ended with me, then..."

But he trailed away at a knock on the door.

"Expecting company?" I asked him coolly.

"All the ghosts of Christmas owe me a visit today."

There would be no escaping consequences now. If I opened that door, I might lose my chance at catching him alone. I tugged my gloves, securing them more tightly. Not that it mattered. Too many people knew where I had gone; even Alexander couldn't cover this up for me. The press would be all over the story as soon as it broke, and undoubtedly the House of Commons would be more fanatical in their pursuit of Hammond's killer than they were of him.

In the end, I didn't have to make a choice. The door opened, and Belle stepped inside. It took a moment to process that she was here. I'd spent the last hour trapped with Hammond in my past, and my future had just walked through the door. In the dimly lit room, her hair glowed, making it seem as if an angel had descended to save me from the darkness. But this was one hell I couldn't escape—not until its gatekeeper was dead.

Her bright eyes flickered to my hands, widening when she saw my leather gloves. If she'd had any doubt about what I was doing here, she didn't now. "You don't have to do this."

"That's where you're wrong, beautiful," I said softly, sadness filtering into my blood. I wished there was another way to protect her, but there wasn't. "You should leave."

"I'm not going anywhere." She planted her hands on her hips and stared me down. "Whatever you're planning, I'm part of it, too. I suppose it's not worth it to kill in order to protect me if I end up in jail, too." She pressed her lips into a thin line that dared me to challenge her on this.

"If I might interrupt," Hammond said.

For a moment I'd forgotten all about him.

"I don't really give a damn what you have to say," Belle told him. "I'm not here to save your life. I'm here to save his."

"You really chose an exceptional woman," he said to me.

An exceptionally headstrong one. How she'd managed to stay out of trouble before we met was beyond me.

"Could you shut up?" she snapped.

I probably should have set Belle on him months ago. He would never have stood a chance against her.

She crossed the room and dropped to my side. Reaching into her pocket, she withdrew a small object and set it on the desk.

The copper bullet.

All our eyes focused in on it.

"I found that in your trousers," she whispered. "I knew why you had it."

It had been a symbol. Nothing more. In our haste to leave Stuart Hall, I'd left behind the hunting rifle. But I'd kept the bullet—as a reminder that I'd made my choice.

"Do you know what that means to me?" I asked her. "It was a decision I made, to leave Stuart Hall and find Hammond."

I had no doubt she could fill in the rest of my plan.

"It's not that simple, Price. Wouldn't it be easier if it was?"

But it was that simple. "I would commit any crime to secure your safety. That's my choice."

"And you think I wouldn't do the same?" She grabbed my hands, squeezing them. "If you're in, I am, too."

"No." I closed my eyes and wrenched my hands from her grasp. Protecting her wasn't just a matter of security, it was about keeping her pure. In my world of sin, she'd been the only innocent person in my life. I refused to compromise that.

"You have a choice," she reminded me, "and so do I. We can walk away from here. We can leave, go to New York or Paris or Minnesota."

I crooked an eyebrow, smiling despite myself. "Have you ever been to Minnesota?"

"Focus," she commanded with a sigh. "You forgot about that bullet. Have you even looked for it?"

I hadn't, but it hardly proved anything. I'd chosen to believe that Hammond was actually going to pay for his crimes. Now I knew that wasn't the case. She was right. I hadn't gone looking for the bullet because I needed nothing more than my own two hands to end his life.

"You changed, Smith, and no matter what he's done, you deserve more than being pulled back into his world."

I glanced up, meeting Hammond's gaze.

"Listen to her. You have a conscience. You have something to live for. Don't throw that away," he advised.

"You are the last person I'm interested in hearing from." He would say anything to survive. After all, it was what he'd always done.

"And I'm the first," Belle said, gently calling my attention back to her. "At least, I better be."

"You are," I assured her, grinning.

"Then stop letting him have a say in our lives," she pled.

I stroked her pale cheek, torn between the man I wanted to be and the man I needed to be. "I'm not sure what I need or what I want."

"Me."

"Cocky," I accused as I picked the bullet up from the desk and shoved it into my pocket.

"Killing him is choosing him, not me." Her throat slid as she stood up. She stared down at me wordlessly and then headed toward the office door.

Him or her—that wasn't even a choice.

The door clicked shut behind her and neither Hammond nor I spoke. After a moment, I got up and walked across the room.

"You're making the right choice," Hammond called after me. "You'll understand that soon."

But I didn't care what he thought. The chill of the night air stung as wind whipped across my face. Belle was standing at the end of the street, staring at me. She didn't move as I strode toward her, increasing my pace until I was running. Catching her in my arms, I swung her around before I lowered her back to the ground.

"You. I choose you," I told her as the first snow began to fall, coating the world like a soft, wintery baptism.

We'd chosen each other.

CHAPTER TWENTY-SIX

We spent the next morning eating toast and jam in bed. After the last few weeks, all I needed was a proper lie-in with my wife, and after last night, I needed the rest. She hadn't told me she was ready to try again, but we'd already begun to practice. If anyone deserved a Christmas miracle, it was us.

Around midday, Belle crawled out of bed and returned fully dressed. "We should do something."

"I couldn't agree more, beautiful, but I don't think we need clothes for what I have in mind." Tossing off the sheets, I stroked my dick in invitation.

"Outside the house," she said dryly.

"Sex in public." I shrugged. "Works for me."

"Has anyone ever told you that you're a sex fiend?"

I shot her a crooked smile. "Coming from you, that's a compliment."

"Get dressed," she demanded.

"A month of marriage and you're already immune to my best panty-dropping grin." I shook my head as I pushed myself out of bed. "I guess the honeymoon is over."

"It's just beginning," she promised, darting out of the room before

I could drag her ass back into bed, "and if you need incentive, I didn't bother with knickers."

"That's not incentive," I called after her. "That's meeting expectations."

Walking into the closet, I stared at the suits hanging neatly on the racks. After a moment, I bypassed them and pulled a pair of jeans out of a drawer. Grabbing a button-down, I threw on the clothes. Later I would strip off her clothes and make her join me in the shower, where I could punish her for making me skip one now. My dick perked up at the thought of lathering up her perfect ass and spanking it until it glowed.

"Where are you taking me?" I asked as I joined her downstairs.

"I have a very dangerous mission for you," she murmured, nuzzling my jaw. "After-holidays sales."

I smirked at the idea. "Beautiful, you don't have to bargain shop."

"You are recently unemployed," she reminded me.

"Did I forget to mention that I really don't need to work another day in my life and I can still support your Louboutin habit?"

"Wrong answer." She shook her head. "You do have to work, because Bless is going to need legal counsel."

"I'll have to take a look at the benefits package before I commit." I ran a hand over her backside before giving it a quick smack.

"I think you'll find it's very..." She shifted, allowing her hands to drop to *my* benefits package. "Competitive."

I had no doubt I would. "I'd be happy to look over that now."

I didn't wait for her to respond before I'd thrown her over my shoulder and headed for the stairs. She didn't resist, which meant I'd be spanking her ass even earlier than I thought. Apparently Christmas was coming twice this year. But before I'd reached the second step, an insistent rapping on the door stopped me.

"If that is anyone short of Jesus Christ himself..." I grumbled.

Belle wriggled free and scurried over to the door.

Brexton Miles was on the other side. Yesterday he'd played the part of Edward's friend well. Today there was no question that he was all business. His black wingtips had been recently polished and his black wool coat fell just above his knee. He smiled politely, even as Belle rolled her eyes. Apparently she'd figured out why he had come over the day before.

"I don't suppose you two have read the paper?" he asked.

"Are you selling subscriptions?" I asked in a flat voice.

"Hammond is dead."

I'd known it was coming, and I searched for some sort of emotional response: relief, sadness, concern. But there was nothing. I'd given that man more than he deserved for far too long.

"Shot," Brexton continued. "The press found out somehow. It's a circus. The gun rights activists will be up in arms, if you'll pardon me, and the House of Commons will be conducting an inquisition, considering that his charges hadn't officially been dropped."

"Thanks for stopping by to let us know." Belle crossed her arms and glared at him. We both knew that royal security hadn't started making house calls.

"Can I have a moment?" he asked me.

I tipped my head in agreement. Placing my hand on Belle's shoulder, I leaned in. "I'll be right in."

"You know, I think I'm going to call Clara and set up a time to see Elizabeth."

I raised an eyebrow. "Are you certain that's a good idea?"

"I'm ready. I'm not going to miss out on my goddaughter's life. It won't change anything."

That was the woman I loved, but I hated to see her going through this. I had mourned the loss of our baby, but I knew I'd never felt it as strongly as she did. I couldn't. I'd barely had time to process the reality before it was stripped from me.

I stepped onto the front stoop and pulled the door shut behind me.

"I'm afraid I have to ask you a very delicate question." He glanced down the quiet street before finally leveling his gaze at me. "Did you kill Hammond?"

"I'm not sure if I should answer that without a lawyer present." I knew I hadn't. Belle did as well, but it was our word against a mountain of evidence until someone figured out who had pulled the trigger. Once they did, I would be the first to shake the killer's hand.

"Honestly," he suggested, "I have no interest in pursuing you, Price. I've seen the files. I know what you did for this investigation. You put yourself in grave danger. Some people might be able to overlook that, but I'm a military man. We live by a code."

"I'm afraid I'm a civilian."

"Don't sell yourself short," he stopped me. "You were willing to join our ranks. You sought out justice. That puts you pretty high on my list."

"I didn't kill him. I can't offer you more than my word." I stuck my hand in my pocket and pulled out the bullet Belle had brought me the night before. "And this. I've carried this with me for weeks. I was saving it for him. I had the opportunity last night, Brex. Do you know why I'm carrying this today? Because it represents my choice. Hammond was alive when I saw him last."

Brexton's green eyes narrowed, but a moment later he relaxed, shoving his hands in his coat pockets. "That's good enough for me."

"Do you have any other suspects?" I had my own list and it only had one name. Many people probably wanted him dead, but only one person I knew was capable of getting that close to him.

"Georgia Kincaid," he said as if reading my mind. "She's certainly capable of it. I like her for it, but she has an airtight alibi."

"Which I suppose you aren't interested in sharing." No matter how much I fought, I couldn't seem to free myself from the mud.

"I'll leave that up to her to decide." Brexton crossed his bulky arms.

"I'll be honest with you. I'm ready to wash my hands of this. There was a time when this was a nihilistic pursuit. Now I have something..."

"To live for?" he finished for me. His smile was tight as he considered this.

"Yes." To live for and so much more. "And she's waiting for me right now."

"I suppose you don't care who murdered him then?" he asked.

I placed my hand on the doorknob. "I suppose I only care that the bastard is dead."

"Even if this isn't over?"

I wanted him to take back those words, but he could no more *unspeak* them than I could *unhear* them.

"It's over for me." That was all that counted. Whoever had taken the initiative to shuffle Hammond off this mortal coil had nothing to do with me.

"We could use you," he said. "You have contacts within Hammond's circle. Whoever did this was making a power play."

Hammond had insinuated as much, but he'd also given me a parting gift.

No one will touch you now.

Hammond's words. I could only hope he was right.

"I've spent most of my life in his shadow, I'm stepping into the sun."

"I wish you the best of luck."

He wasn't going to press the issue. I'd opened the door before I realized why; turning back to him, I called out, stopping him on the steps. "She's working for you."

"I'm sorry?" he said casually.

"Never mind." Georgia and I were headed on different journeys. Maybe she was finally ready to go legit. Not that I was certain that Alexander or his new private security team were entirely on the up and up, but who was I to question a king?

He nodded, but I had no doubt that he knew exactly what I'd said. "Happy Christmas."

"You too."

Belle was leaning against the wall in the entry, chewing on her lip, as I stepped inside.

"It's over, beautiful."

"Do they suspect you? I can call Clara. She'll believe me," she said in a rush.

"I'm not a suspect." I didn't bother to tell her that Brexton's visit had been a mere formality. I was the obvious choice for a primary suspect. Now that he knew I wasn't responsible, he'd be forced to look for a bigger fish. It was a witch hunt I wasn't interested in, particularly because I didn't know where to start. Hammond had been the top of my food chain. Last night had been the first indication that his business extended much further than I'd suspected. I'd been privy to most of Hammond's personal and business matters, and I couldn't think of a single shred of evidence that he was working with someone else. There was nothing I could offer Brexton, and if he had Georgia, he didn't need me.

"Then it's over."

I didn't bother to remind her that I'd already told her this.

"Yes, beautiful."

It was over, but our lives were just beginning.

CHAPTER TWENTY-SEVEN

At the end of the week, while the rest of London rushed to the market for last minute champagne and hors d'oeuvres, I was on my way to the office. Lola had summoned me for an emergency business meeting earlier this morning. After fifteen minutes of panic-induced rambling, she finally assured me that she had good news to share. Given that I missed out on most of Bless's initial beta launch, I wasn't about to miss being around to celebrate even a small victory.

Lola was at the entrance, wrapped in a grey cashmere coat. As soon as she saw me, she held up a scarf. "No peeking."

"Seriously?"

"I'm always serious," she said, tying it around my head, "except for when I'm not."

"This feels like some sort of corporate team building exercise," I commented as she guided me inside the studio.

"Do you trust me?" she teased.

"That depends. Is this necessary?" I asked, my hands outstretched in front of me, afraid I'd walk into a rack of designer clothing.

"No," Lola said, "but it's pretty fun to watch."

I could hear the smirk in her voice. Whatever was waiting for me in the office must be pretty amazing if it had her this excited about it.

"Some people take New Year's Eve off," I grumbled good-naturedly.

"Those people aren't workaholics like we are," she reminded me. "Besides, there is no way you want to miss this. Okay, keep your eyes closed."

She tugged the scarf off my eyes and I stood there, feeling a bit idiotic. "This better not be a surprise party."

"It's not your birthday."

She had a good point. I could hear her flitting about the room, and I tried to zero in on exactly where her feet were falling for clues. Before I could decide if she was on my left or behind me, her movement ceased entirely.

"Ready?" she called.

"And more than willing."

"Open your eyes before you get any saucier."

It took me a few seconds of looking about before I zeroed in on where she was standing. The whiteboard where she'd started to count new subscribers read 999. I didn't even have time to start crying before she wiped off that number. Lola wrote 1000 with precise, teasing strokes, then stood back to admire her handiwork.

Within our second month of business, we'd already signed up a thousand clients. Things were moving more quickly than I ever could have imagined, and I knew I had Lola to thank.

"You did this." My hand fluttered to my mouth as I stared in shock.

"We did this. I don't know how many times I have to tell you," she corrected me.

I studied my business partner. She was already dressed for this evening's party in a stunning red gown with a crepe skirt that flowed to the ground. Its lacy top was nearly see-through, covering her breasts while revealing plenty of décolletage. Her dark hair was nearly black against the bright color and her creamy skin. "I take it you're going this evening."

"I am," she said with a sigh. "I can't wait to spend another holiday with all my coupled friends."

I dropped an arm around her shoulder and hugged her to me. "There has to be a few single ones in the lot."

"There are," she confirmed, "and they're wankers. I had to shag an unfortunate number of them to discover that."

"Go to Paris," I said suddenly.

"Right now?" she asked with a laugh.

"For the interview. Meet someone new. Have an affair." I winked at her. I loved London, but I understood how trapped a girl could feel in this city.

"You're the face of Bless, and we need you to start relationships with some of the major brands headquartered there."

"I already told you that I want you to take that job on." I hesitated for a moment before deciding to give her the real reason. "We do need to build relationships in Paris. I don't see how we can be in the industry without having contacts there, but Smith and I are going to start a family."

"Oh my God!" Lola's eyes flashed to my stomach as she reached for it. "Are you...?"

"No." I swallowed. *Choose faith.*

"You will be in no time. I swear Smith could knock a woman up just looking at her." She threw her hands up in surrender. "No offense. I'm just looking."

"None taken," I said dryly. I was well aware of Smith's effect on women. I'd fallen victim to it, after all. I could only hope she was right about the rest. "Anyway, since there's a good chance that I'll have cankles in a few months, I'm going to ask you to reconsider taking on Bless. Don't make me beg."

"You've talked me into it."

We both dissolved into squeals and giggles. If this was what hope felt like, I could get used to it.

"Speaking of tonight's party." Lola's mouth curved into a mischievous grin. "Jenny Packham sent you a Christmas present, and I bet you'll look fabulous in it."

"Couture Christmas presents? I should have started this business years ago." I snatched the box out of her hands. "Maybe we should share."

Lola turned around, her gown swishing elegantly as she spun. "I already got mine."

If that was what she'd received, I couldn't wait to open mine. I considered begging out of tonight's affair. Part of me wanted to hide away at home with Smith and enjoy being able to relax for the first time in a long while. But a girl couldn't resist a night out if there was a new dress involved. Removing the lid, I gasped as I caught sight of the silk charmeuse gown inside. As I carefully lifted, the fabric caught the light, revealing a subtle champagne sheen. Delicately hand-beaded crystals shimmered at the shoulders.

"Wow!" Lola was at my side, studying it instantly. "That's gorgeous. A little bridal actually. Perfect for a newlywed."

I held it up to me, admiring how the neckline dipped, meeting with the elegant twist at the waistline. This was the dress I should have worn for Smith on our wedding day. Tonight I would wear it to ring in the New Year at Clarence House as a symbol of starting over.

For once I had no problems with the security gate at Clarence House, but it was probably easier today given that the guard had a guest list. As I pulled into the private drive, I reconsidered. Guards milled along the perimeter of the house. Apparently Alexander didn't trust the fence to keep unwelcome visitors out anymore. Given what he had been through, I couldn't blame him. I could only hope that now that Hammond was gone, he'd be able to loosen up.

That was probably wishful thinking on my part. My best friend had married one of the most powerful men in the world, so things were never going to return to normal. There would always be security and gates. My own happily ever after hadn't come at the cost of my personal freedom. But through everything that had happened since I met Smith, I'd been seriously neglecting Clara. Of course, having to pass a security check made it a lot more difficult to pop by for a glass of wine. That was just an excuse, though, and I knew it. I'd been so absorbed with Smith that I'd put her on the back burner. She'd done the same when she met Alexander, but I had been there on the day of her wedding. I'd held her hand during her first sonogram. I'd sat with her while Alexander buried his father.

Maybe it was the sheer amount of tragedy and pain she'd experienced in the last year that had made me hesitant to bring my own troubles to her doorstep. Yes, I had been trying to protect her, but I couldn't deny that I'd also been avoiding her, especially since we'd returned from Stuart Hall.

I discovered Clara in her room. Her hair hung around her shoulders and she was rocking Elizabeth frantically. Judging by her tiny, mewling cries, Elizabeth was having none of it.

"I haven't even had a shower yet." She was on the verge of tears, and I leapt into action, gently taking Elizabeth from her arms.

I stood, rocking the baby, until she quieted again. It wasn't much help, but it effectively warded off tears from both parties.

"You're good with her," she said softly.

I swallowed, searching for the strength I'd found this afternoon. How could I love a child this much and still hurt so badly?

"Not as good as you are," I said after a few moments of silence.

Clara dismissed the compliment with a wave of her hand. "I'm her mother. That's hardly magic."

I bit down on my lip. It felt like magic—wondrous and just out of reach of reality.

"Alexander won't budge on getting a nanny?" I needed to change the subject from motherhood. Unfortunately at the moment, the topic seemed to bleed into every possible new discussion we might start.

She shook her head. "Honestly, I'm not ready either. My mother has watched her for a while, but you know how giving Madeline is with her time."

Madeline was light years ahead of my own mother, but she wasn't exactly maternal either. It was something Clara and I had bonded over early on in our relationship.

"Lola's been busy," she said absentmindedly, "and of course, there's Edward, but I think he's in denial over David's desire to have kids. The coronation is in a few weeks, and I think I'm going to be pushing a pram in the church."

My eyes narrowed. I hadn't been around to help. My absence had been the reason Lola wasn't available, and there was no way I would have let Edward get away with running scared. "I'm sorry. It's my fault you haven't had more help."

"How is it your fault?" Clara laughed at me.

"Your sister has been busy helping me, and I wasn't around to kick Edward in the arse." *And I wasn't here at all.*

I should have been the one here with her. I always had been.

"You've had enough going on," Clara said, but her eyes darted around me, avoiding mine.

"And?" I pressed. There was more. I couldn't mend things with her if I didn't know badly I'd broken our relationship.

"You don't seem very interested."

I shrank back, freezing on the spot. Elizabeth released a shriek of protest that we'd stopped moving, but I could only shake my head.

"I love her," I whispered.

"I see it in your face when you hold her." Clara sighed. I understood her hesitation. Considering how rocky our last few encounters had been, was she really going to risk making things worse?

"It's not that."

I'd found the courage to tell Lola that I wanted to have a baby earlier. It had been the first time I'd admitted it to myself, but I wasn't certain I had the strength to talk about the miscarriage. It was still so raw that I was scared I'd reopen the wound by even thinking about it. I'd been surviving it by ignoring it.

"Whatever it is," Clara said, "I'm here for you."

The implication was clear. I'd stood by her through the volatile changes in her life. Why wouldn't I assume she would be there too?

But it wasn't that simple. It wasn't that I wanted to keep it from her. I simply didn't want to relive it.

I forced a smile. "Everything's fine."

"Bollocks," she accused.

I raised an eyebrow. "Someone's ready to be queen."

"Don't start," she warned me, leaving little doubt in my mind that I was right. "Something's up. I know you, Belle Stuart. I mean, Belle Price. Gah, I can't get used to that."

"You really want to know?" I walked to the bed and sat down on the edge next to her, still cradling Elizabeth in my arms.

"I really do. I know some of what happened to you, and I hate that I couldn't be there for you," she said apologetically. "But I know there's more. Edward does, too, and we're both too afraid to ask you."

She didn't seem to be having trouble now.

Clara moved closer to me, reaching to relieve me of the baby, but I turned away. If I was going to face this, I would face all of it.

"I had a miscarriage." To my surprise, it hurt a little less to say it aloud this time. I'd expected pain, and it was there. But instead of the clawing, destructive pain I'd expected, this ache was duller.

She didn't say anything. Instead she wrapped her arms around me silently. We sat that way for a long time. Elizabeth sleeping peacefully in my arms and her mother holding me. The circle of life—mother and daughter—had surrounded me, and after a few minutes the pain faded, as if the broken pieces of my heart had begun to fuse once more.

"I don't know what to say," she finally admitted.

"I think that's okay." My throat was raw but I refused to cry.

"It's better than saying something terrible," she pointed out.

Despite myself, I laughed. She joined me, but our amusement evaporated as swiftly as it had arrived.

"I want to ask you a million questions."

I looked at her and nodded. "And I think I want to answer them."

Clara's hand dropped to mine and she squeezed it. "You don't have to carry burdens alone."

She was right. I didn't. My grief had isolated me, and I'd chosen to believe that it was my responsibility to bear it. Telling Clara had lightened that weight. I didn't have to face this alone. Just knowing that proved I was going to survive this.

"Were you trying?" she asked.

"I think Smith has super sperm," I admitted. "That and I missed some pills what with the death threat and attempted murder."

"That's understandable." She paused. "I wish you would have told me."

"It's just...you went through the same thing, but your story had a completely different ending," I whispered.

"Your story isn't over," she reminded me.

And then it was all coming out. Every fear I'd had since I met Smith. All the ugliness and all the beauty. I recounted our impromptu wedding in detail, down to the fact that I'd been wearing my pajamas.

"I haven't told anyone that."

"It just shows how fashion forward you are," she teased.

A rap at the door startled us from conversation. Alexander poked his head in, smiling widely when his blue eyes fell on his wife.

"You want me to take her so you can get showered?" he asked.

Clara opened her mouth, but I jumped in. "I got her. It looks like you could use one, too."

"Thanks, Belle."

"In fact, how about I come by a bit more often?" I suggested. "I need to spend more time with my goddaughter."

Clara and Alexander glanced at each other.

"Yes," Clara said, raising a hand in his direction. "If you have an objection, I don't want to hear it."

"No objection here," he said in an amused voice. "Especially if it means I can take a shower with you."

"I'm going to pretend I didn't hear that," I called.

But the two of them had already dashed off to the sanctuary of the loo. I looked down at Elizabeth. "I guess it's you and me, kid."

She smiled in her sleep, tugging at my heart. I'd come home, not only to Smith, but to everyone in my life and I was here to stay.

CHAPTER TWENTY-EIGHT

When Alexander and Clara finally reappeared, I was dozing in a chair by their hearth with Elizabeth tucked snugly on my chest. I cracked open an eye as Alexander lifted her off me.

"Did you have fun? I was so bored I fell asleep."

He grinned widely at me. "Thanks for that."

Apparently I'd just volunteered myself to be the sexy times nanny. At least their walls were thick.

"I'm sorry that took so long," Clara chirped as she bustled into the room. There was no mistaking the glow radiating from her cheeks.

"I feel like the fairy godmother of orgasms." I stretched my arms as I stood to ease the stiffness lingering after holding the baby for so long.

"It's all yours," Clara said, tilting her head toward the loo. "Guests are going to be here in an hour so I'm going to be playing Russian Roulette with my closet."

A quick check in the mirror revealed I only needed to touch up my make-up and lipstick. That left the question of my hair, but for now, I did know what I was going to wear. My stomach fluttered as I unzipped the garment bag I'd hung my gown in before I left Bless. I felt instantly glamorous as I stepped into it. I'd excused myself to the ensuite bath, so that Clara wouldn't ask why I wasn't wearing knickers. The body-skimming fabric of my dress wouldn't have allowed for them, but that wasn't the reason I'd left them in my garment bag. If I had my way, I'd be ringing in the New Year with more than a kiss.

When I exited the loo, Clara popped her head out of her closet, poised to ask a question. Instead she stared at me.

I ran my palms down the silky fabric anxiously. "Too much?"

"Not remotely," she said, shaking her head. "You look incredible. Smith isn't going to be able to keep his hands off of you."

"That's the idea." I winked at her.

"You are giving me serious doubts about my postpartum body," she admitted.

I followed her into the closet as she began holding up dresses. The good news was that she had dozens to choose from, but that wouldn't soothe her fears about how she looked.

"Has Alexander stopped shagging you?" I asked.

She snorted as she pulled a velvety black dress off the hanger. "I thought he was going to die after Elizabeth was born and he had to wait six weeks for sex."

"So one of the sexiest men alive, and I'm quoting multiple magazines on that, is obsessed with you." I stared pointedly at her, waiting for my words to sink in before I continued, "Wear sweatpants if you want, you're already winning."

She pressed the velvet gown to her bust, sticking her tongue out at me.

"Very mature," I teased her. I hadn't realized until this moment how much I'd missed just hanging out with Clara. At university, this had been the norm. Now our lives made it difficult to find the time. My list of resolutions for the upcoming year had just gotten a little longer.

"This one?" she asked. "Or do I look like I'm going to a funeral?"

"It's a black tie event, it's perfect. Do you think I should wear my hair up or down?" I asked Clara as she began to dress.

"What does Smith prefer?"

"It's never come up," I admitted. On one hand, my husband liked to kiss my neck. On the other hand, he liked to pull my hair. Either way I was coming out a winner on this one.

"Well, based on the advice you just gave me, you could probably wear a ponytail. That man is head over heels for you."

It was a condition I shared with him. "It's that obvious, huh?"

"In other news, the sky is blue," she said in a flat voice. "Help me zip this up."

Half an hour later, we stood in front of the mirror appraising our reflections. Clara's chestnut locks were pinned up in an elegant twist, revealing the elegant slope of her pale neck. Her raven gown dipped in the front, displaying another sliver of creamy skin.

I'd kept my hair down, allowing it to spill down the back of my silk dress. The fabric skimmed my breasts, and through some peculiar alchemy, I felt sexy and timeless at the same time.

"We are so very doable," I announced.

"Doability? Is that a unit of measurement?" Edward's jovial voice called from the doorway.

I tossed a towel at him, but he ducked. "A gentlemen should knock. What if we were naked?"

"Sorry, ladies, despite your *doability*, I'm still not interested."

Clara glared at him in the mirror. "David will be thrilled to hear that."

He crossed his arms, one eyebrow cocked inquisitively. In his tuxedo, he looked the part of the powerful man. He'd smoothed his usually wild hair and left his glasses at home. The absence of his two signature looks transformed him, showcasing his strong jawline and straight nose.

"You're going to break hearts tonight." I hugged him carefully so as not to smudge make-up on his jacket.

"I'm afraid that's a cross I shall have to bear," he said in mock solemnity. He reached up to fiddle with his bowtie.

"Stop," I ordered him. "You're making it worse."

As I adjusted it, I drank in the moment. Until recently, these two people had comprised most of my world. As I prepared to start the new year with Smith, it meant everything that they would be here as well. We had our separate lives now—loves that each of us had fought for—but we also had one another.

Edward crooked both of his elbows for us. Clara and I each took a side, flanking him. He turned us toward the mirror, and in my best friends' reflections, I saw the same understanding.

No matter what the next year brought, we'd get through it together, just as we'd weathered the storms of this one.

"Forget power couples." Edward's mouth quirked into a grin. "As much as I appreciate looking at us, we should probably make an appearance at the party."

As we reached the hallway, Clara halted mid-step. "I forgot something. You two go ahead. Don't make your men wait."

"She's probably arranged for another quick shag with Alexander," Edward whispered as she disappeared back into her master suite.

"Quick?" I repeated dryly, remembering how long they had showered this afternoon. "We might miss the whole party if we wait for them."

As we reached the stairs, Edward paused and wove his fingers with mine. "I don't think I say this enough, but I'm really glad my brother decided to shamelessly snog your best friend in public."

"It was the start of a beautiful friendship," I agreed.

He shook his head, laughter playing at his lips. Despite his dashing appearance, there was a boyish glimmer in his eyes.

"What?" I asked. "What are you up to?"

"Nothing." It was a lie. He didn't even try to hide it.

"Spill, Your Highness."

"Too late now," he told me, looking over my shoulder.

I twisted my head to follow his gaze. Clara had returned, carrying a bouquet of slender calla lilies.

"What's going on?" I repeated, but I was starting to understand.

When Clara held out the simple bouquet, I knew I was right.

"You tried to get married without us," she told me.

"And we both feel we need to successfully get through a wedding before it's my turn," Edward added.

Clara shook her head. "Don't listen to him."

She leaned in to hug me, leaving enough space so she didn't crush the flowers. I couldn't process what was happening, but when Edward tugged my arm, guiding me toward the top of the steps, I didn't hesitate.

Smith stood at the bottom, beaming up at me. His hands were folded in front of him, as if he was restraining himself. His tuxedo had been perfectly tailored to highlight the broadness of his shoulders, and I spotted a square of champagne silk in the pocket. Our gazes met, and a jolt of electricity shot through me. The first time I'd locked eyes with his stormy green ones, I'd felt it. I hadn't understood then that it wasn't a physical reaction but rather an epiphany.

My life had led me to this man. From this day forward, he would be by my side. The realization swelled in my chest until my whole body ached with my love for him.

There was no point trying to compose myself. Smith had undone me. He'd been doing it since that day in his office. The only way to center myself was through him.

"I can't believe you guys did this," I whispered to Edward as we descended the first step.

"We didn't," he said meaningfully, "but we helped. Your husband is more of a romantic than he lets on."

And that beautiful mystery of a man was mine.

If I hadn't been wearing five-inch heels, I might have ran down the stairs and into his arms. But as I took each one, more came into focus. It wasn't the elite party I'd expected to attend this evening, but it was perfect in its exclusivity. Behind Smith, a small crowd of familiar faces was gathered, but I couldn't bring myself to study the cluster of family and friends. I only had eyes for him.

When we reached the bottom, Edward unhooked my arm with a sigh and took my hand. Smith moved toward us, accepting my hand from him. The simple act stole my breath.

"Marry me?" Smith whispered.

"I already did," I reminded him as he brought my hand to his lips and kissed it softly. "I'm willing to do it again though."

"That's good enough for me, beautiful." He drew me to his side, our hands twining together in an unyielding grip. I wasn't letting go of him ever again.

Alexander stood behind us, and we turned to face him.

"It's come to my attention that the two of you got married in America," he said, his voice booming through the space, "and obviously I can't have that. So let's try this again."

Everyone laughed, setting the perfect tone for our second wedding. I'd chosen Smith before, when the world around us was dark and unforgiving. Then I'd chosen faith that we could see each other through it all. I had faltered in that belief after, but despite that, we'd clung to one another. We hadn't given up.

Now enveloped by the love of those that had seen us to this moment, we spoke our vows once more. We were married again in front of them.

There was no apprehension. No doubt. When Alexander prompted me to speak those two simple words, my voice rang clearly across the room.

"I do."

"I'd ask you two to exchange rings," Alexander said loudly, "but when I asked Smith to get them for me, he said 'You can pry them off our dead fingers.'"

Laughter rippled in waves around us. My own joy bubbled inside me as Smith clasped my hand, rubbing my wedding band. He cocked an eyebrow.

"Can you blame me?" he mouthed.

I couldn't. Once I'd found the courage to wear this ring, I knew I'd never take it off again.

"So show everyone that you've made him an honest man," Alexander prompted.

We raised our clasped hands to the cheers of the crowd. There might have been tears elsewhere in the room, but there was no room for them in my heart. Over the last year, I'd grieved and I'd feared. Today I celebrated.

"You may kiss your bride," Alexander told Smith, adding, "again."

But my husband already had his hand coiled around my neck, and as our lips met, a peaceful certainty settled over me.

I had found my forever.

CHAPTER TWENTY-NINE

The crowd erupted around us, and when I finally forced myself to relinquish my wife, the guests rushed toward us. Everywhere I turned, I was met with a handshake or a tight hug. I hadn't bothered with my own guest list. Before tonight, the only person I could count on was the one standing next to me now.

But none of that mattered as the people who loved Belle welcomed me into all their lives. I'd spent my life paying for my family, and she had given me one freely.

Even as we passed through the small crowd, I held her hand tightly. After the initial flurry of well wishes, I pulled her toward an unoccupied corner. I wanted a moment alone with my wife, but before we reached it, Clara and Alexander caught us.

Clara embraced her in a fierce hug, but she didn't try to draw my wife away. Judging from the hand Alexander kept on the small of Clara's back, she had some experience with a protective lover.

With his free hand, Alexander reached out and clapped me on the shoulder. As the women we loved whispered happily, no words passed between us. He and I hadn't always seen eye to eye, but we had found common ground in our love for our wives.

Soon we were joined by Edward and David. I took one look at the two of them and snatched Belle's bouquet.

She turned to me in surprise, but she couldn't help but laugh when I thrust it into David's hands.

"I thought we'd skip the tossing of the bouquet," I informed the group, "and give it to someone who truly needs it."

"I expect an invitation," a voice cut through the laughter, and we parted to make way for Belle's aunt.

Jane barely knew me, an oversight I'd been working to remedy since Christmas. She had championed me based entirely on instinct. I owed her more than my thanks—I owed her my life. Because Belle was my life.

I braced myself when she beckoned me closer.

"You won her," she whispered.

The implication of her words settled over me. I had—with the help of everyone here. I hadn't always considered these people my friends, and I had a long way to go before I could truly know most of them, but I was as committed to that as I was to my marriage. Because these people were more than friends, they were my family.

"If you don't mind, I'd like a moment with my husband," Belle announced, not bothering to hide the suggestiveness of her request.

More than a few knowing glances were shared before my fledgling family released us. Apparently they all understood the all-consuming appetite that came with true love.

Belle turned and immediately froze. Tearing my eyes from my wife, I looked up to see the only person from *my* past here this evening.

Georgia walked toward us, abandoning Brexton to a group of people I didn't recognize.

The two would never understand each other. I was the pole where the two volatile forces of each woman's nature collided. But as we stood in an awkward cluster, Belle dropped my hand and embraced her.

"Don't hurt him," Georgia said as she broke away. "He's one of the few good ones."

She sighed, as if exhausted from the emotional effort she'd exerted.

"I won't," Belle vowed.

"We're never getting out of here," I murmured to my wife as the first bluesy notes of "Wild Horses" began to play. "But I have an idea."

Sweeping Belle into my arms, we started to dance. A few others joined in, but they faded into the background as I held my wife.

"I can't believe you got Clara to play the Rolling Stones," she said.

"I had to concede on a few other items," I admitted. "There's a band setting up as we speak. We get this one song."

She laughed, and it was the most beautiful melody I'd ever heard. "I'll have to thank her."

"I think we have a lot to thank them for." Pulling her closer to me, I lowered my lips to her ear. "Like the chance to have a proper wedding night."

"We've been married nearly two months," she pointed out, but she swallowed as she spoke. In the midst of everything, we'd barely had time to celebrate our insane decision to elope, let alone enough time spent alone.

"I think it's safe to say we're still in the honeymoon stage." I nipped at her earlobe and she moaned softly; the sound was lost in the beat of the music. Only I had heard it, which was exactly how I liked it.

She belonged to me. I'd fought for her and I'd won her, and I was going to spend every day for the rest of my life proving I deserved her.

"Maybe you'll get along better with my friends now."

I spun her around and dipped her back slightly, stealing her breath for a fleeting beautiful moment.

"I'll consider it, beautiful." I winked at her, unprepared to admit that I'd already made that commitment.

"You're trouble, Price."

"I think that's why you like me, Mrs. Price."

She raised an eyebrow. "I'm not used to that yet."

"Later"—I leaned in and whispered in her ear—"I'm going to make you come so many times that when I call you Mrs. Price, you'll be brainwashed into accepting it."

"I suppose hyphenation isn't up for debate then?" But she wasn't in the least bit put off by my caveman need to possess her. There was a hint of pleasure in her voice.

"You like it, don't you?" I asked as I pressed her tight body against my hardening cock. "That I need to own you."

"It makes me feel like I'm the one in charge," she said with a breathy giggle as I kissed her throat.

"You are, beautiful." I moved down to her collarbone. "Until the ropes and leashes come out."

"We're going to get kicked out of our own party." But she made no move to stop me.

I did it for her, resuming a proper waltzing position and putting enough space between our bodies to keep me from getting too excited. A few more seconds and my primal side was going to have her naked on the dance floor.

"You can keep Stuart if you want," I offered as we moved gracefully around the room, swiftly enough that I couldn't make out any faces except hers, which is exactly how I wanted it to be.

"Honestly, I have no attachment to that name," she admitted in a soft voice. "And now that the estate is gone, I think it's time I liberate myself from the whole sordid family history."

It was an impulse I understood. Despite my misgivings, I'd invited her mother. I hadn't been surprised when she declined.

The music had effectively distracted the crowd, and I whirled Belle in a circle, moving us slowly toward the door to the back garden.

No one noticed as we exited. It was unseasonably warm for this time of year, but still cold.

Against my will, I released my hold on her, but only to slip my jacket off. Placing it around her shoulders, I drew her back to me.

"I'm afraid our only means of escape may be the cold."

"I'm not cold," she whispered.

Neither was I. It was impossible to feel anything but the warmth of her body against mine. We stayed like that, bodies pressed together, as we stared up at the stars.

"You gave those to me," she said in a soft voice.

"I'll give you more than that," I promised.

I would give her my life. My breath. My soul.

But I didn't have to—she already possessed them.

"I think we're going to miss the countdown," I warned her.

"You're the only person I want to kiss at midnight," she said breathlessly. "Actually I was thinking..."

She didn't have to finish the thought.

It didn't matter that it was cold. Neither of us felt the chill as I hitched up her dress to reveal her bare cunt. I lifted her into my arms, and Belle's legs coiled around my waist. She didn't buck or strain to press against me. Even as the final moments of the year ticked to its end, I knew we both sensed the same thing.

We had all the time in the world.

Carrying her into the shadows of the majestic house, I braced her against the stucco's pale facade. Her fingers found my belt and unfastened it deftly, freeing my cock. Belle shifted, opening herself to me, and in one swift motion, I was inside her. We moved silently in the moonlight. My eyes never left hers as two became one.

She was my beginning. My infinity. There was no end to us.

From inside the countdown began, the cries of the crowd carrying faintly on the wind, and with each second, I thrust deep, burying myself inside her.

The new year began as she cried out, her cunt contracting around me. I found my own release in hers as the first notes of "Auld Lang Syne" began to play.

We'd been reborn in one another. I had found myself in her, and she'd given me the strength to leave my past behind. Now as fireworks burst overhead, celebrating the promise of a fresh start, I brought my lips to hers in an unspoken vow.

She was the reward I hadn't deserved, the light that led me out of the shadows.

"You captured my heart," I whispered.

"And I'm never letting it go," she promised.

COMPLETE ME

CHAPTER ONE

WASHINGTON D.C.

THE QUEEN'S BEDROOM, considered well-suited to visiting monarchy by the White House staff, felt as stodgy and antiquated as the name suggested. It had certainly received the title when my grandmother wore the crown, because my own wife was anything save boring. Despite the overtly Victorian femininity of the wall-coverings and lacy bedspread, Clara's presence breathed a vitality into the space. She stirred in her sleep and my breath caught even as I felt a familiar restlessness awakening in me.

Her rich, brown hair fanned over the pillowcase as a serenity passed over her fair features, and her lips began to move silently in her dreams. Propping myself up on my elbow, I studied her and wondered who she was talking to. While it might be pointless to be jealous of the time she spent asleep, I couldn't help it. I couldn't possess her in her dreams. For my irrational side—which too often overrode my common sense—it was unbearable.

Maybe that's why I felt the need to wake her so often for nocturnal activities.

The anatomical center of my irrationality twitched in agreement at the thought, and my hand went to it. I stroked myself absently. How early was too early to wake her for morning sex? It was difficult to determine given how cocked up our sleep schedule had been since arriving in Seattle a little over a week ago. Since then we'd visited three more U.S. cities on our goodwill tour. At least the capitol was our last stop. Between traveling and our daughter's teething-induced crankiness, Clara was perpetually knackered.

Still, she never said no.

"Are you warming up for something?" she murmured. Her lashes fluttered as she eyed me drowsily.

"I didn't want to wake you." I didn't add that I would have woken her anyway. Although I took pride in my self-control, I was glaringly deficient in that avenue where it came to my wife. When I had her alone I needed to be touching her.

Clara's laughter lifted some of the never-ceasing weight from my chest. Perhaps my obsession stemmed from the miraculous balm of her presence. She'd always been able to alleviate the burdens I carried with me, even though the pressures in my life had increased exponentially since she came into it. She bound me as she released me. It was the great paradox of our love that we saved each other by chaining ourselves to lives of duty.

"You would have woken me anyway," she accused, stretching her slender arms over her head as she displayed her uncanny ability to read my thoughts.

The movement caught my attention and I seized my chance. Rolling on top of her, I snatched her hands and held them. "Is that a complaint, poppet?"

Her body responded with a comforting awareness of my dominance. Clara's legs fell open, softening in welcome and her breathing shifted to shallow, eager panting as she purred the only words I needed to hear. "Yes, please."

I accepted her invitation, releasing my grip on her only long enough to pluck free the sash that held the bed curtains to the post. She didn't protest as I gently tied her wrist to the bed. Moving my knee against her bare cunt as a gage, I decided she was more than content by the idea of a morning play session.

"I'm not certain Americans approve of bondage so early in the morning." But she stretched her free arm toward the other post even as she spoke.

I couldn't hold back my arrogance as I smirked down at her. "I don't play by their rules."

I cinched her wrists tighter to prove my point and was rewarded with a warm surge of arousal.

"Should the Queen be tied up in her own bedroom?" She loved to rile me up, knowing that it would pay dividends in how rough I'd get. The saucier she got, the more I needed to dominate her. Like most couples our sex life ran the gamut of slow and sensual to clawing and primal. Unlike most couples, it ran that gamut daily.

"If she's in the King's bed, she should be." Sinking back on my heels, I appreciated the sight of my wife tied up and helpless. Thankfully, the house was large and Elizabeth was with the nanny down the hall, because I felt inspired to make her scream. Clara's breasts spilled from her silky nightgown and I snapped the fragile straps to release them entirely. Moving down her body, I sucked the soft mound, drawing her nipple into my mouth. While I might be impatient to get her beneath me, I never minded taking my time once I had her there. Quiet moans escaped from her and I increased my suction until I was practically biting the soft flesh. Clara arched toward me, her hips beginning to wiggle as she searched for relief. I loved watching my wife come but guiding her toward the edge was arguably even better. Turning this beautiful, intelligent woman into mass of incoherent desire was only fair since she reduced me to that primal state every time she walked into a room.

"Don't you have appointments today?" She pressed her body desperately to mine.

"Not for hours," I said with a mouthful of her creamy breast. I hadn't bothered to tell her how early I'd decided to start my day. I had no doubt that the time would pass too quickly for both of our likings.

"X!" she demanded through gritted teeth.

I withdrew and raised an eyebrow. Questioning my authority in the bedroom would only earn her more time on her back. I suspected she knew that. "You're being impatient."

"And you're being infuriating!" Her hands curled over her restraints as if she was testing them.

"Don't think you're getting out of those so easily," I informed her even as I settled between her thighs. Stroking the head of my cock down her swollen seam, I grinned at the amusement she couldn't quite hide from her answering glare. Hoisting her legs around my hips, I held her there, stretching her long body between the bed posts and my groin, and waited.

"Please." She licked her lips, her eyes going glassy as she asked again. "Please. Please."

I groaned, unable to resist her when she began to beg, and thrust inside her. Her muscles immediately contracted around my shaft as I drove her toward release. She cried out, splitting apart. I'd taken her over the edge, but once again she'd brought me to my knees.

THE OVAL OFFICE LOOKED FAR MORE CEREMONIAL THAN official with the camera crew shooting in front of the President's desk. The room itself was decorated in shades of ivory and yellow, but the color palette did little to warm the cool atmosphere. It wasn't unreasonable for the White House to film my visit, but it didn't lend itself to natural conversation. Having never met the new Commander-in-Chief of the United States, I had to be on my best behavior. I only hoped he would be as well.

"Alexander, welcome." President Williams tipped his head in a small greeting as he rose from his chair. It was acknowledgment of our shared power, but not a bow. For that I was grateful. If there was one thing I loved about America, it was that no one routinely felt the need to prostrate themselves in my presence.

Williams was about the age of my father, but the two had never officially met. He'd taken office shortly before the assassination that claimed the King's life. But age is where the similarities ended. Albert had been quintessentially British in his looks and demeanor. At least, in public. Williams was every bit the American head of state right down to the red power tie. Despite his years, the lines on his face only gave him an air of wisdom that matched his salt and pepper hair, and, like most Americans foisted into the spotlight, he looked more like a movie star than a bedraggled politician. He was the on-camera commander, whose power was limited by the large congress of lawmakers also elected by the people. That was one position we were both in.

"Congratulations on your ascension. I had hoped to share your joy, but after the wedding, it was felt that..." He trailed away, allowing my memory to recall the events of my wedding day.

"Of course." I allowed a tight smile. It was polite to offer his solicitations, naturally, but no matter how much time had passed I had never put my wedding day behind me. Williams had been in attendance for the ceremony. Considering the circumstances, he, along with several other powerful dignitaries, had sent their regrets when invited to my coronation. I couldn't blame them. If I could have skipped the ritual I would have, too. "We've been negligent, as well. Clara and I planned to visit your country much earlier. Life and politics got in the way."

"Don't they always?" He gestured to a chair next to his, and I took it. "What is your lovely wife up to today?"

"Motherhood," I said stiffly. Clara would not always be able to avoid the camera, but for the time being I was content to enable her desire to stay off screen. I still hadn't warmed to the idea of sharing her with the world.

"I feel certain our special relationship would be even more special now that you're married to an American," the president said light-heartedly as he adjusted his suit coat before taking his seat.

Annoyance surged through me, and I did my best to hide it. This man and this country had no claim to my wife. I couldn't exactly tell him that though, especially not during a televised interview. "I think you'll find that Clara is as American as I am."

We laughed, but neither of us were amused. Williams's predecessor had been known for his ease in awkward situations. It hadn't been a strong enough quality to get him reelected. Now the atmosphere in the Oval Office had the same wary tension of an impending cock fight. This was what happened when you put two alpha males into a room. There was no punchline, only a quiet struggle for power.

"I heard she prefers coffee," the Secretary of State joined in, her tone effusive. At least, Williams had appointed someone adept at dismantling tension to his cabinet. It was a particularly keen appointment since she handled most of the administration's foreign policy.

"I'm working on that," I admitted. The good-natured ribbing had the intended effect and the conversation shifted into an easygoing conversation between the heads of two sovereign nations. About an hour later, during a rousing debate between the merits of American football versus European football, the camera crews began to dismantle their equipment.

"This way, please," an aide showed the crews out of the office, and the atmosphere changed again.

Williams slumped in his seat, switching off his on-camera persona and becoming another man. "Scotch?"

"Please."

A moment later, an aide dutifully delivered the drinks as a young, nervous man joined us.

"Alexander, allow me to introduce my press secretary Richard May. He's here to keep us on track for the press conference."

I rose and shook the man's hand as he declined the offering of a Scotch. "I do apologize for sticking you back in front of a camera so soon."

"I was born in front of a camera," I said flatly. It wasn't technically true, but it may as well have been. I'd never known what it was like to be in public without someone filming me. My only real sanctuary from that fact had been during my time on the war front.

"Of course," May said absently as he shuffled through some papers. "I imagine that most of their questions will be fairly soft. They'll ask about Clara and your daughter."

I forced myself to nod. Despite my desire to keep my wife and child out of the spotlight, it was futile. I did my best to keep a firm line when it came to the press though, especially given how vicious the media had been during our courtship. As much as possible, I wanted Elizabeth to have a normal life, however unlikely the possibility was.

"Then there's the Edward issue."

"I hope you're speaking about an upcoming magazine article." This time I didn't bother to hide my annoyance. I'd been warned by own people that this might be brought up abroad.

"We've briefed the corps on the topics that they're allowed to broach," the president assured me, "but freedom of the press means we can't tell them what they can ask."

I didn't miss the none-too-subtle dig. "Britain has it as well."

"Then you know the trouble it can cause." Williams spread his hands apologetically, and I nodded.

There had been some negative attention regarding my brother's engagement in the tabloids. But Edward's decision to come out of the closet had been largely met with enthusiasm. For most it signaled that the monarchy was no longer an archaic relic, but there were always dissenters.

"I'm prepared to take the fifth," I joked, doing my best to sound as if the subject didn't irk me.

"I think he'll do just fine." Williams winked at May. "Are we ready then?"

May trembled a little as he nodded his head. There wasn't enough anti-anxiety medicine in the world to counter the stress of his job. It was remarkable that the man was allowed in front of the camera. As we headed toward the briefing room, Williams lagged behind. I took the signal and followed suit.

"I am sorry that we weren't at your coronation." It was a surprisingly sincere apology for a man who had fought to command the room when we first met. "Our security teams felt the risk outweighed the duty, and, speaking man to man, my first concern is always for my wife."

"It's understandable." I could appreciate a man putting his wife first. Where my own safety was concerned, I rarely cared, but I'd surround Clara with an army if she'd allow me. "If it were up to me, Clara wouldn't have come either."

Williams tugged at his necktie, and I realized he was holding something back. After a few seconds, he continued. "Our reports suggest that there might have been a larger plot in the works."

"Ours as well." So it wasn't just the British Secret Service concerned over the assassination. Our troubles had caught the attention of the CIA, too.

"I'm happy to pass along the intelligence we have. I'm sorry to say that most of the information hasn't panned out."

"Please," I accepted tersely. Then it wasn't just their trails that had gone cold, but ours as well. It was tempting to believe that the threat to my family had ended with the murder of Jack Hammond. The problem with accepting it was that someone had seen fit to murder the man who by all accounts was responsible for my father's death. If Smith Price, my personal source of information within Hammond's network, hadn't been the one to take Hammond's life—as he claimed—then someone else had been.

"Unless you already have him..." Williams left the thought hanging in the air. It seemed whatever information he had was unlikely to provide new insight.

"That's the thing about monsters," I told him as we stopped outside the briefing gallery. "You cut off one head, only to discover there's another one."

"That I understand."

Both our countries had faced dark times of late. I could imagine the threats to his family were as significant and omni-present as my own. Without thinking, I clapped a hand on his shoulder in a show of solidarity—and perhaps, comfort. Williams's face showed he understood.

"They're ready for you, sir," an aide advised.

I couldn't quite prevent the grimace that flashed over my face, but I replaced it with a smile as I stepped in front of the rows of reporters. May stayed by my side to direct the chaos as they began to call out to me.

"Miss Bernstein," May said and a woman shot up from her chair. She didn't bother adjusting her skirt or flipping her hair, instead her eyes zeroed in on me.

This is going to sting.

"Your Highness, will the crown sanction the marriage of your brother?"

I had been warned, so I kept my face passive. It was no surprise that they were going after Edward. I couldn't expect one of the most ruthless free presses in the world to ask what type of biscuit I preferred. My father would have taken the woman's head off, but I'd already decided to take a different approach. I'd kill them with charm. Ignoring the rage coursing through me, I smiled. "I already have."

This incited a barrage of follow-ups from the crowd, but I held up a hand before May could step in. "I'd like to limit topics to policy and my country."

Not my family. They were off-limits—all of them. I'd lost too many of the people close to me to share the ones I had left. If I had to give every part of me away to protect my family, I would.

There was a moment of squirming silence while the journalists regrouped.

"There's a vocal minority in Parliament who would like to see the monarchy abolished. How will you respond if support for the initiative gains momentum?" an intrepid man called out.

"God save the King," I replied, earning a wave of laughter. The dry response shifted the line of questioning to topics sure to produce amusing sound bites. I did my best to stay clever and steer things away from the people in my life. When I finally took my leave, Williams met me at the door.

"All charm and no concrete answers—you were born for politics."

I supposed it was meant as a compliment. "I was born into politics."

"I guess you never have had much of a choice," he mused as we made our way to the residential rooms. "Your destiny was decided for you."

I thought of Clara and my life before I met her. Every moment of my life propelled me to her, and yet I'd tried to push her away. In the end, we'd decided to fight for one another. That had been a choice—as had my decision to take the throne. It had been a personal decision rather than a forced one. Becoming king allowed me to search for those responsible for the attacks on my wife. In the end, there had always been choices—hard ones. "I've chosen my destiny."

"As have I." Williams paused to say goodbye before returning to his office.

He still had a day of work ahead of him, and I had my whole world ahead of me. I entered the small living suite our hosts had offered us quietly, afraid to wake a sleeping toddler. Instead, a babbling ball of joy toppled toward me as Elizabeth misstepped. In one swift move, I scooped my daughter into my arms.

"I'm sorry, Your Majesty!" Penny, the ever-fussing nursemaid we'd brought along, rushed over to save me, but I held my little girl. The poor woman couldn't fathom that a man would want to care for his child. If it killed me, I would show her that I wasn't simply any man.

Clara looked up from her book and rolled her eyes at the scene developing before her, but she didn't step in. Later I'd be more than happy to spank her for being mischievous. Her lips curled into a knowing smirk as if she had read my mind again.

"Penny, why don't you take a few minutes for yourself," I advised her.

"Sir?" She stared at me as if this was a test.

"I'd like to be alone with my family," I clarified.

She continued to look distraught, but she curtsied and took her leave.

"Is it so hard to believe that I want to hold my daughter?" I grumbled when we were alone.

"I suppose most kings are interested in furthering their bloodline, not building blocks." Clara's eyes lingered on the two of us as I settled onto the carpet with Elizabeth, who immediately pulled herself up and began practicing her latest trick: walking.

"Clever girl," I praised her. "Already walking."

"She's nearly fifteen months old," Clara pointed out, even as she dropped onto the floor beside me. Soon she was as captivated by Elizabeth's antics as I was. My hand found hers on the carpet. We stayed like that until a familiar form appeared in the doorway. Norris looked as proud as any grandfather as he surveyed my family, but when I lifted my gaze to his, I immediately knew something was wrong.

"I'll just be a few minutes," I murmured to Clara, brushing a kiss over her forehead even as it wrinkled in concern. Norris had given us a fair amount of space during our limited family time. We both knew that his sudden appearance meant news out of England. Getting to my feet, I crossed the room to him, Elizabeth taking dozens of tiny steps to try to catch up with me.

"There's been a development," Norris said under his breath. We both glanced toward Clara who was watching us with wary eyes. She didn't like to be kept out of the loop, a fact which had been a sore point since the day we married. Her contention that we should keep no secrets from each other was valid, but I couldn't bear to burden her with some of the knowledge I carried. She scrambled up and caught Elizabeth as I stepped into the hallway with Norris behind me. I met my wife's eyes for a moment, hoping she understood my need for privacy, before I closed the door.

"Is it about Hammond?" Nearly a year after his murder and we were no closer to the answers that might lead me to our common enemy. Whoever had murdered him hadn't done so as a favor to me. That was becoming clearer with each stone we turned over.

"No. I'm not even certain what it means."

"You're going to have to give me more to go on," I informed him. It wasn't like Norris to be mysterious, which meant that whatever news he had to deliver wasn't good.

"The team combing through your father's personal effects uncovered something."

"That would seem to be good news." When I'd asked for a discreet team to dig further into my father's personal life, I'd hoped to find links to the people responsible for his death. Whatever secrets he'd kept could be the key to discovering the truth about what happened that day.

"I'm afraid it only raises more questions." Norris looked torn and my pulse ratcheted up as adrenaline surged through my blood.

"What did they find?" I forced the question past gritted teeth.

"Not what," Norris corrected gently. "Who."

"Who?" I repeated. "They found a person?"

"They found your brother."

"Edward?" I asked even as sensation of vertigo gripped me.

"No." Norris paused to allow what he was saying to sink in.

"I have another brother?" My words were so strangled I barely recognized my own voice.

Norris drew a deep breath as if steeling both of us for what came out next. "It seems you do, indeed."

CHAPTER TWO

LONDON

The Christmas season was proving to be less a blessing than a headache for Belle's fledgling company. While the business had seen exponential growth in recent months, subscriptions had tripled in the first week of December alone. Thanks, in part, to a number of editorials her partner had managed to arrange in major magazines, but also due to the number of upcoming holiday parties. It seemed that Belle's brain child, Bless—a couture clothing rental company that kept its clients' closets stocked with the latest high end fashion—was headed for success. The trouble was that their operation was quickly outgrowing their office and their two-woman staff.

Lola, her partner and her best friend's little sister, appeared before her with a clipboard. Unlike Belle, who had paired a creamy cashmere jumper from Prada with tight, black trousers and Louboutin flats, Lola was dressed to the nines in a body skimming black Dolce & Gabbana dress that stopped far too short for propriety. The leggy brunette had mitigated this fact by wearing opaque black tights and suede Jimmy Choo boots that came to her knees. She looked as though she might dash from this meeting straight onto the runway. Her make-up was perfect down to the brilliant ruby lipstick she sported. Belle, on the other hand, hadn't bothered with anything but a little mascara and lip gloss. She was too fair and her lashes too blonde to get away without it. She supposed it was a perk of being married that she no longer felt the need to get dolled up every morning, even if she routinely did.

"I leave from New York right after Christmas." Lola began to rattle off her schedule with such speed that Belle redirected her focus so that she caught all the details.

Lola was the face of their fledgling company. She had pushed Belle to be the one to sit for interviews and attend photo shoots, but the founder had decided against it. In a way, Lola was famous in her own right. Whereas her sister was soft and welcoming, Lola was polished with an edge. She was a formidable business woman, and, in the end, it proved to be a marketing coup. Lola Bishop was an it-girl almost overnight. Of course, it didn't hurt that her sister was the Queen of England. What woman wouldn't take fashion advice from her?

It had garnered her a little more attention than they'd planned, however. Lola had found herself the subject of tabloid fodder ever since. If she walked next to a man in public, all the gossip columns speculated if he was the love of her life. Only Belle knew the truth. Lola had sworn off men for the time being, preferring instead to keep her nose to the grindstone and build an empire. There just wasn't time for dating when a girl was out to rule the world. Thankfully, she didn't mind the limelight, which left Belle free to focus on building the business the way she had wanted. It also made her more comfortable.

She'd had no idea when she got involved with Smith Price that her life would change forever. While many good things had come out of it—like the business and their marriage—Belle had also been the target of several attacks aimed to keep her husband under his crooked employer's thumb. They were free of that now, but she was more than happy to stay behind closed doors.

"I also need you to look at those resumes." Lola pointed to the stack of papers she'd printed from an online search. They'd been sitting there for the better part of the week. Apparently, she felt it would take pointing them out before Belle would acknowledge their existence.

"Wow," Belle said, picking up the stack. "It looks like more than a few people are interested in working with us."

"Those are just the contenders," Lola told her proudly.

Belle sifted through them, trying to find the motivation to look.

"We have to hire people," Lola reminded her.

Belle knew that, but it didn't make it any easier. With more people came more responsibility. Neither Belle nor Lola needed a salary, so there were many months where they'd gone without one in order to continue to grow the business. Lola had her trust fund to fall back on, and Belle had Smith's bank account. Adding employees felt a little like willingly putting themselves in shackles. They'd be responsible for other people's welfare. Not to mention that Belle trusted Lola. That wasn't always an easy dynamic to achieve.

Lola sighed, sensing she was getting nowhere, and gathered her sleek, brunette hair into a pony tail. "I'm going to go grab curry. You want any?"

Before Belle could respond, the door to their studio office opened. There was only one person who had a key to this office besides her and Lola. Belle didn't even have to see him before her body responded. Her nipples beaded tightly beneath her cashmere sweater and she grew damp between her legs.

Lola cast a mischievous glance at her. "On second thought, I think I'll take an actual lunch break today."

Smith grinned as he stepped into the room. Clearly, he had overheard her.

"Take an extra long lunch," he advised.

Belle shifted in her seat at the sight of her husband. He never ceased to have this effect on her. With his dark hair that glinted in the light and the stubble on his jaw line, he could have been a model instead of a lawyer. The weather in London was particularly chilly, and his black cashmere coat hugged his body perfectly. He'd turned the collar up against the wind, and Belle could barely see the knot of his tie peeking behind the buttons. She'd always had a particular fondness for his ties, mostly because he often used them for devious purposes that led to hours of pleasure.

"I'll see you two later," Lola said knowingly. She was smiling as she left, but Belle thought she caught a hint of jealousy on her pretty face. Maybe Lola Bishop wasn't as opposed to finding love as she pretended.

"Do you have any friends?" Belle mused out loud. Even after being married for the better part of a year, she'd only met a few of Smith's acquaintances.

Smith gave a low laugh that sent a tremble racing through her. "I have terrible taste in friends, remember?"

"On second thought, forget I asked," she said.

"Are you planning to play matchmaker?" He glanced over his shoulder at the door Lola had just exited. Was she really so transparent? Maybe her husband simply knew her that well.

"I guess I get sentimental this time of the year." She didn't have to explain herself. They were about to celebrate the second of their two wedding anniversaries. True, they'd only been married for a year, but they had been married twice. They had eloped in November and been remarried with their family and friends by their side last New Year's Eve. One anniversary was legal and the other personal. Still, she couldn't bear not to celebrate both as each meant so much to her.

"I think Lola's not going to have a hard time finding men who are interested," Smith said as he slipped his coat off his broad shoulders and placed it on a hook by the door.

It hung like a streak of black contrast against the white walls. They'd kept the office of Bless purposefully clean and modern. Belle had insisted that the showcase be on the clothes. Now they had had to start renting out a warehouse, but they still had several racks of samples available for their high-end clientèle, the kind they might cater to in person.

To her surprise, Smith continued undressing, removing his suit jacket. She could spot the broad coils of his muscles through his linen shirtsleeves.

"What are you doing here anyway?" she asked, not bothering to squash the hopefulness in her voice.

"I thought I'd grab some lunch," he responded.

"Is that an invitation?" She leaned forward, knowing that her low-cut jumper would put her breasts on display for his enjoyment. His eyes swept down to take them in appreciatively, and then he prowled forward until he was lording over her. With only the desk between them, she'd begun to wonder what pleasure was in store.

"Actually," he explained, "I was trying to decide what I was in the mood for. Curry didn't sound good. Italian? Not what I wanted. As it turns out, there's only one thing I had an appetite for."

Belle ran her tongue over her dry lips to wet them. The discussion had her mind focused on his mouth.

"Then I realized what I wanted," he continued as he circled the desk. Holding out his hands, he waited for her to take them.

Belle knew what it meant to place herself under Smith's control. She craved it, and now was no exception. He helped her to her feet and then immediately swept her into his arms. Lowering her to the desk, he shoved her sweater up to reveal her breasts.

"No bra, beautiful?" He dipped his head to catch her nipple in his mouth. A moan escaped her as he sucked hungrily. When he released it, the pert mounds were swollen and heavy. "Do you like it when the air hits your tits? You like that, don't you? Because you're dirty."

She breathed a yes, and he rewarded her by paying homage to her other breast. Smith knew exactly how to elicit a response from her. As such, she spent most of the time, even when they were apart, humming with want. He'd been right about why she hadn't worn a bra. Part of her was trained to keep her lingerie to a minimum. If Smith caught her without her bra or knickers, he rewarded her. But she also needed the contact. The sensation of the soft knit brushing against her nipples satisfied some of her need until she could have him.

"This was exactly what I needed," he growled, trailing from the valley between her breasts downward. He hooked his thumbs in the waistband and yanked her pants off along with her knickers. "I needed to devour you."

There was nothing gentle about the way he buried his tongue between her slick seam. Belle cried out as it flicked across her aching clit. Her hands shot out, searching for purchase. She held on as he delved deeper. It wasn't enough though. She arched up, wanting more of him. His arms caught her around the waist and pushed her down. Belle groaned in frustration and kicked her legs over his shoulders. If he wanted complete control, he should have tied her up. Smith nipped the sensitive nub of her clit in response. It was enough to send her over the edge. Her thighs clamped around his head, trying to push him away and hold him close at the same time. When it became too much, she pulled at his hair, but the suction on her engorged bud increased. He wasn't satisfied.

He never knows when to stop. It was the only thought she could process. Her body fought against the overwhelming sensations as they crowded through her. But with each wild spasm, he took her closer to the brink again. This time when she reached it, pleasure quaked through her and she cried out, completely overcome. When Belle was finally able to open her eyes, she found Smith grinning between her legs.

"I'm stuck," he informed her. That's when she realized her hands were still clenching his hair in a vice grip.

"Sorry," she murmured hazily as she willed her fingers to loosen. It took a concerted effort with her body fighting her. He'd unmoored her, setting her adrift in a chaotic sea, and her mind wanted the assurance of an anchor. As soon as he was freed, Smith took the seat behind the desk. Then he scooped her onto his lap and held her close.

This is one of the perks of being your own boss, she thought. If she wanted to spend the afternoon being fucked by her husband on top of her workspace, there would be no human resources department to fire her. Once they hired more employees, her rendezvouses with Smith would have to wait. She frowned at the unwelcome thought. Lola always knew exactly when to hightail it out of the office. Perhaps, she would get lucky and the new staff members would have a similar sense of self-preservation. If not, Bless might have to find a new home where Belle could have an office with doors.

"What are you thinking about, beautiful?" Smith's husky voice called her from her thoughts.

"The future," she whispered, her words colored with happiness.

"Like round two?" he asked.

"Slightly farther than that," she said dryly. If she only thought that far ahead, she'd never get anything done.

"That far? I hope I'm part of the vision." There was an earnestness to the statement that surprised her.

"Forever," she promised him. Her fingers were still trembling as she brushed her palm down his cheek. There had been dark moments when she thought she might lose him. Those memories were still too raw for her, so whenever he made any mention of what the future might hold she felt an overwhelming possessiveness take hold of her.

She'd never expected to find true love. Not after her first serious relationship had ended in betrayal. Maybe that was how she had found him: by not looking. However Smith Price had come into her life, she had no plans to give him up. They had been through a lot together. More than most couples faced in a lifetime. Some of it she had been able to put behind her. Other things she would carry with her always. Her solace was that he would be there to help her carry the burden. He nuzzled against her, his whiskers tickling her skin, and she giggled.

"You smell like me," she informed him.

"That is my favorite cologne, beautiful." He licked his lips to drive the point home. "Priceless."

"I think it's full of Price actually. Namely my price." She pointed down.

"Rather mine, I think," he corrected. Slanting his head, he kissed her deeply. His lips tasted of the heady mix of arousal and climax he'd drawn from her body. When she was younger, she would never have allowed a man to kiss her after that. But somehow Smith made the forbidden erotic. It was why she could never say no to him.

Still, if she wanted to get any work done, she'd have to start by cutting him off. Wriggling off his lap, she darted out of his reach and collected her trousers. Smith shook his head with disapproval.

"I think I have some mints in the drawer," she told him, giving him a swift kiss on the cheek and wrinkling her nose.

"I like smelling like you," he reminded her. "I'll enjoy it all day and it will give me all sorts of ideas on what I should do to you tonight."

"Don't you have a meeting? Your clients might take offense." Part of her thrilled at the idea of marking her husband with her scent, but the other part didn't relish the idea of him running around London smelling like sex.

"You're no fun, beautiful. Are they in here?"

She glanced over to see him pulling open the left drawer.

"No, not there," she said in a hurry, but it was too late. He was already rifling through it. Then he stopped, his hand on something and his expression unreadable before he pulled a thin compact out of the drawer.

"What's this?" he asked quietly.

He already knew the answer. It was written in disapproval across his handsome face. Belle tried to think of an explanation that would appease him. She could lie and pretend that she had no idea that they were in there, but he wasn't a stupid man. Plus, she'd tried to stop him from looking. She could say they were old, but it didn't matter. Her silence had already spoken volumes.

Smith collapsed into the desk chair, his shoulders drooping under the weight of disappointment. She'd never seen him like this. It was a quiet anger that rolled off of him. Usually he let his feelings be known in a much more vocal manner. The silence between them grew deafening until she couldn't stop herself from filling it.

"I don't know why," she blurted out in answer to a question he hadn't asked.

"So they are birth control pills," he clarified, as he tossed them onto the desktop. "All these months, I thought that you or that I ..."

Smith trailed away. He had never seemed terribly disappointed when her period arrived each month. After their miscarriage the previous winter, they'd halfheartedly agreed to let nature take its course, but when Belle's doctor had offered her the prescription during her follow-up exam, she'd taken it and filled it.

"If you didn't want to have a baby, you could've told me." Accusation sliced through his words. Apparently, she'd been terribly wrong about his desires. How could she have misread him?

"I d-d-do want to have a baby," she stammered. Didn't she? She hadn't been prepared to have this conversation, but now she knew she'd been avoiding the subject entirely.

"It sure as hell doesn't seem like it." He stood and strode across the room, grabbing his jacket from the hook and tugging it on.

When he reached for his coat, she couldn't stop herself. "I didn't think you wanted to have a baby. I thought you were just trying to make me feel better."

He drew it on before turning to face her slowly. "Birds of a feather, remember? I want to have everything with you, Belle. I thought that was a desire that we shared. Maybe I was wrong."

Then he was gone.

CHAPTER THREE

The study was quiet. He hadn't bothered to turn on any lights. Since he'd given up drinking, he didn't need to see to pour a glass. Instead, all he had to do was find a chair. Smith had driven around for a few hours trying to clear his head. When he got home, he half-expected to find her there, but the house was empty. It felt a lot like a metaphor for his life right now. How could she have lied to him for so long? He knew it was more complicated than that, but that was the crux of the issue for him.

When Belle had told him she was unexpectedly pregnant, something he'd never predicted happened. He fell in love with the future, and that destiny had been taken from him only hours later. At the time, he chalked it up to tragedy. There'd been plenty of reason to wait then and plenty of drama to distract him. Once things had calmed down and the two had begun to enjoy their honeymoon together, the tantalizing prospect of that future reappeared. The last few months had been spent in bed, chasing it. Or so he had thought.

He'd seen how happy she was when she told him she was pregnant. There had been apprehension, of course. Since it hadn't been planned, she'd had no idea how he would react, but he'd wanted that baby from that moment. It had been real to both of them, and as each month passed and her period came, life felt a little bleaker. It was a combination of factors, really. He'd wondered if something was wrong with him. That was rational. Somewhere deeper inside him, though, in an ugly place that he tried to ignore, he questioned if he was being punished for his past mistakes. He hated himself every time he couldn't give Belle a child, convinced it was his sins that kept him from completing their family.

Now, he'd discovered it had all been a charade. He was angry with her even though he didn't want to be. In truth, they really hadn't discussed having a child, and he'd made certain assumptions. Logic told him that this was about a lot more than not being ready or miscommunication, still, he couldn't quite see pass the betrayal. He'd been trying to give her the world, and she was rejecting his offer.

"Don't be an arse, Price," he commanded himself. His wife was a much more complicated woman than he was giving her credit for, and she had to have her reasons. But knowing that did nothing to dissipate the sting of it.

The door to the office cracked open, and a slant of light fell across the floor. Belle tiptoed into the room as if she was afraid of him. He didn't really know what to say to her, so he waited. She cleared her throat, and then she took the package of pills out of her purse and tossed them in the rubbish bin.

"I'm not going to take these," she told him.

Smith let his head fall backward in frustration. Somehow he'd managed to guilt her into doing something she didn't want to do. "Take them, don't take them. It's up to you."

"It's up to us," she said softly. "All those things I told you earlier were true, but there's something I left out." She nearly tripped over her own feet trying to take a chair. His hand reached up and flipped on the lamp so that she could see better. That's when he realized she was shaking. She looked delicate cast in the shadows with her pale hair framing her lovely face. His wife had a petite body that drove him crazy. Most of the time she wore heels with black dresses and scarlet lipstick, but right now, she was still in her low-cut sweater and trousers. Her eyes were rimmed red as though she'd been crying.

Smith knew she was strong, but he also knew she could be fragile. As she sat across from him looking small and scared, he felt his anger begin to soften.

"The truth is," she continued in a low voice, "I'm the one who lost the baby. It's my fault."

"It's no one's fault," he cut in.

She shook her head adamantly. "It was my body. I'm the one that's broken."

"We saw the doctor," he reminded her trying to sound gentle. Instantly, her confession had erased all the rage he'd felt. Now, all he could do was comfort her. How his beautiful, brilliant wife could blame herself for something so far out of her control, he didn't understand, but he wouldn't allow her to do so.

"And we didn't get any answers," she said.

Smith thought about rattling off the statistics the doctor had shared with them. One in four pregnancies ended in a miscarriage they were told, but that didn't seem to be the salve she needed. Her wounds ran deeper than he realized. The only things that could heal her were patience and love. Getting up, he went to her and dropped to his knees beside her. Looking into her eyes, he decided not to offer cursory rationalizations. Not when he had also been victim to his own paranoia. Hadn't he been the one to believe for months that they'd been unable to get pregnant because of his past indiscretions? Was that any more ridiculous than Belle's fear that her body didn't work? No. The problem had been that they had not been on the same page. He took her hands. "Beautiful, there are a million reasons that we might have lost that baby."

"I don't know if I can go through that again," she whispered. "It still hurts. How can it hurt to miss someone I never got to know?"

"It hurts me, too," he admitted to her.

"What if it happens again?" she asked.

"Then, it will hurt more," he answered, "but if we don't try, then we'll never know. And if we don't try, we'll miss out on the possibility. Even though it hurts now, I fell in love with the idea of our child, and I got to have that if only for a few hours. I wouldn't change any of it. You are the best thing that ever happened to me, and I want to share everything with you."

They stared into each other's eyes for a long while. When Belle finally opened her mouth to speak, the trembling was gone. Instead her voice was clear and certain. "I want to have your baby."

Perhaps she didn't mean immediately, but he wasn't going to wait. He stood and reached for her. Their eyes remained locked together as she got to her feet. Sweeping her into his arms, he carried her to the bedroom. This afternoon had been the time for foreplay. Tonight was about connection. When he placed her on the ground, she loosened his tie and tossed it to the ground. There would be no need for that—all they needed was one another. Flesh and bone, body and soul. She fumbled with his buttons and he cupped her face in his hands. He needed to touch her. That wasn't anything new, but the physical urge to feel her skin consumed him. Even the innocent gesture sent a concentrated blast of blood to his dick. It hardened painfully as if it, too, felt the overwhelming compulsion to mate. Belle finished unbuttoning his shirt and slid it off, then she found his cock with her hand.

"No need to rush, beautiful," he murmured.

"I need you inside me," she whispered. "I don't think I've ever needed anything so badly."

He could take his time and still meet her needs, he decided. Moving quickly, he stripped her clothes as she unbuckled his trousers. Within moments they were bared to each other. No matter how many times he saw her body, he would never get enough. The idea that it might change in the coming months—that it might swell and bloom with life—overtook him. Before she could respond, he'd hitched her around his waist and plunged inside her. He didn't care about allowing her time to adjust to his girth. He didn't worry about being rough. Smith knew that the only thing that mattered to either of them was completing one another. Belle cried out as she sank completely onto him. She rocked against him, and he guided her open further. She whimpered as her clit found the friction she sought. He felt it against his skin, proof that she was just as aroused by forging into the unknown as he was.

"Fill me," she pleaded with him.

Oh God, he wanted nothing more. Since the moment he'd seen her, he had known he would never be satisfied until she was dripping with him every waking moment. It was an impossible feat, but he was up to the challenge. Now that impulse was even more undeniable. He carried her to the wall, using it to brace her body as he thrust. His hips pistoned in deep strokes that bumped against her cervix. Belle began to gasp as her muscles clamped around his shaft.

"Harder!"

"Everything for you," he grunted as a sweat broke across his forehead. Somehow this gorgeous creature had chosen him. She had allowed his body to claim hers, and he would never stop giving her everything she deserved. He ground violently against her until her cries rent the air and her pussy milked jet after jet of his seed. Belle collapsed against him, sagging like a limp doll, and he caught her. She clung to him as he took her to the bed, but when he laid her down, she whimpered.

"More," she begged.

Smith stroked his hand down his slick cock, pumping it vigorously as he lowered his body onto hers. Her thighs opened in welcome and he slid inside her in a swift motion that stole her breath. Bracing his palms on the bed, so he wouldn't crush her under his weight, he called to her in a soft voice, "Open your eyes, beautiful."

Belle's lashes fluttered as she struggled to obey his command. She peered up at him through hooded eyelids and murmured dreamily, "Yes, Sir."

"Not tonight," he told her, even though he felt a pang in his balls at her words. She was giving everything to him—her trust, her submission, even her future. His mouth found hers and they kissed languidly, gasping and panting as their bodies moved in a slow, primal rhythm. He lifted his head to marvel at the unbroken circle of their love. "Do you feel that? I'm inside you—giving you life."

She surged around him and he filled her, completing the circle once more.

CHAPTER FOUR

Snow had arrived unseasonably early in London. The delicate flakes grew larger as I watched out the window of my private office. It was yet another reminder that the holidays were only a few weeks away. So was the memo reminding me that we were set to leave for the family home in Balmoral in a little less than a fortnight. And then there was the miniature Christmas tree that a staff member, in their infinite wisdom, had decorated and placed in the corner. The addition would delight Elizabeth when she came to visit Daddy. But no matter what changed, the room still felt like my father's office. In due time, I'd replace the heavy, velvet drapery and send the ostentatious furniture to storage. It was merely a matter of priority. Removing the remnants of my father was less important after we'd been forced to move into Buckingham only a few weeks after the coronation. It didn't feel like home. Perhaps, the holidays would finally change that.

There was a knock on the door and a stammering, young woman peeked in. I rarely noticed the girls on my staff, my eyes completely stuck on my own wife, but I couldn't help but note that the poor thing was practically the shade of a telephone box. That meant that Brexton had arrived for our meeting.

"Show him in." I saved her the humiliation of having to speak.

She nodded and backed up against the door. Her eyes trailed after my old friend as he entered. I'd seen this reaction to him before, even Clara hadn't been immune to his looks the first time they had met. I couldn't be sure if it was the strict, but confident posture he'd developed in the service or the wicked glint of trouble that was omnipresent in his eyes. He was dressed down for the day in jeans and an untucked t-shirt. Judging from the way her eyes lingered it didn't matter if he was wearing this or his uniform as she was preoccupied with undressing him with her eyes.

"Thank you," I called to her as he settled into the chair across from my desk. It took her far too long to realize she'd been dismissed. Curtsying, she quickly shut the door in embarrassment.

"Some things never change," I muttered.

Brexton shrugged as though he had no clue what I was talking about. "Things do change. We used to be out there on the prowl together. Now you don't need a wingman."

"Thank god for that," I said in flat voice. "You were a terrible wingman."

"I resent that. We always went home with a girl," he said.

"You always went home with a girl—usually the one I was eying."

He ran a hand over his closely cropped hair that he still wore in military fashion. "Good thing I was deployed when you met Clara."

I shot him a warning look. Ribbing was one thing. Bringing my wife into it was another.

"What couldn't wait until tomorrow?" he asked, shifting topics before he got into trouble.

"I want you to look into the matter of my father's other son."

"Why?" he asked. It was clear he already knew about the discovery, given how nonplussed he was by my announcement.

"Because it's your job."

He blinked. Brexton Miles had known me far too long to be impressed by my title or authority. Most of the time I appreciated this fact, but today I was immune to the effects of sentimentality. That didn't mean that my good-natured friend and former comrade would simply bow to my will.

Brex relaxed in his seat. Out of uniform he looked like he spent his days in the gym lifting weights, and, no doubt to his tight, black t-shirt, his nights guarding access to night clubs. However, I knew that he'd achieved his formidable physique by carefully adhering to the fitness regime of the Royal Air Force. "Going to boss me around, Poor Boy? I thought we had an understanding."

Despite myself I grinned at the reference to our days on the war front. Brex had treated me no differently then, save to mock my lineage with his tongue-in-cheek nickname. We'd agreed that for him to work on private security team now that our relationship shouldn't change.

"I am your king," I reminded him.

"Bullshit," he called, crossing his arms. "You wanted someone who wouldn't pander to you, remember?"

"I remember," I said in a measured tone. That particular detail had seemed like a good idea at the time. Now I couldn't recall what I had been thinking.

"It was always going to be easier said than done," Brex pointed out. "But that doesn't mean that you are off the hook."

Though I might be inclined to try, I couldn't actually argue with his logic. I needed to switch tactics.

"We don't know where an investigation like this might lead," I explained. "It's possible that this could be connected to my father's assassination."

I swallowed on that final word. Even after a year and a half it was still unfathomable that he had been taken in such a violent manner. Finding out that he had a secret son could be a mere skeleton in the closet or it could be more.

"It seems unlikely—if you want me to be honest." He tacked on the last bit as an afterthought.

"I do want you to be honest," I assured him, "even when I don't like it. But how can we be certain if we don't look into it?"

"We can't," Brex said, "but I suspect the matter of this...discovery is more about curiosity than it is a matter of national security."

"We can't rule it out. Not without knowing more." My gut told me that I was right about this. None of the secrets my father kept were innocent. "He paid the mother of his love child to keep quiet."

"And he was still paying her at the time of her death," Brex reminded me gently. "Look, I'm not telling you to not look into this, but don't divest all your resources. There were other interesting pieces of information in the files the Americans gave us. We need to examine all of it."

"I need someone I trust looking into this. If you're right and this brother is a nobody, his anonymity will be short-lived if the press find out about him." There had been plenty of speculation regarding my father's romantic life after my mother's untimely death. Even the insinuation of this affair would fuel a tabloid frenzy. Until I knew more about why he'd kept this secret I needed to protect it from the outside world.

"If I focus on this, you'll need to put someone else in charge of the assassination investigation."

That wouldn't be a problem. "A temporary shift in focus shouldn't be a problem since we haven't had any new leads in—"

Brex cut me off, "As I mentioned, the CIA gave us some new information to consider. We've been following an important lead."

"That I haven't been informed of?" I roared as the friendliness I usually felt toward Brexton slipped.

"I considered it prudent to look into the matter further before I briefed you—for the sake of Parliament."

"Parliament?" I repeated. Could he be implying that the conspiracy had its roots in our very government? Judging from the placid detachment in Brexton's eyes that was exactly what he was doing. As soldiers, we'd been taught to compartmentalize. By keeping our emotions in check we wouldn't make decisions based on our feelings. Brex still had that ability. I did not.

For the first time, I allowed my control over the room to falter. Dropping my head into my hands, I considered the position I found myself in now. Neither avenue of investigation could be dismissed outright. Both need to be examined—thoroughly and by people I trusted.

"Could Norris?" Brexton suggested as though he could sense my dilemma.

I shook my head, finally lifting it to meet his gaze. "He's in charge of Clara and Elizabeth."

No matter how my situation might change or what information became available, they had to remain my primary concern. No answers and no justice were worth putting the two of them at risk. Clara still ruffled at my security measures, but she'd grown accustomed to Norris's presence. But not only was it a matter of my wife's happiness, it also came down to the fact that he was the only person I trusted with the two people I loved most in the world.

"In that case, that only leaves one other person." We both knew who he was talking about, but there was no missing his hesitation. It wasn't a suggestion he would make lightly given my history.

"You trust her?" I asked. The number of people in a position to take over Brexton's work was limited. That meant that I needed to delegate some of the decisions to him. But even so it was a tough pill to swallow.

"I do. I know the two of you had some issues in the past."

I raised an eyebrow as I tried to decipher what he was really saying. If he knew the true nature of my relationship with his colleague or if he'd merely guessed. I didn't have many secrets from my friend, but I didn't discuss Georgia Kincaid if I could help it.

"She's discreet." It was the most complimentary trait I could find to describe her. Georgia had once helped initiate me into the world of Dominance. As far as I knew she didn't brag that I'd been a past client nor did she share the other men of power she'd submitted to. Our relationship had never been sexual but rather a therapeutic proposition. I'd realized far too late that it had been a power play on behalf of her employer to keep me under his thumb. "But she's also a mercenary. Her loyalty can be bought."

Brexton's shoulders tensed, a vein ticking in his neck, at my words. Even so he was remarkably calm as he responded. "She was a mercenary. She's proven her loyalty to our side."

I bit my tongue before I could ask when he had fallen in love with her. His attachments were none of my business, and Brexton was smart enough to handle her if she proved to still be trouble. I should have seen the inevitability of the romance, but I'd been too caught up in my own affairs to redirect his attention.

"I suppose people change," I offered. I had changed with Clara's help.

"Yes, they do." There was a finality in his tone that even I didn't dare question. "It's your call."

It was my choice. Every possible decision had its disadvantages, but none of them outweighed the danger of inaction. "Brief her."

Brexton nodded, maintaining a professional detachment at my proclamation, but I spotted a gleam of triumph in his eyes. He stood, straightening as if he might salute me. Thinking better of it, he headed for the door.

"Brex," I called before he could leave my office, "tread carefully."

The triumph faded but he managed a much curter nod of acknowledgment.

He might not like to hear it, but it was my responsibility as a friend to warn him. Perhaps my past associations with Georgia had left me prejudiced against her. Still despite our differences, I was certain of one thing: no one ever really knew Georgia.

Except one person.

I was dialing his mobile before my conscious thoughts caught up with my body. Smith answered on the third ring.

"Yes?" The subtle trace of Scot in his tone only underscored his obvious disregard for my position. Then again, an alpha male never bowed to another alpha male, regardless of title.

"My hand has been forced." I explained the situation, taking care to leave out why I'd reassigned Brexton. If Smith was curious about what other matter I found more pressing, he didn't ask. "Keep an eye on Georgia."

"Is that an order?" he asked dryly.

It was a very good thing that we were having this conversation over the phone. The man knew how to get under my skin. We'd achieved a tenuous peace over the last year, but our relationship remained strained at the best times. Like now. I had to remind myself that he was my ally.

"I like to think of it as a mutually beneficial request." When it came to the safety of those we loved, Smith and I saw eye to eye. I was counting on that understanding now.

There was a pause. "Consider it done."

CHAPTER FIVE

"Are you planning to leave your study this evening?"

I startled at the sound of my wife's voice. Tearing myself away from the file I'd been reading for the fifth time, I glanced up. Clara paused in the doorway, the light from the hall cast a glowing silhouette around her. It framed her like an angel, and that's what she was: my own angel sent to deliver me from myself. She stepped forward and came into better view. Her dark hair fell over her shoulders and her face was fresh, free of any cosmetics. She wore a simple white, silk robe that skimmed along her divine body. As I drank her in, the points of her breasts beaded under the thin fabric. I loved how her body responded to me, even at this distance.

"What time is it?" I asked, rubbing the back of my neck absently. What I was really asking was how long I had to fuck her before she pleaded for sleep. If it was up to me, I'd spend every moment of my life making love to her.

Her eyebrow arched as a smile twisted over her face. She knew exactly what I was thinking. "It's ten. Bedtime."

"Would you like me to join you?" I reached for the power button on my computer monitor. She didn't have much of a choice as to whether I joined her if she was going to walk around looking so tempting.

"If isn't too much trouble." She sauntered to the desk and bent over, tapping her fingers on the mahogany. Bending slightly forward, her robe fluttered open enough to reveal a glimpse of creamy breast. "Unless you have something better to do."

"Tonight I'm taking what's mine, poppet." If she wasn't careful, I'd be claiming her on the top of this desk. But as I stood my mobile vibrated in my pocket. I shot her an apologetic smile and she shrugged. She had grown accustomed to quick messages and late night crises. Once I had her naked nothing short of nuclear war would be enough to draw my attention away from her. Slipping the phone from my trousers, I checked the screen. I couldn't stop myself from grimacing when I saw the text from Brexton, and without thinking, I dropped back into my chair. Georgia had gleefully agreed to take the new assignment. That didn't surprise me, but I wasn't thrilled to have her heading up such an important matter.

"What's wrong?" Clara asked, studying my features.

"Nothing," I lied, and my wife frowned. The two of us had been through far too much for me to get something past her. She knew my moods, mercurial as they were, and she loved me anyway. But she had no patience for lies. I shot off a quick response, reminding myself that sometimes the less she knew, the less she had to worry about. Clara might disagree with that assessment but I considered it a marital duty.

Clara came around the desk and carefully climbed onto my lap. Judging from the heat between her legs, the robe was all she was wearing. I couldn't help but enjoy the sensation of her cunt nuzzling against my groin. She pressed a finger to my chin and drew my face up to hers to plant a soft, inviting kiss on my lips.

"Tell me what's on your mind." Apparently her invitation came with a price.

"Nothing you should worry about." This time I wasn't lying. Instead I tried to be reassuring. There was no need for Clara to carry my burdens. She'd given up a normal life by marrying me and I wouldn't pile every matter of state or security on her. "Only one of us should be tasked with dealing with the mundane issues of the country."

"That's not it." Her eyes searched mine for the answer that wasn't forthcoming. "This isn't some Parliamentary issue. You've been preoccupied since we left the States. Talk to me about it. I can help."

"Just being with you helps." It did. Her presence was a comforting assurance that I was acting of her best interest.

"I don't like it when you keep things from me, X," she warned.

I brushed a kiss over her mouth, and she sighed. Her body softened against me despite her hesitance. "Sometimes you have to trust me."

"I could say the same thing." Clara buried her face into my shoulder. "I can handle it. Whatever it is. We said no secrets, remember?"

We had. I promised her that I was through keeping secrets from her, and then I'd proceeded to keep them anyway. Not because I didn't trust her, but because I loved her. If only she could see that. I had to make her understand. "My only concern is with protecting you."

Clara stayed silent and I could see her struggling with how to respond. I suspected the reason I'd gotten away with my past indiscretions had a lot to do with her knowing exactly why I had made the choices I did. Her life had been threatened on more than one occasion. It was a fact that I couldn't live with.

"I'm stronger than you think," she said at last. "I can handle it."

"If you only knew." I laughed under my breath. "If you had any idea how much I struggle with my need to protect you."

"Show me. Let me in. Take what you need from me." She stroked her hand down the side of my face.

It was an offer that I found difficult to refuse. Since the moment I'd met Clara, I'd felt compelled to watch over her. But not simply to just protect her. I wanted to claim her—own her. I'd longed to take that lovely creature and spirit her away where I would be the only one to ever touch her. She would be safe with me, and she would be mine. I tore my gaze from her and the temptation she was unknowingly dangling over me. "You don't know what you're saying."

She caught my face and held it steady. "I am yours. All of me. Take what you need, and nothing less."

"Clara." I swallowed against the longing building inside me. I had to put a stop to this. "I could never."

"You can. I'm asking you to. Whatever it takes. I don't want anything between us. Show me."

Her words vanquished my resistance, and I slid my arms around her. Lifting her into my arms as I stood, I carried her toward our bedroom. Clara exhaled contentedly as I laid her across our bed and plucked open the sash of her robe. It fell open to reveal the luscious curves of her body. I took a step back and surveyed my prize. On another night I would take her right then and there. My cock throbbed as if to second this plan, but I ignored it. I always needed her body. I always wanted it. Tonight, I demanded her freedom.

"Take it off," I commanded her.

Clara wriggled under my watchful gaze until she shrugged the robe from her shoulders. Reaching down, I slid it free from her until it was only her, stripped to nothing for me. She waited, her breath speeding up with expectation. When I moved away from the bed, she remained still. Clara enjoyed it when we played, so when I went to the closet, she made no effort to stop me. At the far end of the walk-in an antique armoire waited ominously. I kept the key with me at all times in an effort to prevent a curious maid from discovering its contents. Opening the black lacquer door, I found what I was looking for immediately. I chose the white, silk rope because it seemed fitting given that I had deprived Clara of her robe. While I loved the sight of red bindings on my wife's fair skin, tonight I wanted the innocence. Despite my tastes, there was a purity to Clara that even my darkness couldn't touch.

I reappeared over her with the rope and surprise flashed over her eyes. Perhaps she thought this was a game. Or a test. I saw it for what it was—for what she had given me. An offering. At times, she forgot what I was. I would remind her of that. I was the predator.

Clara held out her wrists, crossed in supplication. I uncrossed them, meeting her eyes as I took one firmly. She didn't pull away as my grip tightened. This part I would do slowly if only to grant her a second chance. I kept my gaze locked to hers and wondered if she saw the darkness of my thoughts. Leaning down, I found her ankle and urged her leg up. She bent it willingly, even as I brought her wrist to her calf. Then I began to work, looping and tucking until her arm and leg were tied tightly to one another. I repeated the action on the other side. When I was done her legs were spread and bound, displaying the pretty pink gash of her cunt. Her knees pressed into the soft mounds of her breasts, her nipples peeking from above. I wanted to take them in my mouth and suck until she came, but this wasn't about pleasure. She licked her lips, her eyes hooding with want.

"This is what I want, poppet," I murmured. I drew my hand through the air over her naked sex, just enough to stir the air so that she would squirm against her restraints. "I want you helpless to my control. I want to tie you up and lock you away."

"X," she whispered, her eyes widening as she began to piece together what I was saying.

"Shh," I hushed her. "I want you to be mine. I want you to do as I say. Right now you'll do anything I ask, won't you?"

She swallowed, managing to move her head enough for a slight nod.

"All I want is to know that you're here." I didn't wait for my words to sink in before I turned and left her there. Shutting the bedroom door behind me, I walked back to my study and poured myself a bourbon. It should make me feel like a monster for leaving her like that, but instead I took pleasure in it. Some of the weight I'd carried with me since we met had lifted from my shoulders. I took my responsibility for Clara seriously. Since I'd accidentally dragged her into my life, I'd worried for her safety every moment she wasn't in my sight. I was a modern enough man to know that I couldn't reasonably expect my wife to be near me at all times. Even when we were home, her absence from presence needled me. Now there was no question what she was doing or who she was with. I had never known real freedom in my life , and I hated that I savored taking hers now.

I sipped my drink slowly. It burned down my throat. Clara was a wild thing that allowed me to tame her at her pleasure. I had pushed her past her comfort levels before. In every case, she had asked it of me. But that didn't mean she understood when I crossed the line. I had no idea what to expect when I went back to her this evening. She had told me to take what I needed from her, and I had done it. Too often people in my life offered me lip service without devotion. My wife served my pleasure in my bed and I always rewarded her trust. But there had always been the promise of limits coloring our intimacy. I'd abandoned that. Draining the last of my glass, I stood and left it on the table. I paused and listened at the door. No sound came from within. I opened it a crack and caught sight of her on the bed. I had no idea if it had been minutes or hours. I only knew that enough time had passed to call me back to her. My heart pounded in my chest and I strode toward her.

She didn't speak when I reached her. Her eyes were closed but I spotted two dried trails of tears. I undid my cuff links as I waited. She didn't open her eyes. I left them on the nightstand and began to undo the buttons on my shirt. I'd taken off all of my clothes before her lashes fluttered. When our eyes met, they were full—of tears, of accusations, of need.

"I'm here now," I said in a soft voice. There was no way to be sure she would find that comforting, but it was all I had to offer. I took a step closer, careful not touch her. "You know what to say."

Given the hurt shining in her eyes, I knew she needed to be reminded that one word would stop all of this., When her mouth opened she said something I didn't expect. "Please."

My fists clenched into balls as the request processed. My hand dropped to cup the mound of her sex and she moaned. I felt my balls constrict at the sensation of wet heat. Clara tried to push against my touch as if she was desperate for more, but I wouldn't take her this way. I'd always rewarded her trust and tonight would be no exception. Stooping, I undid her bindings and took care to rub the indentations the rope had left in her soft flesh. When she was free and I had massaged away any lingering discomfort, I helped her into a sitting position. Seating myself beside her, I waited. She moved like her limbs were foreign objects until slowly she lowered her body onto my lap. I drew her legs around my waist, encouraging my dick to sink deeper. Clara's breath caught as I impaled her and she released it with a strangled cry as I took her hips and gently rocked her. She stared at me, her expression unreadable, and as we climbed together, she brought her hands to my face to trace the curves of my jawline and my brow. Then she kissed me deeply. She was my air and I released her hips, clutching her body to mine. I would never let her go. I couldn't.

"I love you," I groaned when the kiss broke. Clara's eyes stayed trained on mine, and as I felt the first spasm of pleasure grip my cock, I saw sadness wash over her. We rode out our climax together, but I refused to relinquish her when the waves subsided. She pulled against my hold and I loosened my grip, but only enough to allow her to draw back. She slapped me with a force that vibrated across my cheek.

Shoving me to the mattress, she extricated her body from mine and backed away. "Don't ever touch me again."

"Clara." I sat up, alarmed. Every ounce of me wanted to go to her and hold her while she raged and sobbed. Whatever it would take, I would give—just as she'd given me my darkest fantasy. But I stayed still. Right now the best thing I could do was listen and hear what she was saying. "Clara, I—"

"Don't bother," she advised me, her voice rich with warning. "I asked for it, didn't I? So that made it okay?"

I opened my mouth to speak, but she held up a hand.

"Leave."

If there was ever any question that she was a queen, that command laid it to rest. She lorded over me, too far to touch as I got to my feet. I hesitated and turned to her, but she looked past me as if she couldn't see me. Or perhaps, and the thought left a sick dread in its wake, as if she didn't want to.

I bent and collected my pants from the floor. Sliding them on, I tried to buy myself more time with her. Maybe the more willing I was to meet her demands, the sooner she would unleash the full force of her fury. I didn't look forward to that, but facing the storm would be better than remaining in purgatory. When I slid the buckle of my belt into place, she was still pointing at the door. I guessed I had my answer. I collected my shirt and left the room, shutting the door behind me. A few moments later I heard the lock click in place.

"Good job," I told myself. I couldn't help but feel torn. Had I really expected a different outcome? My eyes clenched shut and before I realized what I was doing, my fist slammed into the wall. The ancient plaster cracked but didn't give way.

Why had she let me touch her if she was that angry? She had every opportunity to use her safe word. Instead she had asked me to touch her. I didn't know what it meant but my heart sank into my stomach.

Penny, the nursemaid, came around the corner and stopped dead in her tracks. She gawked at my half-clothed body and I felt my anger rise to the surface.

"Don't you have somewhere to be," I barked.

The poor girl jumped a little, then scurried away. I could only imagine the rumors that would be circulating amongst the staff in a matter of hours. Wadding my shirt in my hands, I stalked back to the bottle of bourbon I'd left behind.

After an hour, I checked our bedroom door and found it unlocked. I peeked behind it, but the room was empty. The only sign of occupancy were the wrinkles we'd left behind on the damask bed spread. The fireplace was unlit and that fact, combined with Clara's absence from our bedroom, left the space cold and lifeless. If my wife wasn't enjoying the few hours of sleep she could expect before Elizabeth woke us in the night, then she was fuming. I didn't dare think of it as sulking or pouting. She had a right to her anger. What I'd done was inexcusable, even by my standards and since I had no plans to apologize, I knew I shouldn't expect a reprieve. We might find ourselves well into the new year before she forgave me.

Abandoning the empty bedroom, I sought her in the only other place she ever frequented in the short time we had lived here. I'd made certain that the Queen's Sitting Room was updated for her use as soon as I learned that we must move. My grandmother had been the last person to use the parlour regularly and I knew Clara would appreciate neither her decorating or feeling as if she was under the former Queen Mother's thumb. Grandmother had removed herself to Sandringham shortly after the coronation, so none of us would have to keep up the pretenses of civility.

I'd asked the staff to make the room feel light and airy, wanting to give Clara a place that felt entirely different than the rest of our palatial home. It was impossible to cover up the gilded carvings around the room, but they'd been minimized by sheer curtains that allowed sunlight to stream into the room. Now at night ribbons of moonlight slanted across the furniture inside. Clara was tucked into a ball on one, staring out the window into the starless night. I cleared my throat to warn her of my entrance, but she didn't bother to look to me.

"Poppet," I tested the waters with my pet name. Still no response. I debated my options. If I continued to call out to her, it was likely she would continue to ignore me. If I went to her, I could expect a physical response. She'd never had control over her body in my presence. However, given what I'd put her through, it felt wrong to rely on such provocation.

"Are you going to stand there and muse all night?" she said softly, her eyes directed away from me.

The fact that she was talking to me seemed a good sign, but I didn't miss how she kept her body turned from me. It was a message. I crossed an important boundary. Throughout our relationship, I had been the one to insist on precautions to protect her from my unpredictable nature. What was worse that I had disregarded my own rules or that I didn't feel sorry for them?

"Clara, I..." I trailed away, unsure what I should say.

"Don't apologize," she demanded.

"I wasn't going to," I told her softly. Despite her command, she turned a furious gaze on me. It wouldn't be the first time a woman said one thing when she felt entirely the opposite. I'm not certain what it said about the male sex that it still surprised us.

"You should!" she exploded, wrapping her arms tightly around her knees and clutching them to her body.

"You're giving me mixed signals, poppet." It was the wrong thing to say. I knew the moment it left my mouth, and now I would suffer the consequences of two verbal slip-ups.

"I am?" she asked in disbelief, her blue eyes flashing darkly. "I'm giving you mixed signals. Well, Your Majesty, you have a convenient habit of choosing which of your own rules you want to follow."

"I deserve that." But the admission wasn't going to appease her.

"For example, you were the one who insisted that we have a safe word," she continued, "but you have to be in the same goddamn room to know if I'm going to use it."

"You weren't in danger," I reminded her gently. "Be rational."

"Don't you ever tell a woman who's tied up and alone to rationalize her situation. You promised to protect me."

Admittedly her accusation stung. But that was what she didn't understand. I had been protecting her. If I could only make her understand. First, I would have to get a word in edgewise.

"You're also supposed to respect me," she said.

"Clara," I cut her off sharply. There was a time and place for feelings, but I could no longer allow her to misinterpret my actions. "I do respect you."

"Like hell you do."

"I respect you and I was protecting you." I kept going in an attempt to explain myself before she ran away from me. "Will you let me explain?"

"You can try." Her words sliced through the air but her chin dropped to rest on her knees. She was granting me an audience, but I knew I only had one chance to get this right.

"You offered me anything I needed from you." I paused and waited for her to confirm this. All I got was a begrudging tilt of her head. "So, I took what I needed."

"Bravo," she interjected. "That really clears things up."

I had expected that response. I didn't relish how long it might take for her to see the situation through my eyes. "You know that I struggle with my compulsions. You've lived through the bodyguards and the distance and—"

"And the stalking?" she suggested.

I felt a twitch of annoyance in my jaw, but I ignored it. "Since that night in Brimstone I have wanted to take you and lock you away. I've wanted to keep you from the world, so they could never hurt you. I understand that's not the politically correct way to have a relationship." I attempted a small smile but it was met with a glare.

"That's not the sane way to have a relationship, X."

Using my nickname? I decided to take it as another good sign. "I resisted my urges then and focused on less mental ways of protecting you. I know you hate the bodyguards and security sweeps."

"They're part of being with you," she said, "and I accepted that. But if you're going to tell me that you need to lock me away to satisfy your compulsions, then you can kindly go and fuck yourself."

"I don't need that," I reassured her.

"Then what was that?" she cried out. Our eyes met and I saw the moisture pooling near the edges. She blinked, but the tears didn't dissipate. "I told you to take what you needed. I want to give you want you need, but I don't know if I can give you that."

"I don't need you to." I was repeating myself, although I knew it wouldn't reassure her. "I took advantage of your offer."

"You took advantage of my submission," she whispered.

"I was always going to push your boundaries." I felt sick saying it. I thought I'd become a better man for her. Now I realized I was still as fucked up as ever.

"And there will be no apologies for that," she said.

I shook my head. "I took what you gave freely."

Clara stood in a rush, her eyes darting between me and the door. I knew she was calculating whether she could get around me. When she stayed frozen in place, I guessed that she decided she couldn't. That left her with pushing my boundaries: would I be able to let her go? Would I come after her?

History proved I would, and we both knew it.

"Clara, I don't want you to be angry with me."

She laughed mirthlessly and tightened the sash of her robe with a quick yank. "It's a bit late for that. If you wanted to be in my good graces you could have just tied me up and fucked me. I thought we were past this controlling bullshit."

The string of profanities littering her responses told me that she had only gotten more frustrated with me.

"I wish I could be the man you deserve," I admit.

"I do, too." Her words were a slap in the face, but she didn't back down. "But you are the man I want—the man that I chose. That doesn't absolve you from what you did, though. When are you going to see that I'm here with you? You aren't going to scare me away, X. Not if you give me yourself. But you might push me away if you keep taking me without letting me in."

"I want your life to be full of happiness." Not stress or fear. I didn't want to burden my beautiful wife with the secrets that continued to crash down upon me.

"How can it be when you keep resurrecting walls between us?" The softness of her words only made them fall heavier. "I know that we aren't like most couples. You have to guide a country. I can't run out to the market. So much of our lives have been determined for us."

"For that I am sorry." I'd tried to let Clara go when we first met, because I knew that claiming her would only bind her to a life of responsibility.

"I chose that life," she reminded me, taking a tentative step in my direction before she stopped again. If we were too close to one another, we'd fall back on bad habits and wind up in each other's arms. "But the duty should never affect us. There are no security precautions or state secrets. There can't be. You know that."

"Most of what I deal with would bore you," I assured her with a wink.

"Don't you dare!" She pointed a finger at me. "Don't pretend like it's all boring, mundane action items. You are keeping something from me. You have been since we were in DC."

"Clara, I only want to—"

"Protect me?" she guessed with a sigh. "You aren't. You're protecting yourself. Maybe you think I'll be angry or maybe you don't really trust me. Honestly, trying to figure out why you keep secrets is exhausting. I didn't marry you to have secrets between us."

"I won't ask you to carry them."

"Don't you see?" she asked in a weary voice. "You don't have a choice. We're in this together. I can't imagine telling you that I don't need your help."

"You do all the time," I said dryly.

"But you're still there, helping me," she corrected. "It's what we do. Distance doesn't work for us. We might as well try to be abstinent. It will go over about as well as you keep secrets. You don't have to carry your burdens alone, and I don't want you to. That's what I was offering you tonight. All of me. You want to protect me, but when will you see that I want to protect you?"

It took all my resolve not to gather her in my arms and carry her to our bed. I'd overstepped a line tonight and I wouldn't take advantage of her vulnerability in this moment. Especially given that I couldn't tell her what she asked of me. "Some secrets aren't mine to share."

"Then there's our problem. All of me is yours to share." A sob wrenched from her and she shook her head. "At least, it was."

"Clara, please—" I couldn't stop myself from reaching for her then.

"Don't!" She pulled back. "Not tonight. I'll get over it. I'll learn to live with it. Tonight, I need to be alone with the truth."

"What truth?" I dared to ask, even though I didn't want to know.

"That I let myself be swept into the fairytale," she murmured. "I fell under your spell. I let myself believe in happily ever after. I swallowed a pretty story because I fell in love."

"It isn't a fairy tale. This is real." I moved toward her, but she darted past me. "Clara, we're real."

She paused at the door and turned sad eyes on me. "Maybe we were."

CHAPTER SIX

SCOTLAND

The tree would never do. It had been delivered from the village earlier this week, and there were far too many scraggly patches that revealed its crooked brown limbs. No amount of ornaments or decorations could hide that fact. On the off chance that his grandmother decided to join them for the holidays this year, she would send it back immediately, but that wasn't what concerned him. This Christmas had to be perfect. The family had eschewed tradition last year and stayed in London for the holidays. Elizabeth was still a newborn and there had been the chaos surrounding Belle and Smith—knocking off to Scotland hadn't been a priority. That meant this was David's first year celebrating with him at Balmoral, and since Edward hadn't given him a wedding yet, he could give him a proper Christmas morning.

That was easier said than done, given how hard David was pushing back against his preparations.

Strong arms wrapped around his waist as he studied the tree, and he felt David's chin drop to his shoulder. "It's fine."

"It's ugly. What will Belle and Clara say?" He knew David had a soft spot for his best friends, and he wasn't above using it to his advantage.

"They'll be too busy worshiping their husbands to notice," he promised.

David had a point, but Edward didn't miss the edge to his words. Both Clara and Belle had husbands to command their attention; David did not. Maybe he was less obsessed with the perfect Christmas as he was with distracting him from that fact. He hadn't been able to explain to David why he'd continued to push back their wedding date. Just as David didn't know nearly enough about the events that transpired a year ago. Edward had kept the secret out of respect for his friends, but also under the command of his brother.

"I thought we came earlier to be alone," David said pointedly.

"We are alone," he snapped, and David pulled away.

"Alone together, not separately. I can't help but think you've dragged the whole of England's problems with us."

Maybe he had. Edward had brought the Royal Family's problems at least.

"You've been distracted." David stepped closer, frustration blazing in his eyes. "I've been understanding, but you can't keep avoiding your own life."

"I know that you—"

"This isn't about me," David interrupted. "I'm not making threats or ultimatums. Although Christ knows that I should be. I'm simply pointing out that you're only hurting yourself."

They both knew that wasn't true. "And you."

"All things considered, you've come out of the closet, declared your love for me, and upset hundreds of years of tradition just by proposing to me. I shouldn't expect any more miracles in such a short time frame."

"I was the one who proposed," Edward pointed out. He'd made a promise when he asked David to marry him. He didn't take that lightly, but he'd done it when he had no idea about the threat looming over his family. It was possible that whoever was behind the attacks on his brother and father had only been after Alexander. Edward had almost convinced himself as such until Belle had fallen in love with the wrong man. Smith Price, now her husband, had proved his love for her but the secrets he'd revealed had shown that Alexander's paranoia had been warranted. Most of this had been kept from David. In truth, Edward knew very little. His brother hadn't been eager to share his information with anyone. Despite everything, Alexander still believed it was his role to martyr himself for the sake of his family. What bits of information Edward was privy to didn't paint a clear picture. Edward had proposed in good faith and that faith had been slowly stripped away over the last year.

"Yes," David said, drawing his attention back to him, "and if you've changed your mind..."

It took a second for Edward to process what he was saying, but then realization dawned on him. David thought this was about him. How could Edward reassure him otherwise when he couldn't tell him the truth? Alexander had commanded secrecy, and since he wasn't sharing news of the investigation with his own wife, he couldn't breach his trust. "This isn't about you. Or us. It's—"

"Then marry me," David cut him short.

"I will," he promised, but David shook his head.

"Now."

"But the wedding and..."

"Everyone will be here for Christmas. Everyone we care about, and if your brother doesn't have the authority to marry us, no one does. I don't need a big wedding, I just need you."

Edward's heart melted a little at the sincerity shining in his brown eyes. He'd made this man wait for him to be ready for years. "I want to, but there are laws."

"Sod the laws."

"I am the Prince of England," Edward reminded him dryly. If something happened to Alexander, the throne would have to pass to him until Elizabeth came of age. He had to consider his place and responsibility.

"You will always be the Prince of England." There was an implication in David's words that Edward didn't want to consider. "That's not going to change. If you feel that you can't be both Prince and my husband, then maybe it would be best if..."

David absently twisted the ring on his finger, and Edward's heart twisted along with it. Was this really what it would come down to? Choosing between the man he loved and the legacy he'd been born to? It occurred to him that this was how Alexander must have felt when he fell in love with Clara. Although the two had faced scrutiny, scandal, and danger, they'd continued to choose each other. Why couldn't he do the same?

"Yes," Edward said.

"Yes?" David repeated questioningly.

"Yes, I will marry you." Grabbing him by the shirt, Edward drew him roughly to his body. Their mouths crushed together, the air around them charged with an electricity that he'd only felt in his arms. He had shielded himself from it in recent months, trying to keep him safe from unknown enemies by putting distance between them. Now Edward knew he'd only been hurting them by doing that. The love he felt for him transmuted into an intense longing that grew as the kiss deepened. Loosening his grip on him, Edward's hand slipped lower until he found the hardening bulge through David's jeans. David moaned against his mouth as he began to stroke through the thick denim.

The two had always given and taken, each a generous lover, but today Edward wanted to erase any doubts. The idea that David had ever questioned his love wrecked him, and he felt compelled to show his love exactly how much he loved him. Breaking away, he met David's chocolate eyes for a moment before dropping to his knees. Only a selfless act would be enough to show him, even though he took an immense pleasure in performing it. His fingers slid David's zipper down nimbly, and in one practiced motion, Edward freed his cock from the confines of his shorts. It fell heavy and hot into his hands, and Edward began to caress his length as he brought its broad crown to his lips. His mouth closed over the tip, allowing his tongue to swirl languidly until he swallowed it deeply into his throat. David groaned, his hands fisting in Edwards hair as he continued to suck.

"That feels so fucking good," David grunted as he began to rock against Edward's mouth.

They fell into a rhythm and Edward felt his own dick begin to ache. He couldn't stop himself from shoving his hand down his trousers to stroke it as he continued to pleasure his lover.

"It turns you on to have my cock in your mouth, doesn't it?" David growled.

Edward nodded, taking David deeper. He responded by thrusting harder, his balls slapping against his chin, as he fucked his throat. Edward felt the first clench of his own balls, even as he nearly gagged on David's length, and when the first, hot jet shot against his throat, his own release broke free and coated his palm. He licked his shaft as he released him, and David sighed with pleasure.

"My turn?" David asked huskily as he helped Edward to his feet. Edward grinned sheepishly.

"I might have already..." he trailed away as David spotted his sticky hand.

"I don't mind a challenge," David promised him before he crushed his lips to his. When he broke away, they were both panting and rock hard. "Maybe we should take this show to the bedroom before Mrs. Watson comes in and has a heart attack, though."

Edward chuckled at the thought. Balmoral's housekeeper had been in tenure since he was a boy. She was a grumpy, old hen who complained about everything from her arthritic hip to the quality of the village's clotted cream. She had welcomed David with open arms, but she was getting up there in years. The two had already decided that all of this Christmas's house guests needed a gentle reminder not to let her catch them doing anything too shocking. Although it might be easier to lock the fragile Mrs. Watson in her quarters instead of relying on the discretion of any of the couples.

"Lead the way," Edward encouraged him, and David took his hand.

It was beginning to look a lot like Christmas.

CHAPTER SEVEN

In Smith's experience, a phone call from Georgia Kincaid never meant good news. The woman's presence in his life could be most easily described with comparisons to natural disasters. Like hurricanes and tornadoes, she was an inevitability that could not be avoided. No matter how prepared you were.

Smith bypassed valet parking. It was a service he only used in the presence of Belle, whom he wouldn't dare make walk more than a few feet into a building. When he had the option, he generally preferred to keep other hands off the steering wheel of his Bugatti. Even as a grown man, he didn't like to share his toys. He found a particularly secluded spot marked no parking, pulled in and got out of the car. His mobile would alert him if any wanker tried to tow it. That seemed unlikely given the close quarters of London garages and between his smile and his wallet, he could have a boot taken off in no time.

The Westminster Royal hotel was known for ensuring the privacy of its guests. He paused at the revolving door and nodded in greeting to the bell man as he adjusted his tie. Another married man might think twice about meeting a woman, who wasn't his wife in a hotel, but if Belle found out that he had done so, her first concern wouldn't be with the fact that he was meeting up with Georgia. She would never suspect an affair. Instead, she'd interrogate him as to what intelligence he'd gathered. In that regard, he had a united front with his wife. He'd kept her in the loop as much as possible once he'd realized she was the first person in his life he could trust. At times, it had been necessary to keep her in the dark, but she'd always understood that. Still, he preferred to not bother her with any information unless it proved to be of vital importance.

The small bar off the hotel's lobby was relatively busy for a weekday afternoon, but with Christmas only a few days away, more people were taking off work to see to their final holiday shopping. On one hand, this meant their conversation was more likely to be overheard. On the other, it was far more likely that everyone here would be too preoccupied with their own chaotic to-do lists to eavesdrop. He didn't have to look hard once he stepped inside the bar area.

Even with her back turned to him, Georgia stood out in the crowd. Long, black hair swung well past her shoulders and judging from how she flipped it with a toss of her head, she was in the midst of a flirtation. It was the seductive combination of Georgia's looks and her charm that made doors open for her. It was also what had made her a formidable assassin once. Those days were behind her now. Like Smith, she'd chosen to go legit when it became clear that their mutual employer was mixed up in a political game that could destroy them all. Smith had acted based on conscience, but he didn't dare believe that Georgia had acted out of anything other than self-interest. Her beauty may have gotten her behind locked doors, but her survival skills had kept her alive on more than one occasion.

He strode toward her and waited until she finished flirting with the bartender. She paused, winking at Smith so quickly that he almost wondered if he'd imagined it.

"I'm sorry, I have to take this to go," she told the other man, nearly sounding as if she meant it. Smith knew better. Picking up her rocks glass, she tilted her head to a table in the corner.

"That's lucky," Smith said dryly. Given how busy the bar was, it couldn't have been chance that secured a perfect location for a clandestine meeting.

"I rely on many things in my life," Georgia told him. "Luck isn't one of them."

He gestured for her to step in front of him, never mind the fact that Georgia Kincaid was as far from a lady as a woman got. Chivalry must observed. As she sashayed toward the table on four-inch stiletto heels, he noted her strength and confidence. After the attack that had nearly claimed her life a year ago, he'd wondered if she would change. Some things were different now. She had a new job and respectable connections, and, as far as he knew, she'd given up certain unsavory side employment along with her new life. It didn't feel prudent to ask her. Still, despite the veneer of self-confidence, he knew the truth. Smith had seen the scars. He'd read the medical report. Abortions. Suicide attempts. No one would guess the darkness that shadowed her life by looking at her. Georgia's past was as big of a contradiction as she was herself. One moment, she was the most commanding presence he'd ever seen and in the next, she was begging to be dominated. In public she ruled, and in private she submitted, and the face she wore, even to those who knew her best, only hid the pain of her past.

She took the seat against the wall. It was a wise choice. She could see everyone in the room that way, he thought, but it left him to take the chair with the partially obscured view. Georgia always had the high ground. She was always protecting herself.

"So, what's going on?" Smith asked as soon as they were seated.

She swirled the amber liquid in the bottom of her glass and shrugged. "Can't an old friend call someone for drinks? It is Christmas time."

"I had no idea you'd developed a sentimental streak," he said.

A waiter appeared at the table and took his drink order. Georgia raised an eyebrow as soon as he disappeared. "A club soda? Are you pregnant?"

Annoyance shot through him. She had no way to know what a

sensitive subject she'd broached, but he gave her a tight smile. "Everyone changes, I don't need to tell you that."

In truth, he hadn't discussed his recent sobriety with anyone. Belle had noticed, but kept her mouth shut. During his time employed by Hammond, he'd reached all too often for the bottle. It had been a habit of his father's as well. Now that he was attempting to be a better man, drying up seemed like a good idea. He didn't feel the need to explain this to Georgia, and she didn't press him on it. That was why their relationship worked.

"I've been given a new assignment. One that I think you'll find interesting." She tapped her fingernail on her own glass.

"I thought you were going professional these days," he said, tipping his head in thanks as the waiter delivered his club soda. "I'm not on the Crown's payroll."

Was this why Alexander had asked him to keep an eye on her? Did he suspect she would share classified intelligence as soon as she saw it? He'd agreed to do so because Alexander had insinuated that it affected the safety of his wife. He, like Belle, wanted to be in the loop. After working for Hammond he understood the importance of knowing gossip before it became fact. Still, he couldn't stomach being dragged back into the affair. If Georgia was no longer on the right side of the law, he wasn't certain he wanted to know. It would force him to choose between his longtime allegiance to her and his promise to Alexander.

"I'm still a good girl—for the most part. But given the importance of this topic to the both of us, I felt it understandable to share."

He froze, his glass midway to his mouth. There was only one shared interest that would send Georgia calling upon him.

"I'm out," he reminded her. The night that Hammond had died, Smith had gone to kill him himself. Instead, he had walked away after Hammond had delivered a pardon to his adopted son. He had informed Smith that they were all pawns in a much larger game, but since Hammond had been burned, Smith was off the hook. All he had to do to ensure his own safety, and his wife's, was to mind his own business, and he had for the last year. Now both

Alexander and Georgia were trying to drag him into the fray once more.

"No one's ever really out," Georgia murmured.

"I am." Smith's voice was firm. Getting involved in whatever she was investigating would only lead the wolves back to his door. He'd have to speak with Alexander and make his wishes clear. He respected the man's compulsion to protect his wife, but now Alexander would have to respect his desire to do the same. He wouldn't risk Belle to protect Clara.

"You don't care then about the people we lost—about everything we gave up?" she asked. Incredulity was not an emotion that she wore often. It looked as out of place as if she had shown up in a rainbow jumper and pigtails.

"Why are you surprised?" he asked. "I only ever wanted to get out. I wanted my life to be my own. It is now."

"They tried to kill you and your wife," she reminded him.

"Hammond tried to kill my wife," he told her. There have been no more attempts on Belle's life since the last time he spoken with the dead man. That was proof enough to Smith that the threat had died with him. "I'm not interested in revenge."

"Suit yourself." She drained the rest of her drink and placed her empty glass back on the table. "I'll continue to look into this."

She had always had a much stronger need for revenge than Smith but she'd also faced horrors he hadn't. Whatever ghost drove her to pursue revenge were her own to appease. Still he was curious, even if he didn't plan to take action. He had always wondered who was been behind Hammond and his anti-Royal conspiracy. It had been a shock to find out that his ex-employer wasn't the one pulling the strings. The true mastermind had stayed in the shadows, hiding himself so well that this was the first time Georgia had seemed genuinely optimistic in a lead.

He couldn't help but bite. "So, once you have him, will it be the Crown's justice or your own?"

A coy smile snaked across her lips."I haven't decided yet."

"You'll get yourself fired." *Or worse,* he thought to himself. Then again, there were those in high places who might feel inclined to help her out in a pinch—if for no other reason then to protect their own anonymity. If she ever decided to sing the tragic aria of her past, Smith knew there'd be more than a few well-known names included in that melody. "I pity the man when you find out who he is."

"Oh, I already know." She fluttered her lashes, looking anything save innocent.

Leave it to Georgia to drop that bombshell after he'd already sworn his neutrality. Asking for a name couldn't hurt. Could it? The chances that it was anyone Smith knew seemed unlikely, and given she was half the people he cared about in this world—or even spoke to for that matter—he predicted no feelings of betrayal.

"You're dying to know, aren't you?" she guessed when he remained silent.

"It won't change anything," he assured her. He'd made his choice. It was up to Alexander and his men now to concern themselves with this matter. So long as Smith and Belle were of no interest, he held none of his own. "It won't matter."

"Somehow I think it will," she said.

He took a long sip of his club soda, wishing, not for the first time, that it had a higher alcohol content. Or for that matter, any alcohol content. He kept this thought to himself.

"Who is it?" he asked at last.

"We're waiting for confirmation," she prefaced.

He shook his head. She was just teasing him now. She'd gotten him to ask and she wanted to enjoy making him wait. Whatever information they had was enough to catch Georgia's interest. He knew she didn't act rashly, which meant the evidence was damning.

"Who?" he repeated, uninterested in continuing her cat and mouse game.

"Some rising star in Parliament," she said.

"Why would that concern me?" Smith had never been particularly interested in politics. It was a useless fascination that distracted far too many intelligent men. Bureaucracy was a tool for those who preferred red-tape to productivity. "I probably couldn't name a single member of Parliament."

"That's what I thought when I first heard," she said, "but as I learned more about him, I found the connection."

"What connection?" he asked slowly. She hadn't called *him* on a whim. That much he knew. If he was sitting here it was because she had information that would catch his attention.

"He recently bought an estate. Seems he's trying to gentrify himself. We've had a few analysts profile him in an effort to see if he's capable of what we think he's capable of. I didn't need to wait for their reports. I've seen him. He is."

The prickle at the back of his neck told him what she hadn't yet. It filtered into his veins, turning his blood to ice while he waited for the final nail.

"His name is Oliver Jacobson," she continued. "I can't be certain, but given that he's your mother-in-law's new neighbor, I thought you two might have met."

Smith swallowed on the lump forming in his throat, but it had lodged in place. He didn't need her to tell him more. For the most part the man was a stranger. Smith had only spent a few hours in his presence. It had been Belle that Jacobson rubbed the wrong way. At the time, Smith chalked up his wife's dislike of the man to maternal difficulties. Jacobson had made himself useful to Belle's mother. He'd been visiting the Stuart family home for months before the Prices had sought refuge there. The few discomforting moments he'd had with the man, Smith had written off as the subsequent effects of his wife's paranoia. But now things began to click into place: the offhand remarks about the privileged aristocracy, the chilling moment Jacobson had held a gun far too close to Smith's head for comfort, and, of course, Jacobson's interest in the Stuart family.

Belle hadn't walked into Smith's life on accident. She had been sent, and Smith had been given the task of grooming her to be a source of information. His wife was meant to be an unwitting spy on her best friend and the Royal family. But by then Smith had already betrayed Hammond and those behind the conspiracy he was embroiled in. It couldn't be a coincidence that Oliver Jacobson was so well-acquainted with the Stuarts.

When the waiter reappeared and Georgia ordered two bourbons, Smith didn't object. She folded her hands on the table and waited as he processed what she had revealed to him. There was no need to speak. She didn't need to say *I told you so*, although she was barely holding back a smirk.

Georgia had been right. She'd known all along that this would change everything. Smith could no longer stay neutral. The enemy was far too close to home.

CHAPTER EIGHT

Harrods was packed with hundreds of last minute shoppers. It was all Clara could do to keep track of Belle amid the chaos. Their annual Christmas shopping trip had been a tradition since their days in university. Planning it these days was a little trickier than it used to be. It had taken Clara a fair bit of psychological gymnastics to convince Norris, her personal security guard, that she could go somewhere so crowded and public in the weeks leading up to the holidays.

Who was she kidding? These days it took considerable guilt trips for her to leave the palace grounds outside of diplomatic duties. She'd agreed to go in a way that would neither draw attention nor jeopardize her safety. That meant she'd been forced to wear a Burberry scarf around her head. Given how rarely she'd been photographed wearing anything but dresses and heels, she'd opted for Armani jeans and nude flats. She wasn't just shopping with Belle though. Norris was nearby. She couldn't see him. He blended into the crowd too well. She doubted that a woman at the perfume counter could get a spritz off a bottle before he'd be there pulling her to safety.

"Are you sure you don't want sunglasses?" Belle said dryly as they paused at a scarf display. She reached up and fiddled with the fringe on Clara's cashmere scarf.

"Don't remind me how ridiculous I look," Clara pleaded. This was as close as life got to normal for her. She'd have to settle for it. Right now, she needed to pretend that she was just another woman out for a day with her best friend. Otherwise, she'd be forced to think of the situation at home.

Clara had always been hesitant to share her relationship problems with Belle. Alexander was a private man. Every glimpse he afforded her into his own guarded interior was too precious for her to divulge. She'd have to settle for being out and away.

"Is everything okay?" Belle asked, as if she sensed how preoccupied Clara had become.

"Fine," she said absently. Belle's lips pursed. She didn't believe her, but she also didn't push it any further. Clara considered for a moment. "We're fighting," she admitted.

She didn't really have to say anything more. Belle was a married woman herself now. Given that she'd married a lawyer, she was probably no stranger to arguments herself.

"Anything serious?" Belle asked. She was choosing her words carefully, which Clara was grateful for. It was a tactic the two had become accustomed to in recent months. Clara didn't particularly like how the dynamic in their relationship had shifted. Though it had been inevitable, when Belle became involved with Smith Price. She'd begun to keep as many secrets as Alexander, even choosing not to tell Clara when she eloped in New York. They'd managed to both look past their hurt feelings. That was, after all, what best friends did, but nothing had been quite the same since.

"Just the usual," Clara told her. "He's being overprotective and unreasonable. You'd think he was the King of England or something."

Belle giggled appreciatively. "Smith isn't much better, and he doesn't have a title to hide behind."

"I can't stand it," Clara confessed. She wandered over to a display of holiday tea and sniffed the sample. It seemed like an appropriately safe present for her own mother. "I hate the security guards and the constant scrutiny. I hate feeling like a prisoner in my own home."

She left it at that. Belle didn't need to know that her husband had tied her up and left her for an hour in the bedroom. Alexander's proclivities behind closed doors was a subject Clara was fiercely protective of. Plus, she wouldn't put it past her best friend to beat down Alexander's door and let him have it.

Belle remained silent, and Clara realized she had struck a nerve.

"I like it," her best friend finally admitted. "Ever since what happened with Smith, I don't mind that we have a security team. I don't even notice them most of the time, and it makes me feel better."

Clara couldn't help but wonder when the two of them had switched places. Once, Clara had been vulnerable, afraid of her own shadow. It had been a product of the abusive relationship between her and her ex-boyfriend, Daniel. Despite the increased interest in her personal life, she'd railed against Alexander's obsessive need to know where she was, what she was doing, and that she was safe. In all fairness, he had every reason to be concerned, but Clara was determined to remain her own person, even though she'd taken on a life of public service.

Belle had been the wild card at university. Despite being engaged during that time, she could vacillate between dutiful and daring within seconds. It had been something Clara admired about her. Now Belle was the one who preferred to isolate herself. It took considerable effort for Clara to get her to go into public. Clara even knew that her own sister, Lola, who joined Belle's startup company had stepped in to takeover most of the public relations. Belle refused to be the public face of Bless. It was as if she wanted to be a ghost.

Clara decided to respect Belle's wishes, even if she didn't understand them.

"Who do you have left to shop for?" Belle asked.

Clara sensed she was changing the topic. She still had to pick up something for Alexander. Given how angry she was with him, now didn't seem like the best time to buy him a present. He'd done stupid things plenty of times, but for whatever reason, this has crossed a line and she didn't know how to step back over it.

"I need something for Elizabeth," she said, instead. "I know she'll get plenty of things, but I feel like I should get her a special present." Her little princess was already spoiled. She was the first grand baby, the first niece, and the first child. Elizabeth wanted for nothing. Still, Clara had precious few opportunities to purchase something for her child in person.

They headed to the children's department. Elizabeth was petite, taking after neither her mother nor her father, as far as Clara was concerned, so she was still in infant sizes.

"This is darling," Clara cooed, picking up a red velvet cape with a little matching hat. She turned to flash it to Belle but froze when she saw her best friend's face.

Belle was fingering the lacy hem of a christening dress and stopped when she realized Clara was staring.

"I've been thinking about expanding Bless," she explained too hurriedly. "Children grow out of clothes so quickly. At least, that's what I'm told. It might be useful if you didn't have to buy them all."

"Of course," Clara agreed with her. She sensed there was more to this preoccupation than what Belle was sharing. It hadn't occurred to Clara that visiting the children's clothing department might upset her best friend. A considerable amount of time had passed since Belle had confided that she had lost a pregnancy. The subject hadn't come up since. That meant Clara had to make a choice. Belle hadn't pressed for more information when Clara was upset earlier, but that had been an issue of marital difficulty. It seemed that what was on her friend's mind was something that she needed to share.

"Do you want to talk about it?" she asked Belle softly.

Belle began to shake her head, but then thought better of it. She cleared her throat before she began to speak. When she finally did, her words were thick with emotion. "You know I had a miscarriage" Belle began, her words thick with emotion, "It was right after Smith and I were married. It wasn't planned. I didn't mean to get pregnant. So much was going on, I'm not even sure how it happened. I barely had time to process the fact that I was going to have a baby before it was taken away from me. It seems like so much was taken away from me last year."

Clara searched for the right question to ask. She knew a thing or two about unplanned pregnancies, but unlike Belle, she hadn't lost a baby. To know her best friend had been silently carrying this pain for so long broke her heart.

"I know it's been a year," Belle continued, "and I should be over it."

"Love doesn't run on clocks," Clara murmured, recalling the wise words Norris had once shared with her. "I think you get to be sad for as long as you need to be."

"Even if it's forever?" Belle whispered.

"Even then," Clara assured her. She paused. She had already forced her best friend to own up to what was bothering her. Now she had to decide if she should pursue the painful subject. "Are you trying to have a baby?"

"Yes," Belle said after some hesitation, "and no."

"I think that's what's called a conflicting report," Clara said softly. She gave her best friend an encouraging smile as she re-hung the small velvet cape. Maybe this wasn't the best place to be having this particular conversation.

Over her shoulder, she caught sight of Norris, who was staying safely distant. She guided Belle away from petite reminders of what she lost—and what she still stood to lose. They stopped when they found a children's play table tucked in the corner.

"This isn't terribly dignified," Belle noted as they sat in the miniature chairs.

"Who says I have to be dignified?" Clara asked. The joke cut a little bit of the tension and Belle relaxed.

"I said I wanted to try because it was so obvious to me that Smith did."

"But?" Clara prompted.

"I kept taking my birth control pills anyway," Belle confessed.

"So, you didn't want to have a baby."

"No, I do. That's the strange part. I don't know why I kept taking the pills, except that maybe I was scared."

"No one can blame you for being scared," Clara said encouragingly. "Not only did you not plan to get pregnant in the first place, then you lost the baby. That's a lot to deal with, especially given everything else you were going through at the time. How do you feel about it now?"

"Better," Belle said. "Smith found the birth control pills and lost his shit. I had no idea it was so important to him to have a baby."

"Men are funny that way," Clara said in a dry voice. Alexander hadn't had been happy when she found out she was pregnant, but since Elizabeth's birth, she suspected he'd been trying to knock her up every time he took her to bed. She had never quite decided if it was because he adored Elizabeth, which he did, or because he seemed to take pleasure in the proof of his own virility. "Have you talked to him about this?"

"A little." Belle took a deep breath. "I threw away the pills. I told him so. I guess part of me is scared to get pregnant again, but it's not because I don't want to have his baby."

Clara wanted to tell her that everything would be all right, but she knew how damaging a thoughtless, if pretty, lie could be. She wouldn't try to appease her best friend with a platitude. "No matter what happens, I'll be here for you."

It was the only comfort she could offer. Belle smiled gratefully. Apparently, it would be enough.

"Come on," she said to Clara, standing up and wiping away the few tears that had managed to escape during their talk. "I need to buy something for Elizabeth, too."

WHEN CLARA'S MOBILE BEGAN TO RING, SHE IGNORED IT. AMID the crush of holiday shoppers it seemed imprudent to try to have a phone conversation. But when it continued to vibrate in her purse, she decided it couldn't be ignored. Given the number of times it had rang in a minute, she expected Alexander's name to be on the missed call log. Instead, she was surprised to see it was Edward. She flashed the screen to Belle, who shook her head.

"Isn't he supposed to be having a romantic moment alone with his fiancé?" she asked.

Clara didn't want to jinx anything by saying what she was thinking, but she suspected there might be trouble in paradise. Edward had been avoiding choosing a new wedding date for far too long since he'd postponed the original date David and him had settled upon. With all the other stresses of the holiday season, she couldn't help but wonder if matters had finally come to a head. The phone began to ring again and Clara looked to Belle. "I think we're done shopping."

She shot off a quick text message to Edward so he'd stop calling her repeatedly, and then began to search around her for Norris. She caught his eye in no time. He stepped forward and they hurried over to him.

"Edward is having some type of psychotic break." Belle explained. "We need to get to the car and call him back."

"As you wish." He clamped his mouth shut before he could add *Your Majesty*. Clara had asked him repeatedly to stop calling her by that moniker, particularly when they were in public, and she thanked him with a smile. It wasn't easy for Norris to ignore matters of etiquette, but he was more like a father figure to both her and Alexander than an employee. He stepped to one side to make a call and a few minutes later, he led them out the front door.

The arrival of a guarded car caught numerous shopper's attentions, and when the wind caught Clara's scarf and blew it away from her face, she knew it was a lost cause. Mobile phones came out and people snapped pictures. Norris hustled her away from the burgeoning crowd. At least, there were no paparazzi around to make the horror complete. No doubt Alexander would be seeing stories about her impromptu shopping trip from any of the number of the Royal blogs that stalked their every movement.

A twisted thrill ran through her at the idea of pissing him off a little. Every once in a while it was good for him not to get his way.

Belle practically shoved her in the back seat before anyone could take more photos, and when they finally settled in, they abandoned their shopping bags, so Clara could dial Edward. He answered before the phone had even rang on their end.

"Are you dying?" Clara asked him in a flat voice.

"I was wondering the same thing," he retorted. It was easy to see through his mock annoyance. Edward was the more charming of the Cambridge brothers. Being the acknowledged spare to the throne and hiding his sexuality for so long, he'd developed a charismatic wit that ensured his survival amongst the modern day court. It was one of the reasons Clara had warmed to him immediately, and when she'd introduced Edward to Belle the three of them had become the closest of friends.

"If you aren't too busy, I have a bit of an emergency," he announced.

"What's wrong?" Clara's attitude immediately shifted to concern.

"You sound like such a mum when you say that," Belle grumbled next to her. "Honestly, you should see her, Edward. You'd think she was going to burst into tears."

"Do shut up." Clara bumped against her shoulder. "He doesn't care about my emotional whims. Why are you calling us every five seconds?"

"If you're busy," Edward suggested, "I can just call someone else."

"Not bloody likely," Belle said. "Spill."

"Well, David and I are here getting everything ready for Christmas and fighting over the tree."

"Naturally." Clara interjected.

"I know, it's terribly gay of us," Edward said, before continuing, "and...I don't know exactly how to say this, but we've decided to get married."

"Tell us something we don't know." Belle said slowly. She looked to Clara with narrowed eyes.

"Like, *now,*" Edward clarified. "Or over the holidays."

"You're getting married for Christmas?" Clara clapped a hand over her mouth. Tears threatened to spill over. She'd never hear the end of it if she started to cry now.

"We were thinking for the New Year."

"That's hardly a distinction," Belle said. "Were you going to tell us? Or were you worried I'd think you were a copy cat."

"I thought if we had the same anniversary, you could make certain I don't cock up and forget a present every year," he informed them. "Besides, you're supposed to be here in a week, and I was kind of hoping you might come early."

"Of course!" Belle and Clara said at the same time.

"There's a lot we need to do," Edward rambled on, as if he hadn't heard them, "And I know you're both busy. Belle you have your business, and Clara you have—"

"We'll be there." Clara interrupted before he could talk himself out of it. If she had the opportunity, she would get her brother-in-law down the aisle. He'd been dragging his feet far too long not for her to jump at the chance to marry him off at long last.

"I'll need to arrange it with Smith," Belle said. "But of course we can come early."

"And Clara will need Alexander's permission." Edward teased.

"No, I won't." Clara said defensively, earning an awkward silence from both of her friends. It stretched across the phone lines until Edward finally broke it.

"Then it's settled. Call me when as you've cleared everything up." As soon as they hung up, Clara threw her arms around Belle in a tight hug, and the two began to laugh.

"You are an emotional roller coaster," she accused.

Clara pulled back, her eyes bright. She'd been dreading spending the holidays cooped up with her unrepentant husband. Instead, she'd be distracted in the best possible way. "I can't help it. It looks like Christmas is coming early this year."

CHAPTER NINE

Belle blustered into the house in a flurry of activity. She dropped her bags at the foot of the couch before she spotted him. Smith watched with amusement as his wife's cheeks turned pink. It was a lovely shade, and it reminded him of how easy it was to turn her other set of cheeks pink, as well. Her hand fell to her chest as if he'd scared her, but it was what was in his hand that caught her attention. A glass of bourbon. She didn't say anything and he didn't feel the need to offer explanations. One drink with Georgia this afternoon had not been quite enough—not after what she had told him. His prudence in sharing his quest for sobriety now seemed well considered, because today's events required more than a single drink to swallow down.

"Shopping?" he asked. She nudged one of the bags behind the sofa with her foot and nodded, playing the part of the innocent. "Something for me?"

"Something for me to wear for you," she purred. The innocent act disappeared, replaced by a full-fledged vixen.

"Do I have to wait for Christmas?" Right now nothing sounded better than burying himself deep inside his wife. Judging by the way she sauntered towards him, she had the same idea. But when she crawled onto his lap, she bit her lip. Something was on her mind. "Out with it, beautiful."

Belle didn't have to play coy often. They had money, so she never had to ask to spend it. He was obsessed with her, which meant that damn near everything she requested, he found a way to give her. But he didn't mind being in the position of power at the moment. Power was something he rather liked, especially when he could exercise it over his wife.

She hooked an arm around his neck and nuzzled against his jaw and whispered, "I have a favor to ask."

His dick was growing harder in his pants. She could ask for the moon right now and he'd find a way to lasso it. "Anything."

"I need to leave for Scotland in the morning."

That request was unexpected. Now he understood why she was tantalizing him. He popped a lazy eye open and looked at her. "I can't leave for Scotland in the morning."

She knew that already, which was what had brought on her seduction. Although he'd largely retired from legal work, at her provocation he had decided to take on pro bono work. He had a meeting with a client a few days from now. She kept well-informed on his cases, so she knew when he would be home late.

"But I need to go to Scotland," she continued to brush her lips against his jawline.

While it took considerable effort, he managed to grab her by the hips and break away from her spell. Smith wasn't fond of his wife being apart from him. The thought of her being in another country was unbearable, even if it was a neighboring one. However, after what Georgia had told him this afternoon, perhaps it was a good idea.

She took his hesitation as denial and began to pout. "Edward's decided to elope. You can't tell anyone." She rushed to say, as though Smith was about to get on the phone and call the tabloids.

"I was about to phone the press," he said in a flat voice. She stuck her tongue out at him, which only made her look more adorable. This was exactly how the little blonde vixen on his lap had wormed her way into his heart. She'd been wild and uncontrollable and all too eager to sink to her knees for him. He shifted uncomfortably, trying to ignore the steady uptick of interest in his pants at the thought.

"He wants Clara and I to come and help. Clara has already gotten permission."

That was a lie. Smith knew it. Alexander's obsession with his wife made Smith look like a sensitive twenty-first century male.

"Why do you need to go?" he asked. "Doesn't he have a whole staff who could put this together?"

"Because we're his best friends." Belle explained. "And we'll need to plan a bachelorette party or a stag night. I'm not really sure which he'd prefer."

"If you think the idea of you running around town, hopping from pub to pub is going to sell me on this idea, beautiful, you're mistaken."

The flirtatiousness slipped from her face and she began to glare. "If you think you can order me to stay home instead of going to celebrate with my best friend before he gets married, then you're mistaken, Sir."

She added the last bit with emphasis.

"I ought to take you over my knee for being so petulant," he warned. "But you'd like that, wouldn't you?" Belle always enjoyed a little fight before her submissive side came out to play.

"Or," she suggested, leaning forward to employ her feminine wiles again, "I could make it worth your while."

"Beautiful, you make everything worth my while," he assured her. Her hand slipped down and found the rock-hard bulge, he was doing his best to ignore. In actuality, she didn't have to work so hard. He had made up his mind, almost as soon as she'd asked. If Smith was going to follow-up on this information from Georgia, it would be better if Belle was safely out of the way. He had no idea whether Jacobson was in London or in his country home. Not for the first time, Smith was relieved that they wouldn't be spending Christmas with Belle's mother and brother on the family estate. He had helped his wife sell her interest in Stuart Hall to her half-brother earlier this year. That was a decision that was paying off in spades, because it meant that Belle felt no inclination to return there. Now that Smith knew Jacobson had been behind the attacks, she wouldn't be allowed to return; not until Jacobson was dealt with. Sending Belle to Scotland, where there were already armed guards, seemed like a smart move.

Belle pressed her index finger to his chin and drew his attention to her. "What's on your mind?"

"How many hours I'll need to fuck you before I'll be able to let you out of my sight," he said gruffly. She believed him because it wasn't a lie. He just left out some of the other important bits. It made him sick to think that the entire time they'd sought sanctuary from Hammond and his men at her family home, that they'd been in danger.

Jacobson had chosen not to act and Smith didn't understand why. He could have killed Smith that day in the forest, returned to Stuart Hall, and finished the job. Mary Stuart had welcomed Jacobson into her home without batting an eye. Smith couldn't help but wonder how much of the politician's decision to buy the adjoining estate had to do with his wife. It was another matter he'd have to look into.

"Seriously, Price," Belle demanded his attention. "You are in la-la land."

"Do you want me to show you what I'm thinking about?" he asked.

"Yes, Sir." She bit her lip again, but this time it was followed by a shy nod. He loved how her eagerness mixed with vulnerability whenever he shared his plans to take her to bed.

"You can go to Scotland," he said in a husky voice.

"And you'll come next week, right?" she asked, her eyes widening.

"Yes," he promised.

But it was a lie. He had no right to make such promises. Not with what he had to do. Despite that, his responsibilities would wait until morning. "Do you want to go to the bedroom, beautiful?"

She nodded again, a little quicker this time.

"Then show me the way."

Belle needed no further encouragement. Sliding from his lap, she found her way to the floor and began to crawl on her hands and knees toward the staircase. Smith watched appreciatively. It wouldn't be the last time tonight that he enjoyed the sight of his wife on all fours. He licked his lips as she paused at the foot of the stairs and popped back onto her heels. She was such a natural submissive—absolutely breathtaking in her willingness to please.

He stood and removed his belt in one swift motion. Walking toward her he slid it through his open palm. She tensed a little, but he knew she was simply preparing. Pain wasn't what Smith needed tonight, even if she might deserve a little spanking for her games. Instead, he looped it loosely around her throat and tugged.

"Come, beautiful," he commanded. Tonight he needed to possess her. He needed to claim her. No matter what happened in the coming days, he would leave Belle Price with no doubt that she belonged to him.

CHAPTER TEN

A week. I'd rarely spent this long outside Clara's good graces save for the dark periods when we were apart—after we'd first met and in the aftermath of my father's assassination. My wife had been angry with me since, and often. This time she was avoiding me. No doubt owing to the number of arranged and political marriages the monarchy had seen in the past, we both had our own bed chambers. It was a technicality since we took residence. I slept with my wife, and I would have it no other way. Since our fight, Clara had locked the door, forcing me to sleep in my own room. Her bedroom—our bedroom—connected with the nursery, so it was fair. But the dismissal meant that I found myself missing both the comfort of her body pressed against mine and waking to care for Elizabeth in the night. Without the nearness of both of my beloveds, I couldn't sleep. As such I'd found myself taking up temporary residence in my office. Throughout the day, I'd catch myself dozing off in my chair, my naps interrupted by staff members delivering paperwork or afternoon tea.

The more time I spent in the office, the more it felt like it belonged to me rather than my father. It was an unwelcome sensation. I didn't want to belong here. I'd accepted my role as King because it meant I could protect Clara and our children. Without her presence, I'd begun to question if I had become what I'd once hated. Was I my father? A man more obsessed with his own power than his own family?

A fire had been lit in the hearth and its heat warmed the air like a sedative. Abandoning my desk, I took the leather wingback next to it. I was a man who lived for his work. I was a man who bound himself to duty. What further proof did I need but the desire to take a nap in my private study? I clutched the worn, but recently oiled armrests and willed my eyes to open. I stared at the cream, brocade wall-coverings until my irises burned from the effort.

She'd gone shopping this afternoon without telling me. It was a perfectly normal thing for an average wife to do, but Clara was not your average wife. Norris had gone with her, and *he* had told me. I'd been informed, but it didn't change the fact that Clara was living life as she saw fit. Despite the fact that my information came from others, I was receiving her message loud and clear. She would not be ordered about. It would be a wonder if she didn't bring the whole monarchy to a crashing halt on her own. But her going out wasn't what bothered me, it was that she believed she shouldn't tell me. Not only was I concerned that I was becoming my father, now it seemed my wife was, too.

"You can choose the sort of man you become," I said to no one in particular. Even alone, I couldn't bring myself to believe it. It was something Clara might say to me. Would I believe it if she had spoken those words? I closed my eyes and tried to hear them coming from her voice.

A soft knock startled me and I snapped. "Enter."

Norris stepped inside and I relaxed. I couldn't handle the appearance of a timid staffer sent to deliver sandwiches on a silver tray. Not right now. My longtime bodyguard, and if I was being honest the man I considered a true father, didn't look at all ruffled by my tone. He eyed me appraisingly, and although his face betrayed nothing, I knew what he saw. I also knew he disapproved of it.

He looked nothing like what one might imagine a personal security officer looked like. Instead, he looked average with a medium build and a forgettable, if kind, face. In actuality, that made him a formidable presence. It would be unwise to go against him. The last man that had gotten around the security perimeters in place had met his end at Norris's hands. While my old friend considered it a failing that Daniel, Clara's ex-boyfriend, had tricked his way into our wedding, I knew that my wife was alive because Norris had been there that day.

"Might I have a moment?" he asked.

I waved him inside, bracing myself for a lecture. Norris was one of the few men who could get away with chastising a king. Mostly due to the fact that he'd been gently correcting my behavior since I was a child. But also, because I owed Clara's life to him. It was a debt I could never repay given that I held her life in far more regard than my own.

He shut the door behind him before he came to take the seat across from mine. He didn't wait for further permission.

"Please sit," I said dryly. Regardless of his standing within my life, I was in no mood today.

His eyes narrowed at my petulant comment. He took a moment to adjust his cuff links. He would reward my sullen attitude with making me wait even longer for his rebuke.

"Her Majesty plans to depart early for Scotland. She wishes me to pass along the information," he informed me.

"For fuck's sake!" I smashed my fist against the armrest. "Can she tell me nothing herself?"

Norris remained silent, but it was obvious he felt that was answer enough.

I forced myself to regain my composure. "Am I expected to come?"

"I assume that you'll want to discuss that with her, Sir." I didn't miss the insinuation in his words. He was calling me to action. If Clara wouldn't come to speak with me, he would send me to speak with her.

"I doubt it," I grumbled.

"You're not sleeping," he pointed out. There was a time when he would have noticed this much earlier on, but his orders had changed since my marriage. Norris's primary concern was Clara's safety. As Clara refused to be near me, I hadn't seen much of him over the last week.

"I've had a lot on my mind." I folded my hands in my lap. "Why aren't you with Clara?"

"She's in the nursery with your daughter," he said as he settled into his seat. Stroking a hand along his jaw, he studied me for a moment. "In truth, she needs very little by means of protection at the moment. She hasn't left her private chambers for days. She refuses company. And if you will pardon the intrusion of your privacy, she sleeps alone."

"My wife's sleeping arrangements aren't your concern," I bit out. I didn't need a reminder that she was sleeping alone. Not when I was well aware that I was sleeping alone, too.

"Alexander," he said my name firmly. "Do not presume to speak to me like one of the hired help."

"Aren't you?" I asked. But even as I said it, I looked toward the fire.

"I am not." His voice shifted into a softer tone. "I don't need to tell you that. I consider Clara and your child as more than a duty. They are my family, because I think of you as my son."

My eyes flickered to the oil portrait that still hung over the fireplace. Sooner or later I would be forced to replace it with my own. For now, my father looked down at me with disapproval. "Am I as big of a disappointment to you as I was to him?"

"Only when you act like a proper brat," he said. "And you only act that way when you are unhappy in love. Thankfully, that is not very often."

"I regret to inform you then that there is no end in sight to this particular bout of petulance."

"I suspected as much given Clara's behavior."

I wanted to ask him what he meant by that. Had she been crying? Was she still angry? Depressed? I kept the questions to myself. In truth, I thought of Norris as the father I'd chosen rather than the one of my blood. While he knew more about my personal life than most parents might choose, I felt far too possessive of my wife at the moment to share even my thoughts with him.

"I'm not in the mood to discuss my marriage," I warned him.

"That's fine." He shifted in his seat but he didn't rise. "I'll talk. You listen. No discussion."

I might be the King of England but I knew there was no point to refusing him.

"You and Clara have weathered some trying storms since you've met. Often the trouble came from those around you," he began.

It was like a father to overlook my poor behavior when I first met Clara. Norris seemed to sense what I was thinking as he continued.

"You acted in her own interest. I've watched you reject your birthright since you were a child. I know that you wanted to protect her from this life and that you were willing to give her up despite your love for her if it meant giving her the freedom you've never had."

My mouth grew dry and I struggled to maintain my calm. I had tried to give her up. It was what was best for her then, and as Norris spoke, I knew it was what was best for her now. The reality of that realization didn't make it any easier to consider.

"But you can't give her up," he said gently. "Nor can she give you up. You are bound to Clara by more than just a marriage vow. Your souls are bound to one another. Still the two of you fight for control."

"I only want what is best for her," I interjected. How could he accuse me of being power hungry when he knew my true intentions? Norris understood the dangers associated with being a member of this family better than anyone.

"And she you," he said. "But you must learn to give yourself to her."

"I've given myself to her completely." A dangerous anger rippled through me at his insinuation. He should know me better than this, and if he didn't and she didn't, who ever would?

"Have you?" he asked in a soft voice.

"I've given up everything to protect her," I roared. "My freedom.

My choices. She is the only thing I care about. Her safety—her life—is my number one concern."

"That is not giving yourself to her. That is giving yourself for her," he corrected me. "A man must open his heart to the woman he loves. He must bare his soul—his scars and his fears."

"Why?" I asked in a defeated voice. "Why must she bear my mistakes? My sins? My burdens?"

"Because she vowed to share your life—your whole life."

"I want her to be happy."

"You make her happy, Alexander." He leaned forward, shaking his head as if annoyed to have to point out something so obvious. "Your troubles cannot take that from her."

"I haven't told her about my other brother," I admitted. "Without knowing more about why he was kept a secret, I don't want to worry her."

"Why do you think it will scare her?" he asked.

"I'm not certain." I searched for a reason for my own fears but I couldn't find it.

"Has she asked you to protect her from worry?"

I shook my head. "She hates it when I keep what's bothering me to myself."

"A wife takes joy in sharing her husband's troubles. She chose her place at your side, and you chose a place at her side. When secrets creep into a marriage, they push you apart and leave space for lies and distrust."

"I don't lie to her." But hadn't I? I'd kept secrets from her before and Norris was right, it had created distrust between the two of us. I'd worked hard to open myself to her, but here I was still protecting her from myself, even when she begged me not to.

"A secret is a lie to everyone but the one who keeps it," Norris advised. "If I may, have you ever considered that you keep these things from her so that you can ignore your own fears? If you share what scares you, you can no longer control the reality of it."

"I don't know how to tell her," I confessed. I didn't know what any of it meant. I had no idea what the repercussions of pursuing my father's past would be.

"Start at the beginning." Norris stood and straightened his jacket. He took a step toward the door but thought better of it. Pausing, he turned to me and placed a hand on my shoulder. "You married a strong woman with a fierce heart. Believe in her as she has believed in you."

Reaching up I clasped his hand in a show of solidarity. Our eyes met and I nodded before releasing my grip. Norris looked to the painting of my father and sighed.

"You should take that down," he suggested.

"It is rather hard to get things done with your father reproaching your every action," I muttered in agreement.

Norris chuckled softly. "It might feel that way, but you should take it down because you must stop seeing yourself through his eyes. Stop looking at yourself from the past and accept the man you have become."

"What kind of man is that?" I whispered, unsure what his answer would be.

"A good one."

CHAPTER ELEVEN

Luggage waited inside the bedroom, and I stared at it, wondering if Clara had bothered to pack for me. Despite my recent conversation with Norris, I had waited for the morning. She was due to leave for Balmoral in an hour. If she wouldn't speak to me, I wouldn't ruin her Christmas. It was a cowardly thing to wait until the last moment, but the the very real possibility that I would spend the holidays drinking bourbon won out over bravery. Even through the walls I could hear the flutter of activity in the nursery. I took one deep breath to steel myself and followed the convenient passage that led from this room to my daughter's. Inside Clara and Penny were busy checking for all the last minute items they needed to gather for travel.

I watched my wife, her hair gathered into a knot at the back of her neck and her slender body showcasing a lovely navy dress that offset the fairness of her skin. I imagined slipping it from her shoulders and kissing each of the dozens of freckles that dotted them. We'd seen each other in passing, but I had done my level best to give her the space she desired. It wasn't a selfless act. It was one of desperation. I'd hoped time would heal the rift between us, and that if I could show her that I respected her wishes it would undo her pain over that night. But she fled from me in the halls and took her meals in private. She had granted me access to Elizabeth, but on those occasions, she'd left me alone with Penny. With each passing day my resolve to allow her to find her way back to me—if she so chose—weakened a bit.

Penny glanced up and froze. Of course, it wouldn't go unnoticed to the nanny that my wife and I weren't speaking. Her sudden awkwardness caught Clara's attention. My wife swiveled to face me, and we stared across the room at each other.

"Penny, will you go check in with the driver?" I asked her. It was a pointless errand, meant to send her away. We all knew it, but she curtsied and dashed away. I didn't wait for Clara's reaction. Instead, I went to Elizabeth, who was busy gnawing on a wooden block on the floor.

"Come to your daddy, Princess." I picked her up and held her close. Without Clara by my side, our daughter had been the one tangible link I had to my wife.

Clara had made it clear that she had no intention of leaving me. Or had I merely imagined that? The thought of losing either of them was unbearable. I buried my nose against Elizabeth's fine curls and breathed in her baby scent. I'd always known that I didn't deserve Clara, but I knew now that I needed her. I wouldn't survive without them. After a few moments, I decided I couldn't avoid it any longer. "Can we talk?"

She planted her hands on her hips as if considering the request. Finally, she shrugged. "We'll have the entire trip to Scotland to talk."

So, she did expect me to come. I hadn't expected that to be the case, so I hadn't made preparations. "I won't be coming," I told her softly. I felt a small squeeze of hope when disappointment flitted over her face. "Not yet, poppet."

Facing her, I knew that I had to find a way to put the past behind me before I could give all of myself to my family. I planned to take Norris's advice. Clara needed to know what I had been keeping from her. But that wouldn't make the issue go away. If I ran away to Scotland, this mystery wouldn't be solved. Once I laid it to rest, I'd be able to be the father and husband they both deserved.

Clara turned away, but I caught the slide of her throat. Was she swallowing back tears? I couldn't stop myself from going to her. With Elizabeth in my arms, I couldn't touch her but I needed to be near her. I needed her to know I was there. When I reached her, she shook her head. "You have to come! Everyone is expecting you, and Elizabeth will be disappointed."

"She won't know." As much as I'd like to think that my daughter missed me in my absence, she was far too young to realize when I was missing. I couldn't blame Clara for pretending to be concerned for our daughter though.

Clara dared a glance at me, tears swimming in her eyes. "She will, and Edward will want you there."

Apparently, she was going to continue to cast her own desires onto others. I couldn't allow her to suffer over this situation any longer. "Sit down."

"Don't order me around," she snapped.

"Please sit down and talk to me." This was what she wanted. She'd begged me to open up to her. Why did she have to be so infuriatingly stubborn and beautiful and kissable? To my relief, she sat down in one of the nursery's rocking chairs. Crossing her arms, she glared at me. I hadn't expected her to make this easy, but how could facing my angry wife be scarier than addressing Parliament?

"I'm listening."

It was a start. I decided it was best to jump right in rather than risk testing her patience. "First of all, I don't want to push you away, and I don't want to keep secrets from you."

"Then stop keeping secrets from me," she said in a flat voice.

"Okay, I'll try that." I paced in front of her, clutching our daughter. Elizabeth seemed to sense my anxiety and she placed a tiny, reassuring hand on my cheek.

Clara held her arms out. I hesitated, not wanting to give up my lifeline. Then I thought better and handed her the baby. I needed Clara to stay calm. I needed her to listen. There was a better chance of that if her maternal instinct was turned on.

"I've spent most of my life keeping secrets. My secrets. My family's secrets." It was an excuse, but I needed her to understand where I was coming from. "I don't want to keep things from you. I don't think I even mean to most of the time."

Clara raised her eyebrow in doubt. "That might be true, but when I ask you directly, you still refuse to open up. I thought we were past this when we got married..."

"And I keep doing it," I finished before she could. "I wish I had some brilliant insight as to why I'm so thick. I really do. All I can do is try and plead for your mercy when I fail."

"You can start by telling me what has you so worried that you're acting like a git."

This time I raised an eyebrow. "You're sounding more British everyday, poppet."

"God, I hope so. I'm the Queen of England," she shot back. Her eyes followed me as I made another loop around the room. "Will you sit down? You're making me nervous."

"I'm making you nervous." I laughed at the absurdity of that idea. "I've spent the last week going crazy wondering if you still love me."

"It's not a light switch, X. I can't just turn it off." She paused to glare at me before adding, "Even when I wish I could."

I deserved it, but it stung all the same. I never wanted to stop loving Clara. I could no sooner give her up than I could cut out my own heart. I had driven her to this point, and I had to atone for that. I thought of Norris's words of wisdom. I had to start at the beginning and hope that she would hear me through to the end. I cleared by throat and began. "Sometimes I think I keep secrets from you because I don't want to admit that some things are true."

"Do you hear how stupid that sounds?"

Trust my wife to not make this easy on me.

"I've been looking into my father's death." I had told her otherwise, but I'd never believed she was foolish enough to accept that. Judging from her non-reaction to this bit of news, I hadn't managed to convince her. "I told myself I wasn't lying or keeping secrets, but I was."

A smile twitched at her lips. I imagined she was enjoying my admission. I didn't often confess to being wrong. "Continue."

"I felt it was my duty. To him. To our family. I suppose I have a bit of an obsessive personality."

This time the smile broke fully. I could have fallen at her feet. Instead, I took the chair across from hers. "I have a brother."

A weight lifted from me as soon as I said it, but it remained to be seen whether I'd simply handed my burden over to her.

"I've met him," she said suspiciously. It was an understandable reaction. "Are you feeling well?"

"Not Edward," I said quietly, silencing her clever retorts. "My father had another son. He hid it from us."

"Who is he?" She shook her head as if rattling loose cobwebs. I knew exactly what she was feeling. It was one of the reasons I'd kept it from her in the first place.

"I don't know. I asked Brexton to look into it."

There were a million questions she could ask. Why did my father hide it? What would I do when I found him? Did he want to be found? Did he know about me? They were all the questions I asked myself when I found out. Instead Clara asked the one question that hadn't occurred to me. "Does it matter?"

"Of course, it does."

"Why?" she pressed. Elizabeth began to squirm in her arms and Clara released her to the ground. She crawled off, and I couldn't help but note the vacancy in my wife's arms. I didn't dare try my luck though.

"He could be behind everything."

Clara sighed. It was heavy sound as if she'd been carrying it for a long time. "I know the world hasn't given you a lot of reason to have faith in people. But you have to stop expecting the worst."

"I don't expect the worst." It was a ludicrous idea.

"You wouldn't tell me about this because you didn't think I could handle it. How am I doing?" she asked pointedly.

I didn't want to admit that she had a point. Brex had made a similar observation.

"If," she continued, "you wanted to find him because you were curious or because he's your brother, I could understand that. But you don't have to seek out conspiracies everywhere."

"I nearly lost you to a conspiracy," I reminded her. I would never take that chance again. There was good reason for me to be unsatisfied by the findings of the inquest into my father's murder. It had revealed that whoever helped Daniel was still at-large, and he had no problem sacrificing his puppets to keep his identity unknown. I'd thought it would end with Hammond. His untimely death proved otherwise. "I can't chance it."

"Life is too short to chase sorrow." Clara's eyes pleaded with me. "Be here with us. With me."

"I'm trying to," I promised her.

"Why aren't you coming to Scotland?" she asked in a small voice.

"I need to see this through. Maybe you're right, and it doesn't matter. Maybe I need to look at this from a different perspective, but I know I'm close." She turned away from me, and I tried to see the situation through her eyes. "Clara, I am not choosing this over you."

"It feels like you are."

"I will never choose anything over you." I meant it with every fiber of my being. "I will be with you on Christmas morning."

"What about the night before or the day after?" she demanded. A sob wrenched free and she stood, trying to hide her emotions. Now she was the one keeping something from me. I could see it in her eyes. I had no right to demand she share it with me though. Not after I'd been so stubborn about opening up to her. Dashing over to Elizabeth, she picked her up. "They'll be waiting for us."

I blocked her at the doorway. I didn't dare touch her. Not yet. Not while things were still so tenuous between us. She hadn't forgiven me, and I hadn't apologized. But I leaned forward and kissed Elizabeth's forehead. She cooed appreciatively. "You are always with me."

"Prove it," she commanded me softly. "Come back to me. When you've let this go. Find your peace and then find me."

Without thinking I reached out and brushed her cheek. "I will always find you."

Before she could stop me, I bent and captured her lips. After so long without contact, I expected to be driven by my more primitive needs, but as soon as our mouths met, it was enough. The bittersweet contact, full of longing and hope, tugged the shattered pieces of us back together. When she broke away, she didn't turn from me. Instead she allowed me to press my forehead to hers. We lingered like that for a moment.

"I love you," I whispered, "and I will prove I'm worthy of you."

She didn't respond. I watched her leave, feeling ripped apart. Clara was my soul, and as she walked away, I questioned my decision. She might not understand why I had to see this through, but I did. So long as she was breathing, I would give everything, even my own life, to protect her. It was one sacrifice that I would never question, even if she did.

I'd started at the beginning as Norris had suggested. Now it was time to see this to the end.

CHAPTER TWELVE

Christmas had come early to Scotland, indeed. When Edward claimed the tree didn't meet his standards, he had apparently overcorrected to remedy the problem. Now the Christmas tree took up at least half of the estate's family parlor. The rest of the house was dripping to the core: fresh garlands covered mantels and wrapped around stair railings, large arrangements of poinsettias and roses dotted every flat surface. There were so many presents it looked as if St. Nicholas had come early. Clara stared at them, wondering exactly where she would put the presents she had brought. A familiar arm dropped over her shoulder and she leaned against her brother-in-law.

"Did I do okay?" he asked.

"It's perfect," she promised him. "But I don't know how we're going to fit a wedding in here."

Edward swiveled toward her, his teeth biting into his lower lip. He looked guilty as if he was about to deliver bad news. It wouldn't be the first time he called off his wedding, but this time might be his last. Clara was getting as tired of the delays as David. Perhaps, they could stage a coup.

"Nope." She clicked her tongue in disapproval. "You aren't getting out of it this time."

"That's not it." He rushed to assure her. "It's just the more David and I talk about it, the more we want only close family at the wedding."

"Do I qualify?" Clara asked.

"Shut up." He ignored the question rather than pander to her sarcasm. It was further proof that he knew her well. "I know your family will be here for Christmas, and while I love the Bishops—"

Clara cut him off with a raised finger. "You don't need to say any more than that. My lips are sealed."

Planning a clandestine wedding turned out to be harder than she thought. Edward filled her in on the numerous preparations the housekeeper, Mrs. Watson, had been busy making. She insisted that there be a cake, but that meant that they had to hide a cake.

"It's not just any cake," Edward told her. "She went up to the village herself and picked up a pair of lovebirds for the top of it. She was terribly disappointed when they told her they didn't have two grooms."

"If only everyone were as bighearted as Mrs. Watson." Clara couldn't help laughing. Edward had spent nearly every family holiday here since he was a baby, which meant the woman had watched him grow up. It was impossible not to love Edward, and his fiancée, David, was quite lovely, too.

"What will we wear?" Clara asked, motioning toward the couch. She wanted to hear all the details. A wedding was exactly what she needed to take her mind off the bombshell that Alexander had dropped before she left.

Just thinking about it made her twitch. If Alexander had told her, had he told Edward? It didn't seem a good idea to bring it up when he was preoccupied with his wedding but he deserved to know. She pushed the thought out of her mind. It could wait. Everything could wait. Right now, the only thing that mattered was that one of the people she loved most dearly was about to say *I do.*

"I wanted to wear white," Edward said dryly, "but David insists that no one will buy it."

"What about a veil?" Clara teased.

"He said we could go in drag for our second wedding," Edward reassured her. Lounging back into the well-worn leather sofa, he crossed his arms behind his head. "David insisted we pack our tuxedos for New Year's Eve."

"That was forward thinking of him," Clara pointed out.

"Exactly." Edward nodded as if this had not escaped his attention either. "In truth, you can't tell that man he has to miss out on an opportunity to dress up, even if it's only a party of six."

"Six?" she repeated. He had really meant it when he said he wanted to keep it in the family.

"Well, I suppose Elizabeth counts as seven." Edward counted out loud on his fingers. "And then there's Mrs. Watson, so that's eight with you and Alexander, and Smith and Belle."

Clara forced a smile onto her lips, hoping he couldn't see the hint of the pain hearing her husband's name caused her. Thankfully, Edward was too wrapped up in the promise of marital bliss to notice.

Alexander had promised he'd find a way to her. She hadn't wanted to be the one to tell him that Edward was finally going to tie the knot. If Alexander had promised to be there on Christmas, she would plan on it. It would devastate her if he didn't show, but she would step in before she allowed him to miss his brother's wedding. But she wouldn't call him until the absolute last minute. Part of her wanted him to feel as alone as he'd made her feel. Another part of her felt ashamed for that thought. Alexander had opened up to her, and when he had revealed the truth – that he had a brother neither of them knew about — she'd understood some of his hesitance to share. But this was about more than keeping one secret. It was about what was important to her. If their marriage was going to say strong, he needed to learn to compromise, especially when it came to what he chose to share with her.

"Earth to Clara," Edward called, waving his hand in the air until he got her attention. "You're sitting next to me but it seems like you're miles away."

"I just realized that I didn't get you a wedding present," she lied. This was why she couldn't continue to put up with Alexander's secrets. It meant constantly forcing her to keep secrets from the rest of the people in her life. Where did it end?

With her, she decided, and that was final.

"Don't worry about it." Edward dismissed her concern. "It's not as if we need anything, and I didn't exactly give you time to shop."

"You'll have to settle for the pleasure of my company," she told him.

He dazzled her with a boyish grin. In that moment, the difference between him and his brother was clear. It was easy to see their age difference or Edward's curly hair compared to Alexander's black locks, but it was the quickness of his smile that set him apart from his older brother. Edward pushed up his horn rim spectacles. "That's all I ever want."

"Ever?" Belle cried out in mock sadness, interrupting the duo. Edward shot off the couch and ran to hug her. Clara felt a slight pang of jealousy in her chest as she watched the two of them. She had been the one to introduce them, and while she counted them both as her best friends, there was a little part of her that felt left out when she saw them together. Although she had to admit she had given them plenty of crises to bond over through the last couple of years. She shook the irrational reaction away. Between the Christmas season and her fight with Alexander, she was being silly. When the two broke apart, Belle grabbed Edward's hands. "Tell me about the wedding."

He cast a mischievous glance over at Clara. "That seems to be everyone's favorite topic."

They spent the afternoon plotting and planning. They also took turns picking Elizabeth up off the floor after numerous tumbles.

"You've yet to get your sea legs," Edward told his niece, hugging her closely.

"Don't encourage her," Clara warned. "Once she really starts walking it's all over. We'll have to baby-proof everything, and I'll never be able to catch up with her."

"Don't you have a nanny?" He asked her pointedly, looking around the room as if one might suddenly appear. Apparently, Edward presumed the royal family had their very own Mary Poppins.

"We do," Clara said, "but I want to do most of it. I'm her mother, after all."

"She's making up for her own mother," Belle interjected, casting a knowing glance at Edward.

"I think it's nice," Edward said. "I wish I had known my mother."

The girls paused awkwardly and looked to one another.

"Don't be like that," Edward commanded. "You two aren't the only ones who get to be sentimental this time of year."

"Anything is better than my mother," Belle said.

"Mine?" Clara teased.

"I will trade Madeline Bishop for Mary Stuart any day of the week," Belle promised her.

"How is your mother?" Edward asked.

Over the last year, Belle's relationship with her mother had gone from tense to unbearable almost overnight. That largely had to do with Belle's decision to sell her interest in the family estate. The move left Mary without a home. It was merely a technicality, though. Belle had sold her interest to her half-brother, and despite the way his stepmother had treated him over the years, John Stuart had displayed an incredible benevolence by allowing Mary to stay in his home.

"She's spending Christmas with John," Belle informs them.

"Is that safe?" Clara asked. Having known Belle for years, she was well aware of the danger Mary Stuart posed to anyone in isolation.

"She mentioned going to the neighbor's for Christmas morning." Belle shrugged. Whatever suited her mother was fine by her. "He's some politician, and my mother just loves him."

"And you don't?" Edward said.

Belle shook her head furiously. "There's something about him."

"Yes, the fact that he likes your mother," Clara said.

"That might be it," Belle admitted with a laugh.

Mrs. Watson bustled into the room, a flurry of skirts and aprons. She held out a slip of paper for inspection.

"I need one of you to review this, and I don't care which," she said in a thick Scottish brogue. Clara knew the woman less well than most of the others, and she was eager to impress her. Watson was one of the Cambridge men's maternal influences during their youth. Clara dutifully took the sheet and skimmed it.

"I know everyone is busy planning the wedding," Watson continued in a tizzy, "but I need to worry about Christmas supper. There will be far more people here for that."

There would, indeed. This year, the three of them had hatched a plan to revise the typical Balmoral family Christmas. While it had been tradition in Albert's time to extend an invitation to nearly all the branches of the family, Clara had expressed her desire to leave the royal brat pack out of her holiday festivities. Edward had wholeheartedly agreed. Alexander's and Edward's cousins weren't always on their best behavior, and they had never been anything but rude to Clara. Coupling that with the fact that Edward had stayed in the closet longer due to his fear of what they might do, it had been unanimously agreed that they would make their own family this year. It wouldn't be all smooth sailing, though.

After much discussion, it had been decided that all of the Bishops should be invited. Lola was well-loved by Belle and Edward, but David still felt a little annoyance over her misunderstanding with Edward. It had led to an unwanted kiss between the two. Still, she could be counted on to be on her best behavior. Madeline and Harold Bishop were another story. Clara's parents had been in couples counseling for the better part of the last year, and as far as she knew, her father had finally ended his affair with his younger business partner. She hadn't bothered to ask him herself, though. Undoubtedly, there would be tension.

Smith had no living family, and Belle was more than happy to leave her mother off the invite list. The only person representing the newly formed Stuart-Price clan would be Aunt Jane, who had an uncanny knack for knowing when to step in and went to stay out. Clara almost asked Edward if he considered asking her to stay for the wedding, but she wanted to respect his wishes. If it had been up to her when she was planning her own wedding, it probably would have only been close friends, too. As it turned out, she'd gotten just that, but not because she wanted it. Her actual wedding vows had been said in a hospital room. She was determined that Edward's fairytale would be more romantic.

Edward peeked over Clara's shoulder. "This all looks grand to me." He stood and locked his arm to hers. "Now, if we could discuss the filling of the cake."

The old housekeeper might need to worry about Christmas dinner, but everyone else's minds were on the wedding.

CHAPTER THIRTEEN

It had come to this. He had opened his door to a wolf. Georgia looked out of place standing in his foyer. Then again in her leather pants and motorcycle jacket, she looked out of place most everywhere. She certainly didn't belong there. This was his present and his future. She was firmly in his past. She turned in a circle then shoved her hands into her leather jacket and whistled, "You really are a changed man, Price."

"Yes, I am," he assured her.

But just having her here suggested the contrary. This was the second time he had seen her in a month.

He'd taken a few days to consider the information she had given him and to see Belle safely off to Scotland. Knowing who was behind Hammond and the conspiracy that had nearly claimed his wife's life didn't mean he knew what to do about it. There had been a time when Smith Price wouldn't have thought twice. He would have acted on instinct. But, his instincts hadn't always proven wise. Instead, he had digested this news slowly and taken time to consider all of his options.

"I've been thinking about what you told me," he said to Georgia.

She held up a hand. "I have a feeling I need a drink for this. Or are you going to pretend to be sober again?"

His eyes narrowed, but he tipped his head toward the sitting room. Once they reached it, he pointed to the bar cart.

"Not joining me?" she asked.

If someone had told Smith that Georgia was the original serpent in the Garden of Eden, he would have believed it. How many times would he fall victim to her dangling forbidden fruit in front of him? He shook his head. What was the point of any of this if he didn't learn from his mistakes?

"Suit yourself," she shrugged as she uncapped a crystal decanter and poured herself a bourbon. She didn't bother to sit. Instead, she leaned against the wall, sipping slowly. She was here on business and they both knew that. "So, what do you want to know?"

"Has anything changed?" he asked. He doubted it, but it seemed a prudent place to start.

"Not really," she hedged. He sensed she was holding something back. Of course, she would. That was how she operated.

"Has your team found anything new?" he pressed.

"No," she said finally, "because I told them to stop looking."

Smith prided himself on his ability to bluff, but she'd caught him off guard. Surprise passed over his face before he could stop it. She had been so sure that Oliver Jacobson was the one behind the attacks. Had something changed? He cleared his throat. "Why?"

"You asked me the other day if it would be the Crown's justice or my own," she reminded him, and he nodded. "I don't think justice belongs to either of us."

"Who does it belong to?" he asked in a measured voice. This was why it was difficult to accept that Georgia was working for the Crown. She didn't play by their rules. She didn't play by anyone's rules but her own, and it was impossible for an outsider to understand the twisted logic she employed to guide her moral compass.

"It's yours," she told him with a note of finality.

"Mine?" he repeated.

Her lips thinned into a line and she gave him a scathing look of disapproval.

"I don't see how it's my justice," he continued before she cut him off.

"Why am I here, Smith? You called me this time, but I doubt it was for an update."

"I don't know," he said, but it was a bald-faced lie. She'd known him long enough to see right through him, but even if she'd been a complete stranger, his answer was as transparent as glass.

"You want to claim justice as your own," she answered for him when he could not. "No one could blame you for that. I couldn't blame you for that, because it isn't just about justice. It's about protecting her. You have to know that she's still in danger. You have to see that the clock is ticking on your reprieve. He knows her. He chose her. So long as he breaths, Belle will be a target to him."

"You don't know that," Smith growled. But he did. He had already reached the same conclusion. It was what had driven him to this low point. He'd needed Georgia's help to ensure his wife's safety. Now that he knew the truth, he also knew there were far too many variables for him to turn a blind eye. His stomach twisted under the pressure.

"What's stopping you?" she pressured him.

"The night that Hammond died," he looked up to her, "I went to kill him myself."

"I suspected as much," she confirmed.

So, she believed in his innocence. That meant something to him. Even those closest to him, even the people he trusted, had questioned it when he claimed his innocence. They'd let it go because if it had been Smith that had killed Hammond, no one could blame him.

Georgia knew better than anyone the reasons he had to end that man's life. She might have have had even more herself, but she'd been strapped to a hospital bed, fighting for her life.

"I realized I had a choice," his voice was low as he spoke. But it no longer felt that way. Every time he took a fork in the road, it seemed to lead back to the other path. Was this his destiny all along? To be a killer? How had he ever been stupid enough to believe he could escape it?

"Hammond told me I was free. He acted as if he was giving me the option, but I knew in that moment it was my choice. It has always been my choice. I walked away. I didn't want to be him."

"And now?" she said softly, a tone that contradicted her usual demeanor. This was personal to her as well, and she could no longer pretend that it wasn't. Hammond had twisted both of their lives to suit his purposes. He had been responsible for the death of Smith's father and subsequently the slow death that claimed Smith's mother.

But Georgia had been another story. Hammond had groomed her. He had taught her about pain and he had taught her to want it. Smith couldn't imagine what it would take to break a woman like Georgia Kincaid. He didn't want to. It was enough to make him sick. The first time Hammond had ever put a whip in Smith's hands, introduced him to the seedy underbelly of London's bondage scene, he had also given him Georgia to dominate. It was a dynamic that neither of them appreciated or wanted. But, there had been little choice. Maybe that's why it felt like they were still in this together now, because it had been the two of them since the beginning.

"You still have a choice," Georgia told him. "I'm giving it to you now.

"What do you know about him?" Smith asked. He forced the part of himself that felt disgusted for taking part in this man's inevitable death deep inside himself. This was about Belle. His whole life was her now and he couldn't rest until he had ensured her safety.

"He's married," Georgia informed him. "Two kids that they shipped off to boarding school as soon as they were done teething. Everyone we've spoken to suggests his rise to power in Parliament is only just starting. He keeps his anti-Royal sentiments to a minimum, but our sources believe he's swaying more and more members to his side."

"Why doesn't Alexander just go about it like that?" Smith could curse the man despite his own connections with the royal family. Smith himself wasn't particularly fond of the royalty concept. It helped knowing that Alexander didn't exactly love to be King. Smith might not collect Royal memorabilia, but he didn't wish them harm. "And if Jacobson wants to dismantle the Royal Family, why wouldn't he just proceed through legal avenues?"

"I wish I knew," she told him.

"What else?" Smith prompted. What she'd said so far wasn't enough to go on. He needed information, needed facts. Where did Jacobson live when he was in town? Where was he now? Was he a paranoid man? Smith couldn't help but curse himself for not realizing the monster was within his grasp the day they had gone hunting. It would have been so easy, but harder to cover up. A planned attack meant he stood a chance of getting away with the murder. It was unlikely, but the odds were a little better than shooting a man in cold blood.

"Why don't you want to do it?" Smith asked.

Georgia paused as if considering this. Then she poured herself another bourbon. "I suppose in a way, Jacobson did me a favor," she admitted. "I would never have been free from Hammond, not until he was dead. That's why I didn't go after Jacobson myself."

"He was the one who ordered the hit on you," Smith pointed out.

At the time, he thought Hammond had been the one behind the attempt on Georgia's life, but the more he considered it, he couldn't bring himself to believe it. Hammond was obsessed with Georgia. He considered her his adoptive daughter, never mind that he'd been bedding her since she was a teenager. It was a perverse relationship to be sure, but one that Smith knew Hammond held dear. It had to have been Jacobson who ordered her death. It was the only thing that made sense.

"Jacobson tried to have me killed." Georgia shrugged, as if this revelation had rolled off her back like a light rain. "There are worse things than death, believe me." It was the closest she had ever come to opening up to Smith about the past she kept hidden. He didn't blame her for wanting Hammond dead. She'd played her part well, pretending to be the dutiful daughter. She'd accepted her role, and at times she had enjoyed it.

That was the difference in Smith's eyes. Whereas his wife had a natural submissive streak that turned on his dominant side, Georgia craved the pain for much less healthy reasons. She treated her body as a sacrifice, and Smith had always seen the reality behind the submission. The shame, and the guilt had driven her to moments far more depraved than even he could imagine.

"Don't look so heartbroken for me," she said, calling him from his thoughts. "I'm no damsel in distress, remember?"

If only that was true, Smith thought. The best thing that could ever happen to Georgia would be if she allowed someone to save her. He couldn't imagine what kind of man that would take. He had an inkling that she couldn't either. Maybe that's why she continued to seek him out. The trouble with Georgia was that she looked in all the wrong places.

"I want specifics," Smith said, deciding to get back to business. He would never be the one to heal Georgia, no matter the sentimental attachment he held for the woman. He hoped she would find someone who could. If she wouldn't act in regards to Jacobson, he would. There was no other choice. He could see that now. All roads led back to the same decision: to stay under the thumb of an evil man or to destroy the danger once and for all. He'd made his choice long ago, and now it was time for the reckoning.

CHAPTER FOURTEEN

"I am exhausted," Clara announced, flopping onto the couch beside Edward.

Belle sighed heavily. There went her plans. At some point, she felt it was necessary to take Edward on a stag night. There were plenty of pubs in the nearby village, and even Norris wouldn't be able to argue with letting Clara go for such a reason. The trouble was that poor Clara was always tired.

"Why did you leave the nanny at home again?" Belle asked her.

Clara frowned, as if it was obvious. "She has a family, too. There was no need for her to give up her holidays to take care of my child."

When Clara put it like that, Belle couldn't argue with her selflessness. Still, it presented a problem.

"Why so gloomy?" Edward bumped her shoulder.

"I planned to take her to the pub tonight," Belle confessed. "I feel like I should give your bachelorhood a proper send-off as your matron of honor."

"I thought I was the matron of honor," Clara pouted.

"You're both the matrons of honor." Edward stepped in before the two got bent out of shape.

"Regardless," Belle said meaningfully, "I wanted to take you on a stag night. It'll be harder when everyone's here for Christmas."

She respected Edward's desire to keep the whole affair a secret, but that did make it a little more difficult. The extended family didn't plan to depart until right before New Year's Eve. That left no time for a night on the town.

"Go on without me," Clara encouraged.

"We couldn't," Belle said, which earned her an eye roll from her best friend.

"You could," Clara corrected her. "And you will. You two are still young and childless. Enjoy it now." She winked at Belle behind Edward's back.

That hadn't occurred to Belle. Not only were Edward's days as a bachelor numbered, if Smith's and her new hobby panned out, hers might be as well. It was hard enough for her to get away from her husband for the evening. How much more difficult would it be when she had a baby's needs to meet as well?

"I feel like I'm missing out on something," Edward said, looking between the two of them.

Belle plastered a smile on her face and shook her head. "I was just thinking of where I would take you first."

"Norris better drive you," Clara interjected.

"Are you saying we can't handle our liquor?" Edward said in mock horror, grabbing his chest as though she had wounded him.

"Nope," Clara retorted. "I'm saying you can't stay out of trouble."

The Road's End Tavern sat delightfully at the road's end. It wasn't uncommon for locals to spot the royal family here during the holiday season, so no one batted an eye when Belle and Edward stepped through the battered door. They grabbed a table in the corner and ordered a few pints.

"I wanted to take you to a strip club," Belle told him apologetically. "But my options were limited."

"I think there's a fair chance that if you get any of these men drunk enough, they'll take off their clothes." Edward teased. The two of them looked around the room and then back at each other.

"Maybe we should skip that," Belle suggested.

"So, I've never done a stag night before," Belle told him as their beers arrived.

"I think we're supposed to chase women and howl at the moon," Edward informed her. "I'm afraid I'm not a fount of information on it, either."

She laughed at the image. If the two of them were going to chase a woman, it would be to advise her to wear a different type of shoe with her dress.

"Nevermind a bachelor party. What about a hen night?" Edward suggested. "Is that more suitable?"

Belle shrugged. "I don't know. I never really had one."

"We're terrible at this friend thing, aren't we?" Edward pointed out.

"Maybe," she agreed.

"How about we get pissed and you tell me about the dangers of marriage?" he suggested.

"As long as your spouse doesn't have a murderous employer, I think you'll be all right."

She took a long sip of her beer and pondered what he'd said. Were there things she'd wished she had known before she married Smith? She hadn't had time to really consider her decision. They'd eloped on an impulse, and miraculously, it had worked out. Belle supposed that when you have people trying to murder you, you don't sweat the small stuff.

"You've grown dangerously silent," Edward said, lifting his glass and tapping it to hers. "Care to share?"

"I was trying to think of something to warn you about," she said, "But I can't come up with anything."

Edward groaned, and laid his head on the table. After a moment, he lifted it and gave her a crooked grin. "If only every relationship could be as perfect as yours."

"Mine's not perfect," she reassured him, screwing up her face as if the thought was unpleasant. If he knew the half of it, he would never suggest it.

"You never fight, always have a post-orgasmic glow. Your husband is gorgeous and rich. What don't you have?"

It was a rhetorical question, but Belle answered before she could think about it. "A baby."

Edward set his beer glass down. "Is that something we want?"

Belle bit her lip and nodded. She had already come clean to Clara. It was time to open up to Edward as well.

"I suppose my days are numbered," he said sadly.

"What days?" she asked. They would still spend time together. They'd even go out to the bars every once in a while. It took her a second to realize that for the second time this evening, she was treating motherhood as an inevitability instead of an outside possibility. She wanted to slow down, and not get attached to the idea, but it appeared it was too late.

"David will want to adopt," he said, "and then we'll be having play dates instead of pub dates."

Belle scrunched up her nose. "When I think about spending the afternoon with Elizabeth, that doesn't sound so bad." None of them had complained about taking care of Elizabeth because they all adored her. The thought that Belle and Edward could add to the adorable brood didn't scare her.

"At least you can get pregnant," he said casually. "We'll have to adopt."

"You won't have any trouble." She said with a tight smile. "You have the pedigree."

"I suppose I could just walk in and take any baby I like," he said flatly.

"You are the Prince of England," she pointed out.

"I don't think it works that way, but if you're telling me that this whole time I could have been walking in places and taking whatever I wanted, I feel this should have been brought up sooner."

"It will work out," she reassured him. "It will probably be easier."

"Than your getting pregnant?" Edward asked. "I doubt it."

"I've seen both you and Smith. Somewhere, the two of you are at the height of a Darwinian evolution chart. He could probably impregnate you just by looking at you."

Belle's eyes found her glass, and she stared at the tiny bubbles floating to the top of the golden liquid.

"I hope it's that easy," she said in a small voice.

Edward reached over and took her hand. "It will be." He had no reason to believe otherwise.

Belle hadn't shared her miscarriage with him, or her fears about getting pregnant. Maybe if he knew, he wouldn't have said it, but something about the reassurance, the confidence in his voice, made her believe it, too. She squeezed his hand, then lifted her glass.

"I'm not pregnant yet. Let's drink."

CHAPTER FIFTEEN

It felt good to leave the house, although if I were being honest this was like a second home to me. The seat vibrated as the engines roared to life. In another life I'd belonged here. It was strange how easily pieces of who I was had slipped away over the last two years. Nearly all of them had been filled by her, and I would have given up far more of myself if it had been necessary. But while Clara brought out the fighter in me, this was one part of myself that I needed to reclaim. I had been a pilot once, a soldier, a leader in more than name and title, and I had saved men's lives because of it. Clara was still breathing today because of my time on the battlefront.

Brexton's voice filled my earpiece, and I turned to look at my friend.

"I don't think I'm supposed to let you fly, Poor Boy."

"Try to stop me," I said into my mic.

Other people were out doing their Christmas shopping, but nostalgia appealed to me on a very different level. I flipped a few switches and signaled to Brex that we were ready. Then we were airborne. I hadn't flown since that fateful night that nearly claimed Clara's life. Not really. I'd been on private planes and commercial jets. I'd done my fair share of traveling, but that was flying as a passenger, and it was a hell of a lot different than being a pilot.

Brex had put up a minimal fight about letting me take one of the helicopters. Although he had transitioned to my security team, he was still an acting officer of the Royal Air Force. That had certain perks. Whereas my own requests were met with deaf ears and red tape, Brex had gotten a hold of a chopper immediately.

"When I said we needed to talk in private," Brex called over our comms, "this isn't what I meant."

I didn't have to look at him to know he was grinning from ear to ear.

This is how we had met. We had formed a lifelong bond based on our time in the field. I liked to brag that Brex had kept me alive during that time, and he had. All the men I'd flown had kept me alive. I had been in a dark place then, and while I never cared if I came back, I wasn't going to lose any of them. They'd saved me simply by being there. I got the impression that Brex had entirely different reasons for becoming a pilot. Most of them could be found under short skirts.

I couldn't blame him. I'd be lying if I said I'd never used my uniform to catch a woman's attention. Of course, I'd had certain other advantages in that area.

We made our way over London, flying low enough to take in Big Ben and Parliament. It was my turn to grin boyishly as we flew over the London Eye. The romantic in me decided to come out to play when I spotted the place where I had proposed to Clara.

"So," I asked through my mic, "how long have you been seeing Georgia?"

"Every day. We work together," Brex retorted.

"That's not what I meant, brother."

With the heart of London behind us, we headed toward the countryside. I needed to get away and be somewhere where I wasn't surrounded by the constant pressures of my title.

"We're not seeing each other," Brex said after a moment. "You know her pretty well. What's her story?"

I didn't know where to begin with that one. My history with Georgia wasn't up for discussion, but I didn't want to leave Brex out in the cold. There were things he needed to know about her if he wanted to pursue her. Like so many other men, he might have fallen for her attitude and looks without glimpsing what lay beneath. I had to tread carefully. The intimate details of what had happened between Georgia and I in my younger years wasn't something I liked to share, and Georgia prided herself on being discreet. She wouldn't appreciate Brexton finding out that way, either. I did, however, have an out.

"I've known her a long time," I admitted as the wind picked up around us. It was rainy in the countryside today, and it blew in misty sheets against the glass. "I didn't catch up with her until recently, though. She worked for Hammond."

"I know that," Brex said.

Of course he would've been privy to her files, but how deeply had he read up on her?

"What do you know about her, Brex?" I asked him. There was no need to be coy if he already had insight in Georgia's past.

"I know she turned on Hammond. But there's something about her. I didn't want to invade her privacy."

It was a strangely touching gesture for a man who spent most of his time invading knickers. "She owned a club," I told him, "one of Hammond's holdings. It was a BDSM club." Surely, he could fill in the blanks from that.

"You mean like whips and shit?" Brexton asked.

I couldn't decide if it was curiosity or apprehension in his voice.

"And shit," I confirmed. "Really rough shit."

"Damn." Brexton let out a low whistle. "So you think she likes that kind of stuff?"

"Yes, I do," I told him. That was as firm as I would be on the matter. He didn't need any more confirmation from me about what Georgia Kincaid was into.

There was a long, awkward silence.

"What is it?" I asked him.

"So do you think if I said I was into that stuff she'd go out on a date with me?"

If I wasn't in the middle flying an aircraft that weighed several tons, I would've found something to smash my head against.

"I don't think you really date in that scenario." How much more information could I give him without indoctrinating him to the entire world of bondage?

"I don't know."

"Google it."

"I'll take it under advisement."

Despite the wind I could hear the sarcasm in his voice. "There's a good spot."

We put down in a field. It was empty save for a few sheep, but when we got out, rolling green hills smelled of manure.

"Ah, the countryside," I said in a flat voice.

"You were the one who wanted to go for a ride." Brex took off his helmet and tossed it into his seat, and I followed suit.

In case he hadn't realized, I was pretty serious about this whole confidentiality thing. When Brex had informed me he had finally tracked down his special assignment, I decided then and there that I would go to whatever lengths necessary to ensure there would be no leaks, even flying us out to the middle of nowhere to make certain no one could spy on us.

"So you found him," I said, pulling off my gloves.

"I found his mother," Brex informed me. "From the looks of it, that'll have to do."

"He lives with his mum?" I tried hard not to be judgmental, but what kind of a guy was this?

"He seems to be some kind of nomad. He has a couple apartments here or there."

"He has more than one?" This was a surprise, and more than a little disconcerting. I had my suspicions regarding this secret brother of mine. Finding out that he kept houses in more than one place did nothing to allay them.

"He's into some sort of racing," Brex explained. "His mom lives in Silverstone."

"I wonder how he got into racing," I said sarcastically. The little village sat right outside Silverstone Circuit, one of the world's premier race tracks. "Is he any good?"

"I told you he has a couple apartments." Brex grinned. "He can't be that bad."

"Is there any indication that..." I trailed away. Brex didn't share my suspicions regarding my father's secret family, but I think he understood why I had them.

"None, as far as I can tell. They're good, upstanding citizens. The mother's a war widow, and other than his penchant for dangerous driving he hasn't gotten into any trouble."

"But he's gotten into trouble for driving?" I asked.

"He's had a few tickets. And some crashes," Brex added on as an afterthought.

Given his occupation, this wasn't a surprise. I breathed deeply, enjoying the remnants of rain in the air.

"How can you do that, man?" Brex asked, pinching his nose with his fingers. "It smells like shit out here."

"In the city we have smog," I reminded him. Besides, the two of us had smelled much worse things in the time we'd known each other. "So who are they?"

"Her name is Rachel Stone, and we can find nothing on her. And I do mean nothing."

"Nothing?" I repeated. That was impossible. "Did you tell them why we were looking into her?"

"I kept that to myself." Brex shot me an incredulous look, like I'd wounded his pride. "But yeah, no intelligence. No background. It's almost like she never existed."

"My father," I said, and Brex didn't question me. An ordinary woman didn't just *not* exist. She had been covered up, but evidently not well enough.

"He's a little easier to get information on, considering his high-profile occupation."

So he really was a racer. I'd have to look into him further.

"Her name is Rachel Stone," Brex told me. "She's 48 years old, and that's all we know about her. We found a few pictures, but there's no employment history, nothing. She draws a small pension from the armed forces in the name of her husband."

"And a monthly salary from my father," I added with annoyance. Dad had gone to a lot of trouble to make certain no one found her. Why? What had she had on him to guarantee his silence and cooperation?

"I want to meet her," I said after a while.

"That is not a good idea," Brex advised.

I tilted my head back to the helicopter. "And that was?"

"Am I going to talk you out of this?" Brex asked.

"You can try, but it's a waste of breath."

"Can I at least escort you?"

"Send me her files."

"And then we'll talk about this further, right?" Brex prompted.

"And her address," I added. "Tomorrow I'm going to Silverstone."

CHAPTER SIXTEEN

The village of Silverstone had none of the flash of the nearby racing track for which it was known. I couldn't help but chuckle as I passed a sign that read *please drive safely*. It was a well-meant warning that no doubt fell on deaf ears. The area was known for the racing track, and I suspected they had their fair share of local teens angling to become part of the action. The tiny town consisted mostly of 19th-century brick and stone houses. Every few meters sat a tiny pub where the locals went for an evening draught.

Turning the Range Rover onto a slender strip of pavement that barely passed as a road, I found the address I was looking for. I pulled over a few houses down and considered my options. I came all the way here, so it made sense to see this through. But now that the answers I'd sought were within my grasp, I wanted to turn around. A few older gentlemen wearing driving caps and tweed jackets ambled past and nodded their heads. If they recognized me it didn't show. I couldn't expect such luck for long.

"This is what you wanted," I told myself. Had it really come to this? Coaching myself through a confrontation with my father's past while sitting on the side of the road in the middle of nowhere? In that moment, it didn't matter that I was the king of England. It didn't matter that I had faced war and assassins. What did matter was why I was here. I came to find the truth, and I wouldn't find it sitting in a car.

Last night, I had read the file on Rachel Stone. It had been alarmingly brief. There wasn't much to say about this woman who'd commanded so much of my father's attention—or at least his money. She was a widow, and she moved to Silverstone shortly before her son's birth. There were no criminal records or scandalous news articles. If my father had paid for her discretion, she performed that task admirably. There was even less about Anderson Stone. I had ordered Brexton to supply me with information as it came in. That meant we had a lot to learn about the Stone family. It was wise he didn't want me to come. I should have listened to him, but I had never been very good at listening to anyone.

That character flaw left me to wonder if my father had tried to tell me about his other son. I had laid awake in bed, searching my memories for some clue. But if he had left any—other than the mysterious bank account—I had been too dense to see it.

As I sat there, a young man walked by with a Christmas tree braced over his shoulder. I froze, hoping to catch a glimpse of his face. Presumably, Anderson Stone would want to spend the holidays with his mother. I had seen photos of him, mostly on his Facebook account, but I wasn't certain what he'd look like in person. When the man turned, I was relieved and disappointed to see it wasn't him. However, the Christmas tree had been a reminder that I had my own family to think of. I had promised Clara I would see this to the end and then I would find her. The thought of my wife was the catalyst I needed to open the Range Rover's door.

Gravel crunched underfoot as I walked a few paces back to the house. It was an unassuming brick box, a plume of smoke curled from the chimney and a single string of Christmas lights decorated the front door. I paused my hand on the antique knocker and then struck it. Inside a woman's voice called out merrily, "I'll be right there, love."

A few moments later the door opened to reveal an older woman, her sandy blonde hair streaked with gray and her blue eyes shining brightly. She blinked a few times as if she had opened the door to a ghost. Then her mouth fell open. She closed it quickly and stepped to the side. "Won't you come in?"

Her recovery was admirable. Then again, I supposed she had expected this day to come. When I began looking into my father's personal life, I knew I would uncover secrets. She must have known that I would as well. I hesitated on the threshold. I was the one who had questioned her motives and her allegiance. If she was the threat I suspected, I was walking into a viper's nest.

"I won't bite," she assured me. Despite the tension of the situation, she was smiling. I stepped inside, and she closed the door behind me. "I never imagined finding Albert's son on my doorstep."

I raised an eyebrow. If my information was true, she'd had Albert's son under her roof. I kept the jibe to myself.

The house was, for lack of a better term, homey. It still retained much of its historical charm with slightly crooked walls and creaking floorboards. There wasn't much to it, but then again, I lived in a palace. She let me through a quaint hallway into a cheery kitchen with butter yellow walls and checked curtains hanging on the windows.

"Would you like some tea?" She didn't wait for my reply. Instead she began to fill the tea kettle before placing it on the hob. "I'm afraid I don't have any fancy tea to brew. I expect you're used to something a mite better than what I get in town."

"I'm not picky," I said with a shrug. Nothing about this situation was going according to plan. Not that I had a plan. I hated to admit it, I had anticipated more drama.

"You must have questions for me." She took a seat at the small kitchen table and gestured for me to join her. I sat opposite her and searched for what to say.

"You are Rachel Stone?" Now seemed like a good time to clarify that fact, before I started spilling the family secrets.

She nodded. "And you are Alexander. I suppose you don't remember me."

There were a lot of things I expected her to say, but that had not been one of them. Should I remember her? She had obviously played an important role in my father's life, but I had no recollection of her being part of mine. "I thought we hadn't met."

"Not since you were a boy." She shook her head as if recalling some memory that had grown dusty with age. "I worked at the palace."

The high-pitched whistle of the tea kettle interrupted her recollection. She jumped up to take it off the flame, leaving me a moment to collect myself after this revelation. She had worked at the palace? That had not been in her file. Had my father covered it up? Why had he gone to such lengths to protect her? Before I could theorize, she returned with two mugs and a selection of teabags.

I cleared my throat, and asked the first thing that came into mind, "What did you do there?"

"I was household staff. I brought tea and biscuits and the newspaper." She dipped a teabag into water and continued, "It wasn't an exciting job, but most of my family had worked in public service. My late husband included."

I seized my opportunity. Any reluctance I had felt asking about her personal life vanished when she brought it up herself. "I suppose you know why I'm here."

"You want to know about your brother," she guessed, laying to rest any possibility that there had been a mistake. I did have another brother. Even after being told weeks ago, it was difficult to wrap my mind around. The idea that my own flesh and blood had been walking around for the last 25 years without my knowledge seemed impossible.

"Amongst other things. I want to know why he was kept a secret, and how you met my father, and—"

She cut me off. "Maybe I should start at the beginning."

That seemed like a pretty good idea, so I nodded.

"As I mentioned, I worked on the Royal household staff. Initially, I did laundry and worked in the kitchen. After your mother died, I took over some of the domestic duties she had preferred to handle."

Rachel gave me a small encouraging smile as if she knew how I was feeling. "I never took over for your mother, Alexander. But someone had to bring the tea. That's how it started.

"I had just lost my husband, and I needed to keep myself busy. One day your father had been drinking, and I came into his study. He asked me to sit down. I had no idea what to expect. Your father was a private man, and most of the staff considered him aloof at best."

"And snooty at worst?" I offered. This earned me a laugh.

"Yes," she agreed. "I knew a very different Albert. He only wanted to talk. I think he was lonely, which is something I understood. From then on, I took his tea to him every day. At first, we talked about the weather or soccer matches. Trivial things. Slowly, he began to open up to me about losing Elizabeta. I listened, and then one day, I opened up to him about losing Todd. It was less a romance than a friendship."

"I have a half-brother that suggests otherwise," I said dryly.

"You are very like him," she said, not noticing how I cringed at the suggestion. "We comforted one another. I doubt that we were the first adults to find solace in bed. If it had been a romance, it would have been doomed. When we slept together, we were imagining other people."

"And then you got pregnant?" If she was going to accuse me of being like my father, then I would be blunt. I couldn't quite see the picture she was painting, although I knew a thing or two about seeking refuge in sex.

She sighed as if giving up on her trip down memory lane. Rachel squared her shoulders and leveled her gaze at me. "I did. It was unplanned, but not entirely unwanted. My husband and I had planned to have a family when he returned from the Gulf. That never happened. Instead, your father gave me a child and a chance to have the family I thought I had lost forever."

"Does he..." I trailed away. It was the one question I wanted to ask. The question I had come here to ask. Now, somehow, I wasn't certain I wanted to know. Gathering my courage, I forced myself to ask. "Does he know who his father is?"

"As far as Anders is concerned, his father died on the front," she said pointedly.

No man could be that stupid. I didn't say this out loud. Instead, I shifted uncomfortably in my chair. The math didn't add up. If her husband had died in the Gulf and my mother died the same year, that meant she was either lying about her relationship with my father or she was lying to her son.

"Let me guess," she said, interrupting my thoughts, "the timeline doesn't add up. Of course, Anders knows that Todd Stone can't be his father. I suppose everyone does. It doesn't take a genius to look at the date my husband died and the date my son was born and know it's impossible. Todd didn't father Anders, but he's the only father he has ever known, even if it's only my memories. He doesn't ask questions. No one does. I suppose it's considered impolite to question a war widow."

I felt my mouth go dry. If she agreed with that ideal, then I was violating it. "I'm sorry for intruding. I understand your wishes, but I can't help but wonder why you took my father's money?"

I wanted to believe she was the woman she seemed to be, because it meant she was no threat to my family nor was her son. If that was true, I could respect her wishes and move on with my own life. But she had taken money and I could only assume it was for her silence.

"I debated whether or not to tell Albert," she explained. "In the end, I knew I had to leave. It was no secret that the two of us had become friends. If I stayed, there would be gossip and it wouldn't be long before the two of us were linked. I didn't want my pregnancy to become a scandal. I'm certain that people gossiped anyway. It wouldn't be the first time a woman disappeared from a domestic job. But it seemed the better of the two options, considering I wanted to keep the baby. Albert supported my decision. When I asked him to deny paternity, he agreed on one condition: he would be allowed to provide financial support for the child."

"So, he didn't pay you to keep quiet?" I asked.

"No. Children are expensive. You're a father now, so I suspect you know that. They need clothing and shoes and braces and schooling. Albert was adamant that his son not go without. In a way, I think he wanted to give Anders what he couldn't give you."

I tried to swallow this revelation but it lodged in my throat. My father had given me very little. Surely, she knew that. I couldn't quite ignore the twinge of jealousy this produced in me. "Approval? Love? I'm not sure you can send those with a monthly check."

"Your father often worried about the responsibility he would leave you. I'm not surprised that he gave his life to protect you. If he could have given you a choice, he would have."

This was news to me. My father had always loved the power his position afforded, it seemed to me. The idea that he somehow understood the personal sacrifice if required made me question everything. If my father had been the man Rachel claimed he was, then he was a stranger to me. But maybe that was what he wanted. How do you look your child in the eye and tell them that someday they will bear the weight of the world on their shoulders? I dreaded the day Elizabeth discovered the duty laid before her. Unlike my father, I would be behind her for as long as God allowed.

"Tell me about him," I requested in a soft voice. Rachel had made her wishes clear, and after I left here today I would respect them. Whether my father wanted to give Anders a life free from duty or not didn't matter. Not to me. I might never meet this man. But I could do him one service as his brother. I could forget about him. I could give him the life I would never have. Still, I couldn't quite do that without knowing who he was.

"He is responsible for this." She pointed to the gray in her hair, and despite the seriousness of our prior conversation, I laughed. "He's a daredevil. I think that a boy who grows up without his father has something to prove. He's awfully proud of Todd, but I wouldn't allow him to join the service. I like to think I'm a reasonable mother. I just couldn't stomach the thought of him on the front. He respected my wishes and took up motorcycle racing instead."

"I'm not certain that's any less dangerous," I pointed out. I couldn't help but think I might like him. I knew a thing or two about having something to prove. I also understood the rush of danger.

"It's not," she assured me. "I was the one who chose Silverstone, though. He grew up around it. At least he's crashed fewer bikes than cars."

"Is he married?" A wife might be the prescription he needed to finally settle down. It had been what healed me.

She shook her head, a sadness flitting over her features. "A mother can hope. Right now, he seems married to the road. I pray fate will intervene."

"It did in my case," I confessed. We sat there for another hour as she shared stories of schoolyard fights and car crashes. She painted a picture of a brother I had never known and would never know. At noon, I stood to take my leave.

Rachel saw me to the door. But before I could leave, I caught sight of a small table by the entry. A dozen framed photos clustered on it. The older ones I knew were of her husband. In a few, she was young and quite beautiful. No wonder she had caught my father's attention. Then there were the newer photos. I picked one up and stared. Anders and I shared the same eyes, but that was where the similarities ended. He was tall and broad shouldered with light blonde hair and an easy smile. In this photo the scruffy beginnings of a beard appeared on his jaw. In others, he was clean-shaven. But in all of them, he looked happy. I had never had family photos like this. My adolescence had been recorded by tabloids and newspapers. Rachel was right. My father had given him what he couldn't give me.

I placed the frame back on the table, and a strange wave of nostalgia swept over me. Perhaps, it was for a life I had never had. Turning to her, I gave her a hug.

"Watch out for him for me?" I asked her

She reached up and ruffled my hair. For a moment, a fleeting memory darted through my mind, but it was gone before I could latch on. "I always have."

That would be enough for a lifetime. It had to be. Anderson Stone might never know the truth, but that didn't mean he wasn't my brother. With her help, he didn't need to know. Taking one final look at the house, I left this family secret behind.

CHAPTER SEVENTEEN

It was his father's gun. He hadn't kept it for nostalgic reasons, although that would have been understandable. Smith had kept it with him during his employment with Hammond, and after he had been burned by his former employer, he had carried a single round with him.

He was saving it.

The day Brexton Miles showed up on his doorstep asking questions about Hammond's murder, Smith had shown him that bullet and explained its significance. He hadn't been the one to kill Hammond. Smith supposed it was some type of beautiful irony that the bullet he had saved to kill Hammond would now kill the man responsible for Hammond's death. He didn't act out of revenge. He knew he owed Hammond nothing.

Yes, Oliver Jacobson had left Smith and Belle alone for over a year. All signs pointed to the veracity of Hammond's claim that no one would come after him or his wife. But Smith had learned a long time ago not to trust Hammond's word. Everything he touched, the man poisoned. In actuality, Smith had no idea where the conspiracy started. It was like a monster swallowing its own tail, never ending, never beginning, only a horror to behold.

He took Belle's car. The Mercedes was a slick, pretty ride for his wife—and it blended in on the London streets. In this town, a Merc was hardly noteworthy. Smith's Bugatti was an entirely different story. But he didn't leave the Veyron because it was flashy for a getaway car, though of course it was. Simply, if things went wrong, and he imagined they might, he wouldn't have a second thought about disposing of the little sports car.

If he had to choose between the Veyron and his life, he wasn't sure which one would survive.

He pulled into an open spot a few doors down from the address Georgia had given him and turned the car's lights off. It was too cold in London for him to sit in an unheated car and not fog up the windows. The important thing now was not to draw attention to himself.

Smith studied Jacobson's London townhouse and grimaced. He'd been privy to a brief rant straight from his enemy's lips about the privileged class. Apparently, Jacobson didn't hold himself to the same standards as those he preyed upon. Smith knew a thing or two about real estate, and it was easily worth a few million pounds.

"No reasoning with mad men." he said under his breath, as his fingers popped his collar up for added concealment.

He'd gone over the information that Georgia had given him a dozen times this evening, but now he ran through it again. Jacobson's family was in the country. Smith preferred it that way. The body would be found sometime around Christmas when he didn't arrive at the family estate, but not by his wife or children. Jacobson didn't deserve such consideration, but his family did. Some horrors a child could never unsee.

Smith's mind drifted to the swimming pool in the basement of his family's London home. He would never put a child through what he had been through, nor would he put his wife through what his mother had never been able to forget.

According to Georgia and her team of profilers, Jacobson was man of habit. When his wife and children were out of town, he'd retire for a pint at the local pub around 10:00pm. He'd stay for an hour before returning to his empty house. This was where Smith's plan deviated each time he considered it.

The rash side of him wanted to take Jacobson out at his first opportunity. He was ready to be done with this business, but he knew it might not be the best course of action. A far better plan would be to watch and wait for Jacobson to return home. If he did it on the street, there was the possibility it would be written off as a random act of violence. He could snatch Jacobson's wallet and make it look like a robbery. The only trouble was London itself. No city on earth had more surveillance cameras.

That left one final possibility. He could take care of Jacobson in his home and do his best to keep his face obscured. The murder of a member of Parliament would be a national scandal. No matter who Smith's friends were, if he was fingered for the crime, he wouldn't be able to get out of it. He couldn't allow the fantasy of getting away with it to be part of his plan. If he was caught, he would take the blame. No one else.

Alexander would suspect there was more to it, but Smith doubted he would follow up on any inquiries into whether Georgia had shared classified intelligence. Once the King knew that Jacobson was responsible for the attacks on his family, any further interest in the case would disappear. Only one man would have to pay for the crime, and Smith had always been marked for something like this.

Like clockwork, the door to the townhouse opened and Jacobson ambled out in a corduroy field jacket and cap. For a man who claimed to hate the aristocracy, Jacobson didn't mind dressing like them, Smith noted with bemused detachment. Once Jacobson was well down the street, Smith got out of the Mercedes and locked it, then followed on foot. This hadn't been part of any of his plans, but instinct told him it was the right thing to do. He hung back as Jacobson entered the Horse and Hound, then he ducked in after him a few moments later. There were enough regulars in the place that no one seemed to notice a stranger in their midst. Smith took a table in the back corner, taking a page out of Georgia's book, and making sure his back was to the wall. Jacobson on the other hand, sat at the bar, and began a lively conversation with a half dozen or so men.

It was strange to see a predator in his natural habitat. Nothing about Jacobson's behavior belied how dangerous he truly was. It left Smith to wonder what was going on inside his head.

A barkeep wandered over, wiping his palms on the back of a bar towel tucked into his pocket. "Can I get you anything?"

"Scotch." Smith ordered, continuing his steep descent into old habits. The bartender tilted his head in acknowledgement and disappeared, reappearing a few moments later with his drink. Smith handed him a 100 pound bill. Tonight wasn't a night to use credit cards.

Jacobson chatted animatedly as he snacked on a basket of chips. "Enjoy that," Smith thought. It wasn't a proper last meal, but as his executioner, Smith didn't feel he owed him the courtesy.

A few minutes before 11:00, Jacobson raised his hand in the air to call for his bill, and Smith downed the rest of the drink he had been nursing. There would be no way to turn back after this.

He left the tavern before Jacobson had finished paying and returned to the Mercedes. Sliding into the driver's seat, he took the gun out of the glove box. Habit dictated he check the chamber. He knew there was only one round inside, but one was all he would need. There would be no hesitation, and there would be no mistake.

But as the chamber spun open, he found something he didn't expect.

The bullet was there, but where the rest of the rounds should have gone, tiny scraps of paper were lodged. He pulled the first out, recognizing Belle's handwriting immediately.

"If you're reading this," it said, "You think you no longer have choices."

She was right about that. He didn't have any other options not if he wanted to protect her. He withdrew the next slip and read it.

"If I'm not there to stop you, know that I will always trust your judgement."

He took out the next.

"If I'm waiting for you at home, come back to me, and let me help you find the light."

His hands began to tremble as he took out the last slip.

"You always have a choice."

The paper fell into his lap and he dropped the gun into the seat next to him. How could she have known? Or had she always suspected it would come to this?

Listening to her now meant abandoning the assurance Jacobson would never threaten her life again. But if he ignored her, he would refuse the most important request she'd ever made of him. "Come back to me." He could hear her voice saying it.

She could show him the light. Since the day he had met her, Smith had craved everything about her. He would give her anything. But could he step into the unknown with her?

He liked control. He clung to it. But he could never control everything.

Belle was waiting for him in Scotland. Belle, who believed in him, and in his ability to be a good man, even when he did not. Belle, who never questioned that, even when he revealed the darkness of his past. She had stood by his side. That was where he belonged now.

This was his choice, a future he couldn't predict. One that had far more beautiful possibilities than the ugly reality of his past. It was time for him to leave it behind. It was time for him to choose the man he would become, the man he already was.

He started the engine and pulled away from the curb just as Jacobson came into view. The man would never know how close he had come to dying that night, but Smith knew how close he had come to choosing the wrong path. He needed to find Belle and the light within her.

But first, he needed to speak to Alexander.

CHAPTER EIGHTEEN

Smith Price wasn't the sort of man to call at midnight for a chat. I had decided to return to my marital bed, only to be roused from it after a few minutes. My plan had been simple. Get some sleep and head to Scotland in the morning. I had promised Clara I would lay the issue of my brother to rest and then go to her. Now it seemed I was being called on to deal with an entirely different issue. It was a moment I had been dreading and anticipating for well over a year.

Shrugging on a simple black t-shirt, I didn't even bother to find trousers. If Smith had issues with seeing me in my boxers, that was a discussion for another day. My mobile rang on the bedside table, and I scrambled for it.

"I heard you have a visitor." Brexton didn't bother to greet me. Of course he would've been informed that an unknown party had shown up at the palace after hours.

"I do," I said tersely.

"Why is Smith Price coming to visit you?" Brexton asked. Apparently he wasn't going to beat around the bush. Normally, I appreciated his candor. Tonight I had more important things to consider.

"I'll let you know when I know," I promised him. Then I hung up before he could protest. I figured it was about four-to-one odds he would show up within the hour. I'd take those.

Padding into my study, I found Smith already waiting. He was still fully dressed, his hair damp from melting snowflakes. If I thought I hadn't been sleeping, he looked even worse. Bluish marks under his eyes betrayed him. Whatever he had come to tell me, he had known for a while. It had preoccupied him. But despite the weariness of his features, his eyes blazed. They sparked with a ferocity matched only by the fire that had been lit in the hearth. I waited for him to speak. As soon as the door clicked shut behind me, his mouth opened.

"Do we have him?" I asked.

Smith nodded, and it was all I needed to know. It hardly mattered who he was or why.

"Has he been arrested?" I asked. It was a stupid question. Why would Smith Price know that before I did?

But something had brought him here in the darkness to seek me out.

"No," Smith admitted. Then he withdrew a gun from his pocket. If any other man had done so in my presence, I would have rushed him, and tackled him to the ground before he could get off a shot. But although Smith Price and I didn't always see eye to eye, we understood each other.

He turned and set it on the mantle, then drew off his leather gloves. "Would you mind keeping that for me?"

"That depends," I said in a measured voice.

"It hasn't been used," Smith assured me, an answer to an unspoken question. "Not by me. Not for a long time."

"Do you always carry illegal firearms with you?" Of course a man like Price would. He'd seen the depraved side of London that most only imagined. He knew the nightmares and perversions were real, and he had something to protect.

"Why didn't you do it?" I asked him.

I knew why he was carrying the gun, and why he had brought it to me. It was part of why we understood each other. There was only one reason he would ever carry a pistol.

It was the same reason that part of me wanted to pick it up now. Smith had yet to name the man responsible for the murder of my father and the attacks on my wife, but I already wanted my hands around the man's throat. I wanted to watch him suffer. I wanted to watch him beg for his life, and then I wanted to take it from him. Perhaps I had been the wrong person to come to this evening, or maybe Smith had gone to the only person who could understand the contradictory nature of responsibility. My first impulse was to protect my wife, followed closely by the instinct for revenge.

Neither were luxuries I could afford.

"I saw the light," he said simply, as if this was explanation enough for him turning away from the task at hand.

I nodded. Whatever had lured Smith away meant something to him. I wouldn't ask him to share the intimate details of that, but I would ask him for the name. If I couldn't deliver my own personal brand of justice, I could bring the crown to his door.

"Oliver Jacobson," Smith told me. I searched my memory, looking for a connection I couldn't place.

"It's pathetic, really," Smith continued. "He's such a little man that we never even considered him.

"Parliament?" I asked. Brexton had indicated their sources had led them straight to the seat of power within London.

"Yes. I believe I was told he was a vocal minority," Smith said, as though he was recalling someone else's words.

"I hesitate to ask," I added, "but where did you get your information?"

"Do you really want to know?" he asked. "Is this an official inquiry?"

"Consider it off the books," I promised him.

"Our mutual acquaintance."

Smith didn't need to say more. We'd never discussed our own private involvement with Georgia Kincaid. Whether we were linked in more intimate ways hardly mattered now.

"You were right to tell me to look out for her," Smith said. "But not for the reason you think."

I cocked my head and waited. I'd ask Smith to keep an eye on Georgia. Now I needed to know if she could be trusted.

"She came to me. She put the choice in my hands."

"I'm surprised she didn't do it herself," I said in a flat tone. Georgia was capable of it. It was one of the reasons I had hired her in the first place. She had been playing both sides then, and I'd never quite been sure who held her true allegiance. Now I knew it was the man in front of me, the last man I would've guessed.

"She thinks he did her a favor. He killed Hammond, after all. Hammond was always the monster in her closet." Smith's throat slid as if he was swallowing down a disgusting memory.

I knew the kind of perversion Georgia Kincaid craved. If Hammond had been the man to twist her, then I could never blame her for wanting him dead.

Somehow, Smith had walked away tonight. He was a smart enough man to get away with murder. *If* he had come to me in confession, I would have done my level best to help him conceal his involvement. But he had chosen another path, and I couldn't help but ask myself if I would have done the same.

My memories flashed to Clara, and the scent of burnt rubber mixed with rain and oil flooded my nostrils. We'd never been able to prove that the car accident was more than an accident, but after comparing it with several other cases, including the one that claimed Smith's first wife, I had no doubt that foul play was involved.

I could never forget collapsing in prayer over a twisted hunk of metal on a rainy road. Some memories couldn't be erased, but they could be avenged. I glanced up and realized Smith was watching me with wary eyes.

"Georgia gave me the choice," he said in a strangled voice, "and it was difficult for me to walk away. I'm giving you that choice now."

It wasn't a coincidence that he brought a gun. He hadn't done it out of a dramatic need to show and tell about his evening. He was passing the job on to me. It was a show of respect and one I appreciated. I crossed to him and picked up the pistol. Spinning open the chamber, I noted there was only one copper bullet inside.

"It only—" Smith began.

"—takes one," I finished for him.

One shot, and Oliver Jacobson would be held accountable for the reign of terror he had begun. He thought he could play puppet master, but he never realized I was the one holding all the strings.

I held the gun in my hand, allowing the metal to warm to my touch. "I assume you have ample evidence."

"Georgia will show you profiles and notes from meetings. All sorts of *documentation*," Smith said. "But I met the man before tonight, and I can tell you, he's the one. I should have seen it then, but I was blind. I thought Belle and I were safe."

"What do you mean?" I ask.

He filled me in on the particulars of his mother-in-law's new neighbor, and my blood ran cold. The amount of time and effort Jacobson had put into planning this made me question if it would really end with him. He had found Hammond and his network of thugs and spies, and he had utilized them for his own gain. Even a bad guy sometimes grew a conscious. Smith Price was proof of that. I considered the weight of the pistol in my hand, staring at it for a long moment before placing it back on the mantle.

Smith had made a choice, and he did so out of personal duty to himself. I had even less flexibility in that regard. If Jacobson's intent had been to destroy the monarchy, choosing to take his life now might achieve his ends.

Instead, I went to my desk and picked up my mobile. Brexton answered on the first ring. "I want you to bring in Oliver Jacobson now," I ordered him. "No questions. Not until I see him."

I hung up the phone without waiting for his response. Then I went to the decanter of bourbon my father kept on the shelf and poured myself a glass. Raising it, I offered some to Smith.

He shook his head. "No thanks," he said. "I don't drink anymore."

THE CELL BREXTON HAD THROWN JACOBSON INTO WAS THE SORT of thing you expected to see in a movie. Governments like to tell you these places don't exist, but they do. They're for the use of men like me, and we reserve them for the worst kind of traitor.

Oliver Jacobson deserved even less. Not only had he betrayed the will of his country, and those he had been elected to serve, but he had betrayed the safety of my family. He thought I was a man bound by my own duty to British law. He'd soon learn that didn't extend to this place.

Smith had accompanied me against Brexton's wishes, but while my best friend had my interests at heart, he couldn't understand the ties that bound Smith and I together, not in this regard.

Jacobson had come without a fight. Perhaps due to good behavior, someone had bothered to give him a cup of tea. He sat in the dank cell, sipping it slowly as we entered. When he glanced up, he smiled as though we were all old friends meeting at the club. My hands curled into fists, but I did my best to remain in control.

"It's nice to see you again, Price," he said, acknowledging my companion. Jacobson looked utterly serene. He could have been having his conversation on a street corner. "It takes a little bit more than this to rile me up, I'm afraid."

"I wish I could say the same," Smith said flatly.

"Was that you this evening?" Jacobson asked. "At the pub, following me?"

I raised an eyebrow at Price, who shrugged.

"I have no idea what you're talking about." I did, but I kept this thought to myself. Giving Jacobson any information might prove dangerous if things began to go poorly.

"I am supposed to be spending Christmas with your mother-in-law," Jacobson continued conversationally. Next to me, Smith tensed. "It was disappointing to find out you wouldn't be there with your lovely wife. How is the beautiful Belle?"

"Don't say her name," Smith growled.

Before I could stop him, he'd lashed out, smashing his fist against the table and knocking over the hot tea.

"Is your temper going to come out to play, too?" Jacobson mocked me.

I grabbed Smith by the shoulder and helped him straighten up. Then I leaned in and lowered my voice. "Why don't you wait outside?" Smith had already faced his demons tonight. Asking him to do it twice might be too much.

He adjusted his jacket as he left, never turning around to look at the man who had been responsible for so much of the tragedy in his life.

"I suppose you want to ask me why," Jacobson continued as soon as Smith was out of the room.

There had been a time where I wanted that, but now I found it satisfying to know he'd never be free again. It hardly mattered why he did any of it. If I stayed on my best behavior, the audio and video recordings in the room could be used against him later. If I didn't stay on my best behavior, I'd have no problem using every power within my reach to keep him locked away. Either way, Oliver Jacobson would never be a free man again.

"Some of us weren't born with a silver spoon in our mouths," he said.

Apparently, he was going to tell me his sad story, regardless of whether or not I asked him to share it.

"There are those of us who weren't chosen in the lottery of birth, who've had to crawl our way out of the gutter, watching while men like you and your father abuse their power. I know everything about you, Alexander. I know the twisted secrets you keep in your closet. I know why you were sent off to the war."

"Yes, I was very privileged then," I said dryly. I crossed my arms and leaned against the wall. If he wanted to talk, let him. It occurred to me that Brexton might overhear something I had chosen to keep secret from him, but I could no longer afford secrets. Clara had shown me that. I had to learn to trust the people around me. That was the only way I was going to protect my family from men like him in the future.

"Daddy couldn't abide having a perverted son," Jacobson said, "And then he got stuck with a gay one. The lottery of birth, once again. But it never mattered when you sinned, did it? Never did a thing to earn your place, and yet you sit in judgment of me."

My eyes narrowed as I considered what he was saying. To be honest, I had expected more of him. There were questions I had, ones that would need to be answered in the coming weeks to ensure that the threat ended with him.

Perhaps after he told us more, we would understand how he had inspired the treachery of Hammond, but I suspected he simply bought it.

"You don't live in the gutter now," I pointed out. Smith had filled me in on more particulars about our suspect while we waited for Brexton to bring him in.

"As I said, I clawed myself free," he started, but I cut him off.

"Charles Dickens would be proud of you, but the rest of England has no patience for traitors."

"There are more like me," he warned. "Men who want to see the monarchy overturned, men who will enact legislation."

"Let them," I roared, losing my patience. "Do you want to talk about the lottery of birth? You claim to have been born in a gutter and to have fought your way to the top. That might have been admirable if you'd done so for the right reasons, but misplaced obsession only breaks a man."

I knew a thing or two about that, but I wouldn't bother to share it with this scum.

"It's easy for you to say," Jacobson began. "You've never had any choices."

"I have." I cut him off. "I chose to be a good man. You could've done the same. It's too late for that now, so I hope you rot in hell."

He began to talk wildly, but I was past the point of giving him any more of my time. He'd stolen precious moments from my life and from my family. He'd taken away things we could never have back, and I would never give him the satisfaction of a minute more. The heavy cell door groaned shut behind me.

Smith looked up from the floor, mouth opened, but I held my hand up before he could apologize. There was no need. He'd shown amazing restraint this evening. I couldn't hold it against him when he yelled at the man.

"What now?" Smith asked.

"Now we lock him up and we throw away the key," I told him, "and then we go home."

"You are home," Smith pointed out.

"Neither of us are home." I shook my head at the absurdity of the thought. "Our homes are in Scotland with our wives."

CHAPTER NINETEEN

It was Christmas Eve. Guests would be arriving any minute, and David wasn't speaking to him.

It had taken Edward an embarrassingly long time to realize his fiancé was hiding. Once he began to search for him he quickly began to panic. It had been a long time since David ran away, but he'd always had good cause to do so before.

Edward had asked a lot of him in the early years of their relationship. Whereas David had never needed to hide his sexuality, he had done so to protect Edward. Now, once again, Edward had managed to drive him away, and he didn't know why. It didn't help that Balmoral had dozens of rooms for David to abscond to. Checking them all might take the rest of the day. While it might be considered rude not to greet his guests, he wasn't about to spend Christmas without his love.

An hour later he'd checked half of the house and panic was subsiding into frustration. The sound of movement in the west library caught his attention, and he doubled back to check the space again. David didn't bother to hide when Edward entered the room. Instead, he glanced up from a book and frowned.

"I've been looking for you everywhere." Edward spread his hands in concern, but it didn't vanquish the displeasure on David's face.

"I was reading," he said shortly.

"I can see that." Edward willed himself to find a reserve of patience he hadn't yet tapped.

David had never been as comfortable around large groups as Edward was, but he couldn't avoid them forever, not if he wanted to marry into this unusual, dysfunctional family.

"I'm not avoiding guests," David explained to him, "I'm avoiding you."

That was a bad sign. Edward considered his options, finally deciding to take the seat across from David. "And why is that?"

"Don't you have guests to attend to?" David asked.

"No one is more important than you." Edward tried to sound reassuring, but this only seemed to ratchet up the tension between them.

"No one?" David repeated. "Not Belle or Clara?"

Edward's eyebrows furrowed in confusion. "They're here to help with the wedding."

"I'm here to help with the wedding," David cut him off, "But I've barely seen you the last few days."

"I'm sorry. I guess I wanted everything to be perfect." Edward knew it wasn't an excuse, and from the looks of it David wasn't going to let him off the hook so easily.

"And I just wanted to be with you. That's what this is supposed to be about. We said no big wedding. Remember?" David prompted.

He tossed his book on a nearby end table and sighed.

"This is about us." But even Edward couldn't bring himself to believe it. He had been focused on the cake and the flowers. He had poured over the words he wanted Alexander to use when he married them, and he'd been making quiet trips into the village to procure supplies. *I wanted to give you a wedding*, that was what he meant to say.

David deserved one.

He had certainly waited for one.

"I only ever asked for an 'I Do,'" David reminded him. He stood, moving to leave the room, but Edward grabbed his hand.

"Don't go," he urged, "Allow me to apologize properly for being a wanker."

"I'm not sure there are enough words in the English language for that apology," David said, but he paused.

He didn't pull out of Edward's grip. Instead, their hands remained linked.

"Am I really that bad?" Edward asked.

"Sometimes when Clara and Belle are around," David told him. "When they are, you go into girlfriend mode. It makes me jealous."

"Jealous of Clara and Belle?" Edward said incredulously.

"Well, I don't think you're going to run off with them," David's response was dry, but Edward spotted the hurt in his eyes, "You do leave me out though."

"I guess we leave all the men out." Edward held up his hands. "I'm not trying to make an excuse. I'm just trying to understand."

A flicker of a smile betrayed David. "So, I'm the man then?"

"Of course, you are," Edward said, "I'm the one who likes dresses, after all."

David groaned, but before he could come back with another retort Edward stood and pressed his lips to his. "Tell me when I'm being a prick," Edward commanded.

"Notice when I'm being a loner," David suggested.

"You know, I'm told that marriage isn't easy," Edward said, "But I think it will be worth it if you are by my side."

They had encountered rough waters before. There had been storms that nearly tore them apart, but somehow, they had clung together. That's how they survived.

"I couldn't live without you," Edward whispered.

"I just want to live with you," David said gently.

"You are my everything," Edward promised. "And I'm going to give you the world."

David brushed a kiss over his lips. Then he pulled back, grinning impishly, "Anything?"

"Anything," Edward repeated, despite the alert bells ringing inside him.

David grabbed his other hand and pulled him close. "Good, because I'd love to talk about a baby."

CHAPTER TWENTY

I strode into Balmoral Castle like I owned the place, which in point of fact, I did. Unlike my other homes, Balmoral belonged to my family rather than being given to me in trust of my title. Norris met me at the door but he was too late to stop my entry.

"You're getting soft," I informed him good-naturedly.

His head cocked to the side. "You—if you don't mind me saying so —are less paranoid."

"It's a new day," I informed him.

As a matter of fact, it was Christmas Eve. I had made good on my promise to Clara. I would spend Christmas with my wife and daughter. Now I just needed to find them.

Signs of Edward's penchant for decor were all around. The entire castle looked like a Christmas village had been blown up and its remnants scattered throughout. I didn't wait for Smith to follow behind me. We'd traveled together mostly in silence as we contemplated the events of the last day, but instead of tension, the atmosphere had been one of relief. We both knew we had our entire lives ahead of us and our wives waiting for us in Scotland.

Mrs. Watson met me as I passed the kitchen, wiping her hands on an apron, then throwing them around me. "I was wondering when you would get here, sir."

"Do not call me sir," I ordered her. I was fairly certain this woman had changed my nappies, but pride kept me from bringing that up.

"There's so much going on," she explained. "But first, young Edward wants to speak with you."

"And I to him," I said absently. "But first, tell me where my wife is."

"They'll be in the parlor with the wee one."

I pulled away from the old housekeeper, kissing her on the cheek before I left. "Tell me she isn't the prettiest thing you've ever seen," I called over my shoulder.

"The prettiest," Watson confirmed.

I paused in the doorway and took in the scene before me. The Christmas tree was lit, crowded around the base with so many presents that I couldn't imagine where we would put them all—and I lived in a palace. The fire crackled in the hearth, warming the room and casting it in a heavenly glow. This was exactly where I needed to be.

I saw that now.

It had taken me far too long to get here. I had seen to my work and nothing would ever stand between me and my family again. Clara was in the middle of the chaos, her arms wrapped around Elizabeth as she held her up to everyone's delight.

"There aren't nearly enough babies in this scene," I announced in a booming voice. The conversation died down.

Madeline Bishop looked up from her granddaughter. She was a gorgeous, older woman with wavy chestnut hair like her daughters. I imagined Clara would be like that someday. I only hoped she was less high-strung. She called over to me, "Whose fault is that?"

"No one's but my own," I admitted. Striding across the room, I stole my daughter from Clara's arms. Kissing her on the forehead, I passed her off to Belle, who took her with a natural ease. I paused, eying her momentarily. Later on, I'd have to study her for signs. She might be good for bringing more babies into the Christmas scene next year. Regardless, I had plans on filling that need on my own.

Bending down, I took Clara's hand and drew her quickly to her feet. "I think I'll see to it now," I said. Then I scooped her over my shoulder and carried her off. She was too surprised to protest, even as everyone around us began to laugh.

As soon as we hit the hallway, she began to pound on my back. "Put me down. This is undignified."

"Want me to list all the undignified things we've done in our relationship? I can do that, or I can take you upstairs."

She melted at the suggestion, the fight going out of her body. Apparently, I had been right to assume that my wife wanted to see me. We only made it to the private corridor that led to our bedroom before I lost my patience. I lowered Clara to her feet.

"Do you remember the first time you met my family?" I asked her.

She grimaced at the unpleasant memory. "I do."

I caught her hips in my hands and began to slide the fabric of her skirt up to her waist. "Do you remember what happened after?"

"I remember that you gave me some excuses about your compulsions." Fire danced in her blue eyes, and I couldn't stop myself from kissing her. She responded with her body, pressing herself against me as I hooked my thumbs in her knickers and pushed them to the ground.

I couldn't get enough of her. I never would. But, God help me, that wouldn't stop me from trying. Pulling away, I lingered, my lips a breath away from her own. "I told you that some compulsions are healthy."

"Not all of them," she protested, even as she fought to get closer to me.

"This is," I murmured. I dipped my hand between her legs, my fingers spreading her cunt. "Spread wider, poppet."

There was no hesitation. We might need to work on our communication in other avenues, but sex was a language we spoke fluently. Clara responded to my touch as wantonly as the first time we met. I might never give her everything she needed, but I would try—and I would never fail where it came to her body.

"You can't control me," she whimpered, but she didn't protest as I brought my free hand to her stomach and held her against the wall. If that's what she thought this was about then I needed to clarify a few things.

"It's not about control. Not this. Not now." I trailed my lips along her ivory jaw, writing my promises in breath against her skin. "I'm compelled to give you pleasure. I'm willing to compromise everywhere else, but I will fuck you. I will make love to you. I will take you to the edge and hold you as you spill over. Ecstasy is what I demand of you. I can't quiet my need to give it you. It is a healthy compulsion."

Her response hitched in her throat, a strangled mewl of longing escaping past her lips. Finally, she managed two, small words. "Yes, please."

I didn't need her permission, and I wouldn't ask for it. Not when it came to making her come. Watching Clara writhe with pleasure, helpless to resist, was my oxygen. The rest of my life was spent holding my breath until the next time I could gasp for air again. I could compromise on every other issue. I would strive to be the man she deserved and one that she could trust. She would be protected and respected in my arms. But she could never deny this need.

Trailing kisses up her naked thighs, I savored each one as I worshipped her body. I would give her my devotion just as I had given her my life. I slid my tongue slowly to the hollow between them, and her hands tangled in my hair. Her reaction took me back to that night in the hall. I had barely known her then, but I was already her captive. Drawing the tip of my tongue along the wet heat of her seam, I felt my cock twitch with impatience. He would have to wait, because I was exactly where I wanted to be.

"Let go, poppet," I urged, her scent flooding my nostrils as I spoke. "I'm going to fuck you with my mouth. I need to taste you as you come."

She inhaled sharply as if bracing herself, and I thrust my tongue inside her. I stroked hard only pausing on her delicious clit. Her fingers tightened their grip on my hair, and she began to shake. Wrapping my arms around her legs, I held her against me as I continued my assault. She didn't hold back as she came, her arousal gushing against my mouth. When she tried to pull away, I didn't let go. Instead, I idled there, brushing kisses along her trembling cunt.

Finally, she released my head, but she didn't break away. "I need to feel you inside me."

I was on my feet with her in my arms instantly. She sagged against me, her face tucked below my chin so that I could feel the soft heat of her breath. Kicking the door closed behind us, I lowered her to her feet. When she took a shaky step toward me, my arms were waiting to catch her. "Let me help you, poppet."

She clung to me as I lifted her skirt up and drew her dress over her head. Abandoning it to the floor, I studied her body appreciatively. It wasn't the same as when we first met, this body was more beautiful, softened by motherhood and ripened by cultivation. I brought my hands to her breasts and skimmed over them, pausing to flick her nipples. They hardened into two beads that I couldn't resist. Slanting my head, I sucked a mouthful between my lips and Clara cried out. Moving to the other I couldn't help but toy with her. "I could make you come like this with my tongue and my teeth."

"I think you just proved that," she complained through gritted teeth.

"I was willing to prove it again, but..." The back of my head was shoved closer, and I chuckled.

"More," she demanded as I nipped the delicate furls.

I couldn't wait any longer to fulfill her request. Cupping her ass, I lifted her so she could wrap her legs around my waist.

"Slowly," I cautioned her as her sex nudged against the broad crown of my cock. It was as much a reminder to myself as it was to her. I had to fight the impulse to plunge inside her. Even after all this time, her entrance strained to accommodate me. She glided down my shaft, her cunt rippling against the engorged flesh. But it wasn't enough. I needed more. I longed to be brutally deep inside my wife.

Moving toward the bed, I lowered our bodies slowly, never breaking our union.

Clara brushed a strand of hair away from her eyes, and our gazes met. We stayed like that, seeing into one another's souls, as I rocked myself fully inside her. Clara's head tipped back and she struggled to maintain the visual contact as she began to unravel. It was the most beautiful vision in the world—her porcelain body quivering uncontrollably. She bit down on her lower lip, sobs pouring from her, as she came. Her cunt clamped against me, drawing forth my orgasm in punctuated spasms, until I emptied inside her.

I held her for a few minutes or a few hours, her body clutched to mine. We laid in silence, the only movement a brush of the fingers or a soft, fleeting kiss. When I finally withdrew, I watched mesmerized as my seed spilled from her swollen pink mound.

"Everything I am belongs to you," I promised her in a whisper.

"Forever?" she asked, her eyes shining with unshed tears.

"For always."

CHAPTER TWENTY-ONE

Clara snuggled against his chest, releasing a deep sigh of contentment. This was where she belonged. No matter how stubborn she acted or the hoops she made him jump through, she was Alexander's. She had been from the moment she saw him in the lounge at the Oxford and Cambridge Club. Despite her desire that day to write him off as a bad boy, she had been drawn to him, inexplicably so. And nothing had ever been the same since. One brief moment, one stolen kiss and everything had changed. Clara had had a plan for her life and he had come along to upset the destiny she had laid out for herself.

She ran her palm over the slab of muscles that comprised his abdomen, her fingers pausing along the scars that snaked over his torso. Once he had hidden himself from her, showing her only glimpses of the darkness of his past and the burdens he carried inside him. Sometimes he regressed into those habits and it was her job to bring him back to the light. He caught her hand, grasping it with his and lingered over the scars. They were physical reminders of the accident that claimed his sister's life and set him on a trajectory toward her.

"You don't have to," he said, hesitantly.

She wriggled her fingers free and brushed along the damaged tissue. "I want to. I want all of you, X. The beautiful and the ugly. The darkness and the light."

"You already have it," he vowed to her.

She rolled over and climbed on top, straddling his trim waist. Placing her hands over the scars, she rocked her hips until they made contact with his thickening cock. She kept her hands there as the two found each other naturally. His crest knocked gently at her entrance and she lifted herself just high enough to grant him access. Then Clara enveloped him slowly, losing herself to the sensation as he stretched delicate tissues.

In the past, Alexander had been too much for her. He brought too much emotion, too much pain, too much of him for her to handle. Now she accepted the beauty of their bittersweet relationship. She would never have enough of him—physically and spiritually. He completed her. Within her there was a void only he could fill.

Alexander's hands closed over hers as he began to roll his hips in a steady, quickening rhythm.

"Be with me," he called to her. "I want to see how beautiful you are when you're riding my cock."

She opened her eyes to find his trained on hers. As the first, white-hot emissaries of climax stole through her limbs, she cried out, riding through the fire under his lustful gaze. But before she could collapse against him, Alexander's hands found her hips and provided the endurance she no longer had. Her body fought her, as her heart once had, but neither answered to her will any longer. When the friction built again, she exploded, taking him with her.

Clara flopped against the pillow in a boneless heap of limbs. Satiated didn't begin to describe how she felt. Clutching the sheet to her chest, she shot a mischievous glance at her husband.

"It's been a while," she said breathlessly. Clara had grown accustomed to their daily lovemaking. Actually, most of the time, it was damn near hourly. It had been far too long since he had last taken her to bed and now she felt used and strained and sore—all in the best way possible.

"Ten days," he informed her.

"Did you count the minutes, too?" she asked, cocking an eyebrow at him. Trust it to Alexander to know how long he'd gone without claiming her body. She couldn't help taking a little pleasure in knowing that he had missed her as much as she had missed him.

"Speaking of, we need to catch up," he said, propping himself onto his elbow and casting his eyes upon her. "Is there something you want to tell me?"

Alexander's gaze pierced through her, and Clara bit her lip, grinning sheepishly. "Maybe."

It was pointless to hedge. From the looks on his face, he already knew, but his acknowledgement was the first true confirmation she had received. Her suspicions had begun to grow in the last few days but she'd been far too busy to see them through. Alexander reached over and circled her nipple with his fingertip lazily. Even the slight touch set her on edge. He was teasing, or rather, testing her body, and her response might have proven his theory.

"Well," he prompted, "how far along are you?"

She resisted the urge to pull the sheet over her head.

"I don't know," she whispered, daring an embarrassed grin instead.

"You don't know?" he repeated. "This sounds like a familiar story."

"I've been a little busy." Defensiveness overcame her. It wasn't as if she had planned this, and he was the reason she'd been distracted anyway. Maybe he needed a reminder of that. "And I was mad at you."

"That doesn't change the fact that you're pregnant, poppet." Alexander's hand slid to cover her belly and laid his palm flatly against the soft tissue that would soon swell with life.

"For all I know, you *just* got me pregnant." She informed him but with Alexander there to face facts, she knew that wasn't the case. The mood swings, the irritability, and the incessant urge to cry constantly, it was all there. Even Belle had bothered to point it out which made Clara wonder if her best friend suspected before she did.

"Even I'm not that skilled. Though it hurts to admit it."

"How did you know anyway?" Clara asked. She'd had every reason to be upset with Alexander in London, so if he tried to pin it on that, he had another thing coming. No, Alexander hadn't been privy to the emotional gymnastics she'd put on for Belle and Edward. If he had guessed, there had been some other clue she was missing.

He pressed his lips into a bemused smile and shook his head. "No way."

"Now you have to tell me," she cried, picking up a pillow and beating him with it.

He released a tortured sigh before he tilted his head and admitted his source. "I can taste it."

Clara blinked, trying to process this confession. "I'm not certain that's a good thing."

"It is." A smug smile carved over his handsome features. Not for the first time, she hoped the baby looked like him with his inky black hair and crystal blue eyes. *There were worse things than carrying the child of a human sex god who worshiped you*, she thought, *even if he could be an arrogant prick sometimes.*

Her hand found the one resting on her belly and she covered it, holding him there in that sacred spot. Alexander's eyes closed, a reverent calm overcoming his features, as if he was holding vigil.

"Happy Christmas," Clara whispered. Then a terrible thought occurred to her. She hadn't bought him a single present. She couldn't help but wonder if she should plead hormonal insanity in the morning or confess now. "I have to warn you, I don't have anything to give you."

He popped one eye open, then the other and the love reflecting from them nearly blinded her. "Clara, you've given me everything."

CHAPTER TWENTY-TWO

The entire family was gathered into the parlor that evening. Their number had doubled throughout the course of the day, and now they were complete. It was an odd mish-mash of people and a few they suspected might show, like Alexander's grandmother or his friend, Brexton, were nowhere to be found.

But Belle's heart was full. She had spent plenty of Christmas Eves drowning her sorrows with a stolen bottle of wine while avoiding her mother. Last year had been the first holiday that she had not spent at the Stuart family estate. Now getting to spend her Christmas Eve with the people she cherished most, she knew that breaking that tradition had been the right choice.

In the past, she had been desperate for her mother's approval. She'd sought it by agreeing to a marriage that would bolster their family standing and ensure the financial security of Stuart Hall. Now Belle chalked it up to being young and foolish. She knew it ran deeper than that, though. She had wanted to be loved and, without understanding what that really meant, she had been willing to overlook how people like her mother and Philip treated her in return for the illusion of it. When she had ended things with her ex-fiancé, it took her a long time to accept that some people didn't change.

As a girl, she had wanted to believe that if she did the things her mother asked, she would be loved in return. Now as she looked around this room full of people who had been there for her through every up and down, a firm conviction settled over her. She'd heard it said before, but now she truly understood what it meant to choose her own family. They were an imperfect bunch, to be sure, but they were hers and she wouldn't give them up for anything.

Elizabeth crawled over and used Belle's knees to pull herself into a standing position.

"Clever girl," Belle praised, picking her up under her arms and placing the baby in her lap. "You take after your auntie."

Holding her, Belle knew that accepting nothing less than loyalty and unconditional love was her destiny to claim. That seemed a particularly important realization to come to as she considered the leap into motherhood.

Elizabeth caught a lock of her blonde hair and tugged on it, trying to pull it toward her mouth. Belle shook her head, clucking softly and maneuvered it away, only to have Elizabeth catch her palm. The baby seemed content to try to put that in her mouth instead.

Belle couldn't help but laugh as joy flooded through her. When she felt eyes burning across the room, she lifted her own to find Smith watching her with the baby through hooded eyelids. He drank in the sight before him, which was something Belle didn't mind doing herself.

Her husband had opted to dress down in a charcoal sweater and a pair of jeans. He didn't usually wear things that were so casual, and she made it a point to let him know exactly how she felt about the way his ass looked in those pants. As soon as they returned to London, there was going to be a whole new drawer of jeans waiting for him.

His gaze didn't waver from her. Even from a distance, she could see the fierce desire in his emerald eyes. Heat creeped under her cheeks as she recalled welcoming him to Balmoral earlier this afternoon.

It had been easy to slip away, given Alexander's boisterous

entrance. Smith had caught her attention from the doorway, and while everyone laughed as Clara was carried off to her bedroom, Belle and Smith made their way to theirs.

"You're here," she whispered as soon as they were alone.

"There's something I have to tell you." He dropped her hand and paced the length of the room. Her heart leapt into her throat. She'd worried that there was a reason he had insisted on staying behind in London. It couldn't be a coincidence that he was grappling with guilt now.

"Tell me," she pressured him.

"I saw Georgia," he began, but when she opened her mouth to ask questions, he stopped her. "Let me finish. She had information about the man who killed Hammond."

"Whoever killed Hammond did us all a favor," Belle said coldly. She could spare no remorse for a man who had never showed her an ounce of humanity. He had been a monster and they were better off with him gone.

"You and Georgia are so alike," he muttered, but when Belle's eyes narrowed, he hurriedly took it back.

Belle sensed her husband needed to confess, and she would gladly absolve him. She trusted him to do what was right for both of them, even if her heart raced with apprehension. "Did you kill him?"

"I turned him in," he said to Belle's surprise. "I found your notes—in the gun."

She had placed them there on instinct. Smith had given her so much. If the only thing she ever granted him in return was the faith to believe in choice, she might be able to repay him.

There would be a time to ask for particulars, but she wouldn't force him to process all of his feelings at once. Instead, she began to unbutton her blouse. Smith moved to face her and followed suit. They didn't touch each other as they undressed. Instead, they stripped slowly until they stood with nothing between them.

He would have done it—for her. The thought that this man would kill to protect her was almost as hot as the fact that he didn't. If he had any doubt about his choice, she would erase it by placing her body in his hands.

Edward dropped onto the couch beside her, interrupting her daydream.

"You're looking rather heated," he pointed out. "Do I need to turn down the boiler or is this something that can't be helped?" Belle's eyes flickered to her husband, and Edward groaned. "That's what I thought."

"Just wait," she warned him. "You're about to be in your honeymoon period. Then no one will be able to stand to be around you either."

"I hope so," Edward said good-naturedly, giving her a wink over the rim of his glasses. "How did we get so lucky, anyway?"

He had found David across the room and his face was a mixture of love and longing as he studied him.

"I have a favor to ask you," Belle said, tearing her eyes away from Smith. Edward drew in a deep breath, before he nodded. She suspected he would understand what she was asking. "I need you to make more room in your life."

Edward's gaze dropped to her stomach as if his glasses could be used as a sonogram. "Smith works fast," he said with a chuckle.

Belle elbowed him in the ribcage. "I want you to make room for Smith."

She didn't bother to add that with any luck, he'd need to be making a little more room in the future as well.

Edward glanced to David. "I'd like you to do the same."

The two of them had been best friends and while their allegiance would always be to one another, it was becoming increasingly clear that their husbands would be part of their lives forever. Belle didn't want Edward to feel as if he had to choose between Belle and becoming Smith's friend. As far as she was considered, Smith was as permanent an addition to her life as her right arm.

"I think your husband's ears are burning," Edward said as Smith prowled across the room toward them. Belle felt a rush of anticipation thrill through her.

"Take Elizabeth?" she asked.

"Excuse me," Smith interrupted them as Belle handed the baby to Edward, "but I'd like to steal my wife away. I think it's time she heads to bed."

Belle didn't miss the way Edward's eyes rolled a little. Smith's insatiable libido was something he was just going to have to get used to.

Smith took her hand, guiding her through the corridors to their private bedchamber. When they entered, he didn't flip on the light switch.

"You were serious about going to bed?" Sleep was usually the last thing on her husband's mind when he suggested they retire for the evening.

There was only enough moonlight to make out the silhouettes of furniture inside the room, but after a moment her eyes adjusted. Smith stayed close to her. All that mattered was that she could see him, even cast in shades of gray.

"I have something for you." He led her to the bed and handed her a box tied with a long, red ribbon.

"That's not what I was expecting," she said under her breath.

"You'll get that, too, beautiful," he promised her.

She plucked free the ribbon and lifted the lid of the box. Inside, hundreds of feathers cushioned a small black machine. "I knew it was too big to be diamonds," she had teased, "but I'm not sure what this is."

"I have something for you tomorrow," he promised her. "Tonight, you get stars."

He lifted the machine free and flipped the switch. Instantly, a dazzling array of light shimmered across the room, covering the ceiling with constellations. It reminded her of New York and wedding rings and promises made. He had given her the stars then and he was doing so again now.

She cleared her throat, her voice thick with emotion. "I thought I was on the naughty list."

Smith placed the machine on the table and fingered the untied ribbon. "That can be arranged, beautiful. Turn around."

His mouth swept across the arch of her neck and he undressed her. When she was nude, he guided her onto her stomach. His palms flattened on her ass, spreading her to him. She wiggled her legs open, but instead of dipping between them, he picked up each of her wrists and brought them behind her back. A moment later the silky ribbon from her present slid around them, cinching them tightly together. He continued playing with it for a moment.

"You look so pretty, tied in a bow for me." He bent over her to whisper in her ear. "Can I play with my toy now?"

"Yes, Sir," she breathed.

"You are on the naughty list," he informed her, his hand rubbing circles over her ass. "Aren't you?"

He prompted her answer with a firm, stinging smack.

"Yes, Sir."

"It so happens that I prefer the naughty list." This revelation was followed by a quick series of whaps to her bottom that left the tender flesh singing with sensual pain. "Your ass is as red as this bow, beautiful."

He slid a finger down the crack between her cheeks and she writhed under the gentle touch. She wanted more. Since they'd begun to try for a baby, most of their lovemaking had been purely traditional. Belle's preferences, however, ran the gamut.

"Please, Sir," she begged.

"You're dripping for me," he told her. A moment later, she felt the blunt crest of his cock massaging along her seam. "I've been saving this for our future."

"Oh." She couldn't bite back the disappointment. Part of her needed the primal, taboo side of Smith. But she wouldn't say no to him any way she could have him. Smith surprised her, though, bending over to run a tongue along the sensitive pink rosebud. Belle clenched at the contact but relaxed as he continued to circle leisurely.

After a few minutes, a finger pushed inside and began to pump.

"It's Christmas," Smith said with a groan, "I'll give you both."

With a gentle slowness, he guided his dick into her, until he hit resistance. Then he pulled out and did the same. His finger continued the assault of her tight hole and Belle's legs began to shake.

"I love seeing you filled with me," Smith growled, increasing his pace until she shattered beneath him. His warmth flooded inside her and she groaned as he pulled out slowly. His fingers brushed the seed dripping from her upward. He smeared it over the pink circle. "Is this what you want?"

He nudged against the tight pucker, giving her a moment to process the idea. Belle didn't have a safe word. She had never wanted one with Smith, and she never needed it. He knew her body's responses like his own. She circled against the tip in invitation. Smith inched within gradually, giving her body time to adjust. His hands tightened on her hips when he slid in entirely.

They had spent the afternoon making love. There was only one thing on her mind now.

"Fuck me," she begged, her hips beginning to writhe against him.

"I'm sorry?" He didn't move, and she knew exactly what he wanted to hear.

"Fuck me, Sir."

Smith pulled back and thrust inside her with one smooth jab. The sensation was utterly different, and it never ceased to make her feel wanton. In his presence, she was shameless, existing only for his pleasure. That libidinous exchange of power had always guaranteed the same would be returned to her.

"I love fucking your ass, beautiful," he growled as he continued to plunge. He grabbed her tied wrists and jerked until her back arched in the air. Belle craned her neck so see her husband, wanting him to see the ecstatic contradiction of pain and pleasure that consumed her. She felt her eyes rolling back as the first wave crashed over her, dragging her under. He continued to thrust until she went limp.

Belle was barely aware as he untied her wrists and massaged the indentations the ribbon had left. He scooped her up and repositioned her on the bed. A few minutes later, a warm, wet towel wiped along her singing sex. She nearly howled at the contact, her body still overly sensitive, and she saw him bite back a grin.

"Don't look so pleased with yourself," she whispered sleepily.

"I can't help it. You look so pretty with your red cheeks," he told her, climbing onto the bedside beside her. At some point, he had undressed. She felt a twinge of disappointment that she hadn't seen it. But when he cradled her body to his, it evaporated. "I think I'd have to stop screwing you entirely to not look pleased. Giving you orgasms is one of my greatest accomplishments."

"Promise not to stop?" Her eyes were becoming heavy, but as sleep lured her under, she heard his quiet response.

"I promise. Forever."

CHAPTER TWENTY-THREE

If Christmas Eve had been a warm, family gathering. Christmas morning was a frenetic mess of activity. Wads of paper littered the floor from gift wrapping, presents were piled next to each person, and, to Mrs. Watson's horror, plates of food had been sneaked into the parlor.

The Bishop clan hadn't acted like strangers for long. They had made themselves at home almost immediately. That included waiting until everyone was in bed and bringing in enough gifts to nearly double the collection at the base of the tree.

"We'll still be opening presents next Christmas," Lola grumbled under her breath. As soon as she opened her box to reveal an Alexander McQueen clutch, she squealed with delight. "Thank you, Mum!"

Madeline gazed fondly at her younger daughter. "I saw it and knew you had to have it. It's harder to shop for clothes for you these days."

She cast a pointed glance at Lola. Then directed it at Belle Stuart.

"Don't look at me," Lola said. "It was all her idea. I caved to peer pressure." She winked at her business partner. Leave it to the Bishops to complain about not being able to spend more money.

Despite Madeline's success with a start-up web company, she didn't understand the need for Bless. Why would women rent what they could buy? Lola didn't try to explain that not everyone had their bank accounts.

Harold hadn't left his wife's side all morning. The holidays had brought them closer than ever, and playing the part of good old St. Nick seemed to bring a joy to the couple that they hadn't shared for a long time.

Clara watched them across the room, warmth spreading through her chest. She had tried to stay out of her parents' affairs—or rather, her father's affairs—but it hadn't always been easy. She knew better than anyone though that marriages had to be fixed from within. Both parties had to make it want to work in order for there to be compromise and cooperation. Her parents had stayed together this long. She could only that their new-found companionship blossomed into the romance they had once shared.

Alexander appeared at her side and followed the direction of her sight. Then he placed his arm around her, pulling him closer to him. Elizabeth babbled on her mother's hips, still in a plaid sleeper from last night. The two had decided to keep their Christmas surprise a secret for a little while longer. But he couldn't help but grin as he thought of Madeline Bishop's welcome to him the day before. If more grandchildren was what she wanted, he would be happy to oblige.

If only every day could be like Christmas, he thought. Seeing the peace on his wife's face and the giddiness overwhelming his daughter made him wish he could spirit them both away to the Scottish countryside and spend every morning like this.

"We'll need another room to put all of her toys in," Clara said dryly.

"Imagine how bad it will be next year," he whispered. He had yet to decide if he hoped to buy a train set or a doll next year. With any luck, he would get to do both. Twins had run in the Royal family in generations past.

Clara's eyes narrowed as she watched the gears turn in his head. "What are you plotting, X?"

"My Christmas present," he told her in a lowered voice.

A rosy flush heated her cheeks. "What about my Christmas present?"

"You can unwrap that later," he reassured her with a smug smile.

It was his signature crooked grin. The one that had caught her attention the day they met and the one that had held it after subsequent day after. She wanted to kiss that smirk right off his face, but she knew where that would lead. After last night, she was still exhausted.

"Actually," he said, lifting a small box he'd been hiding in his other hand, "I did get you something."

But Clara's eyes didn't fall on the actual present, they zeroed in on the ivory envelope on top that had been sealed with red wax stamped with the letter X. If it was anything like the notes he used to send her, its contents weren't family friendly.

"Maybe I should open that later."

"Open it now." He reached for Elizabeth.

Stepping to the side, so that she was out of sight, she slid her index finger under the flap, breaking the seal, and withdrew the handwritten note inside.

POPPET,

I've been remiss at sending you these little notes. I took for granted having you next to me and forgot the need to romance you. I told myself once that if I ever got the chance to reclaim your heart I would never let a day go by without earning it. I've failed at that. But from this day forward I am going to prove my commitment to you and our children.

CLARA SWALLOWED BACK THE TEARS THAT WERE CREEPING INTO her throat. But it was as if Alexander had suspected this might happen, because as the note continued it shifted from sentimental to sensual.

You should also know that I don't plan to let ten days go by without worshipping your body. I realize that might be difficult, considering your condition, but I'm willing to try. My hands. My cock. My mouth. They exist to serve your pleasure, and I will spend every day for the rest of my life to touch, to lick, to bite, to suck, to kiss, and to make love to you.

For always,

X

"You can open your present now," he told her huskily.

Clara gasped at the sudden interruption. His words had taken her to another place, and she needed a second to recover. Tearing open the paper, she found a long jewelry box. She flipped open the lid to discover a stunning ruby bracelet. The gems were held in place by criss-crossing slashes of gold. They formed tiny *x's* all the way around. It was a message: X was reclaiming his territory.

"Help me put it on," she whispered. It took a moment, given that Elizabeth decided to help her parents out. But when it was safely clasped, Clara studied it. "It's perfect."

"So are you." He brushed a kiss over her forehead.

"Have you ever seen such a disgusting display of affection?" Lola said under her breath to Belle. Both were unabashedly staring at the love scene playing out across the room.

"You're jealous." It wasn't an accusation. But rather a statement. Lola had told her that she didn't want a relationship, but it was becoming obvious that she did.

"So what?" Lola shrugged. "My sister managed to snag one of the sexiest and most powerful men in the world, and he looks at her like he won the prize. Why wouldn't I be jealous?"

"You'll find him," Belle promised.

"I'm beginning to suspect that he doesn't exist." It was the first time she had admitted that part of her was still looking for Mr. Right.

"Trust me, you will. Probably when you least expect it."

"Speaking of..." Lola said dramatically. "I'll leave you two alone."

She hurried off as Smith made his way to his wife. Lola's sense of self-preservation was intact.

Belle couldn't help wondering if that was part of the problem as she watched Lola flee the scene. Then again, Belle herself had sworn off love, and she'd vowed never to go to bed with the cocky lawyer who hired her as a personal assistant.

Smith grinned at her as if he knew exactly where her thoughts were this Christmas morning. The two had a rocky start to their relationship, but that was the thing about love: it survived. Whatever metal love was made of was strong enough to thrive in even the most desolate circumstances. If they could find true love, then she had faith anyone could.

"Alexander beat me to the diamonds," Smith informed her. He wrapped an arm around Belle's waist and drew her to him.

"I don't need diamonds," she said. "I just need you."

That was the only price she had ever demanded of this man. His heart, his soul, his body, and he had given it all to her.

"Then I suppose I can take this back," he said. From behind her back, he drew a thin package.

"It isn't diamonds," he warned her as she opened it.

It was something far more perfect. The delicate charm bracelet, far more elegant than any she had seen before. There were only a few charms so far, but each of them meant something important to them. There was a tiny Empire State Building with incredible attention to details, a small feather and a star.

"I saw a couple more I'd like to add," he told her as he helped her put it on, "but I thought this was a good start."

"I love it."

"The two of you make a gorgeous couple," Aunt Jane interrupted unceremoniously, dropping her arms around each of them and pulling them into a group hug. "And that means you're going to make beautiful babies. So, when can I expect one?"

Aunt Jane was a force to be reckoned with in her own right. She had arrived in Scotland this morning with an overnight bag and a kaftan, only to promptly announce that she had a torrid affair to attend the next day. Belle wished she would stay longer, but she wasn't surprised. She was a woman of means. Although she had flitted from husband to husband and many affairs, she had no children of her own. Belle had become her surrogate daughter, so it only seemed natural for her to ask.

Smith opened his mouth, trying to figure out the gentlest way to tell her to back off. But before he could respond, Belle broke in, "We're working on it."

Jane's eyes glinted wickedly. There had never been any shame in her game. An announcement of a carnal nature might have made another person blush, but it only thrilled her. "I'd ask for details," she said, "but I'll settle for updates."

Alexander shook his head as he walked by. It was nothing new for Aunt Jane to get involved in other people's love lives. He owed her a debt of gratitude for being involved with his own. She had been a voice of reason when Clara needed guidance. For that, he would always be grateful, but he could do more than that. He could pass along the favor to the next couple in line.

Swooping upon Edward, he gripped his brother's arm, "Can I have a moment?"

With all of the guests, the brothers hadn't had a chance to speak since Alexander's arrival the day before. But Clara had made it pretty clear that Edward needed to speak to him.

Edward fidgeted a little before nodding to an empty alcove. It was rarely a good sign when a family member needed to speak to you in private on Christmas, but Alexander's gut told him this wasn't going to be bad news.

"Clara talked to you?" Edward guessed as soon as they were alone.

Alexander nodded. The less he said the easier it would be for his brother to get this out.

"I don't know how much she told you," Edward began.

"Nothing," Alexander answered, "She insisted I speak directly to you." He didn't bother to hide the insinuation in his voice. His little brother wasn't going to get out of coming clean to him.

"David and I would like to get married," Edward said in a rush. This wasn't news to Alexander, but he waited patiently for his brother to continue. "On New Year's Eve, and we'd like you to marry us."

"If this King gig doesn't work out, I suppose I can become a minister," Alexander teased. This was the second wedding he'd been asked to officiate.

"Then you will?" Edward wiped a bead of sweat off his forehead, "And you'll give us permission?"

"I've had that document signed for ages, It's been so long that I can't even remember what I made David the duke of."

"You didn't have to do that," Edward said, his eyes shining.

"It's custom, and who am I to break with tradition?"

"Yes," Edward agreed, "that's my job."

"There's more," Alexander warned him. He didn't want to deliver troubling news to Edward on the cusp of his wedding, but he deserved to know. For the first time in a very long time, Alexander believed he could keep the information brief.

Edward listened quietly as Alexander filled him in on the details of the last few weeks.

"I know you have questions," Alexander said when he finished, "and I'll be happy to answer all of them. You deserve to know and so does he." He nodded to David.

"I haven't really kept him in the loop," Edward admitted.

That was Alexander's fault. He had been the one to dictate what could and could not be shared in his brother's relationship. That was a mistake. "I should never have asked you to keep anything from David."

Alexander had been learning this lesson recently himself, and he wouldn't stand by and force his brother to make the same mistake.

"I'm not sure how he will take it," Edward said. It was clear he was still digesting the news of Jacobson's capture and the existence of Anderson.

"Tell him anyway," Alexander advised. "It's for the best."

He clamped a hand on Edward's shoulder and then left him to consider this.

David found his fiancé still thinking in the corner a few minutes later. "Are you hiding or is something on your mind?"

"Lots of things," Edward said in a measured tone.

"I don't like how that sounds," David admitted.

"It won't change anything between the two of us," Edward prefaced. He needed David to know that. He had put the man he loved through hell, asked him to be patient with little guarantee of a happy ending, and broken his heart far too many times. "I just found out that my family is a little more fucked up than I thought."

David took his hands and squeezed them tightly. "I know the Royals are fucked up. If it bothered me, I would have been long gone a while ago." He tipped his head back toward the rest of the group, "Let's enjoy Christmas. Nothing you can tell me is going to change anything between the two of us, but I'm glad you want to share it with me."

Edward smiled, feeling a weight lift from his chest, "I want to share everything with you."

CHAPTER TWENTY-FOUR

New Year's Eve arrived with a blanket of snow that covered the grounds of the castle. Thankfully, all the guests were in attendance for tonight's festivities, and Edward wouldn't have it any other way. While the extended family had returned to their homes in the city, those closest to him were scattered about Balmoral trying to keep warm. He'd already been down to the kitchen, only to be sent away by Mrs. Watson for attempting to snag a finger full of frosting. Apparently, even the groom-to-be wasn't allowed a taste test.

Much of the holiday decor transitioned nicely to a wedding. Although he'd added a few extra sprigs of holly in places. There wasn't much more he could do but count the hours.

Clara found him staring at a newspaper in the study a few hours later. She took a seat across from him, already dressed in a champagne-colored lace dress that accented the rich chestnut hues of her hair. Although her hair was done, her face was free of make-up. Despite that her pale skin glowed with unmistakable beauty.

"Afternoon shag?" he guessed, tossing aside the paper. He'd been rereading the same article without processing since he sat down. He had higher prospects of being entertained by his best friend.

"A nap," she said with a yawn, "and a shag." She stretched her slender arms over her head as though she was still waking up.

"I won't tell Alexander what order of preference you have for your daily activities," he said dryly. Not that it would matter in the least to his brother.

"What are you doing?" She eyed the abandoned newspaper as if he'd been up to no good.

"David has decided to be a traditionalist, and he refuses to see me before the wedding." Edward thought now was a peculiar time to adopt an ancient custom. They were blowing them all to hell just by getting married. If his entire married life was dependent on an archaic ritual, they were doomed.

Clara glanced around the room. "Where's Belle?"

"I loaned her to David," he explained. "I felt he needed a friend with him. It might be his idea not to see one another, but he's the possessive one in the relationship."

"Oh, really?" Clara couldn't hide her surprise, and Edward felt a slight surge of annoyance.

"In case it hasn't escaped your attention, I am not my brother."

"I noticed," she reassured him. "Well, if Belle has David duty, I get Edward duty."

"You sound like a nanny," he accused. There was nothing like feeling like a third wheel on his wedding day, but Clara shook her finger at him.

"I needed a nap, so I could stay up late," she said, "but now I'm all yours."

"I won't tell Alexander." Her explanation softened him. The truth was he was taking out his nerves on her. She didn't deserve that, especially if she wasn't feeling well. "Did Elizabeth keep you up?"

Clara shook her head, absentmindedly chewing on her lower lip. "She's finally sleeping through the night."

That meant Alexander had. Although he enjoyed teasing her about Alexander's libido, he didn't particularly want to know the details of his brother's intimate life.

"Let's get you dressed," Clara suggested, "and you could use a shave."

Edward felt along his jawline and grimaced. "This is why I need David around. I would have gone to the altar looking scruffy."

"In his future absence, you can use a mirror," she advised him as they set off for his bedroom.

Since David had insisted on tradition, Edward had taken his father's old bedroom. Plaid paper covered the walls in hues of navy and camel, and oak wainscoting lined the room's perimeter. Between the thick, canvas drapes and the hunting portraits, the entire space spoke to a repressed British masculinity that didn't suit him. Although Ralph Lauren might disagree.

"Is this what you're wearing?" Clara studied the tuxedo hanging on the wardrobe door.

"Yes." Edward swallowed a little as he looked at it. He supposed this what most women felt when they looked at their wedding gowns —a curious mixture of apprehension and excitement. It was classically cut with a double breast that reminded him of Cary Grant. He felt like he was stepping back in time whenever he wore it, but unlike the antiquated bedroom, it was into a period of glamour.

"You are going to look dashing."

It was exactly what he needed to hear.

"Are you nervous?" she asked, taking a chair by the door.

He shook his head, moving into the adjoin bath to start the hot tap on the sink. "Not exactly. I can't describe it really. I feel..."

"Ready?" she offered him.

That was exactly it. He was ready. It was strange that he had spent so much of his life denying who he was. It had been David that made him realize he didn't want to be anyone else save a man who could deserve David's love. "Yes, but I'm still anxious. I know that doesn't make sense. I keep thinking David will come to his senses and bolt."

"David has been ready to drag you to the altar for years," Clara reminded him. "He's not going to bolt now."

Still. Edward went to the bar cart his father had always kept well-stocked and poured two glasses of Scotch. A drink couldn't hurt to steady his nerves. It was a tradition he didn't mind observing, but when he held one out to Clara, she shook her head.

"None for me. It will put me to sleep. Alexander kept me up all night." She yawned for good measure, but Edward saw through it.

"Not drinking and afternoon naps?" he pointed out.

She did her best to feign innocence. "It is the holiday season."

"Don't make me read about it on the tabloids." The royal bump watch was due to start up any day now that Elizabeth was walking. Apparently, Clara had seen fit to give them something to actually watch.

"We haven't told anyone," she said in a low voice. "I thought we would wait a little longer."

His eyebrows knit in confusion, and he brushed a rogue curl from his forehead. Then it dawned on him. She didn't want to upset Belle. The third member of the trio wanted a baby as well. While it wouldn't surprise anyone that knew them that Clara was pregnant once more, he understood her desire to keep it to herself.

"Your secret is safe with me," he promised.

"What secret?" Alexander demanded, poking his head into the room.

"It wouldn't be a secret if I told you," Edward explained.

"I'll leave you two for a bit." Clara excused herself, and Alexander's eyes followed her out of the room.

"She's only in the hallway," Edward reassured him. Sometimes he thought his brother might fade into nothing without the presence of his wife, and yet, their love was a comforting reminder that the real thing still existed.

"I came to give you a pep talk since Dad isn't here," Alexander said. "But then I remembered how uplifting his pep talk was when I got married."

"I thought he threatened you." Edward recollected that he'd been asked to leave the room that morning. It was the last time he had spoken to his father until the church. A shiver ran down his spine at the memory. Today would be different. That's precisely why Edward had wanted it this way.

"He did, mostly." Alexander smiled sadly. "But he also told me about marriage. I didn't pay much attention to him, to be honest. I wish I had now." He paused for a long moment as if paying a silent tribute to him. "What I do know is that you and David will be fine."

"Is that it?" Edward couldn't help but laugh.

"I thought about giving you advice about your wedding night duties, but I didn't think I was the expert there." Alexander gave him a meaningful look, and they both laughed. "If you are willing to fight for each other, you'll make it through. All you need is love and a lot of stubbornness."

The Cambridge men had that in spades.

Alexander pulled an envelope out of his pocket. "Your official documentation. I've signed and stamped and decreed."

Edward pulled the papers out and stared at them. This was actually happening.

"I couldn't decide if I could make you both the Duke of York," Alexander explained, "so I thought I'd ask you."

Edward grinned at the thought of the two Dukes of York. It was certainly a new precedent that he was about to set. "I'll ask David."

There was no pressing need to decide right now. For a few blissful days they would be able to keep their marriage private. Eventually, the world would weigh in but tonight was about love. Everything else could wait. He'd struggled a lifetime to get to this place, and soon, with his friends and family, at his side, he would finally be home.

CHAPTER TWENTY-FIVE

Belle didn't like being apart from Smith, especially on their anniversary, but today it couldn't be avoided. Edward had insisted she keep an eye on David, but she had other concerns preoccupying her. That's how the two had wound up in the village only a few hours prior to the wedding.

"I'm glad you don't need your hair or make-up done," she confessed to David as they parked their borrowed Range Rover in front of a row of shops.

"It's my complexion," he teased.

She couldn't disagree. The rich hue of his skin accented his cheekbones and jawline. "It's actually a shame that you and Edward can't have babies biologically. They would be gorgeous."

"Don't I know it?" David said with a blinding grin. He was in a friendly mood today. Although the two had spent time together before, they never had a chance to bond outside the presence of their other friends. When she'd called upon him for help, he had jumped at the chance. Maybe he was as eager to get to know her as she was to get to know him. Of course, it could also have something to do with their secret mission.

"Speaking of..." Belle squared her shoulders and turned to study the shop windows.

"It's over there." David pointed to a small store at the corner. Grabbing her hand, he dragged her toward it.

It was hard to say which of the two of them was more excited.

"You know," Belle said breathlessly as they stepped into the pharmacy, "by next week, you'll be all over the tabloids if you get caught dragging a blonde into a pharmacy."

"Imagine if they caught a snap of this!" He tossed her a long, blue box from the shelf. If the thought of being hounded by the paparazzi bothered him, he didn't show it. Edward had done a fair job keeping the press away from him, but once they were married all bets were off. "Should you do it here or back there?"

"I think I better pay for it," she said with a laugh.

The cashier rang them up, glancing in confusion at the two of them. Belle realized she was wearing a wedding band and David wasn't. Rather than explain herself, she simply crossed her fingers for dramatic effect and dashed out of the shop with the bag.

David followed her, almost doubled over. "She's still scratching her head."

"I don't see why it was so strange." Belle felt inexplicably indignant over the whole thing.

"I've been holding hands with Edward in there all month," he reminded her.

"Well, then, we're just one big, happy family, aren't we?" Belle planted her hands on her hips and tossed her hair.

"I couldn't agree more."

SHE STARED AT THE STRIP, SITTING IN THE LOCKED BATHROOM. Despite his enthusiasm, David had understood why she wanted to tell her husband first. How long could these bloody things take anyway? But within a matter of moments, a second line began to appear. It was faint. Belle turned the test around, trying to make certain it wasn't a trick of the light.

Two lines.

She could see it. She could say it. But she couldn't seem to believe it. There was only one way to make this feel real to her. She needed Smith.

It took her longer than she would have liked to track down a pair of boots and some gloves. When Smith had decided to go out with the gameskeeper, she had thought it would be the perfect opportunity to sneak into the village without him. She couldn't bear disappointing him if the test had come back negative, but it wasn't negative. It was positive.

"I'm pregnant," she said to the empty room as she tugged on the boots. The room didn't respond. The room was not being helpful.

She had less than two hours until the wedding, and maybe it was stark raving mad, but she was going out into the Scottish tundra to track down her husband. She simply couldn't wait any longer. Damn reason and common sense.

Norris gawked at her when she reached the door wearing the galoshes and one of Smith's overcoats. Her own outerwear was more pretty than practical. That would have to change, she realized. Now, she was dressing for two. She couldn't be without hats and socks and other important protection from the elements. Somewhere inside her a tiny voice reminded her that the baby was probably the size of the speck of dust, but it didn't matter. If she read that wearing bubble wrap was good for the baby, she would. It was a very good thing she'd insisted on staying behind the scenes at Bless. She could only imagine what her clients would think of that.

"Mrs. Price, can I drive you somewhere?" Norris offered.

She shook her head. "I need to find Smith."

"I'm sure he will return shortly." Norris tried to steer her from the door. "I don't think he would want you out in the cold."

It hardly mattered what either man wanted. She was going to do this. "Thank you, but I'll be fine."

Either she scared him or he decided it wasn't worth it to upset a woman on a wedding day—even if it wasn't her wedding day—because he backed down.

Outside it was significantly colder than Belle had realized. She prided herself on being an indoor girl. Although she'd spent parts of her youth in the country, she usually stayed out of the cold. Belle could cope with a dusting of snow, this was much more. Her feet sank as she stepped onto the grounds, the snow coming past her ankles. Finding the boots had been a very good idea even if they didn't do much against the cold. She was fairly certain she had frostbite before she even got a hundred meters further.

She had just resolved to turn back when a Range Rover rumbled toward the house. It broke as soon as it saw her, and the door swung open. Smith jumped out and rushed to her.

"What on earth are you doing out here?" The more time he spent with the staff, the thicker the traces of his Scottish accent became.

Maybe this was where they should get a proper house for the baby, Belle thought. Smith seemed at home here. She had never imagined that she would want an estate of her own. Now it seemed necessary. Then again, there was the issue of snow.

"Belle!" Smith grabbed her by the shoulders. "Your lips are blue. Let's get you inside."

It wasn't until he said it that she realized just how frozen her lips had become. She wasn't even certain she could speak. Although she hadn't made it very far from the house, he insisted she ride back in the Rover. As soon as they were through the front door, he swept her off her feet and carried her to their bedroom.

Smith knelt before her and took off her boots, rubbing her toes until blood started to flow again.

"What were you thinking?" he asked, not able to keep a bemused grin from his face.

Belle looked into his green eyes, losing herself for only a moment. Would the baby have those eyes? The thought stirred her back to life and the rest of the chill began to melt away. The trouble was that Smith wouldn't stay still long enough to tell him.

First, he insisted on starting a fire. Then he found her socks. He called to the kitchen for hot tea.

"I am not an invalid," she called after him when he inquired with the butler about a hot water bottle.

"What were you doing out there?" he asked, carrying the cup and saucer to the bedside table.

"I needed to find you," she began.

"I was coming back, beautiful." He tucked a few, loose strands of hair behind her ears.

"We should be together for our anniversary." Why couldn't she just bring herself to say it? Perhaps because the more she saw her outing through Smith's eyes, the more she understood it. Would her whole pregnancy be filled with random acts of insanity?

The butler reappeared with the water bottle and Smith excused himself to the loo to fill it. He was through the door before it registered with Belle. She sat up in the bed. This was the second time in a month that she'd left something lying around that she shouldn't. This time the look on Smith's face when he wandered back into the room was very different than the first.

He was still staring at the test, a curious mixture of wonder and shock plastered on his face.

"Beautiful?" He looked up to her, his eyes full of questions.

She bit her lip and nodded. "I came out to tell you, but I think the words got frozen along with my toes. Happy Anniversary."

"Are your toes okay?" He dropped the test on the bed and reached for her feet. "Do you need me to rub them? Are you hungry? Maybe you should lie down?"

"I don't think we can do the whole nine months in one day," she said with a laugh. Her hands reached out to beckon him to her. Smith climbed into the bed beside her and wrapped his arms around her. They stayed like that for a few minutes until Smith laid down, placing his head in her lap. Turning to her belly, he places a soft kiss where his child grew. Then he slowly began to sing. Tears prickled Belle's eyes as she recognized it. It was as bittersweet as their story, but as filled with promises, too. When he finished, they stayed like that, dreaming of the future.

CHAPTER TWENTY-SIX

With no bride present, the grooms decided to eschew tradition and escort themselves to the altar. Clara led the party with Elizabeth in her arms. Unfortunately, the flower girl was more interested in eating the rose petals than dropping them. I couldn't help but stare at my wife as she made her way across the room. There was none of the pomp and circumstance of our wedding, and somehow the intimacy of the event seemed to erase that fateful day.

When Edward had first shared his plans to marry David, my only concern had been regarding his security. Now I knew that my family was safe, which left me free to focus on the happiness that I'd been robbed of on my own wedding day.

Edward and David entered through doors on the opposite side of the room and walked slowly toward one another, stopping when they reached me. We'd chosen the parlor because the Christmas tree provided a beautiful backdrop. Someone had snuck in earlier in the day and removed most of the ornaments in favor of dozens of white roses tucked into the evergreen branches.

"Please join hands," I instructed the two, shooting Edward a wink. He wanted a traditional wedding, and I would do my best to give it to him. "I was told to keep this short, because Mrs. Watson made a cake."

Edward rolled his eyes, but everyone else laughed. If my little brother thought he was going to get away without being embarrassed, he was mistaken. I considered it part of my official role. My brother looked dashing in his classic tuxedo while David had opted for a more modern cut. Somehow the contrast seemed to fit them as perfectly as they fit one another.

"Over the last few days I've shared some thoughts about marriage with Edward, and he told me I wasn't very helpful. I think Clara might agree with that assessment." She nodded vigorously but she couldn't keep a smile off her face. "So, I decided I wouldn't talk about marriage, I would talk about love. But only for a few minutes, so we can all have cake."

"Thank God," Edward interjected.

"I used to believe that love was a fairytale," I began, "and maybe I was right, because one day, a princess walked into my life. She made me believe in love. She brought so many of us together. Edward once thanked me for showing the courage to choose love over duty or tradition. But she was the one who was strong enough to break away from the expectations and the fear. Before I met her, I felt alone. Now she will always be with me. That's what love is: a constant companion, a best friend who sticks beside you, a soft place to call home. She showed me that. That's why love is so powerful: it can never be broken, even when one of you breaks. Love never loses faith, even when there is nothing left to believe in. Love shines a light, even in the darkest hours. All of us are searching for our happily ever after, but the luckiest of us know that it isn't a place or a destiny. Happily ever after is a person. I know my brother has found his, which is why I couldn't be more proud to stand by him today."

Edward dropped David's hands and hugged me. Pulling back, there were tears in his eyes. "Thank you."

When he had stepped back into place, I couldn't help myself. "I think I'm supposed to ask if anyone objects."

"On with it!" Edward demanded with a laugh.

I led them through their vows, and when the time came, I happily looked to my brother and told him, "You may kiss your husband."

Cheers erupted from everyone, and when Edward and David finally released one another, love shining in their eyes, the crowd gathered for a hug. Clara broke away from the group and came to my side.

"How did I do?" I asked, sweeping her into my arms.

"You made me want to marry you all over again." She pressed up onto her toes and gave me a quick kiss.

"I could do without another wedding," I told her. "Would you settle for a lifetime, poppet?"

"How about a happily ever after?" she whispered.

"Do you think they'll miss us?"

Clara glanced at our loved ones and shook her head. I swept her into my arms and carried her from the room. Pausing at the base of the stairs, I brought my mouth to hers. It was the kiss we should have shared on our own wedding day. Our lips sealed to one another, her breath becoming my own and my life becoming hers.

When we broke apart, I took the stairs slowly, unable to look away from her. In her eyes, I found all the answers I had ever sought. I had been broken until the day she stumbled into my life, and her love fused my shattered pieces. She gave me faith when I deserved none. In all the darkness of my past I found an angel, and she guided me home. When I least expected it, she completed me.

A PREVIEW OF CROSS ME

AVAILABLE IN THE ROYALS VOL. THREE

Whoever said it was good to be King had clearly never had the pleasure.

> *The Royal family has come under increasing scrutiny the last two years due to the controversial actions of Alexander, who recently succeeded his father to the throne. Alexander's decision to marry a half-American was the subject of contentious public debate. The crown seemed intent on making an even bigger statement with Alexander's recent approval of Prince Edward's marriage to Scottish man David McClane. Vocal minorities and religious organizations throughout the world have attacked the king's support for the union. The Catholic Church issued a statement condemning the act and it's been the source of much media speculation in America. Other activist groups, however, applauded the Crown's progressive stance, stating that Alexander and his family are breathing fresh life into stale Royal traditions. Will public opinion swing in favor of the king's choices, or is Alexander threatening the stability of the Crown? Only time will tell, but—*

The television snapped off and I glanced over my shoulder to find my wife leaning against the bathroom's doorframe. "It's too early for bad news, X."

She had voiced opposition to mounting a television in the bathroom, but given that I was expected to be up on world news and that I had very little time in the day to catch up on what the media was saying, I had overlooked her concerns. I reached behind me and took the remote, flipping the television back on, but changed the channel to a cable sports station. "I was just checking the times."

"Since when are you into racing?" She was calling my bluff, but what my wife didn't know was that I had recently become much more interested in racing. When I didn't answer, she hit me with, "You don't even like driving."

"I like driving you."

"Driving me crazy maybe."

I continued to shave, which was a dangerous proposition because my eyes kept drifting from my own reflection to hers. The dawn light had begun to filter into the bedroom, haloing her in a soft glow that accentuated her luscious curves and made her look like God's gift to man. She was certainly God's gift to me. Her dark hair cascaded over creamy shoulders. Last night I'd pressed my lips to them as I rocked her to two climaxes. In the mirror, her own lips twisted into a knowing smirk as if she knew exactly what I was thinking. As I was usually thinking about finding a way to get her naked—something I had never kept secret from her—the smugness was warranted.

She moved towards the counter, hips swaying slightly. Her smile slipped as she studied herself. In the harsher artificial light of the bathroom, I could see what was making her frown. Faint blue smudges circled her eyes and she looked even more pale than normal.

"Have you considered the houses I found for Edward?" she asked.

I'd looked at my wife's list yesterday. She'd been obsessing over his wedding present since we'd returned from the holidays and he'd left on his honeymoon. "I'd like him closer."

"Windsor is close," she gurgled as she brushed her teeth.

"Windsor Castle is a bit extravagant for everyday use, Poppet."

She shot me a look. "Have you seen our house? There's a smaller house in Windsor that sounds perfect and its only half an hour from the city."

"That place?" I shook my head. "It's unacceptable. Practically falling down."

"You need to make a decision soon or they'll never come home from Seychelles."

I wouldn't if I were my brother. I kept this to myself. It would be taken care of, but for now I had more pressing concerns.

"Are you feeling all right? I heard you up earlier this morning." I tried to keep the concern in my voice to a reasonable level, but it was a struggle.

"I'm fine," she said, but it did little to reassure me. At the moment, my wife's moods swung between angelic calm and hysterical rage. I had learned the hard way not to get up and join her when morning sickness hit. I didn't want to allow her to go through it alone, but since my presence seemed to upset her even more, I'd had to keep a restless vigil from the bedroom.

I found other ways to manage her care, though, waking our daughter and doing my best to help Clara get extra rest. That was the hardest, because it usually meant keeping my hands to myself, even when I wanted to spend a few quiet moments together before the rest of the household intruded on our lives.

"Did you get enough sleep?"

"Sure," she said noncommittally as she glared at her reflection. "I look terrible and I have the Child Watch Symposium this afternoon."

She turned the faucet on in the marble sink and bent forward to splash cold water on her face. I took the interruption to quickly wipe remnants of shaving cream from my jaw.

"You know, maybe that's a sign you should stay home," I said, stepping behind her. I stopped my arms around her slender torso, one hand resting over the tiny bump that only we knew about, while the other took a slightly less sentimental path up to her breast. My thumb circled its furl through the thin satin of her nightgown. Clara responded with a soft moan.

"Are you trying to distract me?" Although, even as she pretended to be annoyed, she leaned into me, allowing better access. I slid my hand under the flimsy nightgown and continued my gentle assault. "Because you aren't going to convince me not to go."

We'd been having this argument for some time. After I'd proposed, Clara had struggled with her decision to leave her career behind. When I'd asked her to marry me she had known that one day I would become the King of England. It was inevitable. Before our wedding, I'd promised her plenty of opportunities to continue working on the social programs she'd overseen for Peters & Clarkwell. None of that had gone according to plan. I'd still convinced her to marry me, but both of us had taken on new responsibilities so quickly we might have suffered whiplash. My father's assassination had backed me into a corner, forcing me to ascend to the throne years before I had expected. Clara's discovery that she was pregnant had pushed us both into parenthood, something I'd always thought I didn't want. For the last year and a half, we had been adjusting. I'd had Clara exactly where I wanted her—by my side, in my bed, and, most importantly, home, where I could keep an eye on her personally. Now, despite being pregnant again, she was determined to finally rise to her public responsibilities as Queen. No amount of charm could dissuade her.

"I can think of much better ways for you to spend your day." My other hand abandoned its protective vigil and slid to the hollow between her thighs, working its way past the fabric to the wet heat there.

"You have meetings all day," she breathed. I couldn't help but detect a note of challenge. The message was clear: if I wanted her to abandon her plans for the day I would have to do the same, something we both knew was impossible.

"My meetings are all going to be here." I coaxed her legs farther apart with my knee to give me better access to the prize I was ready to claim. I earned a soft shudder accompanied by a moan of approval as my thumb found its target. "I'm here and you're here. Other people can wait."

My lips whispered temptations as they trailed along the soft skin behind her ear and down to the freckles I'd been fantasizing about only moments ago. I drank in the sight of her languorous body in my arms, the mirror reflecting exactly what I wanted out of life: to possess her completely until she knew nothing but the safety and security I'd promised her.

Clara opened one eyelid, lazily meeting my greedy gaze. "So in this scenario, I'm here waiting naked in your bed—right, X?"

She didn't sound as annoyed about this prospect as she usually might. Of course, I was actively lowering her defenses.

"Something like that," I said silkily.

"No way in hell." She turned her head, though, allowing her face to come a breath away from my own. "But I don't mind if you keep trying to convince me."

"Challenge accepted, Poppet." And then my mouth closed over hers.

Two discussions later and I'd failed to persuade her to stay home. She said goodbye to me, glowing like a lightbulb, which would no doubt contribute to speculation that she was with child again. If she was going to insist on going out in public, we would have to confirm this pregnancy sooner rather than later. It would be easier if she would just stay here. But her defiance was what had first drawn me to Clara Bishop. I'd never take that away from her. I would never want to. Still, it made things more complicated.

My fingers raked through my hair as I buried my head in my hands, wondering what a simple life looked like. What was it like to be a normal guy whose pregnant wife went off to work? I'd never know. Not for the first time I wished I could trade my birthright in for a less regal model.

"Alexander?" A deep voice interrupted my thoughts. I didn't have to look up to know it was my old friend and longtime personal guard, Norris, because he was the only person on my payroll who didn't constantly address me as Sir.

If he was here, that meant my day was about to start. Then again, Norris shouldn't be here. I frowned, not bothering to hide the reproach written all over my face. "I thought you were going with her."

"The Prime Minister's visit today. The household team had to split duty. Brexton is with her."

My frown deepened. It wasn't that I didn't trust my old friend and Royal Air Force buddy, it was simply that I trusted Norris more. If I couldn't be with Clara, I always felt better when he was there. Norris didn't look like a bodyguard. With his thinning blond hair and average build, he blended in, looking more the part of the fatherly advisor than the trained killer. He was lethal and he wouldn't hesitate to protect her. "I'd prefer these decisions were run by me first."

"Her Majesty was quite determined on the point." His lips pressed into a thin line, recalling an unpleasant memory. "She said I fuss over her too much."

My eyebrow cocked at this bit of information. Perhaps my attempts to persuade her this morning had backfired. Now, not only had she gone out, she had sent a defiant message as well. Clara knew that I preferred for Norris to be with her, so sending him away in favor of a team led by Brex was her way of telling me to back off. "I'll discuss this with her later."

"If you don't mind me saying so." Norris finally stepped into the room, his hands behind his back and his expression unreadable. I had no idea what he wanted to say to me, but I suspected I was about to get a lecture. "Clara seems a trifle emotional these days. Perhaps you can trust her to make her own plans. I think she would prefer that."

"Which one of us is the politician?" I grumbled. Norris had chosen his words carefully, but the meaning was clear. I hadn't confided the news of her pregnancy to him yet. She had wanted to keep it private and only begin to tell people once it was confirmed by the doctor later this week. Norris had clearly guessed what was going on. "I don't know why I try to keep secrets from you."

"Well, Alexander, you have been strutting around here like a prize stud for the last week," he said dryly. "She's out to teach you a lesson. I caught her crying twice last week. We've been here before."

I did take an inordinate amount of pride in knowing Clara was carrying my child again. Watching her body transform with the proof of our love and knowing that she had chosen me was a massage for my ego, admittedly.

"Plus," Norris continued, "there's the matter of you both acting like damned fools."

"Excuse me?" His criticism broke me away from thoughts of my wife. It wasn't that he couldn't speak to me that way. It was that he rarely did.

"She's obviously making a point that she won't be told what to do and where she can go, which makes me suspect that you tried to tell her what to do and where to go this morning."

I held my hands up in surrender. "I tried to convince her."

"Are you certain you didn't try to command her?" Norris had been privy to many of our premarital arguments. He'd witnessed the few moments where I'd almost lost her because of my controlling nature. He was well aware of my tendency toward possessiveness.

"I asked. Nicely."

He didn't have to know what I meant by nicely. Clara, however, had obviously seen this morning differently. I reminded myself that my wife was pregnant and therefore prone to mood swings, but despite that, my palm twitched. I had to fight my urge to dominate her outside of the bedroom. If my best efforts were going to be rewarded with passive aggressive actions meant to test me, it would be harder to maintain that boundary.

"It's none of my business," he said with the air of somebody who felt it was very much his business. Norris was like a father to me. Because of the terrible relationship I'd had with my real father, I usually appreciated Norris' insight. Today, with the prospect of a morning meeting with the Prime Minister and briefings all afternoon, I wasn't in the mood.

"Anything else? Are we prepared for Prime Minister Clark's arrival?" My tone shifted to cool business.

His eyes narrowed. He understood when he was being dismissed, but unlike most of the people who worked around me, Norris wasn't prone to sycophancy. Still, he seemed to sense I was on edge.

"Everything is in place and the arrangements for Queen Mary's quarters at Kensington Palace have been made."

Suddenly, I was ready to take my daily meetings. Anything was better than dealing with the family. The Prime Minister wanted to discuss the budget and climate change initiatives, topics I usually found mind-numbingly boring, especially since Parliament was likely to enact whatever budget or legislation they saw fit. The reminder that my grandmother and uncle had decided to return to London was another piece of bad news. Issues of national politics felt positively tame compared to the tangle of family politics that would soon capture me.

"They've chosen Kensington?" I couldn't help but be surprised. I'd expected there to be a fight over Clarence House, the first home I'd occupied with Clara after our marriage. It seemed like the choice my grandmother would make, if only to spite me.

"I believe they were told that Clarence House had potential occupants."

This was news to me. I sat back in my office chair and waited, wondering if it was too early for Scotch.

"It's not official," Norris said. "I thought it prudent to reserve the premises given your brother's new marital status."

"Good thinking. Clara had pitched Windsmoor."

"I assume you told her it was—"

"Falling apart," I finished. "I think she meant to give them more privacy than London might afford them."

Norris and I hadn't had the opportunity to discuss Edward's wedding present, but it was customary for the reigning monarch to gift a residence to close members of the family. I'd been avoiding the conversation, excusing myself from it by reminding anyone who asked, mostly Clara, that Edward and David were still on their honeymoon. Still, I couldn't avoid it forever. I feared my brother would prefer a country estate. It would make sense. It was the choice I would have made had I not been forced to keep a permanent residence in London. Keeping Clarence House open and offering it to Edward felt right. I wanted my brother nearby. He was the only blood relation I trusted and a friend and advisor.

"Will that be all?" Norris's eyes twinkled as he spoke. He was testing me, calling me out for trying to be dismissive earlier.

I leaned back in my seat, crossing my arms behind my head. "I don't suppose I could convince you to go to that symposium."

He levelled an incredulous stare in my direction. "Given Clara's condition, it would be better not to upset her."

"I wish you were with her." This time I wasn't teasing. I was deadly serious. But he had a point. Clara had made her desires known and undermining her would only cause a fight. While I liked making up with her after an argument, I also wanted to see that she was healthy. None of that meant I had to do nothing.

"Keep an eye on the situation," I ordered him. "I want to know if there's someone with so much as a sniffle around her."

Norris opened his mouth as if to respond but then thought better of it. He shook his head as he turned to look into it, but as he crossed the threshold of my office, I could swear I heard him mutter, "Stubborn arse."

The Prime Minister reminded me of my father, which was to say he looked like most Englishmen of a certain age: light hair and skin creased with wrinkles from years of apologetic gymnastics, usually wearing tweed. Next to each other, the two of us looked like night and day. Despite spending most of my time in cabinet meetings and offices, I had my mother's rich olive skin tone. I was suddenly grateful to my mother's Greek heritage for the influx of fresh genes.

Prime Minister Clark was unfailingly gracious and forgiving of the fact I was obviously distracted. With my thoughts on Clara and her event, he'd had to repeat himself several times, making the meeting drag on. We'd taken armchairs by the fireplace in my private office. He was the only politician I met with in closed quarters. No one, not even Norris, attended these meetings. It was meant to encourage a spirit of cooperation. Not for the first time, I wondered if the meetings were even necessary. He had his business and I had mine. We were both busy running very different aspects of the United Kingdom. As he informed me about the latest news on a climate change initiative, I wondered what he would think if he knew the concerns preoccupying me.

"My family stance on climate change is well documented," I reminded him.

"Not everyone will be thrilled with the sanctions," he warned me.

"Do I look overly concerned with my popularity?"

Clark tipped his head, something like a laugh escaping his lips. "The press is crucifying you."

"When I was young, I couldn't do anything right. Now that I'm older, I still can't."

"Welcome to being a politician."

"Isn't that your job?" I only wished it were true. Most of Britain's politics filtered through Parliament and I was expected to simply support or criticize legislation, have a stance on issues affecting my people, and to be up-to-date on all major discussions before Parliament. The government had throttled some of the Crown's powers over the last few years and the monarchy had been turning more and more responsibility over to His Majesty's Government for the last few centuries. That didn't absolve my obligations to my position.

"I should warn you that there are some minority factions in the House of Lords who are questioning the choice to allow Edward to remain in the line of succession."

"That's not really for them to be concerned about." My fist clenching as I imagined getting my hands on one of the dissenters.

"I suppose the authority rests with you—"

"There is no suppose about it. The authority does rest with me. Not that it should be a question at all. I thought Britain was in the twenty-first century."

"It's more about perception. It might strain our relationships with our more conservative allies."

"Sod them." I couldn't help myself. It was my duty to play nice—to act the part of the benevolent king—but I never had much luck hiding my protective streak when it came to my family. That we were still having this argument, even after a year of letting people warm up to the idea of my brother's wedding, pissed me off.

"I'm not sure that should be the Crown's official stance," he said.

"I wasn't planning on releasing a statement to that effect." My lip curled at the thought. The press would have a field day with it, and although there was a time when I would've enjoyed delivering a 'screw you' to anyone who thought they should have a say in my private affairs, I didn't have that luxury any longer.

"Anonymity and freedom from criticism are two expectations only afforded to private citizens." His words were gentle. Not for the first time I suspected the Prime Minister felt a paternalistic responsibility to me, probably owing to the death of my father. He might not feel so inclined if he knew how little I respected my father's advice before his death. I didn't need lectures about the difficulties of being a member of the Royal family. I'd dealt with the media circus for as long as I could remember. My own marriage had been dissected by the tabloids. More than once, my wife's life had been put in danger by overeager leeches who believed exactly what the prime minister had just said: there was no privacy afforded to royals. Of course I knew that, it was why I had been the one to accept the crown. It might've been easier to reject my birthright and make a life on my own. I would never know. The only thing I remained certain of was that my position afforded me the ability to grant some bit of security to those I loved. It also meant bearing the brunt of criticism for my progressive stances.

"Perhaps you could consider another option."

"Which is?" I asked.

"Bring someone in. A publicist of sorts," he suggested. "Someone you can trust to help you maneuver the stickier situations."

"I'll keep it under advisement," I said through gritted teeth.

There were actual matters of state to discuss. Instead we were sitting here worrying about public perception. That was the difference—I realized something. There was a difference between a man who climbed to political office and one who was born to lead. I'd never had a choice of life. In a way, that was turning out to be more freeing. No one could challenge my birthright. No one could vote me out. If anyone had qualms over my choices, it wasn't going to endanger my political career. I would still be King.

No, it would take far more sinister machinations to remove my power. Taking the crown was a much bloodier affair than an election. I had survived my first assassination attempt. My father had not been so lucky. I had no idea how many he'd survived before the one that claimed his life. I suspected that I myself had survived on more occasions than I knew. But those attempts hadn't come from people or journalists or other countries. None of the forces with which the Prime Minister felt so concerned were at play in any of those events. It had been the poison underbelly of Parliament itself. I reminded myself every week, while the Prime Minister sat across from me with a fatherly smile on his face: politicians couldn't be trusted. One member of Parliament had already been arrested in connection with my father's assassination, and despite our best efforts, we still had not discovered how far the plot reached.

Still, perhaps he was right. Maybe I needed someone to handle the public announcements. It would be a load off. If only I could find someone to attend these meetings.

I glanced at the clock, my thoughts slipping away to much more important items on my agenda. I wanted an update on Clara. The longer this meeting continued, the longer I would wait for one.

"There's one final matter I'd like to discuss. The funding for the Sovereign Games."

I grimaced. That had not been on my agenda. "That was my father's pet project."

As far as I was concerned that was the end of that. I'd spent the better part of the last year removing all vestiges of my father's reign from this office. I wasn't about to continue his hobbies.

"It was one of your father's most popular programs. Furthermore, Parliament has approved its half of the funding. There seems to be a general consensus that Britain is feeling more divided than usual." He was choosing his words carefully. It wasn't just the country that felt divided, it was the entire world. Some of my own choices had certainly fractured the unity of the people here, but I didn't see how that mattered in this instance.

"I wasn't even aware the games were moving forward."

"Your grandmother has been quite persistent in—"

"Of course she has." It was starting to make sense. My grandmother, Queen Mary, had left residence here after the death of her son. We weren't exactly on speaking terms. Mostly, because she had called my wife a whore. "So, this has become her baby."

"I suppose in a way. She feels strongly that Albert's memory should be kept alive."

"Doesn't everyone?" I might be the only person content to let my father's memory remain at rest. In his final moments, he had sacrificed himself for me. But while in the end he had granted me acceptance, he had denied it to me for most of my life. His final choices didn't erase the nearly thirty years of disapproval and mistrust between us.

A knock broke the mounting tension in the room, but before I could call the person in, Norris stuck his head through the door. "I apologize for the interruption but I need to speak with you immediately."

"Not a problem." The Prime Minister stood, smoothing wrinkles from his suit. "I need to check in with my secretary. I'll see you this afternoon?"

As if I had a choice.

"I'm looking forward to it," I said in a flat voice.

Norris closed the door behind him and I began to shuffle through the day's agenda, looking to see what unsavory briefing was next on my plate. "Thanks for the save."

But he didn't smile.

"There's been a development. I must warn you that this is likely nothing," he began.

My blood ran cold. It dawned on me too late. Norris wasn't the type to interrupt a meeting with the Prime Minister because I was bored. That was something Brex would do. But Brex was with Clara. If Norris had abandoned his sense of propriety to interrupt a private discussion, something must be terribly wrong.

"This isn't confirmed," he continued, his voice remaining suspiciously even, "but we did receive a message."

He held out his mobile phone and I scanned the screen as the weight of what I read settled onto my chest like a boulder. I couldn't quite digest it—words like bomb and faction and symposium. It didn't matter if there was confirmation. It didn't matter what my wife wanted anymore. It didn't matter if there was only a shred of possibility that what I was reading could be true. "We need to find Clara."

"Alexander, I will handle this."

I was already out of my seat and making my way down the hall. Norris knew better than to try to stop me. Not after I'd received this piece of intel. Not with the threat of an attack on the symposium.

Not before I reached my wife.

ABOUT THE AUTHOR

GENEVA LEE is the *New York Times*, *USA Today*, and internationally bestselling author of over a dozen novels, including the Royals Saga which has sold nearly three million copies worldwide. She lives in Poulsbo Washington with her husband and three children, and she co-owns Away With Words Bookshop with her sister.

ALSO BY GENEVA LEE

THE RIVALS SAGA

Blacklist

Backlash

Bombshell

THE ROYALS SAGA

Command Me

Conquer Me

Crown Me

Crave Me

Covet Me

Capture Me

Complete Me

Cross Me

Claim Me

Consume Me

THE SINNERS SAGA

Beautiful Criminal

Beautiful Sinner

Beautiful Forever

FOUR SEASONS

Fall For You

A Long Winter's Night

Spring Fever

Hot Summer Nights

STANDALONE

The Sins That Bind Us

Two Week Turnaround

His Private Collection

www.ingramcontent.com/pod-product-compliance
Lightning Source LLC
Chambersburg PA
CBHW010356050826
48979CB00052B/2824/J

* 9 7 8 1 9 4 5 1 6 3 5 3 1 *